BY TERRY BROOKS

THE MAGIC
KINGDOM OF
LANDOVER

VOLUME 2

THE MAGIC KINGDOM OF LANDOVER

VOLUME 2

TERRY BROOKS

BALLANTINE BOOKS DEL REY NEW YORK

2009 Del Rey Trade Paperback Edition

The Tangle Box copyright © 1994 by Terry Brooks
Witches' Brew copyright © 1995 by Terry Brooks
Excerpt from *A Princess of Landover* by Terry Brooks
copyright © 2009 by Terry Brooks

Published in the United States by Del Rey, an imprint of The Random House
Publishing Group, a division of Random House, Inc., New York.

DEL REY is a registered trademark and the Del Rey colophon is a trademark
of Random House, Inc.

Originally published in two separate volumes in the United States by Del Rey,
an imprint of The Random House Publishing Group, a division of Random
House, Inc., as *The Tangle Box* in 1994 and *Witches' Brew* in 1995.

This book contains an excerpt from the forthcoming book *A Princess of
Landover* by Terry Brooks. This excerpt has been set for this edition only and
may not reflect the final content of the forthcoming edition.

Map by Russ Charpentier

ISBN 978-0-345-51353-3

Printed in the United States of America

www.delreybooks.com

2 4 6 8 9 7 5 3 1

Book design by Liz Cosgrove

CONTENTS

MISTS and the FAIRY WORLD

Melchor

Deep Fell

Rhyndweir

THE GREENSWARD

The Heart

Sterling Silver

LAKE COUNTRY

Lake Irrylyn

MISTS and the FAIRY WORLD

MISIS and the FAIRY WORLD

Fire Springs

EASTERN WASTELANDS

The
MAGIC KINGDOM
of
LANDOVER

erew

Libiris

MISIS and the FAIRY WORLD

K CHARPENTIER '89

THE
TANGLE BOX

"One evening coming in with a candle I was startled to hear him say a little tremulously, 'I am lying here in the dark waiting for death.' The light was within a foot of his eyes. I forced myself to murmur, 'Oh, nonsense!' and stood over him as if transfixed.

"Anything approaching the change that came over his features I have never seen before, and hope never to see again. Oh, I wasn't touched. I was fascinated. It was as though a veil had been rent. I saw on that ivory face the expression of sombre pride, of ruthless power, of craven terror—of an intense and hopeless despair. Did he live his life again in every detail of desire, temptation, and surrender during that supreme moment of complete knowledge? He cried in a whisper at some image, at some vision—he cried out twice, a cry that was no more than a breath:

" 'The horror! The horror!' "

—Joseph Conrad, *Heart of Darkness*

CONTENTS

SKAT MANDU

Horris Kew might have been a Disney artist's rendering of Ichabod Crane. He was tall and gawky and had the look of a badly assembled puppet. His head was too small, his arms and legs too long, and his ears, nose, Adam's apple, and hair stuck out all over the place. He looked harmless and silly, but he wasn't. He was one of those men who possess a little bit of power and handle it badly. He believed himself clever and wise and was neither. He was the proverbial snowball who always managed to turn himself into an avalanche. As a result, he was a danger to everyone, himself included, and most of the time he wasn't even aware of it.

This morning was no exception.

He came up the garden walk to the swinging gate without slowing, closing the distance in huge, loping strides, slammed the gate back as if annoyed that it had not opened of its own accord, and continued on toward the manor house. He looked neither left nor right at the profusion of summertime flowers that were blooming in their meticulously raked beds, on the carefully pruned bushes, and along the newly painted trellises. He did not bother to breathe in the fragrant smells that filled the warm upstate New York morning air. He failed to give a moment's notice to the pair of robins singing on the low branches of the old shagbark hickory centered on the sweeping lawn leading up to the manor house. Ignoring all, he galloped along with the single-mindedness of a charging rhino.

From the Assembly Hall at the base of the slope below the manor house came the sound of voices rising up like an angry swarm of bees. Horris's thick eyebrows furrowed darkly over his narrow, hooked nose, a pair of fuzzy caterpillars laboriously working their way toward a meeting. Biggar was still trying to reason with the faithful, he supposed. Trying to reason with the *once-faithful*, he amended. It wouldn't work, of course. Nothing would now. That was the trouble with confessions. Once given, you couldn't take them back.

Simple logic, the lesson a thousand charlatans had been taught at the cost of their lives, and Biggar had somehow missed it.

Horris gritted his teeth. What had that idiot been thinking?

He closed on the manor house with furious determination, the shouts from the Assembly Hall chasing after him, elevated suddenly to a frightening new pitch. They would be coming soon. The whole bunch of them, the faithful of so many months become a horde of unreasoning ingrates who would rip him limb from limb if they got their hands on him.

Horris stopped abruptly at the foot of the steps leading up to the veranda that ran the entire length of the gleaming home and thought about what he was losing. His narrow shoulders sagged, his disjointed body slumped, and his Adam's apple bobbed like a cork in water as he swallowed his disappointment. Five years of work gone. Gone in an instant's time. Gone like the light of a candle snuffed. He could not believe it. He had worked so hard.

He shook his head and sighed. Well, there were other fish in the ocean, he supposed. And other oceans to fish.

He clumped up the steps, his size-sixteens slapping against the wooden risers like clown shoes. He was looking around now—looking, because this was the last chance he would get. He would never see this house again, this colonial treasure he had come to love so much, this wonderful, old, Revolutionary American mansion, so carefully restored, so lovingly refurbished, just for him. Fallen into ruin on land given over to hunting and snow sports deep in the Finger Lakes region of upstate New York, not fifty miles off the toll road linking Utica and Syracuse, it had been all but forgotten until Horris had rediscovered it. Horris had a sense of the importance of history and he admired and coveted things historical—especially when yesterday and today could be tied together for his personal gain. Skat Mandu had allowed him to combine the two, making the history of this house and land a nice, neat package tied up at Horris's feet waiting to be opened.

But now Skat Mandu was history himself.

Horris stopped a second time at the door, seething. All because of Biggar. He was going to lose it all because of Biggar and his big mouth. It was inconceivable. The fifty acres that formed the retreat, the manor house, the guest house, the Assembly Hall, the tennis courts, the stables, horses, attendants, cars, private plane, bank accounts, everything. He wouldn't be able to salvage any of it. It was all in the foundation's name, the tax-sheltered Skat Mandu Foundation, and he couldn't get to any of it in time. The trustees would see to that quick enough once they learned what had happened. Sure, there was the money in the Swiss bank accounts, but that wouldn't make up for the collapse of his empire.

Other fish in the ocean, he repeated silently—but why did he have to go fishing *again*, for pity's sake?

He kicked at the wicker chair next to the door and sent it flying, wishing with all his heart that he could do the same to Biggar.

The shouts rose anew from the Assembly, and there was a very clear and unmistakable cry of "Let's get him!" Horris quit thinking about what might have been and went quickly inside.

He was barely inside the house when he heard the beating of wings behind him. He tried to slam the door, but Biggar was too quick. He streaked through at top speed, wings flapping wildly, a few feathers falling away as he reached the banister of the stairway that curved upward from the foyer to the second floor and settled down with a low whistle.

Horris stared at the bird in bleak appraisal. "What's the trouble, Biggar? Couldn't get them to listen?"

Biggar fluffed his feathers and shook himself. He was coal black except for a crown of white feathers. Quite a handsome bird, actually. A myna of some sort, though Horris had never been able to determine his exact lineage. He regarded Horris now with a wicked, gleaming eye and winked. "Awk! Pretty Horris. Pretty Horris. Biggar is better. Biggar is better."

Horris pressed his fingers to his temples. "Please. Could we forgo the dumb-bird routine?"

Biggar snapped his beak shut. "Horris, this is all your fault."

"My fault?" Horris was aghast. He came forward threateningly. "How could this be my fault, you idiot? I'm not the one who opened his big mouth about Skat Mandu! I'm not the one who decided to tell all!"

Biggar flew up the banister a few steps to keep some distance between them. "Temper, temper. Let us remember something here, shall we? This was all your idea, right? Am I right? Does this ring a bell? You thought up this Skat Mandu business, not me. I went along with the program because you said it would work. I was your pawn, as I have been the pawn of humans and humankind all my life. A poor, simple bird, an outcast . . ."

"An idiot!" Horris edged closer, trying unsuccessfully to stop the clenching of his hands as he imagined them closing about the bird's scruffy neck.

Biggar scooted a bit farther up the railing. "A victim, Horris Kew. I am the product of you and your kind. I did the best I could, but I can hardly be held to account for my actions based on your level of expectations, now can I?"

Horris stopped at the foot of the stairs. "Just tell me why you did it. Just tell me that."

Biggar puffed out his chest. "I had a revelation."

Horris stared. "You had a revelation," he repeated dully. He shook his head. "Do you realize how ridiculous that sounds?"

"I see nothing ridiculous about it at all. I am in the business of revelations, am I not?"

Horris threw up his hands and turned away. "I do not believe this!" He turned back again furiously. His scarecrow frame seemed to fly out in half-a-dozen directions at once as he gestured. "You've ruined us, you stupid bird! Five years of work out the window! Five years! Skat Mandu was the foundation of everything we've built! Without him, it's gone, all of it! What were you thinking?"

"Skat Mandu spoke to me," Biggar said, huffy himself now.

"There is no Skat Mandu!" Horris shrieked.

"Yes, there is."

Horris's broad ears flamed and his even broader nostrils dilated. "Think about what you're saying, Biggar," he hissed. "Skat Mandu is a twenty-thousand-year-old wise man that you and I made up in order to convince a bunch of fools to part with their money. Remember? Remember the plan? We thought it up, you and I. Skat Mandu—a twenty-thousand-year-old wise man who had counseled philosophers and leaders throughout time. And now he was back to share his wisdom with us. That was the plan. We bought this land and restored this house and created this retreat for the faithful—the poor, disillusioned faithful—the pathetic, desperate, but well-heeled faithful who just wanted to hear somebody tell them what they already knew! That's what Skat Mandu did! Through you, Biggar. You were the channeler, a simple bird. I was the handler, the manager of Skat Mandu's holdings in the temporal world."

He caught his breath. "But, Biggar, there is no Skat Mandu! Not really, not now, not ever! There's just you and me!"

"I spoke to him," Biggar insisted.

"You spoke to him?"

Biggar gave him an impatient look. "You are repeating me. Who is the bird here, Horris?"

Horris gritted his teeth. "You spoke to him? You spoke to Skat Mandu? You spoke to someone who doesn't exist? Mind telling me what he had to say? Mind sharing his wisdom with me?"

"Don't be snide." Biggar's claws dug into the banister's polished wood.

"Biggar, just tell me what he had to say." Horris's voice sounded like finger-nails scratching on a chalkboard.

"He told me to tell the truth. He told me to admit that you had made it all up about him and me, but that now I really was in contact with him."

Horris's fingers locked in front of him. "Let me get this straight. Skat Mandu told you to confess?"

"He said that the faithful would understand."

"And you believed him?"

"I had to do what Skat Mandu required of me. I don't expect you to understand, Horris. It was a matter of conscience. Sometimes you've simply got to respond on an emotional level."

"You've short-circuited, Biggar," Horris declared. "You've burnt out all your wiring."

"And you simply don't want to face reality," Biggar snapped. "So save your caustic comments, Horris, for those who need them."

"Skat Mandu was the perfect scam!" Horris screamed the words so loudly that Biggar jumped in spite of himself. "Look around you, you idiot! We landed in a world where people are convinced they've lost control of their lives, where there's so much happening that it's overwhelming, where beliefs are the hardest things to come by and money's the easiest! It's a world tailor-made for someone like us, just packed full of opportunities to get rich, to live well, to have everything we ever wanted and a few we didn't! All we had to do was keep the illusion of Skat Mandu alive. And that meant keeping the faithful convinced that the illusion was real! How many followers do we have, Biggar? Excuse me, how many *did* we have? Several hundred thousand, at least? Scattered all over the world, but making regular pilgrimages to visit the retreat, to listen to a few precious words of wisdom, to pay good money for the experience?"

He took a deep breath. "Did you think for one minute that telling these people that we tricked them into giving money to hear what a bird would tell them—never mind who the bird said he was getting the words from—would be something they would be quick to forgive? Did you imagine that they would say, 'Oh, that's all right, Biggar, we understand,' and go back to wherever they came from in the first place? What a joke! Skat Mandu must be laughing pretty hard just about now, don't you think?"

Biggar shook his white-crested head. "He is displeased at the lack of respect he is being accorded, is what he is."

Horris's mouth tightened. "Please tell him for me, Biggar, that I could care less!"

"Why don't you tell him yourself, Horris?"

"What?"

Biggar had a wicked gleam in his eye. "Tell him yourself. He's standing right behind you."

Horris sniggered. "You've lost your mind, Biggar. You really have."

"Is that so? Is that a fact?" Biggar puffed out his chest. "Then have a look, Horris. Go on, have a look."

Horris felt a chill climb up his spine. Biggar sounded awfully sure of himself. The big house suddenly felt much larger than it really was, and the silence that settled into it was immense. The riotous cries of the approaching mob disappeared as if swallowed whole. It seemed to Horris that he could sense a dark presence lifting out of the ether behind him, a shadowy form that coalesced and then whispered with sullen insistence, *Turn around, Horris, turn around!*

Horris took a deep breath in an effort to stop shaking. He had the sinking feeling that somehow, once again, things were getting out of control. He shook his head stubbornly. "I won't look," he snapped—and then added maliciously, "you stupid bird!"

Biggar cocked his head. "He's reeeeeaching for you," the myna hissed.

Something feather-light brushed Horris Kew's shoulder, and he whirled about in terror.

There was nothing there.

Or almost nothing. There was a faint something, a darkening of the light, a small waver of movement, a hint of a stirring in the air.

Horris blinked. No, not even that, he amended with satisfaction. Nothing.

Outside, shouting rose up suddenly from the edge of the gardens. Horris turned. The faithful had caught sight of him through the open door and were trampling through the bedding plants and rosebushes and heading for the gate. They carried sharp objects and were making threatening gestures with them.

Horris walked quickly to the door, closed and locked it, and turned back to Biggar. "That's it for you," he said. "Good-bye and good luck."

He walked quickly through the foyer and down the hall past a parlor and a library sitting room to the kitchen at the back of the house. He could smell fresh wax on the pegged oak floors, and on the kitchen table sat a vase of scarlet roses. He took in the smells and colors as he passed, thinking of better times, regretting how quickly life changed when you least expected it. It was a good thing he was flexible, he decided. It was fortunate that he had foresight.

"Where are we going?" Biggar asked, flying up next to him, curious enough to risk a possible blow. "I assume you have a plan."

Horris gave him a look that would have frosted a small child at play in midsummer. "Of course I have a plan. It does not, however, include you."

"That is mean, Horris. And small-minded as well." Biggar flew ahead and swung back, circling the far end of the kitchen. "Beneath you, really."

"Very little is beneath me at this point," Horris declared. "Especially where you are concerned."

He went to a pantry, pulled open the doors, reached in, triggered the release for the panel behind, and stepped back as the whole assemblage swung open with a ponderous effort. It took a few seconds; the panel was lined with steel.

Biggar swooped down and landed on the top of the open pantry door. "I am your child, Horris," he lamented disingenuously. "I have been like a son to you. You cannot desert me."

· Horris glanced up. "I disown you. I disinherit you. I banish you from my sight forever."

From the front of the house came a pounding of fists on the locked door followed rather swiftly by a breaking of glass. Horris tugged nervously on one ear. No, there would be no reasoning with this bunch. The faithful had become a ragged mob of doughheads. Fools discovering their own lack of wit were famous for reverting to form. Would they be sadder but wiser for the experience? he wondered. Or would they simply stay stupid to the end? Not that it mattered.

He had to stoop to pass through the opening behind the panel, which was well under his six-foot-eight height. He had raised all the other doors in the house when he had renovated it. He had told everyone that Skat Mandu needed his space.

Inside was a stairway leading down. He triggered the release once more, and the heavy steel panel swung slowly back into place. Biggar flew through just as the door sealed and sped down the stairwell after Horris.

"He was there behind you, you know," the bird snapped, flying so close he brushed the other's face with his wing tip. Horris lashed out with one hand, but missed. "Just for a minute, he was there."

"Sure he was," Horris muttered, still a little unnerved by the experience, angry all over again for being reminded of it.

Biggar darted past. "Trying to blame me for your mistakes won't save you. Besides, you need me!"

Horris groped for the light switch against the shadowed wall as he reached the bottom of the stairs. "Need you for what?"

"Whatever it is you are planning to do." Biggar flew on into the dark, smug in the knowledge that his eyesight was ten times better than Horris's.

"Rather confident of that, aren't you?" Horris cursed silently as his searching fingers snagged on a splinter of wood.

"If for nothing else, you need me as a cheering section. Face it, Horris. You cannot stand not having an audience. You require someone to admire your cleverness, to applaud your planning." Biggar was a voice in the dark. "What is the purpose of concocting a well-devised scheme if there is no one to appreciate its intrinsic brilliance? How shallow the victory if there is no one to hail its masterful execution!" The bird cleared his throat. "Of course, you need me, too, to help with your new plan. What is it, anyway?"

Horris found the light switch and flicked it on. He was momentarily blinded. "The plan is to get as far away from you as possible."

The basement spread away through a forest of timbered pillars that held up the flooring of the old manor house and cast their shadows in dark columns through the spray of yellow light. Horris marched ahead resolutely, hearing pounding now on the steel panel above. Well, let's see what they can do with that! he sneered. He wound his way through the timbers to a corridor that tunneled back into shadow. Another light switch triggered a row of overheads, and stooping again to avoid the low ceiling, he started down the passageway.

Again Biggar passed him by, a fleet black shadow. "We belong together, Horris. Birds of a feather and all. Come on. Tell me where we're going."

"No."

"Very well, be mysterious if you must. But you admit we are still a team, don't you?"

"No."

"You and me, Horris. How long have we been together now? Think about all we've been through."

Horris thought, mostly about himself. Hunched down in a crablike stance as he angled through the narrow tunnel, legs bent, arms cranked in, nose plowing through musty air and dusty gloom, ears fanned out like an elephant's, he considered the road he had traveled in life to arrive at this moment. It had been a twisty one, rife with potholes and sudden curves, slicked over with rain and sleet, brightened now and again with brief stretches of sunlight.

Horris had a few things going for him in life, but none of them had served him very well. He was smart enough, but when the chips were down he always seemed to lack some crucial piece of information. He could reason things through, but his conclusions frequently seemed to stop one step short. He possessed an extraordinary memory, but when he called upon it for help he could never seem to remember what counted.

Skill-wise, he was a minor conjurer—not a magician who pulled rabbits out of hats, but one of a very few in the whole world who could do real magic. Which was because he was not from this world in the first place, of course, but he tried not to dwell on that point since his abilities were somewhat marginal when measured against those of his fellow practitioners.

Mostly, Horris was an opportunist. To be an opportunist one needed an appreciation for the possibilities, and Horris knew about possibilities better than he knew about almost anything. He was forever considering how something might be turned to his advantage. He was convinced that the wealth of the world—of any world—had been created for his ultimate benefit. Time and space were irrelevant; in the end, everything belonged to him. His opinion of himself was extreme. He, better than anyone, understood the fine art of exploitation. He alone could analyze the weaknesses that were indigenous to all creatures and determine how they might be mined. He was certain his insight approached prescience, and he took it as his mission in life to improve his lot at the expense of almost everyone. He possessed a relentless passion for using people and circumstance to achieve this end. Horris cared not a whit for the misfortune of others, for moral conventions, for noble causes, the environment, stray cats and dogs, or little children. These were all concerns for lesser beings. He cared only for himself, for his own creature comforts, for twisting things about when it suited him, and for schemes that reinforced his continuing belief that all other life-forms were impossibly stupid and gullible.

Thus the creation of Skat Mandu and his cult of fervid followers, believers in a twenty-thousand-year-old wise man's words as channeled by a myna.

Even now, it made Horris smile.

Horris admitted to only one real character flaw, and that was a nagging inability to keep things under his control once he started them in motion.

Somehow even the most carefully considered and well planned of his schemes ended up taking on a life of their own and leaving him stranded somewhere along the way. And even though it was never his fault, it seemed that he was always, inexplicably, being relegated to the role of scapegoat.

He reached the end of the corridor and stepped into a thirty-foot-square room which housed stacks of folding tables and chairs and crates of Skat Mandu pamphlets and reading material. The tools of his trade, enough fodder for a fine bonfire.

He looked beyond the mounds of useless inventory to the single steel-lined door at the far side of the room and sighed wearily. Beyond that door was a tunnel that ran for almost a mile underneath the compound to a garage, a silver and black 4WD Land Cruiser, and safety. A careful planner was never without a bolt hole in case things went haywire, as they had just done here. He had not expected to put this one to use quite so soon, but circumstances had conspired against him once again. He grimaced. He supposed it was a good thing that he was always prepared for the worst, but it was an annoying way to live.

He glared purposefully at Biggar, who was perched on the crates safely out of reach. "How many times have I warned you against giving in to acts of conscience, Biggar?"

"Many," Biggar replied, and rolled his eyes.

"To no purpose, it seems."

"I'm sorry. I am only a simple bird."

Horris considered that mitigating circumstance. "I suppose you expect another chance, don't you?"

Biggar lowered his head to keep from snickering. "I would be most grateful, Horris."

Horris Kew's gangly frame bent forward suddenly in the manner of a crouched wolf. "This is the last time I ever want to hear of Skat Mandu, Biggar. The last. Sever whatever lingering relationship you share with our former friend right now. No more private revelations. No more voices from the distant past. From this moment on, you listen only to me. Got it?"

The myna sniffed. Horris didn't understand anything, but there wasn't any point in telling him so. "I hear and obey."

Horris nodded. "Good. Because if it happens again, I will have you stuffed and mounted."

His wintry gray eyes conveyed the depth of his feelings far more eloquently than his words, and Biggar's beak clacked shut on the snappy retort he was about to make.

From far back in the cellar came a rending sound—the prying of nailed wood away from its seating. Horris stared. The faithful were tearing up the floorboards! The steel door had not deterred them as completely as he had anticipated. He felt a tightening of his breathing passages as he hurried not

toward the tunnel door but through the crates and furniture to a series of pictures bolted to the wall. He reached the fake Degas, touched a pair of studs in
the gilt frame, and released the casing. It swung away on concealed hinges to
reveal a combination safe. Horris worked the dial feverishly, listening to the
sounds of the enraged mob as he did so, and when he heard the catch release,
he swung open the layered steel door.

He reached inside and withdrew an intricately carved wooden box.

"Hope springs eternal," he heard Biggar snicker.

Well, it did, he supposed—at least in this instance. The box was his greatest treasure—and he had no idea what it was. He had conjured it up quite by
accident shortly after coming into this world, one of those fortuitous twists of
fate that occur every so often in the weaving of spells. He had recognized the
importance of the box right from the first. This was a creation of real magic,
the carvings ancient and spell-laden, rife with secret meaning. Something was
sealed inside, something of great power. The Tangle Box, he had named it, impressed by the weave of symbols and script that ringed its surface. It was
seamless and lidless, and nothing he did would release its secrets. Now and
again he thought he could hear something give in its bindings, in the seals that
bound it close about, but conjure though he might the box defied his best efforts to uncover what lay within.

Still, it was his best and most important treasure from this world, and he
was not about to leave it to those cretins who followed.

He tucked the Tangle Box under his arm and hastened on across the room,
weaving through the obstacle course of spare furniture and worthless litera-
ture to reach the tunnel door. There he worked with a steady hand a second
combination dial set close against a lever that secured the door's heavy locks,
heard them release, and shoved down.

The lever did not budge.

Horris Kew frowned, looking a little like a truant caught out of school. He
spun the dial angrily and tried the combination again. Still the lever would not
budge. Horris was sweating now, hearing shouts to go along with the tearing
up of floorboards. He tried the combination again and yet again. Each time, he
clearly heard the lock release. Each time, the lever refused to move.

Finally his frustration grew so great that he stepped back and starting kicking at the door. Biggar watched impassively. Horris began swearing, then
jumping up and down in fury. Finally, after one last futile try at freeing the inexplicably recalcitrant lever, he sagged back against the door, resigned to his
fate.

"I can't understand it," he murmured woodenly. "I test it myself almost
every day. Every day. And now it won't work. Why?"

Biggar cleared his throat. "You can't say I didn't warn you."

"Warn me? Warn me about what?"

"At the risk of incurring your further displeasure, Horris—Skat Mandu. I told you he was displeased."

Horris stared up at him. "You are obsessing, Biggar."

Biggar shook his head, ruffled his feathers, and sighed. "Let's cut to the chase, shall we, Horris? Do you want to get out of here or not?"

"I want to get out," Horris Kew admitted bleakly. "But . . ."

Biggar cut him short with an impatient wave of one wing. "Just listen, all right? Don't interrupt, don't say anything. Just listen. Whether you like it or not, I am in fact in touch with the real Skat Mandu. I did have a revelation, just as I told you. I have reached into the beyond and made contact with the spirit of a wise man and warrior of another time, and he is the one we call Skat Mandu."

"Oh, for cripes sake, Biggar!" Horris could not help himself.

"Just listen. He has a purpose in coming to us, a purpose of great importance, though he has not yet revealed to me what that purpose is. What I do know is that if we want out of this basement and away from that mob, we must do as he says. Not much is required. A phrase or two of conjuring, nothing more. But you must say it, Horris. You."

Horris rubbed his temples and thought about the madness that ran deep within the core of all human experience. Surely this was the apex. His voice dripped with venom. "What must I say, O mighty channeler?"

"Skip the sarcasm. It's wasted on me. You must speak these words. 'Rashun, oblight, surena! Larin, kestel, maneta! Ruhn!'"

Horris started to object, then caught himself. One or two of the words he recognized, and they were most definitely words of power. The others he had never heard, but they had the feel of conjuring and the weight of magic. He clutched the Tangle Box against his chest and stared up at Biggar. He listened to the sounds of the mob's pursuit, louder now, the flooring breached and the basement open. Time was running out.

Fear etched deep lines in his narrow face. His resistance gave way. "All right." He rose and straightened. "Why not?" He cleared his throat. "Rashun, oblight, sur—"

"Wait!" Biggar interrupted with a frantic flutter of wings. "Hold out the box!"

"What?"

"The Tangle Box! Hold it out, away from you!"

Horris saw it all now, the truth behind the secret of the box, and he was both astonished and terrified by what it meant. He might have thrown down the box and run for his life if there had been somewhere to run. He might have resisted Biggar's command if there had been another to obey. He might have done almost anything if presented with another set of circumstances, but life seldom gives you a choice in pivotal moments and so it was now.

Horris held out the box before him and began to chant. "Rashun, oblight, surena! Larin, kestel, maneta! Ruhn!"

Something hissed in Horris Kew's ears, a long, slow sigh of satisfaction laced with pent-up rage and fury and the promise of slow revenge. Instantly the room's light went from white-gold to wicked green, a pulsing reflection of some color given off deep within a primeval forest where old growth still holds sway and clawed things yet patrol the final perimeters of their ancient world. Horris would have dropped the Tangle Box if his hands would have obeyed him, but they seemed inexplicably locked in place, his fingers turned to claws about the carved surface, his nerve endings tied to the sudden pulse of life that rose from within. The top of the box simply disappeared and from out of its depths rose a wisp of something Horris Kew had thought he would never see again.

Fairy mists.

They rose in a veil and settled across the steel door that blocked entry to the tunnel, masking it like paint, then dissolving it until nothing remained but a vague hint of shadows at play against a black-holed nothingness.

"Hurry!" Biggar hissed at his ear, already speeding past. "Go through before it closes!"

The bird was gone in an instant, and his disappearance seemed to propel Horris Kew on as well, flinging himself after, still carrying the once-treasured box. He could have looked into it now to see what was hidden there. It was lidless, and he could have peeked to discover its secret. Once he would have given anything to do so. Now he dared not.

He went through the veil, through the web of fairy mists come somehow out of his past, eyes wide and staring, thinking to find almost anything waiting, to have almost anything happen. There was a sudden vision of vanishing gold coins and fading palatial grounds, the bitter tally of his losses, the sum total of five wasted years. It was there and then gone. He found himself in a corridor that lacked floor or ceiling or walls, a thin light that he swam through like a netted fish seeking to escape its trap. There was no movement around him, no sound, no sense of being or time or place, only the passage and the frightening belief that any deviation would see him lost forever.

What have I done? he asked himself in terror and dismay.

No answer came, and he struggled on like a man coated in hardening mud, the freeze of night working down to the marrow of his bones, the cold of his fate a certainty that whispers wretchedly of lost hope. He thought he could see Biggar, thought he could hear the bird's paralyzed squawk, and took heart from the fervent hope that the miserable creature's suffering was greater than his own.

And then abruptly the mists were gone, and he was free of the paralytic light. It was night, and the night was velvet black, the warm air filled with pleasant smells and reassuring sounds. He stood upon a plain, the grasses thick and soft against his feet and ankles, their windswept flow running on like an ocean toward distant mountains. He glanced skyward. Eight moons glowed brightly—mauve, peach, burnt rose, jade, beryl, sea green, turquoise, and white. Their colors mixed and flooded down upon the sleeping land.

It can't be!

Biggar emerged from somewhere behind him, flying rather unsteadily, lighting on the nearest of a cluster of what appeared to be small pin oaks colored bright blue. He shook himself, preened briefly, and glanced around.

When he saw the moons, he jumped a foot. "Awk!" he croaked, forgetting himself momentarily. He spit in distaste and shivered. "Horris?" he whispered. His eyes were as wide as saucers, no small feat for a bird. "Are we where I think we are?"

Horris was unable to answer. He was unable to speak at all. He simply stared skyward, then around at the landscape, then down at his feet, then at the rune-scripted surface of the Tangle Box, lidded once more and closed away.

Landover! This was Landover!

"Welcome home, Horris Kew," a low hiss came from over his shoulder—insidious, pervasive, and as cold as death.

Horris felt his heart drop to his feet. This time when he turned around, there really was something waiting.

CHILD

Ben Holiday came awake slowly, languidly, and smiled. He could feel Willow's deliberate stillness next to him. He knew without having to look that she was watching him. He knew it as well as he knew that he loved her more than his own life. He was facing away from her in the bed, turned on his side toward the open windows where dawn's faint light crept through to dapple the shadowed bedchamber with patches of silver, but he knew. He reached back for her and felt her fingers close over his hand. He breathed deeply of summer air fresh with the smell of forest trees, grasses, and flowers and thought how lucky he was.

"Good morning," he whispered.

"Good morning," she replied.

He let his eyes open all the way then, rolled over on his other side, and propped himself up on his elbow. She faced him from inches away, her eyes enormous in the pale light, her emerald hair cascading down about her face and over her shoulders, her skin smooth and flawless, as if she were impervious to age and time. He was always stunned by how beautiful she was, a sylph born of a woodland nymph and a water sprite, an impossibility in the world from which he had come, but merely a wondrous truth here in Landover.

"You were watching me," he said.

"I was. I was watching you sleep. I was listening to you breathe."

Her pale green skin seemed dark and exotic in the early half light, and when she stirred beneath the covers she had the look of a cat, sleek and silky. He considered how long they had been together, first as companions, then as husband and wife. How mysterious she still seemed. She embodied all the things he loved about this world—its beauty, mystery, magic, and wonder. She was these and so much more, and when he woke like this and saw her, he thought he might have somehow mixed up dreaming with real life.

It was a little more than two years since he had come to Landover, a journey between worlds, between lives, between fates. He had come in desperation, unhappy with the past, anxious for a different future. He had left his high rise in Chicago for a castle called Sterling Silver. He had given up his law practice to become a King. He had buried the ghosts of his dead wife and unborn child and found Willow. He had bought a magic kingdom out of a Christmas catalog when he knew full well that such a thing could not possibly exist, taking a chance nevertheless that perhaps it might, and the gamble had paid off. None of it had come easy, of course. A transition of worlds and lives and fates never does. But Ben Holiday had fought the battles his journey required of him and won them all, so now he was entitled to stay, to lay claim to his new life and world and fate, and to be King of a place that he had believed once upon a time to be only a dream.

To be Willow's husband, lover, and best friend, he added, when he had given up on the possibility that he could ever be any of those things to a woman again.

"Ben," she said, drawing his eyes to her own. There was warmth there, but something else, too—something he could not quite define. Expectation? Excitement? He wasn't sure.

He shifted higher on his elbow, feeling her hand tighten about his.

"I am carrying your child," she said.

He stared. He didn't know what he had expected her to say, but it definitely wasn't that.

Her eyes glistened. "I have suspected as much for several days, but it was not until last night that I was able to make certain. I tested myself in the way of the fairy people, kneeling among the garden's columbine at midnight, touching two vines to see if they would respond. When they reached for each other and entwined themselves, I knew. It has happened as the Earth Mother once foretold."

Ben remembered then. They were engaged in the search for the black unicorn and each had, on separate occasions, gone to the Earth Mother for help in the quest. She had told them then that they were important to her and specifically charged Ben with protecting Willow. When the quest was finished and the secret of the unicorn discovered, Willow had revealed to Ben what the Earth Mother had confided in her—that one day they would share a child. Ben had not known what to think then. He was still haunted by the ghost of Annie and not yet certain of his future with Willow. He had forgotten the Earth Mother's prophecy since, preoccupied with the business of being King and lately of dealing with the old King's son, Michel Ard Rhi, who had almost succeeded in stealing away the medallion that gave Ben power over the Paladin, the King's champion. Without the Paladin, Ben could not continue as Landover's King. Without the medallion, Ben would have a tough time just staying alive.

But all that was past now, the threats posed by the appearance of the black unicorn and Michel Ard Rhi ended, and what surfaced from the memories of those events was the Earth Mother's prophecy, a promise of yet another change in an already indelibly changed life.

Ben shook his head. "I don't know what to say." Then he caught himself, his eyes snapping up. "Yes I do. I know what to say. It's the most wonderful news I can imagine. I thought I would never have a child after Annie died. I had given up on everything. But finding you . . . And now hearing this . . ." His smile broadened and he almost laughed at himself. "Maybe I don't know what to say after all!"

She smiled back, radiant. "I think you do, Ben. The words are mirrored in your eyes."

He reached over and pulled her close to him. "I'm very happy."

He thought momentarily of what it would be like to be a father, to have a child to raise. He had tried to imagine it once, long ago, and had since given up. Now he would begin again. The impact of the responsibilities he faced sent him spinning. It would be hard work, he knew. But it would be wonderful.

"Ben," she said quietly, drawing away so that he could see her face. "Listen to me a moment. There are things you have to understand. You are no longer in your world. Everything is different here. This child's coming to life will be different. The child itself will likely not be what you expect . . ."

"Wait a minute," he interrupted. "What are you saying?"

Her gaze fell, then lifted again, steady but uneasy. "We are from two different worlds, Ben, from two different lives, and this child is a joining of both, something that has never happened before."

"Is the baby in some sort of danger?" he asked hurriedly.

"No."

"Then nothing else matters. It will be ours, whatever the mix of its blood and history. It will be the best of both of us."

Willow shook her head. "But each world remains a mystery in some ways, yours to me, mine to you, and the differences cannot always be easily explained or understood . . ."

He put a finger to her lips. "We'll work it out. All of it." He was firm, insistent. He misread entirely the nature of her concern and brushed her words aside in his haste to experience the euphoria he was feeling. "A baby, Willow! I want to go tell someone about this! I want to tell everyone! C'mon! Let's get up!"

He was out of bed in an instant, springing up and rushing about, pulling on his clothes, charging to the window and yelling wildly with glee, coming back to kiss her over and over. "I love you," he said. "I'll love you for ever and ever."

He was dressed and out the door before she had even left the bed, and the words that perhaps she would have spoken to him were left forever unsaid.

He went down the castle stairs two at a time, bounding as if he were a child himself, humming and talking and whistling, buoyant as a cork. He was a man of average size with a hawk nose and frosty blue eyes. His brownish hair had begun to recede slightly, but his face and hands were smooth and taut. He had been a boxer when he was younger, and he still trained regularly. He was lean and fit and moved easily. He was approaching forty when he first crossed into Landover, but he didn't know how old he was anymore. He sometimes felt as if he had quit aging altogether. This morning he was certain of it. He could feel the pulse of Sterling Silver beneath his feet, the beat of her heart, of her lifeblood, of her soul. He could feel the warmth of her stones and mortar, the whisper of her breath in the fresh morning air. She was alive, the home of Landover's Kings, a thing of such magic that she sustained herself and relied only on the presence of a Master to function. When Ben had first come to her, twenty years of neglect had reduced her to a tarnished wreck. Now she was restored, polished and shining and vibrant, and he could sense her thoughts as clearly as his own when he was safe within her walls.

He could feel her joy for him now as he skipped off the stairs and headed for the dining hall. He could hear her wish for his unborn child's long life and happiness.

A child, he thought over and over. *My child.*

He was getting used to the idea a whole lot more quickly than he would have believed possible.

It occurred to him as he entered the dining hall, with its tapestry-hung walls and its long trestle table already set and occupied, that he should have waited for Willow—that he should still wait, for that matter—before delivering the news. But he didn't think he could do that. He didn't think he could help himself.

Abernathy and Bunion sat at the table. Abernathy, the Court Scribe, was a man who had been turned into a soft-coated Wheaten Terrier by a bit of misguided magic and forced to stay that way. Abernathy was shaggy-faced and splendidly dressed, possessed of human hands and feet and able to talk better than most regular humans. Bunion, the King's messenger, was a kobold who, so far as anyone knew, had never been turned into anything other than what he was. Bunion was monkey-faced and gnarled with sharp teeth and a smile that belonged on an interested shark. The one quality they shared was an unswerving loyalty to Ben and the throne.

They paused in unison with forks raised to mouth as they saw the High Lord's face on entering.

"Good morning, good morning!" he beamed.

The forks stayed poised. A mix of astonishment and suspicion crossed their faces. Two sets of eyes blinked.

Abernathy recovered first. "Good morning, High Lord," he greeted. He paused. "Slept well, I trust?"

Ben came forward, ebullient to his toes. The china and glassware glittered, and the smell of hot food rose from the silver serving trays. Parsnip, the cook and other kobold who served the throne, had outdone himself again. Or at least it seemed that way to Ben in his euphoria. He snatched up a small apple muffin and popped it into his mouth on his way to his seat. He glanced about for Questor Thews, but the wizard was nowhere in sight. Maybe he should wait, he thought. Questor's absence gave him a reason. Wait for Questor and Willow. Call in Parsnip from the kitchen. That way the announcement could be made to everyone at the same time. That seemed like a good idea. Just wait. That's what he would do.

"Guess what?" he said.

Abernathy and Bunion exchanged a hasty glance. "I have to tell you, High Lord, that I am not particularly fond of guessing games," declared his scribe. "And Bunion hates them."

"Oh, come on. Guess!"

"Very well." Abernathy gave a large, put-upon sigh. "What?" he asked compliantly.

Ben took a deep breath. "I can't tell you. Not yet. But it's good news. It's wonderful news!"

Bunion showed a few teeth and muttered something unintelligible. Abernathy went back to eating. "Be sure to let us know when you feel the moment is right."

"As soon as Questor gets here," Ben advised, seating himself. "And Willow. And Parsnip. Everyone. Don't leave until they get here."

Abernathy nodded. "I'm glued to my seat, High Lord. By the way, I hope this announcement will take place before this morning's scheduled land-use planning meeting with the representatives of the Greensward and the River Country?"

Ben slapped his forehead. "I'd forgotten!"

"And the noon lunch with the new district judges you appointed for the northern lands?"

"I'd forgotten that, too!"

"And this afternoon's meeting with the irrigation planning committee to start work on the deserts east of the Greensward?"

"That one I remember."

"Good. Did you also remember the meeting with the kitchen staff to discuss the ongoing disappearance of food from the larder? It is getting worse, I am afraid."

Ben frowned in annoyance. "Drat it, why did you schedule all this for today?"

"I didn't. You did. It is the beginning of a new week and you always like to start off a new week by cramming in as many projects as you can manage."

Abernathy dabbed at his mouth with his napkin. "Overscheduling. I've warned you about this before."

"Thanks for reminding me." Ben reached for a plate and shoveled food onto it from the platters. Bread with jam, eggs, and fruit. "Well, we'll get to it, all of it. There's plenty of time." He put the plate down in front of him, his mind already skipping ahead to the matters Abernathy had listed. Why, in the name of sanity, did anyone feel compelled to steal from the larder? It wasn't as if there was a food shortage. "If Willow isn't down here in a few minutes, I'll go up and get her. And Bunion can find Questor, wherever he's . . ."

At that a door was flung open at the far end of the hall leading up from the lower entry inside the castle gates, and Questor Thews appeared.

"This is the last straw, simply the last!" he declared furiously.

He strode to the table without a pause, muttering with such vehemence that those gathered were left staring. The Court Wizard wore his trademark gray robes decorated with brightly colored patches of cloth and wrapped at the waist with a crimson sash, a ragtag scarecrow figure, tall and thin, all sticks and wisps of flying beard and hair. It was immediately apparent that he might have dressed and groomed himself better—at least to the extent of new robes and a trim about the ears, as Ben had tried to suggest on more than one occasion—but he saw no reason to change what he was comfortable with and so did not. He was mild and gentle and not given over easily to fits of pique, and it was strange to see him so agitated now.

He came to a halt before them and threw back his robes as if to shed himself of whatever it was that so burdened him this beautiful summer morning. "He's back!" he announced.

"Who's back?" Ben asked.

"Back and not a bit repentant for anything he's done! There is not the least shame in him, not the least! He comes up to the gate as bold as you please and announces he's here!" Questor's face was reddening as he spoke, turning dangerously crimson. "I thought we'd seen the last of him twenty some years ago, but like the proverbial bad penny, he's turned up anew!"

"Questor." Ben tried to get a word in edgewise. "Who are you talking about?"

Questor's gaze was fierce. "I'm talking about Horris Kew!"

Now Abernathy was on his feet as well. "That trickster! He wouldn't dare come back! He was exiled! Questor Thews, you've been out in the sun too long!"

"Feel free to walk down and have a look for yourself!" Questor gave him a chilly smile. "He presents himself as a supplicant, come to ask forgiveness from the High Lord. He wants the ban of exile lifted. He wants back into Landover!"

"No!" Abernathy's exhortation came out as something very close to a growl. He wheeled on Ben, bristling. "High Lord, no! Do not see him! Refuse him entrance! Send him away immediately!"

"I wouldn't send him away if I were you!" Questor snapped, crowding forward to stand next to the dog. "I'd have him seized and thrown into the deepest, darkest prison I could find! I'd lock him up and throw away the key!"

Willow had come down the stairs and into the room and was now seating herself next to Ben. She gave him a questioning stare as she listened, but he could only shrug to indicate his own lack of understanding.

"Hold up a minute," he interjected finally. Bunion was the only one who wasn't giving any indication of what he thought, sitting across from Ben with that disconcerting grin on his face. "I'm not following any of this. Who is Horris Kew?"

"Your worst nightmare!" Abernathy sniffed, as if that explained everything.

Questor Thews was only slightly more eloquent. "I'll tell you who he is. Horris Kew is the biggest troublemaker who ever lived! A conjurer of a very minor sort, one with just enough magic to get into mischief. I thought we were rid of him, but I should have known better! Abernathy, remember the cow episode?"

"The cow episode?" Ben asked.

Consumed by his tirade, Questor wasn't listening. "Horris claimed he was trying to establish communication with the cows to permit better control over their milking habits, and things got out of hand. His conjuring efforts drove the poor beasts to a frenzy. They broke loose country-wide and trampled down the entire wheat harvest and several towns in the bargain. It was the same with the chickens. The next thing you know he's subverted the evolutionary process, and they're flying like birds and dropping eggs all over the place."

Ben grinned. "What?"

"And don't forget about the cats!" Abernathy snapped. "He found a way to organize them into hunting packs in some harebrained scheme to rid the country of mice and rats, but it backfired and they ended up hunting dogs!" He shivered.

"That was bad," Questor agreed, nodding emphatically at Ben. "But the worst thing he did, the thing that got him banished, was to conjure up that fast-growing plant that took seed overnight and turned everything within fifty miles of Sterling Silver into a jungle!" Questor folded his arms defiantly. "It took weeks to cut a way through it! And while it was being cut down, while the King and his court were trapped in the castle, Abaddon's demons took advantage of the Paladin's absence to raid the countryside in earnest. Dozens of towns, farms, and lives were lost. It was a mess."

"I don't get it," Ben admitted. "What was all this supposed to accomplish? It sounds like he might have had good intentions."

"Good intentions?" Questor Thews was livid. "I hardly think so! These were schemes of extortion! The cows and chickens and cats and plants were levers with which to pry loose the purse strings of those with money! Horris Kew never cared a thing about anyone but himself! Ten minutes after one scheme collapsed, he was already hatching a new one! Excuse the choice of words."

"But, Questor, this was more than twenty years ago, you said." Ben was trying hard not to laugh.

"There, you see?" Questor snapped irritably, the other's facial contortions not escaping his notice. "Horris Kew always seems harmless enough, just a bit of an annoyance. No one takes him seriously. Even my brother ignored him until that last bit with the demons, and then Meeks wanted him gone, too. Seems the unexpected appearance of the demons interfered with one of his own schemes, and my brother could tolerate almost anything but that."

Meeks—Questor Thews's brother, the Court Wizard before him, the man who had tricked Ben into coming into Landover and thereafter become his worst enemy. Gone, but hardly forgotten. He would surely not suffer a man like Horris Kew to cross up his plans.

"Anyway," Questor finished, "my brother persuaded the old King to banish Horris, so Horris was banished, and that was that."

"Uh-huh." Ben rubbed his chin. "Banished to where?"

Questor looked decidedly uncomfortable. "To your world, High Lord," he admitted reluctantly.

"To Earth? For the last twenty years?" Ben tried to remember reading anything about someone named Horris Kew.

"A favorite dumping ground for rejects and annoyances, I'm afraid. Not much you can do with magic where there's so little belief in its existence, you know."

Abernathy nodded solemnly. They stood staring at Ben, apparently out of steam, waiting for a response. Ben looked at Willow, who was eating now and refused to look back, and he remembered that he had wanted to tell his friends about the baby. He guessed that would have to wait.

"Well, why don't we hear what he has to say," Ben suggested, rather curious about someone who could upset even the normally unflappable Abernathy. "Maybe he's changed."

Questor went from crimson to flaming scarlet. "Changed? When cows fly!" He stopped, apparently thinking that where Horris was concerned perhaps that wasn't qualification enough. "Never, High Lord!" he amended, just to make things perfectly clear. "Don't see him. Don't let him set one foot into this castle. I would have sent the guard to greet him on the road if I had known he was coming. I still cannot believe he had the gall to return!" He paused, suddenly perplexed. "In fact, how *did* he return?"

"Doesn't matter. He is a supplicant," Ben pointed out patiently. "I can't be sending supplicants away without even speaking to them. What sort of precedent would that set? I have to at least speak to him. What can it hurt?"

"You don't know, High Lord," Abernathy said ominously.

"You really don't," Questor agreed.

"Get rid of him right now."

"Don't let him within a mile of you."

Ben pursed his lips. He had never heard his advisors so adamant about any-thing. He did not see how a simple conversation could cause problems for him, but he was not inclined to dismiss their warning out of hand.

"Do you believe that your magic is a match for his?" he asked Questor after a moment.

Questor drew himself up. "More than a match. But he is a very slippery character."

Ben nodded. "Well, I can't just send him away. Why don't we all see him together. That way you can warn me if he tries anything. How about it?"

Abernathy sat down without a word. Questor stiffened even further, but finally nodded his agreement. "Don't say I didn't warn you," he declared curtly, and signaled to a retainer standing at the far end of the hall.

They sat in silence then, waiting. Ben reached for Willow's hand and squeezed it gently. She smiled back at him. At the far end of the room, Parsnip appeared from out of the kitchen, gave a brief greeting to the silent assem-blage, and disappeared back in again. Ben was thinking that he would like to dispose quickly of Horris Kew and get on with his day. He was thinking about the meetings he had scheduled and the work that needed doing. He had be-lieved once that no one worked harder than a trial lawyer, but he had since dis-covered that Kings did. There were constant decisions required, plans to consider, and problems by the score to resolve. So much depended on him. So many people were affected by his actions. He liked the challenge, but was con-tinually daunted by the amount of responsibility. Sometimes he thought about the circumstances that had brought him to this place in his life and wondered that such a thing could happen. It was proof that anything was possible. He would measure where he was from where he had been and be amazed. He would measure, and he would tell himself once again that however severe the pressures and demands he would never exchange his present life for his past.

"You could still change your mind about this, High Lord," Questor advised quietly, not quite ready to let the argument die.

But Ben was still thinking about his life, applied the comment accordingly, and found the wizard's assessment wrong. He was a man who had rediscov-ered himself by daring to take a chance that others would not have, and chang-ing his mind now was not a reasonable option. He was going to be a *father,* he thought with renewed amazement. What would that be like for a man who had passed his fortieth year with no children? What would it be like for a man who'd had no sense of family for so long? He wanted a child, but he had to admit that he didn't know if he was ready for one.

There was a clomping of boots at the far end of the room, and a man entered. He was tall and gangly and strange-looking. He had arms and legs that were akimbo, and a nose, ears, and Adam's apple that stuck out like they were parts attached to a Mister Potato Head. He was dressed in gray supplicant's robes that looked like they had seen service last as floor mats in a stable. His feet were dusty and bare, his hands were clasped before him beseechingly, and his body was stooped. He came forward at something approaching a weary shuffle, his head bobbing. A bird with black feathers and a white crest sat on his shoulder, bright eyes searching.

"High Lord," Horris Kew greeted, and dropped to his knees. "Thank you for agreeing to see me."

Ben rose, thinking to himself that this fellow was the most harmless-looking threat he had ever seen. "Stand up," he ordered. "Let's hear what you have to say for yourself. Your press has been pretty bad up to now."

Horris rose, a pained look on his field-plow face. He had a rather bad tic in one eye that gave him the look of a man flinching from an imagined blow. "I confess everything, High Lord. I have done all that I am accused of doing. Whatever Questor Thews and Abernathy have told you, I admit. I don't propose to argue any of it. I just want to ask forgiveness."

Questor snorted. "What are you up to, Horris Kew? You're up to something."

"Awk! Biggar is better!" the bird squawked.

"That bird looks familiar," Abernathy declared, squinting darkly at Biggar.

"Just a common myna, my companion on the road." The tic in Horris Kew's eye twitched double-time.

Abernathy frowned. "I suppose you've trained him to attack dogs?"

"Awwwkk! Fleas! Fleas!" the bird cried.

Ben came around the table to put himself between Abernathy and the bird. "Aren't you supposed to be in exile, Horris? What brings you back?"

"High Lord, I simply want another chance." A truly penitent look settled across Horris Kew's angular face. "I have had twenty years to repent, to consider my mistakes, to think about my misconduct. I was lucky I escaped Landover alive, as Questor Thews can tell you. But now I wish to come back to my home and start over again. Is this possible?"

Ben studied him. "I don't know."

"Don't do it, High Lord," Questor cautioned at once.

"Don't even think about it, High Lord," Abernathy added.

"Awk! Hooray for Horris, Hooray for Horris!" the bird declared.

"Thank you, Biggar." Horris patted the bird affectionately and returned his gaze to Ben. "I have a plan, should you decide to let me return, High Lord. I ask nothing of you or anyone but to be left alone. I shall live out my life as a hermit, a bother to no one. But should the need arise, I stand ready to serve in any capacity required. I have some little knowledge of magic that may someday be of use. I offer it for when you think it appropriate. You can depend on me to come if called."

"I believe that it was your use of magic that got you in trouble the last time," Ben admonished softly.

"Yes, yes, too true. But I will not involve myself in the affairs of the country or her people unless I am asked," Horris said. Tic, tic went the bad eye. "Should I violate this covenant, you may restore the ban immediately."

"No," Questor Thews said.

"No," Abernathy echoed.

Ben tried to keep from smiling. He should probably be taking this more seriously than he was, he thought, but it was hard to get too excited over someone who looked like this fellow and whose worst offense was making chickens fly and cows rebel against farmers.

"Awk! Pretty lady," the bird whistled suddenly.

Willow smiled and glanced at Ben. He remembered the child.

"I will think about it and give you an answer in several days," Ben announced, ignoring the groans from Questor and Abernathy. "You can come back then."

"Happily, High Lord," Horris Kew responded, bowing deeply. "Thank you, thank you. I am indebted."

He backed quickly from the room and was escorted away. Ben wondered what kind of bird Biggar was. He wondered how many words the bird could say.

"Well, that was a monumentally foolish decision!" Questor Thews snapped in disgust. "If I am permitted to say so, High Lord!"

"You are," Ben replied, since it was already said.

"There's something familiar about that bird," Abernathy muttered.

"Just because a man looks harmless doesn't mean he really is," Questor went on. "In Horris Kew's case, appearances are not just deceiving, they are an outright lie!"

Ben was already tired of the subject, and he held up his hands imploringly. "Gentlemen!" he admonished. He was hoping for looks of chagrin but had to settle for hostile silence. He sighed. You couldn't have it your way all the time, he supposed. That was why most matters required compromise. "We'll discuss this later, all right?"

Willow rose to stand beside him, and he smiled as she looped her arm through his. "Parsnip!" he yelled, and when his cook appeared to stand with his wizard, scribe, and messenger, he asked, "How would you feel about our adding another member to our family?"

"As long as it's not Horris Kew," Questor Thews muttered and looked not the least chagrined for saying it.

GORSE

Horris Kew departed Sterling Silver like a fugitive in the night, hastening away as swiftly as propriety and pride would allow, casting nervous glances left and right with every step he took. He hunched along with purposeful, ground-eating strides, his tall, gawky frame rolling and swaying with the movement, a strange figure in this strangest of lands. The tic he had mysteriously developed caused the corner of his eye to jump like a trapped cricket. Biggar rode his shoulder, an omen of doom.

"I really dislike that dog," the bird muttered, ruffling his feathers in a show of distaste.

Horris Kew's lips tightened. "Shut up about the dog."

"He almost recognized me. Did you see? He'll remember, sooner or later, mark my words."

"Consider them marked." They passed across the bridge that connected the island to the mainland and set out toward the forests west. "What's the difference if he does? Meeks is dead and gone."

Biggar had belonged to the wizard in the old days. It was Meeks who had performed the magic that enhanced Biggar's intelligence, hopeful of using the bird as a spy against his enemies. But Biggar had been as obnoxious and outspoken then as he was now, and Meeks had quickly grown tired of him. When Horris Kew had been exiled to Earth by the old King, Meeks had sent the troublesome bird along for the ride.

Biggar hunched down into a black featherball. "If the dog connects me with Meeks, Horris, you can kiss our chances of ever getting back inside those castle walls good-bye."

Horris tried to look unconcerned. "You're worrying about nothing."

"I don't care. I don't like the way the dog looked at me. In fact, I don't like any of this."

Horris didn't say so, but he wasn't sure he liked any of it either. Nothing had gone the way he had expected from the moment he had mouthed "rashun, oblight, surena, whatever" and that *thing* had come out of the Tangle Box. He shivered just thinking about it, picturing how it had looked when he had turned around on hearing its greeting, thinking of it waiting for them now. It was loathsome beyond description. It was the foulest being he had ever encountered.

And now it had taken charge of his life, ordering him about like a common servant, telling him where to go and what to do. It was his worst nightmare come to life, and Horris Kew didn't think for a moment that he had better try to cross it.

"Why do you think it sent us to see the King?" Biggar asked suddenly, as if reading his mind. They passed up the hillside and into a meadow fronting the edges of the forest trees.

Horris exhaled wearily. "How would I know? It told me to go make this pitch to Holiday, so I did. It said to do it, so I did it. You think I was going to argue?"

Biggar didn't have anything to say to that, which was just as well since Horris Kew's temper was already on edge from the events of the past twenty-four hours. This was all Biggar's fault anyway, he was thinking. The channeling scheme, the concoction of Skat Mandu (Skat Mandu, what a joke!), the releasing of that thing, and the return to Landover. Horris didn't know what game it was they were playing, but he knew it was a dangerous one, coming back to the very last place in the universe they should have come, a place where they were anything but welcome. Except, of course, that the old King was dead and this new one, Holiday, at least seemed willing to consider his petition. No matter. What were they doing here? Sure, this was his homeland and all, but it was not a place that held fond memories. It was a place in which he had been born (luck of the draw, that), had grown up, had gotten himself in considerable trouble, been declared persona non grata, and left under duress. He had been perfectly happy in his new world, in the land of milk and honey and believers of Skat Mandu ready to pay him money for a wisp of smoke and a shimmer of light. He had been well settled, content with himself, his surroundings, and his prospects.

Now what did he have? Nothing. And it was all Biggar's fault.

Except, of course, it really wasn't. It was as much his fault as Biggar's, and that made him even madder.

What was going to happen to him now? What did good old Skat Mandu have planned?

"I really don't like that dog," Biggar repeated, and finally lapsed into silence.

They journeyed on through the morning, and as midday passed they reached the Heart. The Heart was sacred ground, the wellspring of Landover's magic and the touchstone of her life. It was here that all of Landover's

Kings, including Ben Holiday, had been crowned. It appeared as a clearing amid a forest of giant broad-leaved trees, its perimeter encircled by Bonnie Blues, its floor a mix of green, gold, and crimson grasses. A dais stood center-most, formed of gleaming white oak timbers and anchored by polished silver stanchions in which massive white candles had been set. Standards ringed the dais, and from their tips flew the flags of the Kings of Landover in a sea of bright colors. Holiday's was newest, a set of balanced scales held forth against a field of green, a nod back to his years as a lawyer in the old life. All about the dais and across the remainder of the clearing were rows of white velvet kneel-ing pads and rests.

All of it was clean and perfectly kept, as if in anticipation of the next coro-nation.

Horris Kew entered the Heart and looked around solemnly. A country's history winked back at him from every polished timber and post. "Take off your hat, Biggar," he intoned. "We're in church."

Biggar looked about doubtfully, sharp eyes gleaming. "Who in the world takes care of this place?"

Horris stared at him and sighed. "What a philistine you are."

Biggar flew off his shoulder and settled down on one of the velvet rests. "So now you're resorting to name calling, are you, Horris? That's really pa-thetic."

And very deliberately he relieved himself on the white cushion.

Horris went rigid for a moment, and then his lanky frame uncoiled as if part serpent and his long limbs worked this way and that, like sticks pinned to a rag doll. "I've had about all I'm going to take from you, Biggar. How would you like me to wring your worthless neck?"

"How would you like me to peck out your eyes, Horris?"

"You imbecilic jackdaw!"

"You moronic baboon!"

They glared at each other, Horris with his fingers hooked into claws, Big-gar with his feathers ruffled and spread. The rage swept through them, then dissipated, evaporating like water on stone in the midday sun. The tension eased from their bodies and was replaced by wonder and a vague sense of un-easiness over the spontaneity of their embarrassing behavior.

"That *thing* is responsible for this foolishness," Horris announced quietly. "Good old Skat Mandu."

"He's not what I expected, I admit," Biggar declared solemnly.

"He's not even a *he*. He's an *it*."

"A maggot."

"A serpent."

Biggar closed his eyes. "Horris," he said, a note of wistfulness creeping into his bird voice. "What are we doing here? Wait, don't say anything until you've heard me out. I know how we got here. I understand the mechanics. We let that thing out of the Tangle Box where it was locked away in that patch of fairy mist, and it used the fairy mist to open a door into Landover. I got that part. But what are we doing here? Really, what? Just think about it a moment. This is a dangerous place for us."

"I know, I know," Horris sighed.

"All right, then. Why don't we go somewhere else? Somewhere less . . . threatening. Why don't we? Maybe it would listen to a suggestion that we go somewhere else. Maybe it would at least consider sending *us* through, even if *it* still wanted to stay. After all, what does it need us for?"

Horris fixed him with a hard stare. "Where would we go, Biggar? Back to where we came from, where the faithful are waiting to tear us apart? You took care of that option quite nicely."

"It wasn't me, Horris. I already told you that. It was Skat Mandu! Or whoever." Biggar hopped one rest closer. "You want to know where we can go? There are lots of choices. I've read about a few. How about that place with the yellow brick road and the emerald city and all those little people running around, the Munchies or whatever?"

Horris looked at him and sighed. "Biggar, that wasn't a real place. That was in a book."

Biggar tried frowning and failed. "No, it wasn't. It was real."

"No, Biggar. You've short-circuited again. That was Oz. Oz isn't a real place. It's a make-believe place."

"With the wizard and all? With the witches and the flying monkeys? That wasn't a story. That was real."

"It was a story, Biggar! A story!"

"All right, Horris, all right! It was a story!" The bird clacked his beak emphatically. He thought a minute. "Okay. How about going to the place with the little people with the furry feet?"

Horris turned red. "What's the use!" he hissed furiously. He strode past Biggar without looking at him, headed for the trees. "Let's just report back and get this over with!"

He moved away again, disappearing back into the forest, leaving the Heart behind. After a moment, Biggar followed. They passed out of the sunlight to where it was dark and cool, even at midday, and shadows draped their intricate patterns like spider's webs across the woodland. They traveled without speaking, Horris striding on determinedly, Biggar hopping from limb to limb, now flying ahead, now winging his way back. Locked in a brown study, Horris pointedly ignored him.

Less than a mile from the Heart, where the light was all but screened away by the interlocking branches of the trees overhead, they descended a steep slope to a dense thicket of brush backed up against a rocky overhang. Easing their way past the brush, they came to a massive flat stone into which symbols had been carved on both sides and across the top. Horris stared at the stone, sighed his weariest sigh, reached up, and touched various symbols in quick succession. He stepped back quickly as the door opened, stone grating on stone. Biggar landed on his shoulder again and together they watched the black opening of the cave beyond come into focus.

Rather reluctantly, they entered. The stone door grated shut behind them.

There was light in the cave to guide them back into its farthest reaches, a sort of dim phosphorescence that seemed wedded to the rock. It gleamed like silver ore in scattered patches and random streaks, breaking up the gloom sufficiently to allow a relatively safe passage through. It was hot within the cave, an unpleasant sort of warmth that suffused the skin and left it damp and itchy. There was a distinctive smell in the air, too. Horris and Biggar recognized it immediately and knew where it came from.

They reached the deepest part of the cave in moments, the part where the light was brightest, the heat hottest, and the stench rawest. The cave widened and rose some twenty feet at this point, and a scattering of stalactites jutted down from the ceiling like a medieval spear trap. The chamber was empty save for a rickety wooden bed set to one side and an equally rickety wooden table on which a metal washbasin sat. The bed was unmade and the basin unemptied.

Next to the wash basin sat the Tangle Box.

From the deepest corner of the cave came a stirring. "Did you do as you were told?" a voice hissed menacingly.

Horris tried to hold his breath as he spoke so as not to inhale any more of the smell than he had to. "Yes. Just as we were told."

"What was the response?"

"He said he would think it over. But the wizard and the scribe are going to try to convince him not to let me stay."

The speaker laughed. It shifted in the gloom, a lifting of its body, a straightening of its limbs. Really, it was hard to tell what was happening, which was very disconcerting. Horris thought back again to when he had laid eyes on it for the first time, realizing suddenly that he was already unsure of what it was he had seen. The thing that was Skat Mandu had a way of showing only part of itself, a flicker of body or limb or head (never face), a hint of color or shape. What you were left with, ultimately, was a sense of something rather than a definite image. What you were left with, inevitably, was unpleasant and harsh and repulsive.

"Do I frighten you?" the voice asked softly. In the smoky gloom something gleamed a wicked green.

Horris suddenly regretted coming back, thinking that perhaps Biggar had been right after all. What sort of madness was this that they had embraced in releasing the monster? It had been imprisoned in the Tangle Box, and it had tricked them into freeing it, using Biggar as channeler, Horris as conjurer, both as instruments for picking the locks that held it chained. Horris Kew understood in the most secret part of his heart that nothing he had done in creating Skat Mandu had ever really been his idea—it had all come from the *thing* in the Tangle Box, the *thing* that had been locked within the fairy mists, dispatched into exile just as they had been, and consigned to oblivion except for a fate that had brought Horris and Biggar to its unwitting rescue.

"What are we doing here?" Biggar piped up suddenly, a frightened stiffness in his reedy voice.

"What I tell you to do," the voice hissed.

Skat Mandu came out of the gloom, rising up like a cloud of smoke that had somehow coalesced into a vaguely familiar but not yet complete form. Its smell drove Horris and Biggar back a step in response, and its laugh was low and satisfied. It rippled like fetid water as it shifted about, and they could hear the hiss of its breathing in the sudden silence. It was huge and fat and dominant, and it had the feel of something ancient and terrible.

"I am called the Gorse," the monster whispered suddenly. "I was of the people who live within the fairy mists, one of their own until I was trapped and confined centuries ago, imprisoned in the Tangle Box for all time. I was a sorcerer of great power, and I will be so again. You will help me."

Horris Kew cleared his throat. "I don't see what we can do."

The Gorse laughed. "I will be your eyes, Horris Kew. I see you better than you see yourself. You are angry at losing what you had in that other world, but what you want most lies here. You are frightened at what has been done to you, but the courage you lack can be supplied by me. Yes, I manipulated you. Yes, you were my cat's paw. You will be again, you and the bird both. This is the way of things, Horris. The people of the fairy mists bound me within the Tangle Box with spells that could not be undone from within, but only from without. Someone had to speak them, and I chose you. I whispered the incantations in your mind. I guided your conjuring steps. One by one you spoke the spells of Skat Mandu. One by one you turned the keys to the locks that held me bound. When I was ready to come out, I made the bird confess that Skat Mandu was a charade so that you would be forced to flee. But your escape could only be managed by setting me free. But do not despair. It was as it should be, as it was meant to be. Fate has bound us one to the other."

Horris wasn't sure he liked the sound of that, but on the other hand he was intrigued in spite of himself with the possibility that there might be something in this for him. "You have a plan for us?" he asked cautiously.

"A very attractive plan," the Gorse whispered. "I know of your history, the both of you. You, Horris, were exiled for your vision of what conjuring should be. The bird was exiled for being more than his creator had expected."

Oddly enough, Horris and Biggar found themselves in immediate agreement with this assessment (although Biggar didn't much care for constantly being referred to as "the bird").

"You were embarrassments and nuisances to those who pretended friendship toward you but in truth feared you and were jealous of you. Such is the nature of the creatures against whom we stand." The Gorse eased back ponderously into the gloom, smoke, and shadow along the rock. The movement produced a sort of scraping sound, like a knife trimming fish scales. It should not have been possible with something that appeared to be so insubstantial. "Wouldn't you like to gain a measure of revenge on these fools?" the Gorse demanded.

Horris and Biggar would have liked nothing better, of course. But their uneasiness with the Gorse remained undiminished for all the reassuring words. They didn't like this creature, didn't like the sight or smell of it, didn't even like the idea of it, and they were still of a mind that they had been better off back where they had come from. Still, they were not foolish enough to say so. Instead, they simply waited to hear more.

The darkening atmosphere of the cave seemed to tighten down like a coffin lid as the Gorse suddenly expanded into the shadows, stealing the light. "For myself, I will secure dominion over the fairy mists from which I was sent and over those who dwelt free within them while I was imprisoned. I will have them for my slaves until I tire of them, and then I will see them closed away in such blackness that they will scream endlessly for death's release."

Horris Kew swallowed the lump in his throat and forgot about any attempt at backing farther away. On his shoulder, Biggar's claws tightened until they hurt.

"To you," the Gorse hissed softly, "I will give Landover—all of it, the whole of it, the country and her people, to do with as you choose."

The silence that filled the cave was immense. Horris found suddenly that he could not think straight. Landover? What would he do with Landover? He tried to speak and could not. He tried to swallow and could not do that either. He was dry and parched from toes to nose, and all of his conjuring life was a dim recollection that seemed as ephemeral as smoke.

"You want to give us Landover?" Biggar squeaked suddenly, as if he hadn't heard right.

The Gorse's laugh was rough and chilling. "Something even Skat Mandu could not have done for you in your exiled life, isn't that so? But to earn this gift you must do as I tell you. Exactly as I tell you. Do you understand?"

Horris Kew nodded. Biggar nodded along with him.

"Say it!" the Gorse hissed sharply.

"Yes!" they both gasped, feeling invisible fingers close about their throats. The fingers clenched and held for an impossibly long moment before they released. Horris and Biggar choked and gasped for air in the ensuing silence.

The Gorse drew back, its stench so overpowering that for a moment it seemed there was no air left to breathe. Horris Kew was down on his knees in the cave's near blackness, sick to his stomach, so frightened by the monster that he could think of nothing but doing whatever was required to keep from feeling worse. Biggar's white crest was standing on end, the sharp bird eyes were squeezed shut, and he was shaking all over.

"There are enemies who might threaten us," the Gorse whispered, its voice like the scratching of coarse sandpaper on wood. "We must remove them from our path if we are to proceed. You will help me in this."

Horris nodded without speaking, not trusting what the words might be. He wished he had learned to keep his conjuring mouth shut a whole lot earlier.

"You will write three letters, Horris Kew," the monster hissed. "You will write them now." The gloom it occupied shifted, and its eyes (or so they seemed) found Biggar. "And when he is finished, you will deliver them."

--◦∞◦--

Night descended over Sterling Silver, the sun dropping below the horizon and changing the sky to deep crimson and violet, the colors streaking first the patterned clouds west, then the land itself. The shadows lengthened, darkening ever deeper, reflecting off the polished surface of the castle and the waters that guarded it, disappearing at last into a twilight lit by the eight moons in one of the rare phases of the year in which all were visible at once in the night sky.

With Willow on his arm, Ben Holiday climbed the stairs to their bedchamber, smiling now and again at what he was feeling, still caught up by the news of their baby. A baby! He couldn't seem to say it often enough. It produced a giddy feeling in him, one that made him feel wonderful and foolish both at once. Everyone in the castle knew about the baby by now. Even Abernathy, normally not given to displays of emotion of any kind, had given Willow a huge hug on learning the good news. Questor had immediately begun making plans for the child's upbringing and education that stretched well into the next decade. No one seemed the least bit surprised that there should be a baby, as if having this child here and now was very much in the ordinary course of events.

Ben shook his head. Would there be a boy or a girl? Would there be both? Did Willow know which? Should he ask her? He wished he knew what to do besides tell her over and over again how happy he was.

They reached a landing that opened out onto a rampart, and Willow pulled him out into the starlit night. They walked to the battlement and stared out across the darkened land. They stood there in silence, holding hands, keeping close in the silence.

"I have to go away for a little while," Willow said quietly. It was so unexpected that for a moment he wasn't certain he had heard right. She did not look at him, but her hand tightened in warning over his. "Let me finish before you say anything. I must tell my mother about this child. She must know so that she can dance for me. Remember how I told you once that our life together was foretold in the entwining of the flowers that formed the bed of my conception? It was on the night when I saw you for the first time at the Irrylyn. I knew at once that there would never be anyone else for me. That was the foretelling brought about by my mother's dance."

She looked at him now, her eyes huge and depthless.

"The once-fairy see something of the future in the present, reading what will be in what now is. It is an art peculiar to each of us, Ben, and for my mother the future is often told in her dance. It was so when I went to see her in my search for the black unicorn. It will be so again now."

She seemed to have finished. "Her dance will tell us something about our child's future?" he asked in surprise.

Willow nodded slowly, her gaze fixing him, her flawless features carved in starlight. "Not us, Ben. Me. She will tell only me. She will dance only for me, not for someone who is not of her people. Please don't be angry, but I must go alone."

He smiled awkwardly. "I can come most of the way, though. At least as far as the old pines."

She shook her head. "No. Try to understand. This must be my journey, not yours. It is a journey as much into myself as into the River Country, and it belongs only to me. I make it as mother of our child and as child of the once-fairy. There will be other journeys that belong to both of us, journeys on which you will be able to go. But this one belongs to me."

She saw the doubt in his eyes and hesitated. "I know this is difficult to understand. It touches on what I tried to tell you earlier. Carrying a child to term and giving birth on Landover is not the same as in your world. There are differences that run to the magic that sustains the land, that gives life to us all but particularly to the once-fairy. We commune with Landover as a people who have spent all our lives caring for and healing her. It is our heritage and bond."

Ben nodded, but felt something drop away inside him. "I don't see why I can't go with you."

He saw her throat constrict, and there were tears in her eyes. "I know. I have tried to find a way to tell you, to explain it to you. I think that I will have to ask simply that you trust me."

"I do trust you. Always. But this is hard to understand."

And more. It was worrisome. He had not felt comfortable being separated from her since their journey back to Earth to recover Abernathy and the missing medallion, when she had almost died. He had relived all the nightmares of Annie's death, of the death of their unborn child, and of the severing of some part of himself that had come about as a result of their dying. Each time there was a separation from Willow, however necessary, however brief, the fear returned. It was no different now. If anything, the feeling was stronger because the reasons for their separation were so difficult to grasp.

"How soon must you go?" he asked, still struggling to come to grips with the idea. All of his earlier happiness seemed to have leaked away.

"Tomorrow," she said. "At sunrise."

His desperation doubled. "Well, at least take Bunion with you. Take someone for protection!"

"Ben." She held both of his hands in her own and moved so close to him that he could see himself reflected in her eyes. "No one will go with me. I will go alone. You needn't worry. I will be safe. I don't need looking after. You know that. The once-fairy have their own means of protection within Landover, and I will be in the homeland of my people."

He shook his head angrily. "I just don't see how you can be sure of that! And I still don't see why you have to go alone!"

In spite of his efforts to keep calm, his voice had risen and taken on an angry edge. He stepped away from her, trying to distance himself from what he was feeling. But she would not release his hands.

"This child is important to us," she said softly.

"I know that!"

"Shhhh. The Earth Mother told us of its importance, do you remember?"

He took a deep breath. "I do."

"Then accept that our needs must give way to those of the child," she whispered. "Even though it hurts, even though the reasons are not clear, even though we might wish it otherwise." She paused. "I do not want this any more than you do. Do you believe that?"

He was caught off guard. It had not occurred to him that she was not a willing party to this decision. "Yes, I believe it," he told her finally.

"I would have you come if it were possible. I would never leave your side for a moment if it were possible. But it is not. It is not in the nature of life that we can be together in all things."

She waited for him to speak. He stared at her wordlessly for a long time, thinking. Then he said, "I guess that's true."

"It will be all right," she told him.

She put her arms around him and held him close against her. He lowered his face into her emerald hair and found himself aching already from having her gone. His fear was a black cloud that scudded about in the corners of his heart. He realized anew how different they really were, a human and a sylph, and how much there was about her that he still didn't know.

"It will be all right," she repeated.

He did not argue, because he knew there was no point in doing so. But he could not help wondering if he shouldn't try.

ROOTS

Willow's journey from Sterling Silver was a relatively uneventful one. She departed under cover of darkness, slipping from the castle unseen and unheard. The guards of the night watch might have sensed her in some dim, quickly forgotten way, but the once-fairy retained enough of the old ways that she could disappear as surely as shadow into light. Willow went down a back staircase, through the castle's deserted halls, along the darkened walls of several inner courts, and out through the central portcullis, which was always kept raised in time of peace to welcome late travelers and supplicants to a sure and friendly shelter. Forgoing use of the lake skimmer, she instead crossed the bridge that spanned the castle moat, a bridge built by Ben when the monarchy was restored and travelers began to come again to the land's seat of power. She waited until the brightest of the moons were shadowed by clouds and the guards were turned away, speaking of things far removed from duties assigned, and in the blink of an eye she was gone.

She did not wake Ben on leaving. She stood looking down at him in the darkness for a time, watching him sleep, thinking how much she loved him. She did not want any more harsh words to pass between them. It was better that she left now. He loved her, but he was the product of a world that did not accept the existence of fairy creatures, and he was still learning to believe in them himself. That was why she had not told him everything. That was why she couldn't.

She walked for the remainder of that night and all through the next day, winding her way along lesser-traveled paths, not hurrying or attempting speed, keeping herself unseen. She passed farmers in the field, plowing and laying in their second-season crop, harvesting the first. She watched peddlers and traders come and go between the communities of man south and east. There were travelers come from the once-fairy country and from the western hills where trappers and hunters roamed. There were families in wagons with possessions stacked high and tied down en route to new homes. Everywhere, there was activity, the bustle and energy of the warm seasons facilitating the plans made when it was cold. It made her smile. She followed the rolling flow of the forested hills, a small bit of movement in a vast sea of green that undulated like waves against the horizon when the breezes blew out of the west as they did at midsummer. She ate and drank from the Bonnie Blues, Landover's most plentiful source of food and drink, and she sang softly to herself when there were only birds and small animals to hear.

She pondered as well. She weighed the wisdom of what she had done, knowing the consternation it would cause Ben, appreciative of the worry it would engender. But hers was a cause born of primal necessity, and there was no room for debate over what was required. She must have this baby in the way that nature dictated, and the pattern of birth had been established generations ago in a time when humans did not even exist. The birthing of fairy people was complex beyond that of humans in any case, peculiar in each instance to the physical characteristics of the creature involved, different for each depending on the genetics that had spawned them. She might have discussed it with Ben earlier, when the immediacy of their child's birth was removed and the requisite time for acceptance was still available. But she had not and there was no time now, and she knew him well enough to recognize that his reaction to what she would tell him was as likely to be damaging as helpful. Though Landover's King, he remained a man from another world in many ways still, and he struggled constantly to accept what he viewed as strange and unusual. It was especially hard where she was concerned because he loved her and was committed to her and wanted so to be comfortable with who and what she was. She knew that, and she did what she could to make easier the transition he was still experiencing.

In the end it had been the Earth Mother's dream that had decided her. It had not been so much a dream as a vision and not so much a vision as a sense of being. Fairy creatures spoke to each other in that way, coming often in sleep to give counsel and warning, speaking out of distant places, traveling on the back of swift winds to reach the listener, a whisper in stillness, a brightening in the dark. Willow sometimes spoke with her mother that way, her mother a wood nymph so wild that nothing could reach her if she did not wish it, a creature that not even the once-fairy could trace. Willow had slipped away from her old life as she made her new one with Ben, but now and again the old would intrude in some small fashion, and the Earth Mother's coming had been the latest reoccurrence.

The Earth Mother was an elemental, the most powerful in Landover, a creature of great magic. She was as old as the land itself and embodied its spirit. Some believed that she was the creator of the land, but Willow thought her too fundamental in her ethics and too mired in her work to be anything so lofty. Nevertheless, she was a creature to be harkened to. Ben and Willow had both gone to her during their search for the black unicorn, and she had told them then that they were important to her and would share a child that was special. There had been no explanation then or since, and after a time both had ceased to think on the matter. Willow had heard nothing from the Earth Mother in all this time.

Yet now she was summoned, unexpectedly, abruptly, out of dreams. The Earth Mother had come to her twice, calling her back to the River Country, to Elderew, to the once-fairy country where the elemental most frequently surfaced. The calling was urgent and unarguable and so had decided Willow to leave Ben without attempting a full explanation. More than the words themselves, it was the Earth Mother's tone that had compelled the sylph to put aside deliberation and act at once.

She camped that night on the shores of the Irrylyn, close by the cove where she had first encountered Ben and known in the fairy way that he was for her and she for him. She ate despite having little appetite, for her child required her strength. Then she stripped away her clothing and stepped into the Irrylyn's waters. The lake was warm and soothing and drew her into its embrace. She floated in the silence of the night, the skies overhead clear and filled with the light of colored moons and silver stars, and she let her memories of Ben envelop her. She could still feel the rush of excitement his appearance had triggered within her. She could still feel the certainty of her love. They had been chosen for each other, and until death they would be together. She had caught a glimpse of their future, for the once-fairy were so blessed (or cursed), and she had known then their lives would be changed irrevocably.

It had proven to be so. Ben had given up his old life, compelled to stay within Landover, decided by many things but by none more certain than his love for her. He had stayed as King and become a leader of strength and vision, and while he was tormented at times by what being King required of him, he had carried out his responsibilities faithfully. Most thought him fair and effective. Only a few still harbored doubts, and most of those were potential rivals for the power of the Kingdom's magic. Her father was one, the leader of the once-fairy, and a wielder of considerable magic himself. The River Master would have preferred a Kingdom in which he alone controlled the magic, but he was no fool and he recognized the benefits that Ben Holiday provided as King—a stabilizing force, a well-reasoned juggler of diverse interests, and a decisive leader—and while he mistrusted Ben on occasion as an outworlder, he respected him always as a man.

Willow, as the River Master's daughter, had lived an unsettled life in the lake country, the child of a union that had lasted but a single night, a constant reminder to the water sprite of the woman he had loved and been unable to hold. For Willow had been born of a hurried coupling and then left behind by her mother for her father to raise, her mother too wild to stay bound to anyone, even a child. Her father had done what was required and nothing more;

he had many children and liked most better than her. Ben's coming had opened the door to the life she had long known was waiting for her, and she had been quick to step through. He had questioned at first that they were meant to be together or even that he loved her, but Willow had never doubted, the prophecy of their joining immutable and fixed. Eventually what was promised at the moment of her birth had come to pass, and now there was to be a child.

She rose from the waters of the Irrylyn and stood upon its shore, her smooth green skin shedding water and drying in the cooling night air. She had not been entirely honest with Ben. She would let her mother dance for her, but then move quickly on. She would not see her father at all. She did not expect their help in the birth of this child. She might have wished it could be otherwise, but she knew there was little they could offer. She had returned to the lake country to see the Earth Mother. It was the Earth Mother alone who could provide useful insight, she sensed——for that was what the dream had whispered in summoning her. So she would go there and listen, and then she would have her child alone.

She slept long and well that night, her sleep undisturbed by dreams, and when she woke she found the mud puppy looking at her.

"Hello, little one," she greeted softly, lifting to her knees.

The mud puppy regarded her with great, soulful eyes. It was short and long and with a vaguely beaverlike face, and it had great floppy ears and a lizard's tail. It was splay-footed with broad, webbed feet, and its body was colored in various shades of brown as if streaked by dirt. Mud puppies were rare in Landover, being something of a fairy creature, and they were reputedly imbued with magic of their own, though Willow had never seen evidence of it. She recognized this one from her early years. Its name was Haltwhistle, and it served the Earth Mother.

"Good old Haltwhistle," she murmured, smiling, and the mud puppy swung its tail to and fro.

She would have petted it, but the Earth Mother had warned her long ago that you should never touch a mud puppy. No explanation for this piece of advice had been offered, but Willow had learned to trust the Earth Mother. She had known the elemental since she was a little girl growing up in the lake country. The Earth Mother had come to her first when she was still quite small, rising from the ground one day while she was playing, an unexpected apparition that was more intriguing than frightening. The Earth Mother had come to her, she was told, because she was special. The Earth Mother would teach her things that no one else knew, and they would be friends always. Willow accepted this as a child does, a bit wide-eyed, but not disbelieving because when you are a child all things are possible. She found the Earth Mother strange and wondrous, a spirit creature rather than a human or once-fairy, but their friendship seemed natural and welcome. She was one of many children in the home of the River Master and not one to whom much attention was paid or of whom much was expected. Willow was lonely, and the Earth Mother helped fill the void that the absence of her real mother had created. As she grew, the Earth Mother counseled her, coming to her less often as she became more sure of herself and her time filled with other things. She had seen nothing of the Earth Mother after Ben's coming save when she went in search of the black unicorn.

But now she was summoned, and Haltwhistle had been sent to guide her to where the Earth Mother waited.

She rose, washed, ate a little, and, with the mud puppy leading, set out anew. The day was warm and sun-filled, and the forests of the lake country smelled of grasses and wildflowers. As they walked, lake and river waters sparkled like gemstones through breaks in the trees and cranes and herons swooped across the surfaces in flashes of white. They traveled on through the morning and by midday were nearing Elderew. Haltwhistle turned east then, away from the city of the River Master and his people, and entered a stretch of forest thick with old-growth trees. Vines and mosses clung to the barked surfaces in brilliant green strips and patches. Insects skittered here and there, bright-colored birds darted through the canopies overhead, and small, furry-faced animals appeared like apparitions and were gone in the blink of an eye. Dust moats floated in streamers of sunlight, lazy and inconsequential.

On nearing the Earth Mother's refuge, Willow found herself wondering as she did from time to time at the elemental's interest in her. Happy for the companionship and special attention, she had never thought to ask when she was a child. When she had grown, she had accepted the Earth Mother's assurances that destiny had provided an important fate for her, and she had never pressed the matter further. Elementals frequently possessed the ability to read the future, and so Willow never doubted that the Earth Mother could see things yet to come, things hidden from her. Nevertheless, it was disconcerting to know that someone besides yourself knew what was fated for you and would not reveal the specifics. She had thought to ask of her future on more than one occasion, but she could never quite bring herself to do so. Perhaps it was her awe of the Earth Mother's history as the keeper of the lands. Perhaps there was a small part of her that did not want to know her future in any event.

But now, with the impending birth of her child, she thought that she must know, and she determined that this time her reverence for the Earth Mother would not prevent her asking.

Haltwhistle took her on through the thickening forests, back from the sunlit clearings into the deep shadows, and finally to where the silence was complete and unbroken by the sound of any life. The mud puppy stopped finally at the edge of a broad, empty clearing filmed with pond waters collected from streams all about, a still, black, mirrored surface that reflected the old-growth canopy that sheltered everything.

The mud puppy lingered for a soulful look back and then disappeared into the trees. Willow waited in the silence.

After a moment the pond stirred and the Earth Mother rose from the waters, her form taking shape out of the slick mud, lifting to stand within the shadowed silence.

"Welcome, Willow," she greeted. "Are you well, child?"

"I am fine, Earth Mother," Willow answered. "And you?"

"Unchanging. The land is stable and healed since the coming of Ben Holiday. It makes my work much easier." She gestured vaguely with her hand, and the light flickered dimly from the damp. "Does your life with him go well and the love between you continue?"

"Of course, Earth Mother."

"It gives me great pleasure to hear you say so. Now you will share a child, and it is for that reason that I have summoned you. There are things you must know, and I would not tell them to you through dreams. Have you come alone, then? And without the King?"

"I thought it better." Willow's gaze slid away momentarily. "He does not accept easily what he finds strange."

"You have not told him about your birthing? About the cycles of life and the periods of growth and the ways of the once-fairy?"

Willow sighed. "I cannot seem to find a way to do so. I had planned to tell him, but when your dream came, I thought it best to wait."

The Earth Mother nodded. "Perhaps you are right." Her face was young and vibrant, a constant surprise when one considered that she had been alive since the creation of the land. "You will tell him when you think it best. For now, we must concentrate on the birthing. You know it nears?"

"I can feel it, Earth Mother. The child stirs inside me already, anxious to be born. It will happen soon." She hesitated. "It is not like that with humans. Ben expects our child to grow within me for months in the manner of the women of his world. He has not said so, but I can read it in his looks. He thinks the child, since it is his, will be like him. But it will not. I can sense it already, and I do not know how to tell him." She was surprised to find herself suddenly on the verge of tears. "What if he will not accept this child? What if he finds it loathsome?"

The Earth Mother's smile was filled with kindness. "No, Willow, that will not happen. This child belongs to you both and was conceived of the love you bear for each other. His commitment to you, and now to the child, is complete. He will not find the child loathsome. Nor shall it be so. It shall be beautiful."

Willow's eyes brightened. "Is this promised, Earth Mother? Can you see it in my future?"

The Earth Mother passed her hands before Willow's face, and the question fell away, forgotten. "We will speak now of what you must do to prepare for your child's birth, Willow. Conditions will not be entirely as you anticipate. Your child will not be born while you are in your human form. It will be born during your cycle of transformation into spirit form."

"As my namesake," Willow said. "I have sensed this might be so. It was one of the reasons for my worry about telling Ben. I did not think he could conceive of such a thing."

"Do not trouble yourself further about Ben Holiday, child. What must concern you now are the conditions required for your birthing. Listen carefully. When you take root to give life to your child, it must be in a mix of soils from three worlds. The soils must come from Landover, from Earth, and from within the fairy mists. The soils reflect the child's heritage, a mix of bloods. This child is a product of each world, born of the union of a human and a once-fairy. It does not happen often. It is a rare and special occurrence."

The Earth Mother paused, and one hand lifted, a strange and compelling gesture. "The soils must be gathered by you, Willow, and by no one else. You must collect them, you must mix them, and you must take root in them when it is time to give birth. The soils must come from special places in each world, for they must reflect the character of that world, combining what is best and worst about the creatures who inhabit each. There is within your child some part of all three worlds, you see—something of Landover, of Earth, and of the fairy mists. If the child is to grow strong and healthy, if it is to secure wisdom and understanding, if it is to sort through and choose from the seeds of good and evil that exist in all living creatures, there must be a balance of possibilities inherent within it. The soils offer that balance. They offer magic that will sustain and secure."

"Fairy magic, Earth Mother?" Willow asked doubtfully.

"As surely as any other. This child's heritage is long and complex, Willow. Its bloodlines run back to when the people of the River Country were part of the fairy world. You carry both bloods within you; so must your child."

Willow's face was drawn and frightened. "Must I go into these worlds to gain possession of the soils, Earth Mother? I cannot do that. I cannot pass into the fairy mists or even out of Landover to Ben's world if he does not take me there. The medallion he wears as King will be needed. I must take him with me after all."

"No, Willow, he cannot go with you on this journey. Your own words—do you remember?" The elemental's face was kind and sad and hard and certain all at once, such a strange mix of emotions that Willow took a step back. "Listen to me now. Hear everything that I would tell you. This will be difficult, but you will have help. There are things at work here that even I do not yet understand. But one thing is certain. Your child must have the soils I have described. You must gather them, mix them, and take root in them. You alone. You must not be deterred by your fear. You must be brave. You must believe. Your child's life depends on it."

Willow was ashen now, gone cold with the enormity of what she was being asked to do. Ben could not help her. Who then would?

"You will begin at the old pines where you go to see your mother dance," the Earth Mother whispered in the stillness of the glade, her voice a ripple across the muddied waters on which she stood. "I will see you safely there. The first of the soils shall come from the lake country, where the best and the worst that is Landover can be found in a single grain. Take from the clearing where your mother dances a small bag of the soil you will find there. When you have finished, you will be met by someone who will guide you into Ben's world."

"Who will meet me, Earth Mother?" Willow asked softly. "Who will it be?"

"I am not given to see that yet," came the reply. "I am given to see only this. Your guide will come from the fairy people, who are equally committed to the safe birth of your child. I have visited them in dreams and found that it is so. This child, this firstborn of human and fairy, of Landover's King and Queen, is special to them as well, and they will do everything they can to keep it protected. Thus they will provide one of their own as guide, one whose magic will allow you safe passage, first into Ben Holiday's world and then into their own. Your guide will know where to take you to find the soils you need.

"But, child, take warning," she added quickly, her voice gone dark with premonition once more. "The fairy people harbor secrets in all that they do, and nothing with them is ever what it appears. They will have reasons beyond what they reveal for giving you aid. Do not accept everything you are told without question. Do not think that you know the whole truth. Be wary always. They will give you the help they have promised; that much is certain. They will see the child safely born; that is certain as well. But all else remains in doubt, so stay cautious in all that you do."

"Can you tell me nothing more?"

"I have told you all."

"There is too much uncertainty in this journey, Earth Mother," the sylph whispered. "I am frightened."

The Earth Mother sighed, the sound of the wind passing through the trees at eventide. "As I am frightened for you, child."

"Must I go, then?"

"If you wish your child safely born, you must."

Willow nodded, resigned. "I do." She looked away into the trees, as if thinking to see something of what was hidden from her. "How much time do I have to make this journey?"

"I do not know."

"The baby, then. How much time until the baby is born?"

"I do not know that either. Only the child knows. The child will decide when it is time. You must be ready when that time comes."

A sudden desperation tightened Willow's throat. "Can you see where the child is to be born? Can you tell me at least that much?"

"Not even that," the Earth Mother replied sadly. "The child will decide the place of its birth as well."

Willow fought back against her despair. "Little is left for me to choose, it seems. All decisions are given to others." She could not keep the bitterness from her voice. "I am the mother of this child. I am the one who carries it within her body. I am the giver of its life. Yet I have almost nothing to say about its coming into the world."

The Earth Mother did not speak. They stood facing each other in the silent clearing, the sunlight filtering down from the south where it eased toward day's end, the waters of the pond between them reflecting their images as if through poorly blown glass. Willow wondered suddenly if her own birth had been so complicated, if the very complexity of it had contributed to her mother's decision to leave her to her father, to abandon any further involvement, to forgo the pain of raising her when the pain of giving her life had been so intense. There was no way to know, of course. Her mother would never tell her the truth. Willow thought then of how she had left Ben, slipping away without saying good-bye, and she wished now that she had woken him.

She straightened. Well, there were few second chances given in life, and it was best not to dwell on their scarcity.

"Good-bye, Earth Mother," she said, for there was nothing else to say, no other words to speak. "I will remember what you have said."

"Good-bye, Willow. Keep strong, child. All will be well."

It was almost exactly the same thing she had said to Ben. All will be well. The words reached out to mock her. Willow's smile was bleak and ironic. She turned and walked to the edge of the clearing.

When she looked back again, the Earth Mother had disappeared.

ENSORCELLED

W hen Ben Holiday woke that first morning to find Willow gone, he was not a happy man. She had told him she was leaving, of course, so he was not surprised to discover she wasn't there. He even understood why she had left without waking him to say good-bye; he probably would have reacted every bit as badly as she had imagined. But none of that made him feel any better about the situation. He simply didn't like being separated from her, even for the best of reasons—and he wasn't sure this visit was one. He had listened to her explanation and tried to be fair about what she was doing, but in the end he still didn't understand any of it. Why did she have to go alone? Why did she have to go now?

Why did the feeling persist, despite his efforts to suppress it, that she was keeping something from him?

He might have sat about stewing for the entire day or even the rest of the week if it hadn't been for the fact that once again he had scheduled a full day of meetings in his continuing effort to find a way to be a good King. It wasn't as easy as people might suppose. In the first place, there was a decided clash of cultures at work in his stewardship of Landover. This was a place in which the feudal system had been at work for hundreds of years (according to Abernathy's carefully maintained histories), while Ben Holiday was a product of what passed in his world for a democracy. Instinctively almost, he found himself from day one looking for ways to implement the kind of government he knew and believed in. The lawyer in him wanted law and order to be the cornerstone of his government and to guarantee justice of, for, and by the people. But you didn't come into a strange country and simply throw out the system already in place. That was a swift and certain path to anarchy. As they were fond of saying where he came from, you had to work within the system.

So Ben settled early on for working toward the establishment of a benevolent dictatorship (still didn't sound too good when he said it, but it remained the best description he could come up with). The emphasis, of course, was supposed to be on the word *benevolent* and not on the other. The trick in all this was to introduce the changes he wanted without making it too obvious. People always accepted change more readily when they didn't realize it was happening. Thus the need for Ben Holiday as King to constantly walk a tightrope. Of course, after two years he was getting pretty good at it.

The process was convoluted, and only Questor and Abernathy really knew what was going on. As the King's closest advisors (not counting Willow), they were pretty much privy to everything that happened. In most instances, they supported Ben's ideas, arguing mostly on the side of caution and restraint in the introduction of his somewhat-revolutionary ideas. Once Ben had established himself as an acceptable and resilient King, one not likely to be dislodged, the next step was to bring the Kingdom's warring factions into some kind of accord. That meant getting at least a semblance of cooperation from such diverse peoples as the once-fairy, the humans, the kobolds, and the Rock Trolls—not to mention various smaller groups—none of whom wanted much to do with the other. Ben had succeeded in that endeavor through a combination of threats, promises, and bribes. A King had to be something of a magician—apologies to Questor Thews—and there was a great deal of on-the-job training. Thus a hard stand here led to a compromise there. You had to know when to bend and when to hold fast.

Starting out as a lawyer was good training, as Ben was fond of saying, for becoming a King.

So here was how matters stood at present in the reign of Ben Holiday, latest King of Landover, a place every reasonable person who hadn't been there knew couldn't possibly exist. The King still had the final say in all matters, particularly in disputes between lesser rulers and leaders of the various peoples of the Kingdom. Because Ben had finally garnered a solid base of support throughout the whole of the land and because he was backed by the armored might of the Paladin, almost no one ever considered using force against him. Ben, on the other hand, had to be careful not to give any of those lesser rulers and leaders reason to feel that their own stature was in any way being diminished. Thus they had to be left to govern where it was reasonable and sensible to allow them to do so. Where the King's own special brand of magic came into play was in getting them to govern the way he wanted.

Ben established early on a series of advisory committees (his designation) to oversee such matters as resource management (land, water, air, and magic—well, of course, in a magic kingdom!), commerce and travel (trading of goods between peoples and the transportation of same), currency exchange (frequently bartering), public works (road building and repair and management of the King's lands), and judicial review (resolution of civil disputes and criminal violations). He set up administrative officials in each part of the Kingdom to oversee the workings of all this, and periodically he brought them to Sterling Silver for a review of how the process was working and what could be done to make it stronger. It wasn't a perfect system by any means, but it had the added benefit of teaching Landover's many and diverse citizens—whether they realized it or not—how to participate in a government system. It was a learning process that took time, but Ben thought that he could see it building on itself. Where once the peoples of the lake country and the Greensward wouldn't have given each other the time of day, now they were working together to solve such common problems as how to conserve and protect water resources and how most effectively to use crop lands for growing. He had them sharing their knowledge and reconsidering their prejudices. He had them behaving better than they had behaved in centuries.

In some ways it was all very primitive compared to where he had come from. But in other ways it was like being able to start over before so much was poisoned. Ben was careful about choosing what knowledge he introduced from his old world. He kept it pretty basic. Good health habits and improved farming techniques, for example. He stayed away from things that would result in drastic change and possible harm—Industrial Revolution inventions and gunpowder. Some things he didn't know enough about to introduce, and that limited what he could choose from. He was at heart a lawyer in any event—not an engineer or a chemist or a doctor or a manufacturer. Maybe, he reflected now and again, it was just as well.

Besides, Landover had something going for it that his old world didn't, and it was important to remember to add it into the equation. Landover had magic. Real magic, the kind that changed things just as surely as electricity. Landover was infused with it, and many of her citizens practiced it in one form or another, and what they did with it obviated the need for many of the things that science had introduced once upon a time in Ben's old world. So it wasn't as simple as it first seemed, this business of categorizing and defining the pluses and minuses, pros and cons, and good and bad of the Kingdom of Landover.

In any case, Ben Holiday's schedule that first day of Willow's absence kept him from dwelling on his dissatisfaction with the matter of her going in the first place, and it wasn't until he retired after a rather late dinner, alone in their bedchamber, that he found himself confronted by his personal demons once again. He stood on the balcony that opened off the room, staring out across the starlit land for a long time, trying to decide how he should handle the situation. He could go after her, of course. Bunion could probably track her down in nothing flat. But he knew even as he considered the idea that he would never do anything so contrary to what she expected of him. He considered using the Landsview, the strange instrument that allowed him to go out into the land and find anyone or anything to be found there, all without ever leaving the castle. He had used it more than once to see what was happening in a faraway place. That was a tempting alternative, but in the end he discarded it as well. It was too much like spying. What if he were to see something that he wasn't supposed to see, something that she preferred to keep hidden from him? When you loved someone as much as he loved her, you didn't resort to spying on them.

He settled finally for going to bed and lying awake most of the night thinking about her.

The second day passed very much like the first except that he was required to spend an extraordinarily long time with a delegation of Rock Trolls, convincing them of the wisdom of carting a portion of their raw ores down out of the Melchor for sale to others rather than insisting that the forging be done entirely in their furnaces and according to what they decided was needed. This in turn resulted in dinner coming even later, which of course delayed bedtime until well after midnight, so that when he finally crawled beneath the covers he was so tired that he was almost asleep before he happened to turn over one final time on the pillow and so bring his hand into contact with the piece of paper tucked under it.

He sat up at once. He didn't know why, but he was instantly certain of the importance of this paper. He brought light to one of the bedside lamps with a touch of his hand, the castle awake even when he slept and responsive to his wishes. He angled the paper into the circle of the lamp's faint glow. The paper was folded in quarters, and he opened it carefully and read:

Holiday,
    If you would know of an invasive magic that threatens Landover in a way even I cannot tolerate then meet me two nights hence on the eve of the new moon at the Heart. Come alone. I will do so as well. I pledge you no harm and safe passage.
                                  Strabo.

Ben stared. His mind raced. Strabo the dragon can write? How did this get here? The dragon couldn't manage to fit through the bedchamber window, could he?

He stopped himself and reconsidered. The dragon wouldn't have written this. Or delivered it. He would have had someone else do both. Somehow. If the letter really was from him. If this wasn't some sort of trick. Which it likely was. Strabo had never written him before—or even contacted him. Strabo, Landover's last dragon, a reclusive, melancholy curmudgeon of a creature who resided far east in the wasteland of the Fire Springs, didn't even *like* Ben Holiday and had made it abundantly clear on more than one occasion that he would be ecstatic if he never saw the King again in his entire life.

So what was this letter all about?

Ben read it twice more, trying to picture the dragon speaking the words. It wasn't hard. The letter sounded like him. But the sending of it was odd. If the dragon was indeed seeking a meeting, this threat of which he warned must be a serious one. Ben discounted the danger of a personal attack. Strabo wasn't interested in harming him, and even if he was he wouldn't bother sending a note to lure him out—he would just take wing and come after him. Asking Ben to come alone was in keeping with the dragon's personality. Strabo didn't care for humans in general and would want any meeting kept private and personal. He also was quite honorable in his own peculiar way, and if he promised safe passage he would keep his word.

Still, the whole business made Ben uneasy.

Come alone?

Come at midnight?

He read the letter again and learned nothing new. He sat propped up against the massive iron headboard, pillows at his back, thinking the matter through. He knew what Questor and Abernathy would say. He knew what reason dictated. But there was something compelling about this letter, something that refused to let him simply discard it and go on about his life. It kept him reconsidering the matter, insisting that it was imprudent to ignore the warning. A sixth sense whispered that there was indeed something to heed here, something of which to be wary. Strabo did not act without reason, and if he felt there was a danger facing Landover then he was probably right. If he felt Ben should know about it, then Ben probably should.

So what should he do?

He went to sleep finally without having made a decision. He thought about the letter all the next day, mulling it over between meetings and conferences, during meals and while reading documents, and as he ran the perimeter of the castle in the late afternoon hours before dinner, keeping up his training habits even now, Bunion as always his silent, invisible protector.

He retired to bed that third night following Willow's departure with the matter still unresolved.

But by morning he had made his decision. He knew he must go. He must take whatever risk was involved on the chance that the letter and warning were real. Besides, he convinced himself, the risk wasn't all that great. The Heart was only several hours away on horseback. He would take a mounted patrol of King's Guards for protection. He would not tell anyone until just before he was ready to leave. That would keep Questor and Abernathy and the kobolds out of the matter. He would leave the Guards safely back from the Heart, go in alone to check things out, meet with Strabo if the dragon was there, and still be back before dawn. Easy enough, and it would satisfy his need to do something besides stand around wondering what he should do!

There was a deciding factor in all this, although he would not let himself dwell on it. No matter the danger he might actually face in any situation, he was protected always by the Paladin. The King's Champion was the single most powerful being in the realm, and it existed for the sole purpose of seeing that the King was kept safe. It could be summoned at a moment's notice, its appearance requiring nothing more than Ben's grasping the medallion he wore always about his neck, the medallion with the graven image of a knight riding out of Sterling Silver at sunrise. Grasp that medallion, call for the Paladin, and the knight of ghosts and shadows would be there instantly.

The problem with the Paladin, of course, was that the King's armored champion was in truth the King himself. Or another side of the King. Or, more accurately, another side of *whoever* was King at any given moment. In this case it meant that the Paladin was really another side of Ben, a dark, destructive side born out of some well of being that he would rather not acknowledge even existed. But it did, and it hovered somewhere at the edges of his consciousness, waiting. Ben had struggled with the knowledge of what this meant ever since he had discovered the truth about the Paladin. The Paladin was a killing machine that had served in the ranks of the Kings of Landover since the beginning, a creation of the fairy folk to give protection to the ruler they had installed to keep the gates to the fairy world safe. The Paladin had fought in every battle visited on Landover's many and diverse rulers, championing all causes, standing fast against all enemies. It had been challenged time and again. It had never lost. It died only when the King died. It was reborn when a new King was crowned. It was a timeless, eternal being that lived only to fight and fought only to kill.

And it was a part of Ben Holiday, an integral part of who and what he was, not merely by virtue of the office he held and the responsibility he had accepted, but because there existed in every living creature the potential for deliberate, controlled destruction. Ben had discovered early on that the Paladin's infusion into his being, their joining as one, was due as much to the darkness of his human side as to any conjuring of fairy magic. He was the Paladin in great part because the Paladin was in truth another side of him, a side that until he had become King of Landover he had kept carefully closed away.

So he could rely on the Paladin to come to his rescue if required, though he was loath to call the dark warrior out again unless the need was great indeed. Summoning it was a last resort, he constantly told himself, but it was something he could do if he must. It was something he no longer believed, as once he had, that he would never do again.

He went through the fourth day in deliberate fashion, standing just outside himself most of the time, watching as Ben Holiday went through the motions of being King. He felt so peculiar about what he was doing, keeping the knowledge of the coming night's plans carefully tucked away, that he was surprised no one noticed. Questor Thews and Abernathy seemed to find him normal and did not question if something was wrong. No one did. He fulfilled his day's duties, ate his dinner, retired to his room, and sat down to wait.

When it was nearly dark, the twilight easing quickly toward night, he went downstairs to the stables, ordered Jurisdiction, his favorite mount, a big bay gelding, saddled, called for a guard of six men, and rode out. He did so quietly and without advising anyone, and he was able to slip away without being noticed. Patrols came and went from Sterling Silver all the time; one more riding out at dusk attracted no particular attention. Even Bunion would probably be resting by now, anticipating a sunrise run with Ben. It was a typical summer night, lazy and warm, and there was that sense of all being right with the world and sleep being just a yawn and a deep, slow breath away. As Ben and his guard rode over the causeway, Sterling Silver was a shimmer of polished starlight against the hazy darkness, a reflection that lingered as they climbed into the forested hills west, then faded as the trees closed about.

They traveled swiftly, Ben pushing the pace, anxious to reach the Heart before midnight, navigating by the stars and his own sense of time's passage. He had learned to live without clocks and watches since coming into Landover, and he could now tell time in the old way—by a reading of the heavens, by the length and position of shadows on the ground, and by the feel of the air and the condensation that gathered on the grasses. His senses were stronger in this world, he discovered, perhaps because he was forced to rely on them more. He wore black clothing and boots and black chain mail devised by Questor Thews out of magic and iron to be lightweight but very strong. He wore the precious medallion of the Kings of Landover and a long knife. A broadsword was strapped to his back because the King was expected to travel armed on night sorties and patrols. Riding gloves protected his hands, and a dark scarf was wrapped about his throat to ward off the dust.

There was no wind as yet, no air movement of any sort, and the night was thick and sultry. Insects buzzed about his head when he slowed, so he kept the pace at a quick trot or canter when the way was clear enough to do so. The new moon left the land bereft of much of its nighttime light—in Landover, the new moon was a combination of some of its eight moons dropping below the horizon and some entering their dark phases (Ben never had figured out exactly how it worked, only when it occurred, which was about every other month). What light there was came from the stars which gleamed all across the cloudless sky, a maze of brilliant pinpricks that seemed to have been placed there for no better reason than to inspire dreaming in those who gazed up at them. Ben did so when the trees cleared enough to allow, but his thoughts this night were occupied mostly with the meeting that lay ahead.

Time passed swiftly, and it was still almost an hour short of midnight when the riders closed on the Heart. Ben brought the patrol up while they were still some distance away, had the Guards stand down, and ordered them to wait for him there. He rode on until he was within several hundred yards of his destination, then dismounted from Jurisdiction, left the horse to graze unfettered, and walked on alone.

The woods were dark and empty-feeling as he passed through them, and although he listened for familiar sounds in the blanketing silence he heard nothing. The smells of the forest were pungent and intoxicating, causing his thoughts to drift to other times and places, to events that had once seemed momentous and now were only memories of building blocks used in the construction of his life. He walked easily and without concern for his safety; oddly enough, he did not feel threatened. Perhaps it was the sense of peacefulness that the summer night instilled within him. Perhaps it was the presence of the medallion, a constant reminder of the power bequeathed him as King. Perhaps it was simply that nothing actually did threaten. Whatever the case, he traveled on toward the Heart as if undertaking no more than a nighttime stroll in his gardens, one that would end with sleep and a waking into the new day.

He reached the Heart shortly before midnight, entering from the trees and standing momentarily at the edge of the rows of white velvet rests and kneeling pads, facing toward the white oak dais with its polished silver stanchions and limp pennants. The clearing was silent and seemingly empty. Nothing moved; there was not the whisper of a wind in the stillness. Memories of all that had transpired here came and went. Ben looked about a moment longer, then walked down an aisle between the benches and rests toward the dais.

A breath of wind brushed his cheek and was gone. *Careful.*

He was almost to the stage when the dark figure materialized from out of nowhere to his right, lifting, it seemed, from the very earth. He stopped, a chill racing down his spine, a lurch in the pit of his stomach. The dark figure was robed and bathed in shadow, the light behind it unrevealing.

"Play-King," a familiar voice greeted.

Nightshade!

Ben froze, on guard now for the first time. Why was Nightshade here? The Witch of the Deep Fell was no friend of his, and if she was present there was reason to believe that the meeting was a trap after all.

She came forward a few steps, tall and imperious, the light catching her features now, etching out the lean, cold, flawless face, the raven black hair with its single streak of white, the narrow shoulders and long, thin arms. "Why did you send for me?" she hissed at him, her voice cold and angry. "What is all this about a threat of magic to my home?"

Ben stared, speechless. Send for her? What was she talking about? He was here because Strabo had sent for him! What sort of game was she playing?

"I didn't . . ." he began.

"You annoy . . ." she started.

And then a shadow fell over them both, and the sky was filled with Strabo's dark bulk as the dragon settled gingerly down at the edge of the dais, serpent body coiling up, wings folding in. Steam rose from his black-as-pitch, fire-slicked, scaled body, and the stench of him filled the air. Even Nightshade drew back in repulsion as he swung his horned and fearsome head from one of them to the other.

"What is this?" he growled, the sound a deep, unpleasant rumble, the grating of stone against the earth. His huge, implacable bulk was outlined against the forest. "Why is Holiday here, Witch?" he demanded ominously. "What does he have to do with your note?"

"My note?" Nightshade's voice was a rasp of disbelief. "I sent you no note! I came in answer to the play-King's missive!"

"Foolish old crone," the dragon purred, a big cat contemplating dinner. "You waste my time with your idiotic denials. The note was yours, the words all too clearly your own. If you have some treasure you wish to trade, then offer it up and be done with it."

Nightshade's face was livid with fury. "Treasure?"

Ben saw what was happening then, recognized the truth of what had been done to them, and knew instinctively that it was already too late to escape. Separate notes sent to each, seemingly from one another, actually from someone else entirely, meant to lure them to this spot—the bait for a trap. Why? The word screamed at him as he started forward, catching sight suddenly of someone who had appeared just long enough to set something down, a tall, gawky figure, vaguely familiar, backing away from a box that sat open at the edge of the dais, smoke or mist or whatever already lifting from its interior, the box unfamiliar but the figure someone he knew . . .

Horris Kew!

What in the name of sanity was going on?

"Wait!" he managed to yell, pointing at the scarecrow figure. Strabo's scaled head whipped around, the fire leaking from his maw as he hissed in warning. Nightshade's arms came up threateningly, the magic forming streaks of wicked green light on her fingertips. There was a sudden crackling in the air. Ben's hand went instinctively to the medallion, and he called forth the Paladin to his rescue.

All too late. Light flared suddenly from all about, thrusting from the blackness on every side, born of some origin earlier fixed and triggered now as the jaws of the trap set to ensnare them closed tightly about. They were hammered forward toward each other and the box, all three of them, King, witch, and dragon, and there was not a moment's time to react. The light caught and carried them across the velvet benches and rests, across the distance separating them from one another, and locked them in a knot of magic that bound them up with ferocious purpose. Then mist and gloom closed about, rising to receive them as if they were an expected offering. Abruptly they began to fall into a deep, impenetrable void. The void opened beneath them, growing in size as they neared it (or were they shrinking?), a vast, empty sinkhole that sucked them inexorably downward.

But there was something more. All were experiencing an odd sense of loss, as if some essential part of who and what they were was being stripped away in layers. And there surfaced within each a demon, a nameless, formless, terrible beast they had kept sealed away, but was now suddenly, inexplicably set free. All three howled in fury and despair.

Where did Horris Kew get such power? was Ben's last, desperate thought.

Then down he tumbled with the dragon and the witch, voiceless and powerless, to disappear into the interior of the Tangle Box.

When they were gone, the Gorse lifted out of the gloom at the edge of the trees behind the dais and hissed coldly at Horris Kew, "Pick up the box."

Horris was shaking so badly he could not make himself move. He stood with his hands clenched tightly and his size-sixteens rooted in place. He was stunned by the magnitude of what he had just witnessed—Holiday, Nightshade, and Strabo picked up like rag dolls by the magic and hurtled down into the murky depths of the Tangle Box. Such power! Yes, the Gorse had taken great pains to set the underpinnings of its implementation, to cast the nets of sorcery, to speak the spells that would lie waiting for the three. Or rather, to have Horris do all this, for the Gorse still seemed unable to act on its own. Horris had glimpsed the depth of the creature's power even then, sharp twinges and stabs that pricked his psyche, but even so he could not have imagined that all these little conjurings could be brought together to form such a singularly devastating magic.

To one side, the Gorse hissed purposefully.

"The box, Horris!" Biggar whispered in his ear, an urgent plea from his perch on the conjurer's shoulder.

Horris started out of his shock, then hurriedly stumbled forward onto the dais. He stared down at the swirling, misty surface of the Tangle Box. There was nothing to be seen. The box was closed once more.

Horris stepped back, sweating, breathing hard. He exhaled slowly. It had worked just as the Gorse had promised. The Gorse told them the notes would attract the three, their greatest potential enemies, the only ones in Landover who could offer any real threat. It told them the notes were spellbound so that their readers would find them impossible to resist, even should their reason and good sense caution otherwise. It told them the conjurings and magics and symbols of power cast and set about the Heart would ensnare the unsuspecting trio so swiftly that none would escape. It told them finally that the Tangle Box was a prison from which they would never escape.

But Horris couldn't help asking again anyway. "What if they get out?"

The Gorse laughed, a low, humorless sound in the darkness. "They will never get out. They won't even know enough to want to get out. I've taken steps to see to that. By now, they are hopeless prisoners. They don't know who they are. They don't know where they are. They are lost to the mists."

Biggar ruffled his feathers. "Serves them right," he croaked dismissively.

"Pick up the box," the Gorse ordered once more.

Horris was quicker to respond this time. He snatched up the carved wooden container obediently, being careful nevertheless to hold it away from him. "What do we do now?"

The Gorse was already moving. "We take the box back to the cave, and we wait." The voice was smooth and self-satisfied. "After the King's absence has caused sufficient panic, you and the bird will pay another visit to your friends at Sterling Silver."

The Gorse eased through the gloom like smoke. "Only this time you will take them a little surprise."

LABYRINTH

The Knight woke startled and alert, lifting off the ground as if jerked erect by invisible wires. He had been dreaming, and while the dream itself was already forgotten, the impression it had made on him lingered. His breathing was quick and his heartbeat rapid, and it seemed as if he had run a long way in his sleep. He felt a damp heat on his body beneath his clothing and along his hairline. He felt poised on the edge of something about to happen.

His eyes shifted anxiously through the gloom. He was in a forest of huge, dark trees that rose like columns to hold up the sky. Except there was no sky to be seen, only the mist that roiled overhead, blotting out everything, even the highest branches. The darkness of the forest was a twilight that was as much a part of day as night, as much of morning as evening. It was not real, and yet the Knight recognized instinctively that it was the only reality of this place in which he found himself.

Where was he?

He did not know. He could not remember.

There were others. Where were they?

He came to his feet swiftly, aware of the weight of the broadsword slung across his back, of the knife at his waist, of the chain mail that warded his chest and back. He was dressed all in black, his clothing loose-fitting and leather-bound, with boots, belt, and gloves. His armor was somewhere close, though he couldn't see it. It was close, he knew, because he could sense its presence, and his armor always came to him when he needed it.

Although he didn't know why.

A medallion hung against his chest beneath his tunic. He lifted it free and stared at it. It was an image of himself riding out of a castle at sunrise. It was familiar to him, and yet it was as if he were seeing it for the first time. What did it mean?

He brushed his confusion aside, and cast about in the gloom. Something stirred at the clearing's far edge, and he moved toward it swiftly. A figure who lay curled upon the ground straightened as he neared and pushed itself up with both arms extended. Long black hair with a single streak of white through its center hung down across face and shoulders, and robes trailed on the earth like liquid shadows.

It was the Lady. She was still with him. She had not run away while he slept (for she would run if the chance presented itself, he knew). Her head lifted at his approach, and one slim hand brushed back the raven hair. Her pale, beautiful features tightened as she saw him, and she hissed at him in anger and dismay.

"You," was all she said, that single word conveying the depth of her dislike for him and for what he had done to her.

He did not try to go closer. The Knight knew how she felt about him, knew that she blamed him for what had been done to her. It could not be helped. He turned away and scanned the rest of the clearing in which they had slept. It was small and close, and there was nothing about it to suggest why they were there. They had come to this place earlier, he knew. They had come here in flight, pursued by . . . something. He had brought the Lady with him—and one other—fleeing the beast that would devour them all.

He shook his head, an ache developing behind his eyes as he tried to see into the past. It was as misty and gloom-filled as his present, as this forest in which he found himself.

"Take me home!" the Lady whispered suddenly. "You have no right!"

He turned to find her standing with her hands clenched into fists at her sides. Her strange red eyes burned with rage, and her lips were skinned back from her teeth like an animal's. It was said that she could do magic, that she possessed incredible power. You did not want to make an enemy of her, it was said. But the Knight had done so. He was not sure how it had happened, but there was no getting away from it now. He had taken the Lady from her home, from the haven of her life, carrying her off to this forest. He was the King's Champion, and he existed only to do the King's bidding. The King must have sent him to bring the Lady, although he could not remember that either.

"Knight of black thoughts and deeds!" she scorned. "Coward behind your armor and your weapons! Take me home!"

She might have been threatening him now, preparing to use her magic against him. But he did not think so. What magic she possessed seemed lost to her. He had come this far, and she had not attacked him with it. If she had been able to do so, she would have tried long ago. Not that it would have mattered. He was a weapon built of iron. He was less man than machine. Magic had no more effect on him than dust thrown in his eyes; it had no place in his life. His was a world of simple rules and tight boundaries. He was not frightened of anything. A Knight could not allow fear. His was an occupation where death was always as close as life. Fighting was all he knew, and the battles he fought could end in only two ways—either he would kill his enemy or his enemy would kill him. A thousand battles later, he was still alive. He did not believe he would ever be killed. He believed he would live forever.

He brushed the musing aside, the thoughts that came unbidden and were unwelcome. "You are traveling to a new home," he told her, letting her anger fall away from him like leaves thrown against stone.

She shook with her rage, balled fists lifting before her breast, the tendons of her neck as tight as cords. "I will not go with you farther," she whispered, and shook her head back and forth. "Not one step!"

He nodded noncommittally, not wishing to spar with her verbally, feeling inadequate to the task. He turned away again, walked to the far side of the clearing, and peered out into the gloom beyond. The trees were packed together like bundles of giant sticks, shutting out the light and the view, closing everything off. Which way to go? Which way had he been headed? The King would be waiting for him, he knew. It was always thus. But which way led home again?

He turned as the Lady came at him with the knife she had somehow kept hidden, the blade black and slick with poison. She shrieked as he seized her wrist and forced the knife away, then twisted it from her grasp. She beat at him and kicked wildly, trying to break free, but he was far stronger and immune to her fury, and he subdued her easily. She collapsed to the ground, breathing hard, on the verge of tears perhaps but refusing to cry. He picked up the blade and cast it far out into the gloom.

"Be careful what you throw about, Knight," a new voice warned, deep and guttural.

He saw the Gargoyle then, resting on its haunches close by, come from the woods as silent as a shadow at midnight. The creature's eyes were yellow and hooded as they studied him, and there was nothing in their reptilian depths to offer even the slightest hint of what the mind behind them might be thinking.

"You've chosen to stay," the Knight said quietly.

The Gargoyle laughed. "Chosen? A strange word in these circumstances, don't you think? I am here because there is nowhere else to go."

The Gargoyle was loathsome to look upon. Its body was gnarled and misshapen, with its arms and legs bandy and crooked, its body all sinew and corded muscle, and its head sunk down between its powerful shoulders. Its hands and feet were webbed and clawed, and the whole of it was covered in bristly dark hair. Its face was wrinkled like a piece of dried fruit, and its features were jammed together like a child's clay model of something only vaguely human. Fangs peeked out from beneath its thick lips, and its nose was wet and dirty.

From atop its hunched shoulders, wings fluttered weakly, leathery flaps too tiny to be of any use, appendages that seemed strangely out of place. It was as if its forebearers might have flown once but had long ago forgotten how.

The Knight was repulsed, but he did not look away. Ugliness was a part of his life as well. "Where are we?" he asked the Gargoyle. "Have you looked about?"

"We are in the Labyrinth," it replied, as if that answered everything.

The Gargoyle glanced at the Lady, who had looked up again on hearing him speak. "Don't look at me!" she hissed at once, and turned away.

"In what part of our country is the Labyrinth?" the Knight persisted, confused.

The Gargoyle laughed anew. "In every part." He showed his yellowed teeth and black tongue. "In all parts of every part of everything. It lies north and south and east and west and even in the center. It is where we are and where we would go and where we will always be."

"He is mad," the Lady whispered quickly. "Make him keep still."

The Knight shifted the heavy broadsword on his back and glanced around. "There is a way out of every maze," he declared. "We will find the way out of this one."

The Gargoyle rubbed his hands as if seeking warmth. "How will you do that, Sir Knight?" His voice was disdainful.

"Not by staying here," the Knight said. "Do you come with us or not?"

"Leave him!" the Lady hissed, rising suddenly to her feet and drawing her dark robes close. "He does not belong with us! He was never meant to be with us!"

"Us?" the Gargoyle repeated slyly. "Are you bound together now, Lady? Are you joined to this Knight as mate and companion? How unexpected."

The Lady curled her lip at the creature and turned away. "I am joined to neither of you. I would rather be killed now and have it done."

"I would rather you were killed as well," the Gargoyle agreed.

The Lady whirled back upon him once again. "You are an ugly beast, Gargoyle. If I had a mirror, I would hold it up to your face so that you could see how ugly!"

The Gargoyle flinched at the words, and then hissed back at her, "And you would need a mirror inside yourself to see the ugliness that possesses you!"

"Do not fight!" the Knight thundered, and stepped between them. He looked changed suddenly, the man in dark clothing and chain mail suddenly gone even darker. It was as if the light about him had been sucked away. It was as if he had been plated in shadows.

"Do not," he repeated, more softly now, and then the dark cast that had enveloped him disappeared, and he was himself again.

There was a long moment of silence as the three faced one another. Then the Lady said to the Knight, "I am not afraid of you."

The Knight looked off into the gloom as if he had not heard, and in his eyes there was a lost, faraway look that reflected memories of missed chances and lost possibilities.

"We will walk this way," the Knight said, and started out.

---◦∞◦---

They traveled through the remainder of the day, and the forest that was the Labyrinth did not change. The gloom persisted, the mist clung tenaciously, the trees did not thin save at scattered clearings, and the cast and shape of the world did not alter. The Knight led them afoot (where was his mount?), trying to travel in a straight line, hoping that at some point the forest would end and the grasslands or hill country that surely lay beyond would appear and suggest to him where they must go next. He pondered with every step the inconsistencies of his memory. He tried to reason out what he was doing there, what had brought him to this abysmal place. He tried to remember how the Lady and the Gargoyle had come to be with him. He tried to think through the fog that enveloped almost the whole of his past. He was a Knight in service to the King, a champion of countless battles, and that was virtually all he knew.

He clung to that, and it kept him just ahead of the madness that too much thinking would bring.

They found streams from which to drink and did so, but they found nothing to eat. Yet they experienced no hunger. It was not as if they were full, but as if hunger's presence had left them entirely. The Knight was puzzled by this, but did not speak of it. They walked through the day, through the twilight that changed only marginally, and when darkness finally came, they stopped again.

They were in another clearing, a clearing that looked much like the first. The forest about them had not changed. They sat down together in the deepening gloom and stared out at the darkness. The Knight did not think to build a fire. They were not cold, or hungry, or in need of light. They could see quite well in the darkness; they could hear sounds they should not have been able to. The Gargoyle sat a little way off from the other two, not wishing to endure the scorn of the Lady again so soon, not feeling a part of them in any case. The Knight could sense the other's distancing, even when traveling together, as if the Gargoyle understood that there would always be a wall between them. The creature hunkered down in the shadows, then stretched his misshapen body and seemed to melt into the ground.

The Lady sat facing the Knight. "I do not like you," she told him. "I wish to see you dead."

He nodded impassively. "I know."

She had been silent and introspective all day, journeying obediently but without interest. He had glanced at her now and again, and sometimes found her openly hostile and sometimes as lost and searching as himself. She held herself as if armored, tall and straight and unafraid, but there was a vulnerability to her that she could not disguise and did not quite seem to understand, as if it was newly come to her and unexpected.

"Why don't you just take me back?" she pressed, a sudden urgency in her voice. "What difference can any of this make to you? There is no enemy for you to fight. There is no battle to be won. Why are you doing this? Am I your enemy?"

"You have said so."

"Only because you steal me from my home!" she exclaimed desperately. "Only because of that!" She inched forward across the grassy earth until she was quite close. "Why have you taken me?"

He could not answer. He did not know why.

"Your King has ordered you to do so? Why?"

He could not remember.

"What does he want with me? I will never be any good for him, no matter what he thinks! I will be neither wife nor consort! I will be his worst enemy until I am dead!"

The Knight inhaled the forest air, smelling the green freshness of the leaves and grass, the musky damp of the soil, and the pungent dryness of bark and old wood. What were the answers to her questions? Why could he not remember them? He withdrew into himself, thinking to find peace. He took comfort in knowing who he was and what he did. He found reassurance in his strength and skill, in the press of his weapons against his body, in the smooth fit of his battle dress.

Yet his armor was still missing. He had felt its presence when he had been forced to step between the Lady and the Gargoyle, but it had not shown itself. Why was that? It reached out to him, yet stayed hidden, as if playing cat and mouse. His armor—it was lifeless and yet seemingly possessed of life, a paradox. Like the medallion he wore about his neck, it was a part of who and what he was. Why then could he not remember its source?

The Lady was a silent ivory carving before him, watching intently, wanting to come forth from within herself he sensed, but unable to do so. What was she hiding from him? Something frightening. Some deep, secretive admission.

She folded her slim hands within her lap, and the disdainful look crept back upon her face. "You are powerless," she declared bitterly. "You have no self-will, no independent spirit with which to act. You are a tool to be wielded by whoever wears the crown. How sad."

"I am a *servant* of that crown."

"You are a slave to it." She cocked her head slightly, the raven hair shifting in a glimmer of black light. Her eyes fixed him. "You can make no decision that conflicts with your master's orders. You can make no judgment on your own. You took me without asking why. You keep me without wondering why.

You do what you are bidden, and you are careless of the reasons for your actions."

He did not like to argue with her. It gained nothing for either of them. He was not good with words; she was not possessed of his sense of honor and obedience. They came from different lives.

"Who is this King who would have me for his own?" she asked pointedly. "Speak his name."

Again, he could not. He stared at her, trapped.

"Are you so ignorant as to not know it?" she pressed, irony sharpening the edges of her anger. "Or are you afraid to give it to me? Which is it?"

He kept silent. But he could not look away.

She shook her head slowly. She was hard-faced and cold-looking with her dark hair and white skin, with the set of her jaw and the glint in her eyes. But she was beautiful, too. She was as perfect as a fond memory lovingly worked over the passing of time, all the roughness rubbed away, all the flaws removed. She enchanted him without trying, without meaning to do so, drawing him past her anger and despair, carrying him out of what was into what should never be.

"Whatever I would tell you," he forced himself to say, "would mean nothing."

"Try, at least!" she whispered at him, and there was a sudden softness in her voice. "Give me something!"

But he could not. He had nothing to give. He had only himself, and she wanted no part of that. She wanted reasons and understanding, and he had neither. He was as adrift as she was, thrown into a place he did not know, into circumstances he did not understand. The Labyrinth was a mystery he could not fathom. To do so, he must first escape it. That, he understood intuitively, would not be easy.

"Have you no feelings at all for me?" she asked plaintively, but this time the falseness in her voice betrayed her immediately.

"My feelings have no place in what I am about. I do what is required of me."

"What is required of you!" she shrieked, angry and bitter all over again, casting off any pretension of weakness. "You do what you are sent to do, you pathetic creature! You bend and scrape because it is what you know! What is required of you? I would rather be cast into the darkest pit in all the land than spend one moment of my life giving heed to what another would demand of me!"

He smiled in spite of himself. "And so you have been," he told her. "For where else are we if not there?"

She shrank back from him, downcast, in silence. They sat like that for a long time. The Gargoyle was sleeping, his breathing nasal and rough, his crooked limbs twitching as if his palms and soles were prodded by hot iron. The Lady glanced at him once and then glanced away. She did not look back. She did not look at the Knight. She stared at a space upon the earth some six feet to her right where the grass had withered away in shadow and the soil had cracked and turned to dust. She sat that way a long time. The Knight watched her without seeming to, without really wanting to, unable to help himself. She was in genuine misery, but the source of her anguish went beyond what she had told him. It was huge and carefully warded, and it transcended his meager understanding of its source.

He felt a strange stirring inside. He should say something to ease her pain. He should do something to lift her burden. But he did not know what. He wondered then at the words she had spoken to him, at the accusations she had cast. There was truth in them. He was given over to another's service, charged with another's wishes, bound to another's cause. It was the essence of his life as King's Champion. A Knight in armor whose weapons and strength settled all causes—that was his identity. On reflection, it seemed too small a possession. He was defined by it, yet it was given out in a single phrase. Was that the sum of his parts? Was there nothing more to him?

Who was he?

"Do you know what you have done to me?" he heard the Lady ask suddenly. He looked over at once. She was not looking back. She was still staring at that same patch of earth. Lines of wetness streaked her cheeks, trailing from her cold, empty eyes.

"Do you know?" she whispered in despair.

—◦◦◦◦◦—

Night's shadows cloaked Landover as well. All eight moons were down, and clouds layered the sky and masked away the stars. The blackness was intense. The day's heat had left the air windless and damp, and the whole of the land lay hushed and sweltering.

The Gorse felt no discomfort as it moved out of the concealment of its cavern lair and into the forest beyond. It was a fairy creature and at one with nature whatever her disposition. It came forth as a cloud of dark mist, the state to which its long captivity in the Tangle Box had reduced it. But already that substanceless form was beginning to coalesce and take shape anew, freedom returning to it the face and body it had once owned. Quite soon now both would be restored. It would be ready then to exact from those who had wronged it the revenge it so desperately craved.

It had thought about nothing else for centuries. Once it had been a fairy creature of great power, a being whose magic was formidable and feared. It had used that magic in ways that so enraged and disgusted its kin within the fairy mists, the world to which all fairy creatures belonged, that they banded together, seized it when it thought itself invulnerable, and imprisoned it. They cast it down into the mists of the Tangle Box, a device they had constructed from their own magic and from which nothing could escape. Locks were placed upon the box from without where the Gorse could not reach them.

Entombing it thus was meant to wear it down, to destroy its will, to make it forget everything it had known before its confinement and in the end to reduce it to dust. The effort had failed. It had remained trapped a very long time but it had not forgotten and its hatred of those responsible had grown.

It had grown very large indeed.

The Gorse moved easily through the night. It required little time to reach its destination and was in no hurry. It had waited until Horris Kew and the bird were sleeping, not wanting them to discover what it was about, needing them to continue to believe it was their friend. It was not, of course. The man and the bird were pawns, and the Gorse was using them accordingly. If they wanted to believe otherwise, if they chose to do so because they were greedy and foolish, that was as it should be. It was the natural order of things. They were mortal creatures and, so, much less than the Gorse. They were expendable.

It crested a rise and found itself at the edge of the Heart. It paused to send out feelers of sight and sound, taste and smell, and discovered nothing amiss, nothing threatening. It looked out across the rows of white velvet seats and rests, past the burnished dais and its standards, past the encirclement of Bonnie Blues. It savored the presence of the magic that rose out of the earth, here at the wellspring of all the land's life. The power of that magic was enormous, but the Gorse was not yet ready to tamper with it. It would serve a different purpose this night. A greater magic could be used to mask the conjuring of a lesser. It would do so now.

The Gorse gathered itself and sent forth the summons it had prepared. Lines of fire that neither burned nor smoked lanced down into the earth and disappeared. The response was immediate, a harsh, grating rumble, the groan of a great stone wall giving way. After a moment, the rumble faded, and the silence returned.

The Gorse waited.

Then the air before it ripped apart as if formed of fabric, first tearing and then splitting wide. Thunder boomed from within the rent, deep and ominous. A hole opened in the night, and out of that hole rose the clang and scrape of armored riders and the hiss and shriek of their mounts. The sounds heightened to a frightening pitch as the riders gathered speed. A fierce wind whipped across the Heart, tearing at the flags atop their standards and screaming into the trees beyond.

The Gorse held its ground.

With a rush of wind and sound, those it had summoned materialized from out of the warp in time and space. They were formed of armored plates and spikes, bristling with weapons, riding on nightmare creatures that had no recognizable name. There were five of them, massive dark creatures that steamed despite the humid night air and whose breath hissed and rasped through the visors of their helmets. They were lean and shadowy, like dark-hued ghosts, and the reek of their bodies was terrible.

The demons of Abaddon had arrived.

Foremost was the one who was designated as the Mark, their chosen leader, a huge, angular monster with serpents carved into its armor and the severed heads of its enemies hung about its neck. It beckoned to the others, and they fanned out to either side, weapons held ready. As one, they advanced on the Gorse.

The Gorse let them come. When they were close enough to spit on, it disappeared before their eyes in a flash of green light, reappeared as one of them, disappeared a second time, and reappeared finally as a pair of snake's eyes. It stole into their armor and licked at them lovingly, showing them they were kindred spirits. It conjured images of the horrors it had once performed on its own people and let the demons savor its evil.

When they were satisfied that it was one of them, that it was as powerful as they, and that it had summoned them for a reason, the Gorse hissed softly to prick their ears for his words and said, "What if I were to prepare a way for you to come into Landover safely?"

He paused, hearing them growl expectantly. This was too easy. "What if Landover and her people were to be given over to you for good?"

Too easy indeed.

VISION

After parting from the Earth Mother, Willow walked on through the forest for a time toward Elderew, lost in thought. The day was bright and sunny, filled with the smell of summer wildflowers and green grasses, and the forest was noisy and crowded with birdsong. It was beautiful and warm and comforting beneath the canopy of the great hardwoods, but Willow was oblivious to all of it. She walked through unaware, lost somewhere deep within herself, pondering over and over again the Earth Mother's message about her baby.

The words haunted her. She must gather soils from this world, from Ben's world, and from the fairy mists. She must mix them together and take root in them in order for her child to be safely born. She did not know how long she had to do this. She did not know when the child would be born. She did not know where. She could not ask another to gather the soils for her; she must do so herself. Ben could not go with her. He could not help her. No one could.

Well, almost no one. There would be the guide chosen by the fairies to direct her on the last two legs of her journey. But who would they send?

She felt cold inside despite the day's warmth. She had almost died in Ben's world on her one and only visit, so her memories were not fond ones. The fairy mists were even worse for being an unknown; she was terrified of what might happen to her there. A once-fairy was even more vulnerable to their treachery than a human. The mists could so bewilder you, so erode your reason and strength, and so change you from who and what you were that you would end up completely lost to yourself. The mists brought out the dark fears you kept hidden deep inside yourself, giving them substance, giving them sufficient power to destroy you. Life within the mists was ethereal, a creation of the mind and the imagination. It was magical and ever-changing.

Reality was what you created it to be, a bog that could swallow you up without a trace.

Willow's fear of the fairy world was the heritage bequeathed to her by her ancestors, those who had been fairies once, those who had come out of the mists. Not all of her ancestors had left, of course; some had remained behind, content with their immortality. Some yet lived and were fairies still. At times she could hear their voices in her sleep, in her dreams, calling out to her, urging her to come back to their way of life. It had been hundreds of years since the once-fairy had departed the mists, but the whispered call to return never ceased.

It was a fact of life for her as it was for all of the once-fairy. Except that now she would be going back in spite of the warnings against doing so, the cautions that were carefully handed down from parents to children by all of the once-fairy. You can never go back. You can never return. But she would be doing so. She would be risking her sanity and her life for the sake of her child. Her needs versus the needs of her baby—it was a conflict that threatened to tear her apart.

She walked on, debating, arguing with herself. The forest began to change perceptibly, the trees rising higher, the look of the land altering subtly, and she saw that she was drawing near to Elderew. She did not intend to enter the city. Her father was there, and she did not want to see him. He was the River Master, leader of the once-fairy and Lord of the lake country. They had never shared a close relationship and had grown farther apart when she had defied his wishes and gone to Ben Holiday when Ben had first come into Landover. She had known she was meant for Ben and he for her, that they would share a life, and she had decided that whatever the consequences she would find a way to be with him. It had not helped that he had succeeded as King when others who craved power over Landover, her father included, had hoped he would not. It had not helped that she had made her life with him, a human, and left her own people. The relationship was further strained by the closeness she shared with her mother. The River Master was still in love with Willow's mother, the only woman he had coveted and been unable to possess. He had fathered Willow on the single night they lay together, and then Willow's mother, a wood nymph so wild that she could not live anywhere but in the deepest forest, had returned to her old life. The River Master had searched her out repeatedly and had even tried to trap her on one or two occasions, but all his efforts had failed. Willow's mother would not come back to him. That she appeared now and again to Willow and danced for her in the fairy way, sharing emotions and dreams that transcended words, was almost more than the River Master could bear. He had many wives and many more children. He should have been content. He was not. Willow thought that without her mother beside him he never would be.

She eased down a corridor of great white oak and shag-bark hickory leading to the silver ribbon of a tributary that fed into the Irrylin, making her way toward the old pines where her mother would come to her at nightfall. She thought of her old life, her life before Ben, here in the lake country, as a child of the River Master. She had been alone most of the time and had never felt loved. She had kept herself strong with her unshakable belief of what would one day be, the prospect of Ben and her life with him, the promise made to her by the Earth Mother when she was still a small child, the dream that nurtured and sustained her. The realization of that dream had been a long time coming, she thought, but any amount of time would have been worth the wait.

She reached the stream, followed it to a shallows, and crossed. She felt the eyes on her for the first time then and stopped. They were bold and steady. She turned toward them, and they were gone. A once-fairy, like herself, probably in service to her father. She should have known she could not come into the lake country unseen. She should have known that her father would not allow it.

She sighed. Now that he knew she was there, he would insist on speaking with her. She might as well wait where she was.

She turned back to the stream and stooped to drink from a rapids. The water was clean and tasted good. She looked at herself in the ripple of brightness as it passed, a small and slender woman who looked to be barely more than a girl, eyes large and expressive, hair thick and flowing from her head but as thin and fine as gossamer where it ran down the backs of her forearms and calves, all of her colored in various shades of green. She was this image reflected by the waters of the stream, but she was also at regular intervals transformed into the tree for which she was named, a consequence of her genetic makeup and now the cause for this journey she had been sent upon. She thought for a moment about how different things would have been if she had been given other blood, if she had been born of other parents. But a moment of such thinking was enough. She might as well ponder what would have happened if she had been born human.

She rose, and the River Master stood before her. He was tall and lean, his skin an almost silver cast, grainy and shimmering, his hair black and thick about the nape of his neck and forearms. His forest clothing was loose-fitting, nondescript, and belted at the waist. He wore a slim silver diadem on his head, the mark of his office. The features of his face were sharp and small, his nose almost nonexistent, his mouth a tight line that allowed no expression.

"Even for you, that was quick," she greeted him.

"I had to be quick," he replied, "since my daughter apparently did not intend to visit me."

His voice was deep and even. He was alone, but she knew his retainers were close by, concealed back in the trees, staying just within hearing so that they could respond quickly if called.

"You are correct," she said. "I did not."

Her honesty gave him pause. "Bold words for a child to speak to her father. Are you too good for me now that you are the wife of the High Lord?" A hint of anger crept into his voice. "Have you forgotten who you were and where you came from? Have you forgotten your roots, Willow?"

She did not miss the snide reference. "I have forgotten nothing. Rather, I have remembered all too well. I do not feel welcome here, Father. I think that seeing me is not altogether pleasant for you."

He stared at her momentarily and then nodded. "Because of your mother, you believe? Because of how I feel about her? Perhaps so, Willow. But I have learned to put those feelings aside. I find I must. Have you come to see her, then?"

"Yes."

"About the child you are expecting?"

She smiled in spite of herself. She should have known. The River Master had spies everywhere, and there had been no attempt to keep the news of her baby a secret. "Yes," she answered.

"Your child by Holiday, an heir to the throne." Her father's stone face was expressionless, but his voice gave something of what he was feeling away. "You must be pleased, Willow."

"And you are not," she declared softly.

"The child is not once-fairy and therefore not one of us. The child is half-human. I would wish it otherwise."

She shook her head. "You see everything in terms of your own interests, Father. The child is Ben Holiday's and therefore another obstacle in your efforts to gain control of the throne of Landover. You can't just outwait him now. You must deal with his child as well. Isn't that what you mean?"

The River Master came forward to stand directly before her. "I will not argue with you. I am disappointed that you did not intend to tell me of the birth of my grandchild. You would tell your mother, but you would let me find out another way."

"It wasn't so difficult for you, was it?" she asked. "Not with all your spies to tell you."

There was a hard silence as they faced each other, sylph and sprite, daughter and father, separated by distances that could never be measured.

The River Master looked away. The sun glinted off his silver skin as he stared out into the shadows of the great forest trees. "This is my homeland. These are my people. It is important for me to remember them first in all things. You have forgotten what that means. We do not see things the same way, Willow. We never have. I was never close enough to you to find a way to do so. Some of that is my fault. You were ruined for me by your mother's refusal to live with me. I could not look at you without seeing her."

He shrugged, a slow, deliberate movement, a relegation to the past of what was now beyond his grasp. "Yet I loved you, child. I love you still." He looked back at her. "You do not believe that, do you? You do not accept it."

She felt something stir weakly inside, a memory of when she had wanted nothing more. "If you love me," she said carefully, "then give me your word that you will protect my child always."

He looked long and hard at her, as if seeing someone else. Then he placed one hand on his breast. She was surprised to see how gnarled it had become. The River Master was aging. "Given," he said. "To the extent that I can do so, my grandchild shall be kept safe." He paused. "But it was not necessary to ask for my word on that."

Willow held his gaze. "I think perhaps it was."

The River Master's hand dropped away. "You are too harsh toward me. But I understand." He glanced skyward. "Do you go now to your mother or will you come with me into the city, to my home? Your mother," he hurried on, "will not come until night."

Willow hesitated, and for a moment thought she might accept his invitation, for she sensed it was extended in kindness and not duplicitously. Then she shook her head. "No, I will go on," she said. "I have . . . a need to be alone before I see her."

Her father nodded, as if he had expected her answer. "Do you think she . . . ?" he began, and then stopped, unable to continue. Willow waited. He looked away and then back again. "Do you think she would dance for me as well?"

Willow experienced a sudden sadness for her father. It had been difficult for him to ask that. "No, I do not think so. She will not even appear if you come with me."

He nodded again, expecting this answer as well. She reached out then and took hold of his hand. "But I will ask her if she will dance for you another time."

His hand tightened around hers. They stood joined that way for a moment longer, and then the River Master spoke again. "I will tell you something, Willow. Whether you believe me or not is your choice. But my dreams are certain and my vision is true, and of all the once-fairy I am the most powerful and the closest to the old ways. So heed me. Even before I was informed of the birth, I knew of the child. I have dreamed of it before. The dreams show me this. The path of your life is marked by the coming of this child. You must find ways to be strong in the face of the changes it will bring—you and the High Lord both."

Willow swallowed her sudden fear. "Have you seen my child's face? Have you seen anything that you can tell me?"

The River Master shook his head slowly. "No, Willow. My dreams of the child are too large for the specifics you would know. My dreams are shadows and light upon a life path and nothing more. If you would know specifics, speak with the Earth Mother. Perhaps her vision is clearer than mine."

Willow nodded. He would not have known she had already spoken to the elemental. The Earth Mother would not have allowed it. "I will do as you suggest. Thank you."

She released his hand and stepped back. Then she started off into the forest. "You will not try to follow me?" She looked back guardedly.

Her father shook his head once more. "No. If you will remember to ask of the dance."

She turned away. "I will."

She continued on then and did not look back again.

⋯⟨∾⟩⋯

The remainder of the day passed away in a ripple of slow breezes and lengthening shadows, the sun easing west across the cloudless sky and disappearing finally beneath the horizon in a broad sweep of crimson. Willow sat at the edge of the clearing in the middle of the old pines waiting for nightfall and her mother's coming. She had arrived early and spent her time considering the direction of her life. She found she had a need to do so.

When she was still small, she came often to the old pines in search of her mother. She came out of a need to know what her mother was like and a sense that by doing so she would better understand herself. The Earth Mother warned her that her mother might not come for a long time, that she would be reticent and perhaps even fearful of facing the daughter she had abandoned. But Willow was determined, more tough-minded, even then, than anyone expected.

But then Willow had never been what anyone expected. She began life as a small, shy, introspective child, not very pretty, lacking the benefit of a mother's guidance or even a father's interest, and there was no reason to think she would ever be any different. But she surprised everyone. The Earth Mother helped by encouraging and teaching, but mostly it was Willow who managed the transformation, and mostly she did it by being determined. She was quiet about it at first. Because she was left to be on her own a lot of the time, she discovered early on that if she really wanted something she would have to go out and get it on her own. She learned to dig in her heels, roll up her sleeves, work hard, and be patient. She learned that if you wanted something badly enough, you could always find a way to get it. The mental toughness was always there; the rest came later. She became beautiful, though she never thought of herself that way. Others found her striking; she viewed herself as too exotic. Because she had to do so much for herself, she learned confidence and directness. She learned not to be afraid of anyone or anything. She developed her skills and her knowledge with the same fierce determination she brought to everything. She was not that way because she was afraid of failing; it never occurred to her that she might fail. She was that way because it was the only way she knew.

In the end, she waited almost three years for her mother to come. She went to the old pines at least once a week. She waited through the days and sometimes the nights as well. The waiting was hard, but not unbearable. Although she never saw her mother, she sometimes felt her presence. The feeling came in a rustle of leaves, a small animal sound, a whisper of wind, or a scent of new flowers. It was never the same, but always recognizable. She would tell the Earth Mother afterward, encouraged, and the Earth Mother would nod and say, yes, that was your mother. She's watching you. She's judging. Perhaps she will show herself one day.

And one day she did. At midnight, at midsummer, she appeared in a glimmer of moonlight, spinning and leaping from the forest trees into the clearing to dance for the child who had waited so long to see her. There was magic in the dance, and Willow knew then and forever after that her life would be special and wondrous.

Now, after the passing of many years and many visits to the old pines, she had come once again. She had come to tell her mother of the child she was carrying, of the journey she was undertaking, and of the warnings she had received. Her emotions were sharply in conflict. On the one hand she was elated by the anticipated birth of her child with Ben; on the other, she was daunted by the prospect of her journey and frightened by the warnings given to her by the Earth Mother and her father. The latter bothered her most, cautions from two of the most powerful and magical creatures in Landover, both telling her that she must be wary, both warning that this child she so wanted would change everything about her life.

She tried to sort through her emotions as she waited for darkness. She pondered the warnings she had been given. There were no new insights to be gained by doing either. The exercise was merely a means for coming to terms with what she was thinking and feeling. If Ben had been there, she would have talked it through with him. Since he wasn't, she was forced to use what had worked for her when she was small and growing up alone.

Mostly, she was hopeful that her mother would be able to help. They would communicate as they always did through the wood nymph's dance. The dance would provide a vision, and the vision would give insight. It had done so on many occasions. Willow hoped it would do so now.

Twilight deepened and the stars appeared. Two moons were visible in the northern sky, not far above the horizon, one pale mauve, one peach. The night air was fragrant with the scent of pine needles and wildflowers, and the clearing was hushed. Willow sat thinking of Ben. She wished he was with her. It would have made things much easier having him there. She did not like being away from him. She did not feel complete when she was.

It was nearing midnight when her mother came. She leaped out of the

trees in a series of flitting movements that took her from one patch of shadows to the next. She was a tiny, ephemeral creature, with long silver hair, pale
green skin like Willow's own, and a child's body. She wore no clothing. She
darted along the edges of the clearing as if testing the waters of a moonlit
lake, and then disappeared into the trees to hide.

Willow waited expectantly.

Her mother returned in a flash of silver skin, spinning swiftly past her, fingers brushing at her cheek, a light ripple of velvet, and then she was gone once
more.

"Mother?" Willow called softly to her.

A moment later her mother danced out from the trees into the very center of the starlight that cascaded down through the heavy boughs. She spun
and twisted and leapt in the radiant glow, her arms moving fluidly, reaching
out for her daughter. Willow lifted her own arms in response. They did not
touch each other, but the words began to flow between them, heard only in
the mind, visions born out of thought.

Willow remembered her promise to her father and spoke first of his desire
to see Willow's mother dance. Her mother drew back immediately, and she
let the matter drop. She spoke of Ben and her life at Sterling Silver. There was
happiness in her mother's response this time, though it was small and measured, for her mother could not understand life beyond the forest and the
dance, life of any kind beyond her own. In a detached way she was happy for
Willow; she was not capable of anything more. Willow had learned to take
what her mother offered and make the most of it.

She let her mother speak to her then through the dance, let her share in
turn the joy she was feeling. Once Willow had found that joy exhilarating.
Now she found it lacking, an oddly empty, circumscribed happiness bound up
in self-indulgence and personal gratification, bereft of interest in or concern
for others, ultimately puzzling and somehow sad. Neither could ever really
understand the other, Willow knew. Still they shared what they could, giving
back reassurance and gratitude, reaffirming the bond that existed between
them.

Then Willow told her mother of the baby and of the quest that would take
her from Landover to Earth to the fairy mists and back again.

Her mother's response was immediate. The dance grew wilder and more
frenzied. The silence of the night deepened and the world beyond that starlit
clearing slipped farther away into the darkness. There were only mother and
daughter and the dance they shared. Willow watched, awestruck by her
mother's grace, her beauty, her strong presence, and her instinctive response
to her daughter's special needs.

And so out of the strange, impossible spinnings and turnings of the dance
appeared the vision Willow had anticipated, rising up into the light to fill the
space between them.

But the vision was not of her child, but of Ben. He was lost, she sensed—lost in a way that he could not understand. He was himself, but at the same time he was someone else. He was not alone. Two others were with him, and she started as she recognized who they were. Nightshade the witch and Strabo the dragon. All three floundered in a morass of mist and gray light that emanated as much from within as from without. They journeyed onward hopelessly, searching for something that was hidden from her, casting desperately about in a futile effort to find it.

Then she saw herself, consumed by an identical patch of mist and grayness, as lost as they, searching for something as well. She was near them and yet far away, close enough to touch them and yet nowhere she could be seen. She was dancing, spinning through a prism of light. She could not stop.

There was something more. In a subtle shift of sound and light, the vision revealed one final horror. In its telling of what would be, she could see that Ben was forgetting her and that she was forgetting Ben. She could see it happening in the gloom and shadows; they were turning away from each other. They would never find each other again.

Ben, she heard herself call out in despair. *Ben!*

--◦∞◦--

When the vision faded, she found herself alone. The clearing stood empty, and her mother had gone. She sat staring at the space through which her mother had danced and tried to comprehend what she had been shown. There had been nothing of her baby; everything had been of Ben. Why? Ben was safely back at Sterling Silver, not lost in misty darkness. And what set of circumstances could possibly bring him together with Nightshade and Strabo, his sworn enemies?

None of it made any sense. Which made it all the more maddening.

Her dilemma now was acute. She wanted to turn around and go back to Sterling Silver at once to make certain that Ben was safe. The urge was so strong that she came close to setting out without another thought for the matter.

But she knew she couldn't do that. Her commitment now was to her baby and to the quest that would ensure its safe birth. She could not afford to burden herself with other concerns, no matter who was involved, no matter how compelling, until she had fulfilled the Earth Mother's quest. Ben would agree with that. In fact, he would insist on it. She would have to ignore the vision for now. She would have to let events take their course until she could afford to do something to affect them directly.

She rose then, more tired than she had expected, drained by the events of the day, and moved to the center of the starlit clearing. She bent to where her mother had danced and began to dig with her hands. It was not difficult; the soil was loose and easily gathered. She scooped up several handfuls and placed them in a pouch she had brought to carry extra foodstuffs—one portion of the magic her baby required. She laced the pouch tight, hefted it in her hands, and tied it again to her waist.

She looked off to the east. The sky was beginning to lighten. The dance had lasted through most of the night.

She looked about the clearing one final time. It sat empty and silent, the ancient pines solemn witnesses that would never tell what they had seen. So much had taken place here over the years, so much that remained an indelible part of her life. Now this.

"Good-bye, Mother," she said softly, speaking mostly to herself. "I wish you could come with me."

She stood there alone, thinking again of the vision, and she closed her eyes against what she was feeling. What of Ben? What if the vision were true? She squeezed her eyes tighter to make the questions go away.

When she opened them again, she was thinking of what lay ahead. Earth, Ben's world, somewhere through the fairy mists, where the second soil collection must take place. But where in his world? To what place must she go? What kind of soil was required to fulfill her obligation? What form of magic?

And her guide . . . ?

She saw the cat then, sitting on a log to one side, licking its front paw. It was colored silver with black paws, face, and tail. It was slender and well-groomed and did not appear feral. It paused in its licking and regarded her with emerald eyes as brilliant as her own. She had the strangest feeling that it had been waiting for her.

I know this cat, she realized suddenly.

"Yes, indeed you do," the cat said.

Willow nodded wordlessly. She should have guessed. The fairies had sent her Edgewood Dirk.

MIND'S EYE CRYSTALS

Horris Kew trudged along the road to Sterling Silver whistling nervously in the midday sun. Another few miles, two or three at most, and then they would see. Anticipation mingled with trepidation and caused a serious burning sensation in the pit of his stomach. He was sweating profusely, and it was from more than the heat. The tic in his eye jumped wildly. He looked like he was juggling invisible balls.

He gave an anxious glance over his shoulder. No problem, everything was in place. The pack mule was still tethered to the other end of the rope he held, plodding obediently after. The twin chests were still roped tightly in place on the carry rack. Biggar was still perched atop them.

"Keep your eyes on the road, Horris," the myna said.

"I was just checking," he replied irritably.

"Don't bother. That's why I'm back here. You just keep walking. Just keep putting one foot in front of the other. Try not to fall on your face."

Horris Kew turned crimson. *Try not to fall on your face! Ha, ha! Big joke!*

Still looking over his shoulder, he opened his mouth to tell the bird to shut up, tripped, and promptly fell on his face. The road was dusty and dry, and he plowed a fair-size furrow in it with his nose and came up with a mouthful of grit. He heaved himself back to his feet and spit angrily.

"Don't say anything, Biggar!" he snapped, and began brushing himself off. His scarecrow body performed a series of violent contortions as he worked to get clean. "There was a rut! A rut! If you hadn't distracted me, I would have seen it and been all right!"

Biggar sighed wearily. "Why don't you just conjure us up a carriage and we could ride to the castle, Horris? Or maybe a horse. A horse would do."

"A horse! Great idea, a horse!" Horris clenched his hands angrily. "We're supposed to be supplicants, you idiot! Poor, penniless supplicants! Remember the plan?"

The mule yawned and brayed loudly. "Shut up!" Horris screamed furiously.

Biggar blinked and cocked his head thoughtfully. "Let me see. The plan. Ah, yes. The plan. I remember it now. The one that isn't going to work."

"Don't say that!"

"Don't say what? That the plan isn't going to work?"

"Shhhh!" a frantic Horris cautioned, tucking his head down between his shoulders for protection, glancing hurriedly about. His eye jumped. "It could be listening!"

"Who, the Gorse? Out here, in the midday sun, in the middle of nowhere?" Biggar sniffed. "I hardly think so. It's a night creature and not given to prolonged exposure to sunlight. Vampiric, I think they call it."

Horris glowered at him. "You're mighty brave when it isn't around, aren't you?"

"I'm merely making a point."

"I didn't notice you making it last night. I didn't notice you saying anything about the plan not working when it was explained to us."

"So you believe the plan is a good one, do you, Horris? Is that right? You think it will work?"

Horris tightened his jaw defiantly, standing in the middle of the road facing mule and bird, fists on hips. He was a boxer leading with his chin. "Of course it will work!" he declared.

Biggar sniffed in obvious disdain. "Well, there you are. I rest my case. What is the purpose of my arguing with this creature, this Gorse, if you're going to stand around nodding in agreement with every cockeyed idea it comes up with? What am I supposed to do, Horris? I can't protect you from yourself. You won't listen to anyone when you're like this. Certainly not me. After all, I'm just your pet bird."

Horris gritted his teeth. "Pets are supposed to revere their masters, Biggar. When do you think you might start doing that?"

"Probably when I get a master who's worth the effort!"

Horris let his breath out with a hiss. "This isn't my fault! None of this is my fault! The Gorse is here because of you! You were the one who summoned it up in the first place!"

Biggar clacked his beak. "You were the one who did the conjuring, if I recall!"

"You told me what to say!"

"Well, you didn't have to say it!"

Horris threw down the rope to the mule. He was trembling all over. It was hot standing around in the midday summer sun, out of the shade of the forest trees, on a dry and dusty road. The robes he wore—a supplicant's robes—were coarse and sweat-stained and they stank. He had been walking since sometime after midnight because the Gorse wanted him at the gates of Sterling Silver just before sundown of today so that they would have to admit him into the castle for the night. He was tired and hungry (no food if you were a supplicant either, unless you could stand eating those detestable Bonnie Blues), and his patience was exhausted.

"Look, Biggar." He addressed the bird as calmly as he could. "I'm all done arguing with you. You had your chance to say something before this and you didn't. So you listen up. The plan will work, got it? It will work! You might not think so and maybe I don't either, but if the Gorse says it will work, it will!"

He bent forward like a reedy tree in a high wind. "Did you see how easily it got rid of Holiday? And Strabo and Nightshade? Like that, Biggar!" He snapped his fingers dramatically. "It has a lot of power, in case you hadn't noticed. With King, witch, and dragon gone, who's going to challenge it? That's why the plan will work. And that's why I don't intend to ask any foolish questions!"

The bird faced him down. "You ought to listen to yourself, Horris. You really should. Got rid of Holiday and the witch and the dragon like that, did it?" He clacked his beak to mimic the other's emphasis. "Did it ever occur to you that it could get rid of us just as easily? I mean, what does it need with us anyway? Have you asked yourself that? We're errand boys, Horris. That's all we are. We're running around doing things it can't do for itself, but once we've done them, what then? If this so-called plan works, what does it need with us afterwards?"

Horris Kew felt a sudden lurch in the pit of his stomach. Maybe Biggar was right. He could still see Holiday and the witch and the dragon being sucked down into the Tangle Box. He could still see them fighting to get free before disappearing into the mists. When he had picked up the box, it seemed as if he could feel them batting around inside like trapped moths. He wondered what the Gorse had done with the Tangle Box after Horris had carried it back to the cave. He wondered if there was room inside for any more prisoners.

Horris swallowed hard. "Don't worry, the Gorse needs us all right," he insisted, but he didn't sound so sure now.

"Why?" Biggar snapped.

"Why?"

"Don't repeat me, Horris. I've warned you about that. Yes, why? Better ask yourself another question while you're at it. If it plans to give us all of Landover, what does it plan to give itself? And don't tell me it's doing this as a philanthropical undertaking. Don't tell me it doesn't want anything for itself. This plan is leading up to something, and so far it's not telling us what!"

"Okay! Okay!" Horris was on the defensive now. "Maybe there is something more than what we're being told. Sure, why not? Say, I've got an idea! Why don't you ask it, Biggar? If you're so worried, why don't you just ask it?"

"For the same reason you don't, Horris! I don't fancy getting dispatched like Holiday and the others!"

"But it's okay for me to chance it, is that it?"

"While it needs you, it is! Think with your brain, Horris! It won't do anything to you while it needs you! It's afterwards that you have to start worrying!"

Horris stamped furiously. Dusty streaks of sweat ran down his narrow, pointed face. "That hardly helps us now, out here on the road, almost to the gates of the King's castle, does it?" he yelled angrily. "Got any other useful suggestions?"

Biggar ruffled his feathers anew, his dark eyes flat and hard. "Matter of fact, I do. This whole plan depends on whether or not the magic it gave us works. If it doesn't, the wizard and the dog are going to have us thrown into the darkest dungeon they can find. Holiday was our only ally when we were here before, and he's long gone. No one is going to be in a very good mood with him missing. So what if the magic doesn't work, Horris?"

Horris Kew glowered menacingly. "I'm getting tired of this, Biggar. In fact, I'm getting tired of you."

Biggar looked unimpressed. "I say we try one out and see if it works before we walk into the lion's den."

The glower deepened. "The Gorse told us not to do that, remember? It warned us explicitly."

"So what?" the bird pressed. "The Gorse isn't the one taking all the risks."

"It said that whatever we did, we were not to use them! It was pretty emphatic, as I recall!" Horris was shouting. "Suppose it isn't kidding, Biggar? Suppose—just suppose now—that it knows what it's talking about! After all, whose magic is it, you idiot?"

Biggar spit—not easy for a bird. "You are foolish beyond anything I could have imagined, Horris Kew. You are incredibly stupid. And myopic to boot. And, even for a human, exceedingly gutless!"

Horris charged him then, his temper frayed past its limits, his anger exploding through him. Roaring like an enraged lion, he came at Biggar with every intent of tearing him wing from wing. But Biggar was a bird, and birds can escape humans every time simply by flying off, which is what Biggar did now, a casual, lazy lifting into the air so that he circled just out of reach of the leaping, grasping, would-be conjurer. What Horris did succeed in doing was frightening the pack mule within an inch of its life so that it bolted back into the forest to disappear in a cloud of dust with a mighty, terrified bray.

"Oh, drat it, drat it, drat, drat, drat!" Horris mumbled, among other less printable things, when he finally calmed down enough to realize what he had done.

It took him, even with Biggar's help, an hour to round up the mule and the

precious chests it carried. Exhausted, sullen, and bereft for the moment of
any other plan, the conjurer and the bird continued their journey.

It was nearing sunset when they finally arrived at the gates of Sterling Silver.

—◦∞◦—

Questor Thews was at his wit's end. Three days had passed since Ben Holiday
had disappeared and there was still no sign of him. The escort that had accompanied the High Lord to the Heart had ridden directly back to the castle after
losing him, and Questor had been able to dispatch a search party immediately.
Those sent had scoured the area surrounding the Heart and then the whole of
the countryside beyond. There wasn't a trace of the High Lord. Jurisdiction
was found grazing where Holiday had apparently left him and that was it.
There was evidence of a disturbance at the Heart—some frayed banners,
some scorched seats and rests, a little dirt kicked up—but nothing that you
could put a name to and nothing that could help explain what had happened
to Holiday. Questor had gone out himself to take a look. He could feel the
presence of used magic in the air, but there was so much magic concentrated
there anyway that it was impossible to decipher what these odd traces meant.

In any case, Ben Holiday was nowhere to be found. Questor Thews had
moved quickly to keep that fact a secret, ordering the guards of the escort
and the search party not to speak of the matter to anyone. That was like sticking your finger in a leaking dike, however, as Abernathy was quick to point
out. News of this sort could not be kept secret for long. Someone was bound
to talk, and once word got out that the High Lord was really and truly gone,
there would be trouble for sure. If the River Master didn't start it, the Lords
of the Greensward surely would—especially Kallendbor of Rhyndweir, the
most powerful of the Lords and an implacable enemy of Ben Holiday's.
Kallendbor, more than any of Landover's nobles and leaders, had resented
the loss of power that Holiday's coronation had cost him. On the surface, he
acknowledged Holiday's sovereignty and obeyed his commands. Inside, he
simmered like something kept cooking too long. There were others as well
who would welcome news of Ben Holiday's removal, whatever the circumstances, and Questor knew he had to do something to put the rumors to rest
at once.

He came up with a rather ingenious plan, one he shared only with Abernathy and the kobolds, keeping the number who knew the truth to a manage-
able four. What he did was to have Abernathy call off the search and announce
that the High Lord had returned safely. To convince those quartered at the castle that the announcement was valid and not a further rumor, he used magic
to create an image of Ben Holiday passing along the castle ramparts at midday
where he could be clearly seen by those below. He even had him wave. He re-

peated his creation several times, making sure that there were plenty of witnesses. Sure enough, the word got passed along gossip-quick.

In the meantime, Questor used every spare minute available (which
wasn't nearly enough) employing the quick travel magic of the Landsview to
scour the countryside in search of Holiday. His efforts yielded nothing. There
was no sign of the High Lord.

Of course, life at Sterling Silver went on, Holiday or no, and it was important that what needed to be done got done, and that it got done as if Holiday
were doing it. This was a whole lot tougher to accomplish than the conjuring
up of an image or two. Since Holiday wasn't there to see any of a large number of representatives and officials who had come from every quarter of Landover, Questor Thews and Abernathy were forced to see them for him and to
pretend that they had been requested to do so. Some of those visiting had traveled great distances to see the High Lord. Some had been summoned. None
among them was much pleased at being put off. Questor resorted to increasingly desperate efforts to quell any suspicions. He forged the High Lord's
name on orders. He passed out gifts. He issued awards and citations of merit.
He even tried using his magic to throw the High Lord's voice from behind a
curtain. This effort produced a woman's voice and caused those listening to
stare at each other incredulously—who was this woman back there with the
High Lord?—and Questor was forced to salvage the situation by claiming it
was a serving girl who had mistaken Holiday for an intruder. Some of his
magic still needed work.

There was also the matter of Willow's absence, which the High Lord had
failed to explain before disappearing himself, so that now not just one person
was missing, but two. But since Holiday hadn't seemed unduly concerned
about Willow going off, Questor decided he needn't worry either, at least
not just now. Really, the only reason for finding her—since he had no particular reason to worry if she was safe—was to tell her about the High Lord's
disappearance. Questor decided he didn't need that additional complication
in his life. If Holiday hadn't been found by the time the sylph returned,
Questor would break the news to her then. There was, after all, only so much
he could do.

Which, at the moment, wasn't nearly enough. Trying to split his time between the requirements of his duties and the demands of his machinations was
beginning to take its toll. He was hardly in the mood then to hear the news
that Abernathy carried on appearing at the door to his work chamber just before sunset of that third day.

"Horris Kew and his bird are back," the Court Scribe announced with
something less than enthusiasm.

Questor looked up from the stack of paperwork visited on him in the High
Lord's absence and groaned. "Again? What does that wastrel want now?"

Abernathy stepped into the room and closed the door behind him. Even for a dog, he looked put upon. "He wishes to speak with the High Lord—what else? Isn't that everyone's reason for being alive these days? And do not bother telling me to send him away. Although I would love to do so, I cannot. He is cloaked in supplicant's robes; I have to admit him."

Questor pressed his fingers to his forehead, massaging the temples. "Did he say what he wants, by any chance?"

"He said it was important, nothing more. He did not mention his exile, if that is what you are asking."

"To tell you the truth, I don't know what I'm asking! I barely know what I'm doing!" The wizard looked as if he were trying to tear at his beard. "You know, Abernathy, I am very fond of the High Lord. Very. I recruited him myself, if you recall. I saw something special in him, and I was not mistaken. He was the King we had all been looking for, the King Landover needed to become whole again."

He came to his feet. "But, really, I wish he would stop disappearing so often! How many times has he done this now? I don't know how he can be so inconsiderate of us. Going off in the middle of the night, just riding out without a word, leaving us to try to cover for him until he comes back. I must tell you, I find it exceedingly aggravating!"

Abernathy looked away and cleared his throat. "Well, in all fairness, Questor Thews, some of those disappearances were not the High Lord's fault. I am quite certain he would have preferred that they had never happened."

"Yes, yes, I know. My brother and all. The black unicorn." Questor brushed the explanation aside. "Still, a King has responsibilities, and they should not be taken lightly. A King should consult with his advisors on these things. That's what advisors are . . ."

He stopped abruptly. "You don't think he's been kidnapped, do you? Wouldn't there have been a ransom demand by now? Unless Nightshade has him. She wouldn't bother with a ransom demand. She would simply eliminate him! But why wouldn't the Paladin protect him against her? Why wouldn't the Paladin come to his rescue—"

"Questor Thews." Abernathy tried to interrupt.

"—whatever sort of danger he was in? What sort of protector leaves his master—"

"Wizard!" the dog snapped irritably.

Questor jumped. "What? What is it?"

"Stop carrying on so, for goodness' sake! What is the point of it? We have no idea what has become of the High Lord, but it certainly does not help him if we lose our heads. We have to remain calm. We have to carry on as if he were still here and in the meantime hope he shows up." Abernathy took a deep breath. "Have you found anything in the Landsview?"

Questor, duly chastened, shook his head. "No, nothing."

"Perhaps you should send Bunion to look about. A kobold can cover more ground than any twenty search parties and make no disturbance doing it. Bunion can track anyone. Perhaps you should let him try to track Holiday."

"Yes." Questor nodded thoughtfully. "Yes, perhaps so."

"In the meantime," Abernathy continued, resisting the urge to scratch at something low down on his body with his hind leg, "what about Horris Kew?"

Questor pressed at his temples again, as if reminded of a headache he had momentarily forgotten. "Oh, dear. Him. Well, he can't see the High Lord, of course. Confound it, why does he have to see anyone?"

"He doesn't," Abernathy answered, "but if I read the depth of his determination correctly, he will keep trying until he does. I do not think he will simply go away."

Questor sighed. "No, I don't suppose he will." He paused thoughtfully. "Abernathy, do you think I look anything like that man?"

Abernathy stared. "What an odd question."

"Well, it bothers me that I might. I mean, we are both in the conjuring business, aren't we? And sometimes they say that all conjurers look alike. You've heard that, haven't you? Besides, we're both rather tall and slight of build and at times awkward, and we both have rather prominent noses and . . . well, sharp features . . ."

Abernathy held up one paw deliberately. "You look as much like Horris Kew as I look like his bird. Please, no more of this. Just decide if we see them tonight or not. I suggest we do not put it off."

Questor nodded. "No, I agree. Let's get it over with."

They went out of the room, down the hall, and descended two flights of stairs to where visitors were kept waiting until they could be received. They made a strange pair, the white-haired, gangly wizard with his colorful patched robes and the dog with his shaggy coat and fastidious dress. Questor grumbled the whole way, griping about this, bemoaning that, keeping such an edge on things that at last Abernathy was forced to ask him in rather rude fashion to be quiet. Two old friends whose shared history made them inseparable in spite of themselves, they could track each other's life steps as if the paths were already laid out before them.

"You know, Abernathy," the wizard confided, as they reached the ground floor of the castle and prepared to turn into the front hall. "If I didn't know better, I'd think Horris Kew had something to do with Holiday's disappearance. It's just the sort of thing he would precipitate with his unbalanced magic, conjuring up trouble here and there, all willy-nilly. But he doesn't have that kind of power!" He thought it over. "He doesn't have enough brains either."

Abernathy sniffed. "It doesn't take brains to be dangerous."

They walked down the front hall to the anteroom where Horris Kew and his bird would be waiting and stepped inside.

Horris rose from the bench on which he had been sitting. The bird was perched on the back of the bench, sharp-eyed and sleek. Next to them on the floor rested two iron-bound wooden trunks.

"Questor Thews and Abernathy!" Horris Kew exclaimed with what seemed excessive delight. "Good evening to you! Thank you for coming to see me so quickly. I am deeply appreciative."

"Horris, let's skip past the pleasantries, shall we? What are you doing back here? As I recall, you were told to come back when the High Lord sent for you. Has he done so without my knowledge?"

The conjurer smiled sheepishly. "No, regrettably, he has not. I continue to live in hope and expectation." He brightened. "That is not why I have come, Questor. I am here for another reason entirely. I have some very exciting news to share." He paused and glanced past them hopefully. "I don't suppose that the High Lord is about?"

Questor grimaced. "Not at the moment. What is this news you bring, Horris? Nothing dealing with farm animals, I trust."

"No, no," the other answered quickly. "I remember my promise and I will not break it. No conjuring. No, this is something else entirely." Again he paused. "May I confide it to you, to the two of you, as Court Wizard and Scribe, since the High Lord is otherwise occupied?"

Questor said something in response, but Abernathy was looking at the bird. Was he losing his mind or had he heard the bird snicker? He glared at the myna, but the myna simply ruffled its feathers indifferently and looked away.

"Well, then," Horris Kew declared, and cleared his throat officiously. "There are times, more than a few I might add, when stress from work and the burden of our obligations wears us down and we find we need some sort of amusement or diversion to relax us. I am sure you will agree that this is true. I speak now not just of the high-born, but of the common man, the workers in the fields and factories, in the markets and shops of our farms and cities. I speak of every man and woman, of every boy and girl all struggling to make their lives a better and more productive—"

"Get to the point, Horris," Questor interrupted wearily. "It has been a long day."

Horris paused, smiled, and shrugged. "Indeed. A diversion, then. A way of removing stress from our lives for a few hours. I believe I have found something that will provide that relief."

"Very commendable," Abernathy snapped. "But someone already made that discovery quite a long time ago. They are called games. Sometimes they are played in groups, sometimes by a single individual. There are all forms of them. Have you discovered a new game? Is that what you are here about?"

Horris Kew laughed politely, though he seemed to be doing so through clenched teeth. "Oh, no, this is not about games. This is something else entirely." He paused, then leaned forward conspiratorially. "A mind's eye crystal!" he whispered hoarsely.

"A what?" Questor Thews demanded, his brow furrowing.

"A mind's eye crystal," the other repeated carefully. "Do you know of it?"

Questor did not, but he did not want to admit to being ignorant of anything to Horris Kew. "A little something, perhaps." He pursed his lips. "But tell me about it anyway."

"A crystal," Horris said, holding up a single finger. "A crystal that you look into as you would a mirror. And when you do, it shows you images of the past and of the future, images of yourself and those you love. The images are pleasant and welcome, and they take you away from your troubles for a time. The perfect diversion from your cares." He rubbed his hands. "Here, let me show you."

He reached into his supplicant's robes and pulled forth a crystal to hold up before them. It was about the width and length of an average thumb, five-sided, pointed at one end, flat at the other, and clear enough to see through.

"Would you like to try it?" he asked Questor Thews, and held out the crystal for the wizard to take.

"Wait a minute." Abernathy was between them instantly. "This thing is magic, is it?"

Horris nodded calmly. "It is."

"I thought you said you would give up conjuring unless asked. You swore to the High Lord that you would give it up, in fact. What happened to your vow, Horris? Where did this crystal come from if you did not conjure it up?"

Horris Kew held up his hands in a placating manner. "I have not broken my vow, Abernathy. This"—he held forth the crystal a second time—"was shown to me in a dream. I was asleep in the deep woods . . . uh," he hesitated, "north. I was asleep, having fasted and contemplated the misdealings and mistakes of my life all day after returning from my visit here, and I dreamed. In my dream I was shown this mind's eye crystal. It was a vision of great power. It told me of the crystal and where it might be found. It told me to seek it out. When I woke, I was compelled to do so. I did and I found it as promised. Knowing that I have not as yet had my exile lifted, I felt compelled to bring it to you." He paused, looking down at his feet. "I admit I hoped that it might in some small way influence you to take me back."

Abernathy was not impressed. He stood his ground, dog face fixed and dog eyes searching. There was a lie in here somewhere, he was sure of it. "You have never, in your entire life, employed a magic that did not end badly for anyone who came into contact with it. I cannot believe that this mind's eye crystal will be any different."

"But I am not the same man!" Horris Kew protested with a dramatic gesture. "I have changed, Abernathy. I have repented my former life and resolved to follow a different path. This crystal is my first step down that path." He drew himself up. "Tell you what. Why don't you try it out first, instead of Questor Thews? That way if there is a problem, Questor can use his formidable magic to do with me as he will. Surely you agree he is more than a match for me in case this is some sort of trick. And anyway, why would I chance anything so foolish this close to the dungeons into which you have already indicated you would like to see me thrown?"

He had a point. Abernathy hesitated. "I would not put anything past you, Horris," he muttered.

"Hooray for Horris, hooray for Horris!" the bird cawed suddenly, and clacked its beak.

Abernathy glared at the bird. "What do you think, Questor Thews?" he asked, and glanced back at the other.

The wizard's mouth was a tight line. "There are guards all about. If this goes awry, Horris goes into the keep and stays there. I stand ready if there is magic to be combated." He shook his head. "It's up to you, Abernathy."

"You will not be sorry," Horris offered, advancing the crystal another few inches toward the scribe. "I promise."

Abernathy sighed. "Very well. Anything to put this matter to bed. What do I do?"

Horris was beaming. "Just take the crystal, hold it in your hand, look into it, and think happy thoughts."

Abernathy grimaced. "Good grief. All right, give it to me."

He reached out, took the crystal from the other's hands, held it up before him, and stared into it. Nothing happened. Sure enough, Abernathy thought disdainfully. No surprise here. He was supposed to think happy thoughts, though, so he tried to picture something that would make him feel good and came up with an image of Horris and his bird in a dungeon cell. That made him feel better right away, he decided, and started to smile in spite of himself.

In the next instant the crystal brightened and locked him into it, drawing his gaze into its multi-faceted depths, pulling him out of himself and down into its suddenly brilliant light. He gasped. What was he seeing? There was something there, something wondrous, something familiar . . .

Abernathy saw it clearly then. There was a man in the light, striding out to greet the day from his home, waving hello to friends, calling out to passersby. The man was carrying books in his arms and was on his way to his day's work. He wore glasses and was dressed in the ceremonial clothing of a Court Scribe. *No!*

The man was Abernathy as he used to be. Abernathy as a human being. Abernathy before he had been turned into a dog. Himself, once more.

Sudden joy surged through the dog as he watched, a happiness he had not felt for years. He was himself again in the crystal's image! He was restored! It was his greatest wish in life, to become the man he had been—a wish he had not dared even contemplate upon discovering that Questor Thews, having turned him into a dog, could not turn him back into a man. Countless attempts to remedy the situation had failed, and Abernathy had given up all hope. But now, here, in this crystal's image, was a chance to feel again what it was like to be a man! He could sense the other's body—as if it were his own. He could experience anew what it was to be human.

The emotions the magic generated were too powerful to bear all at once. He closed his hand quickly about the crystal and snatched the vision away. He could barely breathe. "How did you do that?" he whispered in disbelief.

"I did nothing," Horris Kew responded promptly. "And we could not see what you saw. Only the holder of the crystal sees the vision. It is his own, personal revelation, private and inviolate. Do you understand now the uses for such a magic?"

Abernathy nodded, thinking of how wonderful it would be to call up that image of himself anytime he wanted to remember what his life had once been like. "Yes, I do," he replied softly.

Now it was Questor who pushed forward. "This thing works?" he asked, turning his old friend about, seeing the look in his eyes. "Well, indeed, I guess it does. Are you all right?"

Abernathy nodded, unable to speak, thinking again of what the image had shown him, of himself restored to who and what he had been. He was fighting hard to stay calm, to keep what he was feeling inside.

Neither saw the brief glance exchanged by Horris Kew and Biggar. *Well, well,* the glance said.

"You can appreciate the enormous potential for this magic," Horris said quickly. "Escape from the drudgery and stress of everyday life is only a moment away if you possess a mind's eye crystal. No group participation required, no equipment needed, no time necessary. Use the crystal on a break from your work and return refreshed!" He smiled benevolently. "Don't you feel happy and rested, Abernathy?" he pressed.

Abernathy swallowed. "Yes," he agreed. "I do."

"There you are, then!" Horris beamed. "Abernathy, this crystal is yours. I want you to have it. A gift, for giving me a chance to fulfill my hopes."

"Thank you, Horris," Abernathy replied, genuinely pleased, already envisioning his next look into the light. All suspicions of the conjurer's motives were forgotten. "Thank you very much."

"You see," Horris continued, anticipating Questor Thews, who was about to offer a further objection, "I have a few more of these to give out. Quite a few more, in fact."

He turned to one of the iron-bound trunks, released the catch, and threw open the lid. The trunk was filled to the brim with mind's eye crystals.

"Thousands of them," he offered, making a sweeping gesture. "The vision showed me one, but when I followed the pathway to where it was hidden, I discovered all these. Two trunkfuls, Questor. I have brought them both. I want you to have them. A little penance, perhaps, for my past misdeeds. I cannot comprehend why I was chosen to find them, but I am grateful that I was and I have decided to accept responsibility for their proper use. So I entrust them now to you. My gift to Landover. Pass them out to her people and let them enjoy the images they find therein. A little happiness to dull the edges of their more stressful moments."

Questor Thews and Abernathy stared at the trunkful of crystals, open-mouthed. "Perhaps with the crystals to occupy people's time there will be less violence," Horris Kew went on thoughtfully, looking off somewhere into the room's rafters as if seeking a higher truth. "Perhaps there will be fewer wars and killings over meaningless things when there are so many more pleasant and harmless ways to gain diversion. Perhaps there will be less time spent fomenting rumors that lead to mischief." He gave the wizard and the dog a surreptitious glance. As he said that, he did not miss the look that passed between them. "Fewer loose tongues wagging on about whether Landover's matters are being handled as they should and whether her leaders are leading as they ought to."

"Hmmm." Questor rubbed his beard thoughtfully. "Yes, perhaps. This really works?" he asked again, looking Abernathy directly in the eye, taking hold of the hand that held the crystal.

Abernathy moved the crystal away, tightening his grip on it.

"Of course, I have one for you, too, Questor," Horris Kew advised quickly. He reached back and closed the lid to the trunk. "These are all yours now." He yawned widely. "Well, enough talk. You should both be in bed, resting for tomorrow's challenges. I have tired you out with all this, I am sure. If you could spare a pallet, I would be most grateful. In the morning I will be off again, waiting to hear . . ."

He stopped. "Unless," he went on, as if he had just thought of it, "unless you would consider letting me help in some small way with the distribution of the crystals?"

He smiled at them hopefully and waited for an answer.

GREENWICH

For two days Willow traveled due west through the lake country with Edgewood Dirk, heading for the fairy mists and the invisible path that would take them out of Landover and into Ben's world. Dirk led the way, mostly without seeming to do so, content to keep pace or even follow, moving to the fore only when her path varied from the one he had chosen. He proceeded in leisurely fashion, dictating the pace by his refusal to be hurried, behaving as if time were inconsequential and their journey no more than a stroll through the park on a sunny afternoon.

Willow had encountered Edgewood Dirk only once before, and almost everything she knew about him she had learned from Ben. Dirk had been Ben's constant companion during the search for the black unicorn after Meeks, older brother of Questor Thews and the former Court Wizard of Landover, had tricked Ben into believing he had lost the medallion that gave him the power and authority to be King. Bereft of his identity, spurned by his friends as an impostor, and replaced on the throne by Meeks, Ben had been turned out into the wilderness and left to die. But the fairies, for reasons known only to them, had sent Edgewood Dirk to help him discover the truth about what had been done. Dirk had accompanied him in his wanderings, offering enigmatic cat advice and a sort of vaguely defined direction for the once-King to follow. Ben was tracking Willow, who in turn was tracking the black unicorn, and matters had climaxed in a violent confrontation between Dirk and Meeks that had proved the catalyst to Ben's recovery.

That had been almost two years ago. No one had seen or heard from Edgewood Dirk since. But now, here he was suddenly, and again he had been sent by the fairies, and again no one but the fairies really knew why.

Edgewood Dirk was a fairy being himself, though one of the more independent ones, as much cat as anything, and therefore likely to do exactly as he pleased despite anyone else's wishes, which made it very hard to determine his purpose in events. He had proved that beyond anyone's doubt during his time with Ben. Dirk was a prism cat, a creature possessed of a very rare sort of magic. He could transform himself from flesh and blood to a crystalline as hard as iron that allowed him to capture light and transform it into a deadly fire. Dirk used this power sparingly, but with great confidence. However distant and aloof Dirk appeared, however removed from what was happening around him, he was no one to fool around with.

So Willow accompanied him with some sense of assurance that if trouble threatened, Dirk was probably its equal. She would have preferred to have Ben with her, but that option had already been eliminated by the Earth Mother. Sometimes you took what you could get. Willow was experiencing enough uncertainty about her quest that she was grateful for any sort of company.

Dirk, of course, seemed indifferent to the entire matter.

"Were you sent because of Ben?" she asked him their first night out. They sat together before a small fire that Dirk had insisted be built to ward off some imaginary chill. She had arranged the deadwood, and he had set it afire. The beginnings of a working partnership, she had thought.

Dirk was licking one paw diligently. "I wasn't sent. I am never sent. I go where I choose."

"Excuse me," she apologized. "Why did you choose to come, then?"

Lick, lick, lick. "I can't remember, really. It seemed like a good idea, I guess." Lick, lick.

"Can you tell me where we are going?"

"West," the cat said. Lick, lick.

"Yes, but . . ."

Dirk stopped preening and gave her his cat look, the one that suggested sly amusement, deep understanding, grave concern, and total amazement all at the same time. "Just one moment, please. You are losing me. Don't *you* know where we're going?"

She shook her head in confusion. "No, not really."

He stared at her thoughtfully. "Oh, dear," he said. "Oh, well. I guess we will just have to find our way as best we can." And he went back to licking himself.

A little while later she grew brave enough to ask him again, taking a slightly different approach.

"We should reach the fairy mists by the day after tomorrow," she advised cautiously. "Once there, what do we do?"

Dirk had finished his bath by now and was seated on a patch of grass close by the fire, paws tucked under himself, eyes closed.

The eyes opened to slits. "We pass through the mists into Holiday's world." The eyes closed.

"How do we do that?"

The eyes came open again, a bit wider. "What kind of question is that? I must say I will never understand humans."

"I am a sylph."

"Or sylphs."

Willow's lips tightened. "It is just that I am concerned for my baby. I am required to do these things to protect its birthing, but I do not know how I am to do them."

Dirk regarded her with genuine interest. "Cats learn early on that very little is accomplished by worrying. Cats also know that things have a way of working out, even when the means are kept hidden from us. Best to deal with things as they arise, and let the future take care of itself."

"That seems very shortsighted," she ventured.

Dirk might have shrugged; it was hard to tell. "I am a cat," he offered, as if that explained everything.

She didn't talk to him about the matter again that night or all the next day, and so by nightfall when they had crossed out of the lake country and passed up into the foothills that bordered the fairy mists, she was surprised when he brought it up again of his own accord.

"Tomorrow morning, I will take you through the mists," he advised as she worked on building the requisite evening fire. She had spread her cloak on the ground close by, and Dirk had taken a comfortable seat on it.

She looked over at him. "You can do that?" she asked.

"Of course I can do that," he replied, sounding a bit put-upon. "I live there, remember? I know all the paths and passageways."

"I suppose I just wasn't sure what you could or couldn't do." She rocked back on her heels. "I didn't know if fairy creatures could pass out of the mists anywhere or into any land. I thought it might be limited somehow."

Dirk yawned. "You thought wrong. Cats can go anywhere. Nothing new in that."

"Do you know where we will come out?" she pressed.

He thought it over a moment. "A city, I think. Does it matter?"

She felt her exasperation with him getting away from her. "Yes, it does. I am going back to a world in which I once almost died. I am doing so against my will and for the sake of my child. I want to go there, do what I was sent to do, and leave again immediately. What are the chances of that happening?"

Dirk rose, stretched, and sat. "I haven't the faintest idea." He regarded her solemnly. "It all depends on you, I suppose."

"Yes, but I don't know where we are going," she insisted. "I know I am supposed to gather soil from Ben's world, but I don't know where that soil is supposed to be found. It is a rather big world to be looking through, you know."

"Well, I don't know," the cat said. "I have never been there. But everywhere is pretty much the same to a cat. I am quite certain we will find what we need without having to look too hard. I have a gift for uncovering secrets."

She went back to building the fire, finished the job, stepped back, and looked over at him. "How many secrets do you know, Dirk?" she asked quietly. "Do you know secrets about me?"

The cat blinked. "Of course."

"And about Ben?"

"Holiday? Yes, a few."

"Can you tell them to me?"

"If I choose." Dirk began washing himself. "But cats are secretive by nature and tell little of what they know. It is because no one listens to us, mostly. I spoke of that often to Holiday when I traveled with him last. He was like everyone else. I would tell him things, but he wouldn't listen. I warned him that he was making a mistake, that cats know many things, but no one ever seems to pay attention. It was a mistake he should avoid, I cautioned."

"I will listen, if you will tell me something," Willow offered. "Tell me anything, Dirk. Any of your secrets. I know so little of what is happening, and I am hungry for even a small bit of knowledge. Can you tell me something?"

Dirk looked at her, then began to wash. He licked himself fluffy and then licked himself smooth, stopping every now and then to see if she was still paying attention. He took his time with the job, but Willow waited patiently, refusing to become perturbed. Finally Dirk was finished, and turned his emerald gaze upon her.

"You are going to have a child," he declared. "But matters will not work out as either you or Holiday expect them to. Expectations are dangerous things for parents to have, you know. Cats have none and are the better for it."

She nodded. "We can't help ourselves. Like not listening to cats."

"I suppose that is true," Dirk agreed. "A shame."

"Tell me something more."

Dirk narrowed his gaze. "Are you sure you want to hear what I have to say? I mean, that is part of the reason no one listens to cats."

She hesitated. "Yes, I want to hear."

"Very well." He considered. "You and Holiday will be lost to each other for a time. In fact, you are lost to each other already. Didn't you know?"

"The vision," she said softly. "My mother's vision."

Dirk looked off into the growing dark. "You spend so much time wondering who you are, don't you think? You flounder about, searching for your identity, when most of the time it is as plain as the nose on your face. You struggle with questions of purpose and need, and forget that the answers are found mostly inside yourselves." He paused anew. "Cats are not included in that analysis. Cats don't waste time wondering about such things. Cats just get on with the business of living."

"Is the vision true, then?" she asked, trying to mask the growing sense of desperation she felt that something terrible was happening to Ben, something beyond her control.

Dirk blinked. "What vision?"

"Is Ben in danger?" she pressed.

"How would I know?" Dirk growled, stretching once more. "Better step back from that deadwood."

She did so, and Dirk shimmered and turned to crystalline in the fading twilight, gone from flesh and blood to liquid glass, drew in the glow of sunset, two early moons, and a scattering of stars, and sent fire lancing from his emerald eyes into the wood. The blaze burned hotly, and the prism cat transformed back again, settled himself down anew on Willow's cloak, closed his eyes, and was instantly asleep.

Willow watched him for a time, then fell asleep as well.

⚬

She slept poorly, haunted by dreams of Ben and their child, of each being drawn away from her, stolen by invisible hands that wrapped about and pulled them from her side until nothing remained but the echo of her voice calling after them. There was an unspoken suggestion in her dream that somehow she was to blame for what had happened to them, that somehow she had failed them when they needed her most.

She had no appetite for breakfast, and since Dirk never showed any interest in food, they washed and were on their way up to the beginnings of the fairy mists shortly after sunrise.

The day dawned hot and still, the summer air a suffocating blanket that clung to the land even in the high country. Dew formed a slick upon the ground, and its dampness glimmered in the hazy first light. They climbed the rest of the way into the hills, found a narrows that led into a pass, and walked back toward the gray gloom of the mists.

They reached their destination in less than an hour and started in. No words passed between them as they did. Dirk had taken the lead now, no longer content to leave matters to chance. He walked directly in front of the sylph, picking his way carefully over ruts, around stones, and across bare ground where lack of sunlight prevented any grasses from growing. They moved into the haze, following the trail until there ceased to be a trail and all the light from the rising sun had disappeared behind them and there was nothing but mist, swirling about them with relentless purpose, twisting first this way and then that, drawing the eyes to one side and then to the other, obscuring any sense of direction, any chance of keeping track of where they were going or from where they had come. Willow ignored the distracting movement, focusing her attention on Dirk, who sauntered along with his usual indifference, seeming to find his way as much by chance as by plan. He glanced neither left nor right and did not turn to see if she was following. He sniffed the air now and again, but otherwise showed no interest in their surroundings.

The minutes slipped away, but it was not clear to Willow how many of them passed. Time and place lost meaning, and everything took on a disturbing sameness. There was silence at first, deep and numbing, and then a series of small sounds, like the scuffling of forest animals in scrub or birds among leaves. After a time, the noises took on definition and began to suggest the presence of something else. Faces began to appear, just at the corners of her vision, just where they could be glimpsed but nothing more. The faces were sharp-featured and lean, with pointed ears and brows, and hair like trailing moss and spiky straw. Eyes as penetrating as an owl's watched her pass. The fairy folk had come out to see her, to consider her, and perhaps to let her pass. She did not look at them, keeping her eyes fixed on the movement of her feet and on Edgewood Dirk. She did not look at them because she was frightened that if she did, she would be instantly lost.

Something brushed at her cheek, and tears filled her eyes. Something rubbed against her hand, and she felt a sudden heat rush through her. Her skin crawled and her mouth went dry. *Don't look,* she told herself. *Don't turn to see what it is.* She pressed on, following diligently after Dirk, thinking of the baby inside her, thinking of Ben waiting somewhere behind, hardening herself against her fear . . .

Until finally the mists began to drop away, and she could see something solid ahead through the haze. A shadowed darkness cloaked a wall of mortared stone, and rain drizzled down out of leaden skies. There were strange mechanical sounds and muffled shouts, and the wall rose high overhead and was lost in gloom. The mists receded behind her, and she found herself standing in the rain in an alleyway that ran like a deep crevice between two towering buildings. Clouds masked the skies and scraped against the tops of the buildings. Shadows cascaded down off the walls to pool underfoot. Smells rose up from the cracked stone surface on which they stood, pungent and rank.

"Where are we?" she whispered in horror.

Something moved to one side. It was a man in ragged clothing, sprawled in the lee of a doorway, curled up and sleeping. He was wrapped in pieces of cardboard to shield himself from the weather. An empty bottle was clutched in one hand.

Dirk sniffed in the direction of the man and turned away. He looked up and down the alley. One end went nowhere. The other led to a noisy street. Turning toward the latter, he stepped daintily over pieces of garbage strewn from an overturned container, flinching with displeasure at what he felt, and started in the direction of the noise. Willow followed.

They walked toward the end of the alley, watching the street beyond come into focus through the rain, seeing movement begin, hearing the sounds grow louder. There were cars and buses streaming past, moving in fits and starts, horns blaring, brakes squealing. Willow knew about these things from her last visit. She had no idea what Dirk knew. What she remembered was not pleasant. She was already cringing from the impact of the sounds and smells. With the dirt and grit it gathered, the rain smeared on the stone beneath her boots and pooled in gutters and low spots amid the garbage. Broken glass glinted everywhere.

They reached the end of the alley and looked out onto the street. The cars and buses were locked close together in the gloom and drizzle, crawling in one direction toward another line of vehicles traveling crosswise. Red and green lights blinked down from lines overhead. Yellow lights shone from street lamps and through the windows of buildings with peeling paint and cracked mortar.

And there were people everywhere, most in long coats, some in boots. They walked with their heads bent and carried strange implements—Willow didn't know the proper name—to shield them from the rain. They shuffled along with a sense of urgency and resignation that was palpable. A few glanced in her direction, but looked quickly away again. They climbed in and out of the buses and cars, and they moved in and out of doorways. A few spoke, but most of what they said was shouted in anger at one another.

Dirk sniffed the air and looked about, seemingly unfazed. Then he moved out from the alley and started left down the walkway. Willow followed. A crush of people caught them up and swept them along. Willow pulled her cloak tightly about her shoulders, hating the closeness of the people and the smell they gave off. She thought of Ben living in such a world and found she could not imagine it.

They reached a corner and stopped because everyone else was stopped as well. A few bold looks were directed at her, but she ignored them. She stared about at the buildings, some of them monstrous stone and glass monoliths that soared into the clouds, featureless and impregnable-looking. Did people live in those? she wondered. What purpose did they serve?

To her surprise she found she could understand what the people about her were saying. She should not have been able to do that unless they were speaking in the languages of Landover, but she could. She looked up at a sign on the street corner beside her. She could read it. It said Greenwich Avenue.

Above her the light changed, and people began to cross the street. She followed with Dirk.

On the other side, about a block away, a woman with a ring through her nose tried to kick Dirk when he walked in front of her. The kick should have connected, but somehow it missed and struck an iron railing in front of a low window and caused the woman to lose her balance and fall down. The woman shrieked in fury and swore violently at Dirk, but the cat went past the woman without a glance. Willow did the same.

"Hey, lady, spare some change?" a sallow-faced man with long hair and a beard asked. She shook her head and walked on. "It's a little late for St. Patrick's, isn't it?" he called after her, and laughed.

She bent down to Dirk. "Do we understand their language?" she asked curiously.

"We do," Dirk replied. "A little fairy magic lets us do that."

They walked for some time through the crowds. The rains diminished and the skies cleared. The cars and buses began to pick up speed. It grew more dangerous at the crossings. The crowds thinned somewhat, changing character as they moved down the street. The men and women in tailored clothing gave way to a more casual and eclectic group. There were people in leather and chains and metal-tipped boots who slouched along with exaggerated movements or leaned against building walls; people in long, peach-colored robes with shaved heads and earnest looks passing out papers; ragged people with dogs and cats and babies carrying small handmade signs that said things like PLEASE HELP and NO FOOD; people with shopping bags and handbags clutched tightly against their chests as they walked; people of all sorts, all possessed of the same uneasy, guarded look, all with eyes that shifted and searched, all with a posture that either challenged or bordered on flight.

Comments were directed openly at Willow from those they passed, some brazen and insulting, some joking and curious. A few people tried to stop her, but she simply moved past them, following Dirk along the walk.

They reached a particularly busy cross street and Dirk stopped. A street sign read Avenue of the Americas. Dirk glanced at Willow as if to say, *See there?* Willow did not see. She did not understand where they were or why. She mostly wanted to get to wherever it was they were going and then get out. Everything about this place was unpleasant and unwelcoming. She wanted to ask Dirk if he had any idea at all where he was going, but she did not think he wanted her to speak to him with all these people about. Besides, he must have some idea; he was certainly moving down the street as if he did.

"Are you lost?" a young woman standing next to her asked. The woman was dark-skinned. She was holding a small child in her arms.

"No," Willow said without thinking, but realized as she did that she could speak the language of Ben's world as well as read and understand it. Dirk must be at work with his fairy magic.

"Are you sure? You look confused." She smiled. "You can get lost in this city pretty easy."

"Thank you, I'm fine," Willow said.

The light changed, and the woman walked away. Dirk and Willow crossed to a new street that read West 8th. There were people everywhere. Storefronts opened onto the walkway, small markets of fruit and vegetables, craft shops with jewelry and bright clothing, doorways leading to food and drink and wares of all sorts. Stands were set up along the street with books and more jewelry. Vendors called to her. Want to buy this, take a look at that? They smiled, some of them, and she smiled back, shaking her head no.

"What a great look!" someone said, and she turned. A young man with a long dark coat, boots, a light beard, and a leather folder stood looking at her. "You aren't an actress, are you?"

"No." She shook her head. Dirk was still moving down the street. "I have to go."

"Wait!" He began walking with her. "Uh, look, I thought that . . . well, because you're colored green, I thought that . . . that because you were dressed up, you might be an actress or something. Like in *Cats*. Sorry, I didn't mean to be rude."

She smiled. "You weren't."

"My name is Tony. Tony Paolo. I live a few blocks away. I'm studying to be an actor. I'm in my second year at American Academy. You been there? Dustin Hoffman went there. Danny DeVito. Lots of people. I just finished a reading for a part on Broadway. A comedy, Neil Simon. This is my portfolio, you know, my pictures and stuff." He indicated the folder. "It's just a small part, just a few lines. But it's a start."

She nodded and kept walking. She didn't have any idea at all what he was talking about.

"Look, can I buy you a cup of coffee or something? If you have some time?"

Ahead of her, Dirk had turned around and come back. Now he moved between her legs and looked up at Tony. "That your cat?" Tony asked. "Hey, kitty, kitty."

"Keep your hands to yourself," Dirk snapped as Tony started to reach down to pet him.

Tony straightened instantly. He stared at Willow. "Hey, that's pretty good! How did you do that?" He grinned. "That's the best I've ever heard that done. Do some more."

"We could use something to eat," Dirk said.

"Man, I couldn't even see your lips move!" Tony declared in amazement. "That's some talent! A bite to eat, huh? Okay, why not? There's a little coffee-house just around the corner. You know the Village? You from around here?"

He led the way through the crowds to a small shop with round tables covered with checkered oilcloth and straight-backed iron chairs with matching checkered cushions. Tony waved to someone working behind the counter and took a table near the entry. Willow and Dirk both sat down with him.

"So what do you want?" Tony asked. He had lank brown hair, dark eyes, and a quick, unassuming smile.

"You decide," Dirk said.

Tony did, ordering food for himself and Willow and a saucer of milk for Dirk. When the food arrived, Willow found herself hungrier than she thought, and she ate everything without bothering to decide whether she liked it. Tony ate with her, talking about how good she was at throwing her voice and about his life as an actor-in-training. Dirk sat in front of the milk and ignored it.

"You know, I forgot to ask your name," Tony said in midbite.

"Willow," she answered.

"Really? What a great name. So, are you a ventriloquist all the time or do you have a job doing something else?"

She hesitated. What was she supposed to say?

"That's okay, you don't have to tell me. But you're not an actress, I guess, right?"

"No, not an actress."

When they were finished, Tony asked her again, "Do you live around here somewhere?"

She glanced at Dirk, who was staring out the door, ready to be off. "No, just visiting."

"From where?"

"Landover." She said it before she could catch herself.

"Sure, Maryland, right? I know Landover. Who are you staying with here? Do you have friends or something?"

She shook her head. "I have to go now, Tony. Thank you for the meal. I hope you become a good actor."

She stood up and started for the door. Dirk was already outside on the walkway. "Hey, wait!" Tony called, throwing some money on the table and charging after her. He caught up with her outside. "Can I see you again, maybe?"

She shook her head and walked on, wondering how to get out of this. Tony walked with her. "I know this is kind of sudden, but . . . well, I really would like to take you to dinner or a play or something. Even if I have to come down to Landover . . ."

"She's married," Dirk announced. "Happily."

Tony stopped in his tracks. "Oh. Sorry, I didn't realize . . ."

They crossed the street in a clutch of traffic and left him groping for something else to say. He carefully watched their progress.

--~∞~--

Nightfall set in shortly after, a sudden darkening of the skies as the sun set and the clouds returned, a fading of the light that brought up the city's lamps. Willow and Dirk were seated on a bench in a park with a large marble arch. It was called Washington Square. It had been filled with people until just a few minutes ago, people with newspapers and babies, people with dogs and toys, but now with the sun gone and with the day ending it was emptying out. There were only a few old men left sitting on other benches and a handful of young boys huddled under a tree at the far end. A ragged man with a dog was holding out a metal cup by the street corner.

Only a few hours had passed since Dirk and Willow had arrived from Landover where it had been early morning, and that meant time did not pass at the same speed in the two worlds. How did that effect aging when you crossed from one world into the other? Willow wondered. Was she aging differently than Ben? She stared out into the gloom, watching the city lights beyond the park brighten. Dirk was hunched down beside her with his paws tucked underneath his body and his eyes closed. He had told her when they were alone that they must wait for night when the park was clear so that they would not be disturbed. It appeared that it was here that she was supposed to gather the soil she needed, but Dirk hadn't volunteered anything specific. Dirk rarely did.

The darkness deepened and the hours passed, and still they sat on the bench and waited. Willow was patient, and the wait did not disturb her. She understood now why Dirk had wanted her to have something to eat. She might have gone this long without food, but her child needed nourishment even if she did not. The cat understood this. She glanced down at him and wondered how much of his indifference was pretense.

Soon they were alone except for the odd passerby. Midnight came and went, and the city showed no sign of shutting down for the night. The wares shops had closed, but the places where food and drink were served remained open. There were still people on the streets, crowds of them, passing this way and that, calling out, laughing and shouting, on their way to or from somewhere. No one seemed interested in sleeping. No one seemed anxious to go home.

Willow watched the people and the lights in the distance, trying to imagine what it must be like to live here. Stone and mortar and glass everywhere you looked, the buildings long lines of soldiers set at march, the roadways flat and endless, the visible earth reduced to small squares of worn green like this park—it was nightmarish. Nothing was real; everything was manufactured. The smell, taste, look, and feel of it assailed her at every turn and threatened to swallow her up like a tiny bit of light in a massive dark.

Someone left the sidewalk across the way and approached—a familiar figure with long coat, boots, lank hair, and a ready smile. Willow stiffened.

"Still here, I see," Tony declared as he came up and stopped in front of her. "Tell me the truth, Willow. Do you have a place to sleep? I've been following you, and you don't seem to be going anywhere."

She fixed him with her emerald eyes. "Go home, Tony."

"You don't, do you?" he pressed. "I've come by a couple times now to see if you were still here, and sure enough, you were. You wouldn't be out in the park this late if you had somewhere to go. Look, I'm worried about you. Would you like a place to crash?"

She stared. "What?"

"To sleep, for the night." He held out his palms. "This isn't some sort of come-on, I promise."

"Come-on?"

"You told me you were married, right? So where's your ring? I think you made all that up, but that's okay. I just want you to know I'm not after your bod or anything. I like you, that's all. I don't want anything to happen to you. This is a dangerous city."

Dirk rose, stretched, and yawned. Without a word, he climbed down off the bench and began walking across the park. Willow glanced quickly at Tony, then got up and followed. Dirk crossed the park north to south, ambling contentedly, sniffing at this and that, seeming in no hurry, appearing to have no purpose in mind.

"It can be dangerous out here," Tony repeated, walking next to her, looking over. "Especially at night. You don't know."

She shook her head. "I'll be fine."

"I can't just leave you out here like this," he declared. "Look, I'll keep you company, okay? And don't tell me to go home. I won't do it."

Dirk had moved to a spot at the far end of the park beneath an old shade tree tucked within a gathering of small vine maples where the earth was worn and so wrapped in shadows that almost no grass was growing. It was here that a mother had read on a blanket with her baby beside her until it was almost dark. Dirk sniffed about a bit, then sat back on his haunches and waited for Willow to come up.

"Here," was all he said.

Willow nodded. She knelt and touched the earth, then drew her hand back quickly, her fairy senses pricked by what she found.

"Much has happened in this place," Edgewood Dirk said quietly. "Great ideas have been conceived and terrible plans laid out. Hopes and aspirations have been shared. Killings and maimings have been perpetrated on innocent and guilty alike. A baby was born here once. Animals have hidden here. Whispered promises have been given and love consummated." He looked at her. "The soil is rich with memories. It is the wellspring and the epiphany of many lives."

Tony crowded close. "What are you talking about? Was that the cat who said all that? Well, of course it wasn't the cat—I mean, how could it be, right? But it sure sounded like it was. What's going on?"

Willow ignored him and began to dig. She used the hunting knife she carried beneath her cloak, stirring up the earth, bringing buried soil to light so that she could have a thorough sampling. The lifeblood and memories of others to sustain her baby—were they intended as a balm, a preventative, or something else entirely? Would they heal or sear? She did not know. She knew only that they would make her child strong, that they would protect, that they would instill something of life's truths as embodied in humankind.

She finished digging and began scooping the soil into the same leather pouch that held the earth from the old pines. Tony was still talking, but she wasn't paying attention to what he said. Dirk had wandered off in the direction of another cat.

She filled the pouch halfway and laced it tightly closed again. She stood up then and faced Tony.

"This is really weird," he was saying. "Creeping about the park in the middle of the night and digging up bags of dirt? I mean, what's the point? Look, are you a witch or something? Are you involved in some sort of . . ."

He stopped abruptly and looked past her, alarm spreading over his face. She turned. A gang of boys stood behind her, watching. They seemed to have materialized out of nowhere, so quietly had they gathered. They were of varying ages and sizes, all dressed in black T-shirts and blue jeans. Some wore boots, some leather jackets. There was writing on the shirts and jackets, but she didn't understand the words. One carried a baseball bat, one an iron bar. Several sported tattoos. They had hard, old faces, and their eyes were flat and mean.

She looked instantly for Dirk, but the prism cat was nowhere to be seen.

"What's in the bag, Witch Hazel?" one said, smirking.

"Hey, look, we don't want any trouble . . ." Tony started to say, and the speaker stepped forward and hit him in the face. Tony dropped to his knees, his nose and mouth bloody.

"I said, what's in the bag?" the speaker asked again, and reached for Willow.

She eluded his grasp effortlessly and moved over to stand in front of Tony. "Get away from me," she warned.

Several laughed. One of them said something about teaching her a lesson. There was muttered approval.

Edgewood Dirk moved out from the shadows to one side. "I don't think you should say anything else. I think you should leave."

The boys stared in disbelief. There was a raucous exchange and more laughter. A talking cat! They spread out guardedly, trapping Willow and Dirk against the trees. The one with the baseball bat started forward. "Hey, cat?" he called. "How about lunch?"

In the next instant Dirk began to glow. The gang members hesitated, shielding their eyes. The glow brightened, and Dirk began to change form. His cat self disappeared and was replaced by something so terrifying that even Willow was repulsed. He became monstrous and huge, rising up like an apparition out of Abaddon, all teeth and claws. The circle of attackers collapsed. Most broke and ran, screaming at their fellows, cursing at Dirk. A handful froze, undecided, and lived to regret their indecision. Dirk hissed at them with such force that he knocked them off their feet and sent them tumbling back twenty feet to land bruised and dazed. When they were able to scramble up, they fled after the others.

In seconds, the park was empty again.

Dirk stopped shimmering and turned into a cat again. He gazed after the boys for a minute, then yawned. He began to wash himself.

Willow helped Tony back to his feet. "Are you all right?" she asked him.

He nodded, but there was blood smeared all across his face. "How did the cat . . . ?" He couldn't finish.

"Go home, Tony," she told him, brushing him off, straightening his coat about his shoulders. "Go on."

Tony stared at her. She did not like what she saw in his eyes. Then he turned and stumbled away into the darkness. She watched after him until he reached the street and disappeared around the corner of a building. He did not look back. She did not think she would see him again.

She turned wearily to Dirk. She felt sick, as if the terrible harshness of Ben's world had found a way to burrow down inside her soul. "I don't want to stay here any longer. Can we go now?"

Dirk blinked, emerald eyes glinting. "It was necessary that you come," he said to her.

"Yes, but are we finished?"

Dirk stood abruptly and moved off. "Such impatience. Very well. The fairy mists are this way."

She felt a chill pass up her spine. The fairy mists. But she would do what she must. For herself, for Ben, for their child. One last leg to her journey and she would be home again.

Resolved, she set off into the night.

HAZE

Three days into their journey through the Labyrinth, the Knight, the Lady, and the Gargoyle came upon a town.

It was late afternoon, the light's wane barely perceptible, a darkening of a gloom that they now knew never brightened beyond twilight. They had walked steadily through a changeless forest world until suddenly, unexpectedly, the town came into view as they crested a small rise. A cluster of ramshackle wooden buildings and worn dirty streets, it hunkered down in a hollow where the trees had been cleared away so that it looked as if the forest had swept around it like the waters of a river around an island. No roads led into it and none away. There were people; the Knight could see them moving on the streets. There were animals, though they were a shabby lot and had the look of creatures beaten down by life. Lights burned in a few of the windows, and as the three stared down more were lit. They gave off a weak and singularly desperate glow, as if they had fought their battle against the coming night too many times and were tired of the struggle.

Overhead, where the trees opened to the skies, there was nothing to be seen of moon or stars, only an endless layer of impenetrable mist.

"People," the Gargoyle said, and there was both surprise and distaste in his voice.

The Knight said nothing. He was thinking that he was weary of his trek through this dismal world where everything looked the same and nothing ever changed. The past three days had dragged away in a mind-numbing crawl, filled with silence and darkness and an implacable sense of hopelessness. Twice the Lady had tried to kill him, once with poison in his drink, once with a sharpened stick when she thought he was sleeping. Her efforts had been wasted, for he sensed everything she was about. She seemed to accept this. She went through the motions as if already resigned to her failure, as if the attempt must be made even when the conclusion was foregone. Yet he was damaged nevertheless. It was what he saw in her eyes that wore at him. He was a warrior and could withstand her physical attacks. But the looks of rage and loathing and sadness were less easily dealt with, and he was made sick at heart by their constancy.

Of course, she hated the Gargoyle as well, but her hatred of him was in-bred and impersonal and somehow more acceptable.

"Why is there a town here?" he asked them quietly.

For a moment, no one answered. Why, indeed? A town, come out of nowhere, materialized as if from a vision, having no purpose or excuse, exist-ing in a vacuum. Where was the trade that would support it, since there were no roads? Where were the crops that would feed it, since there were no fields? Was this a town of hunters and trappers? If so, to where did they carry their goods and from where did their supplies come? The Knight in three days had seen almost no forest creatures, and what few he had seen had been small and furtive and somehow natural to the gloom, existing because and not in spite of it.

"What difference why it is here?" the Lady demanded irritably. "It is here, and that is all that matters. We have a chance to find our way again. What pur-pose is there in questioning that?"

The Gargoyle edged forward a step, stooped and hunched within his dark cloak, keeping as always to shadow. "I mistrust this," he said. "There is some-thing wrong here."

The Knight nodded. He felt it, too. Something was not right. Still, the town was here, and they could not simply pass it by. Someone living there must know of a way to leave the Labyrinth; someone must know of a way back out into the real world.

"We will go down to see what we can learn. We will not stay beyond that." The Knight looked over at the other two.

"If they discover me, they will kill me," the Gargoyle said.

"Remain behind, then," the Lady snapped, unmoved.

"Ah, but I hunger for their words," the Gargoyle murmured, as if ashamed. "That is the puzzle of me. I am loathed by those I would come to know."

"You would be them, you pathetic creature," she sneered. "Admit it."

But the Gargoyle shook his head. "I would not be them. Oh, no, Lady—not for all the gold and silver in the world. They are such uncertain, indecisive beings, all wrapped up in the small measure of their lives. I, on the other hand, am certain, and have the gift of immortality. I am not burdened by the smallness of their existence."

"Nor do you have their beauty. Easy to belittle those whose lives are finite when death for you is so distant you barely need consider what it means." The Lady fixed him with her cold eyes. "I have life beyond that of humans, Gar-goyle, but I treasure beauty as well. I would not be ugly like you even if I could live forever."

"Your ugliness is within," the Gargoyle whispered.

"And yours, always and forever, is plainly stamped so that no one can mistake what you are!"

The Knight moved to stand before the Lady, to draw her hard gaze away from the Gargoyle to himself. He shuddered as those cold eyes found his own and he saw the measure of himself mirrored there.

"We will keep to ourselves and not speak if we do not have to. You and I, Lady, will seek the answers we need. He"—he nodded back toward the slouched, cloaked figure behind him—"will remain silent. But be forewarned that if you attempt trickery or betrayal, you will be silenced. Give me your word."

"I will give you nothing!" She sneered openly at him, drawing herself up haughtily.

"I will leave you here with him then," the Knight said softly. "I will be safer on my own down there."

The Lady paled at the suggestion, and the rage that emanated from her was palpable. "You cannot do that!" she hissed.

"Then give me your word."

She trembled with frustration and despair. "Very well. You have it, Sir Knight. May it rise up within you and devour your soul!"

The Knight turned away. He cautioned the Gargoyle to keep hidden within his cloak and stay back from the light. "Do not be drawn into conversation," he warned. "Do not stray from my side."

They descended rapidly in the failing light, the town beginning to vanish already into the growing darkness, the buildings reduced to glimmers of light framed in windows like pictures hung against a black velvet curtain. They slipped through the cloaking gloom like wraiths come from the trees of the forest, following the line of the cradling slope downward. In minutes they had reached the hollow floor and the beginnings of the town. Their eyes adjusted to the shift in light, and they followed one of the short roadways that ran through the town's center, a rutted, worn stretch of earth that began on one side of the clustered buildings and ended on the other. Men and women passed them in the gloom, but none spoke. The doors and windows of the houses and shops on either side were closed. Dogs and cats prowled the length of the building walls and scooted beneath the walkways where they had been elevated above the earth. Voices were muted and indistinguishable. The Knight listened with his heart as much as his ears, and he found no hint of solace, no measure of comfort. The town was a coffin waiting to be nailed shut.

At the town's center there was a tavern. Here the doors were blocked open, and the people came and went freely. There was the smell of smoke and freshly drawn ale, the clink of glasses and the scrape of booted feet, and the raw heartiness of laughter born of momentary escape from the dreariness of life's toil. The Knight moved toward the doorway, the Lady and the Gargoyle following. He took note of the cloudiness of the interior, a mix of smoke and poor lighting. Faces would not be easily distinguished here; privacy would be valued. He stepped up onto the porch that fronted the building and saw that while the tavern was crowded there were tables empty and seats to be had. They would be recognized as strangers, of course; it was unavoidable in a town so small. The trick would be to draw attention to himself and away from his charges.

They entered amidst a swell of raucous laughter that appeared to have its origins at the serving bar where half-a-dozen workingmen were crowded elbow to elbow over their glasses facing in toward the counterman. The Knight moved through the tables to the very back of the room, drawing the other two with him, and they seated themselves wordlessly. The Gargoyle turned toward the shadows, circumspect and wary, but the Lady faced directly into the room, as bold as a spoken threat with her cloak flung open and her hood lowered. Eyes shifted toward her at once. Some were filled with hunger.

The Knight seated himself, partially blocking her. It was too late to tell her to cover herself now. He must assume his stance as her protector and hope that was enough.

There was a sudden lowering of voices as the room became aware of them, and all present paused to take their measure. The Lady's strange eyes swept the room without settling anywhere, without acknowledging that there was anything worth seeing. The Knight was already regretting his decision to let her come with him; he would have been better off if she had stayed behind. But he had not wanted to let her out of his sight either; he could not chance losing her.

He fixed the counterman with his gaze and signaled for three mugs. The counterman nodded and hastened away to the casks.

The moment passed, eyes shifted away again, and conversation resumed. The room was filled with a mix of men and women, all poorly dressed, all with the harsh, worn look of people who scraped out an existence without luck or skill or the help of others. They might have been anything from farmers to trappers to miners; the Knight could not tell. That they worked with their hands was certain; that they plied some specific trade less so. They were of varying ages, and they sat together in such a fashion that it was impossible to judge who was with whom. Relationships seemed not to matter, as if perhaps they were still forming, as if they were not yet even considered. Now and again people rose and changed tables, but never as couples or in groups. It was as if each man and woman lived a solitary existence and identified only as a singular part of the whole community.

There were no children. There were no signs of any children, no babies, no hint that anyone not grown lived within the town. Not even a sweeping boy worked the floors or mopped the counter.

The counterman crossed the room with the mugs of ale and set them down before the Knight. He glanced at the Knight's weapons and rubbed his hands nervously. "Where do you come from?" he asked as the Knight fished in his pocket for coins he was not even sure he possessed. The Knight finally produced a single piece of gold.

The Knight passed the gold piece over. "We are lost," he answered. "Where are we?"

The counterman tested the gold piece with his teeth. "In the Labyrinth, of course. Right at its heart, in fact."

The counterman was looking at the Lady now, interested. The Lady looked back and right through him.

"Does this town have a name?" the Knight pressed.

The counterman shrugged. "No name. We have no need for one. Did you come from the north?"

The Knight hesitated. "I'm not sure."

The counterman lowered his voice conspiratorially and leaned down a bit, his attention on the Knight now. "Did you see anything strange in the woods?"

"Strange?"

"Yes." The man wet his lips. He seemed reluctant to use a name, as if speaking it might somehow bring what he inquired after through the tavern door.

"We saw nothing," the Knight said.

The counterman studied him a moment as if to make certain he was not lying, then nodded, relief in his face, and walked away.

The Lady leaned forward, and her voice was cool and measured. "What is he talking about?"

The Knight shook his head. He did not know. They sat in silence and drank the ale from the glasses, listening to the conversations around them. There was talk of work, but in a general way. There was mention of the weather and the seasons and the absence of this and that, but it was all vague and indistinguishable. No one spoke of anything specific or made mention of the particulars of their lives. There was something odd about the conversations, about their tone, about the inflection of the voices speaking. It was quite some time before the Knight was able to figure out that woven into the exchanges was a sense of anticipation, of uneasy expectation, of waiting for something unspoken to happen.

An old man edged by the table and stopped. "Come a long ways, have you?" He slurred his words, his speech thick from the ale he had consumed.

"Yes," the Knight replied, looking up. "And you?"

"Oh, no, I don't go nowhere. This is my home, this town. Always and forever. I been here, oh, years and years." He grinned, toothless. "Can't go nowhere else, once you're here."

The Knight felt something turn cold in the pit of his stomach. "What do you mean? You can leave if you choose, can't you?"

The old man cackled. "That what you think? That you can leave? You must be new, son. This is the Labyrinth. You can't leave here. Can't no one leave here ever!"

"If you can come in, you can go out!" the Lady snapped suddenly, anger flaring in her voice.

"You just try it!" the old man replied, still laughing. "Been lots who have before, but they always come back. This is where they have to stay once they're here. You, too. You, too."

He tottered away, mumbling to himself. The Knight signaled the counterman for three fresh mugs, trying to think his way clear of the tangle of the old man's words. No way out, the Labyrinth a trap that no one could escape—he listened to the whisper of the words in his mind.

"Anything to eat?" the counterman asked, coming up with the glasses of ale. "You got some credit yet from that gold piece."

"Can you draw us a map?" the Knight asked perfunctorily.

The counterman gave them his patented shrug. "A map to where? Maps all lead to the same place, eventually. Right back here."

"I need a map that will show us a way out of the Labyrinth."

The counterman smiled. "So does everyone else here. Trouble is, no one can find it. Some—like that old fellow—been trying for years. He can't get out, though. None of us can. We try, but we always end up coming back here."

The Knight stared at him in stunned silence.

"It's all right, really," the other continued quickly, worried by the look that appeared on the Knight's face. "You get used to it. We don't have too many worries. Just the . . ." He shook his head.

"The what? What are you talking about?" the Lady demanded.

The counterman took a slow breath. When he spoke again, the words were barely a whisper. "The Haze."

The Knight glanced quickly at his companions. Neither spoke. He turned back to the counterman. "We don't know what that is."

The counterman was suddenly sweating, as if the temperature in the room had just risen to a midday heat. "Best if you never do!" he hissed. "There's stories. It lives in the woods. It comes out when you least expect it and devours everything! Eats it right up, and when it's done there's nothing left!" His mouth tightened. "I've never seen it myself. No one here has. But we hear it sometimes. More so recently, like maybe it's looking us over. They say a monster always precedes its coming—a thing out of myth and legend, a beast out of the old world."

He shook his head. "I've said enough. It's bad luck to even talk about it. It doesn't come often. But when it does . . ."

He shook his head again, then wheeled about and walked hurriedly away. The Knight stared after him, then turned back to his companions. "Do you know of this?" he asked quietly.

"I have heard rumors," the Gargoyle offered, his voice a disembodied growl from within the shadows of his hooded cloak. "An ancient legend, thousands of years old. Men see the Haze as divine retribution for their sins."

"What rubbish!" the Lady sneered. "Would you give credence to the superstitions of these common people? Is this how you would identify with them?"

The Gargoyle said nothing, keeping his gaze fixed on the Knight. The Knight drank his ale and tried to think. No one knew of a way out of the Labyrinth. Whatever direction you went, they claimed, you ended up back at this nameless town. Was this belief commonly accepted by these people or was there at least one among them who knew differently? The Knight had not spoken with anyone beyond the counterman and the oldster. Perhaps he should try.

"Stay here," he ordered.

He rose, glass in hand, and walked to the counter. He was aware for the first time of the notice being taken of his weapons and light armor, for none of the townsfolk wore either. He began asking questions of those men gathered at the bar. Had any of them ever been outside the Labyrinth? Did any of them know of a way? Was there anyone who might know? The men shook their heads and looked away.

"River Gypsies might," one said. "They been everywhere there is to be. 'Course, you got to find them first."

There was a burst of shared laughter, a private joke. The Knight glanced back at the table where he had left the Lady and the Gargoyle and froze. Two men had moved over and were taking seats, one on either side of the Lady. She had pulled her cloak tight around her body and was staring straight ahead while they talked and smiled at her. The Gargoyle was shrinking farther back into the shadows.

The Knight moved away from the counter and began to cross the room. He was too slow. One of the men touched the Lady, and she wheeled on him, nails raking at his face. He surged to his feet with a yowl and stumbled back into the Gargoyle. The concealing cloak fell away, revealing the Gargoyle, and the other man lurched to his feet screaming. Instantly, the room was bedlam. Men and women shrieked in terror and loathing as the Gargoyle tried to cover himself. Weapons flashed into view, long-handled hunting knives and daggers of varying shapes. Fighting to keep his balance in the surging melee, the Knight bulled his way past those separating him from his charges. Mugs crashed to the floor and lamps went out. Men rushed for the doors.

"Look what you've done!" the counterman shouted wildly, pointing at the

Knight. "You've brought a monster into our town! You've doomed us! Damn you forever!"

The Knight reached the table, snatched up the Lady, and threw her over his shoulder. He had his broadsword free, and he swung about to level it between himself and those threatening. The Gargoyle crouched behind him, his ineffectual wings beating frantically, his breath hissing through his sharp teeth. The Knight swung the broadsword downward with all his might and splintered the table before him. Men fell back quickly as he made his way toward the door, the Lady kicking and screaming over his shoulder, the Gargoyle hunching close against his back for protection. One man tried to rush him from behind, but the Gargoyle's claws laid his arm open to the bone.

Then they were through the door and back out into the night. The screams and shouts followed after them, but the street had cleared as the people fled to the protection of their homes. The Knight moved quickly through the town, his eyes readjusting to the gloom. Nothing to do but to try to find the way on their own. He cursed their misfortune and the ignorance of the townsfolk.

At the base of the hollow's slope, he set the Lady on her feet, keeping hold of her wrist to make certain she did not try to flee.

"Let me go!" she snarled, pulling back against him. "How dare you touch me!" She spit at him. "I hate you! I will see you cut apart while you are still alive for this!"

He ignored her, heading for the darkness of the trees, ascending the slope toward the concealment of the forest beyond. Behind, the lights of the town burned weakly from the windows of the buildings, and the shadows of the people milled about in their glow. The Knight spared them only a glance, his attention focused on the line of the trees ahead. Pursuit was not improbable.

They had reached the edge of the forest when the Gargoyle wheeled about and went into a guarded crouch. "Something comes!" he warned, his voice thin and breathless.

In the same instant, new screams of terror rose from the townsfolk. The Knight and the Lady turned to look. A towering wall of wicked green light had appeared within the trees on the far side of the hollow. It flickered like fire and hissed like acid, eating away at the silent dark. It moved steadily forward, and as it came it seemed to change appearance, taking on the look of a heavy rain, a rush of shadows and light that tore mercilessly at everything in its path.

The screams of the people below heightened. *The Haze! The Haze! It's here! Run! Oh, run!*

But there appeared to be nowhere to run and no time left in which to do it. The greenish rain came out of the trees and descended the slope toward the town. The world disappeared in its wake. Not a tree, not a shrub, not a hint of life remained. All were consumed. The Haze reached the town and began to tear at the buildings. One by one, they were drawn into its strange curtain. The townsfolk went, too, shrieking in frenzy, unable to escape. The Haze claimed them as they fled, and they did not come out. Even their screams were swallowed.

On the ridge of the hollow, the Knight tensed as the last building and inhabitant of the nameless town disappeared and the Haze came on. But suddenly, without reason, the Haze began to draw back. In a matter of seconds, it had reversed itself—a storm front that had suddenly shifted, its thunderheads turned by an unexpected head wind. Slowly, deliberately, it climbed back up the slope of the hollow, melted into the trees, and vanished.

The Knight, the Lady, and the Gargoyle stared down into the empty hollow. The town they had fled was gone—every building, every person, every beast, every trace that any of it had ever been. Bare earth alone remained, steaming like scalded flesh. The Haze had burned it bare.

The Knight looked over at the Gargoyle. The Haze was more than legend, it seemed. But what had brought it from the woods this night? Was it in fact preceded by a monster as the counterman had warned? Was that monster the Gargoyle? Was there some link between the two, a terrible pact to ravage the earth and devour the life that lived upon it? The Gargoyle was, after all, a monster come out of the most ancient of times. The Knight pondered the possibilities. The Lady was looking at the beast as well, and there was a hint of fear in her cold eyes. Staring off into the dark, the Gargoyle did not return their looks.

The Knight turned away. All those people gone, he thought. All. He could see them vanish anew in his mind. He could hear them screaming still. The sound was horrific, but familiar. He had heard such screams before. He had heard them all his life. They were the screams of the men he had fought and killed in battle. They were the screams of his victims. The screams were captured in his memory like trapped souls in a net, and he would carry them with him forever.

He wondered then, in the terrible aftermath of the destruction he had witnessed, if the burden of these newest screams was his to bear as well.

RIVER GYPSIES

They walked all that night, too nervous to sleep. They did not speak of what had happened, but each knew that the others were thinking of it. The endless forest closed about them again, a vast impenetrable canopy of leafy boughs and misty skies. The Labyrinth stretched on once more, and after a time it seemed as if the town and her people might never have been at all.

When it was morning and the darkness lightened to gray, they found a clearing and slept for a time. The Knight rested in the half doze that he had long since mastered for when there was need, a sort of trance in which some small part of him, some singular instinct, remained awake and alert against danger. He might have dreamed, but he was haunted by the screams of all those he had seen die and by his inability to rid himself of them. They were the shades of the dead, all that remained of what had once been human. They lived on in him, as if they had attached themselves and would not release until death came to him as well.

When he did not doze, he lay thinking on the Gargoyle, wondering still what part the creature had played in what had happened to the town. He was bothered anew by the fact that he could not remember how the Gargoyle had come to be with him, why it was that they were traveling together. He could remember nothing of the beast beyond knowing that he should be there. Where had the Gargoyle come from? What reason had he to be with the Knight and the Lady in the Labyrinth? The Gargoyle might belong here, the Knight kept thinking. He had known first of the common belief that the Labyrinth was a maze without an exit. He had said first what the towns-folk had said later. The Gargoyle had known of the Haze. There was so much that the Knight did not know that the Gargoyle did. It was troublesome. The Knight did not fear the creature, but was wary of his purpose. There seemed a fundamental honor and fairness to the beast, but try as he might the Knight could not bring himself to trust him.

On waking, they went on. They traveled now because they had little choice. If they did not go on, they would be admitting defeat. The Knight would not allow that. He could sense his control of things slipping away, his self-assurance and certainty of purpose slowly eroding. Little by little he was coming to see how fragile was his place in the scheme of things. Here, he was a pawn of circumstances he could not fathom or control. There was nothing recognizable in the Labyrinth, and what he remembered of life before was a shadowy play of figures against a too-vague and distant backdrop. Try as he might to concentrate and remember, nothing of his former life would come into focus for him. It was as if he had been born here, and only the presence of the Lady—and perhaps the Gargoyle—reassured him that there was some-thing that had gone before.

The Lady talked to him this day, almost as if she were compelled. She did not converse as a friend or intimate, merely as his charge and companion on the road. She questioned him repeatedly about who he was and why he was there. She questioned him about what he remembered of his life before. She wanted to know why he had taken her and for whom. He avoided her ques-tions, turning each aside as deftly as he could manage. He avoided them be-cause he could not answer them. He had no answers to give. She pressed him until she grew weary, and then she fell silent once more.

"You toy with me," she said, the sadness and despair come back into her voice, replacing the otherwise-always-present anger. "You play games with me because I am your prisoner."

He shook his head, gazing off into the mist. "I would not do that to you."

"Then tell me something of yourself," she begged, just managing to keep her voice level and controlled. "Give me something as reassurance that you do not lie."

He walked without speaking for a moment, then lowered his head. "I do not like it that things must be this way. I wish they could be otherwise. I am sorry for taking you, whatever the purpose, whatever the cause. If there is a way to do so later, I will make it up to you."

He thought she would laugh outright at the suggestion. He thought she would simply scorn him. She surprised him by doing neither. Instead, she sim-ply nodded without speaking and walked on.

It was midafternoon when they reached the river. It appeared as the town had appeared, coming into view as they crested a rise and the trees broke apart. The river was broad and slow, and it ran in either direction across their path for as far as the eye could see. On the far bank, the forests of the Labyrinth resumed, stretching away forever. Overhead, the skies remained shrouded and empty.

They walked down to the river's edge and stopped, looking first across, then upstream, then downstream. There was no sign of life. The water was cloudy and smooth where rapids and rifts did not churn it to foam amid rocky outcroppings. No debris floated in it, nor did fish jump to mar the glassy surface.

"If there is a river, there must be a town somewhere along it," the Lady said hopefully.

"But does the town lie within the Labyrinth or beyond?" the Knight queried. He looked at her. "We shall follow it and see. Which way shall we go?"

Again, she surprised him. "You decide. You are the one who leads us."

He took them downstream. The riverbank was broad and grassy and easily traversed. The trees of the forest ended some hundred yards back at most points, and the way was clear and open for travelers. As gray daylight waned toward nightfall, the mist moved out of the trees and settled down across the river and its banks. It crept to their boot tops and then to their knees. By darkness, it was waist-high and they could no longer see where the bank ended and the river began.

The Knight had just decided to move back into the trees for the night when they heard the singing. They stopped as one, listening. The sound came from just a little farther ahead, around a bend not two hundred yards away. The Knight took them back to the fringe of the trees so that they would escape a fall into the river, and they continued from there. When they reached the bend and rounded it, they saw light from several fires. The singing came from there. They moved toward the fires, peering intently through the gloom. As they neared, a handful of painted wagons came into view. There were mules tethered nearby, and tents of bright cloth that had been tied to poles and the ends of the wagons and made fast by rope stays. The singers were more than a dozen in number, men and women both, all dressed in colorful garb with many sashes, cloaks, and headbands, all gathered about the fires as they sang.

The Knight and his companions approached and were seen, but the singing continued as if their appearance did not matter. The Gargoyle was hanging back, wrapped in his cloak for concealment, but one of the singers rose and beckoned them all forward, making certain that the beast was included. They came up slowly, cautious by nature and circumstance, even in these seemingly friendly surroundings.

"Welcome to our camp," the one who had encouraged them to join in greeted. "Will you sing with us? Sing for your supper, perhaps?"

The man was heavy and round and had great, gnarled hands. His hair and beard were thick and black. He wore several gold earrings and a chain with a locket. A brace of daggers were tucked in a sash at his ample waist, and another protruded from the top of his boot.

"Who are you?" the Knight asked.

"Ah, ah—no names, my friend," the other said. "Names are for enemies we would avoid, not for friends we would make. Will you sit with us?"

"River Gypsies," the Gargoyle said, come to a full stop, and the Knight looked quickly at him.

The big man laughed. "That's us! Well, look at you, my friend. A Gargoyle! Not many of your kind left in the world, and none have been seen in my lifetime, I think, within the Labyrinth. So, now. Don't be shy, don't lurk about at the edges of the light. You are all welcome. Come sit with us and sing. Come share the fire."

He shepherded them forward to join the others. Space was made, drinks were brought, and the singing went on. Smiles passed from face to face as songs were begun and finished. One man played a stringed instrument of some sort. One played a flute. The Knight and his companions listened to the songs, but did not join in. They drank the wine they were offered, but only a little at first. They looked about at the assemblage and wondered how they had gotten there.

"Have you come far?" the big man asked of the Knight after a time, leaning close to be heard.

"Five days' walk," the Knight answered. "We cannot seem to find our way out."

"A common enough problem here," the other replied, nodding.

"Do you know a way?" the Knight pressed.

The other began to clap along with a song. "Perhaps. Perhaps."

The singing went on for a long time. The Knight began to grow sleepy. The Lady had drunk more than he had and was already stretched out upon the grass, eyes closed. The Gargoyle sat hunched down within his cloak, featureless in his hood's shadows. Some of the Gypsies had begun to dance, leaping and spinning in the firelight. The women had fixed bells to their fingers, and the silvery tinkle lifted above the singing. The men trailed scarves that were crimson and gold. Wine was drunk freely. There had been mention of food earlier, the Knight thought, but none had appeared.

"Is this not the way life should be lived?" the big man asked suddenly, leaning over once more. He was flushed and smiling. "Give no thought to tomorrow until it comes. Do not worry about that over which you have no control. Sing and dance. Drink and laugh. Leave your troubles for another time."

The Knight shook his head. "Troubles have a way of catching up with you."

The other laughed. "Such a pessimist! Look at you! You neither sing nor dance! You drink so little! How can you enjoy yourself? You must give life a chance!"

"Is there a way out of the Labyrinth?" the Knight asked again.

The Gypsy shook his head merrily, climbed to his feet, and shrugged. "Not this night, I think. Tomorrow, maybe." And off he went, dancing lightly for all his size across the firelight.

The Knight drained away the last of his wine and looked over for his companions. The Lady was still sleeping soundly. The Gargoyle had disappeared. The Knight cast about for him in vain, even beyond the firelight. He was gone.

The Knight tried to rise and found he could not. His legs would not work, and his body felt encased in iron. He struggled against a weight that seemed to chain him down, managing to come almost all the way up before falling back. The River Gypsies danced and sang about him, oblivious. Colors and shapes spun past him as he turned toward the darkness. Something was wrong. Some trick had been played.

He was still wondering what was amiss as he toppled over into blackness.

⸺◦∞◦⸺

When he came awake, he was alone. The River Gypsies were gone—the men, the women, the wagons, the mules, everything. All that remained were the ashes of the fires, still smoldering faintly in the hazy dawn. The Knight was stretched full length upon the grassy earth. He rolled over weakly and came to his knees. His head throbbed from the wine, and his muscles were cramped from his sleep. To his left, the river flowed past, smooth, soundless, and undisturbed. To his right, the forest was a dark curtain filled with mist.

The Knight rose to his feet and waited for the dizziness to pass.

The Lady was gone as well.

He felt his breath quicken and his chest constrict with anger and disbelief. Where had she gone? He cast about through the early morning gloom for some sign of her, but there was none. She had disappeared.

He was still in the process of regaining his bearings when the Gargoyle emerged from the trees and came toward him. The Knight realized suddenly that his weapons were missing as well, all of them. He was defenseless.

"Sleep well?" the Gargoyle queried as he reached the Knight, the sarcasm in his voice unmistakable.

"Where are my weapons?" the Knight demanded angrily. "What has become of the Lady?"

The Gargoyle hunched down before him, dark-featured. "The River Gypsies have them both. They took them while you were sleeping."

"Took them?" The Knight was stunned. "You mean they stole them?"

The Gargoyle laughed softly. "The Gypsies do not look at it like that. To them, the weapons and the woman are our payment for last night's pleasures. Fair is fair, they think. They relieved you of what you do not need."

The Knight glowered. "And you did nothing to stop them?"

The Gargoyle shrugged. "Why should I? What difference does it make to me what happens to the Lady or your weapons? I care for neither. In truth, you are better off without them. There is no need for weapons within the Labyrinth—only wits and patience. The Lady was a millstone about both our necks, an annoyance that no sane man should have to bear."

"That was not your decision to make!"

"Nor did I make it." The Gargoyle was unruffled, his ugly face lifting slightly into the light, his yellow eyes calm. "I let events take their own course and nothing more."

"You could have warned me!"

"You could have warned yourself if you had been thinking straight. There is no mystery to Gypsies of any kind—they are the same the world over and always have been. They live by their own rules, and if you choose to drink and sing with them you accept that this is so. Consider it a lesson, Sir Knight, and let it pass."

The Knight forced down his rage. Fear lurked just beneath, the feeling that he was losing control and could do nothing to stop it. The Lady and his weapons were gone, and he had been powerless to prevent it. Why hadn't he seen better what might happen? Why hadn't he taken the precautions he knew were necessary?

He breathed in deeply and looked up and down the river. "Which way did they go?" The Gargoyle did not respond, and the Knight turned on him quickly. "Do not give me reason to mistrust you further!" he snapped.

The Gargoyle held his angry gaze. "I have given you no reason ever."

"Haven't you?" The Knight squared himself. "When I woke in the Labyrinth, you were already there. You knew where we were; you called the Labyrinth by name. You said that there was no way out, before anyone else had even mentioned it. When we reached that town and we were told of the Haze, you knew the story. The counterman identified you as a monster that preceded its coming. Last night, when we came upon the River Gypsies, you knew who they were when the Lady and I did not. You seem to know a great deal about a place which you do not claim to come from. I cannot help but wonder what cause you serve in all of this."

The Gargoyle stared at the Knight, and for a long moment he said nothing. "You have cause to be suspicious, I suppose," he replied finally, reluctantly. "I would be suspicious as well, were I you. It must seem as if I am duplicitous. But I am not. What I know comes from living for a very long time and having been to a great many places. I have acquired knowledge for which I can no longer name the source. I remember things that I heard about or discovered centuries ago. I am very old. Once, as the River Gypsy said, there were many of my kind. Now there is only me in all the world."

He paused, as if reflecting. "This place and those who live here and the things that happen within are familiar to me, known from another time, one for which my memory has long since been erased. I sense, as well, some of what will be. I know this place; I recognize it. I anticipate some events. But I am not from here, and I am not sure I have ever visited before." The Gargoyle scowled. "It bothers me that this is so. My memory is quite fragmented, and I confess that nothing of my previous life is clear to me anymore. Save," he added darkly, "that I am no longer who or what I was."

The Knight nodded slowly. He sensed truth in the Gargoyle's words. "Nor am I. The past seems long ago and far away."

"But there are associations that trigger memories, as with the River Gypsies last night," the Gargoyle said. "I knew them without ever having met them. I knew what they were about. I could have told you, it is true. I did not. I wanted them to take the Lady. I wanted her gone." His gaze was direct. "I am not ashamed."

"I must get her back from them," the Knight said.

"Why? What reason is there to do so?" The Gargoyle seemed genuinely interested.

The Knight was silent. His hands clenched as he struggled to speak. "Because it is what I was given to do before I came here. It is the only certainty I possess. Without her, I am lost. She is all that keeps me going. She is the reason for my being. I exist because of her. Do you see?"

The Gargoyle thought for a moment and then nodded. "I think I do. You have no cause beyond taking her to your master, no cause that you can remember. But do you remember anything even of that, Sir Knight?"

The Knight shook his head. "This place seems to have stolen my past."

"And mine." The Gargoyle's voice was bitter. "I wish my life back again. I wish my memories restored."

"Did you see which way they went?" the Knight repeated.

"You are better off without her," the Gargoyle replied. There was no response from the Knight, no change in his expression. The Gargoyle sighed. "Upstream, back the way we came." He shook his head wearily. "I will go with you."

⎯⎯⟨∞⟩⎯⎯

They set out at once, moving through the long grasses of the riverbank, following the earth-colored ribbon into the misty gray. They found tracks almost immediately, and it wouldn't have been hard for the Knight to have discovered for himself which way the River Gypsies had gone. It made him suspicious anew of the Gargoyle's place in the scheme of things; after all, the Gargoyle might have told him simply to serve his own purpose. But that was harsh thinking, and the Knight was not comfortable with it. He believed the Gargoyle to be a fundamentally honorable creature. He did not sense lies in what he had been told. They had both come into this world from some other, and their destiny here, along with that of the Lady, was of a single piece.

They pushed on through the day, moving steadily ahead in the wake of the wagon tracks, pausing infrequently to rest themselves, intent on completing their chase by sunset. The river broadened after a time, growing so large that the far bank was little more than a dark line against the clouded skies. The Knight was growing depressed by the constant grayness, by the absence of any sunlight, by the oppressive lowering of the sky toward the earth. He missed people and animals and the presence of other life. He had enjoyed those once, he knew. Mostly, he felt the loss of his identity beyond the vagueness of his present existence. It was not enough to sense who and what you were; memories were needed as well, clear pictures of the life you had lived and the things you had done while you lived it. He had almost none of those—fewer, it seemed, than the Gargoyle. He was cast adrift in a limbo, and the emptiness he felt was beginning to breed madness.

It was after sunset when they came upon the River Gypsies again. They were fortunate to see the firelight well before they were close enough to be seen themselves. The Gypsies were encamped on the riverbank once more, and the sound of their singing rose into the twilight stillness with careless disregard. The Knight and the Gargoyle moved back within the trees and edged along within the protective fringe until they were close enough to see what was happening. There were no surprises. The River Gypsies sat about their fires drinking wine, letting the night close in about them. The Lady sat with them. She did not appear to be restrained in any way. She held a cup in one hand and sipped at it. Her face was cold and empty, but she did not appear afraid.

"Perhaps she wants to be with them," the Gargoyle whispered. "Perhaps she is freer with them than she was with you."

The Knight ignored him. "I need my sword back."

The Gargoyle shook his head reprovingly. "You are of a single mind, aren't you? No deviation in your life." His laugh was deep and soft. "We are both cast in a mold that can never be changed."

He rose abruptly. "Wait here for me."

He disappeared into the trees. The Knight waited, watching the camp. Darkness deepened until everything beyond the glow of the firelight disappeared. The drinking and singing went on, uninterrupted, unabated. All other sounds and movements disappeared behind the gaiety, submerged as deadwood in a river's flow. Time passed, and the Knight grew anxious.

Then the Gargoyle was there beside him again, holding out the broadsword, sharpened teeth gleaming along the edges of a smile. The Knight accepted the sword, balanced it in his hand to study its condition, then slipped it back into the sheath he wore across his back.

"Now we will ask them to give the Lady back," he said, rising.

"Wait." The Gargoyle's clawed hand restrained him. "Why ask when there is no need? Wait until early morning, then slip down and take her while they sleep. It might be the easier way."

The Knight thought it over a minute and nodded. "We will wait."

They sat together in silence within the concealment of the forest trees. The River Gypsies began to dance, and the merriment went on. It did not end until the night was mostly gone and the fires burned away. Then the men and women rolled themselves into their blankets and were still. The Lady slept with them. She had not moved from the place she had been sitting; she had merely eased herself down onto the grass. Mist edged in about the wagons and animals, no longer kept at bay by the heat of the flames, and soon it covered the sleepers.

The Knight and the Gargoyle rose then and slipped from the trees. They made their way in silence through the long grasses toward the camp. They searched for a sentry and found none. When they reached the wagons, they paused again, listening. There was only the sound of the Gypsies sleeping and the distant rustle of the river against her banks. They edged along the wagons until they were close to where the Lady lay. Then the Knight went forward alone.

He found her, knelt close, and placed his hand over her mouth. She came awake at once, looking up at him with cool, appraising eyes that were free of any fear. He started to help her up, then saw the chain that ran from a clamp fastened about her ankle to a wagon wheel.

The Knight stood, fury racing through him. He'd had enough. He walked through the sleepers heedlessly until he found the one who had spoken so enticingly to him of leaving one's cares for another day. He reached down, fastened his fingers in the man's tunic, and hauled him to his feet.

"I will cut you end to end if she is not freed at once," he hissed.

The man looked him in the eye and nodded wordlessly. The Knight steered him back across the camp to where the Lady waited. The bearded Gypsy reached into his pocket, produced a key, released the lock, and stood back.

"You should not be angry at us," he said quietly.

The Knight pulled free the clamp from the Lady's leg and brought her to her feet. She reached down to rub her ankle, then turned and strode out of the camp for the trees.

"Wine and entertainment come at a price," the Gypsy declared. "You owe us."

The Knight turned. "Be grateful I do not kill you."

The Gypsy put his fingers to his lips and whistled, a shrill, piercing sound. Instantly the camp was awake, and there were armed men all about. They held daggers and short swords and axes, the metal blades gleaming wetly in the damp air. They took in the situation at a single glance and edged toward the Knight.

"Do not be foolish," the Knight warned, placing his back to the nearest wagon.

"It is you who have been foolish, I think," the bearded Gypsy replied.

They came at the Knight in a swarm, but he scattered the rush with a huge sweep of his blade. His chain mail protected him from the dirks thrown at his chest, and he turned and moved swiftly past the wagons for the woods. Where was his heavy armor? he wondered suddenly. Where were his plates and greaves and helmet? He sensed them somewhere close at hand once more, but still they would not come to him. This was twice now that he had been forced to stand and fight without them. He had never had to do so before. His armor had always been there when he needed it. Why didn't he have it now?

Again the Gypsies rushed him, and this time he was forced to defend himself. He cut two of them down and wounded a third, taking no injury himself. He could hear the Gargoyle calling. When he glanced back, he saw the Lady standing at the edge of the trees, watching him.

Rage at the stupidity of the River Gypsies washed through him. He braced himself for another rush.

It never came. A familiar, wicked green light lifted off the river in a towering curtain and began to advance on the camp. The Gypsies turned at its coming and screamed in recognition. The Haze swept out of the mist and dark, a terrible hissing rain that ate away the landscape. The Knight turned and ran for the woods, taking advantage of the Gypsies' terror and confusion. He gained the trees as the Haze reached the camp. It ate its way through the wagons and animals and people so quickly that they disappeared in seconds. Even the screams lingered only an instant. No one seemed able to escape.

It was over in moments. The Haze advanced until the camp was devoured and then it drew back. As with the town, it retreated across the scorched, barren earth and disappeared from view. As with the town, nothing of the River Gypsies remained behind.

The ravaged ground steamed in the early dawn light. The Knight stared out from the trees in shock. The Lady stood at one elbow, the Gargoyle at the other. No one spoke. The Knight was wondering how this had happened, how it was that the Haze had come again, how it could be that it took only the camp and left them alone. What had brought it? What had kept it from destroying them as well? Something in all of this was not right. There was a surreal aspect to everything that had happened—in their discovery of that nameless town, in their encounter with the River Gypsies, in the coming of the Haze. There was an unmistakable skewing of reality that lacked identity, but not form. Ignorant of its source, he was nevertheless aware that it existed.

An unpleasant suspicion began to form at the back of his mind, one so terrible that he could not give it voice. He buried it away deep inside himself in despair and disbelief.

"What monstrous thing is this," the Lady whispered, stepping forward to stare out across the river. "Does it track us like dogs at hunt?"

"It does," the Gargoyle growled softly. "I can sense its hunger."

The Knight could sense it, too. And while he would not say so, while he could not bring himself to speak the words, he thought that its hunger had not yet been sated.

COSTS YOU NOTHING

They must have seemed an odd sight, Abernathy thought as they approached the gates of Rhyndweir, castle fortress of Kallendbor, the most powerful of the Lords of the Greensward. A tall, scrawny, gangly man with a bird on his shoulder, a smallish, wiry beast that looked a little like a crazed monkey, and a dog with human hands and wearing reading glasses—Horris Kew, Biggar, Bunion, and himself. Up the roadway through the town surrounding the fortress they trudged, carrying before them (well, Bunion carrying, actually) the banner of the current and still absent King of Landover. Their horses trailed on a line behind them, grateful no doubt to be rid of riders who didn't much care for the beasts anyway. The mule with the chests of mind's eye crystals plodded along with them. The day was hot and humid, the air still, and the prospect of a bath and a cold drink was foremost in everyone's mind.

Townspeople gathered to watch them come, standing in the shade of doorways and awnings, nudging one another and whispering. Perhaps they knew, Abernathy thought. Perhaps by now, everybody knew.

They had departed Sterling Silver three days earlier, a delegation of King's emissaries dispatched for the particular purpose of distributing mind's eye crystals to the people of the Greensward, both high-born and low. The decision to allow the crystals to be shared had been reached with some reservations, but reached nevertheless. Questor Thews was growing desperate in his efforts to cover for the missing King. It was getting harder and harder to invent excuses to explain why the King refused to see anyone personally, delegating all meetings to his chief advisor. A diversion of some sort was needed to keep the more persistent questioners at bay. If nothing else, perhaps the crystals could provide this. Take them out, spread them around, let them amuse for a time, and hope the novelty wouldn't wear off too fast.

Questor, of course, could not go himself. So Abernathy, despite his objection to the idea, was the logical choice to go in his place. Someone had to represent the King besides Horris Kew and his bird. Someone had to keep an eye on Horris and maybe the bird as well. So Abernathy was pressed into service, and Bunion was sent along for protection and support. An escort of soldiers was offered as well, but no one wanted them, including Abernathy, who preferred to keep matters simple and straightforward. Visit the Lords of the Greensward with an escort and you called immediate attention to yourself. That was a bad idea, Abernathy had decided, and therefore the escort was unnecessary.

Besides, this was a time of peace. What sort of trouble would they run into with the King's banner paraded before them?

So off they had gone, marching out of the castle gates and heading northeast through the forests and across the hills to the grasslands of the Greensward. Everyone they met along the way was offered one of the crystals. Most accepted them gladly, entranced by what they could do. One or two, more curmudgeonly than their fellows, wouldn't even consider such nonsense. There were a great many farms and small communities between Sterling Silver and the castles of the Lords of the Greensward, so hundreds of crystals were distributed. Word began to spread, and before long there were people waiting for them on the road. More crystals were passed out, and more people went away happy. So far, so good.

Abernathy had to give credit to Horris Kew. The conjurer made certain that each person given a crystal knew that it was a gift from the King and that he was acting solely as the King's representative. There was no attempt to take credit for anything, no hint of self-promotion. It was very unlike the Horris Kew Abernathy remembered, and it made him suspicious all over again.

But the faithful Court Scribe was compromised on the matter. As much as he distrusted Horris Kew and his schemes, including this one, he was desperately attached to his own, personal crystal. When he could admit it to himself, which was less and less often, he worried that his attraction bordered on addiction. He seemed to have been snared from the first moment he had looked into the crystal's wonderous depths. What had he been shown, not once, but each time he looked? Himself, restored to who and what he had once been, a man with a man's features, the dog body in which he was trapped forever gone. It was his deepest, fondest wish in life, the dream he lived to fulfill, and when he gazed into the faceted light of his mind's eye crystal, it all came to pass. He could stay there and watch himself for as long as he chose—an increasingly longer period of time each day. He could not only see but feel himself as a man; he could remember what it had been like before Questor Thews invoked his unfortunate incantation and consigned him to his present fate.

It was a wickedly pleasurable pastime, and Abernathy could not get enough of it. It was not as good as being himself again, as looking as he once had, but it was as close as he was likely to get. It was immensely satisfying. And he owed it all to Horris Kew.

Even now, as he approached the towering gates of Rhyndweir and thought gratefully of the bath and cold ale that would be waiting, he was thinking as well of his crystal and the prospect of time alone in his room to look into its depths once more.

The gates opened to receive them, and they marched through and past the handful of guards standing watch. A single minor court official waited to receive them and guide them on. No trumpeted greeting, no turning out of the garrison, no personal attendance by Kallendbor as there would have been for the King, Abernathy thought. Minimal respect was accorded to envoys, and less-than-minimal interest. Kallendbor had never liked Holiday, but he was growing more open in his disdain. Memories of Holiday's triumphs and accomplishments were growing dim, it seemed. Holiday had faced down Kallendbor on several occasions and done what the Lords of the Greensward had been unable to do—defeat the Iron Mark, disperse the demons back to Abaddon, and unite the kingdom under a single rule. He had defeated every opponent sent against him and overcome every obstacle. All this had been accepted by Kallendbor, if never appreciated. Now, perhaps, even acceptance was in question.

Kallendbor met them at the palace doors, resplendent in crimson robes and jewels, accompanied by his advisors and current favorites. He was a tall, well-built man with hair and beard so red they shone almost gold in the sunlight. His hands and forearms were callused and marked with battle scars. He stood waiting for them to approach, arrogant head held erect, giving the impression that he was looking down on them, that he was lending them his time and attention out of the generosity of his heart. His attitude did not bother Abernathy; the scribe was well used to it. Nevertheless, he did not appreciate the deliberate insolence.

"Lord Kallendbor," Abernathy greeted, foremost of the three as they came up to him, and inclined his head slightly.

"Scribe," the other replied with an even slighter bow.

"Awk! Mighty Lord! Mighty Lord!" Biggar squawked.

Kallendbor blinked. "What's this we have here? A trained bird? Well, now. Is this gift for me, perhaps?" He was suddenly beaming. "Of course it is! Very well chosen, Abernathy."

Now here was an opportunity that Abernathy would have given almost anything for—a chance to get rid of Biggar. Abernathy had not liked the bird from day one and the bird had not liked him—and each knew how the other felt. There was something about Biggar that bothered Abernathy more than he could say. He couldn't define what it was exactly, but it was most certainly there. He had not wanted the bird on this trip; he had argued against it vehemently. But Horris Kew insisted that the bird must accompany them, and in the end—in large part because the mind's eye crystals were the conjurer's offering and the entire reason for the journey—the bird went.

Abernathy opened his mouth to speak, to tell Kallendbor that, yes, indeed, the bird was all his. He was too slow.

"My Lord, forgive me for letting this poor creature distract you from our purpose in coming to see you," Horris Kew interjected quickly. "The bird, alas, is not a gift. He is my companion, my sole treasure in this world from my old life and the people who meant so much to me, who gave me all that I have and made me what I am. You understand, I am sure." He was speaking very quickly. "The bird, truth be told, is an unpleasant sort, given to fits of temper and biting. You would not be happy with him."

As if to emphasize the point, Biggar reached over and pecked hard at Horris Kew's ear. "Ow! There, you see!" Horris took a swipe at Biggar, who flew off a few yards before settling back down on the other's shoulder, alert for further attempts.

"Why am I not offered this bird if I wish it?" Kallendbor demanded, his face darkening. "Are you saying I cannot have this bird if it pleases me?"

Abernathy was thinking that this was the end of the crystal distribution program, that they might all just as well turn around and go home right now—except for Biggar, who, it appeared, was destined to stay.

"My Lord, the bird is yours if you wish him," Horris Kew declared at once. Biggar squawked anew. "But you should know that he speaks very little, and what he said just now—'Mighty Lord'—is a phrase he learned from the King. In other words, the King taught him to say that about himself."

Abernathy stared. There was a very long silence. Kallendbor flushed and straightened further, looking as if he might explode. Then slowly the dangerous color drained away.

"Never mind, I don't wish him after all," he said disdainfully. "If he is mine to take, that is enough. Let Holiday keep him." He took a steadying breath. "Now, then. Since we have dispensed with the matter of this bird, what is it you wish?"

"My Lord," Horris Kew said, jumping in again before Abernathy could speak, "you were right in your assumption. We do bring you a gift, something far more intriguing and useful than a bird. It is called a mind's eye crystal."

Kallendbor was interested once more. "Let me see it."

This time Abernathy was quicker. "We would be happy to show it to you, my Lord, perhaps inside where it is cooler and we can be shown to the quarters that I am sure you have arranged for us as envoys of the King."

Kallendbor smiled, not a pleasant sight. "Of course, you must be exhausted. Riding is hard for you, I expect. Come this way."

Abernathy did not miss the intended snub, but he ignored it and the little company followed Kallendbor and his retinue inside to the great hall. Glasses of ale drawn from casks kept cooled in the deep waters of the Bairn and the

Cosselburn, the rivers bracketing Rhyndweir, were brought and arrangements were begun for rooms and baths. Kallendbor took them over to an area before a series of doors that opened onto a training field and seated them in a circle of chairs. Most of his retinue was left standing, gathered at their master's shoulder.

"Now, then, what of this gift?" Kallendbor asked anew.

"It is this, my Lord," Horris Kew declared, and produced from his clothing one of the mind's eye crystals.

Kallendbor accepted the crystal and studied it with a frown. "It doesn't look to be precious. What is its worth? Wait!" He leaned forward, looking now at Abernathy. He pointed at Horris Kew. "Who is this?"

"His name is Horris Kew," the scribe answered, resisting the urge to add more. "He is at present in service to the King. He is the discoverer of these crystals."

"*These* crystals?" Kallendbor turned back to Horris Kew. "There are more than one? How many are there?"

"Thousands," the conjurer replied, smiling. "But each is special. Hold it before you, my Lord, so that it catches the light and then look into it."

Kallendbor studied him suspiciously for a moment, then did as he was bidden. He held the crystal out to catch a streamer of sunlight, then bent down to peer into its depths. He remained that way until the crystal seemed to ignite with white fire, then gasped and jerked back sharply, but kept his eyes fixed. Suddenly he was open mouthed, bending close once more, a bright gleam in his eyes. "No, is it so?" he muttered. "Is it possible?"

Then he snatched the crystal from view, shutting off its light and whatever the light had shown him. "All of you, out!" he demanded to those peering over his shoulder expectantly. "Now!"

They disappeared with surprising quickness, and when they were gone Kallendbor looked again at Horris Kew. "What are these?" he hissed. "What power do they command?"

Horris seemed confused. "Why, they . . . they offer visions of many things, my Lord—visions peculiar to each holder. They are a diversion, nothing more."

Kallendbor shook his head. "Yes, but . . . do they show the future, perhaps? Tell me that."

"Well, yes, perhaps," Horris Kew went along, no fool he. "To some, of course, not to everyone."

And suddenly Abernathy found himself wondering if perhaps it was so. Horris himself did not seem to know the truth of the matter, but what if Kallendbor's guess was right? Did that mean that the visions shown might come to pass? Did it mean that Abernathy might be seeing himself not as he had been but as he would be again?

"The future," Kallendbor whispered, lost in thought. "Yes, it might be so."

Whatever he had seen had certainly pleased him, Abernathy thought, barely interested in what that might be, too caught up in considering his own use of the crystal. His chest constricted with the emotions that gathered at the prospect that he might become a man again. If it could only be true!

"How many of these do you have?" Kallendbor demanded suddenly.

Horris Kew swallowed, not sure where this was leading. "As I said, thousands, my Lord."

"Thousands. How much do they cost?"

"Nothing, my Lord. They are free."

Kallendbor seemed to choke on something. "Have you given many out yet?"

"Yes, my Lord, many. It is our purpose in coming to the Greensward—to give these crystals to the people so that they may be amused by what they see in them when their daily work is done. Of course, for you, my Lord," he added quickly, not missing an opportunity when he saw one, "they perhaps offer something more."

"Yes, something more." Kallendbor thought. "I have an idea. Allow me to distribute those crystals intended for the other Lords of the Greensward. I shall pass them about in the King's name, of course. That would save you visiting each stronghold and leave you free to visit the common people."

It was not a request. Horris Kew looked at Abernathy for help. Abernathy surmised what Kallendbor intended. He would not give the mind's eye crystals to the other Lords for nothing; he would charge dearly. Probably he would tell them that these crystals, unlike those given for free to the working people, foretold the future. But Abernathy frankly didn't care one way or the other. News would travel fast enough. Let Kallendbor deal with his neighbors as he chose.

Abernathy shrugged. "Of course, my Lord," he replied. "Whatever you wish."

Kallendbor stood up abruptly. "Your rooms are ready. Wash and rest until dinner. We will speak more of this then." He turned from them, and it was apparent that he could barely restrain himself from peering once more at his crystal. "Oh, yes. Ask my servants if you require anything."

He went out the door as if catapulted, and was gone.

Alone in his room, Abernathy bathed, dressed, drank another glass of the fine, cold ale, and settled back in his bed, stretched full-length across its covering. He took his crystal from where he kept it hidden, held it up to the light, and stared into it. He was practiced in its use by now, to the extent such practice was needed, and the light and images came at once. He watched himself appear in his old form, a young man with a bright, happy smile and an expectant look, rather handsome for his bookish appearance, rather appealing. He was playing with children and there was a woman watching, pretty and shy. Abernathy felt his breath catch in his throat. There had never been a woman in his life before, no wife, no lover, and yet here one was now. The future, perhaps? Was it possible he was seeing what would be?

He closed his hand over the crystal abruptly and focused everything on the idea. The future. Anything was possible, wasn't it? What would he give if it were so? He knew the answer without asking. He stared up at the ceiling, at the cracks in the old mortarwork, at the faded paint that had once clearly detailed a pageant of some sort. Like his past, time had faded the event. So much of what once was had been lost in the passing of the years and in the changes wrought. He would not wish to recapture much, he told himself. Just the essence of who he was. Just the whole of who he had been.

He thought suddenly of Ben Holiday, who had been so anxious to leave his past behind. The King had few memories to sustain him, and the changes he had sought had been not of lifestyle but of life. It was not so with Abernathy, but there were parallels to be drawn. He wondered where Holiday was, what had become of him. There remained no trace of the King, no sign of him anywhere, though the search had been long and thorough and was continuing still. It was disturbing that he should vanish so utterly; it did not bode well for any of them if he was gone for good. Another King could bring changes that were not necessarily welcome. Another King would not possess Holiday's strength of character and determination. For another King, the magic might not work.

He drank the last of his ale, sitting on the edge of his bed, dejected. Nothing seemed right with Holiday gone. Everything seemed disrupted and out of joint. He wished that there were something he could do to change things.

Bunion had gone out to scout the surrounding countryside, to see if there was anything to be learned of the missing King. Perhaps he would find something in his quest. Perhaps something good would come of this trek through the Greensward. Perhaps.

Abernathy lay back upon his bed once more and held his crystal out to catch the light.

Kallendbor did not appear for dinner. Neither did Bunion. Horris Kew and Abernathy ate dinner alone with Biggar looking on from the back of the conjurer's chair like some foul omen of doom. Abernathy tried to ignore him, but it was difficult since the bird was sitting directly across the table, staring down malevolently from his perch. Abernathy couldn't help himself. At one point, when Horris wasn't looking, he bared his teeth at the bird.

Biggar told Horris about it later, but Horris wasn't interested. They were back in their room, sitting in near darkness with but a single candle burning on the bedside table. Horris was seated on the bed, and Biggar was hunched down on the deep window ledge.

"He growled at me, I tell you!" the bird was insisting. "He practically snapped at me!"

Horris was looking about the room nervously. The tic was working furiously at the corner of his eye. "Growled at you? I didn't hear anything."

"Well, all right, maybe he didn't actually growl." Biggar was not up to hair-splitting. "But he showed all of his considerable teeth, and there was no mistaking his intent! Horris, pay attention, will you? Quit looking all over the place!"

Horris Kew was indeed scanning the room end to end. He stopped long enough to stare at Biggar in a rather harried, suspicious manner. Tic, tic went the eye. The bird cocked his head. "Are you all right, Horris?"

Horris nodded doubtfully. "I keep seeing something . . ." He gestured vaguely. "Out there." He shrugged. "Sometimes in the shadows of trees and buildings, and sometimes at night in dark corners I think I see it. I feel like I'm being watched." He took a deep breath. "I think *it* might be here."

"The Gorse?" Biggar sighed. "Don't be ridiculous. How could it be here? It never leaves the cave. You're imagining things."

Horris hugged his lanky frame as if cold. His plow-blade nose thrust forward. "I keep thinking about Holiday and the witch and the dragon and what it did to them. I keep worrying that you were right, that it might do the same to us."

"Well, you can't say I didn't warn you." Biggar felt an immense satisfaction at the admission. "On the other hand, we've gone a bit far with this crystal business to be worried about that now."

Horris rose and walked about the room uneasily, checking into corners and behind furniture. Biggar cocked his white-crested head. A waste of time, he was thinking. If the Gorse doesn't want to be seen, it won't be. Not a creature like that.

"Will you sit down and relax?" he said irritably. Horris was making him nervous.

Horris moved back to the bed and seated himself once more. "Do you know what the Gorse said when I asked what would become of Holiday and the others in the Tangle Box?"

Biggar couldn't remember and didn't care. But he said, "What, Horris, tell me."

"It said they would become entangled in the fairy mists. It said that the spell of forgetfulness would start them down a road that had no end. They would not know who they were. They would not remember from where they had come. They would be sealed away in the mists, and the mists would play with them and eventually drive them mad." Horris shuddered. "The Gorse said it would take a very long time to happen."

"None of this is our concern," Biggar sniffed. "We have enough to worry about as it is."

"I know, I know." Horris fidgeted and looked off into the shadows as if he had heard something. "I just can't stop thinking about it."

Biggar was disgusted. "Well, you better find a way to stop thinking about it. We have a lot to lose if this crystal-giving program doesn't work out the way the Gorse expects. On the other hand, we have a lot to gain if it does. For the Gorse, Landover is a stepping-stone to other things, but for us it's the pot of gold at the end of the rainbow. If we stick to business, we can do a lot better than we did with Skat Mandu."

"I know, I know."

"Stop saying that—I hate it when you're condescending!"

Horris came to his feet, shaking with anger. "Shut up, Biggar! I'll be condescending if I choose!" He wrung his hands and swept the room with his eyes. "I know what to do, and I'll do it! I've been doing it right along, haven't I? But I don't like being watched! I don't like the idea of someone being there when I can't see them!"

Biggar spit. "Horris, for the last time, the Gorse isn't here!"

Horris clenched his fists in frustration. "But what if it is?"

"Yes, what if I am," the Gorse said from the shadowy depths of the clothes cabinet, and Horris fainted dead away.

When it was done with them, when it had frightened them both so thoroughly that it was satisfied they would do exactly as it wanted them to and not step one inch outside the lines it had directed them to follow, the Gorse went down the outside wall of the castle like a spider. Once on the ground, it changed to a man and went out through the gates to the town beyond. It was getting easier to move about, its magic growing stronger the longer it was free of the fairy mists and the Tangle Box. It was now able to assume different forms. It could be anything or anyone it wished.

It smiled inside to think of the possibilities.

Horris and the bird were idiots, but useful idiots, and the Gorse intended to keep them just long enough to complete its plan for Landover's destruction. After that, it would dispense with them.

They had not expected it to come with them on their journey. They could not fathom how it had managed to do so. Well, a few more surprises awaited them on this trip. It was best to keep them just a little off balance, a little uncertain. They could say what they wished about it as long as they worried when they did. A little fear was a useful thing.

Once outside the castle and the town, the Gorse shape-changed once more and moved off toward a darkened stretch of woods in the countryside beyond, becoming barely more than a shadow skimming over the land. Worried for Holiday, the witch, and the dragon, were they? Well, they should worry. It could happen to them just as easily. It could be as terrible as they imagined. Surely his three captives in the Tangle Box must be wishing they could escape their nightmare existence just about now. They must wonder what it would take. Too bad they would never know.

It reached the woods and gathered its magic to summon up the demons of Abaddon. Time for another conference. Their entry into Landover was not far off. The Gorse wanted them ready and waiting. Lines of fire speared downward from its hands into the earth.

The answering rumble of discontent came almost immediately.

GRISTLIES

The Knight, the Lady, and the Gargoyle followed the river downstream through the Labyrinth for the remainder of that day and all the next. It broadened at times so that the far bank disappeared entirely in the mist, and the flat, gray surface stretched away like smooth stone. No fish jumped from its depths; no birds flew over its surface. Bends and twists came and went, but the river flowed on unchanged and unending.

They encountered no other people, River Gypsies or otherwise. They saw no animals, and the small movements that caught their attention came from the deep shadows of the forest and were gone in the blink of an eye.

The Knight searched often for the Haze, but there was no sign of it. He thought long and hard on its origins, compelled to do so by his certainty that it was somehow tied to them. There was, as the Gargoyle had said, a hunger in the way it came after them. It tracked them for a reason, and the reason was somehow connected to why they were trapped in the Labyrinth. He could not see or hear the Haze, but he could sense its presence. It was always there, just out of sight, waiting.

But what was it waiting for?

On the evening following her rescue from the Gypsies, the Lady asked the Knight why he had come after her. They were seated in the gloom as the last of the day's faint light filtered away into darkness, staring out at the mist as it crawled out of the trees toward the river. They were alone; the Gargoyle had gone off by himself, as he frequently did at night.

"You could have left me and gone on," she observed, her voice cool and questioning. "I thought you had done so."

"I would not have done that," he replied, not looking at her.

"Why? Why bother with me? Am I really so important to your master that you would risk your life for me? Am I such a rare treasure that you would die before losing me?"

He stared off into the dark without answering.

She brushed at her long black hair. "I am your possession, and you would not let anyone take your possessions from you. That is why you came for me, isn't it?"

"You do not belong to me," he said.

"Your master's possession, then. A chattel you dare not lose for fear of offending him. Is that it?"

He looked at her and found derision and bitterness in her eyes. "Tell me something, my Lady. What do you remember of your life before waking in the Labyrinth?"

Her lips tightened. "Why should I tell you?"

He held her gaze, not looking away this time when the anger sparked and burned at him. "I remember almost nothing of my own life. I know I was a Knight in service to a King. I know I have fought hundreds of battles on his behalf and won them all. I know we are tied together somehow, you and I and, I think, the Gargoyle as well. Something happened to me to bring me to this place and time, but I cannot recall what it was. It is as if my whole life has been stolen away."

He paused. "I am tired of not answering your questions because I have no answers to give. I do not know the name of the master I serve. I do not even know my own name. I do not know where I came from or where I was going to. I came for you not out of loyalty to a master I do not remember or to fulfill an obligation that I cannot recall, but because you are all I have left to hold onto of my life before coming here. If I lose you, if I give you up, nothing would remain."

She stared at him, and the anger and bitterness dimmed. In their place there showed understanding and a hint of fear. "I cannot remember anything either," she said softly, speaking the words as if it caused her pain to do so. "I was important and strong, and I knew what I was about. I had magic once."

Her voice caught in her throat, and he thought she might cry. She did not. She regained control of herself and continued. "I think that magic sent me here. I think you are right, that we were together before and sent here for the same reason. But I think, too, that it was your fault that it happened, not mine."

He nodded. "That may be."

"I blame you for this."

He nodded again. "I am not offended."

"But I am glad that you are here and that you came for me, too."

He was too astonished to reply.

On the second night, when the Gargoyle had disappeared into the growing darkness and they were hunkered down by the riverbank, she spoke to him again. She was wrapped in her cloak as if cold, although the air was warm and humid, and there was no wind.

"Do you think we shall escape this place?" she asked in a very small voice.

"We shall escape," he replied, for he still believed they would.

"The forest and this river go on and do not show any sign of ending. They show no change. The mists still wrap us about and close us away. There are no people or animals. There are no birds." She shook her head slowly. "There is magic everywhere; it controls everything in the Labyrinth. You may not be able to feel it, but I do. It is a place of magic, and without magic to aid us we shall not escape."

"There will be a town or a pass through mountains or—"

"No," she interrupted, her slim white hand coming up quickly to stop him. "No. There will be nothing but the river and the forest and the mists forever. Nothing."

He woke early the following morning, having spent an uneasy, mostly sleepless night. The Lady's words haunted him, a grim prophecy he could not forget. She was sleeping still, curled into her cloak in the tall grass, her face serene and smooth, no trace of anger or despair, no hint of bitterness or fear. She was very beautiful lying there, all pale skin and dark hair, flawless and perfect, the coldness that sometimes marked her when she was awake replaced in sleep by softness.

He looked down at her, and he wondered what they had been to each other before coming into the Labyrinth.

After a moment, he rose and went down to the river's edge. He splashed water on his face and wiped himself dry. When he rose, the Gargoyle was standing next to him. The beast had cast off his cloak. Dew glistened on the bare patches of his bristly hide, like water on a reptile newly risen from the river's depths. His wings hung ribbed and listless against his hunched back. His face, so ugly and misshapen, seemed contemplative as he looked out over the river. He did not speak at first, but simply stood there.

"Where do you go at night?" the Knight asked him.

The Gargoyle smiled, showing his yellow teeth. "Into the woods where the shadows are thickest. I sleep better there than in the open." He looked at the Knight. "Did you think I was off hunting down and eating small creatures too slow and soft to escape me? Or that I was performing some diabolical blood rite?"

The Knight shook his head. "I did not think anything. I simply wondered."

The Gargoyle sighed. "The truth is, I am a creature of habit. We spoke of what we remembered—or did not remember? I remember my habits best. I am ugly and despised by most; it is a fact of my life. Since I am loathsome to others, I take comfort in keeping to myself. I search out the places others would not go. I conceal myself in darkness and shadows and the privacy of my own company. It works best for me when I do."

He looked away again. "I did eat other creatures once. I ate whatever I chose and traveled wherever I wished. I could fly. I soared the skies unfettered, and there was nothing that could hold me." The yellow eyes shifted back. "But something changed that, and I think it is tied somehow to you."

The Knight blinked. "To me? But I do not even remember you."

"Odd, isn't it? I heard what the Lady said to you, about how she believes the Labyrinth is magic. I was listening from the trees. I think she is right. I think we were somehow transported by magic, and that magic keeps us prisoners. Do you feel it as well?"

The Knight shook his head. "I don't know."

"The Labyrinth does not feel like any real place," the Gargoyle said. "It lacks the small things that would make it so. It feels artificial, as if it were created by dreams, where everything happens a short step out of time from how we know things to be. Did you not sense it to be so with that town and after the Gypsies? Magic would do that, and I think it has done so here."

"If so," the Knight said quietly, "then the Lady is also right when she says we shall not escape."

But the Gargoyle shook his head. "It only means that since magic brought us in, magic must take us out. It means we must look for our escape in a different way."

The Knight stared off again. What other way was there? he wondered. He could not think of any. They lacked magic themselves; to sustain them they had only the weapons he carried and their wits. That didn't seem enough.

They followed the river again that day, and nothing changed. The river rolled on, the forest stretched away, and the mist and gray permeated everything. The Labyrinth's sameness was growing almost unbearable. The Knight found himself imagining that the ground they were covering now was the same ground they had covered before. He found himself catching sight of landmarks he recognized and geography he knew. It was impossible, of course. They had gone on the same way without once turning back, so there was no chance that they could be repeating their steps. Still, the feeling persisted, and it began to wear at the Knight's resolve.

They camped at a bend in the river where the forest came almost to the water's edge and they could settle themselves back within its shelter. They did so because the Knight wanted the Gargoyle to be able to sleep with them and not have to go off by himself. The creature was scarred already by his hideous appearance, and it seemed cruel that he should be compelled to hide himself away from them each night. They were companions on this journey and had only themselves for support. They must do what they could to keep the bond between them strong. Even the Lady had quit baiting the Gargoyle, had ceased referring to him in derogatory terms, and had begun to speak to him in a civil tone now and again. It was a start, the Knight believed.

His thoughtfulness was rewarded when the Gargoyle did not go off into the dark, but curled up only a few feet off, in the shadow of an old shade tree. For this night, at least, he would sleep with them.

—◦∞◦—

Rough hands brought them awake, pulling them from their sleep as if they were logs from a woodpile. The Knight came to his feet with a bound, staring about wildly. How had they managed to get so close without his hearing them? The Lady was pressed against him, and he could hear the harsh sound of her breathing. The Gargoyle was hunched down a few feet off, yellow eyes gleaming in the faint new light.

There were monsters all about them, ringing their camp and closing off any avenue of escape. There were at least a dozen huge, gnarly brutes, standing upright on two legs, but bent over in a half crouch as if they might be just as comfortable going down on all fours. They were vaguely manlike in appearance—two legs, two arms, a torso, hands and feet, and a head—but their bodies were knotted and muscled grotesquely and covered with some sort of rough hide. Their faces were almost featureless, but their eyes and snouts gleamed wetly as they peered at their three captives.

One of them spoke, his mouth splitting wide to reveal huge fangs. He gibbered at them, a mixture of snorts and grunts. He gestured vaguely, first at them, then at the river, and finally at the forest.

"They want to know where we come from," the Lady said.

The Knight stared at her in surprise. "Do you understand them?"

She nodded. "I do. I can't explain it. I've never seen them before. I don't speak their language. I am not even able to put words to all of the sounds. But the meaning is clear. I can decipher it. Here, let me see if I can make them understand me."

She made a few deft motions with her fingers and hands. The creature who had spoken grunted some more. Then he looked about at his fellows and shook his head.

"They want to know what we are doing here. They say we don't belong, that we are intruders." The Lady had stepped away again from the Knight, her composure recovered. "They don't like the look of us."

"What sort of things are they?" the Gargoyle growled, his own teeth showing.

There was another exchange. "They call themselves Gristlies," the Lady reported. Her face tightened. "They say that they are going to eat us."

"Eat us?" The Knight could not believe he had heard right.

"They say we are humans and humans are to be eaten. I can't make all of it out. It has something to do with custom."

"They had better keep away from me," the Gargoyle hissed. His muscles bunched into iron cords, and his claws came out. He was on the verge of doing something that would doom them all.

The Gristlies had engaged in a new discussion, all of them grunting loudly and gesturing. There was apparently some sort of disagreement. The Knight made a quick appraisal of the beasts. All of them were huge, and any two more than a match for him in a contest of strength. He felt the weight of his broadsword on his back. The sword would give them a better chance, but still there were too many to stand against. He had to find a way to even the odds.

The Gargoyle had been thinking the same thing. "We will have to make a run for it," he rasped.

"Stay where you are." The Lady's voice was cool and calm. "They are arguing over what is to be done with us. They are very primitive and superstitious. Something about us bothers several among them. Let me try to determine what it is."

The argument continued, sharper now. Fangs bared, claws unsheathed, two of the Gristlies began growling at each other. They were ferocious-looking creatures, and the Knight began to suspect that they were much quicker and stronger than he had first believed.

"We have to get out of this circle," he said quietly, and his hand stole back toward the handle of his sword.

In that instant, the two combative Gristlies attacked each other, tearing and ripping and shrieking horribly. Their fellows fell back before the onslaught, and the circle about the Knight and his companions collapsed. Instantly the Gargoyle bolted for the river. The Knight followed, pulling the Lady after him. To their surprise, the Gristlies did not give chase. The Knight looked back over his shoulder as he ran, but no one was there. From the shadow of the trees came the sounds of the battle between the two who had argued. Improbable as it seemed, the captives no longer appeared to matter.

They had reached the river's edge and were looking for a way to cross over when the Gristlies reappeared. It was immediately apparent why they had been in no hurry. They bounded from the trees like cats, covering ground so fast that they were upon the three in seconds. There were only seven now, but they looked formidable in the dim light, massive bodies uncoiling, claws and teeth gleaming like knives.

"Draw your sword!" the Lady cried in warning, and, when he was too slow to act, seized the weapon in her own hands and tried to draw it free.

"Don't!" he snapped, breaking her grip and thrusting her away.

She held her ground furiously. The Gristlies slowed and began circling. "Listen to me!" she snapped. "Your sword does more than you think! Remember the townsfolk? Remember the Gypsies? It was when you drew your sword and did battle that the Haze appeared!"

He stared at her in disbelief. "No! There is no connection!"

"There must be!" she hissed. "We have seen the Haze no other time. And when it comes, it never comes for us, only for those who threaten us! The two must be joined in some way! The Sword and the Haze, both weapons that eliminate our enemies! Think!"

She was breathing hard, and her pale face was bright with perspiration.

The Gargoyle had moved close to them, keeping his sharp eyes fixed on the circling Gristlies.

"She may be right," he said quietly. "Take heed of her."

The Knight shook his head stubbornly. "No!" he said again, thinking, *How could that be, how could it possibly . . . ?*

And suddenly he knew. The truth appeared like a beast come out of hiding, monstrous and terrible. He should have recognized it earlier; he should have seen it for what it was. He had suspected a link between the Haze and themselves, known there was a tie he could not fathom. He had thought all this time that the Haze hunted after them, a stalker awaiting its chance to strike. He had been wrong.

The Haze did not track after them; it traveled with them.

Because it belonged to *him.*

The Haze was his missing armor.

He went cold to the bone. His armor had not been there when he awoke in the Labyrinth, and yet he had sensed it close at hand. His armor had always been like that, hidden, awaiting its summons. It came on command and wrapped itself about him so that he could do battle against his enemies. That was how it worked.

But here, in the mists of the Labyrinth, its form had been altered. Magic had subverted it, had poisoned it, had made it over into a thing that was unrecognizable. His armor had become the Haze. It must be so. Why else would the Haze come to their rescue each time they were threatened and then retreat back into the mists? What other explanation was there?

He could not breathe, the cold so deep inside him that he was paralyzed. It was true, as he had feared, that he was responsible for the deaths of all those people, that he had destroyed the townsfolk and the River Gypsies, that he had killed them all in his warrior's guise without even realizing what he was doing.

He stood there, stunned by the impact of his recognition. "No," he whispered in despair.

He felt the Lady's hands on his shoulders, bracing him, trying to give him strength. The Gristlies were edging closer, emboldened by his indecision, by his inability to act.

"Do something!" the Lady cried.

The Gargoyle made a quick feint at the Gristlies, but the foremost only snarled in challenge and held its ground.

"I have no magic!" the Lady wailed in despair, shaking the Knight violently.

He shook her off then, come back to himself, recognizing their danger. The Lady was powerless. The Gargoyle was overmatched. They needed him if they were to survive. But if he drew his broadsword the Haze would come, destroying these creatures as it had destroyed the townsfolk and the River Gypsies—and he could not bear that.

But what other weapon did he possess?

In desperation, almost without thinking about what he was doing, he reached into his tunic and pulled out the medallion with its graven image of a knight riding out of a castle at sunrise. He yanked it free and held it forth before him, as if it were a talisman. What he hoped it would do, he did not know. He knew only that it was all he possessed from his former life, and that it had the same feel of strangeness and remoteness as his armor.

The effect of its appearance on the Gristlies was astonishing. They cringed away from it instantly, some dropping to their knees, some shielding their eyes, all shrinking from it as if it were anathema to them. Whining, weeping, shivering with fear and awe, they began to withdraw. The Knight lifted the medallion higher and took a step toward them. They broke and ran then, bolting for the trees as if pursued by demons, all the fight taken out of them, anxious only to put as much distance between themselves and the medallion as they could manage. They bounded away on all fours and were gone.

Why? the Knight wondered in amazement.

In the silence that followed, his breathing was audible. His hands lowered to his sides, and he lifted his face to the mists.

The Lady went to the Knight and stood so that her face was directly before his. He did not see her, he was staring straight ahead at nothing, his eyes dangerously fixed and empty.

"What did you do?" she asked quietly.

He did not answer.

"You saved us. Nothing else matters."

He made no response.

"Listen to me," she told him. "Forget about the people of that town, and forget the Gypsies. What happened to them was not your fault. You could not have known. You did what you had to do. If you had acted otherwise, we would be dead or imprisoned."

The Gargoyle hunched down at her elbow, his cloak pulled about him, his face hidden away. "He does not hear you."

The Lady nodded. Her voice hardened. "Would you abandon us now? Would you give up on yourself because of this? You have killed men all your life as a King's Champion. It is the essence of who you are. Can you deny this? Look at me."

His eyes did not move. There were tears in them.

She reached out and slapped him hard three times, each slap a sharp crack in the silence. "Look at me!" she hissed.

He did then, the life coming back into his eyes as they turned to meet hers. She waited until she was certain he saw her. "You did what you should have done. Accept that sometimes the consequences are harsh and unforeseen. Accept that you cannot always allow for every result. There is nothing wrong in this."

"Everything," he whispered.

"They threatened us!" she snapped. "They might have killed us! Is it wrong that we killed them first? Is your guilt such that you would give them their lives at the cost of ours? Have you lost all reason? Where is your great strength? I would not have you for my keeper if it is gone! I would not be taken by such a man! Give me my freedom if you are so compromised!"

He shook his head. "I acted out of instinct, but I should have used judgment. There is no excuse."

"You are pathetic!" she sneered. "Why do I waste my time with you? I owe you nothing! I am trapped in this world because of you, and I don't even know why that is so! You have stolen away my life; you have stripped me of my magic! Now you would deny us the protection of your own small measure as well! Don't use it, you would say, because it might cause harm! You would pity those who try to destroy us because we must destroy them first!"

His lips tightened. "I pity anything that must die at my hands."

"Then you are nothing! You are less than nothing! Look about you and tell me what you see! This is a world of mist and madness, Sir Knight! Could it be that you have failed to notice? It will destroy us quickly enough if we underestimate its dangers or show weakness in the face of its considerable strengths! Stand on your hind legs, or you are just another dog!"

"You know nothing of me!"

"I know enough! I know you have lost your nerve! I know you are no longer able to lead us!" Her face was as cold and hard as ice. "I am stronger now than you. I can make my own way! Stay on your knees, if you must! Stay here and wallow in your pity! I want nothing more to do with you!"

She started to rise, shoving past the Gargoyle. The Knight reached out, grasped her arm, and pulled her back down before him. "No!" he shouted. "You will not leave!"

The Lady swung at him with her fist, but he blocked the blow. She swung again, but he caught her wrist. She looked into his face and found it hard-edged and taut. The weakness was gone from his eyes.

"When you leave," he hissed at her, "you will leave with me!"

She stared at him without speaking. Then her free hand came up slowly and touched his cheek. She felt him flinch, and she smiled. She let her fingers trail down to his neck and drop away.

Then she leaned forward and kissed him on the mouth.

HANDFUL OF DUST

Abernathy stopped halfway down the stairs leading from his bedroom to the great hall of Rhyndweir and listened in dismay. At the foot of the stairs, Kallendbor was screaming at Horris Kew. At the gates of the fortress, the people of the Greensward were trying to break through. Across the countryside, there was chaos.

It was not a happy time.

From the start Abernathy had known that something would go wrong with Horris Kew and the great mind's eye crystal giveaway. He had known it as surely as he had known his own name. It was so predictable that it could have been written in stone. Horris Kew had been involved in a lot of schemes over the years, had come up with a whole bushel full of ideas for quick fixes and cure-alls, and not a one of them had ever worked. It was the same story every time. Things would start out in promising fashion and then somewhere along the way go haywire. No matter what the circumstances, the result was always the same. Somehow, some way, Horris Kew invariably lost control of the events he had set in motion.

In this instance, however, knowing it was so was not enough to save Abernathy. Knowing didn't do you any good if you didn't also believe. In truth, Abernathy needed to believe the exact opposite, because once he accepted that nothing had changed with Horris Kew and his schemes, even twenty years later, he had to acknowledge that the mind's eye crystals weren't what they seemed, and he couldn't possibly bring himself to do that. Abernathy was in the throes of serious denial. His own wondrous crystal had captivated him totally. Its visions had enslaved him. He was a prisoner of the prospect of being forever able to recapture glimpses of his former self and to live with the hope that what he was seeing might be a promise of what one day would be again. The visions were his private ecstasy, his own secret personal escape from the hard truths of life. Abernathy had always been a pragmatic sort, but he was helpless before this particular lure. The more he called the visions up, the more entranced he became by them. His addiction progressed from mild to severe. It wasn't just that he found pleasure in the visions; it was that they offered him the only escape that meant anything.

So he ignored his suspicions, his innate distrust, and his common sense, and he accompanied Horris Kew and his hateful bird down the path to chaos.

Hard evidence of where things were going surfaced quickly enough. The little company had progressed from Kallendbor and Rhyndweir to the other parts of the Greensward and to other people who had learned of the mind's eye crystals and were waiting to see if what they had heard was true. Crowds gathered at every crossroads and hamlet, and crystals were passed out by the handfuls. When Horris Kew failed to visit the remaining Lords—in deference to Kallendbor's false promise to deliver their crystals himself—the Lords quickly came to him. Where were their crystals? Was there to be none for them? Were they to be deprived of a treasure given so freely to common folk? Fearing personal harm and silently cursing Kallendbor for his duplicitous nature, the conjurer quickly gave them what they wanted. It became clear to Abernathy that Kallendbor hadn't taken those extra crystals to sell them. He had taken them to be certain that if his own was lost or stolen or broken, he would still have others. His greed was pointless, though. There were more than enough crystals to go around. The supply appeared inexhaustible. No matter how many were given out, the number remaining never seemed to diminish. Abernathy noted this phenomenon, but as with everything else connected with the great crystal giveaway, he blithely ignored it.

Then the rumors started. There were only a few at first, but the number quickly grew. People were starting to balk at doing their work. Farmers were letting their lands lie fallow and their stock go untended in the fields. Fences broke and barns collapsed, and repairs went unmade. Shopkeepers and merchants were opening and closing when they felt like it and showing little interest in selling their goods. Some were simply letting their wares be stolen, some were giving their merchandise away. Road and construction crews were failing to show up for their jobs. Building had come to a halt. The courts were down to half-day sessions and sometimes less than that. Justice was being dispensed in a cavalier and disinterested manner. Couriers with important dispatches were arriving days late. The dispatches themselves were being written in haphazard fashion by scribes. Home life was no better than the workplace. Husbands and wives were ignoring each other and their children. Housecleaning was being left for someone else, and unwashed dishes and cookware were piling up. No one had clean clothes. Dogs and cats were going hungry.

The cause of this mass neglect was no secret. Everyone was spending every free moment gazing into their newly acquired mind's eye crystals.

It was astonishing how quickly things began to fall apart once the obsession with the crystals set in. One failure led to another, one moment of disregard to the next, and pretty soon it was like toppling a line of dominoes. Work could wait, the reasoning went; after all, there was always tomorrow. Besides, work was boring. Work was hard. Gazing into the crystals was infinitely more interesting and enjoyable. It was amazing how quickly time passed when you peered into their depths. Why, entire days seemed to disappear in the blink of an eye!

So it went. And the loss of one day led to the loss of the next. Everyone quit doing everything, and soon no one was doing anything except sitting around staring into the crystals. Abernathy knew, somewhere in the back of his mind, where the truth of things still flickered with a candle's dim glow, that what was happening to the people of Landover was also happening to him. But he could not accept it. He could not give up his use of the crystal, not even for a single second. Not today—maybe tomorrow. Anyway, things weren't really so bad, were they?

They were, of course. And they quickly got worse. Abernathy was the first to discover how bad they would get. One morning, two weeks out of Rhyndweir, he awakened, reached into his pocket, pulled out his crystal, summoned up his favorite vision, and watched the gem turn to dust in the palm of his hand. He stared at it in disbelief, then in shock, and finally in despair. He waited for it to come back together again, but it stayed a pile of dust. He carried it to Horris Kew, desperate to have it restored. But Horris didn't have a clue about what was happening. Maybe it was a bad crystal, he suggested. He would give Abernathy another.

But when he opened the chests to get one, they found both empty. Not a crystal remained, although Abernathy was certain there had been crystals the day before or at least the day before that—no one was quite sure. Had they somehow given them all away without realizing it? Where had all the crystals gone?

They were far out on the eastern border of the Greensward by now, having visited most of that land and some parts of the Melchor, and they quickly turned for home. Maybe more crystals could be found on their return, Abernathy suggested hopefully, trying the very best he could not to sound too anxious, conscious of Horris and that stupid bird hanging on his every word. Maybe so, Horris agreed. Yes, quite possibly so. But he didn't sound like he believed it.

As Abernathy, Bunion, Horris, and the bird journeyed back, new rumors began to crop up. Crystals everywhere were turning to dust. People were furious. What was happening? What were they supposed to do without their visions? Lethargy gave way to violence. Neighbors turned on one another, looking to beg, borrow, or steal crystals to replace the ones they had lost. But no one had any to give. Everyone was in the same terrible position, deprived of what had been seen initially as a diversion but had evolved all too rapidly into a necessity of life. The people milled about and bumped up against each other for a few days in anger and despair, searching for crystals. Then they did what people always do when they get frustrated enough—they turned on the government. In this case, they turned on the Lords of the Greensward. Hadn't they authorized and facilitated the dispensing of the crystals in the first place? Surely they must be able to get more.

With single-minded resolve, the people marched on the castle fortresses of their Lords, determined to seek redress for their perceived wrongs.

Abernathy should have seen then where things were headed, but he was still so traumatized over the loss of his own crystal that he could not think of anything else. He trudged along despondently, trying to imagine what life would be like if there were no more crystals and the visions were really gone for good. It was a prospect too awful to contemplate. He was barely aware of the others and what they were doing. When Horris and his bird began whispering anxiously at each other and casting uneasy glances over their shoulders, he failed to pay attention. When the black-cloaked stranger joined them—absent one moment, there the next—he didn't see. Even when Bunion reappeared from one of his frequent scouting patrols and hissed in warning that there was something wrong with the stranger, Abernathy only just heard him. He was beyond such concerns, consumed by private grief, on the edge of slipping away completely.

They arrived at Rhyndweir and found matters in such turmoil that they almost bypassed the castle completely. But they were without supplies by now and anxious to discover if Kallendbor still had his own crystal supply intact. They had heard nothing to suggest otherwise, and indeed by the time they worked their way past the crowds jammed up against the gates and gained the interior of the fortress they discovered that, yes, things were apparently just fine. Kallendbor met them with self-absorbed indifference, provided a brief greeting, and then immediately disappeared again. His crystals were fine, it seemed. Why they remained unaffected when all the others were turning to dust was a mystery, but it was a mystery they thought it wise not to pursue. The plan was to spend the night, replenish supplies, and leave at first light for Sterling Silver. No lingering about, they decided. None of them wanted to be there if anything went wrong with Kallendbor's crystals.

Abernathy retired to his room and stayed there. He wasn't hungry, so he didn't go down for dinner. He wanted to spend as little time with Kallendbor as he had to. Bunion disappeared almost immediately after they arrived, and Abernathy neither knew nor cared where the kobold had gone. Bunion had escaped the trap of the crystals and their visions. Like most kobolds, he was disinterested in and mistrustful of magic and had refused the offer of one early on. Leaving Horris and Abernathy to manage the great crystal giveaway, Bunion had spent his time scouring the countryside in search of the missing

Ben Holiday. He had found nothing so far, but he refused to give up looking. Sooner or later, he was convinced, he would find some trace of the missing King.

So Abernathy was alone when night set in and the mob at the gates began to light huge watch fires before the castle, fueling them with the thatched roofs and wooden walls of the closest of the city's shops and market stalls. As the fires rose and the heat built, the mood of the people began to grow uglier and uglier. Soon they were throwing things against the gates and over the parapets. Shouts turned mean and threatening. Something had to be done, they cried, and it had to be done right now! Where were their crystals? They wanted their crystals back! The castle guards hunkered down and waited out the storm, their own mood a bit uncertain. Many among them had lost crystals as well and were sympathetic to the crowd's demands. Many had friends and relatives out there yelling up at them. There were some who were leaning toward opening the gates. The only thing that kept them from doing so was a threadbare sense of duty, an ingrained force of habit, and a healthy fear of Kallendbor. It was not clear how long such barriers would keep them in check.

Kallendbor seemed oblivious to the problem. There had been no sign of him since they arrived, and Abernathy had been just as grateful. But when the sound of the mob without began to undergo an ominous change, he found himself wondering what the Lord of the manor house was planning on doing about it. Boiling oil would be a likely choice, if temperament dictated Kallendbor's reaction. But maybe Kallendbor was ensconced in his private chambers, curled up alone with his wondrous crystal, gazing into its depths, absorbed in what he found there, in the kind of visions that Abernathy himself had once enjoyed . . .

Abernathy squeezed his eyes shut and gritted his teeth. It was too much, really. He was suddenly furious at the prospect of Kallendbor and his mind's eye crystals. It wasn't enough that he enjoyed the use of one; he was hoarding several dozen! Shouldn't he be willing to share one or two with his guests, especially emissaries from the King himself? Shouldn't custom and good manners dictate it? Shouldn't a complaint be lodged and a demand be made?

Abernathy went out of his room in a huff, driven by an itch in his soul, compelled by a need he could barely comprehend.

So it was that he was halfway down the stairs when he heard the sound of Kallendbor and Horris Kew arguing over the din of the crowds outside the castle walls.

"They're gone, charlatan!" Kallendbor was screaming in fury, his voice echoing up the stairwell from the great hall below. "Every last one of them, gone! Turned to dust! What do you know of this?"

"My Lord, I don't—"

"You listen to me, you idiot!" Kallendbor wasn't interested in explanations. "You are responsible for this! I hold you responsible! You had better find a way to restore them right now, right this instant, or I will inflict such pain on your body that you will beg me to put you out of your misery! You and your bird both!"

Abernathy caught his breath. So Kallendbor's crystals had turned to dust as well! He felt both satisfaction and disappointment. Steeling himself, he crept slowly down the stairs, one cautious step at a time.

"Well?" Kallendbor's patience had the life span of a moth caught in a candle's flame.

"My Lord, please, I shall do what I can . . ."

"You shall do what I tell you!" Kallendbor screamed, and there was the sound of shaking, of teeth rattling together, and of Biggar squawking and flying off in a rush.

Abernathy gained a bend in the stairs that allowed him to look down on what was happening below. Kallendbor was holding Horris Kew off the floor by his supplicant's robes and shaking him as hard as he could. The unfortunate conjurer was whipping back and forth in the big man's grasp like a rag doll, his feet kicking wildly, his head snapping on his skinny neck. Biggar circled overhead, crying out in dismay, swooping here and there, looking decidedly undecided about what to do.

"Give—me—back—my—crystals!" Kallendbor spit out the demand like a curse, giving Horris Kew a punctuating shake with each word uttered.

"Put him down," a voice said from the shadows.

Kallendbor turned, startled. "What? Who speaks?"

"Put him down," the voice repeated. "He isn't to blame for any of this."

Kallendbor threw Horris Kew to the floor, where the conjurer lay twitching and gasping for breath. The Lord of the Greensward wheeled toward the voice. His hand dropped to his broadsword, the weapon he always carried. "Who's there? Show yourself!"

A black-cloaked figure detached from the wall to one side, materializing out of nowhere. It glided into view rather than walked, all darkness and smooth motion. Abernathy shrank back instinctively. It was the stranger who had joined them on the road. How did he come to be here? Had he entered the fortress with them? Abernathy could not remember him doing so.

"Who are you?" Kallendbor asked sharply, but the edge had disappeared from his voice and been replaced by a hint of uncertainty.

"A friend," the stranger answered. He stopped moving a dozen feet away. Although Abernathy tried, he could not see the man's face. "You can shake Horris Kew until his bones come out of his skin, but that won't get your crystals back. Horris Kew doesn't have them to give."

Kallendbor stiffened. "How do you know this?"

"I know a good many things," the stranger said. His voice had an odd hissing quality to it, as if the vocal cords had once suffered some severe injury. "I know that Horris Kew and his companions are dupes in this matter, that they do only what they were instructed to do, and that they have no more crystals to give you. I know as well that they did not realize that the crystals they were giving you would turn to dust after only a short period of use. You have been cheated, my Lord. You have been tricked."

Kallendbor's hand tightened on his sword. "Who is responsible for this? If you know so much, tell me that!"

The stranger was motionless, enigmatic, impenetrable in the face of the other's rage. "Take your hand away from your weapon. You cannot hurt me."

There was a long moment of silence. Horris Kew inched carefully away from Kallendbor, crawling on his hands and knees. Biggar sat on the edge of the stair banister as if carved from stone. Abernathy held his breath.

Kallendbor's big hand dropped away. "Who are you?" he repeated once more, confused.

The stranger ignored the question. "Think a moment," he said softly. "Who sent you these crystals? Who sent the conjurer and his bird? Who sent the scribe and the runner? Who do they serve?"

Kallendbor went rigid. "Holiday!" he hissed.

Oh, oh, Abernathy thought.

The stranger laughed, a curiously grating sound. "Do you see now? How better to weaken your position, my Lord, than to make you seem a fool? You have been a thorn in the King's side from the beginning, and he would have you removed for good. When the crystals turn to dust, the people turn on you. You are their Lord and therefore must answer for their misery. The plan works well, don't you think?"

Kallendbor could not seem to manage an answer. He was choking on whatever he was trying to say.

"There are more crystals to be had," the stranger was saying, his voice gone smooth and persuasive. Abernathy was leaning forward to hear every word now. Who was this lying troublemaker? "There is an entire chamber full of them at Sterling Silver, hidden away for a time when they are needed. I have seen these crystals myself; there are thousands and thousands of them. Shouldn't they be yours?"

For just a moment Abernathy was persuaded. All he could see was a shimmering pile of the precious crystals, hoarded away like gold, selfishly kept from those who needed them. But in the next instant he saw the argument for the lie it was, knowing that Ben Holiday would never do anything like that, remembering in fact that the crystals had come from Horris Kew and not until after the King had disappeared.

He wondered suddenly and for the first time if the two events were connected somehow.

"There is a simple solution for your problem," the stranger was saying. He had walked over to Horris Kew and pulled him to his feet again, seemingly without effort. "Tell your people the truth of the matter. Tell them that the crystals are being kept secretly at Sterling Silver by the King. Tell them to march on his castle and demand that he give them up! Call together all the Lords of the Greensward. Have them gather their armies and their subjects and march them down to the King's doorstep. He cannot refuse all of you. He cannot withstand you even if he tries."

Kallendbor was nodding, persuaded. "I have had enough of Holiday—enough of his interference!"

"Perhaps," the stranger whispered thoughtfully, "it is time for a new King. Perhaps it is time for a man who would be more responsive to those like yourself, a man who would not behave so intractably toward his betters."

Abernathy almost barked. He was not proud of the reaction, but it was an honest one. He swallowed the sound in a muffled gasp.

"There are those who appreciate the proper uses of power." The stranger's voice was low and compelling. He made a brief, encompassing gesture toward Horris Kew. "There are those who understand the nature of loyalty, who comprehend the realities of its implementation. In other words, Lord Kallendbor, there are those who would serve any master who paid the right price."

Horris Kew was staring at the stranger, openmouthed. There was another long moment of silence.

Then Kallendbor nodded thoughtfully. "Perhaps so. Yes, why not? If he would agree to certain terms, of course. Yes. Why not make another King?" Then he shook his head abruptly. "But there is still Holiday to contend with. It is one thing to demand the release of the crystals and another altogether to remove him from the throne. He commands the services of the Paladin, and none can stand against him."

"Ah, but what if Holiday were to simply vanish?" the stranger asked in response. He paused meaningfully. "What if he already has?"

Abernathy felt his heart drop. So there it was—the truth at last. Ben Holiday's disappearance was indeed tied to Horris Kew and his mind's eye crystals, and all of it was tied to this mysterious stranger. Something terrible was going on, something that Abernathy still didn't fully comprehend, but the stranger was most definitely behind it.

What was he going to do?

He exhaled softly. He didn't know, but whatever it was he would have to get out of here to do it.

He began to back carefully up the stairs.

Not carefully enough, however. His boot scraped on the stone as he turned. It was a small noise, but one pair of ears was sharp enough to hear it.

"Awk! Someone's there!" Biggar rasped out in warning.

They all wheeled toward the stairs. "Find him!" the stranger hissed at once.

Abernathy bolted, deciding that it would not be a good idea for him to be

captured at this juncture. He remained upright on two legs for the first couple of steps, then gave it up and went down on all fours. Speed took prece-
dence over dignity, and after all a considerable part of him was dog. He raced
up the stairs and down the hall for his room, not knowing where else to go.
He could hear the flapping of wings behind him and the pounding of boots farther back. All chance of slipping away quietly in the dead of night was gone.
What was he going to do? If they found him they would throw him into the
darkest hole in the castle keep. If he was lucky, that was. Otherwise, they
would just eliminate him on the spot.

He reached his room and raced inside, slamming the door shut behind him
and throwing the bolt. The room was shadowed and dark, the candles not yet
lit. He stood gasping for breath with his back to the door and listened to the
beating of wings as Biggar flew past, shrieking, "Up here! He's hiding here!"

Stupid bird talks a lot better than he lets on, Abernathy thought darkly, and
found himself staring through the gloom at a pair of yellow eyes that stared
back.

"Arf!" he barked, unable to stop himself this time. He flattened back
against the door, frozen in place. He was trapped now on both sides. He
groped through his clothing for a weapon, but he didn't have one, so he bared
his teeth instead. The yellow eyes blinked curiously, and a familiar face came
into view.

"Bunion!" Abernathy gasped in relief, for it was indeed the kobold. "Am I
glad to see you!"

Bunion chittered something in response, but Abernathy wasn't listening.
"We have to get out of here, Bunion. Kallendbor and Horris Kew and that
stranger caught me listening in on them. They want Holiday off the throne!
They have done something to him already, I think. I will tell you all about it
later if you can just get us out!"

Bunion jumped down off the window ledge where he had been perched,
sped across the room to the door, threw it open, and made a diving grab for
Biggar, who was trying to fly inside. Biggar shrieked and swooped aside, but
Bunion came away with a handful of black feathers. The bird flew off, crying
out in pain and indignation. Bunion beckoned hurriedly to Abernathy, and the
scribe followed him out the door. Kallendbor and Horris Kew were just
rounding the head of the stairs. There was no sign of the stranger.

Bunion and Abernathy fled in the opposite direction, both of them down
on all fours. Like whipped curs, Abernathy thought as he ran.

They went down a back stairs and along a lower hall and into a small storage room. There was a hidden passageway behind a section of the wall, and in
seconds they were groping their way through the dark—or at least Abernathy
was, since he lacked Bunion's extraordinary eyes. It took them a long time,
but when the passageway ended they were outside the castle walls once more.

From there, they made their way back through the mostly sleeping town and out into the countryside. As they traveled, Abernathy remembered anew the loss of his crystal. It made him cry, and he hid his tears from Bunion. But the pain faded after a while, lessened considerably by the knowledge that the recapturing of his past had been the gift of a false prophet. Horris Kew had used him, and that hurt far more than the loss of his visions. As unpleasant as it was to admit, his self-indulgence had allowed a travesty to take place, and now perhaps Ben Holiday was paying the price for it. Certainly he must do what he could to salvage the situation, and that meant getting word to Questor Thews as quickly as possible. It would be hard to face the wizard after what had happened. It would be hard to tell him the truth. Questor had not taken one of the crystals, after all. He was too stubborn and proud to accept anything from Horris Kew, Abernathy guessed—and right in being so, as it turned out. Yes, facing him would be terribly hard. But it was necessary. Perhaps there was still a way to put things right.

They slept that night in an old barn some miles south and west of Rhyndweir. The straw they used for bedding was rife with fleas and smelled of manure, but Abernathy reasoned that it was minimal penance to pay for his gross stupidity and a small price for his freedom. As he lay squirming and shifting in the dark, listening to Bunion breathe easily next to him, Landover's Court Scribe promised himself that one day soon there would be a reckoning for all this, and that when that day came he would make certain that Horris Kew, his bird, and that black-cloaked stranger got what was coming to them.

DREAM DANCE

Night waned toward morning, a slow, dull ebbing of sound and motion, and the streets of Greenwich Village grew empty and still. A few cars and trucks crawled by, aimless and solitary, and people still meandered the walks, but that was all. The traffic lights blinked through their sequence of green, yellow, and red with steady precision, and their colors glared off the concrete where a light rain had left its gritty sheen. In the doorways and alleys there were homeless sleeping, ragged lumps of clothing, shadows hunched down against the gloom. The rank smell of garbage wafted on the air, mingling with the steam and mist that rose out of the sewer and subway grates and off the newly washed streets. Somewhere out in the harbor, a fog horn blew.

Willow walked in silence with Edgewood Dirk, feeling trapped and alone. She should not have felt that way. Her confidence should have been higher, her expectations greater. Two-thirds of her journey to gather the soils of three worlds for the birth of her child was complete. Only one leg remained. But it was the one she dreaded most. For as much as she disliked and abhorred Ben's world with its sprawling cities that ate away at the land and its almost compulsive disregard for the sanctity of life, it was the fairy mists that frightened her most.

It was a difficult fear to reconcile. It grew out of the history of her people and their deliberate distancing from the mists, their choice to accept the burdens and responsibilities of reality over fantasy, their decision to embrace mortality. It grew out of the stories of what happened to mortals who ventured into the fairy mists, of the madness that claimed them because they could not adjust to the dictates of a world where everything was imagined and nothing fixed. It grew as well out of the Earth Mother's warning to beware the motives of the fairy people in offering their help, for in all things they kept their real purposes hidden, secret from those like her.

She glanced at Edgewood Dirk and wondered what secrets the prism cat kept from her. How much of what he did was for reasons known only to him? Was there duplicity in his accompanying her to this world and the next? She could ask him, but she knew he would not answer. Neither the part of him that was fairy nor the part that was cat would let him tell. He was an enigma by nature, and he would not give up his identity as such.

So she walked and tried not to think too hard about what would happen next. They left the main streets and maneuvered their way down alleys clogged with garbage bins, debris, and rusting vehicles. They passed out of street light into misty gloom, the way forward marked faintly by faraway lamps, a dimly reflected glow on the building walls. Mist and steam mingled in the close corridor, shrouding the passageway, cloaking the night. Willow shivered with its touch and wished she could see the sun again.

Then they were at a gap in the buildings where the haze was so thick she could see nothing of what lay beyond. Dirk slowed and turned, and she knew instantly that all her choices were gone.

"Are you ready, my lady?" he asked deferentially, unusual for Dirk, and she was instantly afraid all over again.

"Yes," she replied, and could not tell afterward if she had spoken the word.

"Stay close to me," he advised, and started to turn.

"Dirk," she called quickly. He glanced back, hesitating. "Is this a trap?"

The prism cat blinked. "Not of my making," he said. "I cannot speak for what you might intend. Humans are known well for stumbling into traps of their own making. Perhaps this will happen to you."

She nodded, folding her arms about herself for warmth. "I am trusting you in this. I am afraid for myself and my child."

"Trust not the cat," Dirk philosophized, "without a glove."

"I trust you because I must, glove or no. If you deceive me, I am lost."

"You are lost only if you allow it to happen. You are lost only if you quit thinking." The cat regarded her steadily. "You are stronger than you think, Willow. Do you believe that?"

She shook her head. "I don't know."

A veil of mist blew between them, and for a moment the cat disappeared. When he was back again, his eyes were still fixed on her. "I told Holiday once that people should listen more closely to what cats would tell them, that they have many useful lessons to teach. I told him it was a failing common to most humans—that they did not listen as closely as they should. I tell you the same thing now."

"I have listened well," she said. "But I am not sure I have understood."

Dirk cocked his head. "Sometimes understanding has to wait a bit on events. So. Are you ready?"

She came forward a step. "Do not leave me, Dirk. Whatever happens, do not. Will you promise me that?"

Edgewood Dirk shook his head. "Cats do not make promises. Are you ready or not?"

Willow straightened. "I depend on you." The cat stayed silent. "Yes," she said then. "I am ready."

They moved into the narrow passageway and the mists that clogged it and were immediately swallowed up. Willow kept her eyes lowered to where Dirk walked before her, vaguely visible in the haze. The mists were dark at first, and then lightened perceptibly. The walls of the buildings fell away, and the smells of the city disappeared. In the blink of an eye, everything about them changed. They were in a forest now, a world of great old trees with canopied limbs that hid the skies, of thick brush and tall ferns, and of smells of an ancient, forgotten time. The air was thick with must and rot and with a misty gloom that shrouded everything, turning the forest to shadows and half light. There was a suggestion of movement, but nothing could be certain where everything was so dim.

Dirk walked steadily on, and Willow followed. She glanced back once, but there was nothing left of the city. She had come out of that world and into this. She was within the fairy mists, and it would all be new again.

She heard the voices first, vague whisperings and mutterings in the gloom. She strained to understand the words and could not. The voices rose and fell, but remained indistinct. Dirk walked on.

She saw their faces next, strange and curious features lifting from the shadows, sharp-featured and angular with hair of moss and corn-silk brows, eyes as penetrating as knife blades when they fixed on her, and bodies so thin and light-seeming as to be all but ethereal. The fairy folk darted and slowed, came and went, flashes of life in the shifting gloom. Dirk walked on.

They arrived at a clearing ringed by trees, fog, and deeper gloom, and Dirk walked to its center and stopped. Willow followed, turning as she did to find the fairy people all about, faces and bodies pressed up against the haze as if against glass.

The voices whispered to her, anxious, persuasive.

Welcome, Queen of Landover
Welcome, once-fairy, to the land of your ancestors
Be at peace and stay with us awhile
See what you might have here with the child you bear . . .

And she was walking suddenly in a field of bright red flowers, the like of which she had never seen. She carried a baby in her arms, the child wrapped carefully in a white blanket, protected from the bright light. The smells of the field were wondrous and rich, and the sunlight warm and reassuring. She felt impossibly light and happy and filled with hope, and below where she walked the entire world spread away before her, all of its cities and towns and hamlets, all of its people, the whole of its life. The child moved in her arms. She reached down to pull back the blanket so that she could peek at its face. The baby peeked back. It looked just like her. It was perfect.

"Oh!" she gasped, and she began to cry with joy.

She was back in the clearing then, back within the fairy mists, staring out into the gloom.

The voices whispered once more.

It will be so, if you wish it

Make your happiness what you would, Queen of Landover. You have the right. You have the means

Keep safe within the mists, safe with your child, safe with us, and it shall be as you were shown

She shook her head, confused. "Safe?"

Stay with us, once-fairy

Be again as your kind once were

Stay, if you would have your vision come true . . .

She understood then, saw the price that she was being asked to pay for the assurance that her child would be as the vision had shown. But it was not really so, for they would both end up living in an imaginary world and the vision would be nothing more than what they created in their minds. And she would lose Ben. There had been no mention of Ben, of course, because he was not to be included in this promised land, an outsider, an other-worlder who could never belong to the fairy life.

She looked down at Dirk, but the prism cat was paying no attention to her. It sat turned slightly away, washing its face carefully, lick, lick, scrub, scrub. The indifference it showed was studied and deliberate.

She looked back at the sea of faces in the mist. "I cannot stay here. My place is in Landover. You must know that. The choice was made for me a long time ago. I cannot come back here. I do not wish to."

A grave error, Queen of Landover

Your choice affects the child as well. What of the child?

The voices had changed in tone, turning edgy. She swallowed back her fear of what that might mean. "When my child is old enough to decide, it shall make its own decision."

There was a general murmuring, and it did not sound supportive. It whispered of dissatisfaction and thinly veiled anger. It whispered of bad intent.

She held herself stiffly. "Will you give me the soil my child needs?" she asked.

The whispers died into stillness. Then a voice answered.

Of course. You were promised this soil in coming. It is yours to take. But to take it, it must first be made your own

Fairy earth cannot pass out of the mists until it has been celebrated and embraced by its taker

Willow glanced again at Dirk. No response. The cat was still washing as if nothing else in all the world could be quite so important.

"What must I do?" she asked of the faces.

What is in your blood, sylph child. Dance as your wood nymph mother has taught you to dance. Dance across the earth on which you stand. When you have done so, it will be your own, and you may take it with you and depart these mists

Willow stood transfixed. Dance? There was something hidden here. She could feel it; she was certain of it. But she could not fathom what it was.

Dance, Queen of Landover, if you would have the soil for your child

Dance, if you would complete your journey and give birth

Dance, Willow of the once-fairy

Dance . . .

So she did. She began slowly, a few cautious steps to see what would happen, a few small movements to test if all was well. Her clothes felt heavy and cumbersome, but she was not persuaded to take them off as she might have done otherwise, anxious to stay ready to flee if something should go wrong. Nothing did. She danced a bit further, increased the number of her steps, the complexity of her movements. Her fear and caution eased a bit in the face of her joy at doing something she loved so much. The faces of the fairies seemed to recede into the mist, sharp eyes and thin noses, stringy hair and sticklike limbs, bits of light and movement gone back into the gloom. One minute they were there, and the next they were gone. She was alone.

Except for Dirk, who had moved away from her and was watching carefully. He sat as if carved from stone.

She danced faster, caught up suddenly in the flow of the steps, in the rhythm of the movements, in the joy that swelled and surged inside. It seemed to her as if she could dance more quickly, more lightly, more precisely here in the fairy mists than in the real world. All of her efforts were rewarded with success beyond anything she had ever known. Her joy increased as she performed ever more complicated movements, spinning and twirling, leaping and twisting, as light as air, as swift as the wind. She danced, and she could tell that she was suddenly far better than her mother had ever been, that she had mastered in seconds that which her mother had worked for all her life.

She shed her clothes now, her inhibitions forgotten, her promise of caution and restraint abandoned. In seconds, she was naked.

Across the clearing she flew, alone in her flight through mist and half light, oblivious to all else. Yes, the dance was everything she had ever wanted it to be! Yes, it would give her things she had never thought possible! She rose and fell, rose again, and sped on. Colors appeared before her eyes, rainbow-bright and as fresh as flowers in a vast, limitless garden, all carefully arranged and fragrant beyond belief. She was flying over them, soaring in the manner of a bird, as free as air. There were other birds with her, all brightly colored and singing wonderfully, sweeping about her, showing her the way. She lifted from the garden into the sky, rising toward the sun, toward the heavens. Her dance carried her, bore her on, gave her wings.

She was dreaming anything she wished, any possibility, any hope. It was all there, and it all belonged to her. She danced, and all else was forgotten. She no longer remembered where she was or why she had come. She no longer remembered Ben or her child. The dance was everything. The dance was all.

From the mists surrounding the clearing, the fairies watched and smiled among themselves, unseen.

Willow might have been lost then, caught up forever in her dance, had Dirk not sneezed. There seemed to be no reason for it; it just happened. It was a small sound, but it was enough to draw her back from the precipice. For just a second she caught a glimpse of the prism cat somewhere at the corner of her vision and remembered. She saw him looking at her, his steady, impenetrable gaze an open accusation. What was it he had told her? She had asked him of traps, and he had warned her that humans mostly stumbled into those of their own making. Yes, like this one. This dance.

But she could not stop. She was too deep in the throes of its pleasure, of its wonder, to cease moving. The dreams it induced were too compelling to give up. She had done what he had warned her against and trapped herself, and now she could not get free. It was the fairies' plan for her, she saw—that she should dance and keep dancing and never leave. Here is where her child would be born, here in the fairy mists, and when it was born it would belong to them. They would both belong to the fairies for all time.

Why? Why did they wish it so? She had no answer.

Her thoughts scattered, and for a moment she was in danger of slipping back into her dreams. But she kept her eyes on Dirk as she spun across the clearing, watching him watching her, desperately trying to think what to do. Dance forever. She would never stop. But she must. She must! She would not let this happen to her, she told herself. She would find a way to break free.

Ben. If Ben were there, he would help her. Ben, who she could always rely upon to stand with her, who had pledged himself to her forever. Ben, the strength that sustained her when all else failed. He would always come. Always.

But how could he come this time?

Ben!

Had she called out loud to him? She couldn't be sure. She felt Dirk beginning to slip away. She could barely see him through the haze of her dance, through the magic that ensnared her.

Ben!

And for just an instant, he was there—a glimpse of his face, of his eyes come out of time and distance. He was there, still a long way off, but within reach.

Suddenly she saw a chance for escape. She would use the fairy magic to her own advantage, turn it to her own use. It had been set to trap her and she had allowed it to do so, but there was still a way out. The dance was a dream, and the dream could be altered if she was strong enough. She was not completely lost, not yet. Not if she didn't wish it. Not if she didn't forget.

She closed her eyes and in the sweep of her dance called out to Ben Holiday. She could imagine him as she could imagine everything else. That was the magic of the fairy world. Banish her fear, and she would be able to control her vision, to make it her own, to affect its direction. That was the lesson Ben had once learned. It was the one Dirk had cautioned her to. Use the magic to free yourself. Use the dance to escape.

Ben! She called to him, her voice strong and steady.

And then something wondrous and completely unexpected happened.

The Knight lay sleeping in the Labyrinth, stretched full-length upon the ground within the cover of a grove of hardwood that canopied overhead like a tent. The Lady lay pressed against him, curled to his body, her head resting on his shoulder, her arm draped across his chest. She was smiling, the hardness that so often marked her features absent this night. Mist and gloom hung all about, shrouding the world and those who stalked it, but for the moment at least the Knight and the Lady had left it behind.

The Gargoyle sat hunched down within his cloak a few feet away and watched them uneasily. It did not feel right to him. He could not explain it, but there was a lie in what was happening. That was unmistakable. These two were enemies and this new alliance lacked wisdom and reason. Their impetuousness would catch up to them, he believed. Perhaps it would destroy them.

His misshapen features wrinkled in distaste, and he looked purposefully away.

As he slept, the Knight began to dream. At first the dream lacked focus, a blurring of sound and movement as he was carried across time and space toward some unknown destination. He was at peace, and so he did not resist the pulling that bore him on. Then he began to hear voices—no, a single voice—calling out a name. He could hear it repeating, over and over. He recognized the voice, but could not place it. The name seemed familiar, too.

Ben.

He listened to the sounds as he traveled, knowing he was closing on them, that he was being drawn, that he was called deliberately.

Ben.

Then he was jolted as if by a massive hand and found himself earthbound once more and upright. The voice was distinct now and quite close. It was a woman, and she called with need. She was someone he knew, someone to whom he was bound, and she called for his protection.

The Knight went to her at once, drawing forth the great broadsword as he pushed through the trees of a forest that loomed about him. It was the Labyrinth and yet it was not. He could not explain it, but while the two were separate they were also somehow joined. All of the elements were the same. He brought the broadsword before him, prepared to do battle. He lacked his heavy armor still, cloaked only in chain mail, in his leather clothing, in his belt and boots and gloves. He gave it less than a passing thought. He felt no fear of what waited for him. The certainty he felt for his cause overwhelmed any doubts. He was meant to give aid to those to whom he was pledged, and the woman who called was foremost of these.

He reached a clearing, the light where it widened to the skies a vague brightness in the smoky haze. Figures scattered at his coming, small creatures that were thin and angular, all sharp edges and bits of moss and stick. They fell back from him as if he bore a plague, hissing and muttering like cornered rats. He went through them without slowing to the clearing's center and stopped.

The woman who danced through the shadows and half light spun into his arms and held him as if he were a line to safety from a raging sea. Naked, she shivered as if chilled to the bone, and her face and body pressed up against him.

"Ben," she whispered. "You came."

The Knight held her close in an effort to still her shaking, and as he did so recognition flooded through him.

"Willow!" he whispered back fiercely.

He knew then. The deception that had shackled him fell away at her touch, at the sound of her voice, at the sight of her face. Though he dreamed, in some way the dream was real. He had been called to her in sleep, but they were joined as surely as if awake and together in the flesh. She clung to him, whispering his name, telling him things he could not understand. They were within the fairy mists. She was imprisoned by the fairies in a dance and could not break free. Their child was to be kept from them, kept here forever. But all was reality if you could imagine it, and so she had imagined him coming to save her in a desperate effort to break free. And come he had, but not as she had believed he would. He was really there. How had this happened? How had he breached the fairy mists?

All about the fairies swarmed like maddened bees, hissing and darting through the gloom, enraged. He saw Edgewood Dirk sitting close by, watching in his cat way. Edgewood Dirk? What was he doing here?

Ah, but more important, what had been done to the Knight of the Labyrinth, who knew himself now to be Ben Holiday? Memories flooded through him, the spell of forgetfulness broken. He had been snatched away from the Heart by magic and imprisoned in a rune-carved box. It was the last thing he remembered had happened before his waking in the Labyrinth. Except that Horris Kew had been standing there, had set the box down, had stepped away just before Ben fell into it, tumbling down with . . .

His heart stopped.

With Nightshade and Strabo.

With the Lady and the Gargoyle.

The truth stunned him so that for a moment he could not breathe or move. He held onto Willow as if their positions had been reversed and now she was the lifeline that kept him from being swept away. She sensed his shock and looked up at him quickly, and her hands came up to hold his face.

"Ben," she whispered anew. "Please. It's all right."

With a massive effort he shrugged off his immobility. There was a tearing at the corners of his vision. The dream that bound them was fragmenting, coming to a close, the magic expending itself. Willow could feel it as well. With the ending of the dance, the dream could not sustain itself. She moved to dress, ignoring the small sounds of fury that emanated from the mists, come back to herself once more and determined that she would not be tricked again. Clothed, she bent to the earth across which she had danced and scooped a handful of the soil into the pouch she carried.

Ben watched her without understanding. He started toward her, then found he could not move. He looked down at himself and saw to his horror that he was fading away.

"Willow!" he cried out in warning.

She rose at once and hurried toward him. But he was already losing shape and definition, returning to his dream, to his sleep, to the prison that still held him. He heard her call out to him, saw her reach for him, watched her try to hold him back. But she could not. The magic that had joined them from the fairy mists of two worlds was breaking up.

"Willow!" he cried out again, desperate now, unable to slow his going. "I'll find you somehow! I promise! I'll come for you!"

"Ben!" he heard her call to him one final time, and then he was lifting away, transparent in the mists, a bit of air and wind borne back across the gap that separated them in waking, back into the sleep from which he had come.

⸺⊷∞⊶⸺

Alone once more in the silent clearing, Willow stared skyward at the roiling gloom. Ben was gone. The magic of her vision had been strong enough to bring him, but not to hold him. He had set her free of the dance, but could not stay to help her further. She felt a renewed desperation settle through her and fought back against her tears. But there was no time for grief, for anything but her child, and she used her anger as armor and wheeled on Edgewood Dirk.

"I want to go home," she said quietly, deliberately. "Right now."

The prism cat blinked. "Then go, Queen of Landover."

"You will not stop me?"

"Not I."

"Nor the fairies that ring this clearing?"

Dirk yawned. "They have lost interest in playing this particular game. Interesting, don't you think, how they failed to challenge Holiday?"

She considered. It was interesting. Why had they let him go? And her. What was it that stopped them from interfering?

"What path do I take, Dirk?" she asked him.

Edgewood Dirk rose and stretched. "Any path will do. All lead to where you are meant to go. Your instincts will guide you. As I said earlier, you are stronger than you think."

She did not respond to him, too angry with what had been done to her to accept compliments. He had helped her in his own peculiar way, whether by accident or on purpose she still wasn't certain, but the prism cat was no friend in either case. The fairy mists and the creatures who lived within them, Dirk included, were anathema. She wanted gone from them all.

"You are not coming with me?" she questioned.

"No," he answered. "You have no further need of me. Your quest is finished."

So it was. She had the soils she had been sent to gather, the soils of the three worlds to which her child's blood could be traced. If the Earth Mother spoke the truth, the birth of her child could take place now. There was nothing more for her to do, nothing else required. She could go home.

Folding her cloak about her, clutching her pouch of soils close against her body, she turned and began to walk. She did as she was told and followed her instincts. Surprisingly, they seemed quite clear. They took her in a straight line through the trees.

They took her deep into the mists until she disappeared.

WAKENING

Ben Holiday awoke with a start. His eyes snapped open, and he stared straight ahead through the predawn gloom into the trees of the Labyrinth. He did not move; he could not make himself. He was frozen in place as surely as if he had been encased in ice. Questions raced through his mind, one after the other, whispers and dark teasing. Had he dreamed of his meeting with Willow or had it actually taken place? Was it truth or a wild concoction of his imagination? How much of anything that had happened to him that he could remember was real?

The Lady lay pressed up against him, still sleeping. The Gargoyle sat hunched down at the edge of the trees several yards away, head bowed. Ben blinked. Nightshade? Strabo?

He closed his eyes and kept them shut for a moment, thinking. Something had happened to reveal the truth—that much was certain. He was not the Knight; he was Ben Holiday. The Knight was some personification of his real identity. It was so with the Lady and the Gargoyle as well. They had been changed by the Labyrinth and its magic, or by the magic that had sent them here, or by some foul deception they did not yet understand. They had been given identities that mirrored some part of who they were but concealed the rest. They appeared significantly different than they were. Strabo had been changed most; he was not even a dragon anymore. Nightshade was recognizable, yet she was different, too, in a way he could not quite explain. Neither had the use of their magic. Neither possessed the strength and power that was theirs in Landover.

He opened his eyes again. Mist hung amid the trunks and limbs of the trees. It carpeted the grasses on which he lay. The Labyrinth was a vast, endless mirage their vision could not see through.

What had been done to them?

Horris Kew. The conjurer had something to do with this, though in truth it was hard to believe he possessed power enough to imprison them in this otherworld. But he had been there watching. He had provided the box into which they had been lured, in which they were now trapped. Ben repeated the words. Trapped in a box. How, he wondered abruptly, had that been done? Horris Kew. He breathed slowly, carefully, trying to think. Did knowing Horris Kew was involved help in any way? Where were they? Oh, yes, the Labyrinth, but where was that?

His mind sideslipped. Willow. He had gone to her. He had not dreamed it—or if he had, there had been a large piece of reality in the dream. All was possible if you went into the fairy mists, where reality was fluid and anything could be brought to pass. Magic had brought him to her, magic born of her dance and of her imaginings. She had called him to her because she could not break free. Was she free now? Had he helped her escape before the dream had ended? What was she doing in the fairy mists in the first place?

There were no answers for his questions, only more questions. He could not allow too many. Too many would strangle him. Only one thing mattered now—that he break free of the Labyrinth and find her. There must be a way. Magic had been used to conceal the truth about who he was, and there was a reason for that. Somewhere in that concealing there was something that would help him, that would help them all.

He looked back at them again, at their silent, sleeping forms.

Once they knew, of course. Once they were told.

He eased himself away from Nightshade, thinking of what had passed between them as the Knight and the Lady, recognizing the damage they had inadvertently done to themselves. He remembered how she had kissed him. He remembered her touch. His eyes closed in dismay. How could he tell her that it was all a lie? How could he tell her that she was not his charge as he had believed, that the magic of their prison had misled them, had tricked them into thinking that their relationship was something other than what it really was and caused them to . . .

He could not finish the thought. Only one thing mattered. There was now and had always been only Willow.

He climbed to his feet, not yet ready to do so. He walked away from her, moving toward the trees, trying to assemble the fragments of what he knew into some recognizable whole. He thought of how he had been made to appear, a Knight with no past and no future, a nameless warrior, a champion for a master with no name and of a cause without identity. His worst nightmare. His worst . . .

Fear.

He saw it then, the truth that had been hidden from them all this time. They were in the fairy mists, too!

The Gargoyle was next to him suddenly, a dark shadow moving out of the haze. Gnarled hands balanced his disjointed body as he leaned forward. "What is it?" he asked, seeing Ben's face.

Ben looked at him, trying to see past the ugliness, past the mask the magic had created. He could not. "I know what has been done to us," he said. "I know where we came from. I know who we are."

The Gargoyle's face twisted and froze, his eyes glittering like candles. "Tell me."

Ben shook his head. He motioned to the Lady. "We must wake her, too."

They walked to her, and Ben reached down and touched her arm. She awoke at once, flawless, cold features softened by sleep, a smile upon her face. "I dreamed of you," she began.

He placed a warning finger to her lips. "No, say nothing. Don't speak. Sit up and listen to me. I have something to tell you." He moved back from her, letting her rise. "Listen carefully. I know who we are."

She stared at him for a moment, then shook her head quickly. "I don't want to know." There was fear in her voice, recognition that something was about to be stolen away. "What difference does it make to us here?"

He kept his voice calm, even. "By knowing who we are and where we come from, we give ourselves a chance to escape. Our only chance, I think."

"How is it that you know and we do not?" she snapped at him, angry now, defensive.

"I was given a dream," he told her. "In the dream I discovered what had happened to us. We have been trapped in this place by magic. We were sent here from another world, our world. Magic was used to make us forget who we are, to make us seem different. We were sent here to wander about forever, I think—to spend what was left of our lives futilely attempting to find a way out. But there is no way out of here except by using magic. You were right—magic alone can save us. But first we have to understand how that magic works. To do that, we have to understand ourselves, who we are, where we came from, what it is we do."

"No," she said quietly and shook her head back and forth. "Don't say anything else."

"I am not the Knight," he said, pressing quickly ahead, anxious to get this over with. "I am Ben Holiday, King of Landover."

Her hands flew to her mouth, shaking. She made a noise deep in her throat.

Unable to bear her look, Ben turned to the Gargoyle. The monster was staring at him, expressionless. "You are called Strabo. You are a dragon, not a Gargoyle."

He turned back to the Lady, determined. "And you are . . ."

"Nightshade!" she hissed in fury. She shrank from him, and her smooth face contorted with despair and recognition. "Holiday, what have you done to us? What have you done to *me?*"

Ben shook his head. "We have done it to ourselves, each of us in turn. This place has made it possible. Magic stole our memories when we were sent here from the Heart. Do you remember? There was a man with a box. There were notes purportedly sent by each of us to the other, bait for the trap that was used to ensnare us. Some sort of spell wrapped us about and sent us here, into the box . . ."

"Yes, I remember now!" Strabo growled, who in spite of having his identity uncovered still did not look like the dragon. "I remember the man and his box and the magic netting us like fish! Such power! But why was it done? Look at me! How could I have been changed so?"

Ben knelt before him. The clearing was hushed and closed about. It was as if their world had stopped moving.

"We are in the fairy mists," he said quietly. "Think about how we appear. We have become the things we most fear we might really be. You are a monster, loathed and despised, an outcast that no one wishes to look upon, hunted by all, blamed for everything that cannot otherwise be explained. And you cannot fly, can you? Your wings have been stripped away. Haven't you always feared being earthbound? Flying has always provided you with a form of escape, no matter how terrible things were. Here, you have been cheated even of that."

He paused. "And look at me. I am what I feared most to become. I am the King's Champion, his handpicked destroyer, his butcher of enemies, nameless and empty of everything but my fighting skills and my desire to use them. Even my armor has become a weapon, a monstrous apparition called the Haze that eliminates any enemy who threatens. I fear killing more than anything, and so for me it comes to pass."

He stopped himself, unwilling to say more. They did not know he was the Paladin, only that the Paladin served the King. He would not have them know more.

"Nightshade," he said softly, turning back to her again. She crouched down like a cornered beast. "What is it you fear most? What frightens you? Loss of your magic, certainly. You have said as much. But something more . . ."

"Silence!" she screamed.

"Being human," Strabo snapped. "She loses power when she acknowledges her humanness. Her emotions make her weak; they steal away her strength. She must not let herself feel. She must not be tender or soft or give love . . ."

Nightshade flew at him, nails raking at his face, but Ben pushed her aside, bore her to the ground, and pinned her there while she spit and screamed like a madwoman. Nightshade had been changed in more ways than one, he thought as he held her. He would never have been able to do this in Landover, for Nightshade had ten times his strength. She was indeed without her power.

She went quiet finally and turned her head aside from him, tears coursing down her pale face. "I will hate you forever," she whispered, the words barely audible. "For what you have done to me, for what you have made me feel—all of it a lie, a monstrous deceit! That I could care for you, could love you, could have you as a woman would a man—how could I have been so stupid? I will hate you forever, Holiday. I will never forget."

He stood up and left her lying there, still turned away. There was nothing he could say to her that would help. That she had been made to feel something for him was unpardonable; that she had been deceived into thinking him her lover unforgivable. It did not matter what she had felt before. The chasm that had opened between them would never be bridged now.

"The Labyrinth is a part of the fairy mists." He straightened his cloak, knocked askew in his struggle. "It was Willow who called to me in my dream. She called from another part of the mists. When I went to her, I could sense that where she was and where I was were joined. I was reminded how the mists work on those who are human or have left that world. They use fear against us, to change who we are, to make us over, to confront us with that which will drive us mad. Where there is no reality but that which we create, imagination plays havoc with our emotions. Particularly fear. We are lost when that happens. We cannot control it as the fairy people do. They told me so once. They warned me against it."

He took a deep breath. "What we have done in our travels, where we have gone, who we have encountered, is not real. Or not real beyond the Labyrinth. Do you see? We made it up, all of it! Together or separately, I don't know which. The townsfolk, the River Gypsies, the Gristlies—they were all representations of creatures from Landover. The people of the Greensward, the once-fairy, Rock Trolls, G'home Gnomes, or whatever. They don't exist outside our minds or these mists or this prison in which we are confined."

Strabo shook his head. "The fairy mists would not affect me or the witch as they would you. We are fairy creatures ourselves. Yet look at me. I am more changed than you! And no less riddled with the fear you describe. And I did not sense it! I should have been able to do so, having access to the mists in my passage from world to world. Nightshade might be banned from the mists, but I am not. No, Holiday. There is more to this."

"There is the box!" Ben snapped. "The box is something more than a container for the mists. It is a trap strong enough to hold such as we. Another magic works within it."

"It is possible," the other agreed thoughtfully. "But if so, then what magic can free us?"

"I've been thinking about that," Ben said. "When I remembered who I was, I remembered something else, too. I think that our identities were stripped from us to wipe out any chance that we might remember anything that would help us escape. This trap was set up to work two ways. First, to make us forget who we are. Second, to steal away any magic we commanded, to render us impotent. Well, we've overcome the first, so that leaves the second. No magic. And we can't escape this trap without magic."

He glanced from one to the other. Nightshade was back on her feet, ramrod straight, her expression flat and set. "But I think that Horris Kew or whoever it was who put us here might have made a mistake. The magic intended to be stolen from us was innate. That's why we were changed in different ways. You were changed most of all, Strabo. Your magic is inherent in what you are—a dragon—so you were changed to something else entirely. Otherwise, you could use your fire to escape this trap, because your fire is your greatest power and among other things it lets you cross between worlds."

He turned to Nightshade. "And you were stripped of your magic for the same reason, although it was not necessary to change your appearance because how you looked made no difference to whether your magic worked. But the result was the same. Like Strabo, you were trapped without a means of escape because the magic you relied on most, the magic inside yourself, was gone."

He paused. "But it is different with me. I have no innate magic. I came to Landover without any and still possess none. So I was not affected. My memory was stolen, and that was enough. As long as I didn't remember who I was, what danger did I pose?"

"Get to the point," Nightshade snapped coldly.

"This is the point," Ben replied. He reached into his tunic and pulled forth the medallion with the graven image of the Paladin riding out of Sterling Silver at sunrise. "The medallion of the Kings of Landover, given to me when I was brought over from my own world. It invests me with the right to rule, it gives me command over the Paladin, and it does one thing more. It lets me pass through the fairy mists."

There was a protracted silence. "Then you think . . ." Strabo began and stopped.

"It is possible that the magic of the talisman was not leached away in the same manner as your own, that our prison is designed to render the magic of living creatures useless, but not the magic of inanimate things." Ben paused. "Beyond Landover, the medallion lends no authority to rule and will not summon the Paladin. But it will allow passage through the fairy mists. Perhaps it can do so here. It has retained its link to the armor of the Paladin, even though that armor comes in the form of the Haze. It was recognized by the Gristlies and warded us from them. Perhaps it can set us free as well."

"If we are indeed imprisoned in some part of the mists," Strabo pointed out dourly.

"If," Ben agreed.

"This is a very slim chance you offer us," the other mused.

"But the only one we have."

Strabo nodded, his ugly face almost serene. "The only one."

Nightshade came forward then, all black anger and hard edges, and stopped before Ben. "Will this really work?" she demanded, her voice dangerously quiet.

He met her gaze and held it. "I think so. We will have to take the medallion into the mists and test it. If it does what it should, we will emerge from the mists where we entered them."

"Restored to ourselves?" Her eyes glittered.

"I don't know. Once we are beyond the prison and its magic, we should be."

She nodded. Her face was white marble, her eyes gone almost red. There was such fury mirrored there that he shrank inwardly from it.

"You had better hope so, play-King," she said softly. "Because if we do not escape this madness and I am not made whole again, every part of me, every piece of who and what I am, I will spend the rest of my days waiting for a chance to destroy you."

She drew her long cloak close about her, a dark ghost in the misty dawn. "You have my word on that. Now get us out of here."

Time seemed stopped.

Willow walked slowly, steadily through the mists, placing her feet carefully with each step. She could not tell where she was going. She could barely see the ground she trod. If this was a trap, she was finished. The haze was so dense that she would be on top of whatever snare might be waiting long before she could identify it. She was proceeding on trust, and where the fairies were concerned this was not particularly reassuring.

But after a while, the air began to clear. It thinned gradually, like dawn coming out of night, a slow giving way of greater shadows to lesser. The light strengthened from black to gray, but still there was no sun. Gradually the mist receded until it was entwined within a wall of trees and scrub. Willow looked about. She was in a jungle of tangled trees and vines, damp and fetid earth, and silence. There was no sound about her, no movement, as if all life had been destroyed.

She moved forward a few tentative steps and stopped. She looked about again. A sinking feeling unsettled her stomach. She knew where she was. She was in the Deep Fell, the home of Nightshade.

For an instant she thought she must be mistaken. How could she possibly have come here, of all places? She moved forward again, searching the jungle about her, trying to peer through the thick canopy of the trees, to see beyond the shadows, to convince herself she was wrong. She could not. Her instincts and memory were quite clear on the matter. She was in the Deep Fell.

She took a slow breath to steady herself. This might be another fairy trick, she thought. It might be their revenge on her, letting her wander into Night-shade's lair. Trust your instincts, Edgewood Dirk had advised. Trust not the cat. She exhaled. Whatever the case, she must escape quickly or she would be discovered.

She moved swiftly through the thick, green tangle of the Fell, anxious now to gain the rim of the Hollows while it was still light. Though morning was not yet here, it was quite conceivable that she could wander the Fell until night-fall without getting free. Many had. Many had never come out. She kept silent in her passage, using her skills as once-fairy, taking heart in the fact that at least she was back in Landover. She wondered how her instincts could have misled her so. She had to have been deceived by fairy magic. How cruel and spiteful of them, she thought angrily.

Then sudden pain shot through her stomach and limbs, and she doubled over. She dropped to one knee, gasping. The pain lasted only a moment and was gone. She came back to her feet and hurried on. Within minutes, it re-turned. It was stronger this time and lasted twice as long. She knelt in the tall grass and clutched at herself. What was happening to her?

A jolt of recognition snapped her head up.

It was the baby! It was time!

She closed her eyes in frustration and disbelief. But not here! Please, not here!

She struggled to her feet and continued on, but in seconds the pain re-turned, dropping her back to her knees, so strong she could barely breathe. Her teeth clenched, she tried to rise one final time and then gave it up. The baby would decide, the Earth Mother had said. Apparently the baby was doing so now. Willow knelt on the floor of the Deep Fell and cried. Her child should not be born in this foul place! It should not be born in shadows and darkness, born out of the sunlight! Did the fairies have anything to do with this? Had they planned it this way, their spite so great at losing the child that they now wished it harmed?

Tears continued to leak from Willow's clenched eyes as she groped at her waist for the pouch containing the precious soils. She found it and pulled it free. She loosened the drawstrings. The pain was coming in sudden spurts that wracked her body. No preparation for this birth, no time to adjust. It was hap-pening quickly, coming so fast that there was no time left for thinking.

She crawled a few feet farther to a patch of bare ground and clawed at the soil with her fingers to loosen it. It was not difficult to do; the Deep Fell's earth was damp and soft. When she had cultivated a small patch, she opened the pouch and spread the soils she had gathered in a wide swath about her, reaching down to mix them in. The pain was continuous now, rising and falling in steady waves. She wished she knew more about what to expect, wished she had asked the Earth Mother. Giving birth for the once-fairy was an inconstant and differing experience with each child conceived, and she knew so little of how it worked. She gritted her teeth harder, mixing the soils to-gether, those of the old pines in the lake country, of the place called Green-wich in Ben's world, and of the fairy mists, working them into the soil of the Deep Fell.

Please, she thought. Please don't let this harm my child.

Then she cast down the empty pouch and with an effort came to her feet. Wracked with pain, feeling the child stirring anxiously now within her womb, she prepared to give herself over to the change. The child would come when she was in tree form. She had not been able to tell Ben that. She did not know that she ever could.

She shed her clothing and was naked. Then she placed herself at the very center of the soils she had mixed and dug her toes into the earth.

At the moment of her transformation, she was at peace. It was out of her hands now. She had done all she could do to assure her child's safe birthing. She had kept the trust of the Earth Mother; she had brought back the soils that were required. There was nothing left for her to do but to let her child be born. She wished suddenly for Ben. She wanted to feel his presence, to have him touch her, to hear some small words of reassurance. She did not like being alone now.

Her eyes closed.

Slowly she transformed, fingers and toes lengthening to twigs and roots, arms splitting into branches, legs fusing to a trunk, the whole of her body changing shape and color and look. Her hair disappeared. Her face vanished. She twisted sinuously as bark covered her over. She sighed once, and then she was still.

Hours passed and nothing moved within the Deep Fell where the willow tree rooted. No wind rustled its leaves. No birds flew onto its branches. No small creatures climbed its smooth trunk. The air brightened to a dull, hazy gray, and the summer heat intensified, trapped within the jungle's dank tan-gle. A rain passed through and faded. Water dripped from the supple limbs onto the ground.

Noon approached.

Then the tree seemed to shiver with some inner turmoil. Slowly, agoniz-ingly, where the trunk began to branch skyward, the skin split apart and a broad shoot pushed out into the light. It appeared quickly, as if its growth were accelerated, thrusting and twining upward. It broadened as it grew and changed shape.

In moments, it had become a pod.

Within the pod, there was movement.

STASH

Questor Thews and Abernathy stood together on the parapets of Sterling Silver and looked out across the lake that surrounded the castle island to the throngs of people streaming onto the grasslands. They had been coming all day, tens growing to hundreds, hundreds to thousands. Most had come from the Greensward, though there was a scattering of Trolls from the Melchor, wights from the barren wastelands east, and villagers and farmers from some dozen or so small communities directly north and south. They came as if vagabonds, bearing no food or blankets or even the most rudimentary implements for firemaking. They seemed not to care. Men, women, and children, some with old plow horses and mules, some with a ragtag following of dogs and cats, they had trekked their way here from wherever, as diverse a gathering as ever there was. Now they milled about across the lake from the castle and stared over at it as if hoping someone might invite them in for a good meal.

It was not food they sought, however. What each of them craved, what every single one of them had come to obtain, what all of them were determined to have at any cost, was a mind's eye crystal.

"Look at them," Abernathy muttered, then shook his head so that his dog ears flapped gently. "This is truly dreadful."

"Worse than what we had anticipated, I'm afraid," Questor Thews agreed solemnly.

They had been anticipating some sort of trouble ever since Abernathy and Bunion had returned from Rhyndweir with the story of the black-cloaked stranger and Horris Kew. A vast stash of mind's eye crystals awaited them at Sterling Silver, the stranger had insisted. It was there for the taking. Abernathy had dutifully reported every last word to Questor Thews, and so they had braced themselves. But it was Kallendbor and the other Lords of the Greensward they had expected to face, appearing with their armies to exact an accounting, marching up to the gates to force an entry. Instead they found themselves confronted by thousands of farmers and tradesmen and their families, simple people who bore no weapons and wore no armor, all of them hungry and tired and misguided, all of them standing about like cattle waiting for someone to lead them to the barn.

Well, the barn was back the way they had come, of course, but none of them wanted to hear that. They didn't want to hear anything that didn't involve the words "mind's eye crystals" and that was the sad but inescapable fact of the matter.

They certainly weren't listening to anything Questor Thews or Abernathy had to tell them. When the first of them had arrived, quite early that morning, they had come onto the bridge that linked the island with the mainland. The portcullis had been lowered during the night, so they halted at the gates and shouted up for Ben Holiday to come down. Questor Thews had appeared on the ramparts and shouted back that the King was absent at the moment— what did they want? Mind's eye crystals, they declared vehemently, one for each of them. Well, there weren't any to be had, Questor had replied. They called him a liar and a few other names, and started making disparaging remarks about his lineage. Abernathy had appeared beside his friend, still feeling very responsible for the whole mess, and assured the people massed on the bridge—the number growing even as they argued—that Questor Thews was telling the truth, that there were no mind's eye crystals inside the castle. That didn't fly with anyone. The threats and name-calling continued. The mob grew larger.

Finally Questor sent a squad of King's soldiers out to move the people back off the bridge and to set up a picket line on the far side of the lake. Amid much pushing and shoving, the soldiers cleared the bridge, but no one turned about and started for home as the Court Wizard had hoped. Instead they held their ground just beyond the picket line and waited for something to happen. Nothing did, of course. Questor wasn't entirely sure what they thought might. In any event, the number of people swelled into the thousands by midday, all crammed down off the high plains and surrounding hills onto the lower grasslands fronting the castle. The summer heat worsened on a day that was gloriously clear and cloudless, and tempers grew short.

Then someone on one side of the picket line said something and someone on the other side said something else, and as quick as that the mob rushed the line, overpowered the soldiers, and threw them into the lake. Then they charged across the bridge for the castle gates.

This might have been the start of real trouble except that Questor was still standing out on the battlements with Abernathy trying to decide what else he could do. When he saw the mob rush the castle, he pushed up the sleeves of his old gray robe and called on his magic. This was a precipitous act if ever there was one, since Questor's conjuring never worked well when rushed (or even when it wasn't, for that matter), but no one was really thinking too clearly by now. He meant to send a bolt of lightning flashing down into their midst, something to scatter them or to fling them into the waters of the lake. Instead, he sent down the equivalent of several gallons of oil—not the flaming kind, the plain old greasy kind—right into the foremost of those leading the charge. The oil splashed down across the wooden surface of the bridge and the entire leading edge of the mob went down in an oily tangle of arms and legs. Those following stumbled over their fellows while trying to slow themselves or break past, and they went down, too. In seconds, the entire bridge was awash in oil-slicked bodies.

Questor Thews ordered the gates closed, and the castle was summarily sealed up. The mob dragged its collective self back off the bridge, cursing and threatening with every step. This isn't finished by any means! You watch and see if it is, Questor Thews! Just wait until the Lords of the Greensward arrive! You'll see what real trouble is then, all of you!

True enough, Questor Thews had agreed silently, but there wasn't much he could do about it. So here they were, some long hours later, the day edging toward night, waiting to see which would arrive first, Kallendbor or sunset.

Sunset seemed a pretty good bet. The skies east were already darkening and the skies west turning gold. Several of the moons were out to the north, hanging low in the horizon, lifting gradually toward the stars. There was no sign of Kallendbor and the Lords of the Greensward—no shouts announcing their imminent arrival, no dust upon the approaching plains, no thud of horses' hooves or clank of armor. It looked as if any further trouble was going to be delayed until morning.

Abernathy hoped so. It had been difficult telling Questor Thews how he had been tricked by Horris Kew. It had been like pulling teeth to admit that he had been duped so thoroughly that he had aided and abetted the dissemination of the wretched mind's eye crystals to the people of Landover, thereby permitting the present situation to come to pass. He was still struggling with the loss of his own crystal and the visions it had presented, and in the end he told that to Questor Thews as well. Might as well admit everything, he decided. What difference could it make now?

As it happened, Questor had been extraordinarily understanding and supportive. Quite all right, he had said. Who could blame you? I would have done the same if it were me. He actually thanked Abernathy for putting aside personal feelings in favor of the greater well-being of the Kingdom of Landover and of the missing Ben Holiday in particular.

"I was as much a fool as you," he said solemnly, his wispy hair stuck out as if he were a porcupine taking a defensive stance. "I accepted Horris Kew's word as gullibly as you. I did not question the worth of these crystals he presented to us. They seemed the perfect answer to our dilemma. To tell you the truth, I was on the verge of asking for one myself."

"But you did not," Abernathy observed sadly. "I have no such excuse."

"Nonsense!" Questor shook his head vehemently. "I practically forced one on you when he asked for a trial. I could have tried it out myself, but I let you take the chance. Anyway, it was not too long ago that I stood in your shoes, old friend. I was the one who conjured the magic that sent you and the King's medallion back to his old world. No, I can't allow you a bit of the blame in this."

All of which made Abernathy feel not a minute's worth better about what he had done. Still, Questor was trying to make him feel less guilty, and Abernathy appreciated it. What would make him feel a whole lot cheerier was finding out what had become of Ben Holiday. Questor had used the Landsview anew just that morning, Bunion had scoured the countryside close at hand once more, and neither had a thing to show for their efforts. Wherever Ben Holiday was, he was well hidden. Abernathy wanted to get his teeth on that black-cloaked stranger and bite down real hard on his ear or some such. He was ashamed that his animal side was coming to the fore in this matter, but he was desperate to redeem himself for the harm he had caused.

"Uh-oh," Questor Thews said suddenly, and put an end to the scribe's contemplation. "Look over there."

Abernathy looked. A gang of men had emerged from the trees of the forest west bearing a huge log that had been fashioned into a battering ram. They lugged the log down the hillside and onto the grasslands. They bore it across the flats toward the lake. They were chanting and huffing as they came, and those thousands of their fellows gathered about cheered them on lustily.

"They can't be serious," the wizard gasped.

But they were, of course. They were dead serious. There were thirty or more, evenly split to either side of their makeshift ram, trotting slowly across the grasslands and up to the bridge. All about them, people had come to their feet and were thrusting their fists into the air.

"You, there!" Questor Thews shouted, white hair flying. "Turn back right now! Drop that log!"

No one could hear him; they were shouting too loud. They were practically screaming in anticipation. The gang of men and their ram turned onto the bridge and started across, picking up speed. A howl of determination burst from their lips.

Questor Thews rolled up his sleeves once more atop the parapets. "We'll see about this!" he muttered furiously.

Abernathy stood frozen in place. What should he do? His ears twitched, and he let out a growl.

The men on the bridge crossed in a final rush and slammed their battering ram into the castle gates. There was a monstrous thud and a splintering of wood. The ram and the men carrying it bounced back a few feet and collapsed on the causeway. It seemed to Abernathy as if he could feel the force of the blow on the gates all the way atop the wall where he stood in his half crouch, hands clamped over his muzzle.

"All right for you!" Questor Thews cried out, arms and robes flying. He looked ready to do something. He looked poised to strike. White light gathered at ends of his fingertips. Abernathy clenched his teeth. Something bad was about to happen.

The men with the ram picked themselves up and charged once more, undaunted.

Questor's arms windmilled wildly. Too wildly. He was working so hard at whatever spell he was conjuring that he lost his balance. When he tried to regain it, he tripped on his robes. He stumbled forward dangerously close to the edge of the ramparts. Abernathy reached out hurriedly and grabbed him. As he did so, Questor's magic released from his fingers and flew down into the mob. From the sound that emanated from the wizard's lips, Abernathy could tell that something unexpected was about to happen.

He was not wrong. The magic fell onto the bridge like silver rain, soft and gentle. Perhaps it was meant to be a bolt of lightning that would scatter the men with the ram. Perhaps it was supposed to be another dousing of oil. Neither happened. Instead the magic fell upon the causeway and disappeared into its wooden surface as if water into sand, and a moment later the bridge shuddered and arched as if a sleeping snake awakened. Down went the men with the ram a second time, only yards from their objective, cursing and screaming. The bridge heaved, throwing the men about like rag dolls. The ram flew up into the air and rolled off the bridge and into the moat. The men screamed and cursed some more. Questor and Abernathy hung onto each other and stared downward in disbelief. The bridge was writhing now. It detached from the castle and the far shore and began to twist back on itself. The few men still clinging to its surface abandoned their perch and dived for safety. Boards cracked and snapped apart. Iron nails popped. Bindings frayed and gave way. Up rose the bridge one final time, a serpent breaching from the deep, then it broke into a million pieces and collapsed into the lake and was gone.

There was a long moment of stunned silence. The men who had carried the battering ram were pulling themselves back ashore with the help of friends and relatives. The rest of the ragtag mob was gathered on the shoreline, staring. The waters churned and roiled like a kettle set to boil.

Questor looked at Abernathy and blinked. "Well, what do you know about that!" he said.

Sunset arrived and there were no further incidents. The mob had apparently had enough for one day and now turned its attention to building cooking fires and scrounging for food. With the causeway destroyed, the last open link with the mainland was severed, and Sterling Silver was truly an island in the middle of a lake. No way to reach her now, it was clear, unless you wanted to swim. Most of those gathered couldn't swim and in many cases distrusted water in general. Questor was inclined to congratulate himself on a well-executed bit of magic, but he refrained from doing so since the whole business had gone completely awry and Abernathy knew it.

Abernathy, for his part, had gone back to wondering how ever in the world they were going to get out of this mess without Holiday.

It was still light when, despite Questor's and Abernathy's fondest hopes and unspoken predictions, Kallendbor and a substantial army arrived to take up a position directly across from the castle gates. Peasants and common folk were shoved aside and room was made for the fighting men and their leader. Close by Kallendbor's side was Horris Kew and his bird, the former shuffling about distractedly, the latter riding his shoulder like the proverbial omen of doom. Abernathy watched them bleakly. The cause of all of this, he thought darkly. Horris Kew and his bird. If he could just reach them. If he could just get his hands on them for five seconds. The image lingered.

There was no sign of the black-cloaked stranger. Questor and Abernathy both searched for him without success. Maybe he had stayed behind, but neither of them believed so.

Darkness fell, the sun disappeared, and the fires brightened against the night. Sentries took up positions on the banks of the lake, visibly placed so that those in the castle could see that a siege had been laid. Questor and Abernathy remained on the ramparts where they had stood all day and brooded.

"Whatever are we going to do?" Abernathy muttered disconsolately.

The camp milled about below, people jostling for room in the crowded meadow. The smell of meat cooking wafted up. Cups of ale were being passed about, and laughter grew loud and raucous.

"A regular picnic, isn't it?" Questor replied irritably. Then he started. "Abernathy, look there!"

Abernathy looked. Kallendbor was standing at the edge of the lake with Horris Kew and the bird. Right next to him was the black-cloaked stranger, bold as you please. They stood apart from everyone else, staring out across the water at Sterling Silver.

"Making plans for tomorrow, I'll warrant," the wizard said. He shook his head wearily. "Well, I've had enough of this. I'm going up to the Landsview to see if there is anything new to be learned of the King. I shall scour the countryside once more, and maybe this time something will reveal itself." He made a dismissive gesture with his hands and started away. "Anything is better than watching those idiots."

He departed in a sweep of gray robes, leaving Abernathy to keep watch alone. Contemplating the unfairness of life and the stupidity of men become dogs and wondering anew what he could do to redeem himself, Abernathy continued standing there despite Questor's assessment of the act as a waste of time. There seemed little he could accomplish so long as he was penned up in the castle. He thought vaguely about swimming the lake and sneaking up on Horris Kew and his bird, but that would only get him taken prisoner or worse.

On the far bank, Kallendbor, Horris Kew, Biggar, and the stranger continued to huddle in the near dark, coconspirators of the night.

Abernathy was trying quite unsuccessfully to read their lips when a commotion from behind brought him sharply about. Two of the castle guards had appeared from out of the stairwell holding in their burly hands two small, grimy, struggling figures.

"Great High Lord!" one moaned pitifully.

"Mighty High Lord!" the other wailed.

Well, there you are, Abernathy thought as the two were brought forward. Just when you think things can't get any worse, somehow they always do. There was no mistaking these two—the stout, hairy, dirt-encrusted bodies; the bearded, ferretlike faces with pointed ears and wet noses; the peasant-reject clothes topped off with ridiculous leather skullcaps and tiny red feathers. They were as familiar and unwelcome as deep winter cold and sweltering summer heat, unavoidable visitations that came and went more frequently than the weather. They were G'home Gnomes, the most despised people in the entire kingdom of Landover, the lowest of the low, the final step down the evolutionary ladder. They were thieves and pilferers who lived hand-to-mouth and by the deliberate misfortune they brought to others. They were that variety of creature that scavenges what it consumes and thus cleans up what all others leave behind—except, of course, that G'home Gnomes also cleaned up much of that which was not intended to be left behind in the first place. They were particularly fond of pet cats, which was all right with Abernathy, and pet dogs, which was decidedly not.

These two Gnomes, in particular, were a source of unending distress to the members of the court of Ben Holiday. Ever since they had appeared unexpectedly to pledge their fealty to the throne some three years earlier—a decidedly mixed blessing if ever there was one—they had been underfoot. Now here they were again, the same two troublemakers, back for another shot at making Abernathy's life miserable.

Fillip and Sot cringed when they saw him. They were still whining for Holiday, who at least would tolerate them. Abernathy had no such compunction.

"Where is the High Lord?" Fillip asked immediately.

"Yes, where is the King?" Sot echoed.

"Found them messing about in the King's bedchamber," one of the guards advised, giving Fillip a good shake in an effort to still his struggling. The Gnome whimpered. "Thieving, I expect."

"Never, no never!" Fillip cried.

"Never from the High Lord!" Sot cried.

Abernathy felt a headache coming on. "Set them down," he ordered with a sigh.

The guards dropped them in a heap. The Gnomes fell to their knees, groveling pitifully.

"Great Court Scribe!"

"Mighty Court Scribe!"

Abernathy rubbed his temples. "Oh, stop it!" He dismissed the guards and motioned the Gnomes to their feet. They rose hesitantly, glancing about with worried looks, thinking perhaps that some terrible fate was about to befall them, thinking perhaps of trying to escape.

Abernathy studied them wearily. "What is it that you want?" he snapped.

The G'home Gnomes exchanged a hurried glance.

"To see the High Lord," Fillip answered hesitantly.

"To speak with the High Lord," Sot agreed.

They were terrible at lying, and Abernathy saw at once that they were being evasive. It had been a very long, disappointing day, and he had no time for this.

"Eaten any stray animals lately?" he asked softly, leaning forward so that they could see the faint gleam of his teeth.

"Oh, no, we would never . . ."

"Only vegetables, I promise . . ."

"Because every so often I have this craving for roast Gnome," Abernathy interrupted pointedly. They went as still as stone. "Now give me the truth, or I shall not be responsible for what happens next!"

Fillip swallowed hard. "We want a mind's eye crystal," he answered miserably.

Sot nodded. "Everyone has one but us."

"We just want one."

"Yes, just one."

"That is not asking too much."

"No, not too much."

Abernathy wanted to throttle them. Was there no end to this nonsense? "Look at me," he said, a very real edge to his voice. They met his gaze reluctantly. "There are no mind's eye crystals here. None. Not a one. There never were. If I have anything to say about it, there never will be!" He almost checked himself on that last statement, but then decided he really meant it. He reached out and caught them by their skinny, gnarly arms. "Come here."

He dragged them over to the parapets, ignoring their moans and cries about being thrown to their doom. "Look out there!" he snapped irritably. "Go on, look!" They looked. "See that man with the bird? Next to Lord Kallendbor? Next to the man in the black cloak?"

They hesitated, then nodded as one.

"That," Abernathy declared triumphantly, "is the one who has the mind's eye crystals! So go talk to him!"

He let go of them and stepped away, hands on dog hips. The G'home Gnomes looked at each other uncertainly, then back at Horris Kew, then back at Abernathy.

"There are no crystals here?" Fillip asked, sounding hurt.

"None?" Sot asked.

Abernathy shook his head. "You have my solemn word as Court Scribe and servant to the King. If there are any crystals to be found, that is the man who can find them."

Fillip and Sot wiped dirt-encrusted fingers across damp snouts and teary eyes and stared down at the conjurer with increasing interest. They sniffled rather anxiously, and their jaws worked to no discernible purpose. They stepped back.

"We shall speak with him, then," Fillip announced, taking the lead as always.

"Yes, we shall," Sot reinforced.

They started to turn away and move back toward the stairwell. In spite of himself, Abernathy called them back. "Wait!" he hailed. "Hold on a moment." He walked over to them. He didn't owe them this, but he couldn't let them go unwarned either. "Listen to me. These men, the one in black particularly, are very dangerous. You cannot just walk up to them and ask for crystals. They are likely to cut you into tiny pieces for your trouble."

Fillip and Sot looked at each other.

"We will be very careful," Fillip advised.

"Very," Sot agreed.

They started away again.

"Wait!" Abernathy called a second time. Something had just occurred to him, something he had missed before. The G'home Gnomes turned. "How did you get in here?" he asked suspiciously. "You did not come over the bridge. And you do not look like you swam the lake. So how exactly did you get in?"

They exchanged another in that endless series of furtive looks. Neither spoke.

Abernathy came right up to them then and bent down. "You tunneled in, didn't you?" Fillip bit his lip. Sot clenched his jaw. "Didn't you?"

They nodded. Reluctantly.

"All the way from the far bank?" Abernathy was incredulous.

Fillip sulked. "The forest, actually."

Sot sulked harder. "Back in the trees."

Abernathy stared. "No, how could you? That would take days, weeks." He stopped himself. "Wait a minute. How long has this tunnel of yours been in place?"

"Awhile," Fillip muttered, and scuffed the stone rampart with the claws of his feet.

"And where does this tunnel come out?"

Another pause, this one longer. "The kitchen larder," Sot admitted finally.

Abernathy straightened once more. Memories of food mysteriously disappearing from the larder surfaced like dead fish at moonrise. Cooks' helpers had been blamed. Accusations had been made. No resolution had ever been reached.

"So," he said softly, drawing the word out like a hangman's noose. "The kitchen larder."

Fillip and Sot cringed and waited for the blow to fall. But Abernathy wasn't even looking at them. He was looking away, toward the ramparts and beyond. He was not considering retribution against the G'home Gnomes; he was weighing instead the prospect of getting even with Horris Kew. With the glow of the watch fires dancing off the shadowed stone of Sterling Silver, he stood poised on the brink of a decision that would either redeem him or cost him his life.

It took him only a moment to make up his mind.

He bent down again and asked pointedly, "Is this tunnel of yours big enough for me?"

GNOME TIME

Abernathy was not by nature compulsive in his behavior or even remotely venturesome, so it was with some surprise that he found himself contemplating squeezing into the narrow tunnel hollowed out by Fillip and Sot far back in a corner of the kitchen larder, intent on crawling its length to the woods behind the siege lines ringing Sterling Silver, there to undertake some precarious and probably foolhardy effort to capture and squeeze information out of Horris Kew. It wasn't that he didn't realize what it was he was doing or appreciate the danger involved that disturbed him; it was that he would even consider such madness in the first place.

He consoled himself by determining it was his dog side taking over and therefore entirely the fault of Questor Thews.

The wizard had no idea what Abernathy was about. If he had known, he would have put a stop to it at once or insisted on going himself, neither of which the Court Scribe could permit. After all, this was Abernathy's mess to clean up, his pride to redeem, his self-esteem to regain. Besides, Questor was needed where he was, within the walls of the castle where he could present at least a semblance of a defense against the inevitable assault Kallendbor and his army would mount. Questor's magic might be erratic, but it was a force to be reckoned with nevertheless and would give the castle's assailants at least some pause in their efforts.

Meanwhile, he hoped, he would be able to find out what had become of Ben Holiday.

He was forced to strip off his clothes to get into the tunnel; it was that tight. Nudity was an indignity he was prepared to endure. The G'home Gnomes had made the tunnel for themselves, after all, and not for him. In the shadows of the larder, the kitchen staff dismissed summarily and without explanation to other parts of the castle, Abernathy pulled off his clothing and thought for a moment about what he was doing. He did not think about Horris Kew or his bird or Kallendbor or the black-cloaked stranger this time. The danger from that quarter was known. He thought instead about placing himself in the hands—and possibly teeth—of Fillip and Sot: They were dubious allies at best, given their history as scavengers and consumers of cats and dogs. He was quite certain that if the opportunity presented itself they would not hesitate to eat him. Why not? It was in their nature, wasn't it? Since that was so, however, it was incumbent on Abernathy, given his present precarious circumstances, to give them a very good reason not to make a meal of him.

He decided to appeal to the one character virtue he was able to accord them.

"Listen carefully to me," he told them, crouching naked at the tunnel entry, trying hard not to feel foolish. "There is something I have not told you. What we are doing is very important to the well-being of the High Lord. We have not given out the news, but something bad has happened to him. He has disappeared. Those men out there, the one with the mind's eye crystals and the black-cloaked one, are responsible. I have a plan to save Holiday, but you will have to help me. You want to save the High Lord, don't you?"

"Oh, yes!" Fillip declared.

"Yes, indeed!" Sot insisted.

They nodded so hard he thought their heads might shake loose from their shoulders. He was stretching the truth here concerning Holiday and any plan for his rescue, but in a good cause. The one thing he could count on where the G'home Gnomes were concerned was their unswerving loyalty to the High Lord. It had been set in concrete from the time of their first meeting, when Ben Holiday had done what no one else would have even considered doing— he had gone to their rescue in a cause that was recognizably questionable, determined that a King must serve all of his subjects equally. He had saved their lives, and they had never forgotten. They continued to be thieves and scavengers and acted in misguided ways more often than not, but as they had shown already on more than one occasion, they would do anything for the High Lord.

Abernathy was counting on that now. He was counting on it quite heavily.

"Once we are through the tunnel, I will tell you my plan," he continued. "But we must work together on this. Holiday's life is at risk."

"You can depend on us," Fillip advised eagerly.

"You can," Sot agreed.

Abernathy hoped so. His life was at risk as well.

They went down into the tunnel, Fillip first, Abernathy second, Sot trailing. They crawled in headfirst, stretching out full-length along an earthen passageway that twisted and burrowed down into blackness. Abernathy found that he could not see a thing. He could hear Fillip moving ahead of him and followed the sound of his squirming. From behind, Sot nudged his feet to prod him along. Roots scraped his belly and back. Insects skittered past him in a flurry of legs. In places, patches of damp soaked into him and matted his fur. Everything smelled pungent and close. Abernathy hated tunnels. He hated anything that confined him (another dog trait, he assumed). He wanted out of there very badly, but he forced himself to go on. He had initiated this venture and he was determined to see it through.

The Gnomes must have tunneled all the way under the lake, a feat that Abernathy could not comprehend, given its well-known depth. He envisioned the earth collapsing on top of him; he imagined the lake waters pouring in. The crawl went on endlessly, and at more than one point he thought that he had reached the limit of his endurance. But he refused to quit.

When he emerged once more into the light of moons and stars within a clump of bushes behind the siege lines, there to brush dirt and insects away and to breathe anew and with much gratitude a cool night air which smelled and tasted sweeter than anything in recent memory, he vowed that whatever happened from here on out, he was not under any circumstances going back into that tunnel.

His composure regained, he followed the G'home Gnomes out of the bushes and through the trees to the rise that looked down on the meadow and the makeshift army besieging Sterling Silver. Cooking fires were dying out, and people were stretched out on the grass sleeping. Sentries from Kallendbor's war party still patrolled the shores of the lake, keeping close watch over the island castle, and small knots of men still drank and joked restlessly, but for the most part everyone had settled in for the night. Abernathy searched the meadow, particularly along the shoreline, for some sign of Horris Kew or the black-cloaked stranger. There was none to be found. Not even Kallendbor was visible.

"What do we do now?" Fillip asked anxiously.

"Yes, what?" Sot echoed.

Abernathy wasn't sure. He licked his nose worriedly. Somehow he had to find Horris Kew. But how was he supposed to do that given his present circumstances? To begin with, he looked like a dog, and without any clothes he had little hope of disguising the fact. If he went down into the camp like this, he would be spotted in a moment.

Reluctantly, he turned to the Gnomes. "Do you think you could sneak down there and find the man I showed you from the castle, the one with the bird?"

"The man with the mind's eye crystals," Fillip announced brightly.

"That one," Sot declared.

Abernathy had hoped they might focus on something besides the crystals. It was Ben Holiday he was after, and G'home Gnomes were easily distracted from what mattered in favor of what interested. It was Abernathy's biggest fear that they would get sidetracked. They just couldn't seem to help themselves.

"We can find him," Fillip said.

"Easily," Sot said.

Abernathy sighed. "All right, give it a try. But just find him, then come right back and tell me where he is. So I can tell you my plan. Do not do anything else. Do not let him know you are there. Can you remember that?"

"Yes, we can remember," Fillip said, nodding.

"Easily," Sot repeated.

They slipped away into the darkness and disappeared from view. We can remember, they had promised. Abernathy wished he could be sure.

Not too far away, back somewhat from the rabble that crowded the meadow, Horris Kew and Biggar sat conversing quietly in the dark. Horris was crouched within the shadows of an old spreading maple that edged out from the forest behind, coming halfway down the slope like a scout. Biggar was perched on the trunk of a tree that had once been the maple's companion but had fallen victim to lightning. Horris sat with his back against the maple, the trunk of the other tree close by his legs where they stretched out before him like tent poles.

"You are a coward, Horris," the bird sneered. "A pathetic, craven coward. I would never have thought it of you."

"I am a realist, Biggar." Horris was having none of this coward business. "I know when I am in over my head, and this is definitely one of those times."

It was a bitter admission, but not an unfamiliar one. Sooner or later Horris Kew always found himself in over his head in his machinations. Why these things never worked out as he intended, why they always went wrong somewhere along the way, was a mystery that continued to baffle him. But it was clear that this time, just as all the other times before, things had gone dangerously haywire.

He had been convinced of it since the Gorse had showed itself to Kallendbor and instigated the march on Sterling Silver. *At least* that long, he corrected. Perhaps he had been convinced of it before, given the nature of the being with which he had become entangled. The Gorse was just what Biggar had warned it was—an incredibly powerful monster that could turn on them in a moment. That it would do so sooner or later was no longer in doubt. Since the march from Rhyndweir, Horris could see his usefulness to the creature coming to an end. For one thing, the Gorse had regained its human form and could walk among men, night or day. That meant it no longer relied on Horris to run its errands. Worse, it was beginning to disregard the fact that Horris was even there. When siege was laid to Sterling Silver, it addressed Kallendbor as an equal and barely deigned to notice Horris. Forgotten were all the promises of the role Horris would play in the new order. There was no longer any mention, veiled or otherwise, of Horris becoming King in Holiday's place. Horris was being shoved aside, no mistake about it.

"So you simply plan to give it all up once again?" the bird snapped, bringing him out of his reverie. "Just walk away from the chance of a lifetime? What's the matter with you? I thought you had some backbone about you!"

Horris glowered. "Just exactly what is it that you expect me to do, Biggar? Tell that monster I don't like how I'm being treated and I want what's fair? That should prove interesting. Given what we now know, I should say we will be lucky to get out of this alive even if we keep our mouths shut!"

Biggar spit, an ugly sound. "You can tell it you want to be King, Horris! You can tell it that! The Gorse suggested it, after all! It's a good plan. You be King for a day, we get our hands on as much wealth as we can, then we get out of here. But we don't cut and run with nothing!"

Horris folded his arms across his bony chest and huffed. "Tell it I want to be King, you think? Haven't you been paying attention to what's going on? Haven't you been listening? This isn't about mind's eye crystals or Sterling Silver or being King! There is something else going on here, something infinitely more complex and devious. The Gorse is simply using us—Kallendbor included—to get what it wants. It spent a lot of time getting free of that box, and it wasn't happy about being put there in the first place! Think about it!"

Biggar's beak clacked shut. "What do you mean?"

Horris leaned forward. "For a bird possessed of enhanced intelligence, you can be awfully dense. Revenge, Biggar! The Gorse wants a healthy measure of it, don't you see? There are old debts to be paid for injuries suffered, and the Gorse is doing all this to collect on those debts. It practically told us as much. Landover for us, it said, and the fairy mists for itself—remember? I didn't realize what that meant then, but I do now. We have always followed a very sound rule of business, Biggar, and it has served us well. If there isn't any money to be made, we get out. Well, there isn't any money involved in the revenge business, and it's time to fold our tent and get while the getting's good!"

"But there *is* money, Horris," the bird insisted. "That's just the point. There's all kinds of money, just across that lake, just inside those walls. If we can hang on for a few more days, we have a chance to take a good chunk of it with us. The Gorse can help us—maybe without even knowing it. Let the beast have its revenge, what do we care? What we need is what's inside those walls. That, and a way out of Landover. Or have you forgotten we're trapped here? The Gorse can give us both."

"What it can give us is a quick trip into that box with Holiday and the others." Horris shook his head stubbornly. "You saw what it did. It dispatched Holiday like a child. Down into the Tangle Box and out of Landover in the blink of an eye. No more King. It'll do the same with us when it's ready, and I don't think that time is too far off."

Biggar hopped onto the end of Horris Kew's boot. His claws dug in. "Maybe we should hedge our bets a bit, Horris. Suppose you're right. What we need is a little something to keep the Gorse from harming us. Like the box."

Horris blinked. "The Tangle Box?"

"We slip away right now, tonight," said the bird. "We can reach the cave on horseback and return before morning. Take the box and hide it. Use it as a lever to make certain we get what we want." The sharp eyes gleamed.

Horris stared at the bird for a moment, then he shook his head in disbelief. "You've gone round the bend, Biggar. You really have. Threaten the Gorse? What does it care if we have the box or not? We don't even know how to use it!"

"We know the words," the bird whispered. "We know the spell. What if we were to say it again?"

There was a long, terrible silence. Horris wished he had never opened the box in the first place, never spoken the words that released the Gorse, never returned to Landover at all. He wished he had taken up some other less-stressful profession, like leatherworking or weaving. He was suddenly and inescapably fed up with magic in all its forms.

"Come on, Horris, let's go!" Biggar urged. "Don't just sit there. Get up!"

Biggar couldn't see it, of course. Perhaps it was due to the fact that even with enhanced intelligence there was still only a bird's brain inside that tiny feathered cranium trying to sort it all out. Or maybe he simply didn't want to see.

"If we do this," Horris Kew began softly, "if we decide to challenge the Gorse, if we actually go back to the cave and steal the Tangle Box . . ."

He couldn't finish. He couldn't bring himself to speak the words. He slumped back against the tree, his bony frame collapsing in on itself like a deflated balloon.

Biggar hopped back and forth between the other's boot and the tree trunk, hissing like a snake. "You coward! You worm-body! You ridiculous excuse for a wizard! All talk and no action wimp-head! How I ever let myself become involved with the likes of you is more than I can comprehend!"

Something moved behind the tree trunk, barely noticeable, a silent bit of shadow and nothing more, but neither of them saw it.

"Biggar, Biggar, you are not thinking . . ."

"I *am* thinking! I am the only one who's thinking!" Biggar puffed up to twice his size, turning himself into a ferocious black porcupine. "Go on, then! Lie there like a rag doll, a collection of sackcloth sewn up with sawdust brains! Go on!"

Horris Kew closed his eyes and put his hands over his face.

"I'll not spend another moment with such a coward!" raged Biggar. "Not one, single, further, disgusting—"

A grimy hand reached up from behind the log on which he perched, clamped itself over his beak and neck, and dragged him from sight.

After a moment, Horris Kew opened his eyes again and peered about. No Biggar. Just like that, he was gone. Horris sat forward, puzzled. A single black feather lay rocking on the log.

"Biggar?" he called tentatively.

There was no answer.

The hour approached midnight.

Abernathy sat quietly at the edge of the woods and watched the last of the revelers nod off, leaving a sprinkling of fires and the distant, vague shapes of Kallendbor's sentries. The darkness deepened all about. Sterling Silver was a vague bulk against the horizon, almost entirely empty of light. Overhead, the sky was clear and bright with several moons and thousands of stars. It was warm and pleasant and under other circumstances might have assured everyone a good night's sleep.

As it was, Abernathy did not dare even think about sleep, worried sick already over the length of time that had passed since Fillip and Sot had left his side in search of Horris Kew. There had been no outcry, so he didn't think they had been spied, but he was uncomfortable with having them gone this long nevertheless. There were too many ways for that pair to get into trouble, too many missteps they could take before they realized their mistake. He wished he had gone with them. He chided himself for trusting them to go alone.

He had just about made up his mind to go look for them, to slip down into the camp and steal a concealing cloak and search them out, when they abruptly reappeared. They popped up out of the shadows almost in front of him, causing him to start in spite of himself.

"Where have you been?" he asked, irritated.

The G'home Gnomes smiled, showing all their teeth. They looked exceptionally pleased with themselves.

"Look what we have," said Fillip.

"Come, take a look," said Sot.

Abernathy tried to look, for he could see that they did indeed have something—something that appeared to be moving—but they brushed past him without slowing.

"No, no, not here," Fillip said quickly.

"In the dark, away from the camp," Sot said.

So they trekked back into the woods, well away from the meadow and its campers, until there was no one anywhere about but themselves. At this point Fillip and Sot turned back to Abernathy once more, and the former proudly held out his hands.

"Here!" he announced.

Abernathy stared. It was the bird, the myna or whatever it was, the one that belonged to Horris Kew. It was clutched firmly in the Gnome's grimy hands, its neck grasped none too gently, its beak clamped shut so that it could not cry out. Its wings fluttered weakly, but it appeared to have spent itself thoroughly.

Abernathy sighed in despair. "I told you just to look, just to find the bird's owner and come back to me. I did not tell you to take the bird! What good is the bird to us!"

"Much good," insisted Sot, undeterred. He prodded Fillip eagerly. "Show him."

Fillip dropped his fingers below Biggar's beak and gave a small shake. "Speak, bird."

The bird did not speak. It hung there limply, pitifully. It looked half-dead. Abernathy felt a throbbing in his temples and sighed.

Fillip glowered. He bent down close to the bird's face. "Speak, stupid bird, or I will wring your neck and eat you," he said, and he tightened his clawed fingers meaningfully.

"All right, all right!" the bird snapped, coming suddenly alive. Abernathy jerked back in surprise. The bird's head twisted wildly. "I'm talking, okay? What do you want me to say?"

Fillip held the bird out proudly. "See?"

Abernathy bent down for a closer look. "Well, well," he said softly. "You talk a lot better than you pretend, don't you?"

"Better than you, furball," Biggar sneered. "Tell these mole people to let go of me right now or it will be the worse for you."

Abernathy reached out and poked the bird. "What is your name again? Biggar? Well, Biggar, guess what?" There was unmistakable satisfaction in his voice. "It took awhile, but I remember you now. It was a long time ago, wasn't it? You belonged to the old King's wizard, to Questor Thews's brother. One day, you were simply reported missing. What happened? Were you dispatched to Ben Holiday's old world—just like Horris Kew? No, never mind about that. It hardly matters now. Just tell me what you know about the High Lord's disappearance, hmm? And don't leave anything out."

Biggar closed his beak with a sharp clack. But it was too late for stonewalling. Fillip and Sot had overheard most of his conversation with Horris Kew and dutifully repeated it now to Abernathy. They got their facts confused a few times and failed to interpret all the words properly, but it was clear enough for the scribe to figure out what had happened. The Gorse was some sort of monster. It was using Horris Kew and Kallendbor. The mind's eye crystals were its cat's paw against the throne. Most important, Ben Holiday's disappearance had come about through use of a powerful spell that would somehow have to be reversed. That meant finding the Gorse's cave and the Tangle Box hidden within it.

Abernathy turned his attention back to Biggar. The bird had said nothing since his first outburst, withdrawing into silence for the entirety of the time that Fillip and Sot had revealed his secrets. Now he glanced quickly up at Abernathy as the scribe bent down close to look at him.

"Polly want a cracker?" Abernathy coaxed maliciously.

Biggar, despite being firmly held, snapped at his nose.

Abernathy smiled and showed all of his teeth. "You listen to me, you worthless bag of feathers. You are going to lead us to this cave—tonight. When we get there, you are going to take us inside. You are going to show us this Tangle Box, and you are going to teach us the words of the spell. Do you understand me?"

Biggar's bright eyes fixed on him. "I'm not doing anything. They'll find me missing and come looking for me. The Gorse, particularly. Wait until you see what it'll do to you!"

"Whatever it does," Abernathy replied pointedly, "you will not be around to see it happen." There was a long, meaningful silence. "The fact of the matter is," he continued, "if you do not show me where that cave is right now, I am going to give you to my friends and tell them to do whatever they like with you as long as they assure me that I will never, ever see you again."

He kept his gaze and his voice steady. "Because I am very angry about being tricked. I am even more angry about what you have done to the High Lord. I want him back, safe and sound, and I expect you to help me if you have any hope at all of living out the night. Has that penetrated your little bird brain?"

There was another long silence. "Say something quick," Abernathy urged.

Biggar's voice came out a croak. "The cave is west, beyond the Heart." Then he recovered. "But it won't do you any good."

Abernathy smiled and gave the bird another look at his teeth. "We'll see about that," he promised.

BIGGAR'S LAST STAND

While Fillip kept tight hold of Biggar, Sot was dispatched to find horses for the journey west, the word *find* being understood to be a euphemism for the word *steal* by all concerned. Beggars could not afford to be choosers, and the G'home Gnomes were thieves by nature and habit and would readily interpret *find* as *steal* in any event. The hard part of all this was not in reconciling moral principles but in accepting that horses must be used. Neither Abernathy nor the Gnomes had any particular love for horses, and in truth horses didn't much care for them either. It was one of those inbred hostilities that could not be overcome by either reason or circumstance. But the distance involved required at least a good day by foot and only four hours by horseback. Since time was running out for Questor Thews and Sterling Silver—dawn, after all, would find Kallendbor and the black-cloaked stranger working hard to discover ways to shorten the siege—necessity ruled and horses would have to be tolerated.

If only barely.

Sot was back in record time, leading two haltered and blanketed horses, one a bay, the other a sorrel, that he had quite obviously removed from a picket line. He had not thought to acquire either saddles or bridles, which complicated matters. The horses were already shying and snorting with distaste at the small, ragged, dirt-encrusted rodent who led them. In lieu of saddles, Abernathy decided to leave the blankets in place, trimming them with Sot's hunting knife so that they did not hang below the horses' flanks and securing them as best he could with a makeshift girth strap woven out of the pieces trimmed. It was a sad-looking job, but there was no help for it.

They mounted up then, Abernathy aboard the sorrel, which was the more rambunctious of the pair, and Fillip and Sot atop the bay. Fillip held the halter rope and Sot the bird. The horses were dancing and huffing by now, beginning to realize what was in store for them and being none too happy about it. Abernathy had them walk the horses at first, anxious to get as far away from the encampment as possible in case they chose to bolt. This was accomplished with a minimum of fuss. When they were several miles off and well up into the hill country west, Abernathy kicked his mount in the flanks gently and they were off.

At a dead run. Both horses leapt away as if on command and tore through the trees and over the hills like creatures possessed. Abernathy tried to rein his sorrel in, but the horse was having none of it. Free of the constraints of bit and reins, it simply took command. Abernathy gave up trying to do anything but hang on. Behind him, he could hear the Gnomes howling in despair. If they were thrown, they might lose the bird. If they lost the bird, they were finished. He gritted his teeth and resisted the urge to shout back useless advice.

Eventually the horses wore themselves out, slowed to a trot, and finally a walk. All three riders were still aboard and in possession of their faculties, although they felt as if their bones had been rearranged. They had come a very long way in a very short time, as it turned out, and before they knew it they were at the Heart and passing west. Abernathy called back from time to time for directions from Biggar, and the bird grudgingly supplied what was required. The moons shifted languidly along the horizon and overhead across the sky as night eased toward morning. The countryside changed its look as the trees thickened and the forests grew more dense. Soon they were forced to proceed at a careful walk in a woods that offered no trail and allowed no misstep.

It was little more than an hour later when they reached the cave. They dismounted at the top of a steep rise, tied the horses to a tree, and maneuvered their way down the slope to a tangled thicket below. The descent went slowly, as all were stiff and sore from the ride. The Gnomes complained loudly and incessantly, and Abernathy gave thought to gagging them. At the base of the slope, they turned back through a gathering of brush and found themselves up against a huge, flat stone into which intricate symbols had been carved. Abernathy could neither read nor understand the symbols.

"What do we do now?" he demanded of Biggar.

The bird was looking somewhat the worse for wear, having been held tightly by the legs during the entire ride, often upside-down as Sot struggled to keep his seat atop the bay. Feathers were sticking out everywhere, and dust coated the once-sleek black body.

"I don't know that I should tell you another thing," he snapped in reply. "When are you going to let me go!"

"When I see the High Lord safe and sound again!" Abernathy was in no mood for argument.

Biggar spit disdainfully. "That won't happen. Not if I help you get into the cave, not if I show you the box, and not if you speak the spell. It won't happen because you're not a wizard or a conjurer or anyone else capable of summoning magic."

"This from a bird," Abernathy replied testily. "Just get us inside, Biggar. Let me worry about the rest."

The bird sniffed. "Very well. Have it your way. Touch these symbols in the order I direct." And he proceeded to repeat the procedure for opening the cavern door as he had memorized it from watching Horris Kew.

A moment later, the stone swung back, grating against its rock seating, yawning into a black hole streaked dimly with a silver phosphorescence. The little company stood staring uncertainly into the uninviting gloom.

"Well?" Biggar sneered. "Are you going to stand out here all day or are you going in? Let's get this over with."

"How far back does this cave run?" Abernathy asked.

"To its end!" the bird snapped. "Sheesh!"

Abernathy ignored him. He didn't like caves any better than he liked tunnels, but he couldn't risk sending the G'home Gnomes in alone. No telling what might happen. On the other hand, he wasn't anxious to walk into a trap.

"I will go first," Fillip volunteered, providing a solution to the problem.

"I will go second," Sot offered.

"We don't mind tunnels and caves."

"We like the dark."

That was fine with Abernathy. He was content to bring up the rear. The better to keep an eye on everyone. Besides, if there were any traps the Gnomes would have a far better chance of spotting them than he would. Too bad his nose worked better than his eyes, but such was his lot and there was no point in bemoaning it.

"All right," he agreed. "But be careful."

"Do not worry about us," Fillip advised cheerfully.

"Not for a minute," Sot added.

Fair enough, Abernathy allowed. Not that he was inclined to do so in any case. "Just keep a tight grip on the bird," he ordered.

They stepped cautiously through the door, easing their way out of night's darkness and into the cavern's. The phosphorescence gleamed in dull streaks along the corridor walls ahead, like candlelight seen through a rain-streaked window. They paused in the entry, casting about. The air within was surprisingly warm. The silence was immense.

A sudden, terrible thought struck Abernathy. What if the Gorse had come here ahead of them for some reason and was waiting? The idea was so frightening that for a moment he could not move. It occurred to him suddenly that he was in way over his head. He had no weapons, no magic, and no fighting skills with which to protect himself. The Gnomes were worthless in a fight; all they would do was burrow to safety. This whole enterprise was fraught with danger and riddled with the possibility of failure. What had he been thinking in undertaking it in the first place?

Then the momentary fear passed, and he was able to calm himself. He had done what he must do, what was necessary and right, and that was enough to justify any risk. High Lord Ben Holiday depended on him. He did not know how exactly, but he knew that in some way it was true. He reminded himself anew how he had aided and abetted the Gorse and Horris Kew in their efforts to subvert the people of Landover and undermine the throne. He reminded himself of the debt that he must pay for his foolishness.

"Well, then, let's proceed," he announced bravely.

The Gnomes, who had been watching him work his way through his hesitancy, eased through the doorway. Abernathy took a deep breath and followed.

Instantly, the door grated shut behind them.

Abernathy jumped, the Gnomes yelped, and for an instant there was complete pandemonium. Abernathy threw himself instinctively against the door to force it open again. Both Gnomes raced to help and ran into each other for their trouble. As they collided, Biggar pecked as hard as he could on the hand grasping him, and Sot let go.

Biggar broke free instantly, flew up into the air, and in the blink of an eye streaked away into the cave.

Within the Labyrinth, Ben Holiday worked his way slowly through the mist, the talisman of the medallion held carefully before him. Strabo and Nightshade trailed, silent wraiths following his lead. They had all been transformed inwardly since the revelation of their identity, but outwardly each was crippled in appearance and capability and bore the weight of their imprisonment like chains. There was the sense now that they walked their last mile, that if they failed to get free this time they would be trapped forever. There was within them a growing desperation.

None was more acutely aware of it than Ben, who carried in his hands their only hope. The medallion did not speak to him; it did not give off light or provide direction. He walked like a blind man, seeing nothing of the trail he needed, knowing only that the medallion had taken him through the fairy mists before and must somehow do so again if they were to survive. For survival was the issue here, though the word went unspoken. If they remained within the mists, they would eventually go mad. Madness was a certainty they could see as clearly as their desperation, a pall as inexorable as the Haze arising when they were threatened. But unlike the Haze, it came not to protect but to destroy them. It did so gradually, an eroding of confidence, hope, and will. It worked against them as surely as a sickness against health, wearing them down so that in the end death was all that remained.

But it would not have them yet, Ben whispered in his mind. Finding Willow again, even in his dream, even for that briefest of moments, finding her and knowing that she depended on him, that she waited for him somewhere beyond the entangling mists of the Labyrinth, she and their unborn child, was enough to strengthen his determination to live. He would find a way out. The medallion would give them their escape. It must.

"I see no change in anything." Nightshade's cold voice drifted up from behind.

In truth, she was right. They seemed to be making no progress, though they had been walking for hours. Shouldn't they have been clear by now if the medallion was working? How long must it take? Ben peered ahead through the gloom, trying to see some difference in the texture and viscidity of the mist. He did not slow, thinking that if he did they might stop, and if they stopped they were lost. Movement gave hope, movement of any sort.

"There is a lessening of the dampness," Strabo said suddenly.

Ben glanced down. He was right. The ground on which they walked was firmer than it had been at any time since they had come into the mists. Perhaps this was a sign. He took it as one and picked up the pace. Ahead, the trees seemed less dense. Was this possible? Hope blossomed within him. He grew flushed with its brightness. The trees were giving way, opening into a clearing, the clearing opening in turn into a passageway, a hollowed-out tunnel through massive old growth that ran on into a distant dark . . .

"Yes," he whispered aloud.

For it was a recognizable trail they approached now, one familiar to all who had passed through the fairy mists into Landover. They hastened toward it eagerly, even Nightshade brightening perceptibly at the welcome sight. They entered the tunneled gloom in a knot, hurrying down the forest trail. It was the link they had sought, the way back from where they had come. There were no fairies here, no sounds, no movement, no hint of life of any sort save the trees and the brush and the fog that shrouded them. They were still within the fairy mists of the Labyrinth. Yet somewhere close, somewhere just ahead, the door leading out awaited.

But suddenly the gloom closed tightly about before them, turning as dark as ink, becoming a wall that rose and stretched away without end. They slowed as they came up to it, baffled that it should be there. They stopped as they found it would not allow them to go farther, touching its surface and finding it as hard and immovable as stone. They walked its perimeter in either direction for a distance and then retraced their steps. The wall offered no doorway leading through. It allowed no passage out.

"What is this madness?" Nightshade hissed in fury.

Ben shook his head. The medallion would neither part the mists nor show them a way around. This wall, whatever it was, was impervious to the magic. How could that be? If the fairy mists imprisoned them, then the medallion

should be able to take them through. The medallion gave passage through all
of the mists.

Then suddenly he recognized what it was that he was seeing. This black
wall was not formed of the fairy mists. It was the confinement of the Tangle
Box itself, a different form of magic than the mists, a final barrier against escape. And the lock for this door, he feared, did not lie within their prison. It
lay instead without.

He stepped back in frustration and despair. He had been able to pass from
the mists of the Tangle Box in his dream, but he could not do so while awake.

"What are we supposed to do now?" Strabo asked quietly, hunched down
at his elbow, anger seeping into his voice.

Ben Holiday did not have an answer.

It took Biggar only moments to reach the back of the cavern, the chamber
where the Gorse had concealed the Tangle Box. Biggar swooped down to
where the box sat on a rock shelf far back in the shadows, landing on an out-
cropping just above. Now what? He had given no thought to anything but escape up until this point, and now that he had achieved his goal he wasn't sure
what to do next. There was only one way out of the cave and that was back the
way he had come. There were runes carved in the rock above the door, different than those that opened the door from without, but he knew the required
sequence. All that was needed was to lure the dog and the ferrets away long
enough to let him trigger the release.

He could hear them coming already, the scratching of their claws on the
rock, the whine of their voices.

"Here, birdie, birdie," one of them called.

Biggar sneered. Birdie, birdie, indeed.

He waited patiently in the near dark until they came into view. They materialized out of the gloom like hairy pigs, sniffing and snuffling their way
about the cavern floor. How pathetic! It was the ferrets or whatever they
were, creeping about, earthbound imbeciles who had about as much chance
of catching him as they did of mastering physics.

"Come here, birdie," one of them repeated patiently.

"Here, stupid bird," the other snapped.

Must be the one he pecked, Biggar thought. He would have smiled if his
beak had allowed it. He hoped he had hurt the wretched little monster plenty.
He hoped the beast developed gangrene and dropped dead. Precious little
concern he'd shown for Biggar, after all. Carrying him slung down on that
horse! Beating Biggar's head against his leg as he tried to keep his seat! Well,
they'd soon see what messing around with him would get them!

He lifted off his perch and flew back across the chamber. They saw him instantly, eyes sharper than he would have thought, and leapt to catch him as he

whizzed past. Hopeless, of course. He was twenty feet off the floor and twice
as quick as they were. He was past them and speeding for the entrance while
they were still clutching at air. Maybe the dog had come hunting, too. Maybe.

But he hadn't. The dog was stationed directly in front of the stone barrier,
waiting. Biggar banked hurriedly, narrowly avoiding the dog's outstretched
hands and bared teeth. The dog was smarter than the ferrets. He wasn't about
to let Biggar escape so easily.

"Come back here, you little . . ."

The dog's shouted epithets died away into echoes that bounced off the
rock as Biggar flew back toward the main chamber. So it was a standoff. They
were all trapped in the cave. Biggar's mind raced. The trick now was to lure
the dog away from the stone slab, to bring him back into the cavern just long
enough for Biggar to slip past and trigger the lock. Once he was outside the
cave, they would never catch him. Then the Gorse could deal with them. He
wondered suddenly if there was any chance that the Gorse would come back
to the cave that night. Perhaps Horris would go to it with the tale of Biggar's
disappearance. Perhaps. But that was giving Horris more credit for brains
than he deserved. These days, Horris was too stupid to figure out how to tie
his shoes. Since the Gorse had been released, Horris was scared and confused
and generally useless. Biggar was thinking that maybe it was time for a new
partner. What did he need Horris for anyway? He was the real brains of the
pair. Always had been.

He lifted toward the ceiling as he approached the back chamber, but even
so he just narrowly avoided Sot as the Gnome leaped down from a rocky
promontory he had gained high up on the wall to one side. The Gnome plum-
meted past him, hands grasping, and dropped to the cavern floor. Biggar listened to him hit, a dull thud, then heard him groan and start to mutter. Good.

"Nice try, rodent-face," he called out gleefully, and then he ducked as the
other ferret threw something past his head. A metal pan or plate, some piece
of cookware that Horris had carried in. He squawked angrily and rose up as
far as he could go. Time for evasive action.

All sorts of things started flying at him now as the Gnomes attacked in
earnest, trying to bring him down. They threw everything they could lift,
yelling at him all the while, calling him "stupid bird" and worse, growing an-
grier by the moment. That suited Biggar just fine. Anger caused mistakes, and
he was counting on one from them. They had not seen the Tangle Box yet, and
he made a point of staying away from it. Wheeling, diving, soaring out of
reach, he teased and taunted them unmercifully, calling them names back,
daring them to catch him. Total idiots that they were, they just kept yelling
and leaping about and trying to hit him with stuff. Fat chance.

On the other hand, he was growing a tad weary with all this dodging
about, and he still didn't have a plan for getting the dog away from the door.
He needed a distraction that would bring the dog running, something the dog

couldn't ignore. He wondered suddenly what would happen if he spoke the words to the spell that had imprisoned Holiday and the others. Nothing good, he decided and discarded the idea quickly. That box was too dangerous. Besides, suppose it released its prisoners? Better to leave it where it was for now. He scanned the cavern again for another avenue of escape, hoping that maybe he had missed an air shaft or fissure. But there was nothing to be seen.

Below, the G'home Gnomes began pulling blankets off Horris Kew's makeshift bed and tying them together to form a net. Come now, Biggar smirked. He flew at them while they worked, distracting them, taunting them further. He could see the gleam of their yellow eyes as they ducked and hissed up at him. They were really angry, the both of them. Served them right. They completed their net, the whole of it riddled with escape holes—Idiots!—and began trying to maneuver him into a corner where he could be trapped.

"Fatheads! Toads! Stupid groundhogs!" he called down to them, easily evading their pathetic efforts.

He swooped down and picked up some of the lighter implements that had been thrown at him, carried them aloft, and dropped them on the Gnomes' heads. The Gnomes screeched and howled. Maybe that would bring the dog, Biggar thought hopefully. But the dog still didn't come. Not enough noise, maybe. Biggar tried again with something slightly heavier, a wooden ladle. He dropped it squarely on Fillip's head, and the Gnome lost his balance on the perch he had gained some ten feet up and fell headfirst to the floor. It must have hurt terribly, but the Gnome was back on his feet at once. Heads of iron, Biggar thought. No brains to encumber their thick skulls.

The game continued for a time, the Gnomes swinging their net at Biggar, Biggar avoiding the snare and calling out names. No one could gain an advantage. Biggar called the dog names as well, but there was no response. He darted back down the tunnel to where the dog kept watch, trying to draw it after him with insults and nosedives, but the dog stayed put.

It was Biggar who lost patience first. He could not bear that these halfwits had kept him trapped for so long, could not stand the idea of being stymied by idiots. He decided to try something to break the stalemate. He streaked back into the far chamber, past the leaping, grasping Gnomes, and across the room to the Tangle Box. Enough of caution. The one thing that would bring the dog was the box—especially if he thought something dreadful was going to happen to it. Biggar would accommodate him, then.

He teased the ferret creatures back toward the entry, giving them just enough hope that they might catch hold of him to keep them coming, then swooped back across the chamber to the Tangle Box. He landed squarely on top of the container, dug his claws into the crevices where the symbols of power had been carved, secured his grip, and lifted off. It was not easy doing so. The box was heavy and cumbersome. He watched the Gnomes race toward him, yelling more wildly as they realized what he was doing. They were incoherent, however, not yet yelling "Tangle Box" or some such, so the dog still didn't come. Clacking his beak with the effort, Biggar rose into the gloom, the box secured in his claws. His wings flapped madly to keep him aloft. His pinions strained. Below, the ferrets were leaping wildly for him.

He struggled and flapped his way into the highest reaches of the chamber, the Tangle Box bobbing in his grasp. His plan was to carry it about for a few more moments and then drop it. One act or the other was bound to bring the dog.

"Stupid bird, come down!" one Gnome howled.

"Why don't you come up?" he snarled back.

"You'll be sorry for this!" the other shouted.

"Care to see what will happen if I let go of this?" he teased, letting the box jiggle wildly. "I don't think I can hold on much longer."

They shrieked like banshees at that, racing about below him like scampering mice routed out of their nest. He was really enjoying this. He angled from one side of the chamber to the other, drawing them after, a pair of ridiculous, hopeless pawns.

But still the dog didn't come.

He lost patience for the last time. Fine, if this was how they wanted to play it, fine! He was all worn out anyway. He banked away from them to the highest point in the chamber and released the Tangle Box.

Unfortunately, one of his claws caught quite firmly in a seam as he did so.

Down went the Tangle Box, plummeting to the cavern floor, and down went a hapless Biggar with it. The bird struggled wildly to break free, scratching and scraping at the weight about its foot, but it was held fast. Up rushed the stone floor. Biggar shrieked and closed his eyes.

The expected did not come to pass, however. There was no skull-smashing stop on the stone, no splatter of box and bird. At the last possible moment Sot threw himself across the floor and caught both in the cradle of his gnarly, hairy arms.

Biggar had just enough time to open his eyes before a grimy hand closed tightly about his unfortunate neck.

"Got you now, stupid bird," the Gnome whispered.

⸱⸱⸱◦∞◦⸱⸱⸱

Abernathy stood at the cavern entrance and listened as the tumult in the inner chambers died into sudden and unexpected silence. He waited for it to resume, but it did not. The silence lengthened and deepened. Clearly something had happened, but what? He could not leave his post to find out. He knew that Biggar would slip past him and escape if he did. The bird had been trying to lure him away for the past hour, waiting for his chance. Abernathy had sent Fillip and Sot in after the troublesome creature, thinking as he did that they were best suited for the task in any event. He did not know how they would ever manage to catch the bird, but there was little choice other than to allow them to try. The extent of their efforts had been evident from the sounds of their struggle, a continuous, relentless cacophony that suggested all manner of unpleasant happenings.

And now everything was still.

"Fillip?" he called tentatively. "Sot?"

No answer. He waited anxiously. What should he do?

Then finally a pair of dim, but familiar shapes appeared out of the phosphorescence-streaked gloom, bearing between them an intricately carved wooden box. Abernathy's heart leapt with expectation.

"You found it!" he exclaimed, restraining the urge to dance a bit.

The Gnomes trundled toward him, looking somewhat the worse for wear.

"Stupid bird tried to drop it," Fillip said grimly.

"Tried to smash it," Sot embellished.

"Hurt the High Lord," Fillip said.

"Maybe kill the High Lord," Sot said.

They stroked the wooden surface of the Tangle Box lovingly and then passed it carefully over to the dog.

"Stupid bird won't do that again," Fillip said.

"Not ever," Sot said.

And spit out a well-chewed black feather.

DEAD RECKONING

The sunrise over Sterling Silver was a blood-red stain on the eastern horizon that promised bad weather for the day ahead. Questor Thews was back on the ramparts of the castle, looking down over the waking encampment of Kallendbor's professional army and the ragtag collection of villagers and farmers that had preceded it in the quest for the phantom collection of mind's eye crystals. Night's darkness was receding reluctantly west, edged back by the crimson dawn, and the light washed over the huddled forms of the besiegers like blood.

Hardly an auspicious omen, the wizard thought.

He had been up most of the night scouring the countryside with the Landsview in search of Ben Holiday. He had traveled the length and breadth of Landover, north to south, east to west, and found no trace of the High Lord. He was tired and discouraged from his efforts and frankly at his wit's end. What was he supposed to do now? The castle was under siege, two-thirds of the population were in open revolt, and he had been left alone to deal with all of it. Not even Abernathy was to be found, a new and unwelcome source of irritation. Willow hadn't returned yet either. If people kept disappearing, the monarchy would soon run out of responsible leaders and collapse like a deflated balloon.

Bunion moved out of the shadows and stood beside him, looking down at the congregation stirring on the meadow. For once, the kobold didn't offer his toothy smile. Questor sighed, reached down, and patted the gnarled little fellow reassuringly on the shoulder. Bunion was exhausted and discouraged, too. It seemed as if they all had run out of options and must now simply wait to see what would happen.

They didn't have to wait long. As the sun began to rise and the camp to stir, the black-cloaked stranger appeared out of the forest gloom and made his way toward the far end of the meadow where heavy thickets fronted the face of a bluff. No one was camped in this space, the ground rough and uneven, the brush studded with thorns and itchweed, the light veiled, and the shadows thick. Questor watched the stranger move away from the besiegers. No one went with him. No one even seemed to notice he was there. He did not move furtively, but with a purpose that defied intervention from any quarter. Questor glanced back across the broad stretch of the meadow. There was no sign of Horris Kew or his bird or even of Kallendbor.

Keeping clear somehow of the brambles, the black-cloaked stranger eased through the lingering shadows. What was he up to? Questor Thews didn't know, but he was convinced he would be better off if he did. He kept thinking that he ought to be doing something, but he really had no idea what.

Bunion chittered quickly, urgently.

"No, wait here," Questor advised. "No swimming the moat until we know what he's up to. No heroics. We've lost enough people as it is." And he wondered again where Abernathy had gone.

Kallendbor had come into view now, trailed by his officers and retainers. Most were armored and ready for battle. War horses were being saddled. Weapons were being brought down from the heights in wagons and foot soldiers were lining up to receive them. Questor's mouth tightened. Apparently Kallendbor was growing tired of the siege already.

Scarlet light swept over Sterling Silver and its encircling lake and spread across the meadow. It reached the bluff face where the black-cloaked stranger had stepped out of the shadows. It began to climb toward the woods beyond.

Questor squinted against its glare. The stranger had moved well out into the open and was facing the bluff.

"What is he up to?" the wizard muttered suspiciously.

In the next instant the stranger's arms lifted beneath his concealing cloak, his body went rigid, and lines of fire arced downward into the earth. The wizard started. The stranger was using magic! He exchanged a worried glance with Bunion. There were shouts now from the central part of the meadow, where others had seen the flames. Kallendbor was atop his charger, shouting order at his officers. Men were milling about, not certain what it was they were supposed to do. Lines of soldiers afoot and on horseback were drawing up into formation. Farmers and villagers and their families were caught between fleeing and sticking around to see what would happen.

Had they possessed sufficient foresight, they would have chosen flight. There was a deep, ominous rumble from within the earth, and the sound of stone grating, as if an enormous door had swung open.

Uh, oh, Questor Thews thought belatedly.

The bluff face seemed to rip itself apart, torn like shredded paper, obliterated behind the sundering of the air in front of it. Scarlet dawn light poured into the black hole that was left, filling it with shifting color and smoky shadows. Thunder boomed, shaking the earth and those who stared openmouthed from both the meadow and Sterling Silver's ramparts. The hiss of monsters mixed with a clash of armor and weapons. Everything rose to a shriek that sounded of things dying in terrible agony.

Questor went dry-mouthed. Demons! The black-cloaked stranger had summoned demons!

A fierce wind whipped across the meadow, flattening tents and standards and causing horses to rear in terror and men afoot to drop to their knees. Kallendbor had his broadsword out, holding it forth like a matchstick against a hurricane.

Demons emerged from the rent, their armor bristling with spikes and jagged edges, all blackened and charred as if burned in the hottest fire. Their bodies smoked as they leapt from the gap onto the meadow floor, steam leaking from their visors and the chinks where their armor was fastened by stays. They were lean and misshapen beings, all bent and twisted like trees on a windswept ridge stripped bare and turned as hard as iron. They rode beasts that had no name and lent themselves to no description, things out of nightmare and horrific fantasy, creatures out of shadowy netherworlds.

Out from the darkest recesses of Abaddon they came, spreading right and left about the solitary figure of the black-cloaked stranger, sweeping from lake to bluff rise and filling up every inch of ground in between until they covered the far end of the meadow. The dawn's blood hue settled over them so that they had the look of coals on which a bellows had been turned, the heat etched into the fissures and cracks of their black forms like fire burned into metal.

Questor Thews felt his heart move into his throat.

When the black-cloaked stranger turned to face him from across the lake, he knew that real trouble had arrived on his doorstep.

—◆◇◆—

"You ate the bird? You ate him?"

Abernathy stared in disbelief at Fillip and Sot, who stood crestfallen before him, the satisfied smiles slowly melting from their faces.

"He deserved it," Fillip mumbled defensively.

"Stupid bird," Sot muttered.

"But you didn't have to eat him!" Abernathy shouted, furious now. "Do you know what you've done? The bird was the only one who knew how to get us out of here! He was the only one who knew how to open the box! What are we supposed to do without him? We are trapped in this cave and the High Lord is trapped in the box and we cannot do anything about either!"

The G'home Gnomes looked at each other, wringing their hands pathetically.

"We forgot," Fillip whined.

"Yes, we forgot," Sot echoed.

"We didn't know," Fillip said.

"We didn't think," Sot said.

"Anyway, it was his idea," Fillip said, pointing to Sot.

"Yes, it was my . . ." Sot stopped short. "It was not! It was yours!"

"Yours!"

"Yours!"

They began shouting at and then pushing each other, and finally they rushed together kicking and biting and fell to the cave floor in a tangle. Abernathy rolled his eyes, moved over to one side, and sat down with the Tangle Box on his lap. Let them fight, he thought. Let them pull out their hair and choke on it, for all he cared. He sat back against the cave wall, pondering fate's cruel hand. To have come this close and be denied was almost too much to bear. He watched the G'home Gnomes battle across the cave floor and into the shadows. He still couldn't believe they had eaten the bird. Well, maybe he could. Actually, it made perfect sense, given who he was dealing with. For them, eating the bird was a natural response. He was mostly angry at himself, he guessed, for letting it happen. Not that he could have anticipated it, he supposed. But, still . . .

He ruminated on to no discernible purpose for a time, unable to help himself. The minutes slipped by. From back in the dark, the sounds of fighting stopped. Abernathy listened. Maybe they had eaten each other. Poetic justice, if they had.

But after a moment, they emerged, cut and scraped and disheveled, their heads downcast, their mouths set in a tight line. They sat down across from him wordlessly, staring at nothing. Abernathy stared back.

"Sorry," Fillip muttered after a moment.

"Sorry," Sot muttered.

Abernathy nodded. He couldn't bring himself to tell them that it was all right, because of course it wasn't, or that he forgave them, because of course he didn't. So he didn't say anything.

After a moment, Fillip said brightly to Sot, "Maybe there are still crystals hidden back in the cave!"

Sot looked up eagerly. "Yes, maybe there are! Let's look!"

And off they went, scurrying away into the darkness. Abernathy sighed and let them go. Maybe it would keep them out of further mischief. More time passed—Abernathy didn't know how much. He thought about using trial and error to figure out the rune sequence that would open the door, but there were dozens of markings about the door and he had no hope of finding the right combination. Still, what else could he do? He set down the Tangle Box and started to rise.

Just as he did, the locks on the cave door triggered, and it began to open.

Abernathy froze, then flattened himself against the wall to one side. The door swung slowly inward, grating and squealing as it went, letting in a faint twinge of reddish-gray light from the approaching dawn.

Abernathy caught his breath. What if it was the black-cloaked stranger? He closed his eyes involuntarily.

"Biggar?" a familiar voice called tentatively.

Horris Kew's plow-nosed face shoved into view as he waited for his eyes to adjust to the gloom. Abernathy stayed perfectly still, unable to believe his good fortune.

"Biggar?" the other called once more, and came inside the cave.

The stone door began to close behind him. Abernathy moved between the door and the conjurer, and said, "Hello, Horris."

When Horris turned, Abernathy leapt on him and bore him to the floor. Horris shrieked and tried to break free, struggling mightily. He was all bony arms and legs, and Abernathy couldn't hold him. Horris squirmed out from under his attacker, dragged himself to his feet, and reached for the door. Desperate to hold him, Abernathy fastened his teeth in the other's worn supplicant's robes and braced himself on all fours. Horris tried to pull free, but couldn't quite manage it. Abernathy growled. The two struggled back and forth in front of the door, neither able to gain an advantage.

Then Horris Kew caught sight of the Tangle Box, shrieked anew, tore himself free with a mighty rip, and snatched up the box. He was making for the door and safety, kicking out at Abernathy furiously, when Fillip and Sot charged out of the darkness and catapulted into him, knocking him from his feet and flat on his back where he lay gasping for breath.

Abernathy took back the Tangle Box, started to give it to Fillip, and thought better of the idea. Using his free hand, he hauled Horris Kew back to his feet and shook him so hard he could hear the other's teeth rattle.

"You listen to me, you troublesome fraud!" he hissed angrily. "You do exactly as I say or you will regret the day you were born!"

"Let me go!" Horris Kew pleaded. "None of this is my fault! I didn't know!"

"You never know!" Abernathy snapped. "That's your problem! What are you doing here, anyway?"

"I came looking for Biggar," Horris managed, swallowing his fear in great gulps of breath. "Where is he? What have you done with him?"

Abernathy waited for the other's breathing to slow a beat, then brought them nose-to-nose. "The Gnomes ate him, Horris," he said softly. Horris Kew's eyes went wide. "And if you do not do what I tell you, I am going to let them eat you as well. Do you understand me?"

Horris nodded at once, unable to speak.

Abernathy moved back a fraction of an inch. "You can start by opening the cave door and getting us out of here. And do not attempt any tricks. Do not try running. I shall have a good grip on you the entire time."

He propelled Horris back to the entrance, Fillip and Sot following close behind, and waited while the terrified conjurer worked the rune sequence and triggered a release of the locks. The door opened ponderously, and conjurer, scribe, and Gnomes stumbled back out into the light.

Abernathy swung Horris Kew back around to face him. "Despite what you think, this is indeed all your fault, Horris, everything that has happened, so I do not want to hear you say anything else. You have one chance to set things right, and I suggest you take it. I want the High Lord set free. I want High Lord Ben Holiday back in Landover. You put him in the box; now you get him out!"

Horris Kew swallowed, his Adam's apple bobbing, his cheeks and mouth making a sucking noise. He looked like a scarecrow left out in the field long after its usefulness has reached an end. He looked like he might collapse into a pile of straw. "I don't know if I can do that," he whispered.

Abernathy gave him the meanest look he could muster. "You had better hope you can," he replied softly.

"But what will they do to me once they're free? Holiday might understand, but what about the dragon and the witch?"

"You will have bigger worries if you do not set them free." Abernathy was in no mood to bargain. "Speak the words of the spell, Horris. Right now."

Horris Kew licked his lips, glanced down at the G'home Gnomes, and took a deep breath. "I'll try."

Abernathy, without releasing him, handed over the Tangle Box and moved around behind him. One hand clamped about the conjurer's skinny neck. "Remember, no tricks."

Dawn was a red glare through the shadowy mass of the forest about them as it chased the darkness slowly west. Abernathy did not like the look of it. Bad weather was moving in. He was already thinking about the trip back to Sterling Silver, about the siege, about Kallendbor and the black-cloaked stranger. He gave Horris Kew's neck a sharp squeeze. Horris began to speak.

"Rashun, oblight, surena! Larin, kestel, maneta! Ruhn!"

And the top of the Tangle Box disappeared instantly in a misty swirl of wicked green light.

Ben Holiday saw the crack appear in the blackness of the wall before him and turned toward it instantly. It glimmered as he raced for it, Nightshade and Strabo a step behind, then broadened as if the entire wall had been split apart. Fairy mist spun wildly, drawn to the brightness as if become a living thing. Ben flung himself into the breach, heedless of the consequences, knowing only that an opening of any kind offered a chance to get free. The light seemed to suck him up, to draw him into a vortex that twisted him about like a feather in a great wind. He was conscious of the witch and the dragon being drawn along with him, all three of them caught up in a whirlwind of motion. The gloom and the mist disappeared below him. The Labyrinth faded away. Above, the light took on a greenish glow, and there were shadows that swayed and rippled—tree branches and leaves, he realized—and sky, still dark with night's departure, and the smell of earth and moss and old growth, and the coppery taste of something like sulfur, and the sound of voices crying out . . .

And then he was spit out into the forest gloom of Landover, come back once more into the world from which he had been taken. He found himself standing less than a dozen feet from Abernathy, Horris Kew, and Fillip and Sot, all of whom stared at him wide-eyed and openmouthed.

Then Nightshade appeared as well, become herself once more, the power of her magic radiating off her body in small sparks and glimmerings. She flung her arms skyward, a spontaneous gesture, the white streak in her black hair gleaming like frost on coal, the cool edges of her sculpted face lifted toward the red glow of the dawn.

"Free!" she cried with joy.

Strabo exploded out of the Tangle Box behind her, returned to his dragon form, scaly black body uncoiling, wings unfolding, rising skyward with a huge burst of fire that rolled from his maw, hammered into the cave door, and then burned upward through the trees. Steaming and glistening, all spikes and edges, the dragon gave a huge, booming cough and rocketed away into the departing night.

"High Lord!" Abernathy exclaimed in greeting, the relief evident in his voice. He snatched back the Tangle Box from Horris Kew and hurried over. "Are you all right?"

Ben nodded, looking around, making certain that in fact he was. Fillip and Sot were making small squeaking sounds in his direction while cowering away from the black form of Nightshade. Horris Kew appeared to be looking for a place to hide.

Ben took a deep breath. "Abernathy, what is going on?"

The scribe drew himself up. "Well, actually, quite a lot, as it happens . . ."

A burst of acclaim from the G'home Gnomes cut him short.

"Great High Lord!"

"Mighty High Lord!"

Fillip and Sot were hugging each other and jumping up and down in glee, apparently convinced that it really was him after all. Ben gave them a tentative smile. What were *they* doing here?

Abernathy tried to continue, but Nightshade had spotted Horris Kew and was starting forward in a rush of black robes. "You!" she hissed in undisguised fury.

Ben stepped quickly between them. "Wait, Nightshade. I want to hear from Abernathy first."

"Get out of my way, play-King," the witch ordered venomously. "We are no longer in the Labyrinth and no longer subject to its rules. I have my magic back, and I can do as I please!"

But Ben held his ground, reached into his tunic, and brought forth the medallion. "We are both who we were. Do not test your strength against mine. I will hear from my scribe on what has been happening in our absence before I make a decision about Horris Kew."

Nightshade stood frozen in place, livid with fury. "Start talking, Abernathy," Ben advised quietly.

Abernathy did. He told the High Lord all about the Tangle Box and Horris Kew, the mind's eye crystals, the black-cloaked stranger, Kallendbor, and the siege of Sterling Silver. Ben listened without comment, his eyes fixed on Nightshade. When Abernathy was finished, Ben stepped back to stand beside Horris Kew. "Well?"

"My Lord, I have nothing to say in my defense." The conjurer seemed totally defeated. His tall, skinny frame was hunched over in submission. "The stranger is a fairy being come out of the Tangle Box—my fault, as well—a thing of great magic and evil called the Gorse. It plans revenge of some sort against the people of the fairy mists after it conquers Landover. I am sorry I did anything to help it, believe me." He paused, swallowing. "I would say in my behalf that I did help set you free."

"After you trapped us, of course," Ben pointed out. He looked at Nightshade. "I'll have to keep him with me for a time. I may have need of him in dealing with this fairy creature."

Nightshade shook her black-maned head. "Give him to me."

"He is not the real enemy, Nightshade. He never was. He was used as thoroughly as we were, if not as badly. Put aside your anger. Come with us to Sterling Silver and confront the Gorse. Your magic would be a great help. We worked together in the mists; we can do so again."

"I have no interest in your problems!" Nightshade snapped. "Solve them on your own!"

She stared at Ben challengingly. Ben took a deep breath. "I know that what happened in the mists, what passed between us . . ."

"Stop!" she shrieked with such fury that Fillip and Sot scattered into the trees and disappeared. She was white with rage. "Don't say a word! Don't say anything! I hate you, play-King! I hate you with every bone in my body! I live only to see you destroyed! What you did to me, what you pretended . . . !"

"There was no pretense . . ."

"No! You cannot speak to me!" Her cold, hard, beautiful face was a twisted mask. "Take the conjurer! I want nothing to do with either of you! But . . ."

Here she fixed Horris Kew with her gaze as a pin might a butterfly. "If I should ever see you again, if I should ever catch you alone . . ."

Her gaze shifted back to Ben. She gave him a withering glare. "I will hate you forever!" she whispered, the words a curse that hung in the following silence like razors waiting to cut.

Then she lifted her arms in a sweeping motion, brought smoke and mist about her in a rush, and disappeared into the dawn.

Ben stared after her, mixed emotions running through him as he considered the impact of her anger. It seemed strange that it should be like this after what they had shared—and at the same time inevitable. He wondered briefly if there was any way it might have been avoided and decided there was not.

"High Lord!" Abernathy cried urgently, and grabbed at his sleeve.

Ben turned.

A huge shadow fell over them, and Strabo descended once more out of the sky, snapping off branches and stirring up dust and debris as he settled his great bulk down upon the forest floor.

"Holiday," he rasped in friendly fashion. "We are not finished yet, you and I. Is this the one responsible for what was done to us?"

Ben shook his head. "No, Strabo. The one we want is back at Sterling Silver, engaged in further mischief."

The dragon's great horned head swung about, and the yellow eyes gleamed in the half light. "We started this journey together, though we did not choose to do so. Shall we end it together as well?"

Ben smiled in pleasant surprise. "I think we should," he agreed.

When they had gone from the clearing, Holiday, Abernathy, Horris Kew, and Strabo, the men flying off atop the dragon, and when enough time had passed that it was clear that Nightshade was gone as well, Fillip and Sot emerged from hiding. They crept out of the trees and stood peering about guardedly, ready to bolt at the slightest sound. But there was only silence and the faint, lingering smell of dragon fire where it had burned the trees.

"They are gone," Fillip said.

"Gone," Sot echoed.

They turned toward the cave, measuring the distance that separated them from its opening. The door stood ajar now, knocked off its hinges by Strabo's blast of fire, the locks smashed. Steam rose from its blackened surface in delicate tendrils.

"We could go inside now," Fillip said.

"Yes, we could look for crystals," Sot said.

"There might still be some," Fillip said.

"Even though we didn't find them before," Sot said.

"Hidden in a clever spot."

"Where we didn't think to look."

There was a long pause as they considered the prospect. The dawn's coloring had penetrated the forest gloom and was turning everything crimson. Birds had stopped singing. Insects had stopped chirping and buzzing. Nothing moved. The silence was oppressive.

"I think we should go home," Fillip said quietly.

"I think we should," Sot agreed.

So they did.

REDEMPTION

As he looked down from his perch atop Strabo, flying high above Landover, Ben Holiday found himself pondering on how quickly things could change. An hour earlier he had been imprisoned in the Tangle Box, as far removed from this world as the dead from the living. A day earlier, he had not even known who he was. He had believed himself to be the Knight, a King's Champion, a personification of the Paladin that was in fact his alter ego. Nightshade and Strabo had not existed; his companions had been the Lady and the Gargoyle, and they had been as lost to themselves as he was. Together they had formed an odd company, bereft of any real knowledge of their past, forced to begin life anew in a world about which they knew almost nothing. Thrown together by a common mishap, compelled to share a life filled with unknowns and false hope, they had reached an understanding during their travels that bordered on friendship.

More than friendship, he amended carefully, where Nightshade was concerned.

Now all of it was gone, stripped away with the recapture of their identities and return to Landover. It was as if they had been made over twice, once going into the Tangle Box, once coming out, stripped each time of life's knowledge and forced to learn anew, strangers first in an unknown world, familiars second in a world all too well known. It was the second that would allow no part of the first, the second that demanded that everything from the first be given up because it had all been acquired and nurtured under false pretenses. It made Ben sad. He had shared a closeness with Nightshade that would never be there again. There had been a mutual dependence that was ended forever. Things would be different with Strabo as well. He carried them now to Sterling Silver to settle accounts with the Gorse, but once that was finished he would be gone. Ben harbored no illusions. There would be no further talks as there had been between the Knight and the Gargoyle, no sharing of fears and hopes, no common effort to understand the workings of life. They would go their own ways as they had done before being lured into the Tangle Box, and the time they had spent together in the mists would fade as surely as a dream on waking.

Ben resisted the urge to look back at Horris Kew, who sat immediately behind him and ahead of Abernathy. The instrument of their misfortune, he thought darkly—yet too foolish and misguided to be held responsible. The Gorse was the real enemy. How was he going to deal with this creature? It had a formidable command of magic and would not hesitate to use it, especially once it discovered that Ben, Nightshade, and Strabo were set free again. Why had it imprisoned them in the first place? What sort of threat did they represent that compelled it to place them in the box? Or was it simply a matter of expediency and nothing more?

Whatever the answers to his questions, there was one chilling certainty. In order to deal with the Gorse, he would once again be forced to become the Paladin, the King's knight-errant, the creature he feared he was becoming in fact. His fear had made him see himself as the Knight within the Tangle Box, and he had barely survived what that had initiated—the destruction of the townsfolk, the River Gypsies, and very nearly the Gristlies. His fear of his dark half had worked to destroy him within the fairy mists, but he had escaped. Yet now he must become his dark half if he was to survive. And once again he must worry how much of the Paladin's identity he assumed and how much of Ben Holiday's he gave up with each transformation.

Ben watched the Heart pass away beneath him, white velvet rests outlined in pristine bars against verdant green grasses, the flags of Landover's Kings a swirl of bright color in the wind. A part of him was anxious for the change, eager for the transformation. It had always been so. It was this that frightened him most.

Horris Kew was thinking as well, and his thoughts were not pleasant ones either. A confrontation between the Gorse and Holiday was only moments away, and no matter who won he was in big trouble. Both would hold him responsible for anything the other had done or had tried to do or even had planned to do. Both would want to exact punishment of some sort. In the case of the Gorse, Horris did not want to consider too carefully what that punishment might be. Certainly it would not be pleasant. Holiday might be the better choice. He wished Biggar were there to consult. He found, oddly enough, that he missed the bird. They had shared a common attitude toward life's opportunities and misfortunes, and it was too bad the latter had caught up with Biggar a little earlier than either of them had expected. Horris felt keenly the loss. If nothing else, perhaps he could have blamed some of what had happened on the bird.

He sighed. Thinking like that led nowhere, of course. He shifted gears and tried to decide what he could do to salvage matters. He would have to do something quick. Already Sterling Silver's bright ramparts were coming into view. Take sides with Holiday then, he decided. His chances were better with Landover's King, a fellow human being, than they were with the Gorse. So what could he do to help himself? What could he do that would put him in a better light when it came time to determine his fate?

Ahead, the dawn was a crimson stain all across the horizon, a strange and terrifying sight. The red was so pronounced that it seemed to have seeped into the earth itself, to color grasses, trees, brush, rivers, lakes, roadways, fields, towns, farms, and the whole of every living thing for as far as the eye could see. Clouds were forming all about them. They hadn't been there the previous day; there had been no trace of them last night. They appeared as if by magic, masking the morning skies west to east, threatening to swallow the rising sun, the harbinger of a storm that was quickly approaching.

Strabo started down, a gradual descent out of the retreating night. The approaching sun momentarily blinded the dragon's passengers, and they squinted against its glare. The castle's polished battlements and towers gleamed redly, reflecting the strange light. The portcullis was down and the gates closed. The bridge running from the island to the mainland was shattered. Shadows clustered darkly across the meadow that fronted the castle gates, and the sluggish movement of armies massing was visible. Ben Holiday started. Battle lines were being drawn up between opposing forces. There were Greensward soldiers at one end of the meadow and Abaddon's demons at the other.

"High Lord!" Abernathy exclaimed in horror.

Ben glanced over his shoulder and nodded back. Demons from Abaddon—the Gorse must have brought them out to aid him in his plan. What had he promised them? What lure had he used? They would not have come if they thought the Paladin would be there to stop them; they had always been terrified of the Paladin. So the Gorse must have promised them that with the King gone from Landover, there would be no threat from his Champion. With Nightshade and Strabo dispatched as well, there was little to fear from anyone.

Ben's mouth tightened. Now he must face both the Gorse and Abaddon's demons. Even with Strabo to aid him, he did not much care for the odds.

"Strabo!" he called down to the dragon. A wicked yellow eye locked on him. "Take us down! Land right between them!"

The dragon hissed sharply, flattened out his approach, swept the battlefield once in a high, broad arc so that all could see him, and then settled slowly into the center of the meadow.

Ben, Horris Kew, and Abernathy scrambled down. It was like descending into a bizarre painting, a horrifically rendered version of Hell on Earth. The reddish dawn gave the whole of the grasslands a surreal look. Even the Bonnie Blues were turned to blood. Men, women, and children clustered at the edges of the trees and across the ridgeline north like the ghosts of the dead.

Ben turned toward the demons and exhaled slowly as he took in the size
of their army. Too many. Far too many.

"My Lord, I think that maybe I have——" Horris Kew began, and was cut
short as Abernathy's hand clamped tightly about the back of his neck.

Ben turned to his scribe, who still clutched the Tangle Box tightly beneath
his free arm. "Take the box and Horris and move to the lake," Ben ordered his
scribe. "Call for Questor to bring the lake skimmer and have him ferry you
both across. Hurry!"

Abernathy hastened away, dragging a protesting Horris Kew after. Ben
glanced at the demons anew. The Gorse had moved into the forefront of their
ranks, black-cloaked and featureless even in the strange light. Ben moved out
from the shadow of the dragon to face the demons. He reached into his tunic
and held forth the medallion of Landover's Kings. At his side, Strabo widened
his maw and coughed sharply, an explosive sound. There was movement all up
and down the clustered black ranks, an uneasiness, a hesitancy. It was one
thing to face a Lord of the Greensward and his army. It was something else
again to confront Holiday and Strabo as well.

"Kallendbor!" Ben called over his shoulder into the ranks of the
Greensward army.

Almost immediately there was the sound of a rider approaching from behind. Ben turned. Kallendbor, armored head to foot with only his face showing beneath his lifted visor, wheeled to a stop atop his charger.

"High Lord," he greeted, his red-bearded face pale, his eyes darting nervously to the dragon.

Ben stalked to meet him. "I know of your part in all this, Kallendbor," he
said curtly. "You will have to answer for it when this business is done."

Kallendbor nodded. There was no apology in his piercing blue eyes. "I'll
answer if I must and if we are both alive at the end of this day."

"Fair enough. For now, let's concentrate on finding a way to dispatch the
demons back to where they belong and the black-cloaked trickster with
them. Do your men stand ready to fight?"

"We are at your service, High Lord." There was no hesitation.

"Ride back then and wait for my signal," Ben ordered.

Kallendbor saluted and galloped away. Unrepentant to the last, Ben
thought. Some men refused to change.

He turned back toward the Gorse and the demons. A huge black rider had
moved out in front of the others. The Mark. The others would follow its lead
into battle. The demon leader stopped and stared across at Ben and Strabo.

The dragon's crusted head swung about. "Call up the Paladin, Holiday. The
demons grow edgy."

Ben nodded. He was resigned to what must happen now, but despaired of
it as well. Once again, he must summon the Paladin to do battle for him. Once
again, there would be killing and destruction, and much of it would come at

his hands. Another terrible battle, and he was powerless to stop it, helpless to do anything other than participate and hope that somehow he could find a way to shorten it. Faint hope, born of desperation and lack of choice. He felt Strabo's eyes watching him. The Gorse was responsible for this and should be brought to account, but how could that be done? How powerful was this fairy creature? Very, he guessed, if the fairy people had gone to such extremes to lock it away in the Tangle Box and keep it there.

"Holiday!" the dragon rasped impatiently.

Lock the Gorse back into the Tangle Box—that was what he should do. Lock it away for good. But how? What magic would it take?

There was no time to wonder about it further, no time to decide what help could be found. The demons had begun to advance, coming across the meadow in a dark mass, slowly, deliberately, inexorably.

"Holiday!" Strabo hissed furiously.

Paladin's sword and dragon's fire—would they be enough to save Land-over?

Ben Holiday reached for the medallion that would give him his answer.

Horris Kew was practically beside himself with frustration. He stood glumly next to Abernathy at the water's edge, watching the approach of Questor Thews in the lake skimmer, thinking that his last chance to save himself was about to be taken away.

He had tried to tell Holiday, but Landover's King did not have time for him. He had tried to tell Abernathy, but the scribe had heard all he wanted to hear. He considered telling Questor Thews when the wizard arrived to convey them back across to the comparative safety of the castle fortress, but he was reasonably certain that he would find no help from that quarter either. No one wanted to listen to Horris and that was the hard truth of the matter.

Except that for once Horris had something important to say.

He shuffled his size-sixteens, hugged himself like a rag doll, and tried to remain calm. But it was hard to stay calm knowing what was going to become of him if the Gorse and the demons prevailed over Holiday. If Holiday won, his circumstances would still be precarious, but acceptable. If Holiday won, he had a reasonable chance of staying alive. But if the Gorse came out of this the victor, Horris Kew was stew meat. It didn't pay to dwell on exactly what recipe would be used, but the result would be the same. The Gorse had seen him standing with Holiday and the dragon; it had seen him quite plainly. The inference was obvious. Horris had joined the enemy. There could be no forgiveness. No excuses would be allowed. The Gorse would grind him up and spit him out, and that would be that.

Horris recalled how the creature had made him feel when they first

started out together in this hateful venture. He remembered the silky, dangerous voice and the lingering smell of death. He could still feel its power threatening to strangle him with invisible fingers. He did not relish experiencing
any of it again. The tic was gone from his eye for the first time since he had set
the Gorse free. Here was his chance to keep it from coming back.

Thunder rolled out of the west, building on itself where the clouds
massed. The heavy bank was spreading rapidly toward the sun, swallowing up
its light as it came, turning everything black. Wind whipped across the
meadow and over the confronting armies. Horses shied, and armor and
weapons clanged. The air began to smell of rain.

Horris had been thinking about the Tangle Box. How had the Gorse been
put into it in the first place? Surely the renegade fairy had not gone willingly—
no more so than Holiday, the witch, and the dragon. Twice now, Horris had
been called upon to speak words of power that released captives of the box.

Could the spell be reversed?

He thought about the way that Holiday and the others had been dispatched. The Gorse had constructed an elaborate net of magic upon the spot
to which his three victims had been lured. Then Horris had appeared with the
Tangle Box, spoken the words of power, triggered the net, and the trap had
been sprung.

Simple enough. It would seem at first glance then that a similar approach
would be necessary to snare the Gorse. Except that something was nagging at
Horris Kew. Wasn't the Tangle Box constructed for that particular purpose? If
so, then the entrapment of Holiday and the other two was an unnatural use of
the box, an aberration of that for which it was intended. Besides, if the Gorse
knew this was how the magic worked, how had it allowed itself to be trapped
in the first place? And if it didn't know then, how had it learned since?

And what about this? The Gorse had known the words that would free it,
but couldn't speak them. It had been necessary to manipulate Biggar through
the Skat Mandu charade to have Horris speak the words instead. Didn't this
suggest something? Didn't this mean that the Gorse found the words anathema for some reason and so required that another use them?

Didn't it mean, Horris wondered, that the same spell—the spell that the
Gorse was so careful to avoid using himself—might work both ways?

The more he considered the possibility, the more sense it made. The
fairies, having built the Tangle Box, would have employed a special, cus-
tomized magic to trap the Gorse within, a magic that it could never use to effect its own escape. And it would not be a magic that would trap away
others—like Holiday, Nightshade, and Strabo—so that, to subvert the purpose of the box, something different would be required to ensnare them. And
perhaps, in the bargain, to protect the Gorse from being recaptured. Hence
the carefully conceived net of magic the Gorse had employed.

Sure, it was a stretch. But Horris Kew was desperate and his conjurer's op-
portunistic mind was grasping at straws because that was all that was left him.

They should listen to him, he believed. Holiday, Abernathy, Questor
Thews, all of them. They should try his suggestion out. What harm could it do
at this point? But he might as well be asking to be made King. No one was
going to try any idea he suggested.

Thunder rolled once more, a long, booming peal that shook the ground on
which he stood. In the meadow's center, Kallendbor had ridden back to his
army and Holiday was turning toward the Gorse and the demons. The Mark
had moved to the forefront of his horde and was beginning a slow advance.
The dragon had lifted itself into a crouch and was venting steam through its
nostrils as the fire built in its belly. Horris glanced over his shoulder. Questor
Thews was almost ashore. Abernathy had turned to meet the wizard, his back
momentarily to Horris.

Biggar had always accused him of indecision. He hated to think that the
bird had been right.

Horris Kew swallowed, his throat dry. Now or never, wasn't it? He
glanced again at Holiday. Landover's King had removed the medallion of his
office from within his dark tunic and was holding it up to the light.

Do it!

Horris yanked the Tangle Box out from under Abernathy's arm, then lowered his shoulder and knocked the astonished scribe backward into the lake.
Then he ran as fast as his long legs could carry him toward the Gorse. He was
thinking he had gone mad, he was a fool, he had just made the worst mistake
of his life. Shouts rose up as he was sighted. Angry cries assailed him from
every side. Out of the corner of his eye, he saw the dragon's black-horned
head swing quickly about, and he envisioned himself encased in fire. A moment more, he thought. One moment more.

The Gorse had not moved. It was watching him come, thinking he was
bringing the Tangle Box back again, an unwitting pawn to the end. The
demons shifted like shadows in the enfolding black of the storm. Weapons
glinted darkly. Horris Kew tried not to think about them. His gangly body was
shaking, and his scarecrow limbs were flying out all over the place. He was
sweating and gasping from the strain of his flight. He had never been so terrified.

He heard Questor Thews shout his name. A bolt of ragged fire zipped past
his ear. He dropped to one knee in a panic and set the Tangle Box on the
ground before him. He looked across the meadow at the Gorse, and he could
see in its terrible eyes that it recognized the truth at last. The monster's black
cloak billowed as it charged toward him in rage.

Quickly, Horris began to chant.

"Rashun, oblight, surena! Larin, kestel . . ."

---◦∞◦---

Ben Holiday stood frozen in place, the medallion still clutched in his hand, momentarily forgotten. He had not seen Horris Kew until just a moment ago. Questor Thews was pulling Abernathy from the lake, both of them shouting angrily and gesturing. Strabo was uncoiling his huge, dark length, spreading his wings, and preparing to lift off. Fire leaked from between his jagged teeth.

All of them too late to intercede, Ben thought in frustration and despair.

Mist blossomed in a dark cloud from the Tangle Box, the lid disappeared, and the tunnel back down into the Labyrinth opened anew. Wicked green light shot forth to mingle with the red glare of the sun and the dark of the approaching storm. Thunder boomed, and a scattering of raindrops began to fall. The meadow had gone suddenly still, the clamor of the opposing armies disappearing into a hush of expectancy.

Out from the Tangle Box appeared a swarm of shadows, misty forms that twisted and writhed in the strange mix of light, dark specters set free. They rose in a cluster and then shot across the meadow toward the demons. The Gorse cried out, a terrible wail of despair. Webs of protective magic spun from its hands, encircling its black form to ward off its attackers. The shadows went right through the webs, seized the Gorse, and dragged it into the open. The Gorse thrashed and tore futilely. It spit like a cat. It fought with every ounce of strength and every weapon of magic it possessed. But the shadows were relentless. They hauled the renegade fairy back across the meadow to the box. They wrapped it about with their cloaking forms and pulled it down.

Down into the prison it thought it had escaped forever.

Down into the frightening darkness of the fairy mists.

They disappeared inside, the shadows and the Gorse, and the lid to the Tangle Box closed for good.

The wind broke loose across the meadow in a howl. Airborne, Strabo passed over the box and Horris Kew like death's shadow, but then flew on to descend instead upon the demons of Abaddon, breathing its fire into their midst. Dozens disintegrated. The rest, bereft of the promised protection of the Gorse and its magic, had no interest in a fight. Led by their Mark, they turned back toward the bluff out of which they had come, back into the rent in the air that had given them passage into Landover, and descended down again into their netherworld home. In seconds, the last of them had gone, and the space they had briefly occupied in the world of light stood empty.

Strabo swung back toward the army of the Greensward, hissing in triumph and challenge.

Standing at the center of the meadow still, the rain falling into his face in sheets, the wind ripping at his frozen body, Ben Holiday exhaled slowly and slipped the medallion of the Kings of Landover back inside his tunic.

GREEN EYES

Willow came awake in the faint, gray dawn light, the dampness of the Deep Fell seeping through her naked body. She was lying on the ground, curled into a ball, the baby resting in the crook of her arm. At first she wasn't aware of it. She blinked against the sleep that still clouded her mind, trying to remember where she was. Then she felt the baby move and looked down at it.

Her child.

She studied it for a long time, and tears came to her eyes.

She remembered everything then—coming out of the fairy mists into the Deep Fell, transforming into her other self, forming the pod, drifting into sleep. She cradled the child to her, giving it what warmth she could, lending it the small shelter of her body.

Then she rose, slipped back into her clothes, and wrapped the baby in her cloak. It was sleeping still, not yet hungry enough to wake, not disturbed by its surroundings as Willow was. The Deep Fell had not been her choice for where the baby should be born, and she did not intend to remain there any longer than necessary. Mist rolled through the branches of the jungle trees and snaked down along the trunks. Silence blanketed everything. Nothing moved. It was a dead world, and only the witch who had made it so belonged here.

Willow began to walk, moving toward the light—east, where the sun rose over Landover. She must get clear quickly, before she was discovered. She was weak still from giving birth, but mostly she was fearful. She was not so frightened for herself as she was for her child, the measure of her life with Ben, the culmination of their bonding. She peeked down at it again through the folds of the cloak, making certain she had seen it right on waking, that nothing had changed. The tears came anew. There was a tightness in her throat. She wanted to find and be with Ben, to make certain he was all right, and to let him see their child.

She walked for what seemed a long time, but probably was not. Her body ached in strange ways—a dull, empty pain in her loins, a constriction in her chest, a soreness that laced the muscles of her arms and legs. She did not know how much to attribute to the birth and how much to sleeping naked in the chill of the Fell. Movement helped ease the pain in her arms and chest, loosening muscles that were cramped and tight. The pain within her loins persisted. She ignored it. She could not be too far from the wall of the hollow, she told herself. If she just kept moving, she would get free.

She came out of a stretch of old growth laced with mist and gloom, entered a clearing, and stopped. Nightshade stood before her, wrapped in her black cloak, drawn up as straight and immutable as a stone statue, her red eyes gleaming.

"What are you doing here, sylph?" she demanded softly.

Willow's heart sank. Having been forced to give birth to her child in this forbidding place, she had wanted only to escape without encountering the witch, and it seemed she was to be denied even this.

She managed to keep the fear from her voice as she answered. "I entered through the fairy mists and by mistake. I want no trouble. I want only to depart."

Nightshade seemed surprised. "Through the fairy mists? Have you been imprisoned, too? But, no. You were elsewhere in his dream, weren't you?" She stopped talking, collecting herself. "Why would you come out here? Why would you come out at all, for that matter? The fairies release no one from the mists."

Willow gave a moment's thought to lying, but decided against it. The witch would know, her magic strong enough here in her lair to detect another's deception.

"The fairies were forced to release me when the High Lord came to me in his dreams and set me free of their magic. They released me from the mists. They did not tell me where I would come out. Perhaps they sent me here as punishment."

Nightshade's gaze lowered to the bundle she cradled in her arms. "What is that you carry?"

Willow's arms tightened about the baby. "My child by the High Lord, newly born."

Nightshade took a quick, harsh breath. "The play-King's child? Here?" She laughed. "Fortune does indeed play strange games with us. Why do you carry the child about so? Did you carry it into the mists as well?" She stopped abruptly. "Wait, I have heard nothing of this child. I have not been gone that long from Landover. I should know of this. Newly born, you say? Born where, then?"

"Here," Willow answered softly.

Nightshade's face twisted into something grotesque. "Born here, in my home? Holiday's child? While I was locked in the fairy mists with him, trapped in that cursed box? Trapped with him, girl—did you know? Together for weeks, drained of memory, made over into creatures we did not even recognize. He came to you in a dream? Yes, he told me so. It was the dream that released him from his ignorance, that led him to divulge the truth about both of us."

Her voice was a hiss. "Have you seen him since his return?" She smiled at Willow's reaction. "Ah, you didn't know he was back, then, did you? Back from his other life, a life with me, little sylph, in which I was his charge and he my protector. Do you know what happened between us while you were carrying his child?"

She paused, her eyes gleaming with expectation. "He bed me as if I were his—"

"No!" Willow's voice was as hard as iron, the single word a forbidding that cut short the witch as surely as a cord about the throat.

"He was mine!" the witch of the Deep Fell screamed. "He belonged to me! I should have had him forever if not for his dream of you! I lost everything, everything but who I am, the power of my magic, the strength of my will! Those I have regained! Holiday owes me! He has stripped me of my pride and my dignity, and he has incurred a debt to me that he must pay!"

She was white with rage. "The child," she whispered, "will satisfy that debt nicely."

Willow went cold. She was shaking, her throat dry, her heart stopped. "You cannot have my child," she said.

A smile played across Nightshade's lips. "Cannot? What a silly word for you to use, little sylph. Besides, the child was born in my domain, here in the Deep Fell, so it belongs to me by right of law. My law."

"No law condones the taking of a child from its mother. You have no right to make such a claim."

"I have every right. I am mistress of the Deep Fell and ruler over all found here. The child was born on my soil. You are a trespasser and a foolish girl. Do not think you can deny me."

Willow held her ground. "If you try to take my child, you will have to kill me. Are you prepared to do that?"

Nightshade shook her head slowly. "I need not kill you. There are easier ways when you have the use of magic. And worse fates for you than death if you defy me."

"The High Lord will come after you if you steal his child!" Willow snapped. "He will hunt you to the ends of the earth!"

"Silly little sylph," the witch purred softly. "The High Lord will never know you were even here."

Willow froze. Nightshade was right. There was no one who knew she was in the Deep Fell, no one who knew she had returned from the fairy mists. If she was to disappear, who could trace her footsteps? If her child was to vanish, who could say it had ever existed? The fairies, perhaps, but would they do so?

What was she to do?

"Someone will discover and reveal the truth, Nightshade," she insisted desperately. "You cannot keep such a thing a secret forever! Not even you can do that!"

The witch gave a slow, disdainful shrug. "Perhaps not. But I can keep it a secret long enough. Holiday's life is finite. In the end, I will be here when he is gone."

Willow nodded slowly, understanding flooding through her. "Which is why you want his child, isn't it? So that he will leave nothing of himself behind when he is dead. You would make the child yours and wipe away all trace of him in doing so. You hate him that much, don't you?"

Nightshade's thin mouth tightened. "More. Much, much more."

"But the child is innocent," Willow cried. "Why should the baby be made a pawn in this struggle? Why should it suffer for your rage?"

"The child will fare well. I will see to it."

"It isn't yours!"

"I grow tired of arguing, sylph. Give the child to me and perhaps I will let you go. Make another child, if you wish. You have the means."

Willow shook her head slowly. "I will never give up my baby, Nightshade. Not to you, not to anyone. Stand aside for me. Let me pass."

Nightshade smiled darkly. "I think not," she said.

She was starting forward, arms lifting within her black robes, intent on taking the child by force, when a familiar voice spoke.

"Do as she asks, Nightshade. Let her pass."

The witch stopped, as still as death. Willow looked around quickly, seeing nothing but the trees and misty gloom.

Then Edgewood Dirk stepped into view from one side, easing sinuously through the heavy brush, silver coat immaculate, black tail twitching slightly. He jumped up on the remains of a fallen tree and blinked sleepily.

"Let her pass," he repeated softly.

Nightshade stiffened. "Edgewood Dirk. Who gave you permission to come into the Deep Fell? Who gave you the right?"

"Cats need no permission or grant of right," Dirk replied. "Really, you should know better. Cats go where they wish—always have."

Nightshade was livid. "Get out of here!"

Dirk yawned and stretched. "Shortly. But first you must let the Queen pass."

"I will not give up . . . . !"

"Save your breath, Witch of the Deep Fell." A hint of weary disdain crept into the cat's voice. "The Queen and her baby will pass into Landover. The

fairies have decided, and there is nothing more to say about it. If you are unhappy with their decision, why don't you take it up with them?"

Nightshade shot a withering look at Willow, then turned to face the cat.
"The fairies cannot tell me what to do!"

"Of course they can," Edgewood Dirk said reasonably. "I have just done so
for them. Stop fussing about this. The matter is settled. Now step aside."

"The child is mine!"

Dirk gave one paw a short, swift lick and straightened. "Nightshade," he
addressed her softly. "Would you challenge me?"

There was a long pause as witch and prism cat faced each other in the half
light of the Deep Fell. "Because if you would," Dirk continued, "you must
surely know that even if I fail, another will be sent to take my place, and another, and so forth. Fairies are very stubborn creatures. You, of all people,
should know."

Nightshade did not move. When she spoke, there was astonishment in her
voice. "Why are they doing this? Why do they care so about his child?"

Edgewood Dirk blinked. "That," he purred softly, "is a good question." He
rose, stretched, and sat back down again. "I grow anxious for my morning
nap. I have given this matter enough of my time. Let the Queen and the child
pass. Now."

Nightshade shook her head slowly, a denial of something she could not ar-
ticulate. For an instant Willow was certain that she intended to lash out at
Dirk, that she would fight the prism cat with every ounce of strength and
every bit of magic she possessed.

But instead she turned to Willow and said softly, "I will never forgive this.
Never. Tell the play-King."

Then she disappeared into the gloom, a wraith simply fading away into the
shadows. The baby woke, stirring in its mother's arms, blinking sleepily. Willow glanced down into the cloak's deep folds. She cooed softly to her child.
When she looked up again, Edgewood Dirk was gone as well. Had he been
with her all the way? The fairies had sent him once again, it appeared, although
with the prism cat you could never be entirely certain. He had saved her life
in any case. Or more to the point, saved her child. Why? Nightshade's question, still unanswered. What was it about this child that mattered so to everyone?

Cradling the baby in her arms, she began to walk on once again.

—◦◦◦—

It was nearing midmorning by the time Ben Holiday reached the country just
south of the Deep Fell. He would never have gotten there that fast if Strabo
had not offered to trade him a ride for possession of the Tangle Box. The
dragon had wanted the box from the first, but Ben had refused to give it up,
not convinced that it should be in anyone's possession but his own.

"Let me have it, Holiday," the dragon had argued. "I will keep it in a place no one can reach, in a fire pit deep within the Wastelands where no one goes."

"But why would you want it at all?" Ben asked. "What would you do with it?"

The dragon had flown back from his assault on the demons. They were alone in the center of the meadow. Horris Kew slumped on the ground some yards away. Questor Thews and Abernathy had not yet reached them.

The dragon's voice was wistful. "I would take it out and look at it from time to time. A dragon covets treasures and hoards precious things. It is all we have left from our old life—all I have left, now that I am alone." Strabo's horned head dipped close. "I would keep it hidden where it could never be found. I would keep it just for me."

Ben had interrupted the conversation long enough to intervene between a sodden, angry Abernathy, who had just come rushing up, and a terrified Horris Kew, and assisted by Questor Thews had restored some small measure of peace between them. The conjurer had saved their lives, after all, he reminded his much-distressed scribe. He went on then to dismiss Kallendbor and his army, exacting an oath from the Lord of Rhyndweir to appear before him in one week's time for an accounting of his actions. He ordered his Guard to disperse those people who had come looking for mind's eye crystals and found a great deal more than they had bargained for, back to wherever it was they had come from.

Then he remembered Willow. He went immediately to the Landsview and found her just as she was climbing free of the Deep Fell. Nightshade's domain, he thought in horror, and no place for the sylph. He was thinking of Nightshade's parting words to him. He was thinking what the witch might do to Willow if she were given half a chance.

It was a two-day ride to the Deep Fell—far too long under the circumstances. So he struck a bargain with Strabo. A ride to the Deep Fell and back in exchange for the Tangle Box, if the dragon promised that no one else would ever set eyes on it and no one, including the dragon, would ever attempt to open it. Strabo agreed. He extended his firm and unbreakable promise. He gave his dragon's oath. It was enough, Questor Thews whispered in a short aside. A dragon's word was his bond.

So off Ben went aboard Strabo, winging through the storm winds and rain, finally passing out of black clouds and into blue skies. The sun shone anew on the land, spilling golden light across the grasslands and hills running north, cutting a swath of brightness through the fading dark.

"She is there, Holiday," the dragon called back when they grew close, its sharp eyes finding the sylph much quicker than Ben's.

They swooped down onto the crest of a hill, a scattering of woods running right and left. Willow appeared from across a meadow of wildflowers and

Bonnie Blues, and Ben ran to meet her, heedless of everything else. She called to him, her face radiant, tears coming into her eyes once more.

He raced up to her and abruptly stopped, the bundle in her arms a fragile barrier between them. What was she carrying? "Are you all right?" he asked, anxious to be reassured that she was well, eager just to hear her voice.

"Yes, Ben," she answered. "And you?"

He nodded, smiling. "I love you, Willow," he said.

He could see her throat constrict. "Come see our child," she whispered.

He came forward a step, closing the small distance between them, expectation and disbelief racing through him. It was too quick, he thought. It was not yet time. She had not even looked pregnant. How could she have given birth so fast?

The questions vanished in the afterglow of her smile. "The baby?" he said, and she nodded.

She parted the folds of her cloak so he could see. He bent down and peered inside.

A pair of dazzling green eyes stared boldly back.

BESTSELLER

The interviewer sipped a pineapple-strawberry smoothie in the living room of Harold Kraft's palatial Diamond Head home and looked out across the vast expanse of lanai and swimming pool to the only slightly vaster expanse of the Pacific Ocean. It was late afternoon, and the sun was easing westward toward the flat line of the horizon, the gradual change in the light promising yet another incredibly beautiful Hawaiian sunset. The granite floors of the living room and lanai glittered as if inlaid with flecks of gold, the stone ending at the pool, one of those knife-edge affairs that dropped into a spillover as if falling all the way to the ocean. A Jacuzzi bubbled invitingly at one end of the lanai. A bar and cooking area dominated the other end, complete with hollow coconut shells used for tropical drinks at the frequent parties the author gave.

The home was conservatively valued at fifteen million, although the price of real estate is always subject to what the market will bear and its measure is not an objective exercise. Homes around it had sold for ten million and up and lacked both the extensive grounds and the unrestricted view that took in most of Honolulu. Bare land went for five million in this neighborhood. The numbers were unimaginable for most people. The interviewer lived in Seattle in a home he had bought fifteen years ago for somewhat less than what Harold Kraft earned in a month.

Kraft wandered in from his study where he had gone to answer a private phone call, leaving the interviewer to sip his perfectly mixed drink and admire the view. He strolled over to the bar with a brief apology for taking so long, fixed himself an iced tea, crossed the room to the couch where the interviewer was patiently waiting, and sat down again. He was tall and slender with graying hair and a Vandyke beard, and he moved like a long, slow, elegant cat. He wore silk slacks and shirt and hand-tooled leather sandals. His tanned face was aquiline, and his sandy eyes were penetrating. There were rumors of reconstructive surgery and a rigorous training regimen, but that was fairly commonplace with the rich and famous.

"Good news," he announced with a smile. "Since you're here, I can share it with you. Paramount just bought rights to *Wizard*. Two million dollars outright. They want Sean Connery for the title role, Tom Cruise for the part of the Prince. What do you think?"

The interviewer smiled appreciatively. "I think you're two million dollars richer. Congratulations."

Kraft gave him a short bow. "Wait until the merchandising kicks in. That's where the real money is."

"Do you write your books with an eye toward movie sales?" the interviewer pressed. He wasn't getting nearly enough out of Kraft to satisfy either himself or his magazine. Kraft had published three books in two years and dominated the bestseller lists for most of that time, selling more than five million copies in hardcover. But that was practically all anyone knew about him. For all his notoriety and success, he was still very much a mystery. He claimed to be in exile, but he wouldn't say from where. He claimed to be a political refugee.

"I write to be read," the author replied pointedly. "What happens after that is up to the consumer. Sure, I want to make money. But mostly I want to be happy."

The interviewer frowned. "That sounds a bit . . ."

"Disingenuous? I suppose it does. But I've done a lot of things and been a lot of places, and I don't have much to show for any of it. What I have is myself, and my writing is an extension of myself. It is very hard to separate the two, you know. A writer doesn't just punch a clock and go home at the end of the day. He carries his work around with him, always thinking about it, always polishing it up like the family silver. If you're not satisfied with it, you have to live with your dissatisfaction. That's why I want to be happy about what I do. More important to be happy than to be rich."

"Doesn't hurt to be both," the interviewer pointed out. "You've had an amazing string of successes. Do you ever think about what it was like before you were published?"

Kraft smiled. "All the time. But I sense an attempt at an end run. I have to remind you that try though you might, you won't get me to talk about my earlier life. Ground rules for this interview, right?"

"So you've said, but my readers are quite curious about you. You must know that."

"I do. I appreciate the interest."

"But you still won't discuss anything about yourself before you were published?"

"I made a promise not to."

"A promise to whom?"

"A promise to some people. That's all I intend to say."

"Then let's discuss your characters and try coming into your life through the back door, so to speak." The interviewer harbored hopes of publishing a book himself one day. He fancied himself very clever with words. "Are they based on real people from your old life? For instance, the misguided King of your magic land, his inept court wizard, and the snappish dog who serves as his scribe?"

Kraft nodded slowly. "Yes, they exist."

"How about your protagonist, the renegade wizard who saves the day in each book? Is there some of you in him?"

Kraft cleared his throat modestly. "A bit."

The interviewer paused, sensing he was finally getting somewhere. "Have you ever dabbled in magic? You know, played at conjuring spells and the like? Has that been a part of your life?"

Harold Kraft was lost in thought for a moment. When he came back from wherever he had been, his face turned serious. "I'll tell you what," he said. "I'm going to make an exception to my rule of never talking about my past and tell you something. There was a time when I did play about with magic. Small stuff, really—nothing serious. Except that once I did stumble quite inadvertently on something that turned out to be very dangerous indeed. My own life as well as those of others was threatened. I survived that scare, but I made a promise to certain people that I would never use . . . that is, dabble, in magic again. I never have."

"So the magic in your books, the conjuring and the invocations of spells and the like, has some basis in real life?"

"Some, yes."

"And the tales you weave, those spellbinding stories of monsters and elves, of mythical creatures and wizards like your protagonist—do these have a basis in real life as well?"

Kraft slowly raised and then lowered one eyebrow. "A writer writes what he knows. Life experience enters in. It usually takes a different form than the reality, but it is always there."

The interviewer nodded solemnly. Had he learned anything from this exchange? He wasn't sure. It was all rather vague. Like Harold Kraft. He covered his confusion by checking the tiny tape recorder sitting on the coffee table. Still spinning. "Would it be fair to say that the adventures you write about in some way mirror your own life?" he tried again.

"It would be both fair and accurate, yes."

"How?"

Kraft smiled. "You must use your imagination."

The interviewer smiled back, trying not to grit his teeth. "Do you have other stories left to tell, Mr. Kraft?"

"Harold, please," the author insisted with a quick wave of his hand. "Three hours together in the journalistic trenches entitles us to conclude our conversation on a first-name basis. And to answer your question, yes. I have other stories to tell and some time left to tell them, I hope. I'm working on one now. *Raptor's Spell* is the title. Would you like to see the cover?"

"Very much."

They rose and walked from the living room down a short hall to the study, which served primarily as Kraft's office. Word processors and printers sat at various desks, and books and paper were piled all over the place. Framed book covers hung on the walls. A koa-wood desk dominated the center of the room. From the stacks of writing on the top of this desk, Kraft produced a colored photo and handed it over to the interviewer.

The photo showed a bird that was all black save for a crown of white feathers. The bird was in the act of swooping down on a malevolent being that resembled a mass of thistles. Lightning streaked from the bird's extended claws. Dark things fled into a woods at the bird's approach.

The interviewer studied the photo for a moment. "Very dramatic. Is the bird representative of someone from your earlier life?"

Horris Kew, who now called himself Harold Kraft, nodded solemnly. "Alas, poor Biggar, I knew him well," he intoned with a dramatic flourish.

And gave the photo a nostalgic kiss.

WITCHES' BREW

To Lisa.
For always being there.
&
To Jill.
Because you must never give up
on yourself.

All children, except one, grow up. They soon know that they will grow up, and the way Wendy knew was this. One day when she was two years old she was playing in a garden, and she plucked another flower and ran with it to her mother. I suppose she must have looked rather delightful, for Mrs. Darling put her hand to her heart and cried, "Oh, why can't you remain like this for ever!" This was all that passed between them on the subject, but henceforth Wendy knew that she must grow up. You always know after you are two. Two is the beginning of the end.

—J. M. Barrie, *Peter Pan*

CONTENTS

—⁂—

MISTAYA

The crow with the red eyes sat on a branch in the towering old white oak where the leafy boughs were thickest and stared down at the people gathered for their picnic in the sunny clearing below. That was what Holiday called it, a picnic. A brightly colored cloth was spread out on the lush spring grass, and the contents of several baskets of food were being emptied onto it. The food, if you were human and possessed of an appetite, would have pleased and delighted, the crow supposed. There were platters of meats and cheeses, bowls of salad and fruit, loaves of bread, and flasks of ale and chilled water. There were plates and napkins set around for each participant and cups for drinking and utensils for eating. A vase of wildflowers had been placed at the center of the feast.

Willow was doing most of the work, the sylph with the emerald tresses and small, lithe form. She was animated, laughing and talking with the others as she worked. The dog and the kobold helped her: Abernathy, who was Landover's Court Scribe, and Parsnip, who did most of the castle's cooking. Questor Thews, the ragtag white-bearded wizard, wandered about looking in amazement at sprigs of new growth and strange wildflowers. Bunion, the other kobold, the dangerous one, the one who could spy out almost anything, patrolled the clearing's perimeter, ever watchful.

The King sat alone at one end of the bright cloth. Ben Holiday, High Lord of Landover. He was staring out into the trees, lost in thought. The picnic was his invention, something they did in the world from which he came. He was introducing it to the others, giving them a new experience. They seemed to be enjoying it more than he was.

The crow with the red eyes sat perfectly still within the concealment of the branches of the old oak, cognizant of the adults but really interested only in the child. Other birds, some more dazzling in their plumage, some more sweet with their song, darted through the surrounding woods, flitting from here to there and back again, mindless and carefree. They were bold and heedless; the crow was purposefully invisible. No eye but the child's would be cast; no attention but the child's would be drawn. The crow had been waiting more than an hour for the child to notice it, for its unspoken summons to be heeded, for its silent command to be obeyed, and for the brilliant green eyes to be drawn upward into the leafy shadows. The child was walking about, playing at this and that, seemingly aimless but already searching.

Patience, then, the crow with the red eyes admonished. As with so much in life, patience.

Then the child was directly below, the small face lifting, the dazzling green eyes seeking and abruptly finding. The child's eyes locked on the crow's, emerald to crimson, human to bird. Words passed between them that did not need speaking, a silent exchange of thoughts on being and having, on want and loss, on the power of knowledge and the inexorable need to grow. The child stood as still as stone, staring up, and knew there was something vast and wondrous to be learned if the proper teacher could be found.

The crow with the red eyes intended to be that teacher.

The crow was the witch Nightshade.

Ben Holiday leaned back on his elbows and let the smells of the picnic lunch bring a growl to his empty stomach. Breakfast had been hours ago, and he had been careful to refrain from eating anything since. Thank goodness the wait was almost over. Willow was unpacking the containers and setting them out, aided by Abernathy and Parsnip. Soon it would be time to eat. It was a perfect summer day for a picnic, the sky clear and blue, the sun warming the earth and the new grasses, chasing memories of winter's chill into the past once more. Flowers were blooming, and leaves were thick again in the trees. The days were stretching out farther as midsummer neared, and Landover's colored moons were chasing each other for increasingly shorter periods of time across the darkened heavens.

Willow caught his eye and smiled at him, and he was instantly in love with her all over again, as if it were the first time. As if they were meeting in the midnight waters of the Irrylyn and she was telling him how they were meant for each other.

"You might lend a hand, wizard," Abernathy snapped at Questor Thews, interrupting Ben's thoughts, obviously peeved that the other was doing none of the work in setting out the lunch.

"Hmmm?" Questor looked up from a strange purple and yellow wildflower, oblivious. The wizard always looked as if he were oblivious, whether in fact he was or not.

"Lend a hand!" Abernathy repeated sharply. "Those who don't do the work don't eat the food—isn't that how the fable goes?"

"Well, no need to get huffy about it!" Questor Thews abandoned his study for the more pressing need of appeasing his friend. "Here, that's not the way to do that! Let me show you."

They went back and forth for a few more moments, then Willow intervened, and they settled down. Ben shook his head. How many years now had they been going at each other like that? Ever since the wizard had changed the scribe into a dog? Even before? Ben wasn't sure, in part because he was the newcomer to the group and the history wasn't entirely clear even now and in part because time had lost meaning for him since his arrival from Earth. Assuming a separateness of Landover from Earth, he amended, an assumption that was perhaps more theoretical than factual. How, after all, did you define a boundary that was marked not by geographical landmarks or proper surveys but by fairy mists? How did you differentiate between soils that could be crossed in a single step, but not without words or talismans of magic? Landover was here and Earth there, pointing right and left, but that didn't begin to explain the distance between them.

Ben Holiday had come into Landover when his hopes and dreams for a life in his old world had dried to dust, and reason had given way to desperation. Purchase a magic kingdom and find a new life, the ad in Rosen's Christmas catalogue had promised. Make yourself King of a land where the stories of childhood are real. The idea was unbelievable and at the same time irresistible. It called for a supreme act of faith, and Ben had heeded that call in the manner of a drowning man reaching for a lifeline. He had made the purchase and crossed into the unknown. He had come to a place that couldn't possibly exist and had found that it did. Landover had been everything and nothing like what he had expected. It had challenged him as he had not thought anything could. But ultimately it had given him what he needed: a new beginning, a new chance, a new life. It had captured his imagination. It had transformed him completely.

It continued to baffle him, though. He was still trying to understand its nuances. Like this business of time's passage. It was different here from his old world; he knew that from having crossed back and forth on more than one occasion and finding seasons out of synch. He knew it, too, from the effect it had on him—or the lack thereof. Something was different in the way he aged over here. It was not a progressive process, a steady rate of change, minute by minute, hour by hour, and so forth. It was difficult to believe, but sometimes he did not age at all. He had only suspected that before, but he was certain of it now. This was a deduction arrived at not from observing his own rate of growth, which was not easily measured because he lacked objectivity and distance.

No, it was from observing Mistaya.

He looked over for her. She stood in front of a massive old white oak, staring upward into its branches, her gaze intense. His brow furrowed as he watched her. If there was one word he would use to describe his daughter, that was probably it. "Intense." She approached everything with the single-mindedness of a hawk in search of prey. No lapses in concentration or distractions were allowed. When she focused on something, she gave it her complete attention. Her memory was prodigious and perhaps required that she study a thing until it was hers. It was strange behavior in a small child. But then, Mistaya herself was strange.

There was the question of her age. It was from this, from his study of her rate of growth, that Ben was able to see more clearly that his suspicions about himself were not unfounded. Mistaya had been born two years ago, measured by the passing of Landover's seasons, the same four seasons that Earth saw in a year's time. That should have made her two years old. But it didn't. Because she wasn't anywhere close to two years old. She seemed almost ten. She had been two years old when she was two *months* old. She was growing quite literally by leaps and bounds. In only months she grew years. And she didn't do it in a logically progressive fashion, either. For a time she would not grow at all—at least, not noticeably. Then, she would age months or even an entire year overnight. She would grow physically, mentally, socially, emotionally, in every measurable way. Not altogether or even at the same rate, but on a general scale one characteristic would eventually catch up with the others. She seemed to mature mentally first; yes, he was convinced of that much. She had been talking, after all, when she was three. That was months, not years. Talking as if she were maybe eight or nine. Now, at two years or ten years or whatever standard of reference you cared to use, she was talking as if she were twenty-five.

Mistaya. The name had been Willow's choice. Ben had liked it right from the first. Mistaya. Misty Holiday. He thought it a nice play on words. It suggested sweetness and nostalgia and pleasant memories. It fit the way she had looked when he had first seen her. He had just escaped from the Tangle Box; she and her mother had escaped from the Deep Fell, where Mistaya had been born. Willow would not talk about the birthing at first, but then, they had both harbored secrets that needed revealing if they were to stay true to each other, and in the end they had both confessed. He had told her of Nightshade as the Lady; she had told him of Mistaya. It had been difficult but healing. Willow had dealt better with Ben's truth than he had with hers. Mistaya might have been anything, given the nature of her birth. Born of a tree as a seedling, nourished by soils from Earth, Landover, and the fairy mists, come into being in the dank, misty deadness of the Deep Fell, Mistaya was an amalgam of worlds, magics, and bloods. But there she was that first time he had seen her, lying in the makeshift coverings, a perfect, beautiful baby girl. Dazzling green eyes that cut to your soul, clear pink skin, honey-blond hair, and features that were an instantly recognizable mix of Ben's and Willow's own.

Ben had thought from the first that it was all too good to be true. He began to discover soon enough that he was right.

He watched Mistaya shoot through infancy in a matter of several months. He watched her take her first steps and learn to swim in the same week. She began talking and running at the same time. She mastered reading and elementary math before she was a year old. By then his mind was reeling at the prospect of being parent to a phenomenally advanced child, a genius the like of which no one in his old world had ever seen. But even that didn't turn out the way he had expected. She matured, but never as rapidly in any one direction as he anticipated. She would advance to a certain point and then simply stop growing. For instance, after she mastered rudimentary math, she lost interest entirely in the subject. She learned to read and write but never did anything more with either. She seemed to delight in hopping from one new thing to the next, and there was never any rational explanation for why she progressed as far as she did and no farther.

She evidenced no interest in childish pursuits, not once, not from day one. Playing with dolls or toys, throwing and catching a ball, and jumping rope were for other children. Mistaya wanted to know how things worked, why they happened, and what they meant. Nature fascinated her. She took long walks, much longer than Ben would have thought physically possible for a child so young, all the time studying everything around her, asking questions about this and that, storing everything away in the drawers and closets of her mind. Once, when she was very young, only a few months old and just learning to talk, he found her with a rag doll. He thought for just an instant that she might be playing with it, but then she looked at him and asked in that serious voice and with those intense eyes why the maker of the doll had chosen a particular stitching to secure its limbs.

That was Mistaya. Right to the point and dead serious. She called him "Father" when she addressed him. Never "Dad" or "Daddy" or some such. "Father." Or "Mother." Polite but formal. The questions she asked were serious, important ones in her mind, and she did not treat them lightly. Ben learned not to do so, either. When once he laughed at something she had said that struck him funny, she gave him a look that suggested that he ought to grow up. It wasn't that she couldn't laugh or find humor in her life; it was that she was very particular about what she found funny and what not. Abernathy made her laugh frequently. She teased him unmercifully, always quite serious as if not intending to put him on at all, then breaking into a sudden grin just as he caught on to what was happening. He bore this with surprisingly good humor. When she was very small, she used to ride him about and tug on his ears. She was not mean about it, only playful. Abernathy would not have tolerated this from another living soul. With Mistaya, he actually seemed to enjoy it.

For the most part, however, she found grown-ups dull and restrictive. She did not appreciate their efforts to govern and protect her. She did not respond well to the word "no" or to the limitations that her parents and advisors placed on her. Abernathy was her tutor, but he confessed in private that his prize student was frequently bored by her lessons. Bunion was her protector, but after she learned to walk he was hard pressed to keep her in sight much of the time. She loved and was affectionate toward Ben and Willow, though in that strange, reserved way she cultivated. At the same time she clearly thought them mired in conventions and attitudes that had no place in her life. She had a way of looking at them when they were offering an explanation that suggested quite clearly that they didn't understand the first thing about her, because if they did, they wouldn't be wasting their time.

Adults were a necessary evil in her young life, she seemed to believe, and the sooner she was fully grown, the better. That might explain why she had aged ten years in two, Ben often thought. It might explain why, almost from the time she began to talk, she addressed all adults in an adult manner, using complete sentences and proper grammar. She could pick up a speech pattern and memorize it in a single sitting. Now, when Ben conversed with her, it was like carrying on a conversation with himself. She spoke to him in exactly the same way he spoke to her. He quickly abandoned any attempt at addressing her as he might a normal child or—God forbid—talking down to her as if she might not otherwise pay attention. If you talked down to Mistaya, she talked down to you right back. With his daughter there was a serious question as to who was the adult and who the child.

The one exception to all this child and adult business was Questor Thews. The relationship she shared with the wizard was entirely different from the ones she shared with other adults, her parents included. With Questor, Mistaya seemed quite content to be a child. She did not talk to him as she did to Ben, for instance. She listened carefully to everything he said, paid close attention to everything he did, and in general seemed content with the idea that he was in some way her superior. They shared the kind of relationship granddaughters and grandfathers sometimes share. Ben thought it was mostly the wizard's magic that bound the two. Mistaya was fascinated by it even when it didn't work the way in which Questor intended, which was all too frequently. Questor was always showing her some little bit of sorcery, trying out something new, experimenting with this and that. He was careful not to try anything dangerous when Mistaya was around: Even so, she would follow him about or sit with him for hours on the chance that he might give her a little glimpse of the power he possessed.

At first Ben worried. Mistaya's interest in magic seemed very akin to a child's early fascination with fire, and he did not want her to get burned. But she did not ask to try out spells or runes, did not beg to know how a bit of magic worked, and she listened respectfully and uncomplainingly to

Questor's admonitions concerning the dangers of unskilled practice. It was as if she had no need to try. She simply found Questor an amazing curiosity, something to study but not emulate. It was odd, but it was no stranger than anything else about Mistaya. Certainly her affinity for magic was consistent with her background, a child born of magic, with an ancestry of magic, with magic in her blood.

So what would come of all this? Ben wondered. Time passed, and he found himself waiting for the other shoe to drop. Mistaya was not the child he had envisioned when Willow had told him that he was going to be a father. She was nothing like any child he had ever encountered. She was very much an enigma. He loved her, found her intriguing and wondrous, and could not imagine life without her. She redefined for him the terms "child" and "parent" and made him rethink daily the direction his life was taking.

But she frightened him as well—not for who and what she was at present, but for what she might someday be. Her future was a vast, uncharted journey over which he feared he might have absolutely no control. What could he do to make certain that her passage went smoothly?

Willow did not seem bothered by any of this. But then, Willow took the same approach to child rearing that she did to everything else. Life presented you with choices to make, opportunities to take, and obstacles to overcome, and it presented them to you when it was good and ready and not one moment before. There was no sense in worrying about something over which you had no control. Each day with Mistaya was a challenge to be dealt with and a joy to be savored. Willow gave what she could to her daughter and took what was offered in return, and she was grateful. She would tell Ben over and over that Mistaya was special, a child of different worlds and different races, of fairies and humans, of Kings and wielders of magic. Fate had marked her. She would do something wondrous in time. They must give her the opportunity to do so. They must let her grow as she chose.

Yes, all very well and good, Ben thought ruefully. But it was more easily said than done.

He watched his daughter as she stood staring up into the branches of that great oak and wondered what more he should be doing. He felt inadequate to the task of raising her. He felt overwhelmed by who and what she was.

"Ben, it is time to eat," Willow announced, her voice a gentle interruption. "Call Mistaya."

He pushed himself to his feet, brushing the troubling thoughts from his mind. "Misty!" he called. She did not look at him, her gaze fixed on the tree. "Mistaya!"

Nothing. She was a statue.

Questor Thews came up beside him. "Lost in her own little world again, it seems, High Lord." He gave Ben a wink, then cupped his hands about his mouth. "Mistaya, come now!" he ordered, his reedy voice almost frail.

She turned, hesitated a moment, then hurried over, her long, blond hair shimmering in the sunlight, her emerald eyes bright and eager. She gave Questor Thews a brief smile as she darted past him.

She barely seemed to see Ben.

—⸺∞⸺—

Nightshade watched the child move away from the oak to rejoin the others. She kept still within the concealing branches in case one among them should think to take a closer look. None did. They gathered about the food and drink, laughing and talking, heedless of what had just taken place. The girl was hers now, the seeds of her taking planted deep within, needing only to be nurtured in order that she be claimed. That time would come. Soon.

Nightshade's long-anticipated plan was set in motion. When it was complete, Ben Holiday would be destroyed.

The crow with red eyes remembered—and the memories burned like fire.

Two years had passed since Nightshade's escape from the Tangle Box. Bitter at the betrayal worked upon her by the play-King, stung by her failure to avenge herself against his wife and child, she had waited patiently for her chance to strike. Holiday had carried her down into the Tangle Box, trapped her in the misty confines of the Labyrinth, stolen her identity, stripped her of her magic, broken down her defenses, and tricked her into giving herself to him. That neither of them had known who he or she was, nor who the other was, did not matter. That the magic of a powerful being had snared them both along with the dragon Strabo was of no concern. One way or the other, Holiday was responsible. Holiday had revealed her weakness. Holiday had caused her to feel for him what she had long ago sworn she would never feel for any man. That she had hated him always was even more galling. It made acceptance of what had happened impossible.

She kept her rage white-hot and close to the surface. She burned with it, and the pain kept her focused and certain of what she must do. Perhaps she would have been satisfied if she had been given the child in the Deep Fell following its birthing. Perhaps it would have been enough if she had claimed it and destroyed its mother in the bargain, leaving Holiday with that legacy as punishment for his betrayal. But the fairies had intervened and kept her from interfering, and all this time she had been forced to live with what had been done to her.

Until now. Now, when the child was old enough to be independent of humans and fairies alike, to discover truths that had not yet been revealed, and to be claimed by means other than force. Mistaya—she would be for Nightshade the balm the Witch of the Deep Fell so desperately needed to become whole again and at the same time the weapon she required to put an end to Ben Holiday.

The crow with red eyes looked down on the gathering of family and friends and thought that this was the last happiness any of them would ever know.

Then she lifted clear of the leaf-dappling shadows and winged her way home.

RYDALL OF MARNHULL

The next morning, the sunrise still a crescent of silver brightness on the eastern horizon and the land still cloaked in night's shadows, Willow jerked upright from her pillow with so violent a start that it woke Ben from a sound sleep. He found her rigid and shaking; the covers were thrown back, and her skin was as cold as ice. He drew her to him at once and held her close. After a moment the shaking subsided, and she allowed herself to be pulled gently down under the covers once more.

"It was a premonition," she whispered when she could speak again. She was lying close and still, as if waiting for something to strike her. He could not see her face, which was buried against his chest.

"A dream?" he asked, stroking her back, trying to calm her. The rigidity would not leave her body. "What was it?"

"Not a dream," she answered, her mouth moving against his skin. "A premonition. A sense of something about to happen. Something terrible. It was a feeling of such blackness that it washed over me like a great river, and I felt myself drowning in it. I couldn't breathe, Ben."

"It's all right now," he said quietly. "You're awake."

"No," she said at once. "It is definitely not all right. The premonition was directed at all of us—at you and me and Mistaya. But especially you, Ben. You are in great danger. I cannot be certain of the source, only the event. Something is going to happen, and if we are not prepared, we shall be . . ."

She trailed off, unwilling to say the words. Ben sighed and cradled her close. Her long emerald hair spilled over his shoulders, onto the pillow. He stared off into the still, dark room. He knew better than to question Willow when it came to dreams and premonitions. They were an integral part of the lives of the once-fairy, who relied on them as humans did on instincts. They were seldom wrong to do so. Willow was visited in dreams by fairy creatures and the dead. She was counseled and warned by them. Premonitions were less reliable and less frequently experienced, but they were no less valuable for what they were intended to accomplish. If Willow thought them in danger, then they would be wise to believe it was so.

"There was no indication as to what sort of danger?" he asked after a moment, trying to find a way to pin it down.

She shook her head no, a small movement against his body. She would not look at him. "But it is enormous. I have never felt anything so strongly, not since the time of our meeting." She paused. "What bothers me is that I do not know what summoned it. Usually there is some small event, some bit of news, some hint that precedes such visits. Dreams are sent by others to voice their thoughts, to present their counsel. But premonitions are faceless, voiceless wraiths meant only to give warning, to prepare for an uncertain future. They are drawn to us in our sleep by tiny threads of suspicion and doubt that safeguard us against the unexpected. Paths are opened to us in our sleep that remain closed while we are awake. The path this premonition traveled to reach me must have been broad and straight indeed, so monstrous was its size."

She pressed against him, trying to get closer as the memory chilled her anew.

"We haven't had anything threaten us in months," Ben said softly, thinking back. "Landover is at peace. Nightshade and Strabo are at rest. The Lords of the Greensward do not quarrel. Even the Crag Trolls haven't caused trouble in a while. There are no disturbances in the fairy mists. Nothing."

They were silent then, lying together in the great bed, watching the light creep over the windowsills and the shadows begin to fade, listening to the sounds of the day come awake. A tiny brilliant red bird flew down out of the battlements past their window and was gone.

Willow lifted her head finally and looked at him. Her flawless features were pale and frozen. "I don't know what to do," she whispered.

He kissed her nose. "We'll do whatever we have to."

He rose from the bed and padded over to the washbasin that sat on its stand by the east-facing window. He paused to look out at the new day. Overhead, the sky was clear and the light from the sunrise was a sweeping spray of brightness that was already etching out a profusion of greens and blues. Forested hills, a rough blanket across the land's still-sleeping forms, stretched away beyond the gleaming walls of Sterling Silver. Flowers were beginning to open in the meadow beyond the lake that surrounded the island castle. In the courtyard immediately below, guards were in the middle of a shift change and stable hands were moving off with feed for the stock.

Ben splashed water on his face, the water made warm by the castle for the new day. Sterling Silver was a living entity and possessed of magic that allowed her to care for the King and his court as a mother would her children. It had been a source of constant amazement to him when he had first come into

Landover—to find a bath drawn and of perfect temperature on command, to have light provided wherever he wished it, to feel the stones of the castle floor warm beneath his feet on cold nights, to have food kept cooled or dried as needed—but now he was accustomed to these small miracles and did not think much on them anymore.

Although this morning, for some reason, he found himself doing so. He toweled his face dry and gazed downward into the shimmering surface of the washbowl's waters. His reflection gazed back at him, a strong, sun-browned, lean-featured visage with penetrating blue eyes, a hawk nose, and a hairline receding at the temples. The slight ripple of the water gave him wrinkles and distortions he did not have. He looked, he thought, as he had always looked since coming over from the old world. Appearances were deceiving, the saying went, but in this case he was not so sure. Magic was the cornerstone of Landover's existence, and where magic was concerned, anything was possible.

As with Mistaya, he reminded himself, who was constantly redefining that particular concept.

Willow rose from the bed and came over to him. She wore no clothes but as always seemed heedless of the fact and that made her nakedness seem natural and right. He took her in his arms and held her against him, thinking once more how lucky he was to have her, how much he loved her, how desperately he needed her. She was still the most beautiful woman he had ever seen, a prejudice he was proud to acknowledge, and he thought that her beauty came from within as much as from without. She was the great love he had lost when Annie had been killed in the old world—so long ago, it seemed, that he could barely remember the event. She was the life partner he had thought he would never find again, someone to give him strength, to infuse him with joy, to provide balance to his life.

There was a knock at the sleeping chamber door. "High Lord?" Abernathy called sharply, agitation in his voice. "Are you awake?"

"I'm awake," Ben answered, still holding Willow against him, looking past her upturned face.

"I am sorry, but I need to speak with you," Abernathy advised. "At once."

Willow eased free from Ben's arms and moved quickly to cover herself with a long white robe. Ben waited until she was finished, then walked over to open the door. Abernathy stood there, unable to disguise with any success either his impatience or his dismay. Both registered clearly in his eyes. Dogs always imparted something of an anxious look, and Abernathy, though a dog in form only, was no exception. He held himself stiffly in his crimson and gold uniform, the robes of his office as Court Scribe, and his fingers—all that remained of his human self since his transformation into a soft-coated Wheaten Terrier—fidgeted with the engraved metal buttons as if to ascertain that they were all still in place.

"High Lord." Abernathy stepped forward and bent close to assure privacy. "I am sorry to have to start your day off like this, but there are two riders at the gates. Apparently they are here to offer some sort of challenge. They refuse to reveal themselves to anyone but you, and one has thrown down a gauntlet in the middle of the causeway. They are waiting for your response."

Ben nodded, stifling half a dozen ill-conceived responses. "I'll be right there."

He closed the door and moved quickly to dress. He told Willow what had happened. Throwing down a gauntlet in challenge sounded quaint to a man of twentieth-century Earth, but it was no laughing matter in Landover. Rules of combat were still practiced there, and when a gauntlet was cast, there was no mistaking the intent. A challenge had been issued, and a response was required. Even a King could not ignore such an act. Or perhaps, Ben thought as he pulled on his boots, *especially* a King.

He rose and buttoned his tunic. He paused to grip the medallion that hung about his neck—the symbol of his office, the talisman that protected him. If a challenge had been issued, the battle would be fought by his champion, the knight called the Paladin, who had defended every King of Landover since the beginning. The medallion summoned the Paladin, who was in fact the King's alter ego. For it was Ben himself who inhabited the body and mind of the Paladin when it fought its battles for him, becoming his own champion, losing himself for a time in the other's warrior skills and life. It had taken Ben a long time to discover the truth about the Paladin's nature. It was taking him a longer time still to come to terms with what that truth meant.

He released the medallion. There would be time enough to speculate on all that later if this challenge was to combat, if the Paladin was required, if the danger was not imagined, if, if, if . . .

He took Willow's arm and went out the door. They moved quickly down the hall and climbed a flight of stairs to the battlements overlooking the castle's main entry. On an island in a lake, Sterling Silver was connected to the mainland by a causeway Ben had built—and now rebuilt several times—to permit ready access for visitors. Landover was not at war, had not been at war since Ben had come over to assume Kingship, and he had decided a long time ago that there was no reason to isolate her ruler from her people.

Of course, her people were not in the habit of casting down gauntlets and issuing challenges.

He opened the door leading out onto the battlements and crossed to the balcony that overlooked the causeway. Questor Thews and Abernathy were already standing there, conversing in low tones. Bunion skittered along the parapets to one side, swift and agile, his kobold's claws able to grip the stone easily. Bunion could walk straight down the wall if he chose. His bright yellow eyes were menacing slits, and all his considerable teeth were showing in a parody of a smile.

Questor and Abernathy looked up hurriedly as Ben appeared with Willow and hurried over to meet him.

"High Lord, you must resolve this as you see fit," Questor said in typically succinct fashion, "but I would advise great caution. There is an aura of magic about these two that even my talents cannot seem to penetrate."

"What irrefutable proof!" Abernathy observed archly, dog's ears perked. He gave Ben a pained look. "High Lord, these are impertinent, possibly demented creatures, and offering them some time in the dungeons might be worth your consideration."

"Good morning to you, too," Ben greeted them cheerfully. "Nice day for casting down a gauntlet, isn't it?" He gave them each a wry smile as he moved toward the balcony. "Tell you what. Let's hear what they have to say before we consider solutions."

They moved in a knot onto the overlook and stopped at the railing. Ben peered down. Two black-clad riders sat on black horses in the middle of the causeway. The larger of the two was dressed in armor and wore a broadsword and had a battle-ax strapped to his saddle. His visor was down. The smaller was robed and hooded and hunched over like a crone at rest, face and hands hidden. Neither moved. Neither bore any kind of insignia or carried any standard.

The armored rider's black gauntlet lay before them in the center of the bridge.

"You see what I mean," Questor whispered enigmatically.

Ben didn't, but it made no difference. Not wanting to prolong the confrontation, Ben shouted down to the two on the bridge, "I am Ben Holiday, King of Landover. What do you want with me?"

The armored rider's helmet tilted upward slightly. "Lord Holiday. I am Rydall, King of Marnhull and of all the lands east beyond the fairy mists to the Great Impassable." The man's voice was deep and booming. "I have come to seek your surrender, High Lord. I would have it peaceably but will secure it by force if I must. I wish your crown and your throne and your medallion of office. I wish your command over your subjects and your Kingdom. Am I plain enough for you?"

Ben felt the blood rush to his face. "What is plain to me, Rydall, King of Marnhull, is that you are a fool if you expect me to pay you any mind."

"And you are a fool if you fail to heed me," the other answered quickly. "Hear me out before you say anything more. My Kingdom of Marnhull lies beyond the fairy mists. All that exists on that side of the boundary belongs to me. I took it by force and strength of arms long ago, and I took it all. For years I have searched for a way to pass through the mists, but the fairy magic kept me at bay. That is no longer the case. I have breached your principal defense, Lord Holiday, and your country lies open to me at last. Yours is a small, impossibly outnumbered army. Mine, on the other hand, is vast and seasoned and would crush you in a day. It waits now at your borders for my command. If I call, it will sweep through Landover like a plague and destroy everything in its path. You lack any reasonable means of stopping it, and once it has been set in motion, it will take time to bring it under control again. I do not need to speak more explicitly, do I, High Lord?"

Ben glanced quickly at Willow and his advisors. "Have any of you ever heard of this fellow?" he asked softly. All three shook their heads.

"Holiday, will you surrender to me?" Rydall cried out again in his great voice.

Ben turned back. "I think not. Maybe another day. King Rydall, I cannot believe that you came here expecting me to do what you ask. No one has heard of you. You bring no evidence of your office or your armies. You sit there on your horse making threats and demands, and that is all you do. Two men, all alone, come out of nowhere." He paused. "What if I were to have you seized and thrown in prison?"

Rydall laughed, and his laugh was as big and deep as his voice and decidedly mean. "I would not advise you to try that, High Lord. It would not be as easy as it looks."

Holiday nodded. "Pick up your gauntlet and go home. I'm hungry for breakfast."

"No, High Lord. It is you who must pick up the gauntlet if you do not accept my demand for surrender." Rydall eased his horse forward a step. "Your land lies in the path of my army, and I cannot go around it. I will not. It will fall to me one way or another. But the blood of those who perish will not be on my hands; it will be on your own. The choice is yours, High Lord."

"I have made my choice," Ben answered.

Rydall laughed anew. "Bravely said. Well, I did not think you would give in to me easily, not without some proof of my strength, some reason to believe that your failure to do as I have commanded will cause you, and perhaps those you love, harm."

Ben flushed anew, angry now. "Making threats will not work with me, Rydall of Marnhull. Our conversation is finished."

"Wait, High Lord!" the other exclaimed hurriedly. "Do not be so quick to interrupt—"

"Go back to wherever it is you came from!" Ben snapped, already turning away.

Then he saw Mistaya. She was standing alone on the parapets several dozen feet away, staring down at Rydall. She was perfectly still, honey-blond hair streaming down her narrow shoulders, elfin face intense, emerald eyes fixed on the riders at the gate. She seemed oblivious to everything else, the whole of her concentration directed downward to where Rydall and his companion waited.

"Mistaya," Ben called softly. He did not want her there where she could be seen, did not want her so close to the edge. He felt sweat break out on his forehead. His voice rose. "Mistaya!"

She didn't hear or didn't want to hear. Ben left the others and walked to her. Wordlessly he grabbed her around the waist and lifted her away from the wall. Mistaya did not resist. She put her arms around his neck and allowed him to set her down again.

He kept his annoyance hidden as he bent close. "Go inside, please," he told her.

She looked at him curiously, as if puzzling something through, then turned obediently, went through the door, and was gone.

"High Lord Ben Holiday!" Rydall called from below.

Ben's teeth clenched as he wheeled back to the wall one final time. "I am finished with you, Rydall!" he shouted back in fury.

"Let me have him seized and brought before you!" Abernathy snapped.

"A final word!" Rydall called out. "I said I did not expect you to surrender without some form of proof that I do not lie. Would you have me provide that for you, then, High Lord? Proof that I am able to do as I have threatened?"

Ben took a deep breath. "You must do as you choose, Rydall of Marnhull. But remember this—you must answer for your choice."

There was a long silence as the two stared fixedly at each other. Despite his anger and resolve, Ben felt a chill pass through him, as if Rydall had taken better measure of him than he had of the other. It was an unsettling moment.

"Good-bye for now, High Lord Ben Holiday," Rydall said finally. "I will return in three days time. Perhaps your answer will be different then. I leave the gauntlet where it lies. No one but you will be able to pick it up. And pick it up you shall."

He wheeled about and galloped away. The other rider lingered a moment, all hunched down and still. This rider had not moved or spoken the entire time. It had shown nothing of itself. Now it turned away unhurriedly and moved after Rydall. Together they crossed the open meadow through the wildflowers and grasses, black shadows against the coming light, and disappeared into the trees beyond.

Ben Holiday and his companions watched them go until they were out of sight and did not speak a word.

Breakfast that morning was a somber affair. Ben, Willow, Questor, and Abernathy sat huddled close at one end of the long dining table, picking at their food and talking. Mistaya had been fed separately and had been sent outside to play. As an afterthought, Ben had dispatched Bunion to keep an eye on her.

"So no one has heard of Rydall?" Ben repeated once again. He kept coming back to that same question. "You're sure?"

"High Lord, this man is a stranger to Landover," Questor Thews assured him. "There is no Rydall and no Marnhull anywhere within our borders."

"Nor, for all we know, anywhere without, either!" Abernathy snapped heatedly. "Rydall claims to have come through the fairy mists, but we have only his word for that. No one can penetrate the mists, High Lord. The fairies would not permit it. Only magic allows passage, and only the fairies or their creatures possess it. Rydall does not seem one of those to me."

"Perhaps, like me, he possesses a talisman that allows passage," Ben suggested.

Questor bent forward with a frown. "What of that black-cloaked companion? I told you I sensed magic in that pair, but it was probably not Rydall's. Perhaps the other is a creature of magic, a fairy being of the same sort as the Gorse. Such a being could secure passage."

Ben thought back to the Gorse, the dark fairy that had been released and brought back into Landover at the time of Mistaya's birth. A creature of that sort was certainly capable of negotiating the fairy mists and visiting as much misery as possible on any who stood in its way.

"But why would a creature of such power serve Rydall?" he asked abruptly. "Wouldn't it be the other way around?"

"Perhaps the fairy creature is in his thrall," Willow offered quietly. "Or perhaps things are not as they appear, and it is Rydall in fact who serves."

"If the black-cloaked one has the magic, it might be so and still appear otherwise," Questor mused. "I wish I could have penetrated their disguise."

Ben leaned back in his chair. "Let's review this a moment. These two, Rydall and his companion, appear out of nowhere. One of them, or maybe both, possesses magic—considerable magic, they claim. But we don't know what that magic does. What we do know is that they want an unconditional surrender of the throne of Landover and that they seem confident that they will have it one way or the other. Why?"

"Why?" Questor Thews repeated blankly.

"Put it another way," Ben continued. He pushed back his plate and looked at the wizard. "They made a demand, offering no evidence that it should be given any serious consideration. They revealed no magic of the sort that might intimidate, and they showed nothing of their vaunted army. They simply made a demand and then rode off, giving us three days to consider. To consider what? Their demand that we have already rejected? I don't think so."

"You think they intend to offer us some demonstration of their power," Willow surmised.

Ben nodded. "I do. They haven't given us three days for nothing. And they made a fairly obvious threat on leaving. Rydall was too quick to back away from his demand for immediate surrender. Why make it if you don't intend to enforce it? Some sort of game is being played here, and I don't think we know all the rules yet."

The others nodded soberly. "What should we do, High Lord?" Questor asked finally.

Ben shrugged. "I wish I knew." He thought about it for a moment. "Let's use the Landsview, Questor, to see if there is any sign of Rydall or his army in Landover. We can make a thorough search. I don't want to alarm the people by giving out word of this threat until we find out if it is real, but it might not hurt to increase our border patrols for a few days."

"It might not hurt to increase our watch here as well," Abernathy growled, straightening himself. "The threat, after all, seems directed at us."

Ben agreed. Since no one had anything further to offer, they adjourned from the table to begin the day's work, much of which was already set by an agenda that had been in place for weeks and had nothing to do with Rydall and his threats. Ben went about his business in calm, unperturbed fashion, but his apprehension about Marnhull's King remained undiminished.

When there was time, Ben went up into the castle's highest tower, a small circular chamber in which the wall opened halfway around from floor to ceiling, to look out across the land. A railing rose waist-high along the edge to guard against falls, and a silver lectern faced out from the center of the railing into the clouds. Thousands of intricately scrolled runes were carved into the metal. This was the Landsview. He closed the door to the room and locked it, then pulled a worn map of Landover from a chest and crossed to the lectern. He spread the map across its reading surface and fastened it in place with clips.

Then he placed himself directly before the lectern, gripped the guardrail, and focused his attention on the map. A warm vibrancy began to emanate from beneath his hands. He centered his concentration on the lake country, for that was where he wished to begin his search.

Seconds later the walls of the tower fell away, and he was flying across Landover with nothing but the guardrail for support. It was an illusion, he knew by now, for he was still within the castle and only his mind was free to roam Landover, but the illusion created by the Landsview's magic was powerful. He sped across the lake country's forests, rivers, lakes, and swamps, all the details of the land revealed to him, his eyes as sharp as an eagle's at hunt. The search revealed nothing. There was no sign of Rydall or his black-cloaked companion or their army. The borders to the fairy mists were quiet.

Ben was still brooding over the matter at midday when Willow took him aside. They walked out into a private garden that opened just off the ground-floor rooms Willow kept for herself and Mistaya. Mistaya was not there. She was eating with Parsnip in the kitchen.

"I want to send Mistaya away," Willow announced without preamble, her eyes fixing on him. "Tomorrow."

Ben was silent for a moment, staring back at her. "Your premonition?"

She nodded. "It was too strong to ignore. Perhaps Rydall's coming was its cause. Perhaps not. But I would feel better if Mistaya were somewhere else for a while. It may be difficult enough protecting ourselves."

They walked down a winding pathway into a stand of rhododendrons and stopped. Ben breathed in the fragrance. He was remembering Rydall's veiled threat about harm coming to those he loved. And Rydall had seen Mistaya on the wall.

Ben folded his arms and looked off into the distance. "You are probably right. But where could we send her that would be safer than inside these walls?"

Willow took his hand. "To my father. To the River Master. I know how difficult he has been in the past, how opposed to us at times. I do not defend him. But he loves his granddaughter and will see that she is well cared for. He can protect her better than we. No one can come into the country of the once-fairy if they are not invited. Their magic, for all that it has been diminished by their leaving the mists, is still powerful. Mistaya would be safe."

She was right, of course. The River Master and his people possessed considerable magic, and their country was secure from those who were not welcome. Finding the way in without a guide was all but impossible; finding the way out again was harder still. But Ben was not convinced. The River Master and his daughter were not close, and while the Ruler of the lake-country people had been pleased by the birth of Mistaya and had journeyed to Landover to visit her, he was still as aloof and independent as he had ever been. He accepted Ben as King of Landover grudgingly and without conviction that the monarchy served any real purpose in the lives of the once-fairy. He had obstructed and refuted Ben on more than one occasion, and he made no effort to hide his own ambitions to extend his rule.

Still, Ben was as worried as Willow that Mistaya would not be safe at Sterling Silver. He had been thinking about it ever since he had taken his daughter down off that battlement. If Willow's premonition was correct—and there was no reason to think it wasn't—then the real danger was here, since the threat that faced the family was principally to him. It made sense to remove Mistaya to another place, and there was no safer place in Landover than the lake country.

"All right," he agreed. "Will you go with her?"

Willow shook her head slowly. "No, Ben. My life is with you. I will remain here. If I can, I will help protect you. Perhaps I will have another sensing."

"Willow . . ." he began.

"No, Ben. Don't ask it of me. I have left you before when I did not want to, and each time I almost lost you. This time I will not go. My father will take good care of Mistaya." Her eyes made it clear that the matter was settled. "Send another instead to see her safely on her journey. Send Questor or Abernathy."

Ben gripped her hand. "I'll do better than that. I'll send them both.

Questor will keep Mistaya in line, and Abernathy will counsel Questor against any rash use of his magic. And I'll send an escort of King's Guards to keep them all safe."

Willow pressed herself against him wordlessly, and Ben hugged her back. They stood holding each other in the midday sunlight. "I have to tell you that I don't like letting her go," Ben murmured finally.

"Nor I," Willow whispered back. He could feel her heart beat against his chest. "I spoke with Mistaya earlier. I asked her what she was doing on the wall, staring down at Rydall." She paused. "Mistaya said that she knows him."

Ben stiffened. "Knows him?"

"I asked her how, but she said she wasn't sure." Willow shook her head. "I think she was as confused as we are."

They were quiet then, still holding each other, staring off into the gardens, listening to the sounds of the insects and the birds against the more distant backdrop of the castle's bustle. A connection between Mistaya and Rydall? Ben felt something cold settle into the pit of his stomach.

"We'll send her away at first light," he whispered, and felt Willow's arms tighten about him in response.

HALTWHISTLE

M istaya's parents told her that evening that they had decided she should
visit her grandfather in the lake country and would be leaving in the
morning. In typically straightforward fashion she asked if anything was wrong,
and they said no. But the way they said it told her there most definitely was.

Still, she was astute enough in the ways of parents to know better than to
contradict them by asking what it was—even though she was quite certain it
had something to do with the man who had come to the gates that morning—
and she was content to let the matter lie until she could speak to one or the
other of them alone. It would be her mother most likely, because her mother
was more honest with her than her father was. It wasn't that her father wanted
to deceive her. It was that he persisted in viewing her as a child and sought
continually to protect her from what he considered life's harsh realities. It was
an annoying habit, but Mistaya tolerated it as best she could. Her father had
trouble understanding her in any event, certainly more than her mother did.
He measured her against a standard with which she was not familiar, a standard conceived and developed in his old world, the world called Earth, where
magic was practically unheard of and fairy creatures were considered a myth.
He loved her, of course, and he would do anything for her. But love and understanding did not necessarily go hand in hand in real life, and such was the
case here.

Her father was not alone in his puzzlement. Most of those who lived in the
castle found her a bit odd for one reason or another. She had been aware of it
almost from the beginning, but it did not bother her. Her confidence and self-
reliance were such that what others thought mattered almost not at all. Her
mother was comfortable with her, and her father, if bewildered, was supportive. Abernathy let her do things to him that would have cost another child a
quick trip to its room for prolonged consideration of what good manners en-
tailed. Bunion and Parsnip were as odd as she, all ears and teeth and bristly

hair, chittering their mysterious language that they thought she couldn't really understand when, of course, she could.

Best of all, there was Questor Thews. She loved that old man the way a child does a special grandparent or a favorite aunt or uncle, the two of them mysteriously linked as if born into the world with a shared view of life. Questor never talked down to her. He never begrudged her a question or opinion. He listened when she talked and answered her right back. He was distracted, and he fumbled a bit when showing her his magic, but that seemed to make him all the more endearing. She sensed that Questor truly found her to be a wondrous person—a *person,* not a child—and that he believed she was capable of anything. Oh, he chided and corrected her now and then, but he did it in such a way that she was never offended; she was touched by his concern. He lacked her mother's fierce love and her father's iron determination and probably their sense of commitment to her as well, but he made up for it with his friendship, the kind you find only rarely in life.

Mistaya was pleased to hear that Questor would be her guardian on her journey south. She was pleased to have Abernathy come along as well, but she was especially happy about Questor. The journey itself would be a delight. She had not been away from the castle since she was a baby, barely able to walk, and then only for day trips. Picnics and horseback rides didn't count. This was an adventure, a journey to a place she had never been. Discoveries would be plentiful, and she would have Questor there to share them with her. It would be great fun.

She had to admit, considering the matter further, that part of the attraction was the prospect of getting away from her parents. When her parents were around, she was always watched more closely and restricted more severely. Don't do this. Don't touch that. Stay close. Keep away. And the lessons they insisted on teaching her were interminable and mostly superfluous to what really mattered. It was when she was alone with Questor that she felt her horizons expand and the possibilities begin to open up. Much of her enthusiasm had to do with the wizard's use of magic, which was a truly fascinating and important pursuit. Mistaya loved to watch what Questor could do with his spells and conjurings, even when he didn't get them right. She thought that someday she could learn to use magic as he did. She was certain of it.

Secretly she tried a spell or two, a conjuring here and there, and found she could almost make them work.

She kept it to herself, of course. Everyone, Questor Thews included, told her that using magic was extremely dangerous. Everyone told her not to even think of trying. She promised faithfully each time the admonition was given but kept her options open.

Magic, she knew, even if they didn't, was an integral part of her life. Her mother had told her early on of her birthright. She was the child of a human and a once-fairy. She was the child of three worlds, birthed out of three soils. She had been born in a witch's lair, the hollow they called the Deep Fell, the haven of Nightshade. All that was in her blood was laced with magic. That was why, unlike other children, she had grown to the age of ten in only two years. That was why she grew in spurts. How she grew was still something of a mystery to her, but she understood it better than her parents did. Her intelligence always grew first, and her emotions and body followed. She could neither predict nor govern the when and how of it, but she was aware of a definite progression.

She also believed that being a child was not particularly desirable or important, that basically it was a necessary step toward becoming an adult, which was what she really wanted. Children were one rung up the ladder from house pets; they were cared for, fed regularly, frequently sent outside to play, and not allowed to do much of anything else. Adults could do whatever they chose if they were willing to accept the consequences. Mistaya had mastered an understanding of the dynamics of growing up right from the beginning, and she was anxious to get through the preliminaries and try out the real thing. She chafed and tugged at the restrictions placed on her both by her physiology and by her parents, unable to exert much control over either. A trip to the lake country and her grandfather came as a welcome respite.

So she dutifully acknowledged her parents' wishes in the matter, secretly rejoiced at her good fortune, and began making her plans. No time limit seemed to have been placed yet on this visit, which meant it might last for weeks. That was fine with Mistaya. All spring or even all summer in the lake country with the once-fairy was an exciting prospect. She liked her grandfather, although she had met him only once. He had come to the castle to see her when she had been very young, only a few months old. The River Master was a tall, spare-featured, stern man, a water sprite with silver skin and thick black hair that grew down the nape of his neck and forearms. He was tight-lipped and cool in his approach, as if disdaining to know her too well, as if suspicious about who and what she might be. She gave no quarter in their meeting. Disregarding his aloofness, she marched right up to him and said, "Hello, Grandfather. I am very pleased to meet you. We shall be good friends, I hope."

Boldness and candor did the trick. Her grandfather warmed to her immediately, impressed that so small a child could be so forthcoming, pleased that she should seek his friendship. He took her for a walk, talked with her at length, and ended up inviting her to come visit him. He remained only a day, then went away again. Her mother said that he did not like to sleep indoors and that castles in particular bothered him. She said he was a woods creature and seldom ventured far from his home. That he had come to see her at all was a great compliment. Mistaya, pleased, had asked when she could go visit him, but the request had been filed away and seemingly forgotten. She had not seen him since. It would be interesting to discover what he thought of her now.

Following dinner she was kept busy packing for her trip and did not get a chance to ask either her mother or her father about the men at the gates. She slept restlessly that night and was awake before sunrise. With hugs and kisses from her parents to remind her of their devotion, she set out with her escort at first light: Questor Thews, Abernathy, and a dozen of the King's Guards. She rode her favorite pony, Lightfoot, and watched the sun chase the shadows back across the meadows and hills and into the dark woods as the new day began. Six Guards rode in front of her, and six behind. Questor was at her side atop an old paint improbably called Owl. Abernathy, who detested horses, rode inside the carriage that bore her clothing and personal effects. A driver nudged the team that pulled the carriage along the grassy trail they followed south.

Mistaya waited until Sterling Silver was safely out of sight, then eased Lightfoot close to Questor and asked, "Who was the man at the gates, Questor—the one Father didn't want to see me?"

Questor Thews snorted. "A troublemaker named Rydall. Claimed he was King of some country called Marnhull that none of us have ever heard about. Claimed it lies on the other side of the fairy mists, but we both know how unlikely that is."

"Is he the reason I'm being sent to see my grandfather?"

"Yes."

"Why?"

The wizard shrugged. "He might be more dangerous than he looks. He made some threats."

"What sort of threats?"

The shaggy white brows knitted together fiercely. "Hard to say; they were rather vague. Rydall wants your father to hand over the crown and let him be King instead. Pure nonsense. But he suggested it might be safer to do as he asked. Your father is looking into it."

Mistaya was quiet for a moment, thinking. "Who was the other one, the one in the black robes?"

"I don't know."

"A magician?"

Questor looked at her, surprise showing on his narrow face. "Yes, perhaps. There was magic there. Did you sense it, too?"

She nodded. "I think I know one of them."

Surprise turned to astonishment. "You do? How could you?"

She frowned. "I don't know. I just felt it while standing there on the wall." She paused. "I thought at first it was the big man, Rydall. But now I'm not sure. It might have been the other." She shrugged, her interest in the matter fading. "Do you think we will see any bog wumps on the way, Questor?"

They traveled steadily all day, stopping several times to rest the horses and once for lunch, and by sundown they had reached the south end of the Irry- lyn. There they set up camp for the night. Mistaya went swimming in the warm waters of the lake, then fished with Abernathy and a couple of the King's Guards for their dinner. They caught several dozen fish in almost no time, causing Mistaya to complain to the scribe that it was all too easy. While the Guards carried their catch back to the camp to clean and cook, the girl and the dog sat alone on the shores of the lake and looked out across the sil- ver waters as the sun sank in a shimmer of red and pink behind the distant horizon.

"Do you think Mother and Father are in danger, Abernathy?" she asked him when they were alone, her face and voice impossibly serious.

Abernathy considered a moment, then shook his shaggy head. "No, Mis- taya, I do not. And even if they are, it will not be the first time. When you are a King and Queen, there is always danger. When you wield power of any kind, for that matter, there is always danger. But your parents are very resourceful people and have survived a good many things. I would not worry for them if I were you."

She liked his answer and nodded agreeably. "All right, I won't. Are you and Questor staying with me once we reach Elderew?"

"Only for a day or so. Then we must go back. Your father will have need of us. We cannot be away for very long."

"No, of course not," she agreed, rather pleased that she would be on her own. Her grandfather knew magic as well. She wondered what he could be persuaded to teach her. She wondered if he would let her experiment a bit.

A shadowy form crept out of the trees to one side and melted into some bushes that ran along the edge of the lake. Mistaya and Abernathy were seated on a cluster of flat rocks elevated above the bushes and could see anything try- ing to approach. Neither missed the furtive movement.

"Bog wump?" she asked in an excited whisper.

Abernathy shook his head. "Some sort of wight. Neither very old nor very bright, judging from its lack of circumspection."

She nudged the scribe lightly. "Bark at him, will you, Abernathy? A good, loud bark?"

"Mistaya . . ."

"Please? I'll not pull your ears for the rest of the trip."

The dog sighed. "Thank you so much."

"Will you?" she pressed. "Just once? I want to see it jump."

Abernathy's jaws worked. "Humph."

Then he barked, a quick, sharp explosion that shattered the twilight silence. Below, the wight jumped straight out of the bushes in which it was hiding and streaked back into the forest as if launched from a catapult.

Mistaya was in stitches. "That was wonderful! That was so funny! I love it when you do that, Abernathy! It just makes me laugh!"

She gave him a big hug and pulled lightly on his ears. "You make me laugh, you old woolly."

"Humph," Abernathy repeated. But he was clearly pleased nevertheless.

The fish cooked up nicely, and dinner was delicious. The members of the little caravan ate together, and everything was quickly consumed. It was better than a picnic, Mistaya concluded. She stayed up late swapping stories with the King's Guards despite Abernathy's clear disapproval, and when she finally rolled into her blankets—refusing the down-filled pad brought along for her personal comfort (the King's Guards, after all, didn't use them)—she was asleep in moments.

Without knowing why, she woke when it was still dark. Everyone around her was sound asleep, most of them, notably Questor Thews, emitting snores that sounded like rusty gates. She blinked, sat up, and looked about.

A pair of eyes stared back at her from only a few feet away, reflecting bright yellow in the last of the dying firelight.

Mistaya squinted, unafraid. The eyes belonged to a mud puppy. She had never seen one, but she knew what they looked like from the descriptions given by Abernathy in his endless lessons on Landover's native species. She waited a moment for her vision to sharpen to make sure. The mud puppy waited with her. When she could see clearly, she found herself face to face with an odd creature possessed of a long body colored various shades of brown, short legs with webbed feet, a vaguely rodent sort of face, great floppy dog ears, and a lizard's smooth, slender tail. *Sure enough, a mud puppy,* she thought.

She pursed her lips and kissed at it. The mud puppy blinked.

She remembered suddenly that mud puppies were supposed to be fairy creatures. They were rarely seen anywhere in Landover and almost never outside the lake country.

"You are very cute," she whispered.

The mud puppy wagged its tail in response. It moved off a few paces, then turned back, waiting. Mistaya rose from her blankets. The mud puppy started off again. No mistaking what it wanted, the girl thought. What luck! An adventure already! She pulled on her boots and crept through the sleeping camp in pursuit of her new companion. The mud puppy made certain never to get too far ahead, deliberately leading her on.

She remembered too late that there was a sentry on watch at either end of the camp, and she was on top of one before she could stop herself. But the sentry did not seem to see her. He was staring out into the night, oblivious. First the mud puppy and then Mistaya walked right past him.

Magic! the girl thought, and was excited anew.

The mud puppy took her away from the Irrylyn and into the surrounding woods. They walked quite a long way, navigating a maze of tightly packed trees and thickets, fording streams, descending ravines, and climbing hills. The night was warm and still, and the air was heavy with the smell of pine and jasmine. Crickets chirped, and small rodents scurried about in the brush. Mistaya studied everything, listened to everything, letting nothing escape her. She had no idea where she was going but was not worried about finding her way back. She was thinking that the mud puppy was taking her to someone, and she was hoping that it was a creature of magic.

Finally they reached a clearing in which a broad swath of moonlight glimmered off a grassy stretch of marsh that marked the end of a stream's downhill run from some distant spring. The water was choked with grasses and night-blooming lilies and was as smooth as glass. The mud puppy moved to within a few feet of its edge and sat down. Mistaya walked up beside him and waited.

The wait was a short one. Almost immediately the waters of the marsh stirred, then parted as something beneath their surface began to lift into view. It was a woman formed all of mud, slick and smooth and dark as she took shape. She rose to tower over Mistaya, much larger than any woman the girl had ever seen, her lush form shimmering with dampness in the moonlight. She stood on the waters of the pond as if they were solid ground, and her eyes opened and found Mistaya's own.

"Hello, Mistaya," she greeted in a soft, rich voice that whispered of damp earth and cool shadows.

"Hello," Mistaya replied.

"I am the Earth Mother," the woman said. "I am a friend of your mother. Has she told you of me?"

Mistaya nodded. "You were her best friend when she was a little girl. You told her about my father before he came into Landover. You help take care of the land and the things that live on it. You can do magic."

The Earth Mother laughed softly. "Some little magic. Most of what I do is simply hard work. Do you like magic, then?"

"Yes, very much. But I am not allowed to use it."

"Because it is dangerous for you."

"Yes."

"But you don't believe that?"

Mistaya hesitated. "It is not so much that I don't believe it. It is more that I don't see how I can learn to protect myself from its dangers if I never get to use it."

The eyes gleamed like silver pools. "A good answer. Ignorance does not protect; knowledge protects. Did you know, Mistaya, that I helped your mother prepare for your birth? I gave her the task of gathering the soils out of which you were born. I did that because I knew something about you that your mother did not. I knew that magic would be a very important part of your life and that you could not protect yourself from its effects if its elements did not constitute a part of your body. You required earth from the fairy mists as well as from your father's and mother's lands."

"Am I a fairy creature?" Mistaya asked quickly.

The Earth Mother shook her head. "You are not so easily defined, child," she answered. "You are not simply one thing or the other but a mix of several. You are special. There is no one like you in all of Landover. What do you think of that?"

Mistaya thought. "I suppose I shall have to get used to it."

"That will not be so easy to do," the Earth Mother continued. "There will be obstacles for you to overcome at every turn. You may think that growing up has been difficult, but it will become more difficult still. There are hard lessons ahead for you. There are trials that may undo you if you are not careful. Experience is the necessary teacher for all children growing to adulthood, filled with revelations and discoveries, with disappointments and rewards, and with successes and failures. The trick is in finding a balance to it all and then surviving to turn knowledge into wisdom. This will be doubly hard for you, Mistaya, because yours will be the lessons and trials of three worlds, and you must be especially careful how you go."

"I am not afraid," Mistaya said bravely.

"I can tell this is so."

Mistaya frowned thoughtfully. "Earth Mother, can you see what lies ahead for me? Can you see the future?"

The Earth Mother's silver eyes closed and opened slowly like a cat's. "Oh, child, I wish I could. How easy life would be. But I cannot. What I see are possibilities. The future may be this or that. Usually it may be a handful of things. I see glimpses of dark clouds and rainbows in the lives of those who inhabit my land, and sometimes I can forestall or alter what might be. The future is never fixed, Mistaya. For each of us it is an empty canvas on which we must paint our lives."

"Mother and Father believe we are in danger," the girl said. "Is it true?"

"It is," the Earth Mother answered. "One of those dark clouds of which I spoke comes toward you. It will test your resolve and challenge your insight. It looks to be a very black cloud indeed, and you must be wary of it. It is for this reason I brought you here to me tonight."

"To warn me?"

"More than that, Mistaya. You have already been warned, and my own warning adds nothing." The Earth Mother shimmered as one arm rose to point. "The mud puppy who brought you to me is called Haltwhistle. He has served me long and well. Your mother has known him since she was a child. Haltwhistle is a fairy creature, come from the mists once upon a time to be my companion. Mud puppies are able to live both in and out of the mists and serve who they choose. They are independent in making their choice and loyal ever after. They have a very powerful form of fairy magic at their command. It is a good magic, a magic of healing. It counteracts magics that are used to harm or destroy. It cannot protect against them completely, but it can alter their effects so that they are not so severe. Haltwhistle's magic does this for those he serves and sometimes for their friends."

Mistaya glanced down at Haltwhistle, who was looking up at her with great, soulful eyes. "He seems very nice," she said.

"He is yours now," the Earth Mother said gently. "I give him to you for the time it takes for you to grow to womanhood. While you grow, Haltwhistle will be your companion and protector. He will keep you safe from some of the harm that might be done by those dark clouds that come into your life."

Her arm fell away in a shimmer of moonlight. "But understand this, Mistaya. Haltwhistle cannot protect you against everything. No one can do that. If dark magic is used to harm you, he can become your shield. But if the dark magic is your own, he can do nothing to help you. What you choose to do with your life must be your responsibility. The consequences of your acts and decisions must be your own. You will make mistakes and engage in foolish behavior, and Haltwhistle will not be able to stop you. These are the lessons of growing up that you must endure."

Mistaya's brow furrowed, and her mouth tightened. "I shall not make mistakes or behave foolishly if I can help it," she insisted. "I shall be careful of my choices, Earth Mother."

The other's strange eyes seemed suddenly sad. "You will do the best you can, child. Do not expect more."

Mistaya thought. "Have I magic that will help me?" she asked impulsively. "Magic of my own?"

"Yes, Mistaya, you do. And perhaps it will help you. But it may also cause you harm. You are at some risk should you choose to use it."

"But I don't even know what it is. How can I use it? How can it hurt me?"

"In time," the Earth Mother said, "you will learn."

Mistaya sighed impatiently. "Now you sound like Father."

"It is time for you to go back," the Earth Mother advised, ignoring her complaint. "Before you do, there are a few things you must know about Haltwhistle. He will always be with you, but you will not always see him. He keeps watch over you as he deems best, so do not despair if from time to time you cannot find him. Also, you must never try to touch him. Mud puppies are not meant to be touched. Be warned. Finally, remember this. Haltwhistle requires neither food nor water from you. He will look after himself. But you must speak his name at least once each day. It may be spoken in any way you choose, but you must say it. If you fail to do so, you risk losing him. If he does not feel needed, he will leave you and come back to me. Do you understand all this?"

Mistaya nodded firmly. "I do, Earth Mother. Haltwhistle will be well cared for." She caught herself. "Earth Mother, I am traveling to see my grandfather in the lake country. What if he will not allow Haltwhistle into his home? He is a very stern man and quite strict about some things."

"Do not worry, child," the Earth Mother assured her. "Mud puppies are fairy creatures. They come and go when and where they choose. They cannot be kept out of any place they wish to visit unless powerful magic is used. Halt-whistle will be with you wherever you go."

Mistaya glanced down at the mud puppy and smiled. "Thank you, Earth Mother. Thank you for Haltwhistle. I love him already."

"Good-bye, Mistaya." The Earth Mother began to sink back down into the ooze. "Remember what I have told you, child."

"I will," Mistaya called back. "Good-bye." Then she shouted, "Wait! When will I see you again?"

But the elemental was already gone, disappeared into the earth. The marsh shimmered faintly with small ripples in the moonlight where she had stood. The clearing was empty and silent.

Mistaya was suddenly sleepy again. It had been a wonderful adventure, and she was looking forward to more. She yawned and stretched, then smiled down at Haltwhistle. "Are you tired, too?" she asked softly. Haltwhistle stared at her. "Let's go back to sleep. Okay, boy?"

Haltwhistle wagged his tail tentatively. He didn't seem all that sure it was.

But Mistaya was already walking away, so the mud puppy dutifully followed after. Together, they went back through the woods toward the camp and the fate that was waiting for them.

SPELL CAST

The crow with the red eyes, who in human form was Nightshade, sat high in the branches of a shagbark hickory and watched Mistaya return out of the nighttime woods. The girl materialized abruptly, a silent, stealthy shadow. Made blind to her presence by the Earth Mother's magic, the sentries did not spy her, staring right through her as she passed, as if there were nothing to see. The girl moved quickly to her blanket, wrapped it about herself, lay down, and closed her eyes. In seconds she was asleep.

The crow cast a sharp eye across the clearing and into the woods beyond. There was no sign of the mud puppy. Well and good.

The presence of the mud puppy had upset Nightshade's plans. She had not anticipated its appearance and still did not know its particular purpose. She was aware that it served the Earth Mother, of course, but that did not explain what had brought it to the girl. A summons from the Earth Mother? Possibly. Probably, as a matter of fact. But why had the Earth Mother summoned the girl this night? Did she know of Nightshade's intent? Had she warned the girl in some way? None of this seemed likely. Just as Nightshade could not penetrate the Earth Mother's magic to discover why she had dispatched the mud puppy, neither could the Earth Mother penetrate Nightshade's magic to reveal what lay in store for the girl. Either could gain a *sense* of what the other was about, but no more than that. It was a stalemate of sorts. So any attempt to follow the mud puppy and the girl in an effort to discover what the Earth Mother intended would have been quickly thwarted. Worse, it would have revealed Nightshade's presence in the lake country, and that could easily have ruined everything.

In any case, the girl had returned alone, so the Earth Mother must have finished with her. The fact that she had returned at all strongly suggested that she knew nothing of Nightshade's plans, so there was probably no reason to worry. Not that the Witch of the Deep Fell would have worried much in any

event. Had the Earth Mother or her four-legged messenger chosen to interfere, Nightshade would have found a way to make them regret the decision
for a long time to come. The witch's magic was much stronger than the Earth
Mother's, and she could have sent the elemental scurrying for cover in a
hurry.

The crow with the red eyes blinked contentedly. All was as it should be.
The Earth Mother had probably summoned the girl to pay her respects as a
longtime friend and protector of her mother. Now the girl was right back
where Nightshade wanted her, sleeping amid her decidedly ineffectual pro-
tectors, blissfully unaware of how her life was about to change.

Nightshade had known that Holiday would send his daughter away when
Rydall made his threat against their family. She had known exactly what Holiday would do. The sylph's premonition—the one Nightshade had dispatched
to her in her sleep, as black and terrifying as the witch could make it—had
planted the seed for the idea. Rydall's appearance had brought the seed to
flower. Whatever else might happen, Holiday and the sylph would take no
chances with their beloved daughter. Nightshade hadn't known where the girl
would be sent, although the lake country and the once-fairy had been her first
guess, but in truth it didn't matter. Wherever Mistaya might have gone, Nightshade would have been waiting.

And now it was time.

Using not just vision but instinct as well, the red eyes made a final sweep
of the clearing and the woods surrounding it, a final search of the shadows and
the dark where something might hide. Nothing revealed itself. The red eyes
gleamed. Nightshade smiled inwardly. The sleeping men and the girl belonged
to her now.

The crow took wing, lifting away from the branch on which it had kept
watch, soaring momentarily skyward, circling the clearing, then dropping
down again in a slow spiral. They were in the last few hours of the waning
night, the ones leading into the new day, the ones during which sleep is deepest and dreams hold sway. Darkness and silence cloaked the men and the girl
and their animals, and none sensed the presence of the descending crow. It
passed over their heads unseen and unheard. It swept across them twice to
make certain, but even the sentries, watchful once more now that the girl had
returned and the Earth Mother's vision spell had been lifted, saw nothing.

The crow banked slowly left across Mistaya, then flew back again, its
shadow passing over the small, still form like the comforting touch of a
mother's hand. On each pass a strange green dust that winked and spun in the
moonlight was released from the crow's dark wings like pollen from a flower
and floated earthward to settle over the sleeping girl. Four passes the crow
made, and on each the greenish dust fell like a mossy veil. Mistaya breathed it
in as she slept, smiled at its fragrance, and pulled her blanket tighter for comfort. Slowly her sleep deepened, and she drifted farther from consciousness.

Dreams claimed her, a conjuring of her most vivid imaginings, and she was carried swiftly away into their light.

The crow rose skyward again and circled back into the shelter of the trees. Now the girl would sleep until Nightshade was ready for her to wake. She would sleep and be no part of what was to happen next.

Descending by hops from branch to branch, the crow passed downward through the concealing limbs until it was only a few feet above the ground. Then it transformed into Nightshade, the witch rising out of feathers and wings in a swirl of dark robes to stand again on the earth in the night shadows. Tall and regal, her beauty as dazzling and cold as newly fallen snow, her black hair with its single white streak swept back from her aquiline face, her smile as hard as stone, she gathered her magic about her and stepped out from the trees and into the moonlit clearing.

In her dreams Mistaya was a bird with snow-white feathers flying across a land of bright colors. There were forests of emerald green, fields of butter yellow and spring mint, mountains of licorice and chocolate, hills of crimson and violet, lakes of azure, and rivers of silver and gold. Everywhere wildflowers bloomed, sprinkled across the land like fairy dust.

A bird with black feathers flew next to her, leading the way, showing her the miracle that lay below. The other bird said nothing; it had no need for words. Its thoughts and feelings buoyed Mistaya's small feathered body. She was borne as if on a wind, sailing down their currents, riding atop their gusts, stretching out to soar along their slides. It was wondrous, and it gave her an intoxicating sense of having the entire world at her wing tips.

The flight wore on, and they passed over people looking up from down below. The people craned their necks and pointed. Some called out to her and beckoned. They were people she had known in another life, in another form, and had left behind. They might have loved and cared for her once; they might even have helped nurture her when she was a fledgling. Now they were trying to lure her back to them, to draw her down so that they could cage her. They begrudged her the freedom she had found. They resented the fact that they no longer controlled her destiny. There was anger and disappointment and envy in their voices as they called out, and she found herself eager to get far away from them. She flew on without slowing, without looking back. She flew on toward her future.

Beside her the bird with black feathers turned to look at her, and she could see its red eyes glimmer with approval.

Having come completely clear of her shadowy concealment within the trees, Nightshade turned her attention first to the two sentries who kept watch at either end of the little clearing. She let them see her, all cloaked and hooded, a tall black shape as menacing as death. When they turned their weapons toward her, knowing instinctively that she was trouble, she brought up her hands and sent her magic lancing into them in twin flashes of wicked green fire. The sentries were engulfed before they could cry out, and when the fire died, they had been transformed into rocks the size of bread loaves, rocks that steamed and spit like live coals.

The Witch of the Deep Fell came forward another few steps. She pointed at the line that tethered the caravan's animals, and it flared and turned to ash. The horses, Lightfoot and Owl among them, bolted away. Nightshade gestured almost casually at the camp's cook fire, now no more than a clump of dying embers, and it flared alive, rising upward toward the heavens as if it had become some fiery phantasm risen from the earth. A moment later Mistaya's carriage burst into flames as well.

Now the remaining members of the King's Guards woke, blinking against the sudden light, scrambling clear of their blankets, and reaching instinctively for their weapons. They were pitifully slow. Nightshade transformed five of them before they even knew what was happening, catching them up in her magic, turning them to stones. The others were quicker, a few even swift enough to leap up and start toward her. But she pointed at them one after the other, a dark angel of destruction, and they were struck down. In seconds the last of them were gone.

Now the clearing was empty of everyone but Nightshade, the sleeping girl, and the astonished and confused Questor Thews and Abernathy. The latter two stood in front of Mistaya to protect her from harm. Everything had happened so quickly, they had barely had time to wake and come to her side. Questor Thews was weaving some sort of protective spell, his hands, as old and dry as twigs, making shadow pictures in the glare of the revived fire. Nightshade collapsed the spell before it could form and came forward to stand within the light. She swept back her hood and revealed herself.

"Don't bother, Questor Thews," she advised as he prepared to try again. "No magic will save you this time."

The old man stared at her, trembling with rage and indignation. "Nightshade, what have you done?" he exclaimed in a hoarse whisper.

"Done?" she repeated, indignant. "Nothing that I did not intend, wizard. Nothing that I have not planned for two long years. Do you begin to see now how hopeless things are for you?"

Abernathy was edging away, searching for a weapon to use against her. She made a sharp gesture, and he froze in his tracks.

"Better, scribe, if you stay where you are." She smiled at him, contented by the feeling of power that washed through her.

Questor Thews straightened himself, attempting as he did so to regain his dignity. "You overreach yourself, Nightshade," he declared bravely. "The High Lord will not tolerate this."

"The High Lord will have his hands full just trying to stay alive, I think," she replied, her smile growing broader. "Oh, I think he will have them quite full. Too bad you won't be there to help him. Either of you."

Questor Thews saw the truth of things then. "You have come for the girl, haven't you? For Mistaya?"

"She belongs to me," said the witch. "She has always belonged to me! She was born out of my soil, in my haven, from my magic! She should have been given to me then, but the fairies intervened. But not this time, wizard. This time I will have her. And when I am finished, she will not ever wish to leave me."

The fire roared and crackled in the night's deep silence, an enthusiastic accomplice to the witch's scheme. Questor Thews and Abernathy were scarecrow figures trapped within its light, helpless to escape. But they refused to crumble.

"Holiday will come for her," the old man insisted stubbornly, "even if we are gone."

Nightshade laughed. "You do not listen very well, Questor Thews. Holiday must deal with Rydall first, and Rydall will see him destroyed. I have planned it, and I will see it come to pass. The King of Marnhull is my creature, and he will bring about Holiday's destruction as surely as the sun will rise on the new day. Holiday will struggle against his fate, and that will give me great pleasure to watch, but in the end he will succumb. Stripped of his child, his friends, and eventually his wife as well, he will die all alone and forsaken. Nothing less will satisfy me. Nothing less will serve to repay me for what I have been made to suffer."

"Rydall is your doing?" the wizard whispered in shock.

"All of it is my doing—all that has come about and all that will be. I have made it my life's work to see the play-King reduced to nothing, and I will not be disappointed."

Abernathy edged forward a step. "Nightshade, you cannot do this. Let Mistaya go. She is only a child."

"Only a child?" The smile fled from Nightshade's face. "No, scribe, that is exactly what she is not. That is where you have all been so mistaken. I should know. I see myself in her. I see what I was. I see what she can be. I will give her the knowledge that you would keep hidden. I will shape her as she was meant to be shaped. She harbors within her soul demons waiting to be unleashed; I will help her set them free. She has the power of a child's imagination, and I will use that. Let this be your final thought. When I am done with her, she will become for me the instrument of the play-King's destruction! One more time will he see her, will he clasp her to him, a snake to his breast, and on that day he will breathe his last!"

She saw the hopelessness in their eyes as she finished and waited for them to react. Questor Thews was already trying furtively to gather back his scattered magic in a spell of protection, his gnarled fingers working in the shadow of his skinny body. She smiled at the futility of his effort.

None of them saw Haltwhistle edge out of the forest shadows to stand just within the clearing far to one side, splayed feet padding gingerly, sad eyes watchful.

"What do you intend to do to us?" Abernathy demanded, risking a quick glance over his shoulder at Mistaya. He was wondering why she did not wake up.

"Yes, Nightshade, what?" Questor Thews pressed. He was trying to give them more time so that he could complete the forming of his spell, not realizing that he was already far too late. "Would you turn us into rocks as well?"

Nightshade smiled. "No, wizard, I would not bother with anything so prosaic where you are concerned. Nor you, scribe. You have been a constant source of irritation to me, but you have interfered for the last time. Your lives end here. No one will ever see either of you again."

There was a moment in which time froze, the witch's words drifting away on the crackle of the fire. Then Questor Thews's hands came up, magic flaring in a wide arc before him. Abernathy turned swiftly toward Mistaya and reached down in an attempt to snatch her up. Nightshade laughed. Her arms extended, green fire exploded from her fingertips, and her magic rushed forward in a surge of energy and dark intent to engulf her victims.

As all this was happening, Haltwhistle's head drooped, his body slumped, the hackles on the back of his neck rose, and something akin to a mix of moonlight and frost rose off his cringing form and rocketed across the clearing. An instant before Nightshade's magic struck Questor Thews and Abernathy, smashing the wizard's flimsy shield to smithereens, the moon/frost reached them first.

Then the witch fire consumed them, and they were gone in an instant's time. Nothing remained but smoke and the stench of something charred and ruined.

Nightshade wheeled about. What was it she had seen? That odd glow come out of nowhere? Her eyes swept the clearing quickly, then reached into the woods beyond. Nothing. She narrowed her gaze. There had been something, hadn't there? She lifted her hands and sent witch light deep into the trees, seeking out any living thing concealed there. Small rodents, insects, and a handful of ground birds scattered before her power. But there was nothing else.

She turned back finally, vaguely dissatisfied. The clearing was empty of everyone save herself and the girl. The King's Guards had been turned to stones. The wizard and the dog were gone, never to be seen again. Everything had happened as she had intended. She was free to continue with her plans.

Still . . .

She brushed aside her misgivings in annoyance, walked over to the sleeping girl, and stared down at her. So much to be done with you, little one, she thought in satisfaction. So many lessons to be taught, so many secrets to be revealed, so many tricks to be played. Can you hear what I am thinking?

The girl stirred within her blankets, dreaming.

Yes, sleep on, the Witch of the Deep Fell urged silently. Tomorrow your new life begins.

She bent down then and lifted the girl into the cradle of her arms. Light, like a feather quilt, she was. Nightshade stared down at her new child and smiled.

Then she turned the air about them to icy mist. A moment later the clearing was deserted.

CHALLENGE

Exactly three days after his first appearance Rydall of Marnhull returned to Sterling Silver. This time Ben Holiday was waiting.

Ben never doubted that Rydall would come to make good on his promise. The only unanswered question was, What form of coercion would Marnhull's King employ to persuade Ben to accede to his ludicrous demands? Awake before sunrise, Ben had thought to take a run in an effort to clear his mind. A carryover from his boxing days, he still trained regularly, a regimen of running, weights, and workouts on the light and heavy bags. Sometimes he boxed with members of the King's Guards, but there was no one sufficiently skilled at the sport to give him much competition. Or maybe they thought it better for him to think as much. So mostly he trained alone. This morning he prepared to run, then lost interest. Instead, he climbed atop the battlements with Willow and Bunion to watch for the sunrise and Rydall.

The night had been chilly, and when the darkness began to ease to the west and the east to brighten, he found that during the night a low fog had moved out of the trees and down into the meadow fronting the castle. It lay across the damp grasses in a thick gray smudge that ran from the woods all the way to the waters of the lake. When the sun broke against the eastern horizon in a silvery splash, the fog inched back from the water's edge where the causeway bridged to the castle, and there was Rydall. He sat atop his charger, all armored and bristling with weapons, his silent black-cloaked companion hunched atop his own dark steed, the two of them looking just as before, just as if they had never left.

Ben stared down from the castle walls without speaking, waiting them out. The gauntlet cast down by Rydall three days earlier still lay in the center of the causeway. Ben had ordered it removed, but no one had been able to comply with his demand. It was as if the gauntlet had been nailed to the bridge. No one could lift it; no one could budge it, for that matter—not even

Questor Thews. Some form of magic held it in place, and nothing short of tearing up the bridge was going to get it out of there. Ben was not that desperate, so the gauntlet had stayed where it was.

It lay there now, gleaming faintly with the damp, a reminder of what Marnhull's King had promised.

"Holiday!" Rydall called out sharply. No use of "King" or "High Lord" this time. No pretense of respect. "Have you given further thought to my demand?"

"My answer is the same!" Ben shouted back. He felt Willow move in close beside him. "You knew it would be!"

Rydall's horse stamped impatiently. Rydall's hand lifted in a dismissive gesture. "Then I must ask you to change it. Rather, I must insist. You no longer have a choice. Things have changed since we last spoke. I have your daughter."

There was a long silence. Willow's hands fastened tightly on Ben's arm, and he heard her sharp intake of breath. Ben's throat constricted in response to the words. *I have your daughter.* But Mistaya was safe. She was two days gone into the lake country with her grandfather, safely beyond Rydall's reach.

Wasn't she?

"I told you I would find a way to convince you to listen to me," Rydall continued, breaking the momentary silence. "I think now that you must. Your daughter is important to you, I assume."

Ben was trembling with rage. "This is another of your games, Rydall! I have had just about all of you I can stand!"

The dismissive gesture came again. "That remains to be seen. I don't expect you to take my word for what I tell you, in any case. Not you, Holiday. You are the sort of man who demands proof even when the truth is staring him in the face. Very well, then."

He whistled, and a pair of horses appeared from out of the blanket of low-lying fog. Ben felt his heart sink as they came closer. One was Lightfoot, and the other Owl. There was no mistaking their markings. They came past Rydall and started across the bridge.

"Send someone down and have them bring you what they find tied to the pony's saddle," Rydall called up once more.

Ben looked over at Bunion. The kobold raced away instantly, a dark blur against the castle stone. Unable to speak, burning with anger, Ben stood with Willow pressed close against him. A moment later Bunion was back. There was no expression on his strange, wizened face. He handed Ben a necklace and a scarf. Ben studied them closely and, sick at heart, handed them to Willow. They belonged to Mistaya. She had been wearing them when she had left for the lake country.

"Oh, Ben," Willow whispered softly.

"Where are Questor Thews and Abernathy?" Ben shouted down to Rydall. "Where are the men of their escort?"

"Safely tucked away," Rydall answered. "Are you ready to hear my demands now, High Lord of Landover?"

Ben choked back the emotions that threatened to steal away his good sense. He put his arm around Willow as much to steady himself as to steady her. He was still not willing to accept what he was being told. It was not conceivable that Rydall could have taken Mistaya so easily. How had he managed it? How could he have overcome her escort? Questor Thews and Abernathy would have died before giving her up.

"Rydall!" he called down suddenly, shocking himself with the strength he found in his voice. "I will not surrender Landover's throne or her people for any reason. I will not be blackmailed. You seem comfortable with preying on small children, and that makes me doubt your claims of conquest with armies numbering in the thousands. I think you are a coward."

Rydall laughed. "Brave words for a man in your position. But I do not begrudge them. Nor, in fact, do I expect you to hand over the throne now any more than I did before. I took your daughter not to blackmail you into accepting my demands but to persuade you to hear me out. You would not do so before. You must now. Listen well, then. You can ill afford not to, I think."

Rydall pointed to the gauntlet. "The challenge I offer is not the one you have anticipated. As I said, I do not expect you to hand over your throne. I made the demand because, of course, I must. A King must always try what is easiest first. It is in the nature of conquest. Sometimes an opponent will accede. I did not think you would be one who would, but it was necessary to find out. Now we are past that, past game playing, past negotiation, and are face to face with reality. I have your daughter and your friends. You have my kingdom. One of us must give something up. Which of us is it to be?"

Rydall brought his horse forward onto the edge of the causeway. "I think it must be you, King of Landover, but I am willing to settle the matter in an honorable way. A challenge, then, as I have said. The challenge is this. I will send seven champions to face you. Each will come at a time of my choosing. Each will be of a different form. All will come to kill you. If you prevent them from doing so, if you are able to kill them first, all seven of them, then I will free your daughter and friends and abandon my claim to Landover. But if any of them succeeds, then your kingdom will be forfeit and your family will be sent into exile for all time. Do you accept? If you do, walk out upon the causeway and pick up my gauntlet."

Ben stared down at the other in disbelief. "He's crazy," he whispered to Willow, who nodded wordlessly.

"You have a champion of your own to defend you," Rydall continued. "Everyone knows of the Paladin, the King's knight-errant and protector. You shall have some form of defense against the creatures I send." Creatures now, Ben thought. Not champions. "I understand that no one has ever defeated the Paladin. That means you have a more than reasonable chance of winning, doesn't it? Do you accept?"

Still Ben did not respond, his mind racing as he considered the proposal. It was ridiculous, but it was the only chance he had to get Mistaya back. It gave him time to find out where she was and perhaps rescue her. And Questor Thews, Abernathy, and his soldiers. But the bargain itself was insane! His life measured against Rydall's seven killers? If he accepted this challenge, if he went down on the causeway and picked up that gauntlet, he would be bound as surely as by his most sacred oath. There were witnesses to this—members of his castle staff, King's Guards and retainers—and Landover's laws would not allow him to forsake his word once it was given. He might kill Rydall and be relieved of it, but the options offered were extreme and narrowly drawn.

"If you do not accept," Rydall shouted out suddenly, "I shall have your daughter and your friends tied to horses and set before my armies as we sweep into your kingdom. They shall die first, before any of my men. I would regret this, but it would be necessary if I were to ask my men to give up their lives as the price of your stubbornness. I told you once before, I prefer to gain your kingdom without bloodshed. You might prefer the same—if for different reasons. My challenge gives you that chance. Do you accept?"

Ben was thinking now that if he did, he must also accept the fact that he would be required to become the Paladin in order to stay alive—not once or twice but seven times. It was his worst fear. He struggled constantly with what giving himself over to his alter ego meant. Each time it became increasingly more difficult to keep from losing his own identity. Becoming the Paladin meant complete submersion into the other's being. Each time it was a little harder coming back out of the armored shell, out of the memories, out of the life that was his champion's. If he accepted Rydall's challenge, he would be facing the prospect not only of being killed in combat but of being transformed forever into his darker half.

"High Lord, do you accept?" Rydall demanded again.

"No, do not!" Willow exclaimed suddenly, seizing his arm. "There is more to this than what you are being told! There is something hidden behind Rydall's words! I can sense it, Ben!" She moved in front of him. There were tears in her eyes. Her voice was so quiet, he could barely hear her speak. "Even if we must lose Mistaya, do not accept."

What it must have cost her to say this, Ben could not begin to guess. She was fiercely protective of Mistaya. She would do anything to keep her safe. But she was giving him a chance to save himself anyway. She loved him that much.

He folded her into his arms and held her close. "I have to try," he told her softly. "If I don't, how will I live with myself afterward?"

He kissed her, then turned away. Beckoning Bunion to follow, he crossed the parapets to the stairway leading down. "Wait for me here," he called back to Willow.

He went down the stairway thinking of what he must do once he picked

up the gauntlet. His options were few. He must find Mistaya, Questor, Abernathy, and his Guards and set them free. That was first. Then he must persuade
Rydall to withdraw his challenge and his threat to Landover. Or, if he was unable to do that, kill him. The alternative was to face Rydall's seven challengers
and hope that he killed them before they killed him. Or was he required to kill
them? Perhaps he could simply defeat them. But Rydall had not made it seem
as if that were an option. "Creatures" Rydall had called them the second time.
Ben found himself wondering what sort of creatures they would be.

He crossed the courtyard to the main gates, Bunion a step behind, the
kobold's teeth clenched in a frightening grimace. It was clear what he was
thinking. "Let them be, Bunion," Ben cautioned softly. "We need Mistaya and
the others back first."

The kobold grunted something in response, and Ben hoped it was the answer he was seeking.

He walked through the main gates and out onto the causeway. The day was
brightening, the sky clear and blue, the last of the fog dissipating on the
meadow fronting the castle's lake. Rydall and his silent companion sat atop
their horses and waited. Ben moved out onto the causeway, alert for any
treachery, his anger growing with every step he took. Perhaps Bunion had the
right idea. How hard would it be to summon the Paladin and put an end to
Rydall once and for all? Easy enough if he chose to do it, he thought. But
where would that leave Mistaya?

He wondered suddenly if this was all an elaborate trick, if the horses, the
necklace, and the scarf were lures to bring him out into the open. He wondered if Rydall really did have Mistaya and her escort as his prisoners. He surmised that it could all be a clever lie.

But he knew in his heart it wasn't.

He reached the far end of the causeway and stopped. The riders stared
down at him from atop their chargers. Wordlessly Ben reached down for the
gauntlet. It came away from the bridge easily, as if nothing more than force of
will had held it in place those three days past. Ben straightened and looked directly at Rydall. Marnhull's King was much bigger than he had first thought,
a man of surprising size and undoubted strength. His black-cloaked companion, on the other hand, seemed smaller. The faces of both were carefully hidden beneath helmet and hood, respectively.

Ben flung the gauntlet back at Rydall. The big man caught it easily and
waved it in mock salute.

"Do not mistake this for anything but what it is, Rydall," Ben said quietly.
"And know this. If anything happens to Mistaya or Questor Thews or Abernathy or one of my Guards, I will hunt you down even if I am required to descend into the fires of Abaddon!"

Rydall bent forward. "You will never have to search that far for me, Holiday. Nor think for one moment that I would be afraid of you if you did." He

tightened his reins and swung his horse about. "Three days, High Lord of Landover. The first of my creatures comes for you then. If I were you, I would start thinking about how to stay alive."

He kicked his mount sharply, and the warhorse leapt away. Once again his black-cloaked companion lingered. Ben could feel eyes studying him from within the hood's deep shadows, as if trying to discover something. Fear, perhaps? Ben held his ground, staring back determinedly. Then Bunion was beside him, hissing furiously at the rider, all teeth and claws as he advanced.

The second rider wheeled away then and galloped after Rydall across the meadow. Ben stood with his kobold protector and watched until they had disappeared into the trees.

---<∞>---

Safely back within the forest shadows where even the new light had not yet penetrated, the riders reined to a halt and dismounted. Nightshade threw off the cloak that had concealed her and, discarding the cramped and hunched form she had assumed as her disguise, restored her body to its normal shape. Her hands lifted then to form a brief spell of invisibility, protection against the unlikely event that someone would stumble across them. When the spell was in place, she used her magic a second time to change the horses back into tiny green and black striped lizards that quickly skittered up her arm and into the folds of her robes.

Rydall stood watching, his visor still lowered. "He does not seem afraid," he offered petulantly.

Nightshade laughed. "No, not yet. His anger shields him for the moment. He still doubts that we really have his daughter. He will need to make certain of that before fear can take hold. Then my creatures will come for him, one after the other, and the fear will build. He will begin to imagine all sorts of things coming to pass, none of them good. He will search for us and fail to find even the smallest trace. He will despair of hope. Then, I promise, the fear will have him."

"He has the sylph for support, don't forget."

There was a flash of anger in Nightshade's red eyes. "Do not mock me, King Rydall, who never was Rydall or King. You serve at my pleasure; do not forget that."

The other stood motionless before her and said nothing, a wall of iron. But she could sense his hesitation and was satisfied. "He has her for now, yes," she admitted. "But in the end I'll see her stripped from him as well. In the end he will be left alone."

Rydall shifted impatiently. "I would feel better about this if I knew the whole of your plan. What if something goes wrong?"

She straightened so that she seemed to grow before his eyes. "Nothing will go wrong. I have planned too carefully for that. As for knowing what I intend, it is better for now that I keep some things to myself. You know as much as you need to know." She gave him a coldly appraising look. "I'll send you back now. Tend to your affairs and await my summons."

Rydall looked away, his armor creaking. "I could have killed him on the bridge and the matter would have been finished then and there. You should have let me."

"And spoil what I have worked and planned for these two years past?" Nightshade was incredulous. "I think not. Besides, I am not so sure you are his better. You have never given proof of it."

He started to object, a grunt of anger rising from his throat, but she cut him off with a wave of her hand. "Stay silent. You will do as I say. Holiday's demise is to be left to me. Your part in this is settled. I want no dispute. You are not trying to dispute me, are you?"

There was a long silence from the other. "No," he replied finally.

"Good. If you want Holiday dead, and I know you do, then leave it to me to arrange. Now go."

She wove her hands through the air before her, and Rydall disappeared in a rising column of mist. She waited until she was sure he had been dispatched back to where he had come from. She neither liked nor trusted him, but he was useful in this matter and would do as a cat's-paw until she was finished. Until Holiday was dead.

She closed her eyes in pleasure as she envisioned the play-King's final moments. She had pictured it over and over again in her mind, shaping it, honing it, polishing it until it was perfect. She could see every detail of it. She could see him breathing for the final time, see the look in his eyes as he realized what had been done to him, hear the despair in his voice as he tried to cry out.

Oh, it would happen. It most definitely would. For now, however, there were other matters that needed her attention.

She brought up her hands one final time. A rush of dark mist engulfed her, and she was gone.

Ben Holiday was already thinking furiously as he walked back across the causeway and reentered Sterling Silver. Willow had come down from the battlements and was waiting for him. She rushed up, and he held her close in an effort to still the trembling inside them both.

"We'll get her back," he whispered, feeling her fists tighten against his back. "I promise."

Then he turned to Bunion, who was trailing behind. "Leave for the lake country right away," he ordered the kobold. "Tell the River Master that his granddaughter has been kidnapped by Rydall of Marnhull and ask for his help in searching for her. Tell him any assistance he chooses to give will be greatly appreciated. Be sure he understands that she was traveling to his country for safekeeping when she was taken. Keep an eye out for any sign of what might have happened on your journey down. And Bunion," he added, "be careful yourself. Don't take any chances. I've already lost Questor and Abernathy. I don't want to lose you as well."

The kobold grinned and showed his teeth. It wasn't likely that anything would happen to a creature that could dispatch a cave wight or a bog wump without breaking a sweat, but Ben was spooked by how easily Rydall had overcome those he had sent to protect Mistaya. If that was what had really happened, of course. He still wasn't sure, but he had to assume the worst. Bunion's visit to the River Master was necessary.

Bunion turned and was gone so swiftly that Ben had to remind himself why he had dispatched his royal messenger in the first place. Kobolds were the fastest creatures alive. A trip to the lake country would take a kobold barely a day. They were strange beings, their bodies all gnarled and bristly, their legs bowed and their arms crooked, their faces monkeylike, and their teeth as numerous and sharp as an alligator's, an amalgam of bizarre and diverse features. But kobolds had served the Kings of Landover for many years, and they were loyal and tough. Ben knew he could depend on Bunion.

He started across the entry court, Willow at his side. "I'm going up to use the Landsview. Maybe I can find some trace of Misty. Will you cancel all my appointments for the day? I'll be down as soon as I can."

He climbed to the castle's highest tower and boarded the Landsview, the magical instrument that allowed its user to travel from one end of Landover to the other without leaving Sterling Silver. He invoked the magic, rose out of the tower as if actually flying, and in his mind's eye scanned the whole of the countryside without finding his daughter or his friends or any indication of what had happened to them. He made a quick visit to Elderew, the home of the River Master, but there was nothing to show that the once-fairy were aware that anything had happened.

He went from there to the eastern borders, searching the fringes of the fairy mists from the Fire Springs south, but there was no sign of Rydall or Mistaya or anything that would have led him to either. He looked for Strabo, but the dragon was not to be found. Probably sleeping in one of the fire pits it called home. He moved on to the Melchor north and finally to the Deep Fell, whose hollows were the one place he could not enter from the Landsview. Nightshade's magic would not permit it. He paused momentarily, thinking that those he searched for could easily be hidden there and he would never know. But it was reaching to imagine that Nightshade was involved in any of this. As much as she hated him, she hated outsiders more. She would never conspire with anyone who intended to invade Landover. Besides, no one had even seen her in months. Ben moved on.

He spent the whole of the morning searching the countryside for Mistaya and his friends and found not a single trace of any of them. It was as if they had disappeared off the face of the earth. When he finally came back into the chamber and stepped down off the lectern, he was exhausted. Use of the Landsview's magic had worn him out, and he had nothing to show for it. He was discouraged and frightened. He went down to his bedchamber and fell asleep.

When he woke, Willow was seated next to him, anxious for any news. But he had none to give her. They spent the remainder of the day going over the agenda of meetings and appointments for the week and ended up canceling most. Some had to be kept because there were obligations that could not wait. But it was a desultory effort at best, and Ben could think of little besides his missing daughter and friends. He did not know what to do next. It seemed there was nothing he could do other than wait on Rydall's challengers. Three days he had been given. Then the first would appear. He did not speak of it with Willow, but he could see in her eyes and hear in her voice that she was thinking of it, too. A battle to the death seven times over if he was to survive. A use seven times of the Paladin's armored body and battle skills. A giving over of himself seven times to the life and memories of a being whose only purpose was to destroy the King's enemies. It was a thoroughly terrifying prospect.

They slept poorly that night, waking often to hold each other, lying close in the silence and thinking of what the days ahead promised. Ben had never felt so empty. It seemed on reflection that he had betrayed Mistaya by sending her away, that he should have kept her close beside him. Perhaps that way he could have protected her better from Rydall. He did not say so to Willow, of course. It was easy to engage in second-guessing now, when it was too late to matter, when things were over and done. There was nothing to be gained by rehashing the "what ifs" of the situation. All that remained was to try to find some way to make things right again. But how was he to do that? What was left to try?

By noon of the following day Bunion was back. He had met with the River Master. Mistaya and the others had never reached Elderew. No one among the once-fairy had any idea what had happened to them. There was no sign they had ever passed that way.

Ben Holiday and Willow exchanged a long, helpless look and tried to hide their despair.

SEDUCTION

Mistaya woke to find herself shrouded in hazy light and deep silence. She lay upon the ground, still wrapped in her blanket but far from the place where she had fallen asleep. She knew that instinctively. She knew as well that she had slept for a long time. She was still drowsy, her limbs were stiff, her eyes were blurry, and her entire body was filled with the sort of heaviness that comes only after a deep sleep. Something had happened to her. Something unexpected.

She rose to a sitting position and looked around. She was alone. There was no sign of Questor, Abernathy, or the King's Guards. There was no trace of Haltwhistle. The animals were gone, and her baggage and carriage were missing. She was not surprised. She had been taken away from all that while she slept. She did not think she was even in the lake country anymore. The look of things was all wrong. She glanced skyward. There was no sky to be seen. There were trees all about, but they were ancient and webbed with vines and moss. The light was gray and thick with mist. It smelled and tasted of damp earth and decay. Strangely enough, it seemed familiar.

She stood up and brushed herself off. She was not afraid. She should have been, she supposed, but she was not. At least not yet. There was a strangeness to things that she could not explain, but she had not been harmed in any way. She wondered what had happened to her friends, but she was not yet ready to conclude that she was in any danger.

She peered about carefully, turning a full circle to spy out anything that might be spied, and discovered nothing but the old-growth trees and the misty silence.

When she had completed her circle, she found herself face to face with a tall, regal woman.

"Welcome, Mistaya," the woman said, smiling. A cold smile.

"Where am I?" Mistaya asked, thinking as she did, *I know this woman. I know her. But how?*

"You are in the Deep Fell," the woman answered, calm and still against the half-light. She was cloaked in black. Her hair was black with a single white streak down the middle. Her skin was alabaster white. Her eyes . . .

"You remember me, don't you?" the woman said, making it more a statement of fact than a question.

"Yes," Mistaya answered, certain now that she did, yet unable to remember why. This was the Deep Fell, the woman had said, and only one person lived in the Deep Fell. "You are Nightshade."

"I am," Nightshade answered, pleased. The eyes, silver before, turned suddenly red.

"You are the bird, the crow," the girl said suddenly. "From the picnic. You were watching me."

Nightshade's smile broadened. "I was. And you were watching me, weren't you? Your memory is excellent."

Mistaya looked about uncertainly. "What am I doing here? Did you bring me?"

The witch nodded. "I did. You were asleep when your camp was attacked by those in service to King Rydall of Marnhull, the man who came recently to your father's castle. Do you remember him?"

Mistaya nodded.

"The attack was sudden and unexpected. It was made in an effort to kidnap you. If you were in Rydall's power, then he might force your father to do as he seeks—to relinquish the crown of Landover and go into exile. Your parents thought Rydall would not know of your journey to the lake country and your grandfather, but he is more dangerous than they suspected. It was fortunate that I was keeping an eye out for you, that I was concerned for your safety. I was able to spirit you away before you were taken. I brought you here, to the Deep Fell, to be with me."

Mistaya said nothing, but her eyes gave her away.

"You do not believe me, do you?" Nightshade said.

Mistaya's lips compressed into a tight line. "My father would not want me here," she said quietly.

"Because we are not friends and he does not trust me," the witch acknowledged with a shrug. "That is true. But the fact of the matter is that he knows you are here and can do what he chooses with the information."

Mistaya frowned. "He knows?"

"Of course. I have already sent word. Secretly, of course, so that Rydall will not know. I was forced to act swiftly when the attack came, so I could not leave word with your friends. I think they are well, but I could not stay to make certain. Questor Thews seemed to be holding his own, and I suspect that with you gone, the attack would have been withdrawn rather quickly. After all, there was no point in continuing it."

"Because I was with you."

"Exactly. But Rydall does not know that. He thinks you are returned to Sterling Silver or gone on to Elderew to be with your grandfather. Neither place is safe, of course. He will be looking for you there. He will not think to look for you here. You are better off with me until this matter is resolved. Your father will agree with that once he thinks it through."

Mistaya shuffled her feet, thinking hard. None of this seemed right to her. "How do you know about Rydall? Why have you been watching me?"

"I am interested in you, Mistaya," Nightshade answered slowly. "I know things about you that even you do not know. I wanted to tell them to you, but I wasn't sure how to do so. I was following you, waiting for a chance. I know how your father and mother feel about me. We have not always been on good terms. At times we have fought. But we share a common interest in you." She paused. "Do you know, Mistaya, that you were born in the Deep Fell?"

Mistaya's brow furrowed. "I was?"

"Your mother didn't tell you, did she? I thought not." Nightshade moved to one side. She seemed unconcerned with everything as she gazed off into the trees. "Did she tell you that you can do magic?"

Mistaya's mouth dropped. Interest flickered in her emerald eyes. "I can? Real magic?"

"Of course. Every witch can do magic." Nightshade glanced over, and her red eyes glittered. "You knew you were a witch, didn't you?"

Mistaya took a very deep breath before answering. "No, I didn't. Are you lying to me?"

Nightshade gave no answer. Instead, she gestured vaguely at the air before her, and a table and two chairs appeared. The table was covered with a scarlet cloth and laden with fruit, nuts, bread, cheese, and cider. "Sit down," said the witch. "We shall have something to eat while we talk."

Mistaya hesitated, but hunger won out over reticence, and she took the chair opposite Nightshade. Still cautious, she tried a nut and then a slice of cheese. Both tasted wonderful, so she went on to the rest of the food-stuffs and a cup of the cider. Nightshade sat opposite her and chewed absently on a slice of bread.

"I will tell you something, Mistaya," she said. "I brought you here because the opportunity presented itself, and I was afraid it would not come again. It was chance, of course. If I had waited for you to come on your own or for your parents to send you—if I had been bold enough to make the request, for there would have been no offer from them—you probably would not have come at all. I do not begrudge that. I understand the way of things. I am not well thought of in many quarters and by many people. I am sure you have heard bad things about me."

Mistaya glanced up from her eating, a flicker of concern in her green eyes. But there was no threat in the witch's voice and none mirrored on her face.

"You needn't be afraid of me," Nightshade assured her. "You are here to be kept safe, not to be harmed. You are free to leave whenever you wish. But I would like you to hear me out first. Will you agree to that?"

Mistaya thought it over, chewing on a handful of nuts, then nodded.

"Good. You are perceptive. I meant what I said about you being safer here than with your family." Nightshade made a dismissive gesture with her hand. "Rydall is an outsider, a pretender to the throne, a conqueror of lesser lands who would add Landover to his holdings. Whatever differences your father and I have shared, we agree on one thing. Landover should not be ruled by Rydall. I am a witch, Mistaya, and witches know things that others do not. They hear of them first and comprehend them more fully. Rydall was known to me the moment he crossed out of the mists with his black-cloaked companion. His wizard, I discovered. A very powerful being, one who is, perhaps, as powerful as me. I knew of them and shadowed them on their visit to your home. I heard their demands. I knew what they would do. When they came for you, I was waiting."

She looked off into the trees again, contemplative. "But I had other reasons for intervening at the time I chose. I wanted to bring you here. I wanted you to spend time with me in the Deep Fell. The chance would not come again, I felt. So I was anxious to take advantage of it. I think it is important that you hear the truth about yourself—important to you and to me."

"To you?" Mistaya looked doubtful.

"Yes, Mistaya." Nightshade's hands caressed each other like small white mice. "I am the Witch of the Deep Fell, the only witch in all of Landover, and I have waited a long time for there to be another. I want to reveal what I know. I want to talk with someone who shares my passion for magic. You are that person."

Mistaya had stopped eating. She was staring at Nightshade, entranced. "I thought I might have magic," she said quietly, hesitantly, thinking of the Earth Mother. "Sometimes I could almost feel it. But I wasn't sure."

"You are unschooled in its use, untrained in its calling, and the truth of its existence has been kept from you. But the magic is yours," Nightshade said. "It has always been yours."

"Why wasn't I told?" Mistaya was still not convinced, but she was beginning to explore the possibilities. "Why did my parents and even Questor tell me that use of the magic—of any magic—was dangerous? Are you saying they lied to me?"

Nightshade shook her head. "Of course not. They would never do that. They simply kept from you what they felt you were not yet ready to know. In time they would have told you everything. I think they were mistaken in keeping it from you for as long as they did, of course. But now there are other reasons to tell you, ones that have nothing to do with a difference of opinion between your parents and me, ones that have everything to do with the coming of Rydall and the danger he poses to your father."

"What danger?" Mistaya asked at once. "Tell me."

But Nightshade shook her head and held up one slim hand. "Patience, Mistaya. Let me tell you things in my own way. You can make up your mind when I am finished."

She rose again, and Mistaya rose with her. Nightshade gestured briefly, and the table with its food and drink disappeared. The clearing in which they stood was empty again, save for them. Nightshade smiled at Mistaya. The same cold smile. But it seemed more comforting to the girl this time, more acceptable. She found herself smiling back almost without being aware of it.

"We shall be friends, you and I," the witch said, arching one eyebrow toward the beginning of the white streak in her black hair. "We shall tell each other all our secrets. Come with me."

She moved across the clearing and into the woods without looking back. Mistaya followed, curious now, anxious to hear more of what the other would tell her. She was no longer thinking of the circumstances that had brought her to the Deep Fell. She was not even thinking of her parents or Questor Thews or Abernathy. She was thinking instead of her magic, the magic she had always known she possessed, the magic she had so desperately coveted. Now, at last, it was going to be revealed to her. She could sense it in the tall woman's words.

When they had gone a short distance into the trees, back where the haze was thick enough to cut and the light was drawn thin, Nightshade stopped and turned to face the girl.

"You are not easily frightened, are you, Mistaya?" she asked. Mistaya shook her head. "You do not find the use of magic a cause for tears and huddling under covers as some children do when a storm comes with its lightning and thunder?"

Mistaya shook her head again, this time looking absolutely defiant. "I am not frightened of anything!" she said bravely, and almost meant it.

Nightshade nodded, eyes silver and serene once more. "I brought you here to the Deep Fell because you are a witch. A witch," she repeated emphatically, "like me. You were born in the Deep Fell, born of soil which has been consecrated time and again by my magic, born of a heritage of fairy blood, born into a world in which the strong and the certain are blessed with the use of power. You are something of an enigma to your parents because of this. An enigma. Do you know the word?"

Mistaya nodded. "A mystery."

"Yes, a mystery. Because there is not another like you in all of Landover. You have abilities they do not even suspect. You have magic that only I can comprehend. I can teach you to harness your power and use it well. No one else can do for you what I can. Not your parents. Not Questor Thews. Not anyone. None of them share in being what we are—witches—and so none of them can give you what you need. Yes, use of the magic can be very dangerous indeed. There is no secret in that. But the danger comes in not understanding what it is the magic can do and in making certain that you always know how to control it. Do you see?"

Mistaya nodded once more, eager now, excited by the implicit promise of the other's words.

"Good. Here, then." Nightshade bent down and plucked a wildflower with its buds still unopened. She held it up before Mistaya. Then she lifted one finger and caressed a tiny bud. The bud shuddered and blossomed into a crimson flower. "See? Magic brought it to life. Now you try."

She handed the stalk with its multiple buds and single open flower to Mistaya, who took it tentatively and held it before her as if it were made of glass.

"Concentrate on one bud," the Witch of the Deep Fell said. "Concentrate on how it will look as it opens into a flower. Bring the feeling of its coming to life deep within your body, deep down where there is only darkness and the pictures we form in our imaginations. Concentrate on the flower you would make and then reach up slowly and touch the bud."

Mistaya did as she was told, focusing every ounce of energy on a mental picture of the bud opening into a flower. She reached up and touched the bud gently, hesitantly.

The bud opened halfway and stopped.

"Very good, Mistaya," Nightshade offered, taking the stalk from her hand and casting it aside. "Was that so hard?"

Mistaya shook her head quickly. Her mouth was dry, and her heart was pounding. She had actually performed magic. She had felt the bud respond to her touch, had watched it shudder slightly, just as it had for Nightshade. But there had been more. There had been a ripple of something smooth and silvery deep down inside her that caressed like a cat and left her warm and anxious for more.

Nightshade's slender hand brushed her own. Mistaya did not mind the touch. It seemed familiar and therefore comfortable. "Try this," the witch said.

She reached down and picked up a black and orange striped caterpillar. The caterpillar rolled into a ball in the palm of her hand, then unrolled again after a moment and began to inch its way to safety. The witch reached down and touched the caterpillar, and it was turned instantly to gold.

"Now you change it back again," she instructed, holding out her open palm with the caterpillar to Mistaya. "Concentrate. Picture in your mind what it is you intend to do. Reach down inside yourself for the feeling of it happening."

Mistaya wet her lips, then compressed them. She focused as hard as she could on the caterpillar, envisioning it alive, seeing it turn from metal to organic matter. She saw it in her mind, then felt it in her heart. She reached down and touched the caterpillar.

The caterpillar turned orange and black once more and began to crawl away.

"I did it!" she breathed excitedly. "Did you see? I did it! I used magic!"

She forgot everything in that instant: her doubts, her questions, her parents, and her friends. Nightshade brushed the caterpillar away and bent down quickly in front of the girl, her eyes as sharp as cut glass.

"Now you understand, Mistaya. Now you see the truth of what you can do. But that was nothing, that little bit of magic you just performed. That was only the beginning of what you can accomplish. But you must listen to what I tell you. You must study the lessons I give you. You must practice what I show you. You must work very hard. Are you willing to do that?"

Mistaya nodded eagerly, blond hair shimmering with the jungle damp, eyes as bright as a cat's in a cave. "Yes, I am. But . . ." She stopped then, catching herself as she remembered anew the circumstances of her being in the Deep Fell. "My father . . ."

"Your father knows you are here and will come for you if he feels you should not stay," Nightshade answered smoothly, quickly. "The question you must answer is whether or not *you* wish to stay. The choice is really yours now. But before you make that choice, there is something else you must know. Remember I told you there was another reason for your being here with me, for being told of your potential, for exploring your magic?"

She waited expectantly. Mistaya hesitated, then nodded. "I remember. You said you would tell me later."

Nightshade smiled. "Close enough. In my own time and way, I said. So listen carefully now. Rydall of Marnhull has come to your father again since your leaving. He has told your father that he will use the magic of his wizard to destroy him. Questor Thews will try to protect your father, but he lacks sufficient power to do so. Rydall's wizard is much more powerful."

She raised one slender finger and touched Mistaya gently on the tip of her nose. Like a snake's kiss. "But you have the potential, Mistaya, to be even more powerful. You have the magic, still latent but undeniably contained within you, to defeat Rydall and his wizard and save your father. I sense that power, and it is for this reason that I thought it right to bring you here and prepare you for your destiny. For you will be a witch of no small consequence, and a King's daughter as well, and your mastery of your heritage as both will determine the course of your life."

Mistaya stared openmouthed. "I will be able to save my father? My magic will be that strong?"

"As strong as any you could possibly imagine." The witch paused, smiling anew, suddenly intense. "Didn't the Earth Mother tell you any of this?"

"Yes, she . . ." Mistaya hesitated, thinking all at once that she should not reveal everything to someone who already knew so much. Her meeting with the Earth Mother, after all, was supposed to be a secret. "She told me something of my heritage but left me to discover for myself the nature of any magic I possessed or for my parents to tell me of it when they were ready."

She wondered suddenly about Haltwhistle. Where was the mud puppy? Had he, too, been left behind in the attack when Nightshade had brought her to the Deep Fell? She wanted to ask the witch, but once more something kept her from speaking. Nightshade had not mentioned Haltwhistle when she spoke of the others. Perhaps she did not know of the mud puppy.

"The Earth Mother is your friend, as she was your mother's," Nightshade continued. "A good friend, I expect, isn't she?" Mistaya nodded. "She brought you to her just before the attack. I was watching. Did she warn you it was coming?"

"No," Mistaya answered, again thinking, *Why doesn't she know this?*

"What was it that she wanted with you, then?" the other softly asked. "Tell me."

Mistaya shrugged, a reflex pure and simple. She was outwardly calm, inwardly cold. Something was happening here that she didn't understand. She managed a small smile. "She warned me that there would be danger ahead and that I must be wary of it. She said I would need to keep my wits about me."

She waited, the smile frozen on her face as the witch stared deep into her eyes. *She doesn't believe me!* she was thinking, and wondered all at once why that mattered and what it was that frightened her so.

Then Nightshade's eyes lowered, and she rose. Her slim white hands came to rest on Mistaya's small shoulders. "Do you want to stay with me in the Deep Fell, Mistaya? Do you want to study magic with me?"

Mistaya was soothed by the touch, encouraged by the words, and reassured as swiftly as she had been made to doubt. "How long would I stay?" she asked tentatively, still thinking of her father.

"As long as you wish. You may leave at any time. But," the witch said, and bent down again, her face close, "once you leave to go back to your home, you leave for good. That is the way of things. Once you begin your training, you must remain until it is completed or give it up entirely."

"But if my father comes for me, then what?"

"Then we will speak with him, and a decision will be reached," the other answered. "But Mistaya, you must understand this. Magic is a fragile vessel, one that carries great power but can shatter like glass. It cannot be left untended once it is brought out into the open. So if we are to begin your lessons, you must agree to see them through to their completion. Can you do that?"

Mistaya thought of the way the bud had flowered and the caterpillar had come to life. She thought of the feeling of the magic simmering inside her, smooth and silky. Her misgivings about her circumstances in coming to the Deep Fell seemed inconsequential compared to that.

"I can," she answered firmly.

"So you agree to stay?"

Mistaya nodded, a child's determined affirmation. "I do."

Nightshade smiled down at her benevolently. "Then we shall begin at once. Come with me." She turned away and started back toward the clearing. "Now, there are rules to be heeded, Mistaya," she said as they walked through the haze. "You must listen to me and do as I say. You must never use your magic without me. You must use your magic in the ways I tell you even when you do not understand what it is that I am trying to teach. And——"

She glanced back to make certain Mistaya's eyes found her own. "You must never leave the Deep Fell without me." She let the words sink in. "Because Rydall will be looking for you, and I would never forgive myself if you were to fall into his hands through my carelessness. So we shall stay close to each other while you remain in my charge. Never leave the hollow. Do you understand?"

Mistaya nodded. She did.

The witch turned away, and although Mistaya could not see, there was a satisfied smile on her smooth, cold face. There was triumph in her red-tinged eyes.

They spent all that day working on Nightshade's lessons. Some were incomprehensible to Mistaya, just as the witch had warned. Some were exercises that lacked any discernible purpose. Some were charged with power that Mistaya could feel flowing out of her like the pulse through her body when she ran. Some were so gentle and serene that they lacked any feeling at all and were only words or small gestures on the air.

When the day ended, Mistaya was left with mixed feelings about what she had accomplished. On the one hand, she had felt and seen the magic that lay buried within her, a strange, ephemeral creature that stirred to life and flashed brief glimpses of its visage as she sought to lure it from its den. On the other hand, the ways in which it appeared and was used were enigmatic and unrevealing. Nightshade seemed satisfied, but Mistaya was left confused.

Once, for instance, they had worked at creating a monster. The monster had been one of Mistaya's own choosing, the girl urged on in her creativity by her new mentor, encouraged to make her creature as invulnerable as she could imagine it. Nightshade had been particularly pleased with her efforts there. She had said it was very good. She had said they would try another tomorrow.

Monsters? Mistaya did not understand, but then, she had been told she would not at times, hadn't she?

Rolled up in the blanket by the fire that the witch had allowed her for warmth—Nightshade herself seemed to need no nurturing of that sort—she stared out into the darkness of the Deep Fell, out into the silent gloom, and wondered if she was doing the right thing. Discovering the magic she possessed was exciting, but there was a forbidden quality to its study that she could not ignore. Would her father really approve? He must, if he did not come for her. But then, perhaps he did not know what it was that she was doing with Nightshade. If he did and wanted her to stop, what would she do? She wasn't sure. It was true that she was safer here than in places where Rydall would know to look for her. It was also true that it was much more interesting here. Nightshade was fascinating, filled with strange knowledge, possessed of exotic lore. Although she was clearly the teacher, she treated Mistaya as an equal in their studies, and Mistaya liked that. She coveted the respect she was accorded here, something that had been denied her at home.

She would stay awhile, she decided. Long enough to see what would happen. She could always leave, after all. Nightshade had said so. She could leave whenever she wished if she was willing to pay the penalty of losing her instruction.

Yes, she would stay on a bit longer.

She thought again of Haltwhistle. He would always be with her, the Earth Mother had promised. Was that so? He did not require food or drink or looking after. Mistaya needed only to say his name at least once each day to keep him close.

Her hand came up to her mouth. She had not done that. She had not said his name even once. She had not thought to do so.

She opened her mouth and stopped. Nightshade did not know of the mud puppy. What would she say? Would she send Haltwhistle away? And Mistaya as well?

Mistaya's mouth tightened. Well, it didn't make any difference if the mud puppy wasn't there. She might as well find out before she worried about any of the rest of it.

"Haltwhistle," she said softly, almost inaudibly.

Instantly the mud puppy was next to her, staring down at her from out of the darkness with those great, soulful eyes. Elated, she started to reach for him and stopped. You must never touch a mud puppy, the Earth Mother had warned. Never.

"Hey, boy," she whispered, smiling. Haltwhistle thumped his odd tail in response.

"Did you call, Mistaya?" Nightshade said from out of the darkness in front of her, and Mistaya's head jerked up sharply. Abruptly, the Witch of the Deep Fell appeared, bending over her. "Did you say something?"

Mistaya blinked and looked down for Haltwhistle. The mud puppy had disappeared. "No, nothing. I must have been talking in my sleep."

"Good night, then," the witch said, and slipped away again.

"Good night," Mistaya said.

She took a deep breath and let it out slowly. She looked again for Haltwhistle. The mud puppy appeared anew, materializing out of the night. She watched him for a moment, smiling. Then she closed her eyes and was asleep.

BUMBERSHOOT

The instant Nightshade's witch fire enveloped them, Landover disappeared and time stopped. Soft, gauzy light cocooned Abernathy, and he lost sight of Questor Thews completely. He drifted, suspended in the light, wrapped in silence and consumed by a numbness that emptied him of all feeling. He did not know what was happening to him. He supposed that he was dead and that this was what dying felt like, but he wasn't sure. He tried to move and couldn't. He tried to see beyond the white brightness surrounding him and couldn't do that, either. He could barely manage to form a coherent thought. He didn't even know if he was breathing.

Then the light disappeared in a sudden rush of wind and brilliant colors, and the sights, sounds, tastes, and smells of life rushed back into focus with brilliant clarity. The lake country was gone. He was pretty sure that Landover itself was gone, as well. He was sitting on a grassy flat that spread all around a great stone basin. A fountain at the center of the basin spouted a plume of water that arched high into the air in a feathery spray. Light caught the water and created small, shimmering rainbows. People were seated all across the lawn and at the edge of the fountain. Children played in the fountain, having ventured down into the shallow stone bowl, darting in and out of the spray, laughing and teasing one another. It was summer, and the day was sunny and hot.

Abernathy sat up straight and looked about. There were people everywhere. It was some sort of festival, and everyone was celebrating. Across the way were a pair of jugglers. A clown walked by on stilts. At a nearby table a small boy was having his face painted. Walkways bordered the lawn, the one nearest him packed end to end with makeshift booths selling the works of artisans and craftsmen: glass prisms, wood carvings, metal sculptures, and clothing of all sorts. Other walkways were jammed with carts and stands selling food and drink. Garish signs proclaimed the types of edibles and libations offered. Abernathy did not recognize the names.

But he could read the signs. If he was not in Landover, he should not have been able to do that.

His first thought was, Where am I, then?

His second was, Why aren't I dead?

A man with long, tangled black hair and a full beard streaked with purple dye stood next to a woman with her hair braided in tight beaded rows tipped with tiny bells. Both wore gold earrings and neck chains and sported matching face-painted roses framed in red hearts. They were staring at Abernathy in disbelief.

"Hey, man, that was awesome!" the man declared reverently. "How did you do that?"

"Was it some sort of magic?" the woman asked.

Abernathy had no idea what they were talking about. But he could understand them, and that was as mystifying as being able to read the signs. He looked around in confusion. Music rose from all about, mingling with shouts and laughter. The walkways ran past large stone buildings and pavilions jammed with people. The buildings did not look familiar—and yet they did. The music was of all sorts, none of it immediately recognizable. It was loud and decidedly discordant. One group of musicians occupied a stage that had been erected across the pavilion on the far side of the fountain. The music they played was raucous and amplified so that it sounded as if it were coming out of the air itself. Flags and pennants and streamers flew at every turn. People were dancing and singing. There was something going on everywhere you looked.

"Hey, that's not your whole act, is it?" the man with the purple-streaked beard was asking.

"C'mon, do something more!" his companion pressed.

Abernathy smiled and shrugged, wishing the man and woman would go away. What was going on here, anyway? He wasn't dead, obviously. So what had happened to him? He ran his hands over his body experimentally, checking for damage. Nothing seemed out of place. Two arms, two legs, a body, fingers, and toes—he could feel them inside his boots. All present and accounted for. He ran his fingers through his hair, smoothing it back. He rubbed his chin and found that he could use a shave. He adjusted his glasses on his nose. He seemed to be all right.

He turned the other way then and found himself face to face with Questor Thews. The wizard was staring at him. He was staring at him as if he had never seen him before in his life.

"Questor Thews, are you all right?" he asked anxiously. "Whatever in the world is going on?"

Questor's mouth opened, but no words came out.

Abernathy was immediately irritated. "Wizard, what is the matter with you? Has the witch's magic rendered you speechless? Stop looking at me like that!"

The other's gaunt arm lifted as if to ward off a ghost. "Abernathy?" he asked in obvious disbelief.

"Yes, of course. Who else?" Abernathy snapped. Then he realized that something was seriously wrong with the other man. It was in his eyes, the sound of his voice, the way he seemed unable to accept the obvious, not even recognizing his oldest friend, for goodness' sake. Shock, perhaps. "Questor Thews, would you like to lie down for a moment?" he asked gently. "Would you like me to bring you some water or a glass of ale?"

The wizard stared a moment longer, then quickly shook his head. "No, it's not . . . it's . . . I'm all right, really, but you . . ." He stopped, clearly perplexed. "Abernathy," he said quietly. "What has happened to you?"

Now it was Abernathy's turn to stare. Happened to him? He looked down at himself once more. Same body, arms, legs, familiar clothing, everything in place. He looked back at the other, shaking his head in confusion. "What are you talking about?" He had to speak loudly to be heard over the music.

The gaunt, white-bearded face underwent a truly incredible series of contortions. "You've . . . you've changed back! Look at yourself! You're not a dog anymore!"

Not a dog . . . Abernathy started to laugh, then stopped, remembering. That was right—he *was* a dog! He was a soft-coated Wheaten Terrier, made so by Questor Thews when the old King's spiteful son, Michel Ard Rhi, had sought to do him serious harm, then left that way because Questor could not change him back again.

Yes, a dog.

Except, he realized suddenly, shockingly, he wasn't a dog anymore. He was a man again!

"Oh, goodness!" he breathed softly, unable to believe it. "It can't be! My heart and soul . . . !"

He reached down hurriedly and examined himself all over. Yes, those were arms and legs and fingers and toes. His body was back! His human body! He patted wildly at himself, reaching inside his clothing. No fur, but skin, like any normal man! He was beginning to cry now, tears running down his cheeks. He scrambled for something to look into, finally grasping one of the silver buttons that fastened his ornate tunic. He peered down into its tiny, carved surface, and his breath caught in his throat.

It was his human face he found staring back at him, the face he had not seen in more than thirty years.

"It's me!" he whispered, swallowing. "Look, Questor Thews, it's really me! After all this time!"

He was crying so hard and at the same time laughing that he thought he might simply collapse. But Questor Thews reached forward and braced him with hands on both shoulders. "My old friend," he declared in delight, and he was crying, too. "You're back!"

Then, in a spontaneous and quite out of character display of affection, they were hugging and clapping each other on the back, rendered unable for the moment to speak a word.

The audience that had gathered while all this was going on watched uncertainly. It was sizable by now, drawn initially by the odd costumes and the obvious interest of the man and woman who had first approached, then held there by what everyone presumed was a drama of some sort being played out as open-air theater. Really, they were thinking, it was quite good, if somewhat inappropriate for the occasion.

There was a scattering of polite applause.

Abernathy continued to cling to Questor Thews, as if letting go would change him back again. He could feel the air and the sun's warmth, and he could smell the food and hear the music as if he had never been able to do any of those things before in his life. If he could be born again, he thought, it would feel like this!

"What's happened to us?" he managed finally, drawing away from the other's grasp. "How did I change? How did it happen?"

Questor released him reluctantly, then shook his head, wispy hair sticking out all over the place, the result of his enthusiastic embrace. "I don't know," he declared wonderingly. "I don't understand any of it. I thought we were dead!"

The crowd applauded some more. Abernathy became aware of them now, three and four deep all around the wizard and himself. He was startled in spite of himself—and deeply embarrassed. "Questor Thews, do something!" he demanded heatedly, gesturing at the knot of people ringing them.

The wizard glanced about in surprise but somehow managed to maintain his equanimity. "Hello, there!" he greeted. "Can anyone tell us where we are?"

There was laughter from the crowd.

"Bumbershoot," came a tall, lanky boy's quick answer.

"Bumbershoot?" repeated Questor Thews doubtfully.

"Sure. You know, Bumbershoot, festival of the arts." The boy grinned. He was enjoying whatever game it was they were playing.

"No, no, he means the city," a burly fellow said. He was enjoying the game, too. "You're in Seattle, Washington, fellows."

"United States of America," another voice added.

Other names and places were shouted out, spectators now having decided that this was an audience participation performance. Everyone was quite enthusiastic, and the crowd grew larger still.

"Questor!" Abernathy said sharply. "Do you realize where we are? We're in the High Lord's old world! We've been transported through the fairy mists once again!"

The wizard's jaw dropped. "But how could that have happened? Nightshade meant to destroy us! What are we doing here?"

"Ask Scotty to beam you up!" someone shouted.

"Are they Trekkies?" someone else asked hopefully.

The crowd howled with laughter and engaged in some rhythmic clapping to urge the two on. The music from the pavilion had ceased momentarily, and it seemed as if everyone at the festival had suddenly converged on them, anxious for a new show. Belatedly, Abernathy realized that their unexpected appearance had been the trigger for all this attention, materializing as they had out of nowhere as if . . . well, as if by magic—which was exactly how they *had* gotten there, of course, but that was beside the point. This was Earth, the High Lord's old world, and magic was not practiced here. Not tolerated, really. Not even believed in for the most part. The crowd thought the two were part of the festival, like the jugglers and the stilt walkers and what have you. Whatever magic they possessed was illusion. It was meant to entertain.

"We have to extricate ourselves from this situation right now!" Abernathy insisted in an anxious covert whisper. "These people think we are offering them some sort of performance!"

He scrambled quickly to his feet, looking down at himself as he did so, at his human self, wondering in amazement that he was there, restored once more, miraculously, impossibly. His voice caught in his throat. "We have to talk this out . . . this whole business! But alone, Questor Thews!"

The wizard nodded in emphatic agreement, rising with him. They were both dressed in Landover clothing, looking very out of place unless you accepted their appointed roles as entertainers. The wizard quickly decided that it was better to go along with perceptions than to try to argue or explain them away. He was as confused as Abernathy about what had happened and just as anxious to sit down in a quiet spot and attempt to reason it all out.

"Ahem! Ladies and gentlemen! Could I have your attention, please." He addressed the crowd in his most authoritative voice, lifting his arms in an encompassing gesture to gain their undivided attention. They quieted at once. "My colleague and I require a few moments of preparation before we can proceed with the next act. So if you will just go about your business—enjoy the rest of the festival—we will see you back here in, oh, perhaps an hour. Or not," he added under his breath. "Thank you, thank you very much."

He lowered his arms and turned away. The crowd did not move. No one was prepared to leave just yet, not prepared in some cases to believe that they were even supposed to. This might all be part of the act. Two strangers from another world come mysteriously into this one—it was intriguing. What might happen next? No one wanted to miss out. There was some shuffling of feet but not much lateral movement.

"This isn't working!" Abernathy complained, irritated, confused, and overwhelmed by the entire business. "Confound it, wizard, get us out of here!"

Questor Thews sighed, not at all sure how to do that, then scrunched up his face with determination, took Abernathy by the arm, and marched him directly through the crowd. "Please excuse us, thank you, yes, that's very kind of you, excuse us, please." The crowd parted, polite if somewhat disappointed. Questor Thews and Abernathy escaped untouched and moved swiftly away across the festival green toward a clump of buildings and food stands.

"Where are we going?" Abernathy asked, not daring to look over his shoulder to see if anyone was following.

"Wherever we can, I suppose," Questor answered with a shrug. "Since we have no idea where anything is."

They moved down onto a walkway, past the face painter, past a fellow spinning tops, past several carts selling food and drink, and onto a square of grass fronting a cavernous glass and metal structure out of which rolled a particularly vile-sounding form of music.

"What is that noise?" Questor demanded, shaking his head in dismay.

"Rock and roll," Abernathy answered absently. "I heard a good deal of it the last time I was here." Memories were triggered in his mind, but he brushed them aside. He turned, grabbed Questor by the shoulders, and brought him about so that they were face to face. "Wizard, what is going on? Look at me! I don't know whether to laugh or cry! I'm a man again, for goodness' sake! How did that happen? Surely Nightshade didn't intend it! She was trying to kill us! Why aren't we dead? Why are we here?"

Questor's mouth tightened, and he blinked rapidly. "Well, either something went wrong with her magic or another magic intervened and changed the intended result. I favor the latter." Questor reached up and touched the other's face. His hand was shaking. "Goodness gracious, here's something new! Abernathy, are you aware of the fact that you haven't aged a day from the moment I transformed you from a man into a dog all those years ago?"

"That isn't possible!" Abernathy exclaimed in disbelief. "Not a day? No, I must have aged! Why wouldn't I have aged? It must be the magic, mustn't it? The one that you think intervened? It changed me back again not only to a man but to the man I once was. Questor, why? Why would it do that?"

They stared at each other in confused silence, the sound of the music in the hall washing over them, the laughter and gaiety of the festival rising up all around, outworlders in a foreign land, exiles by means they could not fathom. *Oh, but I am a man again!* Abernathy thought in joy and with a smidgen of terror. *Whatever else, I am changed back to who I was and want always to be!*

Questor Thews shook his head. "I don't mind telling you that this is all very strange," he declared solemnly.

"Excuse me?"

They turned on hearing a girl's voice and found her standing a few feet away, staring at them. She was somewhere in her middle teens, Abernathy guessed, rather small, with curly blond hair and a scattering of freckles across her nose. She was wearing short tan pants, a rather tight sky-blue blouse with some writing on it, and sandals. She looked perplexed.

"I was in the crowd a moment ago," she said, studying them intently, particularly Abernathy. "I followed you afterward because your voice . . . I know this sounds silly, but because . . . you remind me of someone . . ."

She stopped, and her brow furrowed. She looked suddenly at Questor Thews. "I do remember you. I'm sure of it now. Your name is Questor Thews."

Questor and Abernathy exchanged a quick glance. "She overheard us talking," Abernathy said at once.

"No, I didn't." She shook her head emphatically and came forward a step. "Abernathy, that's you, isn't it? You're not a dog anymore! That's why I was confused. But your voice is the same. And your eyes. Don't you remember me? I'm Elizabeth Marshall." She smiled helpfully. "I'm Elizabeth."

He remembered then. Elizabeth, twelve years old when he had last seen her, a child wandering the halls of Graum Wythe, the castle fortress of Michel Ard Rhi, once a Prince of Landover and son of the old King in the days before Ben Holiday. Abernathy had been dispatched to Earth through another of Questor's inept spells, consigned to the trophy room of his worst enemy, and fated for a swift end when Elizabeth had found him and saved his life. Together they had struggled to conceal Abernathy's presence from Michel and help the scribe find a way back into Landover. Elizabeth had stuck with him every step of the way. Even when she was discovered and her own safety was threatened, she had refused to betray her friend.

"I never thought I'd see you again," she said softly, as if still not certain it was really him.

"Nor I," he breathed in disbelief.

She came forward quickly then and hugged him. "I can't believe this," she said into his shoulder, holding him tightly against her. "This is just too weird."

"Well, yes," he agreed, speechless, and hugged her back.

She broke the embrace. There were tears in her eyes. "Look at me, crying like some little kid." She brushed the tears away. "When I saw you, the two of you, surrounded by all those people, I didn't see how it could be true. I mean . . ." She broke off, shaking her head. "Abernathy, what are you doing here?"

He shrugged, embarrassed. "I'm really not sure. We were just trying to figure that out. We don't quite know how we got here. It is rather a long story." He stared at her. "You've grown up."

She laughed. "Well, not all the way, but some from the last time you saw me. I'll be sixteen in a few months. So hello. And hello to you, too, Questor Thews."

"Very nice to see you again," Questor replied. He cleared his throat. "Ah, I wonder, Elizabeth, if we could impose on you—"

"You don't have anywhere to stay, do you?" she declared before he could finish. "Of course you don't. Did you just arrive? Well, you have to have somewhere to stay while you're here. How long will that be?"

Questor sighed, "That is a matter of some speculation at present."

"It doesn't matter; you can stay with me. I still live out in Woodinville, but not at Graum Wythe anymore. We have a house, my dad and me, down the road a short distance. Dad still looks after the estate and manages the castle. But he's away until late next week, so we have the place to ourselves. Except for Mrs. Ambaum. She's the housekeeper. My keeper, too." She giggled. "I'll tell you later. Abernathy, I just can't believe this. Look at you!"

Abernathy turned red. "Well," he managed.

"Maybe we should go now," Questor advised. "To your house, Elizabeth. We really need to sit down and talk."

"Sure," Elizabeth quickly agreed. "Let me tell my friends I'm leaving. I rode down here on the bus, so we'll have to take the bus home. I've got enough money for the three of us, I think. Hope so, because I bet you don't have any. Boy, this sure is strange, isn't it, meeting again like this?"

Questor Thews nodded, looking around absently at the crowds and the festival. Music rolled across the open spaces between buildings. Flags and balloons floated in the warm breeze. Cooking smells filled the air. Laughter and singing rose from every quarter. Bumbershoot, festival of the arts. Seattle, Washington, United States. The High Lord's old world. Now Elizabeth. It was strange, all right. It was also the most colossal coincidence he had ever encountered—or it was something far more complicated. He didn't say so, but he favored the latter interpretation.

He thought they might do well to figure it all out before anything else happened.

GRAUM WYTHE REDUX

After Elizabeth had made excuses to her friends, she guided Abernathy and Questor Thews through the Bumbershoot crowds past a building called the Center House, a collection of mechanical rides filled with screaming children, and a series of food stands to a platform that serviced a monorail—which was something new to Questor, who hadn't spent as much time in the High Lord's old world as Abernathy. After a brief wait they boarded the monorail and rode downtown. Abernathy took great delight in his familiarity with things, his spirits further buoyed by the incredible fact of his transformation. As they sat in the monorail and passed down the track toward the tall buildings of the city, he kept looking at his reflection in the glass window next to him, not yet quite able to believe that it was true, worried deep inside that he might change back again at any moment.

But it was true, and there was no indication that he was going to revert. He was himself once more, a whole man, the exact same man, in fact, he had been when Questor had first changed him into a dog, rather average-looking, medium height and weight, hair dark and lank where it framed his bookish face. His rimless glasses sat comfortably upon his nose, fitting him perfectly, as if it made no difference whether he was a man or a dog. His eyes were wide-set and brown in color. His mouth was full, and his chin firm. An average face, certainly, but still and all a good one.

And it was his. Looking at it in the window glass, he felt as if a huge weight had been lifted from his shoulders. The last time he had passed into Ben Holiday's world, he had been forced to pretend he really was a dog to avoid a good many unpleasantnesses. Magic was not accepted here. Talking dogs were unheard of. Abernathy had been an oddity of monumental importance, and there had been more than one attempt to exploit the fact. So he had crept about like a thief in the night, playing at being something he wasn't, embarrassed and frightened. Now he could walk about like everyone else because he looked like everyone else. He fit comfortably in place. Well, more so than he would have if he had still been a dog. This was, after all, not his own country. But when he finally got back to Landover . . .

It made him smile to think about it.

"How does it feel?" Elizabeth asked him suddenly. She had been watching him. "Being a man again?"

Abernathy had the decency to blush. "I can't seem to stop looking at myself. I apologize. But it does feel wonderful. I can't tell you how wonderful. It has been a very long time, Elizabeth, since I was . . ." He trailed off. "I . . . I'm very happy."

She grinned in response. "Do you know something? You are quite handsome."

His mouth gaped. He could feel his cheeks burn.

"No, really," she insisted. "You are."

He expected at that point to hear a snide comment from Questor Thews, but the wizard was not paying attention to the conversation, his gaze turned away as he stared off into space, lost in thought. Abernathy muttered something unintelligible to Elizabeth and looked out the window at the passing buildings. Enough of admiring himself. He should be thinking, too. He should be trying to figure out what was going on. What was it that had brought them to this place and time, changed him back into a man, and linked him up once again with Elizabeth? Like Questor, he thought it an awfully large coincidence. He had the sense that there was machinery at work that he didn't understand and probably should. But for the moment he was so caught up in his transformation that he could not bring himself to think of anything else.

He looked at himself in the window one more time and almost started to cry. He was entitled to enjoy this feeling for a few moments more, wasn't he? After all, he had waited so long!

At the end of the monorail line they departed their car and entered a tall building set among other tall buildings, the whole of it very imposing, almost overwhelming, and from there they followed stairs, some of them actually moving, to an underground station, where they boarded a bus. Questor didn't know about buses, either, so Abernathy took a moment to explain how they worked and got it wrong. Elizabeth giggled and set them both straight. By now they were far enough removed from Bumbershoot that people were beginning to take notice of their somewhat odd clothing—Questor in his gray, patched robe with its brightly colored sashes and Abernathy in his crimson-lined, silver-trimmed riding cloak—but no one was rude enough to say anything. The bus took them underground for a ways, stopping twice, and then exited from a tunnel back into the sunshine of the late afternoon. They were on a roadway packed with other vehicles spread out in lanes that stretched away into the distance. No one was moving very fast. They sat at the back of the bus and stared out the windows, and for a time no one said much of anything.

"Are Ben Holiday and Willow well?" Elizabeth asked finally, speaking to Abernathy.

He said they were. He told her then about Mistaya. One thing led to another. When Questor didn't give him a pointed look or offer a word of caution, he went on to tell her about Nightshade and the attack on the caravan that had been taking the little girl to stay with her grandfather. He kept his voice low so that no one sitting close could hear. Not that there was much chance of that happening, what with all the noise the bus made. He told her how they had thought themselves finished once Nightshade had summoned her formidable magic but then had inexplicably found themselves in the High Lord's old world, in Seattle, at Bumbershoot. She was aware of the rest.

"It's all very strange," she said when he was done. "I wonder why you ended up back here."

"Indeed," Questor Thews said without looking over.

"I would like to live in your world," she offered suddenly. "There's always so much happening."

Abernathy looked at her in surprise, then looked quickly away.

They rode the bus to a stop in Woodinville, then got off and walked rather a long way out into the country. Houses and traffic faded away, the day cooled, and the sun dropped toward the mountains that framed the horizon. The land was forested and rolling about them, filled with pungent smells and birdsong. The road they followed ran straight and unhindered into the distance, empty of life.

"I should tell you about Mrs. Ambaum," Elizabeth said after a while. She had her face scrunched up, the way she always did when she was addressing a doubtful subject. "She's the housekeeper. She lives with us. Dad's away a lot, and she looks after me while he's gone. She's pretty nice, but she thinks all kids—that's me and anyone else under twenty-five or so—can't stay out of trouble. It's not that she thinks we go looking for it; it's that she thinks we can't avoid it. So she spends a lot of time trying to keep me tucked safely away in the house. She had a fit when I told her I was going by bus to Bumbershoot, but Dad had told her it was all right, so there wasn't much she could do. Anyway, we had better come up with a story that will satisfy her about where you came from or there will be trouble for sure."

"The truth wouldn't work, I suppose?" Questor asked.

Elizabeth grinned. "The truth would blow her mind."

"We could stay somewhere else if we are going to be too much trouble," Abernathy offered.

"Yes, we could stay in a barn or out in a field, perhaps," Questor declared, giving him a reproachful glance. "Really, Abernathy."

"No, no, you have to stay with me," Elizabeth insisted quickly. "We have plenty of space. But we need a story for Mrs. Ambaum. How about this? Abernathy, you can be my uncle, visiting from Chicago. And Questor Thews is your

friend, a professor of . . . geology. You're fossil hunting. No, you're partici-
pating in a forum on extinct species at the university, and you dropped by to
see Dad, not knowing he was out of town, so I asked you to stay with us.
There, that should work."

"We shall rely on you," Questor Thews announced. He smiled bravely.
"With luck, our visit should only be a short one."

"I wouldn't bet on it," Elizabeth said, and neither of her companions presumed to disagree.

They arrived shortly afterward at a two-story home set back from the
road in a grove of spruce and dogwood, the foundation bordered by flower
beds, the walkway lined with petunias, and the yard dotted with rhododendrons. The building was wood-sided and painted white with deep blue trim.
Window boxes filled with flowers decorated its front, and a covered porch
with a swing and rockers ran its length. Dormers jutted out from the slop-
ing roof, the windows brightly curtained, and massive stone chimneys
bracketed the walls at either end. Sunlight streaked the house and yard
through gaps in the trees, and an orange and white cat stalked into view and
disappeared into a wall of bushes. Elizabeth took them up the walk to the
door and rang the bell. There was no answer. Mrs. Ambaum had gone out,
it appeared. Elizabeth fished in her pocket for a key, unlocked the door, and
took them inside.

"We'll have to come up with an explanation for your not having any lug-
gage, too," she declared once she had made certain that Mrs. Ambaum was indeed out. "This might be harder than I thought."

She showed them the second-story bedroom where they would be staying,
then brought them some of her father's clothing, most of which fit after a fashion and was certainly less attention-getting than their own. When they were
dressed, she guided them downstairs to the kitchen, sat them at the breakfast
table, and set about making sandwiches. In short order they were eating. Both
Abernathy and Questor found that they were hungrier than they had thought
and quickly consumed everything they were given.

When they were finished, the daylight fading rapidly now to dusk, they
began to talk about what had happened. They remained at the table, drawn up
close in their chairs, arms and elbows resting on the polished wooden surface,
hands locked before them or cupping their chins, a thoughtful if somewhat
perplexed threesome.

"Well, we can be certain of this much, I think," Questor Thews declared,
opening the discussion. "Nightshade intended to see us destroyed, not transported to this world. We are here, therefore, in spite of her efforts and not because of them."

"Well, yes, of course," Abernathy agreed impatiently. "That much we have
already established, wizard. Tell us something new. What about me, for instance?"

"You were changed at the same time. Transformed back into a man, then sent here, with me." Questor rubbed his whiskers, his brow furrowing deeply. "It is all tied together somehow, don't you think?"

"I don't know what to think," Abernathy admitted. "What do you mean, tied together?"

Questor steepled his fingers before his face. "We must assume, as I said earlier, that magic intervened to prevent the witch from destroying us. Whose magic, then? It could have come from the once-fairy, perhaps from the River Master himself, sent in an effort to save his granddaughter. It could have come from the Earth Mother; she has always been close to Willow and would have reason to want to protect her friend's child."

Abernathy frowned. "Neither sounds exactly right. If the River Master or the Earth Mother had been watching out for Mistaya, how could Nightshade have gotten so close in the first place? Anyway, I saw nothing that would indicate Mistaya was about to be saved once we were dispatched."

"True, it doesn't fit, does it?" Questor agreed.

Elizabeth, who had been listening intently but saying nothing, now said, "Could it have been Mistaya herself who saved you? Does she have magic she can use?"

They both looked at her at once, considering the possibility. "An excellent idea, Elizabeth," Questor said after a moment. "But Mistaya is untrained in the use of whatever magic she possesses, and the magic that was used to deflect or alter Nightshade's was both sophisticated and well practiced."

"Besides," Abernathy interjected, "Mistaya was still sleeping. I saw her when I looked to see if she had been harmed. She was sleeping as if nothing had happened. I think the witch might have cast a spell on her to prevent her from waking."

"Entirely possible," Questor agreed. He leaned back and pursed his lips. "Well, then. Some other magic intervened and saved our lives. It sent us to the High Lord's old world, transformed Abernathy, and gave us the ability to speak and understand the language. But—and this is significant—it sent us here, to the very place we last appeared, where Abernathy was inadvertently exchanged for the Darkling, to the site of Graum Wythe, to what was once the home of Michel Ard Rhi. And," he said, nodding meaningfully at Elizabeth, "to within a few feet of you."

Abernathy stared. "Wait one minute, Questor Thews. What is it you are saying here?"

"What we all have said at one point or another since meeting up at the Bumbershoot festival: that ending up back here, close to Graum Wythe and practically in the arms of Elizabeth, is rather too large a coincidence to be swallowed in one bite. I would be willing to bet that there is a reason for everything that has happened to us. Whoever or whatever saved our lives did not do so haphazardly. It did so with foresight and purpose. We were saved for a reason. We were sent here, to the High Lord's old world, but here to the site of Graum Wythe specifically, quite deliberately."

He paused, considering. "Elizabeth, didn't you say that Graum Wythe is still here?"

"Come look," she offered, getting up from the table.

She took them from the kitchen through a curtained door and out into the backyard, a well-tended lawn that spread away through a scattering of spruce to a split-rail fence. She took them midway to the fence, to where the trees opened up, then stopped and pointed right. There, silhouetted against the skyline by the fading light of the sun, stood Graum Wythe. The castle sat alone on a rise, ringed by its walls and warded by its towers. It sat solitary and immutable, black and brooding as the night swept toward it.

Elizabeth lowered her arm. Specks of sunlight flashed in her curly hair. "Still there, right where you left it. Remember, Abernathy?"

Abernathy shivered. "I could do without the reminder. It is as forbidding as ever, I must say." A sudden thought chilled him further. "Michel Ard Rhi hasn't come back by any chance, has he?"

"Oh, no, of course not." Elizabeth laughed disarmingly. "He moved down to Oregon, several hundred miles away. He gave Graum Wythe to the state as a museum. A trust fund administers the estate. My father is the chief trustee. He oversees everything. No, don't worry. Michel is long gone."

"My magic made certain of that," Questor Thews added pointedly.

"I certainly hope so," Abernathy muttered, thinking as he said it that Questor Thews's magic had never been very reliable.

They went back inside and resumed their places at the table. Darkness had fallen, and the last of the daylight had faded. Elizabeth poured them tall glasses of cold milk and produced a plate of cookies. Questor helped himself eagerly, but Abernathy found that he had lost his appetite.

"So none of this is coincidence; all of it is part of some mysterious plan," the scribe summed up doubtfully. "What plan?"

Questor regarded him as he might an inattentive child, eyebrows lifting. "Well, I don't know the answer to that, of course. If I did, we wouldn't need to have this discussion, now, would we?"

Abernathy ignored him. "An intervening magic saved us from Nightshade and sent us to the High Lord's old world, to Earth, but in particular to Graum Wythe and Elizabeth." He looked at Elizabeth. Then he looked at Questor. "I still don't understand."

"I'm not sure I do, either," Questor Thews admitted. "But assume for a moment that whoever or whatever helped us did so to help Mistaya as well. As far as we know, no one is aware of what happened to the child except for us. We know Nightshade took her. We know that the witch intends to use the child to gain revenge against the High Lord and that Rydall of Marnhull is part of her scheme. If we can get word to Ben Holiday, then he might be able to do something to disrupt the witch's plans. Perhaps that is what we are meant to do. We are alive and here for a specific reason, Abernathy. What better reason than to discover a way to stop Nightshade before she carries out her scheme?"

"Saved to fight another day, is that it?" Abernathy asked, scratching his head with his fingers instead of his hind leg and not thinking twice about it. "Maybe we were sent here simply to get us out of the way. Maybe our rescuer then saved Mistaya as well."

But Questor Thews shook his head emphatically. "No. No, I'm quite certain it didn't happen that way. In the first place, if our rescuer was there all along, keeping watch for just this, as must have been the case given the quick response, why not save Mistaya early on? Why wait until the last moment? If our rescuer was looking simply to get us out of the way, as you put it, why send us all the way here? Why not send us back to Sterling Silver or some such? No, Abernathy, we are here for a reason, and it has something to do with saving Mistaya from the witch."

"You think the answer to all this lies in Graum Wythe, don't you?" Elizabeth declared, making the jump in logic first.

"I do," Questor Thews replied. "Graum Wythe is a vast repository for artifacts of magic, some quite powerful. One of those artifacts could provide a way back into Landover. Or provide us with a means to foil the witch. The fact remains that without magic of some sort, we are trapped here and helpless to aid the High Lord or Mistaya. We do not have a way to pass through the fairy mists. No one knows where we are. No one will come for us. I think we are meant to find our own way home. I think we *must* if Ben Holiday and Mistaya are to be saved."

The three stared at each other, weighing the import of the wizard's words.

"Maybe," Abernathy agreed finally.

"There is no 'maybe' about it. Graum Wythe holds the answer to our dilemma," Questor Thews continued solemnly. "But the key to Graum Wythe is you, Elizabeth. We were sent to you because your father is administrator of the castle and all its treasures. You have lived in the castle and are familiar with its holdings. You have access to places where others are not permitted. What we require is somewhere in that castle. I'm certain of it. We simply have to search it out."

"We can start tomorrow morning when the castle opens," Elizabeth promised. "That's the easy part. The hard part will be finding what it is you need when you don't know what it is you're looking for."

"True," Questor Thews admitted with a slight shrug.

"But what does all this have to do with my being changed from a dog back into a man?" Abernathy asked once more.

He was still waiting for an answer to his question when there was the sound of a key turning in the front door lock and of the door opening. Three heads turned as one.

"Elizabeth, are you home?" a woman's voice called.

"Mrs. Ambaum!" Elizabeth announced, making a face.

For the moment at least, Abernathy's question was left unanswered.

Mrs. Ambaum proved to be less formidable than anticipated. She was a large, straight-backed woman with graying hair, a bluff face, and a suspicious mind, but she was not a villainous sort. Elizabeth offered her explanation of how Abernathy and Questor had come to visit and had been invited to stay, and Mrs. Ambaum, after a few perfunctory questions and a general disclaimer of responsibility, accepted their presence without further argument, retiring to her room at the back of the house for some herbal tea and television. Questor and Abernathy went to bed much relieved.

They were up early the next morning and came down to breakfast to find Mrs. Ambaum already gone to her sister's for the day. They ate hurriedly, anxious to get under way with their search of Graum Wythe, then cleared off their dishes and, with Elizabeth leading the way, headed out the door.

It was a beautiful, cloudless, sun-filled day. Birds sang from the trees, and the air was fragrant with the smell of flowers and spruce. The company of three smiled agreeably as they departed the house, came down the walkway to the edge of the yard, turned left, and began following the road toward the castle.

Elizabeth linked arms with Abernathy, grinning conspiratorially. Abernathy felt stiff and uncomfortable. "You look very nice in Dad's clothes," she told him. "Very distinguished. You should dress like this all the time."

"He should smile more, too," Questor Thews added before he could think better of it.

"This is so incredible, Abernathy, you being here again," the girl continued, hugging his arm affectionately. "Look at you, just look! Who would believe what's happened? Isn't it wonderful? Aren't you happy?"

"Very," Abernathy acknowledged, putting on his best face, though in truth he was still wondering what the price would be for his remarkable but still unexplained transformation. There was always a price for those things. He thought back to the mind's eye crystals of Horris Kew. Always a price.

Elizabeth was wearing a powder-blue sweatshirt that said something about Seattle grunge, a pair of jeans, and worn sneakers. Her hair was tousled artfully, and she was wearing violet eye shadow and dark magenta lipstick. Abernathy thought she had grown up awfully fast, but he kept it to himself.

"Do you have family?" she asked him suddenly. "A wife and children?"

He shook his head, a tad downcast.

"Father and mother?"

"Not for many years." He could barely remember them.

"Brothers and sisters?"

"No, I'm afraid not."

"Hmmm. That's rather sad, don't you think? Maybe I should adopt you!" She grinned brightly. "Just kidding. But you really could be part of my family, since it's rather small and could use another member or two. What do you say? An unofficial adoption, okay?"

"Thank you, Elizabeth," he replied, and was really quite touched.

They strolled up the road, the older man with the electric white hair and beard, the younger man with the rimless glasses and the pensive face, and the curly-haired girl who seemed in charge of them both, closing on Graum Wythe like Dorothy and her companions at the Emerald City of Oz. Except, of course, that Graum Wythe, though castlelike and imposing, was in no other way anything at all like the Emerald City. It was not green or bright but stone-gray and dreary. No yellow brick road led to its entry, just blacktop. No fields of poppies surrounded its walls, although its working vineyards still showed touches of green. It was medieval and fortresslike with no pennants flying from its parapets, only the flags of the United States and the state of Washington to announce its entrance.

Not that either Abernathy or Questor Thews knew anything about Oz or the Emerald City. Had they given the matter any consideration, they probably would have contrasted the drabness of Graum Wythe to the brightness of Sterling Silver, for instance. They were thinking, in fact, of very different things entirely. Abernathy was trying to conceive of what his life would be like now that he was no longer a man in dog form but a man for real. He was trying to picture himself in his new role in various situations. Questor Thews, on the other hand, was recalling his friend's question of the previous night concerning what his change from dog back to man had to do with their coming to the High Lord's world and hoping that his suspicions, unvoiced as yet, would be proved wrong.

The little company came to the low stone wall that encircled the castle and passed through the open iron gates to the drawbridge. Graum Wythe loomed before them, a massive cluster of towers and parapets. The drawbridge was down and the portcullis up, so they moved into the shadow of the castle wall, through the gate entry, and out to the castle's parking lot. Graum Wythe seemed empty of life. A single car was parked in the rear of its visitors' lot. The souvenir stand, ensconced in what used to be a guardhouse, was closed and shuttered. Graum Wythe seemed deserted.

"It's all right," Elizabeth assured her companions. "The museum hasn't opened to the public yet, but we can get in."

She took them across the parking lot and up the steps to the iron-bound front doors. She rapped the heavy knocker on its plate and waited. A moment later the door opened, and a man she greeted as Harvey smiled in recognition and let them inside. They entered the same foyer where several years earlier Ben, Willow, and Miles Bennett—Ben's old law partner, pressed into service for the occasion—all three dressed for Halloween night, had engineered Abernathy's escape from Michel Ard Rhi's dungeons. Abernathy looked around with foreboding, but the menace of Michel and his guards was long absent and the foyer itself had been redecorated with bright tapestries, pamphlet stands, and an admission desk where Harvey held forth. After giving the same explanation about Questor and Abernathy that she had given Mrs. Ambaum, and exchanging a few pleasantries with Harvey, Elizabeth led the wizard and the scribe into the bowels of the castle.

They spent the rest of the day searching. Their search was confined at first to the corridors and rooms left open for the public and to the artifacts and collectibles on display. Most of the items Questor Thews recognized for what they were. Almost all possessed no inherent magic. But a few did, and once or twice the wizard felt obliged to comment on an item that really had no business being exposed to the public, so dangerous was its potential for misuse.

Nowhere, however, did he find the elusive and still unidentified item he was looking for.

Midday passed without result. They ate lunch in the little sandwich shop situated in what used to be the castle kitchen. Visitors were arriving by the carload now, and there were buses filled with touring groups. Business was picking up. To avoid the crowds, Elizabeth took them into the back rooms and storage areas of the castle, those kept closed to the public, looking at the things either deemed unworthy or unready for display. Crates were stacked everywhere, but they managed to get most down for a look inside. Cabinets were filled with odd rocks and minerals, carvings and sculptures, paintings and crafts of all sorts, and none of them were of any recognizable use.

An hour after the castle closed Harvey advised them that they would have to leave and come back tomorrow. Reluctantly they trudged homeward with nothing to show for their efforts. Questor Thews was particularly frustrated.

"It's there, I know it," he muttered, shaking his ragged white head. "I cannot be wrong about this. It's there, but I'm not seeing it, that's all. We'll just have to come back and try again tomorrow. Drat!"

Abernathy and Elizabeth exchanged a quick glance. Neither of them was bothered by the prospect of the hunt going on another day. If Questor had been paying attention, he would have noticed that Elizabeth was holding Abernathy's hand. If he had been paying attention, he would have noticed that Abernathy no longer seemed to mind.

WHAT YOU SEE

The first of Rydall of Marnhull's champions appeared exactly as promised three days after Ben Holiday had accepted the King's challenge.

By the time the sun rose, it was waiting outside the gates of Sterling Silver, a strong, solitary figure standing at the far end of the causeway, looking over at the castle. It was a man of great size and obvious strength. In a land where warriors often reached seven feet, this man was easily eight. A giant of massive girth, broad shoulders, and tree trunk legs, he wore animal skins tied with leather thongs about his muscular body. Boots linked to greaves ran to midthigh, and iron-studded wrist guards laced into leather gloves. A black beard and coarse, thick hair obscured most of his face, but his eyes could be seen to glint brightly in the rise of the morning sun.

He bore but a single weapon, a battle-scarred wooden club bound with strips of hammered iron.

Ben Holiday stood with Willow and Bunion on the ramparts of the castle and stared down at Rydall's champion. His coming was no surprise, of course. Ever since Mistaya had disappeared along with Questor Thews and Abernathy, Ben had been convinced that Rydall was for real. The fact that no one had ever heard of him or of Marnhull, or could begin to discover where he came from or where he had gone to, or, more important, what he had done with Ben's daughter and friends did nothing to lessen the certainty of his threat. Using the Landsview, Ben had scoured Landover from end to end for all three days given to him after Rydall's departure and had found exactly nothing. There was no trace of Rydall, no sign of his passing, and no clue as to where he had gone to earth. Bunion had searched as well, using his kobold speed and extraordinary tracking powers. He, too, had failed. In the end the only conclusion left, however improbable, was that somehow Marnhull's King indeed had managed to penetrate the fairy mists from a land without. Having done so, he had snatched away Mistaya and her guards, Abernathy and Questor included, and had gone back the way he had come, leaving Ben Holiday to face the challenge he had issued, to stand alone against the seven he would send to destroy him.

Ben shook his head resignedly. He had been awake since shortly after midnight, anticipating the arrival of this first destroyer. He was not tired, not even weary, only sad. He would be forced to fight this creature, whoever and whatever it was, and probably would destroy it. He would do so as his alter ego, the Paladin, but it wouldn't change the fact that he would still be the one doing the fighting and perhaps the killing. It wouldn't change the necessity of his transformation into the iron-clad warrior who protected the Kings of Landover, a transformation he feared and despised, because each time it happened a little more of him slipped away into the abyss of dark madness that shrouded the life of the Paladin. Warrior and knight-errant, protector and champion, the Paladin was before all things a destroyer to which no sane man could ever wish to be joined. But Ben Holiday was. And would forever be from now until the end.

But I made that choice when I gave up my old life for this new one, he chided himself. *The decision was mine.*

"Perhaps we can simply ignore him," Willow said quietly. Ben looked over at her, but she kept her eyes focused on the giant. "If we keep him locked outside the gates, what can he do? He might grow weary of his vigil. Time favors you, Ben. Let him be."

Ben thought it over. He could do that. He could leave the giant where he was and see what happened. It wasn't a bad idea, though it would inconvenience those who might wish to enter or leave the castle. But it did nothing to enhance his image as King. It left him a prisoner in his own palace.

"He has made no demands?" Ben asked Bunion, still weighing the possibilities.

The kobold chittered softly. No, the giant had not spoken.

"Well." Ben tightened his mouth. "We'll let him wait a bit. A little breakfast first, now that we know he's here. Then we'll see."

He started to turn away, and abruptly the giant's arm lifted and pointed directly at him. There was no mistaking the gesture. *Do not turn away,* it said. *Do not turn your back on me.*

Ben wheeled about and came back to the wall. The giant's arm lowered, and he resumed waiting, one hand resting on his belted waist, the other on the butt of his massive club. The strange eyes glinted. The huge figure looked to be carved of stone.

"It appears he does not approve of your idea, Willow," Ben murmured, feeling her hand close over his. He could tell what she was thinking: Be careful. Do not rise to his goading. Do not be drawn into this fight until you are ready.

She did not say to him, "Do not go." She knew he must. She knew he could not avoid this confrontation or any of those which must follow if they were to see Mistaya alive again. She hated the situation as much as he did, but they had understood from the moment of Rydall's coming with the news of their missing daughter that they were trapped in this deadly game and that somehow they must find a way to win.

"What is his strength?" she asked suddenly, indicating the giant with an irritated wave of her hand. "He is large and strong, but he is no match for the Paladin. Why has he been sent?"

Ben had been wondering that, too. The Paladin was better armed and protected. How could the giant hope to defeat him?

At his side Bunion chittered softly. He wanted to go down and test the giant's strength, to see what his edge might be, to probe for his weakness. Ben shook his head. He would risk no one but himself in this struggle with Rydall. Not when the lives of Mistaya, Abernathy, and Questor were at risk already.

"He forbids us to leave the wall," he said finally. "What will happen if we disobey? Perhaps we should see. Bunion, stay put and keep watch for us."

Keeping tight hold of Willow's hand, he turned from the wall and walked over to the open stairs that wound downward about the watch house to the courtyard below. He was barely to the first step when he heard Bunion hiss in warning.

The giant was beginning to shimmer like a mirage in the midday summer heat. The air all about it was as damp as liquid, rainbow colors sliding across its surface like autumn leaves across glass.

Ben hesitated, waiting. Then Bunion started and looked quickly over.

The giant had disappeared!

Ben stared at the kobold, undecided about what to do, then started toward him once more, needing to see for himself. At the same moment he heard Willow gasp. He wheeled back, following her gaze to the courtyard below. Soldiers and retainers had scattered as light filled the yard's center in a blaze of shimmering color.

The giant reappeared, come out of the ether, come now into the walls of the castle itself. It rose up out of nothingness, huge and dark. The massive club was shouldered, and there was a new menace about it. A squad of soldiers approached it warily, placing themselves between the giant and their King. In a moment the battle would be joined.

But Ben already knew he could not let that happen.

"Stand where you are!" he called down.

The soldiers looked up at him expectantly. The giant's gaze lifted as well.

Ben felt Willow release his hand, but he could not bring himself to look at her. He reached into his tunic and withdrew the medallion of Landover's Kings, the talisman that warded them from danger. Holding it forth so that it caught the morning sun, he reluctantly summoned the Paladin.

Brilliant white light flared instantly at the foot of the gatehouse stairs, and from out of its brightness the Paladin appeared. He was afoot and armed with his unsheathed broadsword and an iron-tipped mace strapped to his waist. He was armored in silver, shining with the intensity of the sun at midday.

Ben instantly felt a connection between them, locks snapping into place, a picture forming in his mind, a strange combination of fire and ice mixing into something else altogether. Tendrils of feeling and thought began to link them, to join them as one. He was carried out of his body and into the Paladin's armor on a wave of light. He was clasped to the other as if by dozens of hands, wrapped about and encased in the iron, and made one with his protector's weapons. He was submerged in memories of battles fought and won over a thousand lifetimes. He was joined with times and places long past and all but forgotten. He was made over into his other self, and that other self rose up in fury and blood lust to confront Rydall's giant.

They came together in a rush, weapons clashing and grating as metal and iron-bound wood caught, held momentarily, then slid away. They parted grunting, then clashed again. The giant was powerful and determined, using leverage and his awesome strength in an effort to overpower his quarry. But the Paladin was too battle-tested to be taken down so easily. A moment later he had thrust the giant aside, knocked the club from his hands, and thrown him to the earth.

The giant struck heavily, rolled free of the sword blade that hovered over him, and came back to his feet, club in hand once more, unharmed. He came at the Paladin instantly. The Paladin parried another monstrous blow and struck the giant alongside the head. The giant went down, tumbling away, blood smearing the dusty earth where he struck.

Then he was back on his feet yet again, the blood drying and the wound closing. For the first time the Paladin hesitated. The giant should be hurt, but its wounds had healed immediately. Either blow should have slowed or weakened him; neither had.

The giant attacked anew, stronger now than before, thrusting into the Paladin with such force that the King's champion was driven backward to the castle wall. The giant pinned him there, wresting away his sword and bringing the massive club up under his chin to break his neck. The Paladin tried to twist free of the killing hold and could not. The giant grunted with the effort of pushing forward against the Paladin's neck. The dark eyes glinted. The great body heaved mightily. The Paladin's breath was cut off. He could not break loose.

In desperation he hammered both iron-gloved fists into the giant's midsection. The giant grunted in pain. The Paladin struck at him again, this time where his ribs joined. The giant fell back, clutching himself, the club falling away. The Paladin struck him once more, this time squarely between the eyes. The giant reeled backward and collapsed.

But then, impossibly, he came to his feet again, righted as if he had never fallen, his club hefted eagerly as he advanced anew. The Paladin had lost his sword, and now he freed the mace he wore tied to his belt. It was shorter than the giant's club, though just as deadly. Still, there was no weapon to match the speed of the giant's recovery each time he was felled. It was as if the blows gave him new strength.

The giant attacked the Paladin again, hammering at his armored body with blows so powerful that they knocked the mace aside as if it were a toy. The Paladin grappled with his adversary, leaping inside the killing arc of the club. With his arms locked about the great body, he heaved upward to throw the giant down. The giant roared in dismay. Something about this attack clearly bothered him. The Paladin pressed forward. Together, the combatants staggered across the courtyard, grunting and straining from the effort of their struggle. The giant was trying to break free, the club abandoned, both massive arms hammering down on the Paladin's armored body. But the Paladin had discovered something useful. When he lifted upward on his adversary, the giant weakened noticeably. He lost the fury and intensity of his effort. He howled in obvious frustration. He wanted to be put down again, and so the Paladin fought to hold him aloft, to break his connection to the earth, for it was from the earth, it now appeared, that the giant gained his strength.

Finally the Paladin brought the giant to the steps of the watchtower and threw him down upon the stone. The giant kicked and fought to roll from the steps to the earth of the courtyard, but the Paladin would not let him break free. The giant roared anew, and now there was blood spurting from his nostrils and mouth, leaking from his wounds at every turn. The Paladin thrust his adversary farther up the steps, farther from the courtyard dirt, and the giant fell back with a sudden convulsive gasp. Up another few steps the Paladin heaved the great body, and now the giant could no longer breathe. His arms fell back, and his legs sprawled askew on the steps.

The Paladin held him there, pinned and helpless, until he was dead. When his life departed, the giant turned to dust.

⁘⦿⁘

Afterward, when the Paladin had vanished and Ben had come back to himself, he wondered if he could have saved the giant's life. It was not a simple matter to resolve. There was the question of whether the Paladin would have permitted it, for when Ben was the Paladin, he was subject to the knight's ethics and life rules, and they were far different from his own. The Paladin had no interest in saving the life of an enemy. Enemies were to be killed swiftly and remorselessly. Ben was not certain he could exercise sufficient control over his alter ego to permit even a small consideration for the sparing of a life. There was also the question of whether the giant would have cooperated or whether he would have disdained compassion as thoroughly as the Paladin had and gone on fighting until he was killed. There was the question finally of whether the giant was even real. It had turned to dust on dying, and creatures of flesh and blood did not do that so swiftly. It seemed probable that the giant was a thing of magic and that its destruction was inevitable in the face of a stronger magic.

All of which did nothing to make Ben feel any better about what he had been put through. The impact of having killed the giant was not lessened by the fact that the giant might not have been a mortal man. His dying had been real enough, and it had come at Ben's hand. He could still feel the giant's struggles weakening as he held him pinned fast on the tower steps. He would remember for as long as he lived the other's eyes as the life went out of them.

He went back to his bedchamber with Willow and slept for a time, seeking escape from the experience. She stayed with him while he rested, lying close beside him on the bed, her cool hands running across his chest and arms, her voice whispering to him compassionately, soothingly. He did not know how he could live without her, so close was she, so much a part of him. If the Paladin was his dark side, then she most certainly was his light. He took heart from her radiance and drifted in warmth and peace.

When he awoke, it was midday. He ate then, hungry again and anxious to get on with matters that required his attention. He did not speak to Willow of what had happened. He had never told her—never told anyone, for that matter—the truth about the Paladin. No one knew that Landover's King and her champion were one and the same, joined by the magic of the medallion, bound irrevocably in the defense of the realm. No one knew that when the latter surfaced, the former was submerged, one supplanting and repressing the other, one dominant. But it was becoming increasingly difficult for Ben to keep this secret from his wife. The strain of holding himself together after each transformation, of keeping whole when bits and pieces of himself were being ripped away, was beginning to tell. He could not avoid the fact that when he was the Paladin, he gloried in the power of the magic that transformed him and did not want to change back again. One day, he feared, he would succumb to its lure.

Visitors to the castle included officials of the land reformation committee he had appointed to oversee changes in the application of agricultural techniques and irrigation in various parts of the kingdom, particularly the arid Eastern Wastelands, and he met with them at length to discuss their progress in convincing the Lords of the Greensward to commit manpower and materials to his project. The meeting produced mixed results but encouraged him sufficiently to plan a visit to a few of those who remained recalcitrant, notably but not surprisingly Kallendbor of Rhyndweir. Kallendbor resisted everything Ben proposed and two years ago had been persuaded to rise up against him in rebellion through the machinations of a dark fairy called the Gorse. Kallendbor had been all too willing to participate, so Ben Holiday had punished him severely. One year in exile and the loss of certain titles and land had been the punishment decreed. Kallendbor had accepted the verdict without complaint, recognizing perhaps that his punishment could—and some said should—have been much worse. His year in exile had been served, and some of his land and titles had been restored. But he continued to be obstreperous and challenging at every turn, and it was clear to Ben that for all Kallendbor had suffered, he had learned almost nothing.

Ben moved from the committee meeting to a reception with several of his judicial representatives that lasted only a short time, then on to a perusing of law documents concerning disputes over property. Having to deal with those matters without Abernathy's able assistance made him think again on the kidnapping of Mistaya. He pondered anew the inadequacy of his efforts to find her, warding off the despair he felt every time he envisioned losing her. His already white-hot hatred of Rydall grew measurably. That Marnhull's King should use such despicable tactics to force him to play this ridiculous game of pitting Kings' champions against each other was unforgivable. But it was puzzling as well. It lacked balance somehow; it lacked good sense. Something about it suggested that there was more to the puzzle than Ben was seeing.

He would have considered the matter further perhaps, but Bunion arrived in a rush to announce that another of Rydall's champions had appeared.

Ben was stunned. A second, so soon? He had barely bested the first! It seemed that Rydall was determined to have the matter of Landover's Kingship resolved quickly.

Ben headed for the battlements, Bunion scurrying ahead. Guards stepped aside with his passing, uttering words of encouragement and disdain for this latest challenge. By now everyone realized what was happening, knew that an unknown outside force was attempting to wrest control of the throne. There had been peace in Landover since the defeat of the Gorse two years earlier, but now here was a new threat. Ben acknowledged the kind words with a nod and an occasional word of encouragement back. He was joined by Willow, emerald hair streaming out behind her, beautiful face hardened by her iron will, as he mounted the watchtower steps. King's Guards were assembling in force in the courtyard, readying to march forth. Retainers were bringing up a line of warhorses. Everyone was preparing for battle.

Ben climbed to the top of the wall overlooking the drawbridge, Willow and Bunion at his side, and stopped dead.

Armored all in silver, its lance tilted upward in salute, a solitary knight waited at the far end of the causeway. It was instantly recognizable even from this distance. Ben Holiday found himself looking at the Paladin.

He stared in speechless shock, unable to believe what he was seeing. The Paladin? Here, unsummoned? Had it come to do battle with its master? Had Rydall somehow subverted it?

"This can't be possible," he muttered.

"That isn't the Paladin." Willow was the first to say it. "It can't be. You haven't summoned it, and no one else can. This knight is a fraud, a pretender."

But a realistic-looking one for all that, Ben thought darkly. Well, there was no help for it. He was faced with the same dilemma that he had confronted when the giant had appeared. Waiting was pointless. If he refused to meet the knight without, he would all too soon find it within.

Ben put his hands on the stones of the castle wall and tried to decide if he was strong enough to do battle again so soon. For while his transformation into the Paladin required little of him physically, it was excessively demanding mentally and emotionally. When the battle was finished and another challenger lay dead, it was his psyche that the shards of battle would have damaged. He stared down grim-faced at this newest threat from Rydall. This one, at least, was faceless, but the prospect of doing battle with himself—or a part of himself—was unnerving, even if it wasn't really a part but only something that seemed to be . . .

He gave up on his ruminations. Too much of that could be deadly. There was no choice offered him in this matter. If Rydall sent three champions this day, he would still have to fight them all.

"Ben," Willow said softly, her arm linking into his.

He nodded. "I know; you don't have to say it. But I can't make that thing down there go away by ignoring it."

"There will be another trick to winning," she said, "just as there was with the giant."

She released him reluctantly then, and he brought forth the medallion. A moment later he summoned the Paladin. He felt a measure of relief when it appeared in a flare of light from out of the forest at the edge of the meadow; now he could be certain that it was not the real Paladin who served Rydall. His protector wheeled toward the pretender, lance lowered for the attack. Ben felt himself transported once more, flowing easily with the change this time, used to it since this morning, almost welcoming it. The Paladin's armor closed about him, its memories stirred in his blood, and the expectation of battle was a rush of heat that flooded through bone and muscle and into the iron of his weapons.

The Paladin kicked his warhorse in the flanks, and the beast surged forward to the attack. Ahead, the false knight turned and spurred toward him in response. Lances lowered, they raced across the grassy stretch of the meadow in a thunder of hooves and met with a clash of iron and splintered oak as both lances shattered into pieces.

Still mounted, shields cracked and scarred, the combatants wheeled back toward each other, battle-axes in hand. They rushed together a second time, weapons swinging. The Paladin deflected the other knight's heavy blade, and his adversary did the same with his. A second blow got through, but so did one of his adversary's. The knights hammered at each other, and then both axes snapped at the hilt and fell away, broken and useless.

Reining their warhorses about savagely to get into position, the combatants reached for their broadswords.

A third time they came together, the blades of their broadswords striking
fire in the late afternoon sun, sparks exploding from their weapons and
armor. Their horses were weakening, snorting and huffing from the strain of
bearing their armored riders and absorbing the shock of the blows dealt. Finally both went down together, throwing their riders free, rising shakily, and
standing with heads lowered and blood on their muzzles, unable to continue.

The twin Paladins rose as well, broadswords still in hand, and advanced to
the attack on foot. If they were tired, they did not show it. They went at each
other with single-minded determination, and it was clear to everyone watching that neither would give quarter until the other was down for good.

Atop the castle wall Willow observed the struggle with growing apprehension. For every blow landed, a matching one was dealt. The Paladins were
exact duplicates of each other, wheeling and charging, striking and blocking,
moving with synchronized movements in a bizarre dance of destruction. Soon
it became impossible for her to tell which was which. The real Paladin should
have been able to distinguish itself from the pretender through its experience
and battle skill, but it did not seem able to do so. The longer the struggle went
on, the more impossible it became to tell one from the other. They attacked
and defended exactly the same—blow for blow, wound for wound, damage
for damage—no difference in their looks, no variation in their strategies, no
counters that were not instantly imitated. Something was wrong with the way
in which the struggle was progressing, and she realized soon enough what it
was. The Paladin could not gain an edge in this battle because it was fighting
itself. It was like watching yourself in a mirror, seeing your image reflected
back at you, seeing everything you did imitated exactly. Your reflection never
tired and never slowed sooner than you did. While you stood before the mirror, you could never escape it . . .

She caught herself. She realized the secret of Rydall's champion then. She
recognized, too, how it could be defeated.

"Ben!" she shouted above the clash of armor and weapons. She clutched at
him, but there was no response. He stood beside her, looking out at the battle, motionless, voiceless, seemingly entranced. "Ben!" she shouted again,
shaking him harder.

He turned toward her, a barely perceptible movement. He seemed to be
looking at her from a great distance off.

"Ben, send the Paladin back!" she cried out. "Send him away! Rydall's
champion is stealing his strength. He's using him up! Listen to me, Ben! If you
send the Paladin away, Rydall's champion will disappear, too!"

From somewhere in the back of his mind Ben heard the plea. But he was
too far away to respond, trapped in the Paladin's body, caught up in the terri-

ble struggle with his twin, an adversary that seemed to know his every move, to anticipate his every attempt at surprise, to counter his every strategy.

Ben! he heard the voice call frantically. *Ben, listen to me!*

The Paladin brushed aside the plea and renewed his attack. He thought he sensed a weakening in his enemy. He refused to accept that it reflected his own.

In desperation, Willow released her grip on the unresponsive Ben and went down off the wall in a rush. Ben did not seem to be able to act; something was happening with him that she did not understand. Since he could not respond to the Paladin's need, it was left to her to do so. She gained the courtyard below, snatched a spear from a weapons rack, crossed to where a knot of King's Guards stood before the open gates watching the struggle taking place beyond the castle walls, vaulted onto the back of the closest warhorse, and, heedless of the cries that immediately sprang up around her, kicked the horse forward and went out through the gates.

She thundered across the drawbridge and onto the grasslands beyond, heading for the combatants. Shouts of alarm trailed after her, but she was heedless of them. She knew what was needed. The Paladin and Rydall's champion were locked in a battle of twins that was intended to destroy them both. The only thing that would save the Paladin was a disruption of the magic Rydall's champion relied on. This time it was not the earth that sustained it, as had been the case with the giant, but the Paladin's own strength and skill. Rydall's champion was a form of succubus, a reflection in the mirror that fed off its original, imitating it, copying its every move, draining it of its life.

But if the mirror were darkened . . .

She reached the combatants and swept by them without slowing, her lowered spear raking their armored bodies. It was enough to get their attention. They turned as one, seeing her for the first time. She reined in her horse and swung the beast about, spear lowered in challenge, preparing to charge again. Confusion was evident in both Paladins, an uncertainty over what her presence meant. She had to hope that this was disruption enough of the magic that bound them, that Ben somehow could communicate still with the Paladin, and that his protector would find a way to act on the plea.

"Withdraw!" she shrieked in fury, and flung the lance at them.

The closest of the two brushed the weapon aside as it flew past, swatting at it as if it were nothing more than a fly. The other, standing a few paces behind, pointlessly mimicked the action.

There, she thought triumphantly, that one is Rydall's creature!

She spurred as close as she dared to the real Paladin and reined in once more. The meadow had gone quiet.

She looked down at the Paladin. "Sheathe your sword and withdraw!" she said. "Only then can you win!"

There was a long moment of silence and uncertainty, of confrontation between the sylph and the two armored knights. Then, abruptly, the true Paladin sheathed his great broadsword. A motion of one metal-gloved hand brought his exhausted warhorse to him. He looked back at Willow momentarily and then mounted.

Sunlight flared off the silver armor as he wheeled toward Sterling Silver. A sliver of brightness lanced away toward the castle battlements and reflected off the medallion that hung from Ben Holiday's neck, turning it molten.

Then horse and rider disappeared in a flash of light, and the Paladin was gone.

Willow turned quickly to the other knight, held her breath, and waited.

Rydall's creature stood staring at the air into which the Paladin had faded. With its enemy gone, its purpose in life was finished. Bound by the dictates of the magic that had created it, it mimicked its original one last time. Sheathing its sword, it walked to its warhorse and mounted. But there was no provision for its leaving. There was no magic to sustain it beyond this moment. And so it simply fell apart, collapsing in a veil of windblown ash.

Willow stood alone in the meadow. She had guessed right. Once the Paladin had gone, whatever the reason, Rydall's champion could not survive. Permitting herself a smile of satisfaction and relief, she rode slowly back toward the castle and to Ben.

ARDSHEAL

It was still light, the sun hovering at the horizon's crest in the shadow of the mountains to the west, when the River Master's messenger appeared to Ben and Willow at the door of their bedchamber. They had retired to wash and dress for dinner, physically exhausted from the day's events but mentally and emotionally on edge and unable to contemplate rest until after they had calmed down. How the creature knew where to find them or got as far as it did without being seen was a matter best left for the speculation of others. Ben knew by now that the once-fairy, Willow among them, could pass almost anywhere among humans without being seen.

The messenger knocked softly, and when Willow opened the door, he was standing there, stone-faced and motionless. He was a wood sprite, as lean and gnarled as a fence post and with eyes as bright as gemstones in a face almost devoid of any other features. He bowed respectfully to Willow and waited for Ben to join her at the door.

"High Lord," he greeted, and gave a second bow. "My Lord the River Master asks that his daughter and her husband come at once to Elderew to speak with him. He would hear more of his missing granddaughter and would give counsel and assistance to her parents. Will you come?"

Ben and Willow exchanged a brief glance. Neither felt much like going anywhere at present, but both recognized instantly that there were reasons to accept the invitation. If they stayed where they were, they would soon enough receive a visit from another of Rydall's champions. Perhaps by being somewhere else they could forestall that visit. Buying time in their search for Mistaya and for a solution to Rydall's challenge was one of the few options left to them. It might also be that the River Master, a creature of great magic, meant to offer them a talisman or spell to use for their protection. At least he might have news of his granddaughter, for he had learned of her abduction some days ago and by now must have scoured the lake country and beyond for some sign of her.

No words passed between them, but Ben and Willow frequently communicated on another level, and words were not always necessary.

"Tell the River Master we will come," Ben told the messenger.

The sprite nodded, bowed once more, and was gone. He went down the hallway into the growing twilight shadows and simply disappeared.

They took dinner in their room, preferring to be alone and in as much seclusion as they could manage. The castle still bustled with King's Guards set to watch and preparing to go out on patrol. Two attacks in the same day was unheard of. Even Bunion was out tracking, trying to trace the origins of Rydall's defunct champions, though it was a good bet that there was nothing to be found. Appointments had been canceled for the next few days, and the entire castle garrison was on alert. No one would be allowed in or out of the castle without first being thoroughly checked.

Such precautions were of marginal value, however, where the use of magic was concerned, as the unorthodox appearance of the River Master's messenger had made clear. There was no doubt in Ben's mind that Rydall commanded significant magic of his own, and it would probably allow his champions to circumvent the usual precautions that might be laid to stop them. Probably it was Rydall's black-cloaked companion who wielded that magic and Rydall himself who commanded its use, but just who did what made no difference. The first two champions sent to destroy him had possessed magic, and it was a safe bet that the five yet to come would possess stronger magic still.

So Ben and Willow talked out their situation during dinner and reasoned anew that it would be best for all if they traveled to the lake country for a few days. Maybe Rydall would have trouble finding them. Maybe their movement would cause some disruption in his plans. Staying where they were, waiting helplessly, would play right into his hands. Besides, there was little chance of finding Mistaya or Questor and Abernathy without aid from another source. Use of the Landsview had failed repeatedly. All efforts at searching the countryside had failed as well. But there was always the chance that someone they hadn't thought to talk with yet knew something. Or that someone with powers greater than their own and resources denied to them, such as the River Master, might have knowledge to impart.

They chose to go that night, to leave under cover of darkness and before the coming daybreak. They hoped to leave unseen, without having to encounter another of Rydall's champions. Ben particularly was suffering from the day's encounters. Willow could not determine the reason. Ben was still closemouthed about what had happened during that second struggle, why he hadn't responded to her pleas, why he had seemed so removed from what was happening yet so exhausted by it afterward. He had thanked her for her help, not rebuked her in any way for going out onto the battlefield, and then had dropped the matter abruptly, retreating somewhere deep inside himself until the messenger from the River Master appeared. Willow, for her part, had not pressed him. It was apparent that this was something he would talk about when he was ready, and she was satisfied with having helped defeat Rydall's creature. She was worried, though, about what would happen the next time. She did not like the way he had behaved during the Paladin's battle. She did not like not knowing what was wrong.

They waited for Bunion to return, cautious enough to decide to take the kobold with them for added protection. Leaving instructions with a chosen few as to what should be done in their absence, canceling all remaining appointments into the next week, and declaring the King to be on holiday, Ben and Willow departed from a side door on the east, took the lake skimmer across to the far shore, and met Bunion, who was already in place with Ben's bay gelding, Jurisdiction, and Willow's white-faced sorrel mare, Crane. With Bunion afoot and leading the way, they mounted their horses and trotted off into the night.

They journeyed until it was almost dawn. By then they were well away from Sterling Silver and closing on the lake country. Some miles short of the Irrylyn they turned into a heavy grove of ash and hickory, dismounted, tethered their horses, rolled into light blankets, and fell asleep. While the seemingly tireless Bunion maintained watch, they rested until midmorning of the following day. When they awoke, Willow unpacked the cheese, bread, fruit, and ale she had brought for them, and they consumed it in a sunny space at the base of a gnarled old shagbark. Bunion appeared momentarily to snatch a few bites, then set out again, anxious to let the people of the lake country know they were coming. Once they were within the lake country, they all agreed, Rydall would have a hard time reaching them.

When Ben and Willow had finished eating, they rode out again to the south. Bunion would find them along the way. The morning was sultry and still, and the sun's heat beat down on the forestland like a blacksmith's hammer. No breeze came to cool them in their travels, and when they reached the Irrylyn, Willow pulled Crane into the shelter of a cove along the lake shore, dismounted, tied her horse to a tree, stripped off her clothing, and walked into the water. Ben followed. They swam in the lake for a time, floating on their backs, looking up at the tree limbs and the sky, not saying anything. Ben was reminded anew of how impetuous Willow was. He remembered the first time he had met her, here in the waters of this lake just after sunset, waiting for him without knowing who he would be. *You are for me,* she had told him. *It was foretold at the time of my conception. I knew you would come.*

She swam over to him now, embraced him, kissed him, and said, "I love you." Then she swam away again.

They emerged from the lake cool and refreshed, dressed anew, remounted, and started out again. They rode until after midday, when they were closing on the old growth that marked the boundary of Elderew and the country of the once-fairy. Bunion was waiting where the trail began to melt away into weeds. The River Master was expecting them, he reported. Guides would meet and escort them into the city a little farther on.

They left the trail where it ended and began to snake their way through monstrous fir and spruce, shagbark hickory and white oak, red elm and ash. The trees towered overhead, shutting out the sky, closing off the light. It was dark and chilly in spots, some of which never saw the sun. It was still, as if nothing lived in these woods. But already Ben could feel the eyes watching.

When the ground turned soft and the air began to smell of swamp and bog, the guides they had been promised appeared, creatures with green hair trailing off their heads and limbs like tree silk, lean, wiry figures that blended with the forest and could ease through any opening, no matter how narrow and obstructed. Their guides took them on a lengthy circuitous path through the great trees and across uncertain ground. To either side faces appeared out of newly formed mist, eyes bright and curious, there one moment and gone the next. Swamp closed about to either side, and water creatures lifted from the mire and out of the grasses to watch them pass.

Time ebbed. Elderew lay deep within the old growth, warded by elements of nature and magic, and no one passed within unless invited. The once-fairy were a secretive people, suspicious of the world without, cautious of the creatures who inhabited it. Ben had gone a long way toward removing that suspicion and fear, and the people of the lake country now traveled forth into other parts of Landover and on occasion brought outlanders back. But old habits and deep-rooted doubts died hard, and it would be some time yet before the barriers came down completely.

Ben could have found his way to Elderew using Willow or Bunion, but it would have been rude to ignore tradition and hospitality. The River Master's guides were a courtesy extended to those who were welcome. Ben forced himself to be patient. Soon the swamp areas were behind them, and they were climbing back toward solid ground. The trees were larger here, older and more established, hardwoods that had been alive for two hundred years and more. The air turned fresh and warm with the smell of sun and wildflowers. A scattering of people appeared. A few offered shy greetings. Children were among them, darting boldly between the horses, laughing and teasing. The trail reappeared, starting up again out of nowhere, well worn and broad where the trees opened up for it. Ahead, the city of Elderew came into view, a marvel of engineering and ingenuity that never failed to impress Ben.

The city was situated in a stand of massive old hardwoods that were even larger than the redwoods of California. The boughs of these trees were interlocked to form pathways above the earth, and the city rose in levels from the ground to the middle branches of the old growth, cradled like a series of toys in a child's arms. Homes and shops lined roads and tree lanes, an intricate webwork of pathways. Sunlight spilled through the canopy of limbs in long streamers that dappled the shadows and lit the natural gloom brightly. People scurried everywhere, the once-fairy an industrious folk who understood the importance of hard work. Much of that work was with small magics, their stock-in-trade. Much of it dealt with healing and sustaining their forest world. It was intriguing to discover how many aspects of their life they could affect with their efforts. Ben Holiday, as Landover's King, was still just beginning to learn.

Willow gave Ben a reassuring smile, her promise that her home city was still a friend to them. They rode on in silence, Bunion afoot before them with their guides, watching Elderew's complexity unfold as the trees spread wider and the city levels grew more visible. Ahead, the amphitheater that served as the site for the many celebrations of the once-fairy opened out to them in greeting. Formed of trees interlaced in a vast horseshoe, with seats on branches that started high up and ran downward to the arena floor, the amphitheater was as impressive as the city it served.

The River Master was waiting for them at its entry, standing amid his retainers, dressed in simple, nondescript clothing. If you did not know who he was, you would not have been able to pick him out by what he wore. You might have done so by his bearing, however. He was a tall, slender, impressive-looking man, a water sprite with silvery skin so grainy that it resembled fish scales, with thick black hair that, like Willow's, ran down the underside of his forearms and the back of his calves, and with features so stark and sharp that they might have been hewn from stone. His face was an expressionless mask, but his eyes were bright and quick, and Ben had learned to read the River Master's thoughts from what he found there.

The River Master came up to them as they slowed and dismounted, moving at once to Willow, embracing her stiffly, whispering to her that he was glad she had come. Willow embraced him back, equally uncomfortable with the greeting. Their relationship remained an uneasy one, distant and mired in mistrust. Willow's mother was a wood nymph so wild that she could not survive anywhere but in the forest, and Willow's father had never gotten over her refusal to live with him. Willow had been a constant reminder to him while she was growing of the woman he had loved and had not been able to hold for more than a single night. He had resented his daughter for what she represented, abandoning her emotionally from childhood on, leaving her to grow up alone. Even after she was grown, he found her a source of disappointment. He had not approved of her marriage to Ben, a human and an outlander despite being named Landover's newest King. Willow, he thought, had betrayed her people. It had taken time for him to accept her decision. He was less cool and aloof toward her these days than he had once been, but the old memories died hard for both.

Yet the River Master genuinely cared for Mistaya, the differences between father and daughter somehow bypassed in his bonding with his granddaughter. If there was anything he could do to help the little girl, it was certain he would spare no effort. It was for this reason that Ben and Willow had agreed to come to Elderew.

The River Master turned from his daughter and gave Ben a formal bow. It was as much as Ben could expect. He nodded back.

"There will be a dinner in your honor tonight," the River Master advised, surprising them both. "While preparations are being made, come speak with me a bit."

He led them from the arena, where tables and benches were being set up and colored cloths laid out, to the park that fronted Elderew and ran back to the city's closest buildings. Children raced past them as they walked, heedless of the adults who called after them in admonishment. It reminded Ben of other times and places, of Annie and the children they might have had, of Chicago parks in the summertime, of dreams long since abandoned. But the memory lingered only a moment. He thought seldom of his old world these days. He had little reason to do so.

They passed through the play area to a walkway that followed along a stream, weaving and dodging through shaggy conifers as if looking to stay out from underfoot. The children and their guardians faded behind, reduced to distant shouts and laughter. The three walked alone now, though it was certain that the River Master's guards kept pace somewhere in the trees, silent and unseen. When they reached a deserted glade where a pair of benches faced each other across a pond rimmed with flower beds, the River Master beckoned them to take seats. Ben and Willow sat on one bench, and the River Master automatically moved to the other.

"We will not be disturbed here," he advised, his strange eyes giving a cursory glance about at the sunfilled clearing. He looked back at them. When he spoke, his tone was accusatory. "You should have told me you were sending Mistaya here. I would have sent an escort to protect her."

"There wasn't time," Ben responded calmly, cutting short the retort he was tempted to make. "I thought Questor Thews and a dozen King's Guards sufficient protection. I hoped Rydall would be concentrating on me."

"Mistaya is his tool now to use against you," the River Master declared bitterly.

"Have you learned anything?" Willow asked in an attempt to deflect his anger.

The River Master shook his head. "This is what I know. I was able to discover the place where the attack took place. There was a significant amount of magic used in Mistaya's taking. Traces of it still lingered several days after. I could not determine their source. There were no signs of attackers or defenders. There were no footprints leading away from the battle site."

Ben did not miss the other's choice of words. Battle site. He forced his thoughts away. "No footprints. How could that be?"

The River Master's chiseled features tilted into shadow. "Either everyone was destroyed or travel by foot wasn't necessary for the survivors." He paused. "As I said, there was significant magic employed in the attack."

"Have you discovered anything since?"

The River Master shook his head. "I have never heard of Rydall or Marnhull. They do not exist within Landover's boundaries. Marnhull must lie somewhere without. I have tried to trace Rydall and his black-cloaked companion without success. I have watched for them; I have laid traps. They are nowhere to be found."

"Nor Mistaya and her escort?"

"No."

Ben nodded. He looked at Willow and read the disappointment in her eyes. She had been hoping that some small bit of good news might be waiting for them.

"So we are no closer to finding Mistaya than before," he finished, trying not to sound bitter. "Why did you summon us, then?"

The River Master sat delicately poised on the edge of his bench, staring over at them with no expression visible on his face and no emotion revealed in his eyes. "I *requested* your presence," he corrected, his voice flat and calm. "I wish to offer my help in returning Mistaya to her home. It is true that I have not been able to do much as yet, but perhaps I can make up for that now."

He paused, waiting for their response. Ben nodded in acquiescence. "Any help you might give would be greatly appreciated," he said.

It seemed to reassure the River Master. There was a barely perceptible relaxing of his shoulders. "I know we have not been friends," he said quietly. "I know our relationship has not been a warm one." He looked from Ben to Willow, including them both in this assessment. "This does not mean I wish you any harm. I do not. You know as well how strongly I feel about Mistaya. Nothing must be allowed to happen to her."

"No," Ben agreed.

"Can you find her?" Willow asked suddenly.

The River Master hesitated. "Perhaps." He gave her an appraising look. "I would not discount too quickly the possibility that you will find her yourself. Nor would I discount the possibility that she will find a way to get free on her own. She is a very resourceful child. And very powerful. She has great magic, Willow. Did you know that?"

Willow and Ben exchanged another glance, one of surprise. They shook their heads in unison.

"I sensed it the moment we met," the River Master advised. "Her power is latent but definitely there. She is a once-fairy of extraordinary potential, and once she discovers her talent, the possibilities are limitless."

Ben stared, trying to decide if this was good. He had never considered seriously that Mistaya might have the use of magic. It seemed ridiculous to him now that he hadn't. Her heritage allowed for it, and her odd growth pattern certainly suggested it. But she was his daughter, and the fact remained that he had never wanted to believe that she might be anything different from what he expected.

"You did not tell her?" Willow asked quietly.

The River Master shook his head. "It was not my place. I understand that much about being a grandfather."

"Will Rydall sense her potential for magic?" Ben asked suddenly.

The River Master considered. "If he is a creature of magic himself, as he appears to be—if he is one of us, for instance, a once-fairy, a being who wields magic—then I would have to say that he will recognize her power."

"But she doesn't know, so having the use of magic won't help her," Ben reasoned. "Unless Rydall reveals the truth to her. Or unless she discovers it on her own."

The River Master shrugged. "I only tell you of her magic so you will understand that she is not entirely helpless in this situation. She is a resourceful and independent child in any case. She may find a way to save herself."

"But you will continue your own search for her," Willow pressed. "You will not abandon your efforts to help her."

The River Master nodded. "I will not stop looking for her until she is found. I will leave nothing to chance, Willow. You know me better than that." He sounded rebuked. "But the immediate help I can offer is not to her but to you. Or, more correctly," he amended, looking at Ben, "to you."

A small yellow-and-black speckled bird flew down out of the trees and landed at the far edge of the pond. It regarded them solemnly, bright-eyed and watchful, then stopped quickly to drink. It bobbed up and down a few times, then took wing and was gone. The River Master watched after it thoughtfully.

"The danger is to you, High Lord," he advised, returning his gaze to Ben. "Rydall, whoever he is and wherever he comes from, is looking to destroy you. He uses Mistaya to this end, and whoever stoops to using a child to devise the death of an enemy is dangerous indeed. I heard about the attacks of yesterday. The risk to you is great, and it will not lessen until Mistaya is recovered and Rydall defeated. But this may take time. It will not come easily. Meanwhile, we must find a way to keep you alive."

Ben was forced to smile. "I'm doing the best I can, I promise you."

The River Master nodded. "I am quite certain. The problem is, you lack sufficient resources. You have no magic to ward against Rydall's, save that of the Paladin. Rydall knows this; I expect he is counting on it. Something is strange about this challenge he has set you. Seven champions sent to destroy the Paladin, and if one succeeds, you agree to abdicate. Why? Why play this game? Why not simply order you from the throne now or kill your daughter?"

"I have wondered about that as well," Ben acknowledged.

"Then you will appreciate it when I tell you that there is more to this game than is being revealed. Rydall is keeping something important from you. He is hiding a surprise." The River Master looked away. "So perhaps you should have a surprise for him."

He stood up abruptly. "I have one I think you might appreciate. Come with me."

Ben and Willow rose, and the three of them walked from the glade farther into the forest. They went only a short distance, weaving down a small pathway that led back into a thickly grown mass of spruce and fir. The ground was carpeted with needles, and the air was heavy with their scent. It was exceptionally quiet within those trees, sounds cushioned by the forest floor and the heavy green boughs that swept downward about them.

The sun was sinking to the west into the trees, a red orb in a purple haze. Twilight filled the woodlands with long shadows and cool places that whispered of night's coming.

They reached a second clearing. A figure stood there waiting, cloaked and hooded. It did not move as they came into view. It stayed perfectly still.

The River Master took them to within six feet of the figure and stopped. He lifted his arm and beckoned. The figure raised its hands in response and lowered the hood. It was a creature of indeterminate sex and origin, its skin wood-color, its mouth, nose, and eyes slits on its flat, nearly featureless face. There was a glimmer of light behind the eyes but nothing more. It was of average size and build, but its body was all smooth and lean and sleek and hard beneath the cloak.

Ben glanced at Willow. There was recognition in her eyes and something he hadn't seen for a long time. There was fear.

"This is an Ardsheal," the River Master said to Ben. "It is an elemental. It does not need food or drink or sleep. It requires nothing to survive. It was created by the magic of the once-fairy for a single purpose: to protect you. Willow knows. An Ardsheal is a match for anything alive. Nothing is more dangerous."

Ben nodded in response, not certain what to say. He was not expecting this gift. He was not certain he wanted it. He glanced at the Ardsheal. It made no response. It seemed comatose. "This creature will protect me?" he repeated.

"To the death," the River Master said.

"An Ardsheal is very dangerous, Father," Willow observed softly.

"Only to its enemies. Not to you. Not to the High Lord. It will serve as it is directed. In the absence of specific direction, it will do the one thing it has been set to do—it will protect you." He looked at Willow curiously. "You are frightened of them still?"

She nodded, a strange look on her face. "Yes."

Ben was thinking and missed the look. "Why have you chosen to give me this?" he asked finally. "I mean, the Ardsheal as opposed to another form of magic?"

"A good question." The River Master turned to face him, the Ardsheal now become his shadow. "Rydall expects the Paladin to defend you. He must have reason to believe that at some point it will fail to do so adequately. Perhaps that will happen. The Ardsheal will be there if it does. You defend yourself against an enemy you neither know nor understand. You require a defense your enemy does not expect in return. The Ardsheal will be that defense. Take it. It will give you a measure of reassurance. It will give you time to look for Mistaya, time for all of us to look."

He came forward a step, chiseled face bent close. "You are needed alive, High Lord Ben Holiday. If you die, there is a good chance your daughter will die with you. She serves only a single purpose: to draw you on. Once that purpose is served, what reason do you have for believing that she will be allowed to go on living? Consider carefully for a moment the nature of your enemy."

Ben held the River Master's gaze and did as he was bidden.

"He is right," Willow said quietly, almost reluctantly.

Ben found himself in immediate agreement. It did not require a great deal of thought to recognize the value of a second protector. Perhaps it would give him an edge against Rydall's creatures. If it saved him even once from having to call up the Paladin, it would have served a valuable purpose.

"I will accept your gift," he said finally. "Thank you."

The River Master nodded in satisfaction. "A good decision. Now come to dinner."

The feast was a sumptuous, extravagant affair, very much in keeping with the nature of celebrations among the once-fairy. There were tables laden with food, pitchers of iced ale, garlands of flowers, children and adults dressed in bright clothing, and music and dancing everywhere. The River Master placed Ben and Willow at the head of his table, announced their presence to those assembled, welcomed them to the lake country, and toasted them on behalf of the once-fairy. All evening, while the celebration wore on, the people of Elderew came up to greet them personally, some bearing small gifts, some offering good wishes. It made Ben and Willow smile and helped them relax. For a few hours they forgot about Rydall of Marnhull and the misery he had caused them. They ate and drank and laughed with the once-fairy, caught up in the merriment and feasting, soothed by the cool breezes that blew out of the trees and by the warmth of the people surrounding them.

At midnight they retired to a small guest house provided for their lodging. They fell into bed, exhausted but smiling, lying together, holding each other against a return of the fears and doubts they had managed to put aside, falling asleep finally as exhaustion overtook them.

Sometime afterward, several hours before morning, Ben woke, extracted himself from Willow's arms, rose, and walked to the window. The world without was lit by a single half-moon and stars that peeked down through a scattering of low-slung clouds and interlocked tree limbs. He stared out into the darkness, looking for the Ardsheal, wondering if it was there. He had not seen it since the River Master had presented it to him. It had been real enough then but now seemed somehow to be an imagining conjured in a dream.

An Ardsheal is very dangerous, Father, Willow had said.

He saw it then, back within the trees, another of the night's shadows. He would not have seen it at all except that it moved just enough when he was looking so that he would know it was there, standing guard, keeping watch.

Why was Willow so frightened of it? Was that a good thing or bad, given its purpose?

He didn't know. He put both questions in the cupboard in his mind that held all his unanswered questions and went back to bed. Tomorrow he would try to find out. He pressed himself tight against Willow's body, wrapped his arms around her, and lay awake holding her for a very long time before he slept.

NIGHTSHADE'S TALE

Mistaya's days in the Deep Fell slipped by so quickly that she was barely aware of their passing. Enthralled by her lessons on the use of magic, caught up in the exploration of her newly revealed powers, and consumed by the intensity of Nightshade's demands, she gave little notice to any expenditure of time. It might have been only days since she had arrived; it might have been weeks. In truth, it didn't matter. What mattered was what she was doing and the progress she was making in doing it. In that she was delighted, if never satisfied. She had learned a great deal; she had not yet learned enough.

She almost never thought of her parents and home. They were an extraneous and inconsequential consideration for her. Once she had determined that they knew where she was and that therefore she had no need to worry, she had dismissed them completely. Her growing trust in Nightshade and her enthusiasm for her studies made it easy for her to do so. In the beginning she had not been sure that it was all right for her to be here. She had not been sure her parents really did know where she was. But Nightshade's reassurances and her own desire to believe soon convinced her that her fears were misplaced and that all was well. Nightshade had said she could leave when she wished, so it was easy enough to discover whether the witch was lying. That was proof enough for Mistaya that she was being told the truth. Besides, her growing mastery of her magic would help her father in his battle against Rydall, and that provided an extra incentive for her to stay. Her father needed her; she must not fail him.

Time's passage was also affected by where she was. The Deep Fell had a tendency to blur day into night, light into darkness, then into now, making all seem very much alike. The Deep Fell's thick jungle canopy kept everything beneath it gray and misty. Sunlight did not penetrate. The moon and stars were never seen. Temperatures seldom changed more than marginally, and the look of Mistaya's surroundings was constant and unremarkable. What color and brightness were to be found came solely from her magic, from the wonders she performed and the marvels she uncovered. Nightshade gave her new insight with each lesson, turning the focus of Mistaya's attention inward so that she saw only what she created and almost nothing of the world about.

Nightshade was an effective teacher, endlessly patient with her pupil, praising and correcting by turns, offering small insights where needed, never disparaging or condemning a failed effort. It seemed to Mistaya that in the beginning Nightshade was interested primarily in results, but as her involvement in uncovering the girl's latent magic increased, the witch became more and more caught up in the mechanics of how the magic was performed. It seemed to surprise the witch as much as the girl; it also served to draw them closer.

And they were remarkably close by now, so close that Mistaya was beginning to think of Nightshade as a second mother. This did not seem odd to her. No one would ever replace her real mother, of course, but there was no reason why she could not have more than one, each fulfilling certain functions in her life. Nightshade was a strong presence, and her command of magic and revelation of its secrets were powerful inducements to the girl. Mistaya was very young and easily impressed. Nightshade had rescued her from Rydall. She had brought her to the Deep Fell to keep her safe. She was training her in the magic arts so that she could help her father. She was proving herself a good friend and a wise counselor. Mistaya could not have asked for more.

Yet there were still times when she experienced small twinges of doubt. Most of them were inspired by the appearance of Haltwhistle, who came to her in secret each night. While she no longer agonized over her parents or even Questor Thews and Abernathy, she was reminded by the continued presence of the mud puppy that there was another life waiting for her beyond the confines of the Deep Fell. Try though she might, she could not make the memories of that life go away, and while Haltwhistle never said or did anything to interfere, she knew somehow that he was there to make certain she did not forget. It was disconcerting to have to endure this, but she was mindful of the Earth Mother's warning of the dangers she would face and the promise given that the mud puppy would help protect her if she kept him by her side by remembering to call him once each day. So she conducted a balancing act, immersing herself in Nightshade's teachings by day while each night suffering small glimpses of what she had left behind.

Haltwhistle never gave her away. It was a risky thing she was doing, keeping the mud puppy's presence a secret. Nightshade would not approve, though was it really the witch's place to give that approval? Now and again Mistaya thought she could see Haltwhistle watching her while she worked, concealed by the mist and gray, hidden back in the jungle. Small bits and pieces of him would appear: eyes one time, feet the next, ears or nose another. At night he came at her smallest whisper, sitting just out of reach in the misty dark, barely more substantial than the haze out of which he materialized. Good old Halt-whistle, she would say. And smile when his tail thumped.

Doubt surfaced at other times as well, though, when its coming had noth-ing to do with Haltwhistle. The most troublesome was Nightshade's insistence on creating monsters. At first there were only the two, and Mistaya accepted the task as a natural part of her learning experience. After all, creating the un-usual was at the heart of her endeavors. Together the girl and the witch had turned stones to liquid metal, flowers to butterflies, and dust motes to rain-bows. They had made tiny insects speak and mice fly. Mistaya had even discov-ered a way to sing so that the sound of her voice filled the air with colors. Creating monsters wasn't all that different, she decided. She had been told she would be asked to do things she did not understand and to accept it without question. So she did. Try to imagine things against which there is no defense, Nightshade encouraged. Mistaya began with creatures she had read about in a book her father had brought with him from his old world, a book she had found tucked back in his personal library, all but forgotten. The title was something about mythology or myths or some such. The book was intriguing for its subject matter and the strangeness of its language, and Mistaya had mas-tered it quickly and then had set it aside. But her memory of its creatures had remained with her. The giant who took his power from the earth. The changeling who could duplicate anyone or anything. She built her first two monsters based on those. They were not even monsters, really, only things that evidenced inhuman powers.

Nightshade had seemed happy enough with her efforts until today. Today she announced, rather abruptly, that she desired Mistaya to create a third monster, this one less human and more powerful than the original two. For the first time since she had arrived, Mistaya questioned a command. What was the purpose of creating a third monster? What was the reason for this exer-cise, since she had performed it twice already? For just a moment she thought that Nightshade was going to be angry. There was a darkening of her strange eyes and a tightening of the tendons along her slender neck. Then she turned away momentarily, her face lost from view, and just as quickly turned back again.

"Mistaya, listen to me," she said. She was calm, poised, still. "I hoped to spare you this, but it seems I cannot. Your father is already under attack from Rydall and his wizard. Creatures are being sent against him, and he is being forced to use the magic of Questor Thews and the Paladin to survive. Thus far he has been successful. But Rydall's wizard will summon ever greater forces. Eventually your father may not be able to defend himself. Then it will be up to you. The best defense against one monster is another. That is the purpose of this exercise."

Nightshade's logic won out over Mistaya's doubt. So the girl worked hard at her creation all that day. Sunset approached, and she was exhausted. Nightshade's coaching had taken her far in the use of her magic, and some of what she did frightened her. Some of what she envisioned and brought to life was truly terrifying. But Nightshade was quick to sweep it all up, to gather it into the closet of first efforts, and to close it safely away. Mistaya was relieved. She did not want to see any of it again.

Now she sat alone in front of a small cooking fire—the only light the Witch of the Deep Fell permitted after dark—rolling dough into bread to fry with vegetables. Parsnip had taught her how. She cooked mostly for herself since Nightshade ate less than Haltwhistle. In truth, Nightshade rarely lingered once the day's lessons were complete, disappearing back into whatever place she occupied when she wanted to be alone. Sometimes she stayed close, just out of sight; Mistaya could feel her presence when she did that. The closer they became, the more aware the girl was of the witch. It was as if something in their shared use of magic brought them closer physically as well as emotionally, as if ties were being formed that allowed the girl to know more of what the other was about. She could not read Nightshade's thoughts or know her mind, but she could sense her presence and movements. Mistaya wondered if it was the same for Nightshade, and knew somehow it was not.

On this night the witch did not retire as usual, but came instead to sit with Mistaya before the fire. In silence she watched the girl work, watched her knead and roll the dough, form it into patties, wash and peel the vegetables, and place all of it in a pan with oil to cook. She continued to watch after Mistaya removed the meal from the fire and ate it. She sat as still as stone, looking over as if what she was observing were the most interesting thing she had ever seen. Mistaya let her sit. She knew that when Nightshade was ready to speak, she would do so. She knew as well that Nightshade had something to say.

It wasn't until the pan and dishes were washed and put away in the large wooden chest that sat out in the middle of the clearing as if it belonged there that the witch finally said, "I am pleased with you, Mistaya. I am encouraged by your progress."

The girl looked up. "Thank you."

"Today's effort was especially good. What you created was quite wonderful. Are you as satisfied with it as I am?"

"Yes," Mistaya lied.

Nightshade's cold white face lifted to the haze as if searching for stars and then lowered again to the fire. "I will tell you the truth. I was not certain you were equal to the task I set for you. I was afraid that you might not be able to master the magic."

Her eyes shifted, fixing on the girl. "It was clear to me from the first that your magic was strong. It was clear that your potential for using it was virtually limitless. But possession of the magic is never enough. There are intangibles that limit the user's success. Desire is one. Determination. Focus and a sense of purpose. Magic is like a great cat. You can harness and direct its energy, but you must never look away, and you must never let it see fear in your eyes."

"I am not afraid of the magic," Mistaya declared firmly. "It belongs to me. It feels like an old friend."

Nightshade gave her a brief, small smile. "Yes, I can see that. You treat it as you might a friend. You are comfortable with it yet do not regard it lightly. Your sense of balance is very good." She paused. "You remind me of myself when I was your age."

Mistaya blinked. "I do?"

Nightshade looked through and past her into some distant place. "Very much so. It seems odd to contemplate now, but I was your age once. I was a girl discovering her latent talents. I was a novice in search of a life, in quest of my limits as a witch. I was younger than you when I first discovered I possessed magic. It was a long time ago."

She trailed off, still looking away into the darkness. Mistaya shifted closer. "Tell me about it," she encouraged.

Nightshade shrugged. "The past is gone."

"But I would like to hear. I want to know how you felt. It might help me understand myself. Please, tell me."

The strange red eyes shifted back into the present, fixing on the girl. They penetrated with such ferocity that for a moment Mistaya was frightened. Then the glare changed to something worn and faded.

"I was born in the fairy mists," the Witch of the Deep Fell began, her tall, spare form as still as moon shadows on a windless night. She brushed at her raven hair with her slender fingers. "Like you, I inherited the blood of more than one world. Like you, I inherited the gift. My mother was a sorceress come out of one of the worlds that border on Landover, a world where magic is feared. She was very powerful, and she could cross back and forth between worlds through the mists. She was not a fairy creature, but she could walk among them comfortably. One day, while she was crossing between worlds, she met my father. My father was a changeling, a creature who had no true form but adopted whatever form he chose to suit his needs. He saw my mother and fell in love with her. He made himself into something that attracted her. A wolf, all black hair and teeth. In the end he seduced her and made her his own."

Her voice was flat and devoid of emotion, but there was an edge to it that Mistaya did not miss. "He kept her with him for a time, then abandoned her and went on to other interests. He was a fickle and irresponsible creature, like all of the fairy folk, unable to comprehend the demands and responsibilities of love. I was born of that union, conceived in the madness of spring light when the second cycle rounds and the shards of winter spill into melting ice."

Her gaze went away again. Her words, though poetic and lyrical, were nevertheless incomprehensible to the girl.

"My father took the shape of a wolf when he conceived me with my mother. My mother embraced him as a beast and was, I think, his equal in fury and passion." She blinked once, dismissing some picture that formed in her mind. "I took from their coupling a part of each, beast and madwoman, fairy and human, magic of one world and magic of the other. I was born with eyes that could freeze you alive. I was born with the ability to transform myself into a beast. I was born with disdain for life and death."

She looked at Mistaya. "I was a child still, and I was soon alone. My father was gone before I came into the world. My mother gave birth to me, but then she was taken away."

She trailed off, the echo of her words lacing the silence with bitterness. Mistaya waited, knowing better than to speak.

"The fairies condemned her for her efforts to become one of them. She had mated with a fairy and conceived a child, and that was not allowed. She was an outcast for this. She was sent from the mists and forbidden to return. She begged the fairies to reconsider. She wanted me to have the training and experience that only they could offer. She wanted me to have my father's life as well as hers. She wanted everything for me. But she was turned away. She was sent back into her own world. It was a death sentence. She had been able for too long to travel the mists, to cross from one world to another, to fly where she chose. Confinement in one world was unbearable. She bore it as long as she could. Then she threw caution to the winds and tried crossing once more through the mists. She went in, and she never came out. She disappeared like smoke on the wind."

Nightshade's gaze was gathering focus once more. The force of her words was palpable. "Do you see how alike we are? Like you, it was left for me to discover on my own who I was. Like you, the truth of my birthright was hidden from me. I was given over to other people to raise, a man and a woman who did not understand my needs, who did not recognize the magic growing within me. They kept me for as long as I would let them, and then I ran away. I had begun to sense my power, but I did not yet comprehend its uses. There were stirrings, but I could give them no voice. Like you, I grew in the fairy way, in spurts that eclipsed human measure. The man and the woman were frightened of me. If I had stayed, they might have killed me."

Like you, she was on the verge of saying, but did not. Nevertheless, Mistaya could hear the whisper of the words in the silence, and she was startled by them. She was not like Nightshade, of course. Not in that way, at least. She could see it quite plainly. Yet Nightshade felt an overwhelming need to believe that they shared more than they did. There was something happening here that the girl did not understand, and it made her uneasy and cautious.

Nightshade's eyes glittered in the firelight. "I escaped into a forest that bordered on the fairy mists, a shelter for those who were part of both worlds and accepted in neither. I found companions there, some of one species, some of another. We were not friends, but we had much in common. We were outlaws without reason; we were condemned for who we were. We taught each other what we knew and learned what we could. We explored our talents. We uncovered the secrets hidden within us. It was dangerous to do so, for we were unskilled, and some of our secrets could kill. More than a few of us died. Some went mad. I was fortunate to escape both fates and emerge the mistress of my talent. I came away a full-grown woman and a witch of great power. I found and mastered knowledge."

Wood from the fire crackled suddenly, sending sparks flying into the air. Mistaya started, but Nightshade did not move. She stayed frozen against the firelight, rigid with concentration.

Her eyes fixed on Mistaya. "I was younger than you when I learned of my power. I was alone. I did not have another to guide me, as you have me. But we are alike, Mistaya. I was hard inside, and nothing could break me. I was stone. I would not be lied to. I would not be cheated or tricked. I understood what I wanted, and I set about finding ways to obtain it. I see all that in you. I see such determination. You will do whatever you set your mind to, and you will not be deterred. You will listen to reason but will not necessarily be dissuaded from a course of action because of it, not if what you covet is important to you."

Mistaya nodded not so much in agreement, for she was not at all sure she agreed with this assessment, as in encouragement. She wanted to hear more. She was fascinated.

"After a time," Nightshade said slowly, "I determined that I would go into the fairy mists. I had been banished, but that was before I had discovered the extent of my powers. Now, I felt, things were different. I belonged among the fairies. It was my right to travel between worlds as my mother had once done. I went to the edge of the mists and called. I did so for a very long time. No answer came. Finally, I simply entered the mists, determined that I would confront those who had banished me. They found me at once. They gave me no hearing. They refused me out of hand. I was cast out, unable to prevent it despite my magic."

Her mouth had grown tight and hard. "I did not give up. I went back again and again, unwilling to accede to their wishes, determined in the end that I would die first. Years passed. I lived several human lifetimes but did not age. I was impervious to time's dictates. I was more fairy than human. I belonged in the mists. Still, I was not allowed to enter.

"Then I found a rift that let me come into the mists unseen. I changed shape to disguise myself, to keep from being discovered. I entered the mist and hid among its lesser creatures. No one recognized me. I stayed first as one thing, then as another, always keeping carefully back from the light of discovery. I became accepted. I found I could pass freely among the fairies. I began to use magic as they did. I worked my spells and performed my conjuring, and I lived as they did. My deception had worked. I was one of them."

She smiled, cynical and bitter. "And then, like my mother, I fell in love." Her voice was suddenly very small and brittle. "I found a creature so beautiful, so desirable, that I could not help myself. I had to have him. I was desperate to be his. I followed him, befriended him, companioned with him, and in the end gave myself to him completely. To achieve this, I was forced to reveal myself. When I did so, he spurned me instantly. He betrayed me. He exposed my presence. The fairies were not kind. I was banished out of hand. Because I fell in love. Because I used poor judgment."

One eyebrow arched in bitter reflection. "Like my mother."

She was almost crying, Mistaya realized suddenly. There were no tears, but the girl could feel the knife edge of the witch's pain, sharp and close against her skin.

"I was sent here," Nightshade finished. "To the Deep Fell. Banished from the fairy mists, banished from my homeland. Banished to Landover to live out my life. I had used my magic and left my mark upon their world, and I wasn't one of them. I had transgressed. So I was punished. I was placed at the gateway of all the worlds I could never enter. I was placed at the edge of the mists I could never pass through." Her hands clasped, and her fingers tightened into knots. Her head shook slowly from side to side. "No, the fairies were not kind."

"It seems very unfair," Mistaya offered quietly.

Nightshade laughed. "The word has no meaning for the fairy people. They have no conception of it. There is only what is allowed and what isn't. If you think about it, the whole idea of fairness is a fool's fiction. Look at our world, here in Landover. Fairness is determined by those who wield the power to deny it. Invocation of its use is a beggar's plea for help when all else fails. 'Be fair with me!' How pitiful and hopeless!"

She spit out the words in disgust. Then she bent forward with sudden intent. "I learned something from what was done to me, Mistaya. I learned never to beg, never to expect kindness, never to rely on chance or good fortune. My magic sustains me. My power gives me strength. Rely on these and you will be protected."

"And do not fall in love," Mistaya added solemnly.

"No," the witch agreed, and there was such fury in her face that she was momentarily unrecognizable, a beast of the sort into which she claimed she could transform herself. "No," she repeated, the word bound in iron, and Mistaya knew she was thinking of someone in particular, of a time and place quite close, of an event that still burned inside her with a white-hot heat. "No, never again."

Mistaya sat motionless in the dwindling firelight and let Nightshade's rage drain away, willing herself to be little more than another shadow in the dark, nonthreatening and inconsequential. Had she revealed herself to be anything else, it seemed that the witch's rage might have swallowed her whole.

Nightshade looked at her as if reading her mind, then gave her a disarming smile. "We are alike," she said once more, as if needing to reassure herself. "You and I, Mistaya. The magic binds us, witches first and always, born with power that others can only covet and never possess. It is our blessing and curse to live apart. It is our fate."

Her hand lifted and filled the air with emerald light, a dust that spread against the darkness and fell away like glitter.

⸻∞⸻

Later, when she rolled herself into her blankets, Mistaya was still thinking of what Nightshade had revealed to her. So much misery, bitterness, and solitude in the other's dark life. So much anger. *Like me,* the witch had repeated over and over again. *You and I.*

Mistaya's uncertainty grew as she pondered the words. Perhaps there was more truth to their claim than she was willing to allow. She had not thought so, but she was beginning to wonder. Since she was a witch, too, perhaps she belonged here with Nightshade.

She was so troubled by the possibility that she only just remembered to call Haltwhistle before she fell asleep.

JUGGERNAUT

Dawn brought a change in the weather in the lake country, and when Ben and Willow awoke, a slow, steady rain was falling. They dressed; ate a light breakfast of fruit, bread and jam, and goat's milk; wrapped themselves in their travel cloaks; and went out to find the River Master. Elderew was misty and shadowed beneath a ceiling of dark clouds, and the city's canopy of rain-drenched boughs shed chilly droplets on them as they moved along the deserted trail toward the city. They did not hurry. The River Master would have been advised by now that they were awake. He would come to meet them before they were required to ask for him, because that was the way he was.

Ben glanced about surreptitiously for the Ardsheal but did not see it. He could feel its presence, though. He could sense it watching from the gloom.

The River Master appeared as they neared the city center, standing alone in a clearing through which the trail passed. He greeted Ben with a nod and Willow with a brief embrace, neither gesture offering much in the way of warmth, and advised them that their horses were waiting. He did not ask if they would like to stay longer. Now that he had given them the Ardsheal, he expected them to continue the search for Mistaya. He elicited their promise to keep him advised on their progress. Bunion appeared with Jurisdiction and Crane, his gnarled body hunched and dripping in the gloom, eyes narrowed to yellow slits. As Ben and Willow mounted, the River Master put aside his reserve long enough to declare that if he was needed in the effort to reclaim his granddaughter, they had only to send for him and he would come at once. It was an unexpected deviation from his deliberate distancing of himself from them. Ben and Willow were surprised but did not show it. They took him at his word and rode out.

Wood sprites met them at the edge of the old growth leading down from Elderew to guide them back through the swamp and timber mass that warded the city. Rain continued to fall, a drizzle that turned the ground beneath their horses' hooves sodden and slick. When their guides had returned them to the more lightly forested country below Elderew, they paused to rest before continuing on.

"Have you seen it yet this morning?" Ben asked Willow as they passed an ale skin back and forth while standing down from their horses beneath the canopy of the trees.

"No," she replied. "But Bunion has. He said it is tracking us back in the shadows, keeping pace. Bunion doesn't like having it along any better than I do."

Ben glanced over. Bunion was crouched to one side in a covering of trees, looking disgruntled. "He certainly appears unhappy, even for him."

"He considers himself your bodyguard. The presence of the Ardsheal suggests that he isn't capable of doing his job."

Ben looked at her. "You don't think the Ardsheal should be here, either, do you?"

"As a matter of fact, that isn't what I think at all. I think the Ardsheal will do a better job of protecting you than anyone." She gave him a long, cool look. "That doesn't mean I like having it along, though."

He nodded. "You said as much last night. Why is that?"

She hesitated. "I will tell you later. Tonight." She was silent for a moment. "I told Bunion that the Ardsheal was a gift from my father and that it would have been impolite and possibly dangerous to refuse it. Bunion accepted that."

Ben looked at the kobold again. It was staring back at him, yellow eyes glittering. When it saw Ben looking, it smiled like a hungry alligator.

"Well, I hope you're right," he said absently. His gaze shifted to meet hers. "I've been thinking. Should we try to contact the Earth Mother? She always seems to know what is happening in Landover. Perhaps she could give us some insight into what's become of Mistaya and the others. Perhaps she knows something of Rydall."

Rain dripped off the edge of Willow's hood onto her nose, and she pulled the hood forward for better protection. "I gave thought to that. But the Earth Mother would have come to me by now in my dreams if she had any help to give. Mistaya is important to her, a promise of some special fulfillment. She would not let her be harmed if there was anything she could do to prevent it."

Ben prodded a bit of rotting wood with his boot. "I wish some of these people would be more consistent with their help," he muttered sourly.

She gave him a small smile. "Help is a gift that one must never grow to expect. Now, where do we go from here?"

He shrugged and looked off into the trees again. He hated that he couldn't see the Ardsheal. It was bad enough being shadowed by his enemies. Did he have to put up with being shadowed by his protector as well?

He sighed. "Well, I can't see any reason to go back to Sterling Silver. If we do, Rydall will just send another monster. And we won't be any closer to finding Mistaya." He frowned as if questioning his own reasoning. "I thought we might go into the Greensward. Kallendbor knows every adversary Landover has ever faced. He has fought against most of them. Perhaps he will know something of Rydall and Marnhull. Perhaps he will have heard something that will help us find Mistaya."

"Kallendbor isn't to be trusted," she advised him quietly.

He nodded. "True. But he has no reason to favor an invading army. Besides, he owes me for sparing him worse punishment than I gave when he sided with the Gorse. And he knows it. I think it's worth a try."

"Perhaps." She did not look convinced. "But you should be especially careful where he is concerned."

"I will," he assured her, wondering how much more careful he needed to be now that he had the Paladin, Bunion, and the Ardsheal all standing guard over him.

They remounted and rode on. Bunion, advised of their new destination, scurried ahead through the trees, scouting the land they would pass through, leaving them to the temporary care of their invisible bodyguard. The Ardsheal, however, stayed hidden. The day stretched away with languid slowness, morning turning into midday, midday into afternoon. Still the rain continued. They moved northeast toward the Greensward, the trees thinning as the lake country gave way to the hills below Sterling Silver. They stopped for lunch at a stream, where they took shelter beneath an old cedar. Rain dripped off the sagging limbs, a steady patter on the muddied ground. The world around them was cool and damp and still. When the meal was finished, they rode on. They didn't see another traveler all day.

Nightfall brought them to the edge of the Greensward, where the grasslands spread away through the provinces of Landover's lesser Lords to the Melchor. Sunset was an iron-gray glimmer in the west above the distant mountains, its light hammered tin reflecting off the advancing night. Ben and Willow made camp in a grove of cherry and Bonnie Blues on a rise that overlooked the plains. Bunion returned to share dinner, a cold meal prepared without the benefit of a fire, and then he was gone again. The Ardsheal did not appear at all.

When night had fallen and they were alone in its deep silence, the rains having abated to a damp mist that floated across the grasslands like ghost robes, Ben put his arms around Willow, pulled her back against him so that they were both staring out at the gloom, and said, "Tell me about the Ardsheal."

She did not say anything at first, resting rigid and unmoving against him as his arms cradled her. He could feel her breathing, the rise and fall of her breast, the small whisper of air from her lips. He waited patiently, looking past the veil of her hair to the thickening roil of mist beyond.

"There have always been Ardsheals," she said finally. "They were created to protect the once-fairy after they left the mists and came into the world of humans. The Ardsheals were an old magic, one born of earth lore, and because they were elementals, they could be summoned from anywhere. The once-fairy used them only rarely, for they were destroyers, cast of harsh purpose and desperate need. When the threat was so great that the once-fairy feared there would be loss of life among their people, the Ardsheals were called in. A few were usually all it took. In years long past, before the old King, when Landover was newly conceived and birthing yet its lands and peoples, there were wars between humans and once-fairy. Humans occupied Landover first; the once-fairy came after and were regarded as invaders. In the battles fought, Ardsheals were summoned to do battle against creatures conjured by wizards who served the humans."

She stopped, gathering her thoughts. "That was a long time ago. Since then, Ardsheals have been used only rarely. The last time was not long ago. It happened when one of Abbadon's demons penetrated the wards of Elderew disguised as a once-fairy. It was a sorcerous being, a changeling who sought entry for its fellows through the heart of the lake country. The magic harbored there, it reasoned, would then belong to them. So it disguised itself and came into the city, and it tried to kill my father."

"Because he was the River Master?" Ben asked softly.

"Yes, because of that. Because he was the leader of his people." Willow's words were almost inaudible. "The demon tried and failed. But in its attempt to kill my father, it destroyed a handful of others, including several children. The demon escaped. There was terrible panic among the once-fairy. And rage. My father and the elders summoned five of the Ardsheals and sent them in search of the demon. The Ardsheals tracked the creature from house to house, caught it at last in one of its many disguises, and killed it."

She took a deep breath. "It was my house it was hiding in when they found it. It had disguised itself as one of my sisters. It was very clever. It had worked its way back to the one place it thought it might be safe: the River Master's own house. But the Ardsheals were relentless. They could track by touch, smell, taste, the smallest sound, even by a change of heat caused by the casting of a shadow. Nevertheless, they were not infallible. Not this day. They had been conjured quickly and imperfectly. Haste led to carelessness. The demon took several shapes before he took the one in which they caught him. The one he took before that was of my sister Kaijelln. The Ardsheals were closing on it by then, and when they came into our house, bursting through the entry, tearing apart the doors as if they were cloth, they thought the demon was Kaijelln still.

"And so," she whispered, her voice shaking now, "they killed her without taking time to discover the truth. They acted on instinct. They killed her right in front of me."

Ben swallowed against the dryness in his throat. "Your father couldn't stop them?"

Willow shook her head. "They were too quick. Too powerful. An Ardsheal, when it attacks, is unstoppable. It was so that day with Kaijelln. She was gone in the blink of an eye."

They were silent for a long time then, Ben holding the sylph tight against him, neither of them moving, eyes staring out into the darkness. Somewhere a night bird called, and another responded. Water dripped from leaves in the stillness.

"We should have left it behind," Ben said finally. "We should have refused it."

"No!" Willow's voice was hard and certain this time. "Nothing can stand against an Ardsheal. Nothing! You need it to protect you against whatever else Rydall chooses to send. Besides, my father will have taken great pains to make certain that this one does what it is supposed to do and nothing more."

She twisted suddenly in his arms and looked directly at him. "Don't you see? It doesn't matter that I am afraid of it. It only matters that it will keep you alive." She leaned forward until her face was only inches away. "I love you that much, Ben Holiday."

Then she kissed him and went on kissing him until he forgot about everything else.

At dawn they rode out once more. The day was gray and misty, but the rains had moved on. Bunion had come back during the night and this time traveled with them as they moved out onto the open grasslands, the kobold skittering ahead eagerly to lead the way. The Ardsheal appeared as well, emerging from the forest to take up a position some twenty yards to their rear. It stayed there as they journeyed, attached to them like a shadow. They watched it for a while, glancing back over their shoulders, marveling at the easy, fluid motion of its stride. It wore nothing, and its body was virtually featureless—arms, legs, feet, hands, torso, and head smooth and slick with the damp, skin stretched seamless and taut, eyes black holes boring straight ahead into the gloom. It did not acknowledge them as it traveled; it never spoke. It stopped when they did, waited patiently for them to begin moving again, then resumed its steady pace.

By midmorning they quit looking for it. By midday they stopped thinking about it completely.

The grasslands were carpeted thickly with mist, and the towns and farms of the people of the Greensward and the castle fortresses of the Lords materialized with ghostly abruptness before them. They skirted all, intent on reaching Rhyndweir and Kallendbor by nightfall. They bought hot soup from a vendor at a market on the edge of a small town and sipped it from tin cups while they rode. Bunion finished his in the blink of an eye and was off. The Ardsheal stayed back in the gloom and ate nothing.

Ben and Willow traveled in silence, riding side by side, content to be company for each other, not needing to speak. Ben spent much of the day thinking on the tale of the Ardsheal and Kaijelln. He found himself comparing the Ardsheal to the Paladin, both destroyers, both perfect fighting machines, both in his service and therefore his responsibility for whatever damage they might do. The comparison bothered him more than he could say. It made him ponder anew what his transformation into the Paladin was doing to his psyche. Would he someday reach the point where the difference between them was no longer discernible? Would he then become like the Ardsheal, a passionless, remorseless killing machine, a creature without a conscience, serving only its master? He found himself thinking about how he had felt when, as the Paladin, he had been trapped within the Tangle Box, how he had lacked identity beyond his role as King's champion, how he had been lost to everything but his skills as a warrior. The thoughts spun and twisted together with insidious intent, making him question anew his strength of purpose in the battle with Rydall's monsters. He struggled with his thoughts but kept the struggle carefully to himself.

By late afternoon they had come in sight of Rhyndweir. The castle of Kallendbor rose on a bluff at the juncture of the Anhalt and Piercenal rivers, walls, parapets, and towers lifting darkly above the grasslands. A town lay below the castle gates, bustling and crowded, filled with buyers and sellers of goods: tradesmen, farmers, trappers, and craftsmen of all sorts. Rain had begun falling again, a gray drizzle that mingled with the mist and shrouded buildings and people alike, turning them to dark, uncertain images in the gloom.

Ben and Willow had come with no fanfare, no escort, and no advance notice. There was no one expecting them and no one to guide them to the palace. But this fit with Ben's intent. He wanted to surprise Kallendbor, to catch Rhyndweir's Lord unprepared so that he would be forced to improvise a response to Ben's coming. There was a better chance of enlisting his cooperation if he was not given time to weigh the gain and loss.

Ben slowed when they reached the Anhalt and the bridge that spanned it to the castle. He called Bunion back to him, then turned to the Ardsheal and beckoned it close. To his surprise, it did as it was asked. It came to stand directly next to him, face flat and expressionless, eyes staring straight ahead. Ben arched his eyebrow at Willow, told them all to stay close, and nudged Jurisdiction forward.

They crossed the bridge and entered the town, riding through the people and rain as the afternoon light faded toward murky dark. People were hurrying home now, so few paid much attention to the riders and their footmen. Those who did looked quickly away. An Ardsheal and a kobold were not something they wished to ask questions about.

The little company reached the castle gates and was quickly halted by the guards. There were wide eyes and protestations of all sorts, but Ben simply ordered the nearest functionary to guide them to the palace. Word would be sent ahead in any event, and he did not care to wait for its arrival. One commander, braver than his companions, questioned the presence of the Ardsheal and was silenced by Ben's curt reply. The Ardsheal was the High Lord's personal guard. Where the High Lord went—or his Queen—so went the Ardsheal. The commander gave ground, and they were allowed to enter.

They rode through gateways and cobblestone passages, up several levels of defenses, and past quarters for the soldiers who served Kallendbor to the grassy flats on which the palace sat. Their guide tried to slow the pace to give time for word to reach his Lord and for his Lord to prepare, but Ben pushed Jurisdiction ahead and almost rode the lagging functionary down. In minutes they were before the palace entrance and dismounting.

To his credit, Kallendbor came out immediately to greet them. He was alone save for the doorman who stood waiting nervously at the entrance; apparently there had been no time to summon retainers. The Lord of Rhyndweir was a tall, rawboned man with fiery red hair and a temper to match. Battle scars crisscrossed his hands and forearms and marred an otherwise handsome face. He wore a broadsword strapped to his waist as if it were a natural part of his dress. He was flushed as he approached and his eyes were angry, but he gave his guests a deep, respectful bow.

"Had I known you were coming, High Lord, I would have prepared a better welcome," he added, almost hiding his petulance. He took in Bunion with a glance and then for the first time saw the Ardsheal. "What is the meaning of this?" he snapped, and now his anger was obvious. "Why do you bring this creature here?"

Ben glanced at the Ardsheal as if he had forgotten it was there. "It was a gift from the River Master. It serves as my protector. Shall we go inside where it's dry and talk it over?"

Kallendbor hesitated and looked as if he might object, then apparently thought better of it. He led them out of the rain into the front hall and then down a long corridor to a sitting room dominated by a vast stone fireplace that rose from floor to ceiling. The blaze from the logs burning in the hearth threw heat and light from wall to wall and made their shadows dance as they crossed to chairs to sit before it. Bunion had remained to see to the horses. The Ardsheal stopped by the door and merged with the shadows that crowded forward from the hall.

Kallendbor seated himself across from Ben and Willow. His anger had not abated. "Ardsheals have been the enemy of the people of the Greensward for centuries, High Lord. They are not welcome here. Surely you must know that."

"Times change." Ben looked at the empty glasses set next to the decanter of amber liquid on the table between them and waited for Kallendbor to fill two and pass them to himself and Willow. The Lord of Rhyndweir's lips were set in a tight line, and his great hands were knotted into fists.

"Are you quite settled now, High Lord?" he snapped.

Ben nodded. "Thank you, yes." He ignored the other's curt tone. "I apologize for bringing the Ardsheal into Rhyndweir, but circumstances dictate unusual caution just now. I assume you have heard of the threat against my life."

Kallendbor brushed at the air dismissively. "By Rydall of Marnhull? I have heard. Has he pressed the matter?"

"Two attacks so far."

Kallendbor studied him. "Two. With five more promised, I understand. But nothing can stand against the Paladin. And now you have an Ardsheal as well. They should keep you safe enough."

Ben leaned forward. "Will you be terribly disappointed if they do?"

For the first time Kallendbor smiled, a bitter and sardonic grimace. "We are not good friends, High Lord. I have no particular reason to wish you well. But Rydall of Marnhull is no friend, either."

"Do you know him, then?" Ben pressed.

Kallendbor shook his head. "I know nothing of him. He must come from somewhere outside Landover."

"But if so, how did he cross through the fairy mists?"

"As you did, I suppose." Kallendbor shrugged. "He used magic."

Ben sipped at his drink. A rather sweet wine. He would not have expected it of Kallendbor. At his side Willow stirred, impatient with the conversation, anxious to be finished with it. She did not like Kallendbor or Rhyndweir or much of anything about the Greensward. She was a once-fairy, and the Lords of the Greensward had never been their friends.

Ben looked over at the fire momentarily, then back at Kallendbor. "This is a brief visit. One night to dry out from the rains, and then we will be on our way. We will take our meals in our rooms, so you won't have to trouble yourself with entertaining us. The Ardsheal will stay close to us and out of sight. Bunion can join us as well."

Kallendbor nodded, and there was a look of obvious relief on his face. "Whatever pleases you, High Lord. I'll send hot water for baths."

Ben nodded. "There is one thing." He leaned forward so that the full weight of his gaze was resting on Kallendbor. "If I thought for one minute that you knew anything of Rydall and were keeping it from me, I would have you in chains."

Kallendbor stiffened, and his face went hot with rage. "High Lord, I do not have to—"

"Because I am reminded of how you sided with the Gorse against me not so very long ago," Ben continued, cutting him short. "I had every cause to have you exiled for life and stripped of your holdings. I had cause to have you put to death. But you are a strong leader and a man who can bring considerable weight to bear among your peers, and I value your service to the throne. I did not want the Greensward to lose you. Besides, I believe you were misguided in that matter. All of us were to some extent."

He paused. "But if it were to happen again, I would not hesitate to rethink my position where you are concerned, Lord Kallendbor. I want you to re-member that."

Kallendbor gave a curt, barely perceptible nod. He could barely bring himself to speak. "Is that all, High Lord?"

"No." Ben held his gaze. "Rydall has taken our daughter. Your spies may not have told you that. She is a hostage until the Paladin either defeats or is de-feated by the creatures he sends to do battle. I search for her now. But there is no sign of Rydall of Marnhull. No one seems able to help, yourself included. I am determined to get my daughter back, Kallendbor. If you can help, it would be wise for you to do so."

He waited. Kallendbor was silent for a moment. "I do not need to take children as hostages to do battle with my enemies," he managed finally.

He seemed to have trouble speaking the words. Ben wondered why. "Then you will send for me if you hear anything that will help me find Mistaya?" he pressed.

Kallendbor's face closed down, flat and expressionless. There was a hard look in his eyes. "You have my word that I will do whatever I can to see your daughter safely home. I can promise no more."

Ben nodded slowly. "I will take you at your word."

There was a long, harsh silence. Then Kallendbor shifted uncomfortably in his seat and said, "If you are ready, I will show you to your rooms."

For the moment at least they had each had enough of the other.

—◦◦◦—

Midnight came and went. Rain poured down out of the heavens, brought to the grasslands by thunderheads that had broken free of the barrier of the mountains and had crossed in the dark. Lightning seared the black skies in white-hot streaks that dazzled and stunned. Below Rhyndweir's walls the turgid waters of the Anhalt and the Piercenal churned against their banks, swollen and clogged with debris.

Ben Holiday slept uneasily. Twice already he had awakened and risen to look about. Silence had woken him the first time, the storm's fury the second. Both times he had crossed to the doorway and stood listening, then had walked to the windows of the bedchamber tower and looked down. They were housed in the west tower in rooms reserved for important visitors, high up in the palace, away from the household staff and other guests. From their windows it was well over a hundred feet to the rocks of the bluff and the waters of the Anhalt. From their door it was a long climb down a winding set of stairs past several other floors and unoccupied rooms to the hall that led back to the main part of the castle. As was the custom, the rooms selected for the High Lord of Landover were separate and secure, offering but a single approach.

On this night, however, Ben could not stop thinking that they also offered only one way out.

Still, he was safe here. Bunion kept watch just outside the door, and the Ardsheal roamed the stairs and hall below. Without, lightning flashed, thunder boomed, and the wind howled across the plains, a vast immutable force. But the storm did not penetrate to where Ben and Willow slept, save for the sound of its passing, and there was nothing else to make the High Lord wakeful.

Yet he was.

And when the heavy thudding came from the stairs and Bunion shrieked in warning, he was already awake and sitting up in the bed. Willow lifted herself beside him instantly, her face stricken, her eyes wide. The ironbound oak door flew inward, splintered into shards that barely managed to hang together from the shattered bindings. Something huge and dark filled the doorway, tearing at the stone walls that hindered its passage. Bunion clung to the thing, ripping at it with teeth and claws, but it didn't even seem to notice the kobold. Into the bedchamber it came, hammering apart stone and mortar, shredding the lintels and the last of the mangled door. Lightning flashed and lit up the monstrous apparition as Ben and Willow stared in disbelief.

It was a giant encased in metal from head to foot.

My God, Ben thought in stunned surprise, it's a robot!

Iron creaked and groaned as it swung toward them, arms lifting, fingers grasping. The creature was formed of metal plates and fastenings. A robot! But there were no robots in Landover, no mechanical men of any kind! No one here had ever even heard of such a thing!

Willow screamed and tumbled from the bed, looking for room to maneuver. Ben scrambled back, slipped on the bedding, and fell. His head cracked hard on the wooden headboard, and his eyes were filled with bright lights and tears. "Ben!" he heard Willow scream, but he could not make himself respond. He knew he should do something, but the blow to his head had shaken him so that he could not think what it was.

A weapon! He needed a weapon!

Through the blur of his tears he saw the robot fling Bunion away as if the kobold were made of paper. Massive iron feet thudded in heavy cadence as the monster closed on the bed, reached down for the footboard, and tore it away. The bed dropped with a lurch, and Ben rolled free, trying to gain his feet. Bunion attacked again, and this time the robot slapped him away so hard that the kobold struck the wall with an audible crunch, crumpled to the floor, and lay still.

"Ben, call the Paladin!" Willow cried out, throwing loose bedding and broken pieces of wood at the monster in a futile effort to slow it.

Then the Ardsheal appeared, flying through the doorway out of the darkness beyond, slamming into their attacker from behind. The force of the blow caused the robot to sway momentarily before turning back. The Ardsheal closed fearlessly with the giant, grappling with it in an effort to bring it down. Lightning flashed once more, outlining the combatants as they fought for footing across the chamber floor. Willow darted past them, trying to reach Ben. Ben was on his feet, leaning dazedly against the far wall. Blood ran down his temple. He groped for the medallion so that he could summon the Paladin, but to his horror he couldn't find it. The medallion and the chain that had bound it about his neck were gone!

Back against the stone wall crashed the robot and the Ardsheal, locked together in mortal combat, caught up in their terrible struggle like great bears. The Ardsheal fastened its hands on one of the robot's great metal forearms and wrenched at it with terrific force. There was a frightening screech of metal giving way, and suddenly the lower arm and hand separated and fell to the floor with a crash. Instantly the robot wrapped both arms about the Ardsheal, locked its good hand to the remnants of its shattered arm, and tightened its arms in a crushing grip. The Ardsheal stiffened and threw back its head. Something inside it broke with an audible series of snaps.

Willow grabbed up a piece of the shattered door, charged forward with a cry, and slammed the makeshift club across the robot's face. The robot did not seem to notice, still concentrating all its efforts on the Ardsheal. Able to see again, Ben surged forward, his head clear. He pulled Willow away, snatched up a large piece of the bedding, threw it over the robot's head, and yanked back on the ends. The metal giant twisted its head, then started to swing about, still grasping the stricken Ardsheal.

But one boot caught on the bedding, and it tripped. To regain its balance, it was forced to release its grip.

Instantly, the Ardsheal broke free. A dark liquid ran from its mouth and nose, and its joints looked to have come loose from their pinnings. Yet it did not seem to feel its injuries. It attacked anew, hammering into the robot with both fists and knocking it backward toward the open windows. As the robot reeled away, the Ardsheal catapulted into it with a ferocious charge that carried both combatants into the metal-barred opening. Stone and mortar gave way beneath their combined weight, and the iron bars broke loose. The window frame and part of the surrounding wall shattered.

Then the Ardsheal locked itself about the robot, drove it through the opening, and both creatures tumbled out into the night.

Ben and Willow reached the rain-swept opening a moment later, too late to see them fall but in time to hear them smash against the rocks below and tumble into the river. Rain drenched their faces and shoulders as they leaned out into the dark, peering down. Lightning flashed, revealing the water-slick castle walls, the empty rocks, and the surging river. Nothing moved on the rocks. Nothing could be seen in the river.

Ben drew Willow back into the room and hugged her close. She buried her face in his shoulder, and he could feel her drawing in great gulps of air.

"Damn Rydall!" he swore in her ear, trying to keep from shaking.

Her fingers dug into his arm as she nodded in fierce, voiceless agreement.

DRAGON SIGHT

It was afterward that Ben discovered he was still wearing the medallion. He looked down and there it was, hanging by its chain from his neck. For a moment he couldn't believe it. He held it up and stared at it. The familiar graven image of the Paladin riding out of Sterling Silver at sunrise glimmered back. He had been so certain he had lost it. He had looked for it, and it wasn't there.

"Ben, what's wrong?" Willow asked quickly, seeing the look on his face.

He shook his head, letting the medallion fall back into place. "Nothing. I was just . . ."

He trailed off, confused. The blow on the head when he had stumbled must have stunned him worse than he thought. But he had been so sure! He had reached for the medallion, and it hadn't been there!

Willow let the matter drop, moved to the clothes chest, and brought out clean robes. Seconds later a contingent of palace guards came charging up the stairs, weapons at the ready, responding finally to the attack. Ben and Willow were working on Bunion by then and ignored them. The kobold was banged up considerably but otherwise appeared to be all right. Kobolds are tough little fellows, Ben thought admiringly, relieved that his friend had not been seriously injured, thinking that almost anyone else would have been killed.

The palace guards poked around the room, stared out through the gap in the wall into the rain-streaked night, and mostly looked uncomfortable with the fact that they were forced to be there at all. It was a reflection on them that the attack had almost succeeded, and they were wary of both the High Lord's and Kallendbor's reactions to their failure to prevent it.

Ben, for his part, was too preoccupied to concern himself with casting blame; he was still mulling over the suddenness of the assault and the circumstances that had surrounded it. But Kallendbor, bare-chested and broadsword in hand when he burst into the room, was less charitable. After hearing a shortened version of the attack from Ben, he berated everyone within shouting distance. Then he dispatched one search party to the riverbanks below to discover if any trace of the Ardsheal or Rydall's monster could be found. Others he sent throughout the castle to make certain nothing else threatened. Ben, Willow, and Bunion were moved to other rooms, and guards were ordered to keep close watch over them for the remainder of the night. Obviously ill at ease with what had happened and anxious to avoid staying longer in their company, Kallendbor bid them a gruff good night and went off to sleep.

An exhausted Willow and Bunion were quick to follow.

Ben, however, stayed awake for a long time thinking about this latest monster. Two things bothered him, and he could reconcile neither.

The first was how the creature had gotten into the castle in the first place. How had it managed to slip past Kallendbor's guards and the Ardsheal as well? Something that big and cumbersome should never have been able to do so. It should not even have gotten past the front gates. Unless, of course, it hadn't come through them in the first place but had gotten into the palace by use of magic, which was the only conclusion that made any sense. And that made him wonder—although admittedly this was more of a stretch—if magic had also been used during the attack to make him think the medallion was lost. Otherwise, why hadn't he been able to find it—even stunned by the blow to his head, even in the frenzy of the moment—when it was hanging right there around his neck?

The second thing bothering him was that something was vaguely familiar about that robot, and he didn't see how that could be. There weren't any robots in Landover or even, so far as he knew, any idea of what robots were. So he must have seen it in his old world in a movie or a comic or some such, since even there robots were still mostly conceptual. He raked through his memories in an effort to recall where, but nothing came to mind.

When he finally fell asleep close to morning, he was still trying unsuccessfully to place it.

Willow woke him sometime around midmorning. The skies were clear again; the rains had moved east. He lay quietly for a moment, watching her sitting next to him, looking down, smiling in that particularly wonderful way, and he made an impulsive decision. Willow was suffering from Mistaya's loss and Rydall's threat as much as he was. It was wrong to keep his thinking to himself. So he told her all of it, even part of what he had never revealed before to anyone: that the medallion and the Paladin were linked, that the one summoned the other to the defense of the High Lord. They were alone in the room, Bunion having gone off much earlier on business of his own, the nature of which he had not disclosed. Willow listened carefully to everything Ben had to say, then took his hands and held them:

"If the medallion was tampered with," she said quietly, sitting close on the bed beside him, "then whoever did so would have to know that it provides your link to the Paladin." She stared at him steadily a moment. "Who, besides me, would know that?"

The answer was no one. Not even Questor Thews, and after Ben he knew more than anyone about the medallion. Most knew that it marked and belonged to whoever ruled Landover as High Lord. A few knew that it allowed its wearer passage through the fairy mists. Only Ben, and now Willow, knew that it summoned the Paladin.

He was almost persuaded at that moment to tell her everything about the medallion, the last of his secrets, the whole of the truth. He had told her how it linked him to the Paladin, how it allowed him to summon the High Lord's champion. Why not tell her as well how the Paladin and he were joined, how the Paladin was another side of himself, a darker side that took form when he was brought to combat? He had thought to tell her several times now. It was the last secret he kept from her about the magic, and the burden of it suddenly seemed almost unbearable.

Yet he kept silent. He was not ready. He was not certain. The immensity of such a revelation could have unexpected results. He did not want to test Willow's commitment to him by giving up so terrible a truth. He was afraid even now, even after so long, that he might lose her.

"Where do we go now, Ben?" she asked suddenly, interrupting his thinking. "You do not intend to remain here longer, do you?"

"No," he replied, relieved to be able to move on to another subject. "Kallendbor does not appear to have any help to give us, so there's no reason to linger. We'll leave as soon as I dress and we have something to eat. Where's Bunion, anyway?"

The kobold returned to the bedchamber just as Ben finished washing and putting on his clothes. Willow's bandage from the previous night, which had been applied to the worst of his injuries, a severe head cut, was gone. Bunion had been able to retain a strong scent from the robot, and he had gone down the stairway, backtracking its progress from the previous night. It had been a short trip. Much of the scent had been obliterated by the trampling of guards up and down the stairs, but there was enough left to determine that Rydall's monster had materialized out of nowhere on the landing of the floor just below their own. Ben looked at Willow, then back at Bunion. They all knew what that meant.

Bunion also advised them that a thorough search of the Anhalt and its banks by Kallendbor's soldiers had revealed no trace of either their attacker or the Ardsheal.

They summoned breakfast and ate it in their room, then had their belongings gathered and went down to the main hall. Kallendbor met them there, stern-faced and subdued from the previous night's events. Ben advised him that they were leaving, and there was veiled relief in the other's eyes. Ben had expected as much, since they were hardly friends under the best of circumstances. He offered his thanks for the other's hospitality and made him promise anew that he would send word if he learned anything of Mistaya or Rydall. Kallendbor walked them to the palace doors, where their horses were already saddled and waiting. Ben smiled to himself. Kallendbor would never make a good poker player.

They mounted and rode out the fortress gates and back through the town. They crossed the bridge over the Anhalt and headed southwest, retracing their steps in the direction of Sterling Silver. Willow gave Ben a questioning look, wondering anew at his plans, but he just cocked an eyebrow and said nothing. It was not until they were well beyond the castle and deep into the grasslands beyond that he swung Jurisdiction about and stopped.

"I didn't want Kallendbor to see where we were really going," he offered by way of explanation.

"Which is?"

"East, to the Wastelands, to the one other creature who might know something of Mistaya."

"I see," Willow replied quietly, way ahead of him by now.

"He'll talk to you. He likes you."

She nodded. "He might."

They worked their way back toward the Anhalt and followed it for the remainder of the day. By nightfall they had reached the beginning of the Wastelands. They camped there, taking shelter in a grove of ash on a hill that provided a good view in all directions of the surrounding countryside. They ate dinner cold. Bunion offered to stand watch for the entire night, but Ben would not hear of it. The kobold needed his rest as well, particularly if he was to be of any use when the next attack came—and there was no longer any pretense that it wouldn't. Since they were all dependent on one another, they would share the responsibility, he insisted.

There were no monsters this night, and Ben slept undisturbed. By morning he was feeling revitalized. Willow seemed rested, too. All three were anticipating what lay ahead. Even Bunion had figured it out. He went on ahead to scout while Ben and Willow followed at a more leisurely pace. They left the Greensward behind and entered the Wastelands. The day was cloudy and gray once again, but there did not appear to be any immediate threat of rain. Even without sunshine the air was hot and dry, the ground parched and cracked, and the country about them empty of life and as still as death.

By midday they were deep into the Wastelands, and Bunion came back to report that the Fire Springs were directly ahead and that Strabo the dragon was at home.

"If anyone knows of Rydall, it will be Strabo," Ben said to Willow as they rode into the craggy hills surrounding the Springs. "Strabo can go anywhere he wishes, and he may have flown through the fairy mists into Marnhull at some point. It's worth asking, in any case. As long as you're the one who does the asking."

Strabo did not much care for Holiday, although they were somewhat closer now after their shared experience in the Tangle Box. But the dragon genuinely liked Willow. He was fond of declaring that dragons had always had a soft spot for beautiful maidens, even though from time to time he thought that he was mistaken in this and that it was eating them that dragons really enjoyed. Too vain to admit his confusion, he had allowed himself to be charmed by the sylph on several occasions. Still, each visit to the Fire Springs was a new and uncertain experience, and Strabo the dragon was nothing if not temperamental.

When they were close enough to feel the heat of the pits, long after they had spied the smoke and inhaled the smell, they dismounted, tethered the horses, and proceeded on foot. It was a difficult walk over rugged, barren hills and across rock-strewn gullies. Bunion led the way as always, but he stayed close to them now. They had gone on for some minutes when they heard the crunching of bones. Bunion glanced over his shoulder and showed all his teeth in a humorless smile.

The dragon was feeding.

Then they crested a ridge, and there it was.

Strabo lay coiled about the mouth of one of the Springs, his forty-foot bulk as black as ink, all studded with spines and spikes, his sinewy body gnarled and sleek by turns. He was lunching on the remains of what appeared to have been a cow, although it was hard to tell since the dragon had reduced the carcass to legs and part of one haunch. Wicked blackened teeth glimmered as it gnawed on a large bone, stripping it of a few last shreds of flesh. Yellow eyes hooded by strange reddish lids focused on the bone, but as the newcomers topped the rise and came into view, its massive horned head lifted and swung about.

"Company?" it hissed none too pleasantly. The yellow eyes widened and blinked. "Oh, Holiday, it's only you. How boring. What do you want?" The voice was low and guttural, marked by a sibilant hiss. "Wait, don't tell me, let me guess. You want to know about this cow. You've come all the way from the comforts of your shiny little castle to reprimand me about this cow. Well, save your breath. The cow was a stray. It wandered into the Wastelands, and that made it mine. So no lectures, please."

It always surprised Ben that the dragon could talk. It went counter to everything life experience had taught him in his old world. But then, there were no dragons in his old world, either.

"I don't care about the cow," Ben advised. He had made Strabo promise once upon a time that he would give up stealing livestock.

The dragon's maw split wide, and it laughed after a fashion. "No? Well, in that case I'll confess that perhaps it wasn't quite inside the boundaries of the

Wasteland when I took it. There, I feel much better. The truth shall set you free." The eyes narrowed again. "Well, well. Is that the pretty sylph with you, Holiday?" He never called Ben "High Lord." "Have you brought her to me for a visit? No, you would never be that considerate. You must be here for some other reason. What is it?"

Ben sighed. "We've come to ask—"

"Wait, you're interrupting my dinner." The dragon's nostrils steamed, and it gave a rough cough. "Politeness in all things. Please take a seat until I've finished. Then I'll hear what you have to say. If you keep it brief."

Ben looked at Willow, and reluctantly they sat down on the knoll with Bunion and waited for Strabo to complete his dinner. The dragon took his time, crunching up every single bone and devouring every last shred of flesh until nothing remained but hooves and horns. He made a deliberate production out of it, smacking his lips and grunting his approval with every bite. It was an endless performance, and it produced the intended effect. Ben was so impatient by the time the dragon had finished that he could barely contain his temper.

Strabo tossed away a stray hoof and looked up at them expectantly. "Now, then, let's hear what you have to say."

Ben tried to refrain from gritting his teeth. "We have come to ask your help with something," he began, and got no further.

"Save your breath, Holiday," the dragon interrupted with a curt wave of one foreleg. "I've already given you all the help you're getting in this lifetime—more help, in point of fact, then you ever deserved."

"Hear me out at least," Ben urged irritably.

"Must I?" The dragon shifted as if trying to get comfortable. "Well, for the sake of the lovely young lady, I will."

Ben decided to cut to the chase. "Mistaya is missing. We think she has been taken prisoner by King Rydall of Marnhull. At least he claims to have her. We are trying to get her back."

Strabo stared at him without speaking for a moment. "Am I supposed to know what you're talking about? Mistaya? Rydall of Marnhull? Who are these people?"

"Mistaya is our daughter," Willow said quickly, interceding before Ben lost his temper completely. "You helped Ben find us when I was carrying her out of the Deep Fell."

"Ah, yes, I remember." The dragon beamed. "Good of me, wasn't it? And you've named her Mistaya? Very pretty. I like the name. It sings with the promise of your own beauty."

Gag me with a spoon, Ben thought blackly, but kept his mouth shut.

"She is a beautiful child," Willow agreed, keeping the dragon's attention focused on her. "I love her very much, and I am determined to see her safely home again."

"Of course you are," Strabo affirmed indignantly. "Who is this King Rydall who's taken her?"

"We don't know. We were hoping you could help." Willow waited.

Strabo shook his horn-crusted head slowly. "No. No, I don't think so. I've never heard of him. Another in a long line of lesser Kings, I expect There's literally hundreds of them, all parading about, all posturing as if anyone of note could ever for a minute be impressed." He gave Holiday a meaningful glance. "Anyway, whoever he is, I don't know him. And he's from some place called Marnhull? Really? Marnhull? Sounds like what's left after you crack a nut open."

The dragon laughed uproariously, the laughter culminating in a choked gasp as he fell backward into one of the Fire Springs, sending ashs and shattered rock flying everywhere. He hauled himself upright with an effort. "Marnhull! Ridiculous!"

"So you've never heard of either?" Ben pressed, unable to keep silent any longer.

"Never." Strabo snorted dirt and steam from his nostrils. "They don't exist, either of them."

"Not outside Landover, beyond the fairy mists, perhaps?" Ben pressed, disbelieving. "Not even there?"

The great black head swung sharply about. "Holiday, pay attention here. I have traveled all the lands that ever were and a few that weren't. I have been to all those that surround the mists. I have been well beyond. I have been alive a long time, and travel has always agreed with me—especially when I find places where I am not welcome and can feed on the inhabitants."

The yellow eyes lidded. "So. If a land called Marnhull existed, I would have found it. If a King named Rydall existed, I would have heard of him. I haven't. So they don't."

"Well someone calling himself King Rydall exists, because he's come to Sterling Silver twice now to threaten me, claims he's taken Mistaya, and promises to send monsters to try to kill me!" Ben's patience was at end. "Mistaya's disappeared, and I've been attacked three times already—something's happening, wouldn't you say?"

"I wouldn't," the dragon declared with studied disinterest, "since I don't know what you are talking about. I have better things to do than to keep up on the local gossip. If you've been attacked, it's news to me. Rather unimportant news, I might add."

Willow took Ben's arm and gently pulled him back, then stepped forward to face the dragon. "Strabo, listen to me, please. I realize what we are telling you is of little personal interest. You are involved in much larger concerns than ours. And if you say you have never heard of Rydall or Marnhull then it must be so. Everyone knows that dragons never lie."

This was the first time Ben had heard of that, but it appeared to please Strabo, who gave a courtly nod in response.

"Now, I must ask you as someone who has been my friend," Willow continued, "to consider helping me find my daughter. She has disappeared, and we have searched the whole of Landover for her without success. We have spoken with everyone we could think of in an effort to discover where she is. No one can help. You are our last hope. We thought that if anyone would know of Rydall or Marnhull, it would be you. Please, is there anything you could tell us, anything at all that might be of help? Is there anyone you know who might be Rydall? Or any place that might be Marnhull?"

The dragon was silent for a long time. All about him the Fire Springs belched and coughed, spewing forth ashes and smoke. The grayness of the day deepened as the sun drifted west, and the clouds locked together in the skies overhead to form a solid covering. Below the clouds and smoke the landscape stretched away in numbing solitude, bleak and desolate.

"I treasure my privacy," Strabo said finally. "That's why I live out here, you know."

"I know," Willow acknowledged.

The dragon sighed. "Very well. Tell me more of Rydall. Tell me whatever you either know or suspect."

Willow did so, leaving out nothing but the information about the medallion. When she was finished, Strabo thought some more.

"Well, Holiday," he advised softly, "it appears I must help you once again, even though it is against my better judgment. Such help as you receive, however, is due entirely to my considerable affection for the lovely sylph."

He cleared his throat. "Nothing passes through the fairy mists without my knowing. That is simply the way of things. Dragons have excellent hearing and eyesight, and nothing escapes their attention." He paused, considering. "If they deem it worthy of their attention, that is." He appeared to remember his earlier disclaimer of any knowledge about what had been taking place at Sterling Silver. "The point is, no one has come through the mists recently. But even if I were mistaken in this—and a lapse in my attention span could have occurred just as Rydall or whoever was passing through, I suppose—there would still be a discoverable trace of that passing. In short, I could find out anyway."

He gave them a broad smile and added, "If I were to choose to do so." He cocked his ugly head at Willow. "I wonder, my Lady, if you would favor me with one of your exquisite songs. I do miss the sound of a maiden's voice now and then."

It was his favorite thing in all the world, and although once it would have embarrassed him to ask, he seemed to have gotten over his discomfort. Willow had been expecting this. Her success in charming him before had been due in large part to her singing, so she did not hesitate now to do so again.

There was an unspoken bargain being made, and the price the dragon was asking for his help was certainly small enough. Willow sang of meadows and wildflowers filled with dancing maidens and of a dragon who was lord over all. Ben had never heard the song and found it more than a little saccharine, but Strabo lay his horn-crusted head on the rim of one of the springs and got very dreamy-eyed.

By the time she had finished he was almost reduced to the limpness of a noodle. Tears leaked from his lantern eyes.

"When you return from your search," she called over to him, reminding him of his end of the bargain, "I will sing one more song for you as a further reward."

Strabo's head lifted slowly from its resting place, and his teeth showed in a pathetically futile attempt at a smile. "*Je t'adore,*" he advised softly.

Without another word great wings spread from his serpent's body and lifted him skyward, circling up and away until he was lost from view.

They waited through the remainder of the day and all night for his return. Bunion went back for their blankets, and all three took turns standing watch, settled down on the windward side of the Fire Springs so they would not have to breathe the smoke and soot. Flames licked out of the craters, and molten rock belched forth at regular intervals, effectively disrupting attempts to sleep. The heat was intense at times, relieved only when a small breeze blew across them on its way to a better place. But they were safe enough, for nothing would dare to venture into the dragon's lair.

It was nearing dawn when Strabo returned. He came out of a sky in which Landover's moons were already down and the stars were fading into a faintly brightening east, his bulk a massive dark shadow that might have been a chunk of sky unexpectedly broken away. He settled earthward as smoothly and delicately as a great butterfly, without sound, without effort, belying his monstrous bulk.

"Lady," he greeted Willow in his deep, raspy voice. There was weariness and regret in that single word. "I have flown the four borders of the land, from Fire Springs to Melchor, from Greensward to lake country, from one range of mountains and mists to the other. I have searched the whole of the boundaries that mark the passage from Landover to the fairy worlds. I have smelled all tracks, studied all markings, and hunted for the smallest sign. There is no trace of Rydall of Marnhull. There is no trace of your child."

"None?" Willow asked quietly, as if perhaps he might reconsider his answer.

The dragon's gnarled head swung away. "No one has passed through the mists in recent days. No one." He yawned, showing row upon row of blackened, crooked teeth. "Now, if you will excuse me, I need to get some sleep. I am sorry, but I can do nothing more. I release you from your pledge to sing further. I regret to say I am too tired to listen. Good-bye to you. Good-bye, Holiday. Come again sometime, but not for a while, hmmm?"

He crawled off through the rocks, snaked his way down between the simmering craters, curled up amid the debris, and promptly began to snore.

Ben and Willow stared at each other. "I don't understand it," Ben said finally. "How can there be no sign at all?"

Willow's face was pale and drawn. "If Rydall did not come through the mists, where did he come from? Where is he now? What has he done with Mistaya?"

Ben shook his head slowly. "I don't know." He reached down for his blanket and began to fold it up. "What I do know is that something about all this isn't right, and one way or another I'm going to get to the bottom of it."

Taking Willow's hand in his own and with Bunion leading the way, he turned disconsolately from the Fire Springs and the sleeping dragon and started back toward their horses.

WURM

They rode out from the Fire Springs and back into the Wastelands, heading west. The sun crested the horizon behind them in a hazy white ball, obscured by mist and clouds and the thickness of heat on the summer air. Already it was hot and threatening to grow hotter. Clouds rolled in from the west, beginning to build on one another, promising rain before the day was done. Ahead, the land stretched away, stark and unchanging.

Ben rode in silence, his mood as bleak and despairing as the land he traveled. He was putting up a brave front, but he knew he had run out of options. Strabo had been his last chance. Since the dragon couldn't tell him how to find Rydall, he was faced with the unpleasant possibility that no one could. And if he couldn't find Rydall, he couldn't find Mistaya or Questor Thews or Abernathy. If he couldn't find his daughter and his friends, he would have no other choice but to return to Sterling Silver and sit around waiting for the rest of Rydall's monsters to come for him. Three down and four to go; it was not a comforting thought. They had almost had him several times already—almost had the Paladin, he corrected, but it was the same thing. He didn't think he could survive four more, and if he did, he didn't really believe he would get Mistaya back, anyway.

It was a terrible thought, and he cursed himself silently for thinking it. But it was true. It was what he believed. Rydall wasn't the sort to keep a bargain, not this man who devoured countries, who sent monsters to kill their Kings, and who kidnapped children and used them as hostages. No, Rydall played games with his victims, and when you played games of his sort, you made up the rules as you went along so that you didn't lose. It didn't matter if the Paladin survived all seven challengers or not. Mistaya wasn't coming back.

Unless Ben found her and brought her back himself.

Which at the moment he didn't seem to have the slightest hope of doing.

He thought about what Strabo had told him. There was no sign of Rydall's passage through the fairy mists now or any time in the recent past. There was no sign of Mistaya. So what did that tell him? That Rydall was lying? That Strabo had missed something? But Rydall had said he had come through the fairy mists. He had said his army was prepared to follow. Through the mists. Maybe, Ben thought suddenly, Rydall's black-cloaked companion had magic that facilitated this and left no trail. Maybe the magic was such that it could conceal the point of passage. But wouldn't Strabo have found some trace of that magic? Nothing escaped the dragon. Had Rydall been able to do what no one else could and deceive the beast?

Then it occurred to Ben that there was another way into Landover, a way he had forgotten about—through the demon world of Abbadon. Could it be that Rydall had gained entry from there? But in order to do so he would have had to bypass the demons. Or win their support, as the Gorse had done, promising them something in return. Could Marnhull's King have done that? It didn't feel right. The demons hated humans; they never made bargains with them unless they were forced to. It was one thing to ally themselves with the Gorse, itself a creature of dark magic. It was another to join forces with someone like Rydall. Besides, Rydall had said that he had come through the mists, and that was not the same thing as coming out of Abaddon.

Jurisdiction was proceeding at a walk, picking his way carefully over the rocky ground, moving so slowly that they were barely making any progress at all. Ben was oblivious, lost in thought. Willow rode next to him, watching his face, not wanting to distract him. Bunion walked beside them, bright eyes shifting from one to the other, then back to the barren land ahead. It was no concern of his. Behind them the Fire Springs had disappeared into the curve of the horizon, leaving little more than a dark smudge of smoke and ash against the sky.

A crow with red eyes appeared out of the retreating night to the west and circled lazily overhead, unseen.

What was it he was missing? Ben wondered. Surely there was something he had overlooked, or mistaken, or failed to recognize—something that would lead him to Rydall. Maybe he was going about this the wrong way. Assume for the moment that Rydall was lying about who and what he was and where he came from. It was a fair enough assumption given Rydall's disposition toward game playing. Invent the rules of a game, put them in play, and wait to see what would happen—that seemed to fit with what he knew of Rydall. The question he had asked himself earlier and then not gotten back to for an answer was, Why was Rydall doing all this? It had been the River Master's question as well. Why was Marnhull's King sending monsters to challenge Ben instead of simply demanding his life in exchange for Mistaya's? Why was he spending so much time challenging the Paladin to individual duels when he could just as easily have marched his army into Landover and taken it by force? To avoid bloodshed and loss of life? That didn't seem likely.

In fact—and admittedly this was a stretch—Ben was beginning to question if Rydall had any real interest in Landover at all.

Because the truth was that this entire business was beginning to feel very personal. Ben couldn't put his finger on why, but he definitely sensed it. It was something about those monsters, the nature of their magic, and the manner of their attack. Something. The confrontation between Rydall and himself looked to have more to do with the two of them than with Landover. Landover seemed almost an excuse, a pawn to be played and then discarded. Rydall didn't appear to be in any hurry to complete his conquest. No time limits had been imposed regarding the passing of the throne, and no mention had been made of when a transition was expected to take place. All that seemed to matter was the contest.

Why was Rydall wasting so much time if all he wanted was to persuade Ben to give up the throne? Wouldn't Ben do that anyway if it meant getting Mistaya back safely?

Wouldn't he?

He looked quickly at Willow, a pang of guilt lancing through him as he hesitated with his answer. She was staring back at him, but no condemnation or suspicion registered in her green eyes, only concern and sadness and, behind it all, unfailing love. He was suddenly ashamed. He knew the answer, didn't he? When his wife in his old world, Annie, and their unborn child had died, he had thought he would never recover; they were gone, and he could not get them back again. Now he had Willow and Mistaya, and he could not bear losing them as well. He would give up anything to keep them.

Midmorning had arrived, and the Wastelands were hazy—bright and sweltering.

Ben turned to Willow. "Another mile or so and we'll stop and rest," he told her. "And we'll talk things out a bit."

She nodded and said nothing. They rode slowly on.

Overhead, the crow with red eyes wheeled back the way it had come and was gone.

Nightshade flew quickly to the draw through which Holiday and his companions would pass, holding the struggling wurm firmly in her beak. She could barely keep her rage in check. She had waited all night for him to come to her, believing he must, certain that the dragon would offer no help and send him away. Instead, the beast had gone hunting for him—hunting, like some tame dog!—and Holiday had not come back as expected but had camped within the confines of the Fire Springs, a place she could not safely penetrate even with her formidable magic. So she had been forced to wait, to spend the entire night in the Wastelands keeping watch over her prize.

As if in response to her anger, the wurm wrapped itself around her beak and tried to bite her.

She laughed to herself as she watched its tiny teeth gnash. It had been a regular earthworm once, fat and sleek and indolent. Now it was her creature and would undertake the task she had set for it, becoming Rydall's fourth monster.

She was still dismayed that there had been a need for a fourth. The robot should have been enough, would have been enough if not for the Ardsheal. That the River Master should intercede on Holiday's behalf as well, grand-daughter or no, was infuriating. Holiday and he were no more friends than Holiday and the dragon. Why did these obvious enemies keep offering to help the play-King and interfering with her plans? What madness was this?

On the other hand, she thought, trying to put matters in a better light, it had been her intention from the beginning that Holiday survive until the particular end she had devised for him, the end that would come at Mistaya's hands. It would be less enjoyable if he was to die before then. And the appearance of the Ardsheal had provided her with fresh inspiration for playing with Landover's beleaguered High Lord. So nothing had been lost after all, had it?

She swooped down onto the flats and glided into the shadow of a draw that opened between two massive hills that blocked passage to the west and east. Holiday and his companions had come through the draw on the way to the dragon; the hoofprints of the horses made that plain enough. They would return the same way. But this time she would have the wurm waiting for them. She hopped across the ground on her bird feet to the tiny puddle of seepage water that sat back in the shadow of the rocks and had not yet evaporated with the heat of the day. A little water was all it took; a little would be more than enough.

She held the wurm over the water, watching it struggle to get free. She was tired of holding it. It was bad enough that she'd been forced to travel all the way to the Wastelands in nonhuman form, not daring to use her magic for fear it would reveal her presence and give the game away. But having to keep a secure grip on the little monster for so long was really too much. She had been able to put it down last night, safely up in the rocks where the ground was dry and hard and offered the creature no escape. Now she was ready to release it for good. She was thinking that she would like to stay around to see what would happen when she did, but she had been gone from the Deep Fell for a long time now, and she didn't like leaving the girl alone. Mistaya was growing impatient with the direction and limitation of her lessons. In fact, the wurm had been Nightshade's idea, devised when the girl had failed to come up with anything new. She was still obedient, but there were signs that the girl might test the rules Nightshade had imposed on her. Mistaya was incredibly gifted, both with imagination and with talent, and under the witch's tutelage her skills at applying her magic had grown formidable. If she ever chose to challenge Nightshade . . .

The witch brushed the idea aside with a sneer. She was not frightened of Mistaya. She wasn't frightened of anyone.

But it didn't hurt to be cautious.

She made up her mind. It was best that she return to the Deep Fell as quickly as she could. It was best that she make certain Mistaya did not step out of line.

She dropped the wurm into the puddle of water and watched it sink. Then she flew swiftly away.

Ben Holiday peered into the distance, catching sight of the draw that led through the rugged Wasteland hills to the flats beyond. The light was so poor this day, its clarity so diluted by heat and mist, that everything appeared fuzzy and distorted. Even the horizon shimmered as if it were a mirage in danger of disappearing altogether. Ahead, the draw was a mass of impenetrable shadows.

He guided Jurisdiction toward the opening, his mind on other things.

He was thinking again about that robot. Why was it so familiar? Where had he seen it? He was absolutely certain by now that he had, and it was maddening that he could not remember from where. Complicating matters was his growing suspicion that he had seen Rydall's other monsters, as well. And he was now willing to bet, having given the matter considerable thought, that he had seen them since coming into Landover. Yet how could that be? They couldn't have been alive; he would have remembered that. Had Questor or Abernathy told him about them? Had someone described them to him? Had he seen a drawing or a picture?

They reached the edge of the shadows that marked the entrance to the draw. Ahead, the passageway was dark and empty. Ben nudged Jurisdiction forward, his stomach grumbling softly as he savored the prospect of lunch.

Suddenly Bunion chittered in warning. Ben glanced down at the kobold, who was looking back from where they had come. Ben followed his gaze, shading his eyes against the glare of the sun. At first he saw nothing. Then he caught sight of a tiny black speck hanging low against the horizon. The speck seemed to be growing larger.

Ben blinked uncertainly. "What in the heck is—"

That was all he got out before the ground in front of them erupted in a shower of earth and rock and something huge and dark rose out of the draw's deep shadows. Bunion catapulted over Crane, snatching Willow from the saddle an instant before the horse was swallowed whole by the thing before it. There was a terrified scream and the crunching of bones. Dust and heat filled the air. Jurisdiction leapt away in panic, barely avoiding the massive jaws that reached now for him, sweeping past Ben's head with ferocious purpose. Ben hung on as his horse bolted, catching just a glimpse of the thing attacking them—a monstrous snake of some sort, faceless, eyeless, all teeth and maw, its purplish body smooth and ringed like . . .

Like a worm's, for goodness' sake!

Ben reached instinctively for the medallion, but Jurisdiction was shying so badly—skittering up the slope of a steep rise, twisting and bucking in terror—that he had to abandon the attempt and grasp the saddle and reins with both hands to avoid being thrown. He saw Bunion and Willow scrambling up the far side of the draw and into the rocks. The monster dove downward suddenly into the earth, wriggling underground, its great bulk disappearing in the manner of a whale's beneath the surface of an ocean. It burrowed down, the earth rising above it as it tunneled, and the line of the tunnel moved directly toward Ben.

Ben kicked Jurisdiction frantically, trying to make the horse come down off the rise. But Jurisdiction was panicked beyond all reason and could think only to climb higher. It was a losing battle, the horse's hooves slipping badly on the loose rock and earth, its progress stalled. Ben wrenched the horse's head about and sent him scrambling along the side of the slope parallel to the crest, still hoping to turn him downward. Behind them the earth buckled and lifted, the monster turning to follow.

The gap between them closed.

In desperation Ben released his grip on the saddle and tried to reach inside his tunic for the medallion. But the instant he did so Jurisdiction stumbled and went down, throwing him head over heels into the scrub. The terrified horse came back to his feet at once and this time bolted down the slope to safety. Ben was not so fortunate. Dazed and bloodied from his spill, he scrambled up and began racing ahead without any idea what it was he was racing toward, aware only that the subterranean horror was almost on top of him. Rocks and earth split and rumbled as the creature's huge bulk tunneled deliberately in pursuit. Ben groped for the medallion, feeling its hardness through the fabric of his tunic, unable to work it free from where it lodged in the folds. Sweat and blood ran down into his eyes, blinding him. Any moment now his attacker would surface. Any moment it would have him. He could feel the medallion's smooth edge, could touch its engraved surface through the tunic cloth. *Another moment! Just one more . . . !*

Then earth and rock exploded skyward, knocking Ben off his feet and sending him tumbling away. He lost his grip on the medallion and landed on his back with a sharp grunt, the wind knocked from his lungs. The worm-thing towered over him, earth-encrusted body arching forward, jaws opening, mouth reaching down.

Ben twisted wildly in an effort to escape, knowing he was too late, knowing he could not. *The medallion!* he thought. *Have to . . . !*

Then something bigger and blacker and more ferocious than his attacker hurtled out of the sky. Claws fastened on the monster's body, snatching it backward and away. Huge jaws snapped down, severing the sightless head. The head, its maw still gaping, fell away in a gush of ichor, but the body continued to squirm madly. The jaws snapped down again and yet again, and the monster at last fell lifeless.

Strabo dropped what was left, fanned the air once with his great wings, and settled slowly earthward. Willow and Bunion were already running over from the far side of the draw.

"You really are a great deal of trouble, Holiday," the dragon hissed. The great head swung about, and the lantern eyes fastened on him. "A great deal."

"I know," Ben managed, gasping for breath as he pulled himself back to his feet. "But thanks, anyway."

Willow reached him in a rush and threw her arms around him. "Thank you, Strabo," she echoed, releasing her grip on Ben just enough to turn toward the dragon. "You know how much he means to me. Thank you very much."

Strabo sniffed. "Well, if I've given you reason to smile, fair enough," he declared, a hint of pleasure in his rough voice.

"How did you know to come?" Ben asked. "When we left, you were asleep."

The dragon folded his wings against his body, and his eyes lidded. "The Wastelands are mine, Holiday. They belong to me. They are all I have left of what once was unending. Therefore, they are ruled as I determine they should be. No magic is allowed here but my own. If another intrudes, I am warned at once. Even asleep, my senses tell me. I knew of this creature the moment it took shape." He paused. "Do you know what this is?"

Both Ben and Willow shook their heads.

"This is a wurm. W-U-R-M. An ordinary worm turned predator by magic. Expose it to water, and it grows to the size you see now." Strabo glanced down at the severed parts and spit in distaste. "Pathetic excuse for disturbing my rest."

"Rydall again," Ben said quietly.

Strabo's head swung back. "I don't know about Rydall," he hissed softly, "but I do know about witches. Wurms are a particular favorite of witches."

Ben stared. "Nightshade?" he said finally.

The dragon's head lifted. "Among others." He yawned and looked to the east. "Time to be getting back to bed. Try to stay alive long enough to get out of the Wastelands, Holiday. After that you won't be my responsibility anymore."

Without another word he spread his wings, lifted away, and flew out of sight. Ben and Willow watched him go. Bunion stood with them a moment, then left at Ben's direction to hunt for Jurisdiction.

Willow wiped blood from Ben's face with a strip of cloth torn from her shirt. After a moment she said, "Could Nightshade be involved in this?"

Ben shook his head. "With Rydall? Why would she do that?"

Willow's smile was hard and bitter. "She hates you. That's reason enough."

Ben stared off into the empty hills, into the glare of the sun, looking at nothing. Willow finished cleaning off his face and kissed him lightly. "She hates all of us."

Ben nodded. He was thinking suddenly of something else. "Willow," he said, "I remember now where I've seen Rydall's monsters—all three of them."

The sylph stepped back from him. "Where?"

He looked back at her, and there was wonder in his eyes. "In a book."

POGGWYDD

Mistaya woke early that same morning and found herself alone for the first time since she had arrived in the Deep Fell. Her reaction was disbelief; Nightshade never left her alone. She rose in the gray, misted dawn and looked about expectantly, waiting for the mistress of the hollow to present herself. When she failed to appear, Mistaya called for her. When she still didn't show, the girl walked all about the edges of the clearing, searching. There was no sign of Nightshade.

Unexpectedly, Mistaya found herself relieved.

There had been considerable changes of late, and chief among them was her relationship with the witch. In the beginning Nightshade had been a willing, enthusiastic teacher, a companion in the magic arts, anxious to share her knowledge, a secret friend who could instruct Mistaya in the uses of her mysterious, intriguing power. Mistaya was there to discover the truth about her birthright, Nightshade had said. She was there to find ways to help her father in his struggle against Rydall of Marnhull. There was good to be achieved from the skills they would uncover. But somehow all that had gotten lost along the way. There was no longer any mention of Rydall or of her birthright. There was barely any mention of the world outside the hollow. All that seemed to matter now was how swift and compliant Mistaya could be in carrying out the witch's instructions. Patience, once so much in evidence, had dropped by the wayside. Diversity and exploration had been abandoned entirely. For days now all they had done was use the magic for a single purpose: to create monsters. Or if they weren't actually creating monsters, they were talking about it. In the process the student-teacher relationship had suffered drastically. Instead of continuing to grow closer to each other, it seemed to Mistaya that they were now growing farther apart. Praise and encouragement had been replaced with criticism and disgust. Accusations flew. Mistaya wasn't trying hard enough. She wasn't concentrating. She wasn't thinking. She seemed to have reached a point where she couldn't do anything right.

When Mistaya had devised the robot, another of the creatures she had seen in her father's old book, Nightshade had pronounced it wonderful. Then, barely two days later, she had dismissed it as a failure. It wasn't good enough; she wanted something better. Mistaya tried to think of a new monster, but under the intense pressure of the witch's demands and her own growing disinterest in the project, she had been unable to come up with anything. In exasperation, Nightshade had devised a creature of her own—a wurm, she called it—which together they had changed from a harmless crawler to a dangerous predator. This time Mistaya had balked openly, saying that she was tired of monsters, weary of this particular use of the magic, and anxious to try something new. Nightshade had dismissed her complaint with a scathing look and a reminder of the girl's promise to do as she was told in exchange for the privilege of being taught. Mistaya was tempted to remark that the exchange had grown decidedly one-sided, but she held her tongue.

In truth, she didn't understand what was happening. Their differences notwithstanding, she still looked upon Nightshade as her friend. There was a closeness between them that transcended even her present dissatisfaction, but she was discovering that it was grounded in the reality of shared powers and bordered more and more on an increasingly intense form of competition, as if somehow both of them knew that rather than be friends, they were fated to be rivals. Each day there was more tugging and pulling against than with each other, and the breach between them continued to widen inexorably. Mistaya did not want this to happen, but she found herself powerless to prevent it. Nightshade would not listen to her; she would not make any effort to compromise or conciliate. She wanted Mistaya to do as she was told, to not ask questions, and to repress any and all objections. More and more Mistaya found she could not do that.

So this morning she was alone, and she breathed the air as if it were new and fresh. Wary about her unexpected freedom, she cast a simple spell to be certain that Nightshade was not attempting some sort of deception. But no trace of the witch revealed itself, so she called for Haltwhistle. The mud puppy appeared immediately, materializing out of the gloom, eyes soulful, ears cocked slightly, tail wagging.

"Good old Haltwhistle," she greeted him with a smile. "Good morning to you."

Haltwhistle sat back on his haunches and thumped the ground with his tail.

"Shall we do something, you and I?" she asked her four-legged friend. "Just the two of us?"

She looked around the clearing as if expecting the answer to present itself. The familiar misty haze cloaked everything. Trees and brush were shrouded in gloom, the sky was invisible, and the world was a cocoon of silence. She was tired of being confined in so small a space; she wanted to see farther than the edge of the mist. She remembered the world without, and she wanted to look upon it again——on sunlight, green grass, blue skies, lakes, forests, mountains, and living things. She had been thinking about her parents lately, something she hadn't done for a while. She was wondering why they hadn't come to see her or written her or sent word of some sort asking how she was. And what about her friends at Sterling Silver? Why hadn't she at least heard from Questor Thews? They were best friends. What had happened to everybody?

She had not asked this of Nightshade. She knew what the witch would say. They were being careful because Rydall was searching for her. They were making sure she stayed safe. But the answer didn't satisfy her the way it should have. It seemed inadequate somehow. There should have been a way for her parents and friends to contact her, even here. Like it or not, Mistaya was be-coming homesick.

"Well," she declared impulsively. "Enough standing about. Let's go for a walk."

She started out resolutely and without further consideration of her deci-sion. She was about to take a big chance, and she knew it. She intended to walk out to where she could see for more than fifty feet at a time, where there was light and warmth, where there were living things. She intended to go out-side the Deep Fell, and that meant breaking Nightshade's rules.

Oddly enough, she didn't much care.

She conjured up a stalk of Bonnie Blue to chew on, anxious for something she hadn't seen for a while. Travel was easy. Once she would not have been able to find her way out of the Deep Fell. Now she employed her magic with barely a thought and was at the base of the slope leading up to the rim in no time at all. She found a pathway and climbed toward the light. Haltwhistle plodded steadfastly along behind her.

Moments later she emerged from the murky haze into a day filled with sunshine and summer smells. She smiled as the light fell across her face and arms. She blinked away its brightness as she looked first left into forested hills with their deep green shadows and then right across a valley of blue and yel-low wildflowers. Purple-shadowed mountains rose on the distant horizon, clouds scraping across their peaks. Birds flew in the trees close by, and a woodland rabbit darted away through the long grasses of the valley.

"Well, which way shall we go?" she asked Haltwhistle with a bright, deter-mined smile.

Since the mud puppy didn't seem to have a preference, Mistaya made the choice for them. They struck out east into the trees, winding their way through glens and clearings, seeking out small streams and quiet ponds, watching for forest creatures, and smelling out nuts and berries. Mistaya me-andered without concern for where she was going, knowing her magic would allow her to find her way back again when she was ready. She gave Rydall a passing thought, then dismissed him. Her wards were up, the magic lines that kept her alert to anyone who might approach so that she would be warned well in advance of discovery. She did not think Rydall would find her out here in any event. She did not think anyone would.

She was surprised when, in the middle of skipping stones across a small pond, she sensed somebody just a short distance off. She stopped what she was doing and stood perfectly still, using her magic to send out feelers. Nightshade had taught her a lot. She found the other without difficulty. One man, all alone. She sensed no danger from him. She debated what to do, then decided it might be fun to speak with someone. After all, she hadn't talked with anyone besides the witch in weeks. She would have a look at him, and if he seemed safe, she would show herself.

With Haltwhistle in tow, she slipped through the trees, treading soundlessly, cloaking herself in her magic. She found her quarry sitting cross-legged in a clearing before a tiny fire, chewing on the remains of some small animal he had cooked. He was an odd-looking fellow, small-limbed, round-bodied, and hairy all over. He had whiskers that stuck out from his face like the bristles of a brush and tiny pointed ears that were ragged at the ends. His clothes were badly sewn, ill fitting, and frayed from wear. He wore a gold ring in one ear with a dilapidated feather hanging off it. He was encrusted in dirt and grime from his bare feet to his bare head.

She searched her memory in an effort to identify what sort of creature he was and decided finally that he was a G'home Gnome.

Safe enough to talk to, she believed, and she strolled bravely out into the clearing.

"Good morning," she greeted him.

The fellow at the fire started so that he dropped the bone he was gnawing into the dirt. "Jumping junipers, don't do that!" he exclaimed irritably. "Give a person some warning, will you? Where did you come from, anyway?" He reached down hurriedly to pick up the bone, wiping it off with his fingers.

"Sorry," she apologized. "I didn't mean to scare you."

"Didn't scare me! Didn't scare me one bit! No sir!" He was instantly defensive. "Startled me was all. Thought I was alone out here. Had every reason to feel that way, too. No one comes to these woods, you know. Say, who are you, anyway?"

She hesitated. "Misty," she said, no fonder of the name now than before but opting for caution over pride. "What's yours?"

"Poggwydd. That your pet, cute little fellow behind you?" His eyes were suddenly sharp. "What is he?"

She came all the way over and stood looking down at him. Haltwhistle followed. "What are you eating?" she asked in return.

"Eating? Oh, uh, a rabbit, yes, a rabbit. Caught it myself."

"It has a rather long tail for a rabbit, doesn't it?" She indicated the leavings of his meal piled next to him in a bedraggled heap.

Poggwydd frowned petulantly. "Well, I forget. Maybe it's not a rabbit. Maybe it's something else. What difference does it make?"

"It looks like a cat."

"It might be. So what?"

Mistaya shrugged and sat down across from him. "I just didn't want you to get any ideas about Haltwhistle, that's all." She indicated the mud puppy, who was sniffing at the ground. "You're a G'home Gnome, aren't you?"

"Proud to be so," he announced with uncharacteristic boldness for one of Landover's most despised peoples.

"Well, everyone knows G'home Gnomes eat pets."

Poggwydd threw down his bone in disgust. "That's a lie! An outright lie! G'home Gnomes eat creatures of nature and the wild, not those of house and hearth! Now and then a stray gets eaten, but that's its own fault! See here, little girl, we must have an understanding if we're to continue this conversation. I will not be maligned. I will not be reviled. I will not sit here and defend myself. I was here first, so if you feel compelled to impugn the integrity and character of G'home Gnomes, you must leave now!"

Mistaya wrinkled her brow. "You seem awfully grouchy."

"You'd be grouchy, too, if you had to spend your whole life bearing up under the abuse of others. G'home Gnomes have been wrongfully accused since the dawn of time for crimes of which they were not guilty. They have been scorned and ridiculed with never a thought given to the harm that was done. Innocent little girls like you should know better than to follow in the ways of your ignorant, prejudiced elders. Not everything you hear is true, you know."

"All right," Mistaya acknowledged. "I'm sorry for being suspicious. But there are lots of stories about you."

Poggwydd screwed up his whiskered face in distaste. "Humph! Stories, indeed!" He glanced again at Haltwhistle. "So what is he, anyway?"

"A mud puppy."

"Never heard of it," Poggwydd held out one grimy hand. "Come over here, Haltwhistle. Come here, boy. Let old Poggwydd give you a pet."

"You do not pet mud puppies," Mistaya declared quickly. "You never touch them."

Poggwydd looked at her suspiciously. "Why not?"

"You just don't. It's dangerous."

"Dangerous?" Poggwydd looked back at the mud puppy. "He doesn't look dangerous. He looks rather silly."

"Well, you mustn't touch him."

"Suit yourself." The G'home Gnome shrugged. He looked down at the bones gathered in his lap. "Want something to eat?"

Mistaya shook her head. "No, thank you. What are you doing out here?"

Poggwydd ate a sliver of meat off a bone. His teeth looked sharp. "Traveling." He shrugged. "Enjoying my own company for a while, getting away from the noise and bustle of home, escaping from this and that."

"Are you in trouble?"

"No, I'm not in trouble!" He gave her a peevish look. "Do I look like I'm in trouble? Do I? Say, what about you? Little girl wandering around out here in the middle of nowhere. Are you in trouble?"

She thought about it a moment. She was in trouble, she supposed. Not that she was going to tell him. "No," she lied.

"No, huh? What are you doing out here, then, all by yourself? Taking a long walk, maybe? Are you lost?"

Her jaw tightened defensively. "I'm not lost. I'm visiting."

"Hah!" Poggwydd made a face. "Visiting who? The witch, maybe? That's who you're visiting?" The look on her face brought him up short. "Now, now, I was only teasing; no need to be frightened," he reassured her hastily, misreading the look. "But she's right over there, you know. Just a mile or so off in the Deep Fell. You don't want to be wandering about down there. Just remember that." He cleared his throat and tossed away the last of the bones. "So who are you visiting way out here?"

She smiled coyly. "You."

"Me? Ho, ho! That's a good one! Visiting me, are you?" He rocked with laughter. "You must lack much in the way of choices, then. Visiting me! As if that were something a little girl would do!"

"Well, I am."

"Am what?"

"Visiting you. Sitting here having this conversation is visiting, isn't it?"

He gave her a sharp look. "You are too smart by half, little girl. Misty, is it? You tell me now, if we're really friends—who are you?"

She tried her best to look confused. "I already told you that."

"So you did. Misty, out for a walk in the middle of nowhere. Come to visit a new friend she didn't know she had until just now." Poggwydd shook his whiskered face at her. "Well, you look like trouble to me, so I don't think I want to talk with you anymore. I don't need any more trouble in my life. G'home Gnomes have enough as it is. Good-bye."

He rose and brushed himself off, sending dust and crumbs flying. She stared at him in disbelief. He really meant it. She scrambled up with him.

"I don't see what difference it makes who I am," she declared angrily. "Why can't we just talk?"

He shrugged. "Because I don't like little girls who play games, and you're playing one with me, aren't you? You know who I am, but I don't know who you are. I don't like that. It isn't fair."

"Isn't fair?" she exclaimed.

"Not a bit."

She watched him begin to gather up his few belongings. "But I don't really know who you are, either," she pointed out quickly. "I don't know any more about you than you know about me. Except your name. And you know mine, so we're even."

He stopped what he was doing and looked at her. "Well, now, I suppose that's right. Yes, I suppose it is."

He put down his pack with a small clatter of implements and sat down again. Mistaya sat with him.

"I'll make you a deal," he said, holding up a single grimy finger for emphasis. "You tell me something about you, and I'll tell you something about me. How about that?"

She held out her finger and touched it to his, binding the agreement. "You first."

Poggwydd frowned, shrugged, and rocked back. "Humph. Let me see." He looked marginally thoughtful. "Very well. I'll tell you what I'm doing out here. I'm a treasure hunter for the King, for the High Lord himself." He gave her a conspiratorial look. "I'm on a special mission, looking for a very valuable chest of gold that's hidden somewhere in these woods."

She arched one eyebrow. "You are not."

"I am so!" He was immediately indignant. "How would you know, anyway?"

"Because I just do." She was grinning in spite of herself. Poggwydd made her laugh almost as much as Abernathy did.

"Well, you don't know anything!" He dismissed her with a wave of his hand. "I have been a treasure hunter for the King for years! I have found a good many valuable things in my travels, I can tell you! I know more about treasure hunting than anyone, and the High Lord appreciates that. That's why he employs me."

"I bet he doesn't even know you," she persisted, enjoying the game. It was the most fun she'd had in some time. "I bet he has never seen you before in his entire life."

Poggwydd was beside himself. "He has so! I happen to know him quite well! I even know his family. I know the Queen! And the little girl, the one who's missing! Why, I might even find her while I'm looking for that chest of gold!"

She stared at him. *Missing?* She kept her lips tightly together. "You don't know her. You're making this all up."

"I am not! I'll tell you something, since you seem so intent on being rude. The High Lord's little girl is a whole lot nicer than you!"

"She is not!"

"Hah! Fly doodles! How would you know?"

"Because I'm her!"

It was out before she could help herself. She said it in a rush of indignation and pride, but she supposed that she would have said it anyway because this was a game, and he wouldn't know whether to believe it. Besides, she wanted to see the look on his face when she said it.

The look was worth it. He gaped in undisguised amazement, sputtered something unintelligible, and then finished with a monstrous snort. "Pfah! What nonsense! What a heap of horse hunks! Now who's telling tall tales?"

"And I'm not missing, either!" she added firmly. "I'm right here with you!"

"You're not the High Lord's daughter!" he exclaimed vehemently. "You can't be!"

"How would you know?" she mimicked. Then she put her hands to her face and feigned shock. "Oh, excuse me, I forgot! You're the King's personal treasure hunter and know the whole family!"

Poggwydd scowled. He hunched forward, his round body rocking on its stubby, gnarled legs as if in danger of tipping over completely.

"Look here," he said carefully. "Enough foolishness. It's one thing to play at being someone where the playing is harmless but another altogether to make light of misfortune. I know you are just a little girl, but you're a smart little girl and old enough to appreciate the difference."

"What are you talking about!" she snapped, furious at being lectured like this.

"The High Lord's daughter!" he snapped back. "That's what I'm talking about! Don't tell me you don't know." He stopped short. "Well, now, maybe you don't—little girl all alone out here in the woods, bumping up against a fellow like me. Who are you, anyway? You never did say. Are you one of those fairies, come out from the mists for a visit? Are you a sprite or some such from the lake country? We don't see many up this way. Not us G'home Gnomes, anyway."

He paused, collecting his thoughts. "Well, here's what's happened, if you don't already know. The High Lord's daughter is missing, and everyone is looking for her. She's been missing for days, weeks perhaps, but gone for sure, and there were search parties hunting for her from one end of Landover to the other."

He bent close, lowering his voice as if he might be heard. "Word is, King Rydall has her. He's from someplace called Marnhull. He has her. Won't give her back, either. He's making the King's champion do battle with some monsters. I don't know that for a fact, but that's what I've heard. In any case, she's missing, and you shouldn't make fun of her."

Mistaya was dumbfounded. "But I am her!" she insisted, hands on hips. "I really am!"

There was movement in the trees to one side. She caught just a glimpse of it and whirled about, poised to flee, her heart in her throat, her stomach turned to ice. The movement turned to color, a rush of wicked greenish light that filled the shadowed spaces between the trunks and limbs. The color tightened and took shape, coalescing into human form, lean and dark and certain.

Nightshade had returned.

The witch stepped out of the shadows, silent as a ghost. Her bloodred eyes fixed on Mistaya. "You were told not to leave the Deep Fell," she said softly.

Mistaya froze. For a moment her thoughts were so scattered that she couldn't think. Then she managed a small nod in response. "I'm sorry," she whispered. "I wanted to see the sun again."

"Come stand over here," the witch ordered. "By me."

"It was just for the day," Mistaya tried to explain, frightened now of what might happen to her, terrified by the look on the other's face. "I was all alone, and I didn't think—"

"Come here, Mistaya!" Nightshade snapped, cutting her short.

Mistaya crossed the clearing slowly, head lowered. She managed a quick glance back at Poggwydd. He was standing in front of his fire, eyes wide and staring. Mistaya felt sorry for him. This was her fault.

"I am waiting, Mistaya," Nightshade warned.

Mistaya's gaze swung back again toward the witch. She realized suddenly that Haltwhistle was missing. He had been right beside her while she had been talking with Poggwydd. Where had he gone?

She reached Nightshade and stopped, dreading what might happen next. Nightshade forced a smile, but there was no warmth in it. "I am very disappointed in you," she whispered.

Mistaya nodded, ashamed without being quite sure why. "I won't do it again," she promised. She remembered Poggwydd. "It wasn't his fault," she said quickly, looking back over her shoulder at the unfortunate G'home Gnome. "It was mine. He didn't even want to talk to me." She hesitated. "You won't hurt him, will you?"

Nightshade reached out and placed her hands on the girl's shoulders. Gently but firmly she moved her aside. "Of course not. He is nothing but a silly Gnome. I'll just speed him on his way."

"Excuse me?" Poggwydd ventured, his voice small and thin. "I don't need to be here anymore, do I? Any longer, I mean? I . . . I can just pick up my things, and I can—"

Nightshade's hands came up, and green fire blazed sharply to life at her fingertips. Poggwydd squeaked and cringed back in terror. Nightshade let the fire build, then gathered it in her palms and caressed it lovingly as she watched the Gnome. Mistaya tried to speak and found she couldn't. She turned to Nightshade, pleading with her eyes, suddenly certain that the witch meant to harm Poggwydd, after all.

Then she saw Haltwhistle. The mud puppy was crouched at the edge of the trees just out of Nightshade's field of vision. His hackles were standing on end, and his head drooped forward as if he were concentrating. Something white and frosty-looking was rising off his back.

What was he doing?

Abruptly Nightshade sent the green fire hurtling into Poggwydd. But Haltwhistle's moon/frost reached him first. Mistaya screamed at the sound of the impact. The fire and the frost exploded together, and Poggwydd disappeared. All that remained was the Gnome's discarded pack and the smell of ashes and smoke.

"What was that?" Nightshade exclaimed instantly, eyes raking the clearing from end to end. She wheeled on Mistaya. "Did you see it? Did you?"

Mistaya blinked. Her breath came in little gasps. The moon/frost. She *had* seen it, of course. But she would never admit it to the witch. Not after what had happened to Poggwydd. At least Haltwhistle had escaped. There wasn't a trace of him to be seen.

She faced Nightshade down, her voice shaking. "What did you do to Poggwydd? I asked you not to hurt him!"

The witch was nonplussed by the girl's vehemence. "Calm yourself," she soothed. Her eyes were still skittering about uneasily. "Nothing has happened to him. I sent him home, back to his people, away from where he doesn't belong."

Mistaya would not be placated. "I don't believe you! I don't believe anything you say anymore! I want to go home right now!"

Nightshade gave her a cool and dispassionate look. "Very well, Mistaya," she said quietly. "But first listen to what I have to say. You can do that for me, can't you?"

Mistaya nodded, tight-lipped.

"Your friend *wasn't* harmed," the witch emphasized. "But he couldn't be allowed to remain here. What he told you was true, so far as he knew. Everyone thinks that Rydall has you. Your father arranged for them to think that. He started the rumor when Rydall first tried to kidnap you. He even organized a search for you to make the claim seem true. He did this to confuse Rydall and whoever might be trying to find you on his behalf. This way it seemed that no one knew where you were."

She gave Mistaya a sympathetic smile. "But now the little Gnome knows the truth. Suppose he tells someone what you said? Suppose he tells them where he saw you? What if word of this gets back to Rydall's spies? The risk is too great. So I returned him to where he came from, and I used my magic to erase his memory of this incident. I did it to protect you both."

"He won't remember anything?" Mistaya asked carefully.

"Nothing. So no harm is done, is it?" Nightshade bent close. "As for going home, you may do so immediately if you wish." She paused. "Or you may stay with me for three more days and then leave. If you choose to stay, I will make you a promise. I won't ask you to make any more monsters. We've done enough of that, I know. You have been more than patient, and I have been rather demanding of you. So we shall try something else. What do you think about that?"

Mistaya stared at her, surprised by this unexpected turn of events. The witch's eyes were silver again, soft and compelling. Mistaya remembered how things had been when they had first met, how eager Nightshade had been to teach, how anxious she had been to learn. She remembered how excited she had been the first time she had used her magic. She felt a little of the anger and mistrust drop away. She would like to continue the lessons, she supposed. She would like to stay. She didn't have to go home right this instant, not if Poggwydd was really safe and she didn't have to make any more monsters.

"Are my parents all right?" she asked suddenly.

Nightshade looked shocked. "Of course they are. Where do you think I was this morning? I changed form and went to Sterling Silver to make certain. Everything is fine. Your father and mother are well. Questor Thews protects them from Rydall, so we have time to finish your training in the use of magic. Then you will be ready to help protect them as well."

Mistaya stared at the witch without speaking. Nightshade seemed to be telling the truth. And Poggwydd hadn't said anything about her parents being in any danger or having come to any harm. Of course, it was hard to know whether anything the Gnome said was true, she supposed.

She was suddenly very confused. She sighed and looked away from the witch. The clearing was silent and empty save for them. Overhead, the sun brightened the skies and streamed down through the trees. She could almost believe that Poggwydd had never been there at all.

"Well," she said finally, "I guess I could stay for three more days."

"That would be very wise of you," Nightshade encouraged, and Mistaya failed to catch the hard edge that shaped the words or the way the witch's back lost a touch of its stiffness. "But you must not go out of the Deep Fell again."

Mistaya nodded. "I won't." She looked back at the witch tentatively. "What will we study now?"

Nightshade pursed her lips. "Medicine," she answered. "Healing through the use of magic."

She put her arm about Mistaya and began to walk her from the clearing back toward the hollow. "Mistaya," she said softly, "would you like to learn how to use your magic to bring something dead back to life?"

She smiled at the girl, and her eyes were lidded with pleasure.

CONCEALMENTS

After three days of searching Graum Wythe and finding nothing, Questor Thews became convinced that somehow they were overlooking the obvious.

"We're wearing blinders!" he announced abruptly. He sat down on a packing crate with his chin in his hands and a frown on his face, bushy white eyebrows fiercely knit. "It's here, whatever it is, but we're simply not seeing it!"

Elizabeth and Abernathy looked over at him in voiceless contemplation. They were secluded in one of Graum Wythe's many storage rooms, deep in the bowels of the castle, a small windowless room where the sun never penetrated and the air was close and stale. They had searched the room once and were engaged at present in searching it a second time. By now, unfortunately, they had searched everywhere at least once and were growing discouraged.

"It shouldn't be taking this long," the wizard declared forcefully. "If we are meant to find it, if that is why we were brought here, then we should have stumbled on it by now."

"It would help if we knew what we were looking for," Abernathy observed glumly, lowering himself onto a second crate with a weary sigh. He was sick of poking through old boxes and dusty corners. He wanted to be outside, where the sun was shining and the air was fresh. He wanted to enjoy being who he was now that he had finally been restored to himself. All those dog years had fallen away as quickly as leaves from a tree on winter's first storm, as if none of it had ever really happened, all of it a dream from which he had finally awoken.

Elizabeth pursed her lips, causing her button nose to wrinkle. "I don't suppose you could be mistaken about what you are doing here?" she asked Questor Thews tentatively. "Is it possible that your coming was simply a fluke?" She seated herself next to Abernathy. "Or that you were dispatched here for some other reason?"

"It is possible," the wizard acknowledged charitably, "but unlikely. The consequences of magic are seldom haphazard. They almost always have a reason for turning out as they do. Nightshade would not have made the mistake of letting us live when she expected us to die. No, the conclusion is inescapable. Another magic intervened and saved us. We were sent here for a purpose, and I can think of no other purpose than to rescue Mistaya."

"Is it possible you are wrong about the magic being at Graum Wythe?" Elizabeth pressed. "Could it be somewhere else?"

Questor Thews scrunched up his face. "No. It has to be here. It has to be a magic that originally came from Landover. Nothing else makes sense!"

They stared at each other wordlessly for a moment, then looked about the room. "Could there be a second medallion?" Abernathy asked suddenly. "Another like the High Lord's?"

Questor raised a spiny eyebrow thoughtfully. It was a possibility he hadn't considered. But no; Michel Ard Rhi would have found such a talisman quickly enough and would not have gone to such great lengths to force Abernathy to give up the High Lord's when the scribe had been his prisoner at Graum Wythe those several years back.

The wizard shook his head. "No, it is something else, something that Michel would not have recognized. Something, at least, he could not find a way to use." He rubbed at his bearded chin thoughtfully. "This is exceedingly frustrating, I must say."

"Maybe we should have some lunch," Elizabeth suggested, nudging Abernathy playfully. "We might think better on full stomachs."

"We might think better after a short nap," Abernathy observed, nudging her back.

Questor Thews watched them wordlessly. He didn't like what he was seeing. Abernathy was growing complacent in his new life. He was altogether too satisfied with himself, as if getting back to Landover didn't mean anything to him now that he was a man again. He was forgetting his responsibilities. The High Lord and his family still depended on them, and Questor was afraid Abernathy was losing sight of that. He knew he shouldn't judge, but what was happening was obvious. Abernathy was rediscovering himself, and in the process of doing so he was making over his life to fit his new circumstances. It was a dangerous indulgence.

He cleared his throat sharply, causing both of them to jump. "Before we eat or nap, perhaps we could talk this business through one more time." He offered a smile to soften the force of his words. "Just for a few more moments, if you would. I admit to being rather desperate just about now."

Elizabeth smiled back reassuringly. "Don't worry, Questor. You'll find it sooner or later, whatever it is." She ran her fingers through her curly hair. "Even if you don't, this isn't a bad place to be trapped in, is it?"

She sounded altogether too hopeful. Questor did not dare say what he was thinking. "We have to get back to Landover," he insisted quietly. "We have to find the magic that will allow it."

Elizabeth sighed. "I know." She didn't sound convinced. "This magic, whatever it is, has to be something you'll recognize when you see it, doesn't it? If it's really here?"

"We've seen everything at least once already," Abernathy countered, pushing back his glasses on his nose.

"Maybe we're not looking at it the right way," Questor Thews mulled aloud.

Elizabeth swung her feet away from the crate and studied her sneakers. They were silent again, considering.

"Wait a minute," Abernathy said suddenly. "Maybe what we're looking for isn't a thing at all. Maybe that's why we're not seeing it. It was a spell that brought us here, magic conjured out of words. What if a spell is needed to take us back again?"

Questor's eyes widened, and he jumped up instantly from the packing crate. "Abernathy, you are an absolute genius! Of course that's what it is! A spell! We're not looking for a talisman at all! We're looking for a book of spells!"

Abernathy and Elizabeth rose as well, looking decidedly less certain of the matter. "But wouldn't Michel have recognized a book of that sort?" Abernathy asked doubtfully. "Wouldn't he have used it to get back into Landover there at the end, when he wanted to regain the throne? Or wouldn't your brother have searched it out when Holiday defied him? I know it was my idea, but on thinking it through, it doesn't make much sense. If there is a spell that allows passage back into Landover, why didn't one of them use it?"

"Perhaps because they couldn't," the wizard offered, stalking first to one side of the cluttered room, then back again to the other, head lowered, hands swinging animatedly. "Because the spell wouldn't work for them, maybe. I don't know. But I think you have stumbled on something nevertheless. A spell brought us over. It would make sense that a spell would take us back. A reversal of the magic that brought us here. A reworking of the words . . ."

A nasty suspicion crossed his mind, one that had occurred to him earlier in Elizabeth's kitchen when they had been discussing the reasons for what had happened to them. He had discarded it then, refusing to consider it too closely, unable to contemplate the possibility. Now it was back again, looking all too possible to be ignored.

He stopped his pacing and looked at Abernathy with haunted eyes. "Abernathy, this is difficult for me to suggest, but what if . . ."

He never finished. Light flared in the shadows at the far side of the storage room, and all three turned abruptly to face it. The light brightened sharply and then disappeared, leaving in its wake a decidedly ragged and frightened G'home Gnome sitting stunned and shivering on the concrete floor.

When he saw them staring at him, he gasped and threw up his hands defensively. "Don't hurt me!" he begged, blinking rapidly and trying to curl into a ball. "I just want to go home!"

Questor Thews exchanged a startled glance with Abernathy. *A G'home Gnome? Here? What was this all about?*

"Now, now, no one is going to hurt you," Questor reassured the other, starting forward, then stopping again as the Gnome started to gasp for air. "Are you all right?"

The Gnome nodded uncertainly. "If you can call being fried in witch fire 'all right,' then I suppose so."

Witch fire? Questor and Abernathy exchanged a second glance. "What's your name?" Questor pressed. The grimy little fellow was twisted down into an impossible position. "Come, now. We mean you no harm. We are all friends here."

The Gnome sniffled uncertainly, peering out from beneath crossed arms. "G'home Gnomes have precious few friends anywhere," he pointed out sullenly. He lifted his head. He was the scruffiest fellow imaginable, tattered and disheveled and in desperate need of a bath. "You tell me who you are first."

Questor sighed. "I am Questor Thews. This is Abernathy. That is Elizabeth." He pointed to each in turn. "Now, then. Who are you?"

"Poggwydd," the G'home Gnome said. He sounded proud of the fact. He lowered his arms and straightened up a bit. "Questor Thews, the Court Wizard? I heard you were Rydall's prisoner. You and the dog. Is that where we are, in Rydall's prison? Is that where the witch sent me?"

"Wait a minute." This time Questor Thews came right over and brought the Gnome firmly to his feet. "The witch, you said? Do you mean Nightshade?"

Poggwydd nodded. "Who else?" He was a little more sure of himself now. "She's the one who did this to me. Sent me here, wherever that is. Used her witch fire. Say, you didn't answer. Are we in Rydall's prison? What's going on?"

Questor Thews took Poggwydd by the elbow, marched him over to a vacant packing crate, and sat him down. The Gnome was rubbing at his wet nose and trying unsuccessfully to look brave. He kept his eyes fixed on Questor, as if by doing so he could stave off anything worse happening to him.

"Poggwydd," the wizard addressed him solemnly. "I want you to tell us everything that happened, everything you can remember, especially about Nightshade."

"I can do that, all right," the Gnome declared. He paused suspiciously. "You promise me you aren't friends with her?"

"I promise," Questor replied.

Poggwydd nodded, thought it over, then cleared his throat officiously. "Well, I thought she was going to hurt me—the witch, that is. She had that look in her eye. She was real mad at me because of the little girl. Caught me talking with her out there in a clearing about a mile from the Deep Fell. Ridiculous, really. I didn't even know her; she just showed up out of nowhere, way out in those woods, wanting to talk. So we did, and then the witch came, and the little girl asked her not to hurt me, said it wasn't my fault, but the witch didn't look like she believed her, so—"

"Whoa! Stop! Hold on!" Questor held up his hands imploringly. His brow knit furiously. "What little girl are you talking about? What did she look like? Did she tell you her name?"

Poggwydd stared, startled by the look on the other's face. He glanced past the wizard to the other two, found no help there, and looked back again. "I don't know what she looked like. Who can remember? She was . . . small. Not very old, maybe ten. Had freckles and blond hair." He frowned. "She was very clever. Played some games with me while we talked. Pretended to be . . . She said she was the High Lord's . . ." He stopped, no longer certain where to go. "She said her name was Misty."

"Mistaya," Questor breathed, backing away. "So Nightshade has her. Or had her. Did she escape, Poggwydd? Is that what happened?"

The G'home Gnome looked at him blankly. "Escape? I don't know if she did or not. I don't know where she came from. I don't even know who she is for sure. What I do know is that the witch was furious when she found me talking with her and that's why I'm here!" He paused, rubbing at his bristly chin. Bits of dirt flaked off. "Although maybe that's not right, either. You know, she asked the witch not to hurt me, the little girl did. But I don't think the witch was paying any attention to her and meant to fry me like a piece of old meat."

"But she didn't," Questor interjected, trying to hurry the story along, anxious to pin down his suspicions.

Poggwydd shook his head. "Well, there was this mud puppy, you see. I think maybe he stopped it from happening." He looked confused all over again. "Is that possible?"

Eventually they got the whole story out of him although it took a while to do so. They heard about how Mistaya had come upon his camp not far from the Deep Fell and engaged him in conversation. They heard about Haltwhistle and how he seemed to be the girl's companion. Finally, they heard about Nightshade's unexpected appearance, her anger at discovering Mistaya outside the Deep Fell, and her attack on Poggwydd, which appeared to have been thwarted in part by the magic of the mud puppy, resulting in the Gnome's appearance at Graum Wythe.

"Just like us!" Abernathy exclaimed as the Gnome finished. He was standing next to Questor Thews by now, looking quite animated. "Questor, that must be what happened to us, too! The mud puppy intervened, changed Nightshade's magic, and sent us here! It sounds exactly the same!"

"Indeed," Questor agreed, pursing his lips, thinking hard.

"Where is here?" Poggwydd asked once again. "You haven't said yet."

"In a minute," Questor replied, turning away momentarily and then back again. "But who sent the mud puppy to Mistaya? It must have happened that night, while we slept, before the witch came. We were in the lake country, so it could have been the River Master. But the only mud puppy I ever heard of outside the fairy mists is the one who serves the Earth Mother."

"What difference does it make?" Abernathy cut him short. "What matters is that the witch has Mistaya and is using her to hurt the High Lord, just as she promised she would. You were right, Questor Thews. We are here for a purpose, and it must have something to do with helping Ben Holiday. We just have to find out what it is."

"A book of spells," Questor recalled, thinking back to where this conversation had started. "All right, then." He wheeled about, strode quickly to Poggwydd, and placed both hands firmly on the Gnome's narrow shoulders. "Where you are doesn't matter, Poggwydd. What's important is that you are in no immediate danger. But the little girl, Misty, is. We have to get out of here and back to where she is. There is something here, in this place, that can help us do that—if we can find it. That is what we intend to do right now. While we search, I want you to stay right here."

Poggwydd looked around doubtfully. "Why should I do that? Why can't I just go home? I can find my way once I'm outside again."

Questor gave him a sympathetic look. "Not from here, you can't. You will have to trust me on this." He paused, thinking. "If you try, Poggwydd, Nightshade might get her hands on you a second time. Do you understand me?"

The Gnome nodded quickly. He understood, all right. "I'll do as you say," he agreed reluctantly. "How long do I have to wait?"

"I don't know. Maybe quite a while. You must be patient."

Poggwydd sniffled. "I don't have anything to eat. I'm hungry."

Abernathy rolled his eyes. Questor squeezed the Gnome's shoulders and released him. "I know. Be brave. We'll try to find you something to eat and bring it down. But you have to stay where you are, no matter what. This is important, Poggwydd. You must not leave this room for anything. All right?"

The Gnome rubbed at his nose and shrugged. "All right. I'll wait. But try to hurry."

"We'll be as quick as we can." Questor backed away, looking once again at Abernathy and Elizabeth. "We'll have to start over, tourists or no tourists. The common rooms first, then back into storage. But I'm willing to bet the book we need is right out there where we can see it."

"You know," Elizabeth said thoughtfully, "I think there were some books that were kept separate from the others, ones printed in a language that no one here could read. My father mentioned them once."

"Now we're getting somewhere!" Questor exclaimed in undisguised glee. "Books written in Landover's language, carried over by Michel or my brother! They would have to be the ones, wouldn't they?"

And with that, following Questor's final reassuring smile and wave of the hand to Poggwydd, they were out the door and on their way back through the castle.

⎯⎯⎯◆⎯⎯⎯

The search took them longer than they expected, however, extending well into the late afternoon, when the last of the tourists were straggling back to their buses and cars and heading home. They hunted through the rooms of the castle twice before they found what they were looking for. There were books in every room, and most of them were under lock and key. That meant keeping watch and distracting both tourists and guides while the locks were released and a quick survey made to determine if any of the books were what they were looking for. Questor used magic on the locks, which hastened the process, but checking through the books took an inordinate amount of time and for most of the day yielded absolutely nothing.

Until finally, with time running out and the castle closing down, Elizabeth remembered a massive old glass-front cabinet in an upstairs drawing room tucked away in a dormer that was not visible from the roped-off doorway. There were some books there, she thought. Just a few, but she remembered them because her father had remarked once on their covers. Following her suggestion, they hurried to the drawing room as a bell sounded closing time in the downstairs hall. While the girl and Abernathy kept watch, Questor stepped over the ropes and wormed his way through an obstacle course of furniture to the cabinet. He peered inside. Sure enough, there were the books, a dozen of them, all wrapped in dark cloth covers that concealed the titles. The cabinet latch was locked, but a whisper of magic and he was inside.

Excited now, Questor reached past a collection of amethyst glassware that fronted the books and pulled the first out. To his extreme disappointment it was written in English and had nothing at all to do with Landover. He checked another two. It was the same. Another dead end, it seemed. Hope dwindling, he continued on more quickly. Books on gardening, travel, and history.

"Questor Thews, hurry!" Abernathy hissed from the doorway as voices from down the hall rapidly approached.

Questor opened the eighth book in the collection and his eyebrows shot up. It was written in Ancient Landoverian script, in a language the old wizards had commonly used. He paged through it hurriedly to make sure, hearing the voices more clearly: laughter, a quick greeting to Elizabeth, her response. Feverishly, he wedged himself between the wall and the cabinet, where he was out of sight of anyone standing in the doorway.

"Still poking about, Elizabeth?" someone asked, coming to a stop beyond the ropes. "Aren't you getting hungry?"

"Oh, we're almost done," she replied with a nervous laugh. "Is it all right to stay a bit longer?"

"One hour," a second voice advised. "Then *we* leave. Call if you need anything."

The voices continued on down the hall and faded away.

"Questor!" Abernathy warned a second time, his patience obviously at an end.

Questor freed himself from his hiding place and looked down at his discovery. Carefully he pulled back the cloth covering. There were symbols etched in gold leaf on the leather binding that read *Gateway Mythologies.*

"Drat!" he muttered, shoved the book back into place, and pulled out the next one. *Greensward Histories.* He reached for the third.

Theories of Magic and Its Uses.

"Yes, yes, yes!" the wizard whispered in relief.

He could not take time to read it here, he knew. He checked the last of the volumes and found nothing. He would have to hope that the one in his hands held what he was looking for. He moved quickly back across the room toward the door.

"I've got it!" he announced triumphantly as he reached Elizabeth and Abernathy.

Abruptly an alarm went off. They all jumped, and Elizabeth gave a short cry. Questor hurriedly tucked the book into the carry bag he had brought. "What's happened?" he gasped, white hair and beard flying out in every direction. "What did I do?"

"I don't think you did anything at all!" Elizabeth grasped his arm as he whirled this way and that, casting about for imagined attackers. "It's a fire alarm! But I can't imagine what set it off!"

Questor Thews and Abernathy immediately looked at each other. "Poggwydd!" they exclaimed.

They hurried along the corridor to the stairs and started down, jostling and bumping against each other, all talking at once.

"We shouldn't have left him alone!" Questor moaned, clutching the carry bag and its precious contents close against his chest.

"We should have tied and gagged him!" Abernathy snapped. From below came the sound of shouts.

"Maybe it isn't him at all!" Elizabeth encouraged.

But it was, of course. Two security guards were hauling Poggwydd into view just as they arrived at the bottom of the stairs. The Gnome was disheveled and covered from head to foot in a coating of ash. He was struggling and moaning pathetically while the guards held him at arm's length between them, not at all certain what it was they had.

"Boy, I've seen it all!" one of them was muttering.

"Shut up and hold on to him!" the other growled irritably.

Poggwydd caught sight of Questor Thews and started to call for help, but the wizard made a quick motion with one hand and the startled G'home

Gnome was rendered instantly voiceless. His mouth worked in futile desperation, but nothing came out.

"Stand back, folks," one of the guards advised as they carried the struggling
Gnome past.

"What do you have there?" Questor asked, feigning ignorance.

"Don't know." The guard's attention was diverted momentarily as Poggwydd tried to bite him. "Some sort of monkey, I guess. Filthy as a pig and
twice as ugly. Found him in the kitchen, trying to start a fire. It almost looked
like he was trying to cook some food he'd stolen, but c'mon, he's a monkey,
right? Anyway, the fire alarm went off or he might have burned the place
down. Look at him fight! Mean little devil. Must have escaped from a zoo or
something. How he found his way here, I'll never know."

"Well, be careful with him," Questor offered, trying to avoid Poggwydd's
furious look.

"Careful as can be." The guard laughed.

"There, there, little fellow," Questor called after the struggling Gnome.
"Someone will come to claim you soon!"

"Can't be soon enough for me!" the other guard called back, and the unfortunate Poggwydd was dragged kicking and writhing through the front
door and out of sight.

Questor, Abernathy, and Elizabeth stood staring after the Gnome in silence for a moment. Then Questor said, "This is my fault. I completely forgot
about him."

"You told him to wait where he was," Abernathy reminded him, evidenc-
ing a noticeable lack of sympathy. "He should have listened."

"Questor, what did you do to stop him from talking?" Elizabeth asked.

The wizard sighed. "Cast a small spell. I couldn't very well let him tell
them who we are, and that is exactly what he was about to do. Besides, things
would be much worse for Poggwydd if they found out he can talk. He is better off if they think him an animal, believe me."

"He *is* an animal," Abernathy muttered. "Stupid Gnome."

"Stupid or not, we have to help him," Elizabeth said at once.

"What we have to do," Questor announced quickly, "is to go back to the
house, where I can study this book and find out if it is what we are looking
for."

"It better be," Abernathy grumbled. "I have seen all I care to see of Graum
Wythe!"

"Where do you think they will take him?" Elizabeth asked, her brow
creased with worry.

"Wherever they think he came from, I suppose," Questor replied absently.
He was peering down into the carry bag at the book.

"I just don't want us to forget about him a second time," Elizabeth insisted.
They started for the entry. "He looks so helpless."

"Believe me, he is anything but," Abernathy sniffed. He was thinking about the G'home Gnomes' penchant for eating stray pets. "He does not deserve an ounce of your sympathy. He is a nuisance, plain and simple."

Elizabeth took his hand and squeezed it. "You are being difficult, Abernathy. It's not his fault he's here."

"It is not our fault, either. Nor our responsibility."

"She's right, you know," Questor Thews offered.

Abernathy gave his friend a scathing look. "I know she's right. You don't have to tell me that."

"I was just trying to point out—"

"Confound it, Questor Thews, why do you insist on belaboring—"

Still arguing between themselves while Elizabeth tried in vain to reestablish some semblance of peace, the wizard and the scribe passed down the corridor to the front door of the castle and out into the fading light.

In front of them, a King County police car was just pulling away.

···—⟨∞⟩—···

After their return to Elizabeth's house, Questor Thews stayed up all night reading the purloined book. He sat curled up in an easy chair in the far corner of his bedroom with a single light illuminating the pages as he turned them one by one. He was certain early on that this book was what they had been looking for and that hidden within its text lay the answer to the riddle behind their improbable escape from Nightshade. *Theories of Magic and Its Uses.* They were right there, all the discoveries of all the wizards since the dawn of Landover, set out as postulates and axioms, theories proved and suspected, absent only the recipe and ingredients for each specific stew. They were theories, not formulas, but were quite enough to get at the essence of things. Questor even knew what to look for. He hated himself for this, but the obviousness of the truth facing him was inescapable once he accepted its possibility. He worked his way through the book tirelessly, ignoring his exhaustion, suppressing his growing fear, reading on determinedly.

Across the room from him Abernathy slept with his face turned away from the light. It was just as well. His friend didn't want to have to look at him just now.

Sometime during the long, slow hours after midnight Questor Thews discovered what he was looking for. Even so, he kept reading, not wanting to take anything for granted, not wanting to give up his search for a better answer, although he knew already that there wasn't going to be one. He read all the way through the book and back again. He studied individual passages and considered alternative possibilities until his head hurt. Then he went back to the passage he had discovered earlier and read it again slowly, carefully. There was no mistake. It was what he was looking for. It was the answer he had been seeking.

He sighed and put the book down in his lap. He looked over at Abernathy again, and tears came to his eyes. His face crumpled, and his chest ached with need. Life was just so unfair sometimes. He wished things could be different. He wished this could be happening to someone else. His sticklike frame twisted into a clutter of old bones and wrinkled skin, and his heart knotted in his chest.

Finally, exhausted of feeling, he reached up, turned out the light, and sat motionless in the dark, waiting for morning.

SPECTER

"The title of the book is *Monsters of Man & Myth,*" Ben told Willow, speaking directly into her ear.

They rode double atop a still-skittish Jurisdiction, Willow in front, Ben behind. Bunion had retrieved the horse after a lengthy chase, and now they were traveling west again toward the Greensward. Ahead rose the black wall of an approaching thunderstorm. Behind lay the remains of the wurm and the sulfurous stench of ash and gases from the Fire Springs. Overhead, the sun beat down mercilessly, a blinding white-hot flame that turned the arid emptiness of the Eastern Wastelands into a furnace.

Rain will come as a welcome relief, Ben thought wearily, trying to distance himself from his growing thirst.

"And Rydall's creatures were in this book?" Willow asked in response, half turning to catch a glimpse of his face.

He nodded into her emerald hair, breathing the dusty scent of it. "A giant that gained strength from its contact with the earth, a demon that could mimic the look and abilities of whatever foe it faced, and a robotic machine man, armored and indestructible." He looked off into the sweltering distance, trying to make out the geography of the land against the blackness of the storm. "I don't remember the specific stories so much as the picture of the robot. It's right on the cover, and it's exactly the same as Rydall's. But they're all there. It's as if Rydall read the book!"

"But that isn't possible, is it?"

Ben sighed. "You wouldn't think so."

Willow looked forward again. The land shimmered with heat and dust. Bunion was out there somewhere, scouting for further dangers. If he found any, he would try to find a way around them. Another confrontation in their present condition was unthinkable.

"Where is this book?" Willow asked.

"In the library with the others," Ben answered. "It's one of several I brought over with me from my old life, books that I thought I might like to have. I remember why I picked that one in particular. I've had it since I was a boy, and it seemed to represent something of what I was hoping to find here in Landover—as if what wasn't real in my old life might be real in this one." He shook his head. "I got my wish, didn't I?"

Willow was silent for a moment. "But how would Rydall know about it?"

Ben shrugged. "I can't imagine. It doesn't make sense. Why would he know about this book as opposed to any other book? Has he read through my whole library? Does his magic enable him to search out any book at random and read through it without even being there?" He swallowed against the dryness in his throat and kept his temper tightly in check. "What I keep coming back to, Willow, is how personal this all feels. Rydall using my own things against me; striking out at my family and friends; kidnapping Mistaya, Questor, and Abernathy; attacking you and me, chasing us all over the place with this business of pitting his monsters against the Paladin; coming after me over and over again—I just don't get it. Supposedly it's about surrendering the throne to Landover, but it doesn't feel like Landover's got all that much to do with it."

Willow nodded without looking at him. "No," she agreed, and was silent again.

They rode on through the afternoon until the storm met them as they approached the edge of the Greensward. Black clouds swept past, blotting out the sun and blue sky, and a driving, blinding rain enveloped and soaked them to the skin in moments. The dust and grime of their travel were washed from their bodies, and the air about them was cooled. Jurisdiction plodded on, head lowered against the sheets of rain and swirling wind, and soon Bunion reappeared to lead them down into a grove of maple trees that provided good shelter from the damp. They dismounted, stripped off their clothing, wrung it out, and hung it to dry by a fire that Bunion had somehow managed to start. Sitting cross-legged in a soft patch of grass beneath the canopy of the trees, they watched the storm swirl around them and pass on. Darkness descended, and the world beyond their encampment disappeared. They dressed again, chewed halfheartedly on stalks of Bonnie Blue, rolled into their travel cloaks, and quickly fell asleep.

When they woke, it was raining again, a slow, persistent drizzle that fell out of low, empty leaden skies. The whole of the land about them had gone gray and misty in the early-morning light. They mounted Jurisdiction once more and rode out into the weather. Bunion went on ahead, a small, spidery figure skittering into the gloom until he was lost from view. The summer day was warm and filled with the smell of damp earth. Ahead, the Greensward stretched away in a patchwork of greens and browns, of tilled fields and grassy pastures, of mature forests and midseason plantings, all interspersed with rivers and lakes that in the rainy haze took on the look of molten metal, their surfaces stirred by the faint breezes that swept down across the flats.

By midday Bunion had returned with a second horse. He didn't offer an explanation of where he had gotten the beast, and Ben and Willow didn't ask. It was not a farm animal; it was a trained riding horse. Willow stood in front of the horse, a brown mare, and spoke to it encouragingly for a moment, then mounted smoothly and wheeled over beside Ben. She gave Bunion a smile and a wink, and the kobold was gone again.

They rode on through the rest of that day and most of the next. All the while it rained, leaving them wet clear through except for brief periods of dryness when they camped and were able to chase away the damp with the help of the fires Bunion always seemed to be able to construct. They passed Rhyndweir and several of the other castles of the Lords of the Greensward but did not stop to ask for shelter. Ben had no interest in seeing anyone, preferring to minimize the chance of further attacks from Rydall. Surprisingly, there were none. Since Rydall had found them in the Eastern Wastelands with the wurm, Ben had supposed he would be able to find them anywhere. Given the frequency and consistency of the attacks, he had expected another by now. On the other hand, Rydall had used up four of his promised seven challenges, so perhaps he was rethinking his strategy. Ben didn't consider it worth his while to ponder the matter further. He was simply grateful for the respite.

He used the time to think. With his travel cloak a shield against the elements, Willow a silent wraith riding next to him, and the rain a curtain that shrouded everything in damp, gray silence, he shut himself away from his discomfort and tedium and concentrated on the puzzle of Rydall of Marnhull. He was beginning to consider possibilities he had not considered before. Some of this was prompted by his growing sense of desperation. He could feel time running out. Sooner or later Rydall was going to send a monster from which no one could save him—not the Paladin, not Strabo, not anyone. Sooner or later his defenses were not going to be strong enough, and the struggle to survive would be over. The only thing that could prevent that from happening was uncovering the secret behind Rydall, and Ben seemed to be no closer to doing that than ever. So he determined to quit thinking in predictable ways, to be more innovative, more daring. He had to stop being led around by Rydall. He had to refuse to follow the paths Marnhull's King left open to him and start opening a few of his own. There was a net being woven about Ben Holiday, and he could sense it tightening with every new strand laid out. He had to find a way to cut through the webbing.

His thinking, however, was prompted not so much by his desperation as by his realization that there were a few loose threads in Rydall's carefully woven net. First, there was Ben's growing certainty that Rydall's sending of monsters to do battle with the Paladin was part of a game that had far more to do with Ben than with Landover's throne. Second, there was his recognition that three of the four monsters had come from the stories in his *Monsters of Man & Myth* book. Three created in painstaking detail from the writer's descriptions, as if Rydall had copied the creatures directly from the book's pages. Three, but not the fourth. No, the fourth, a wurm, had come from somewhere else.

A witch's favorite magic, Strabo had informed him.

In Landover that meant Nightshade.

He had given no serious consideration before to the possibility that Nightshade might be involved in this. Why would he? Rydall was an outlander, a usurper of power, an interloper whose goals were directly at odds with Nightshade's. On the other hand, no one hated Ben Holiday and his family more than the witch did. Stripped of Rydall's obvious presence, this entire business felt very much like her work. The use of dark magic, the attack on family and friends, and the calculated effort to destroy him all smacked of Nightshade. While he had heard nothing from the witch in more than two years, he did not expect that she had forgotten her promise that she would never forgive him for what had happened to her in the Tangle Box. For what she had been made to feel for him when they had both been stripped of their identities. For what she viewed as the loss of her dignity.

What if there was no Rydall? Oh, there might be someone masquerading as Marnhull's King, but what if Rydall himself was a fiction? No one had ever heard of Rydall or Marnhull—not the River Master, not Kallendbor, not even Strabo, who had traveled everywhere. No one could find Rydall or Marnhull. There was no trace of Mistaya, Questor Thews, or Abernathy. There was no sign of an invading army. The only physical evidence of Rydall at any time in this entire episode had been presented when Marnhull's King and his black-cloaked companion had appeared at the gates of Sterling Silver.

So, Ben mulled, what if this whole business was an elaborate charade? Where, after all, was the one place in Landover that he hadn't searched since Mistaya had disappeared? Where was the one place he had ignored because it wasn't readily accessible to him and because it didn't seem reasonable to look there? Where was the one place none of them had looked?

The Deep Fell, where Nightshade made her home.

Ben Holiday's suspicions hardened. What had begun as a consideration of possibilities rapidly evolved into a careful sifting of facts. Nightshade as Rydall; it made as much sense as anything else he had envisioned. Or Nightshade as Rydall's black-cloaked companion, he amended. He remembered the way the hooded rider had studied him when he had come down onto the causeway to pick up the gauntlet, the intensity of that veiled gaze. He remembered the way both riders had looked upon Mistaya when she had climbed onto the ramparts.

His chest tightened, and his stomach turned to ice.

It was late on the third day of their journey home when they came in sight of Sterling Silver. The castle materialized through the gloom like a vision brought to life from a child's imagining, a gleaming, rain-streaked rise of spires and parapets that hardened into stone and mortar, timber and metal, pennants and flags as they closed on its island surround. They crossed the moat through a misty curtain and passed beneath the raised portcullis. Retainers scurried to take their horses and usher them inside out of the weather. Ben and Willow went wordlessly to their bedchamber, stripped off their sodden clothing, climbed into a tub of steaming water, and lay back to soak. When some of the ache and discomfort of their travel had been eased, they climbed out again, dried off, and dressed in fresh clothing.

Then Ben led Willow down to the library for a close look at his copy of *Monsters of Man & Myth*. It took only moments to locate it. It sat on the shelf exactly where he remembered leaving it. He pulled it out and looked at the cover. Sure enough, there was Rydall's robot. He thumbed through the pages and in short order found a drawing of the giant. Then he found the writer's description of the demon that could mimic any foe.

He showed the book to Willow. "You see? Exactly the same as Rydall's monsters."

She nodded. "But how did he do it? How did he know about this book and these particular monsters? Ben, *I* didn't know about this book. I didn't even know it was here. We've never talked about it, not once. How did Rydall know?"

It was true, he realized. He had never taken it down and shown it to her before. They had never discussed it. There had never been any reason to do so. He had carried it over with him through the mists, unpacked it, placed it in the library, and forgotten it.

Until now. He stood close to the sylph, staring down at the book in silence. Without, the rain continued in dreary, unchanging monotony, the sound of its falling a soft patter on the stone. Ben felt strangely lulled, as if he might fall asleep at any moment. He was more tired than he wanted to admit, but he could not afford to sleep until he had unraveled the secret of Rydall and his monsters. Not until he had found a way to bring Mistaya home.

Mistaya.

He stared at Willow in surprise. "You said you didn't know about this book. But do you know who did? Mistaya. I caught her reading it once, paging through it. I didn't say anything, didn't interrupt her. I don't think she even saw me watching. She was so small, and I didn't think she could even understand it . . ."

He trailed off, his mind racing. "Willow," he said quietly, "I want you to listen to something. I want you to tell me what you think."

Then he told her of his suspicion that Nightshade might be Rydall's creator and that the Witch of the Deep Fell might be behind everything that had happened to them. He gave her all his reasons, laid out all the possibilities, and provided all the underpinnings of his conjecture. Willow listened intently, not interrupting, waiting for him to finish.

"The thing is," he concluded worriedly, "Mistaya could have told Nightshade about the book, could have described the monsters, could even have drawn a picture. She's smart enough to have remembered. She probably understood a whole lot more than I gave her credit for."

"But why would she do this?" Willow wanted to know instantly. "Why would she do anything to help the witch?"

Ben shook his head. "I don't know. I'm guessing about all this. But she has seen the book, and if Nightshade is Rydall, then it was Nightshade who kidnapped her. And has her now."

Willow gave him a long, steady look as she considered the possibility. "Do you remember when we talked about who else knew of the connection between the medallion and the Paladin? Only you and I, you said. But Nightshade knows, too. She was with you in the Tangle Box when you used the medallion."

Ben took a deep breath. "You're right. I forgot about that."

"You said you believed magic was used to hide the medallion when the robot attacked at Rhyndweir. Nightshade possesses such magic." Willow's face was stricken. "Ben, we have to go to the Deep Fell."

Ben slid his book back into its slot on the shelf. "I know. We'll go tomorrow, first thing. It's too late to start out again today. We're exhausted. We need at least one night's sleep in a dry bed."

He moved over to her and put his arms about her waist. "But we're definitely going," he promised. "And if that's where Mistaya is, we'll get her back."

Willow put her arms around him in response and lay her head against his shoulder. They held each other in silence, drawing comfort and strength from their joining, hardening themselves against the feelings of fear and doubt that twisted within.

Outside, the shadows lengthened toward twilight and the rain fell harder.

⸺∽∾∽⸺

They ate dinner alone in the dark silence of the eating hall, two solitary figures hunched close within the candlelight where it pushed back against the gloom. They did not speak much, too tired to attempt conversation, too immersed in their own thoughts. When they were finished, they retired to their bedchamber, climbed beneath the covers, and quickly fell asleep.

It was midnight when Ben woke. He lay quietly for a moment, trying to gain his bearings. He felt a faint burning where the medallion lay against his chest, a warning that something was wrong. He sat up slowly, his ears straining for sounds in the darkness. The rain had ceased finally, but the clouds hung across the sky like a shroud, blotting out the light of moons and stars. He could hear water dripping from the eaves and battlements, soft, small splashes in the inky night. Next to him Willow's breathing was relaxed and steady.

Then he heard something scrape against the stone outside his window, a

barely discernible sound, a whisper of trouble approaching. He slipped from the
bed swiftly, noiselessly, feeling the medallion burn sharply now against his skin.
Panic raced through him. He knew what was coming, and he was not ready for
it. It was too soon. He had convinced himself that Rydall would not strike again
so quickly, that he would deliberate before sending his fifth monster.

Ben glanced about the room, looking for help. Where was Bunion? He had
not seen the kobold since their return. Was he anywhere close at hand? He
turned back to the bed and Willow. He had to get her out of there. He had to
get her to safety, away from whatever was going to happen next.

He reached down for her shoulder and shook her gently. "Willow!" he
hissed. "Wake up!"

Her eyes opened instantly, a brilliant emerald even in the near black, wide
and deep and filled with understanding. "Ben," she said.

Then the room's light shifted as a shadow filled the window, and Ben
wheeled back to face it. The shadow rose into the gap and perched there,
hunched down against the lesser blackness of the night, lean and sinewy and
somehow terribly familiar. He could not see but could feel the shadow's eyes
upon him. He could feel the eyes taking his measure.

He did not move, knowing that if he did so, he would be dead before he
could complete whatever effort he began. His hand was already closed about
the medallion; as if by instinct it had reached for the only help left. He held
the medallion within the clutch of his fingers, feeling the graven image of the
knight riding out of his castle at sunrise, the Paladin from Sterling Silver off to
do battle for his King. He felt the image and stared at the shadow in the window, seeing now that it wasn't all smooth and taut as he had first believed but
was in fact in places ragged and broken, a creature that had suffered some cat-
astrophic misfortune and bore the injuries because there could be no healing.
Bits and pieces of the shadow hung loose, as if layers of skin had been shredded. Bone jutted in cracked shards from joints no longer whole. It made no
sound, but he could hear the silent wail of its inescapable pain and despair.

Then the shadow's head shifted slightly, a tilting to one side, little more,
and silver eyes gleamed catlike out of the black.

Ben's breath caught in his throat.

It was the Ardsheal, come back from the dead.

He had no time to ponder how this could be, no chance to deliberate on
what it meant. His response was instinctive and eschewed reason and hope.
His fingers tightened on the medallion, and the light flared outward in spears
of white brightness. Willow screamed. The Ardsheal launched itself at Ben, a
black panther at its prey, quicker than thought. But the Paladin was there instantly, come out of a sudden, impossibly brilliant explosion of light that
erupted in the dozen yards of space between King and assailant. The knight
rose up in a surge of gleaming silver armor and weaponry, catching the Ardsheal in midair and flinging it aside. The force of the collision sent the Ardsheal

slamming into the stone wall and the Paladin stumbling backward into Ben. A metal-clad elbow hammered into Ben's head, and he collapsed on the bed next to Willow, so stunned that he was barely able to hold on to the medallion.

The Ardsheal was on its feet in a heartbeat, pulling itself upright with the smoothness of a snake, the ease of its recovery belying its ragged condition. Through a haze of pain and dizziness, Ben watched it rise, his vision blurred and his head aching from the blow. But he felt the pain and the dizziness from inside the Paladin's armor, where his consciousness was now irrevocably lodged, there to remain until he triumphed or died. He saw Willow embracing his corporeal body, whispering frantically in his ear. He wondered for the briefest second what she was saying, remembering that he had wanted to get her clear of the room before this battle was joined. He caught a sudden glimpse of the Ardsheal's face in the gloom, one eye gone, a gash opened from forehead to chin, skin crosshatched with cuts and lesions. He saw it tumbling out of the castle window at Rhyndweir, riding the robot to the rocks below and certain death. He wondered how it could possibly have survived.

Then the mind-set of the Paladin closed down like a visor, and all he knew were the knight's long memories of battles fought and survived. He went down into his harder-than-iron other self, the battle-tested veteran of a thousand struggles from which only he had emerged. He withdrew into his armor and his experience, locking away what life there was beyond, shutting out the man and the woman on the bed behind him, the castle in which he now battled, the world beyond, the past and the future, all things but the here and now and the enemy that sought to destroy him.

The Ardsheal feinted right to left, testing. It was a dead thing by the look of its flat silver eyes, by the broken mix of skin and bone, by the gaping wounds that marked its body. But it lived beyond death, fed by magic that wrestled through its once-lifeless tissues and demanded of it one more task before it could rest in peace. The Paladin sensed this, knowing its enemy from knowledge innate and from some spark of Ben Holiday's own reason and memory. He watched the wraith before him shift and shift again, snakelike, looking for an opening. He saw it for the danger it was, a creature created of magic to serve a single purpose; to hunt and destroy. He saw it as he saw so few others he faced—as an equal.

The Ardsheal came at him with lightning speed, so low that it would be hard to take away his legs. The Paladin dropped on the creature in an effort to pin it, his dagger digging futilely into the stone floor as the Ardsheal rolled away, ripping at the knight's visor, twisting at it wickedly. The Paladin shook off the blow and rose to face his enemy once more. Quickness and strength, cunning and experience—the Ardsheal had them all and felt nothing beyond the magic that compelled it. It would not stop; it would not quit. It would keep coming until it could come no more.

An Ardsheal is a match for anything alive. Nothing is more dangerous. The River Master's words.

In the shadows the Ardsheal crouched. The Paladin thought momentarily of drawing forth his broadsword, but the weapon was too cumbersome and unwieldy for this foe. Small weapons would be more effective, until an opportunity presented itself, as it must if he was to survive.

He shifted the dagger to his left hand, reaching with the right for his long knife, and the Ardsheal was on him in a flash, ripping and tearing and wrenching at armor and limbs. The Paladin stumbled back under the fury of the attack, hearing the shriek of fastenings as they tore loose, feeling metal plates threaten to give way. Forsaking the dagger, he jammed both armored hands against the creature's chest and again flung it away. It came back at him at once, animal-wild, crazed beyond sense, a thing insane. It was impossibly strong, and its strength was aided by its lack of feeling and the rush of magic that fed it. It fought without hindrances of any kind; it battled without the complications that emotion and reason demanded. Its efforts were pure and unrestricted, its struggle single-minded. It would win or lose and still be dead either way.

For the third time the Paladin flung it away, and this time snatched free the long knife before it could recover. When it came again, he would skewer it on the blade and rip it in two. His breathing was harsh and unsteady. Though he would not acknowledge it because he could not permit himself to do so, his strength was already beginning to fail. He could not tell if it was the number of battles fought in so short a span of time or the weakened condition of the King he served, for both could play a part in determining whether he survived. He relied on himself, but he was irrevocably attached to the man who commanded his services and lent him his strength of will. If the King failed in his resolve, so might he. But such thoughts were not permitted. So he told himself only that he should end the fight quickly and not speculate further.

The Ardsheal stalked him through the bedchamber's gloom, another of night's faint shadows sidestepping the light. It was no longer attempting a frontal attack; it was looking to do something else. The Paladin shifted, turning to follow its movements, not leaving his place before the King and Queen. His armor hung loosely from the bindings in several places. He was coming undone, as ragged as his attacker. He could feel the other's eyes studying him, searching for an opening. Beneath the armor the Paladin was vulnerable. The Ardsheal sensed this. One strike was all it would take if the strike was deep enough.

It faked a quick rush and retreated. It faked another. The Paladin stayed set, not allowing himself to be drawn out. Then, in a flash of recognition, he saw what the Ardsheal was trying to do. It was trying to pull him far enough away from the King and Queen to leave them exposed. It would kill them, sensing, perhaps even knowing, that this would mean the defeat of the Paladin as well.

As if reading his thoughts, the Ardsheal attacked anew. It came in a slashing, wild charge, so quick that it was almost past the Paladin before he could act. As it was, he barely caught the Ardsheal's arm as it reached for the Queen, snatching the creature back and flinging it aside. This time he went after it, intent on finishing the battle, but again he was too slow, and the Ardsheal was up and away again into the gloom.

Twice more the elemental tried to slip past, and both times it nearly succeeded. Only the Paladin's experience and determination kept it at bay. The Queen was crying on the bed behind him now, small sounds only, almost silent in her misery, her despair. She was strong, but her fear was immense and impossible to conceal. She was terrified of the Ardsheal. The King was awake again. He had placed himself before her, and he held the medallion out like a talisman. Too frail, the both of them, the Paladin knew, to survive if he should fall.

The thought was a mind spike he was quick to wrench free and cast away from him.

The Ardsheal faded into emptiness, leaving the Paladin searching the darkness frantically. Then it reappeared out of nowhere directly before him, a frenzied blackness whipping atop him and beating him to the floor. It sought to break past, but the Paladin collapsed and, momentarily blinded, held on to one leg and dragged it back. The Ardsheal wrenched at the fallen champion, kicked at him, struck at him, tore at his weakened armor. The Paladin felt pain. In desperation, he hauled himself to his knees through the flurry of blows, through a massive effort that came mostly from the heart, and one final time hurled the Ardsheal away.

This time when the Ardsheal came to its feet, one arm hung limp. But the Paladin was a shambles of broken armor and torn bindings, aching muscles and wearied limbs, standing upright through sheer force of will. There was blood in his mouth and on his body. He still gripped the long knife, still waited for his chance to use it. But time was fleeing quickly now. Time was racing away.

The Ardsheal moved forward, an inexorable, implacable force.

Then the door to the room flew open, and a small bristling fury hurtled into the fray. It hammered into the Ardsheal and bore it backward to the wall. All claws and teeth, Bunion appeared to have gone berserk. The Ardsheal was caught off guard, staggered by the force of the kobold's attack. It twisted wildly, trying to dislodge its assailant. The Paladin lunged forward, the chance he had been waiting for there at last. He drove the dagger through the Ardsheal's skull with such force that he buried it to the hilt. The Ardsheal arched upward, silver eyes filling with blood. It tore Bunion free and wheeled toward the Paladin. But the knight had unsheathed the great broadsword, and with every ounce of strength left to him he swung the blade crosswise and down at his enemy. The blade caught the Ardsheal between neck and shoulder and cut straight through. Down it sliced, all the way to the creature's heart.

The Ardsheal slumped into the blow. It convulsed, and in the terrible eyes there was a hint of some ancient recognition that not even the darkest magic could withstand. The eyes fixed, and the magic faded. Death stole the Ardsheal back once more.

Broken, exhausted, a ragged caricature of the silver knight he had been when the battle had begun, the Paladin freed the broadsword and turned to Landover's King where he crouched on the bed. Their eyes met and held. He had the odd sense of looking back at himself. He started to drop to one knee, but he was caught up in the light of the medallion still held outstretched in the King's hand and carried down into healing sleep.

In the silence that followed Ben and Willow could hear the rain begin to fall again.

King's Guards were summoned, and the remains of the Ardsheal were removed. The sounds of the struggle had gone unheard, an impossibility in the absence of magic deliberately employed. When the soldiers were gone and the room had been cleaned and straightened, Bunion took up watch just outside the door. The kobold blamed himself for what had happened. He had been scouting once more, just beyond the castle walls, but somehow the very enemy he had been seeking had slipped past him and entered the castle unseen. No words were spoken, but Bunion's apology was there in the squint of his eyes and the flash of his teeth.

When Ben and Willow were alone again, they clung to each other as if to the last solid grip on a crumbling rock. They did not speak. They stood pressed together in the darkness and took comfort from their closeness. Willow was shaking in the summer heat. Ben, though he appeared steady, was inwardly shattered.

They climbed back into their bed, there in the no-longer-reassuring dark, eyes wandering the room, ears pricked for the faintest of sounds. They could not sleep and did not try. Ben stilled Willow's shivering, chasing momentarily at least her fear of the thing that had come to kill them. He held her tight against him and tried to find words for what he would say, for the confession he now knew he must make if he was ever again to find peace.

Without, the rain pattered on the stone and dripped from the capping on the walls in a steady cadence.

"I have to tell you something about the Paladin," he said finally, speaking in a rush the words he could not seem to organize better. "This isn't easy to explain, but I have to try. We're the same person, Willow. Right now his pain is all through me. I can feel the ache of his body and limbs, the wear on his soul, the hurt that threatens to break him down. I feel it when he does battle, but I feel it now, as well." He took a deep breath. "It's all I can do to stand it. It seems as if it might pull me apart, break all my bones, and flatten me into the earth. Even now it's there. He's gone, but it doesn't matter."

He felt her head lift from his shoulder so that her eyes could see his face. He felt her fingers move along his chest, searching. "He is part of me, Willow. That's what I want to say. He is part of me and always has been, ever since I came into Landover and took up the medallion of Kingship. The medallion joins us, makes us one when I call him up from wherever it is he waits."

He looked at her, looked quickly away. "When the medallion summons him, the magic carries some part of me inside his armor. Not my body or my mind but my heart and will and strength of purpose—those he requires. In some way the King and the King's champion are the same. That's the real secret of the medallion. It's a secret I couldn't tell you."

Her emerald eyes were steady as she stared at him. "Why couldn't you tell me?" she asked quietly.

"Because I was afraid of what it would do to you." He forced himself to meet her gaze and hold it. "I've wanted to tell you. I've felt I should, that it was wrong not to, but I was afraid. What would it do to you to know that every time the Paladin was summoned, it was me—or at least some important, necessary part of me—that would be required to do battle. What would it mean if you knew that the Paladin's death could bring mine as well."

He shook his head, feeling adrift. "But it's worse than that. Every time I go into the Paladin and become one with him, I feel myself slipping farther away from who I really am. I become him, and each time it is harder to get back. I live in constant fear that one time I might not be able to return because I do not want to, because I have forgotten who I am, because I like what I have become. The power of the magic is so seductive! When I'm the Paladin, he's all I wish to be. If the medallion did not bring me back to myself, if it did not take the Paladin away, I do not think I could ever return of my own will. I think I might be lost forever."

The pain in her eyes was terrible to see. "You should have told me," she said quietly. He nodded, emptied of words. "Don't you understand, Ben? I gave myself to you unconditionally when I found you at the Irrylyn. I belong to you, and nothing would ever make me leave. Nothing!"

"I know," he agreed.

"No, you don't, or you would not have hesitated to tell me this." Her voice was soft, but there was iron at the core. "There is nothing you could not tell me, Ben. Not ever. We will be together always, until the end. You know how it was foretold. You know the prophecy. You should never question the strength of its truth."

"I was afraid—" he began, but she hushed him quickly.

"No, let it go for now. Let it go." She touched him gently. "Tell me again. All of his pain comes back into you? All that he bore in your defense?"

He closed his eyes. "I feel as if I am falling apart. I feel as if I'm dying, and I cannot find the wound that's killing me. It's everywhere, inside and out. I am in fragments scattered all over this room—in the air, in the sound of the rain, in my own breathing. I don't know what to do. The Paladin won, but I seem to have lost. Calling him again so soon was too much to bear. It took too much out of me, Willow. I haven't the heart for this!"

"Shhh, no more," she comforted, pressing herself against him. She kissed his mouth. "You have heart enough for all of us, Ben Holiday. It has always been your greatest strength. You survived a terrible struggle. No ordinary man could have done what you did. Do not disparage yourself. Do not demean what you have accomplished. Listen to me. The secret of the Paladin is ours now, not yours alone to bear. Its weight can be better carried by two. I will help you. I will find ways to sustain you when you are weary and sick at heart as you are now. I will help shield you from the pain. If you must go into the Paladin for our sake, I will find a way to bring you back. Always. Forever. I love you."

"I have never doubted that," he replied softly. "I would have been finished long ago if I did."

She stroked his forehead gently, kissing him once more. Gradually he felt himself relax and begin to drift. "Go to sleep," she whispered.

He nodded, his breathing growing slower and deeper. Some of the pain eased. Some of the ache lessened. The memories of his battle as the Paladin lost their hard edge, giving way to the softness of Willow's touch. Sleep would renew his strength, and with morning he would be able to go on. All that would remain was the inescapable knowledge that he must go through this again with each new transformation. And even that could be accepted, he supposed. Even that.

He stilled himself, pushed back the fear and despair. Find Mistaya, he thought. Find her safe and well, and it would all be worth it. Bring back Questor Thews and Abernathy. Put an end to Rydall of Marnhull and his insidious games.

In the inky night's stillness the words were a whisper of hope.

Seek out Nightshade in the Deep Fell. Look there for the truth.

Then he was asleep.

DOG DREAMS

When Abernathy woke the next morning, having slept particularly well considering the trauma of yesterday's events, Questor Thews was sitting in a chair across from his bed, staring at him like Death's coming. It was very disconcerting. Abernathy blinked, reached for his glasses, and gave the wizard a long, slow deliberate look.

"Is something the matter?" he asked.

The wizard nodded, then shook his head, unable to decide. "We have to talk, old friend," he announced wearily.

Abernathy almost laughed at the solemnity of the declaration. Then he saw the look in the other's empty eyes and felt something cold settle into the pit of his stomach. Questor Thews was deeply troubled.

"Well," he said in reply, and went still again, as if that one word had addressed the matter and disposed of it without the need for further conversation.

He rose to a sitting position, taking a moment in spite of himself to admire the smooth line of his arms and legs, pausing then to give critical consideration to the look of his fingers and toes. His fingers were long and slim, but his toes were all scrunched up like those gummy things he had recently acquired a taste for. Elizabeth kept a bag of them down in the kitchen and was forever offering him one. He didn't care for the idea that they reminded him of his toes.

He cleared his throat. "What would you like to talk about?" he asked, hoping it was something other than Poggwydd.

Questor Thews bestirred himself sufficiently to rise from the chair and pace to the window, a tall, bent scarecrow with the stuffing coming out at the seams. He parted the curtain and looked out, squinting against the light. The day was sunny and warm, the sky cloudless, the world coming awake. "Let's go down to the yard and sit in the shade of those trees," he suggested, sounding cheerful in a forced sort of way.

Abernathy sighed. "Let's."

He showered, shaved, and dressed, and in the middle of doing so it occurred to him that what Questor Thews wanted to talk about was the book. *Theories of Magic and Its Uses.* Abernathy had forgotten about the book, all caught up in Poggwydd's unexpected appearance at Graum Wythe and resultant capture, the G'home Gnome another outcast from Landover, trapped now as he was, the difference being, of course, that Poggwydd really didn't want anything at all to do with this world, while Abernathy was growing steadily more comfortable with his exile.

Which meant, he concluded, that the book had revealed something to Questor about leaving. That was why the wizard was still awake: he had found the answer he was looking for and was trying to decide how to tell Abernathy, who he knew wasn't as keen to be getting back. Although, he argued to himself, he really was, because he understood as well as Questor that the High Lord needed them, Mistaya was in the hands of Nightshade, and something awful was going to happen if they didn't get back in time to prevent it.

But what? What was going to happen? He wished he knew. A little certainty in the matter certainly wouldn't hurt.

He finished pulling on his shoes and went out of the bathroom to stand before Questor. The wizard faced him, seemed startled by what he saw, and quickly turned away.

"Well, thank you very much, I'm sure!" Abernathy snapped. "Are my pants on backward? Are my shoes the wrong color?"

"No, no." The other put a hand to his forehead, pained. "In fact, you look quite sartorial." The wizard waved vaguely at the air. "I'm sorry to be so rude. But I've been up all night reading, and I didn't particularly care for the end of the story."

Abernathy nodded, having no idea at all what he was nodding about. "Why don't we go on down and get started with this talk," he pressed, anxious to get it over with. "We can see if Elizabeth is awake and ask her to join us."

But Questor quickly shook his head. "No, I'd rather this discussion was just between you and me." He looked down, then bit at his lower lip. "Indulge me, please."

Abernathy did. They went out the door of the bedroom, along the short hallway, and down the stairs. As they passed Elizabeth's closed door, they heard her singing inside. At least someone was feeling cheerful. They walked from the living room into the kitchen and came face to face with Mrs. Ambaum. She was standing in front of the stove making tea, bluff, hardy, watchful, and decidedly triumphant as she turned to face them.

"I spoke with Elizabeth's father last night. He doesn't recall having an

Uncle Abernathy. Doesn't recall anyone by that name. What do you have to say to that?"

One hand gripped a tea strainer. Armed and dangerous if they were foolish enough to try anything.

Abernathy offered his most disarming smile. "We haven't seen each other in years. We were just boys the last time."

The corner of her mouth twitched. "He said to tell Elizabeth he's flying in tonight. He wants to have a look at you."

Abernathy blinked, conjuring up a picture of the meeting. Mrs. Ambaum cocked her head as if trying to get a look inside his.

Questor Thews quickly took charge. "Imagine that!" he declared. He took Abernathy by the arm and steered him past the startled housekeeper and out the back door. "Don't be worried, now," he called over his shoulder. "It will all get straightened out before you know it!"

They went down the porch steps and into the yard, Abernathy working very hard at not looking back over his shoulder to see if Mrs. Ambaum was staring after them. "I don't much care for that woman," he muttered.

Questor Thews grimaced. "Fair enough. She doesn't much care for you, either."

They moved out into the backyard, well away from the house, where curious ears might pick up what they had to say. Abernathy gazed at the sky and took in the sweep of its vast blue dome. He breathed in the smell of flowers and grasses and fading damp. Mrs. Ambaum was forgotten.

They reached an old bench painted glossy white to protect the wood against weathering and seated themselves, looking east across a broad stretch of empty fields to where the Cascade Mountains rose white-peaked against the depthless sky.

After a moment's silence Abernathy looked at Questor. "Well?" he said.

The wizard sighed, folded his hands in his lap, fidgeted, and sighed again. "We have a problem," he said.

Abernathy waited until it was clear that Questor did not know what to say next. "Could you possibly speak more than one sentence at a time, Questor Thews? That way we won't waste the whole day."

"Yes, all right." The wizard was flustered. "The book. *Theories of Magic and Its Uses.* I read it last night. Read it twice, as a matter of fact. Made a very thorough study of what it had to say. I think it is what we are looking for."

Abernathy nodded. "You think? Not very encouraging for those of us expecting a definite yes or no."

"Well, it's about magic—the book, that is—and magic is never exact. As you know. And this is a book about theory, a general discussion of how various magics work, about their principles, their commonalities. So it doesn't say, for instance, 'Take the eye of a newt, mix with a frog's foot, and turn around three times left' or some such."

"I certainly hope not."

"Well, that isn't a real spell, anyway, of course. But it's an *example* of a specific spell as opposed to general theory. This book is theory, as I said, so you can't be certain about anything until you've tried it out; you can only apply the theory to the situation and be reasonably sure."

Abernathy frowned. "Why do I not feel reassured by this? I wonder. Why does this conjure up memories of other times?"

Questor Thews threw up his hands. "Drat it, Abernathy, this is serious! You are not helping matters by making flippant remarks! Please, no more attempts at humor! Just listen!"

They faced each other in stunned silence. The smile dropped from Abernathy's face. "I apologize," he said, surprised that he could even speak the words.

Questor nodded hurriedly and brushed the apology aside. *Unnecessary between friends,* he was saying. "Theory," he continued, picking up the thread of his conversation. "The book reveals a theory that I remember from the days I studied under my brother in the time of the old King. It goes something like this. When one magic intervenes to change the result of another, to alter that result in a substantive way, then to undo the consequences of the intervening magic, you must use a third magic to put things back exactly the way they were. So magic one is applied, magic two changes the result, and magic three puts everything back the way it was before magic two was applied."

Abernathy stared. "What about the consequences of magic one where the consequences of magic two are negated?"

"No, no, that doesn't have any bearing on things! Magic one is already disposed of!" Questor's thin lips tightened, and his bushy eyebrows narrowed. "Are you following me on this?"

"Nightshade tried to kill us with her magic. She failed because another magic intervened, the one that belongs to the mud puppy, we think. Now we have to use a third magic to put things back the way they were. You lose me there. Put what things back?"

Questor's eyes hooded. "Wait, there's more. The second magic, in order to overcome the first and at the same time facilitate the future possibility of its own negation, must use a catalyst, a powerful hook, a peripheral consequence that can't be mistaken for anything other than what it is. This consequence facilitates the dominance of the second magic over the first. Think of it as a form of sacrifice. In some cases it actually is. One life given to save others, for instance. Pretty hard to reverse that one. Normally the consequence has no meaning in the course of events beyond providing a clear indication of what it is that needs putting back in place." He took a long breath. "I'm sorry. I know this is confusing."

But Abernathy shook his head slowly, his face suddenly gone pale. "You're talking about me, aren't you, Questor Thews? Talking about changing me back again from a man to a dog. Aren't you?"

His friend sighed and nodded. "Yes."

"You think that if magic is used to change me back again, back into a dog, then the consequences of the second magic will be undone and we will all be sent back into Landover. Don't you?"

"Yes."

"That's ridiculous."

But he didn't sound as if it were, and he didn't believe it, either. Some part of him already whispered that it was so. Some part of him had been expecting this from the first moment he had discovered his good fortune. It was an inevitability that he should not enjoy such luck without consequences, not be allowed to escape from his fate so easily. He hated himself for thinking like this, but he could not help it. Damned by fate. Consigned to purgatory. He had been given a vacation from reality, nothing more.

"You could be wrong," he pressed, trying to stay calm, feeling desperation begin to build inside already, feeling the heat of it rise along his neck and into his face.

"I could be," Questor Thews acknowledged. "But I don't think I am. We have already agreed that we were dispatched to the High Lord's old world to save our lives and because something hidden here would help us find our way back again. The magic that sent us, and whoever used it, would have provided us with the key to our prison. Everything fits into place except your transformation—unless your transformation itself is the key. There is no other reason for it to have happened. It is too dramatic a result to be simply a side effect. It must be something more, and what else is there for it to be?"

Abernathy came to his feet—his human feet—and stalked off. He stopped when he was far enough away from the wizard that he felt alone and stared out at nothing. "I am not going to do this!" he shouted.

"I'm not asking you to!" the other replied.

Abernathy threw up his hands in disgust. "Don't be ridiculous! Of course you are!"

He wheeled about in challenge. Questor Thews looked old and frail. "No, Abernathy, I'm not. How could I? I was the one who changed you in the first place. An accident, yes, but that doesn't excuse what happened. I changed you from a man into a dog, and then I couldn't change you back again. I have lived with that failing, that stupidity, every day of my life since. Now I find myself maneuvered into a position where I am expected to change you a second time. I must relive the worst moment of my life, knowing, mind you, that I still cannot undo the magic's consequences once they are in place." There were tears in the old man's eyes, and he wiped at them savagely. "I do not mind telling you that it is almost unbearable to contemplate!"

For both of us, Abernathy thought dismally. He looked down at himself, at his real self, his restored self, and thought for a moment what it would mean to be a dog again. He pictured himself anew as the shaggy-haired, clumsy, laughable creature he had been. He imagined himself trapped inside that alien body, struggling to keep his dignity, fighting every single day of his life to convince those surrounding him that he was as human as they were. How could anyone expect him to make such a sacrifice? *This* was the trade-off for returning to Landover? But he knew it was more than that. It was the trade-off for being alive. Had the mysterious magic not intervened, he would be dead. Nightshade would have put an end to him. To the both of them. And Questor Thews was undoubtedly right, as much as it pained him to admit it. His transformation from a dog back into a man had had a purpose, and the only purpose that made any sense was the one the wizard had revealed after studying the book of magic.

So he could stay or he could go. The choice was his. Questor would not attempt to persuade him either way. The wizard had to live with his own demons in this matter. It was being left to Abernathy to decide. If he rejected the transformation, he was stuck here. Good and bad in that, he supposed. It didn't need detailing. Of course, High Lord Ben Holiday was stuck as well; there would be no help from this end. On the other hand, if he allowed Questor to invoke the magic, he would presumably return in time to help the High Lord. But would he, in fact? Was there some real purpose to be served in going back, or would matters run their course whether he returned or not? If only he knew. It was one thing if by returning he would help save the High Lord and his family from Rydall and Nightshade. It was another if his return would make no difference at all.

He glanced toward the house. Mrs. Ambaum was looking out the window at them, sipping contentedly at her tea. Retribution by nightfall, she was thinking. Still no sign of Elizabeth. Beyond, where the road curved past the front yard and disappeared over a rise, the sunlight was a hazy curtain through the trees.

He walked back to Questor Thews and stopped in front of him, eyes fixed on the worn old face. "I really don't think I can do this," he said quietly.

The wizard nodded, face scrunched into a mass of wrinkles. "I don't blame you."

Abernathy held out his hands and looked at them. He shook his head. "Do you even remember the magic you used to change me that first time?"

Questor did not look up but nodded that he did.

"After so many years. Isn't that something?" Abernathy looked down at himself. He hadn't been changed back all that long, and already he was comfortable with himself in his old skin. "I like myself as I am," he whispered.

Elizabeth appeared in the doorway. "Breakfast!"

Neither moved. Then Questor waved. "We'll be there directly!" he called. He looked at Abernathy. "I am truly sorry."

Abernathy smiled ruefully. "Of course you are."

"I would give anything not to have to tell you this, anything not to have it so." He bit at his lip.

"If it isn't so, for the sake of argument," Abernathy mused, "I will be trapped here not as a man but as a dog."

Questor Thews nodded, holding his gaze this time.

"But it is so. You're sure. As sure as you can be, aren't you?"

The wizard nodded once more, didn't speak.

"I have to make up my mind about this right away, don't I?" Abernathy pressed on reluctantly. "If we are to be of any use to the High Lord and Mistaya, we have to get back quickly. There isn't time to give this a lot of thought."

"No, I'm afraid there isn't."

"Why don't you argue the matter with me, then?"

"Argue with you?"

"Convince me, one way or the other. You choose a side. Argue both ways if you like. But give me some issues I can debate. Give me something to dispute. Give me a voice besides my own to listen to!"

"I have already explained—"

"Stop explaining!" Abernathy was suddenly livid. "Stop being rational! Stop being passive! Stop standing around waiting for me to make this decision all by myself!"

"But it is your decision to make, Abernathy—not mine. You know that."

"I know nothing of the sort! I know nothing at all! I am sick and tired of being ignorant of what is happening in my life! All I want is to be able to go back to the way things were, and I am not being allowed to do that! I am still being required to perform, just as I was when we appeared at that Bumble-whatever festival, only the audience isn't anyone we can see! Why should I agree to go along with this? It would be better just to sit down and refuse to do another thing!"

"Doing nothing is the same as doing something!" Questor was growing a bit heated himself. "A choice is made either way!"

Abernathy clenched his hands in fury. "So it still comes down to the same thing, doesn't it? A choice must be made one way or the other, even if the choice is not really a choice at all?"

"You are babbling!"

"I am trying to make sense!"

Questor Thews sighed. "Why don't we eat some breakfast and then perhaps—"

"Oh, forget it! I'm going back!"

"—things will be a little easier." The wizard caught his breath sharply. "What did you say?"

Abernathy struggled to keep his voice from breaking. "I said I am going back! I want you to use the magic to change me!" He grimaced at the look on the other's ragged face and was suddenly calm. "It isn't so difficult a decision, Questor Thews. When this matter is over and done, I have to be able to live with myself. If I am required to be a dog again, I can adjust. I can accept it knowing that I did everything I could to help the High Lord and his family. But if I stay a man and learn later that by changing to a dog I could have saved their lives . . . well, you can imagine."

He cleared his throat. "Besides, I swore an oath." For a long moment he looked to be the saddest man who ever lived. "I am Court Scribe to the throne of Landover and pledged to serve her King. I am bound to serve in whatever way I can. I might wish it otherwise just now, but I cannot change the fact of it."

Questor Thews stared. The old eyes were fierce. "You really are quite remarkable," the wizard said softly. "Really."

Impulsively, he wrapped his arms about his friend and hugged him, whiskers rubbing roughly into Abernathy's smooth skin. "Well," Abernathy said in reply, overcome by the other's response. He tried to shrug his indifference. "Really, yourself."

❧

They went up to the house to have breakfast with Elizabeth. The three of them sat at the little kitchen table, crowded over bowls of cereal and milk. Mrs. Ambaum bustled about officiously for a few moments as if attempting to supervise in some way, then gave up trying and disappeared out the front door with a promise to be back by noon.

As soon as she was gone, Elizabeth said, "Dad is coming home tonight, flying in from New York."

"So Mrs. Ambaum informed us," Questor advised. He did not look at Abernathy. His friend was eating with his head bent close over the bowl and his hand to his forehead.

"We have to make up a new story," Elizabeth continued. Her curly hair was damp from washing, and her face was freshly scrubbed. "It won't be hard. We'll just say that Mrs. Ambaum got it wrong, and that you . . ."

But Questor was already shaking his head. "No, Elizabeth. That won't be necessary. Abernathy and I are leaving."

"Leaving? When?"

Questor smiled sadly. "Right away. As soon as we finish eating."

Disappointment showed immediately. "You found a way to go back, didn't you?"

Questor nodded. "Last night."

She bit her lip. She looked at Abernathy, brow furrowed. "But you only just got here. Can't you stay another day or so? Maybe I can—"

"No, Elizabeth." Abernathy straightened and met her desperate gaze with kind eyes. "The High Lord needs us. Mistaya needs us. Any further delay is dangerous. We can't stay."

Elizabeth looked down at her cereal and gave it a few stirs with her spoon. "It doesn't seem fair. I don't want to be selfish, and I know it's important you go back. But you just got here." She glanced up, then quickly down. "I've been waiting four years to see you again."

Abernathy couldn't speak. His face was stricken.

There was a momentary silence. "What about Poggwydd?" she asked finally.

Questor cleared his throat. "Poggwydd will go back with us. Abernathy and I will seek his release as soon as we leave here."

"I'll go with you," Elizabeth announced at once.

"No," Abernathy said quickly, thinking it was bad enough that they were going themselves but resigned to the inevitability of it.

"What he means," Questor said, jumping in with both feet, "is that the moment we free Poggwydd, we will be on our way. Poof!" He tried a smile, failed. "If we encounter any trouble, we don't want you involved. Isn't that right, Abernathy?"

"But you might need my help!" Elizabeth didn't wait to hear what Abernathy had to say. "You don't know your way around Seattle! How will you get anywhere? How will you even find Poggwydd?"

"Well, perhaps you *could* help us with that last part," the wizard suggested soothingly.

"Elizabeth." Abernathy folded his hands on the table and sighed. "If we could stay, we would. If we could spend even a little more time with you, we would. You have been our friend. Mine especially. Twice now, not just once. But there are limits to what we can allow you to risk. It will be hard enough explaining us to your father."

"I'm not worried about him! I'm not worried about Mrs. Ambaum or anyone!" She was adamant.

"I know," he replied softly. "You have never let anyone stop you. If you had, I would not be here now." He smiled sadly. "But we worry for you. We worry that something will happen to you, and then we would be responsible. Remember what happened with Michel Ard Rhi? Remember how close you came to being hurt? I was scared to death for you! I cannot take a chance that such a thing might happen again. We have to say good-bye now. Here, at your house, where we know you are safe. Please, Elizabeth."

She took a moment to consider the matter and then nodded. "Okay, Abernathy." Still upset, defensive, angry. "I guess." She sighed. "Well, at least you're a man again, aren't you? At least you're not a dog anymore."

Abernathy smiled bravely. "Yes, at least I'm not a dog."
They finished breakfast in silence.

⸻◈⸻

In an effort to find out what had become of Poggwydd, Elizabeth called the King County police, who referred her to King County animal control, who in turn referred her to the King County animal shelter on Elliott. Because no one had been certain what Poggwydd was and therefore what to do with him, the G'home Gnome had been passed from hand to hand like an old shoe. The final result was temporary as well, she discovered when she spoke with one of the animal shelter employees. A zoologist from Woodland Park and an anthropologist from the University of Washington were both due to pay a visit later that morning. Territorial disputes would be resolved, and Poggwydd would be sent one place or the other for further study.

Elizabeth hung up the phone, gave her report, and said, "You'd better hurry."

A taxi was called to spirit Abernathy and Questor Thews to their destination at the animal shelter. Elizabeth gave them money for the fare. She stood with them at the end of the walk until the cab arrived, giving them final words of caution and encouragement and providing her phone number in case things went horribly wrong and it turned out they needed her after all, secretly hoping they would, hoping they would find some way to come back but knowing they wouldn't. When the cab arrived, she hugged them both and wished them a safe journey. She kissed Abernathy on the cheek and told him that he was her best friend, even if he was from another world, and that she would always wait for him because she knew that someday he would come back. Abernathy said he would try. He said he would never forget her. She cried in spite of saying that she wouldn't, and Abernathy had to work hard at not crying with her.

Then Questor and Abernathy were off, speeding down four- and five-lane highways, zipping around other vehicles, barely missing all sorts of obstacles and barriers. They crossed a bridge, turned down a rampway, sped along a two-lane roadway at a slightly slower speed, and wheeled into a parking area next to a brown brick building with a sign that read "King County Animal Shelter."

They gave Elizabeth's money to the cab driver, stepped back onto solid ground with an unmistakable sense of relief, and headed inside. The walk diverged, and there were entries at either end. They went left through a door to a desk where a bored-looking employee sent them outside again and down the walk to the other door. At the second desk a young woman in a uniform looked up expectantly as they entered.

"Professor Adkins? Mr. Drozkin?" she greeted them.

Questor recognized an opportunity when he saw one. He smiled and nodded.

The young woman looked relieved. "Do you have any idea what this thing is?" she asked. "No one here has ever seen anything like it. It's giving us fits! I've tried everything—we all have—but we can't even get close. After the police brought it in, I removed the restraints and it tried to take my hand off. And it eats everything! Do you know what it is?"

"I have a pretty good idea," Questor Thews said. "Can we have a look?"

"Of course; right this way." She was eager to accommodate them, to rid herself of the burden of Poggwydd. Abernathy understood perfectly.

She brought them around the counter to a heavy metal door, which she unlocked and swung open. From there she led them down a hallway into an area of cages. At the far end was Poggwydd, slumped down at the back of the largest cage. His clothing was torn, and his fur was caked with grime and sweat. Cuts and scratches marked him from head to foot, and his tongue was hanging out. He looked, even for a G'home Gnome, decidedly miserable.

When he saw them, he leapt to his feet and attacked the cage with a vengeance that was astonishing. He shook and rattled and bit at the heavy wire in a frenzy, trying to get at them.

"He's gotten even worse!" the young woman declared in astonishment. "I'd better tranquilize him right now!"

"No, let's wait on that, please," Questor interrupted hurriedly. "I'd like simply to observe him for now. I don't want him sedated. Can you leave us for a few minutes . . . I'm sorry, I don't know your name."

"Beckendall. Lucy Beckendall." She reached out her hand, and he shook it cordially, not bothering with an introduction on his end because he had already forgotten who he was supposed to be.

"A few minutes?" he repeated helpfully. "We can just stand here and have a good long look."

Poggwydd was racing up and down the wire, showing all his teeth, shaking his fist, desperately trying to speak.

"Of course," she agreed. "I'll be right outside. Just call if you need me."

They waited until she went back through the heavy door and closed it securely behind her. Questor looked at Abernathy, then stepped close to the cage.

"Stop that!" he snapped at Poggwydd. "Behave yourself and listen to me! Do you want out of there or not?"

Poggwydd, worn out anyway, dropped to the floor and stood glaring at him. It was very close and antiseptic in the room. Abernathy pictured himself locked away in there for a full day and was suddenly sympathetic toward the Gnome in spite of himself.

"Now, listen!" Questor addressed Poggwydd firmly. "There is no point in leaping about like that! We came for you as soon as we could, as soon as we found out where you were!"

Poggwydd gestured toward his mouth in frustration.

"Oh, of course, you want to say something," Questor furrowed his brow fiercely. "Just keep your voice down when you speak so you can't be heard or I'll silence you again. Understood?"

The G'home Gnome nodded blackly. Questor spoke some words in a low voice, made a gesture, and Poggwydd's voice came back with a gasp.

"You certainly took your time!" he said. "I might have died in here! Those people are animals!"

Questor inclined his head slightly in acknowledgment. "I apologize. But now here we are. We have come to get you out and take you back to Landover."

The Gnome's face scrunched into a mass of angry wrinkles. "Well maybe I don't want to go! Maybe I've had quite enough of you, Questor Thews! And your friend!"

"Don't be ridiculous! You want to stay in there?"

"No, I don't want to stay in here! I want out! But once I'm out, I want to go back on my own. I can find my own way better than you, I'm willing to bet!"

"You couldn't find your way out of an open field, much less another world! Whatever are you talking about?"

"Leave him, Questor Thews!" Abernathy snapped. "We've wasted enough time!"

The three of them began arguing heatedly and were still at it when abruptly the metal door opened and Lucy Beckendall stepped into view. All three went instantly silent. She stared from one to the other, almost certain she had heard the creature in the cage speaking.

"There is some sort of mix-up here," she announced, looking uncomfortable and wary. "I have two gentlemen at the reception desk who had identified themselves as Professor Adkins from the University of Washington and Mr. Drozkin from the Woodland Park Zoo. They have shown me their ID cards. Do you have any identification to offer?"

"Of course," Abernathy declared quickly, smiling and nodding. *Drat!*

He walked quickly down the line of cages, reaching into his pocket, fumbling, and shaking his head. When he reached Lucy Beckendall at the door, he placed his hands firmly on her shoulders, shoved her back through the opening, and yanked the door closed once more. "Questor Thews!" he bawled, bracing himself against the door as pounding immediately began without. "Help!"

The wizard pulled up his sleeves, raised his skinny arms, and sent an electric blue clot of magic zapping into the lock. The lock and handle melted and fused in place.

"There, they won't be getting in that way!" he declared in satisfaction.

"And we won't be getting out, either!" Abernathy stalked back down the walkway. "So you had better know what you are going to do next!"

Questor Thews wheeled on Poggwydd. "There is only one way out, Mr. Poggwydd—with us, back to Landover. If we leave you, they'll have you back in this cage in a matter of minutes. Who will help you then? Now, I'm sorry you're in this mess, but it isn't our fault. And we don't have time to debate the matter." The pounding without had given way to a violent hammering, metal on metal where the lock was fused. Questor's mouth tightened, and his bony finger jutted at the Gnome. "Just think what they'll do to you! Experiments! Tests! Potions of all sorts! What's it to be, Poggwydd? Landover and freedom or a cage for the rest of your life?"

Poggwydd licked his grimy lips, his eyes bright with fear. "Get me out! I'll go with you! I won't make any more trouble, I promise!"

"Good choice," Questor muttered. "Step back from the door."

The G'home Gnome scurried into a back corner. Questor gestured and twisted with his hands, and the door sprang open. "Out!" the wizard snapped.

Poggwydd crawled out meekly and hunkered down like a beaten dog. "Stop that!" Questor ordered. "There's nothing wrong with you! Stand up!"

Poggwydd straightened, his lower lip quivering. "I don't want to see that little girl again! Or her mud puppy, either! Not ever!"

Questor ignored him, already at work marking a circle on the concrete floor with the heel of his boot. When he was done, he motioned the Gnome and Abernathy inside. They stood close together in the heat and silence as the wizard took a deep breath, closed his eyes, and began to concentrate.

"I hope you know what you are doing," Abernathy said quietly, unable to help himself.

"Hush!" the wizard snapped.

Outside, the hammering had been replaced by a large number of voices. Reinforcements, Abernathy thought dismally. Then something heavy rammed into the door. They were trying to break it down! The frame and hinges shook with the force of the blows. Mortar cracked and sifted downward. Whoever was out there would be inside pretty quickly.

Questor began to speak the words of the spell slowly, clearly, deliberately. He had gone somewhere deep inside himself to concentrate, and he seemed oblivious to the hammering and shouting. Just as well, Abernathy thought. It would be just like the wizard to become distracted and get the spell wrong. What would he end up being then? A radish? He looked at Poggwydd. The G'home Gnome had his head lowered and his eyes shut tight. His arms were clasped about his scrawny body. Well, of course, Abernathy thought. We are all afraid.

Questor droned on, sweat beading his forehead. Abernathy could see the tension in his face. Changing me back again, he thought. And hating every moment of it. Abernathy experienced a sudden urge to cry out, to stop him from what he was doing, to make him do something else. But he suppressed that urge, his decision made, his fate accepted. He looked down at himself, wanting to remember everything about how he looked, not wanting to have to wonder again later. It hadn't been so bad being a dog, really. Not so bad.

Light surged upward about them, filling the circle from floor to ceiling, encasing them in its bright cylinder. Questor's voice rose, the words snapping like blankets hung in the wind. Poggwydd whimpered. Abernathy thought of Elizabeth. He was glad she wasn't there to see this happen. It was better that she remember him as he was supposed to be.

The light brightened into a blinding radiance. Abernathy felt himself melting away. The feeling was not unexpected. He had experienced it once before, more than twenty years ago.

He closed his eyes and let it happen.

VENOM

It took Ben and Willow the better part of two days to reach the Deep Fell. They left at sunrise on the first, accompanied by Bunion and an escort of two dozen King's Guards, and made their way north and east out of the hill country to the edge of the Greensward. From there they turned directly north and followed the line of the forested hills toward the witch's lair. The summer heat continued, sticky and damp against their skin, a shimmer of cellophane in the sun's glare. There was little wind to offer relief. There was little shade. Their pace was slow and steady, and they rested the animals and themselves often. All about, the countryside was sultry and still.

They camped where the waters of the Anhalt emerged from the hill country on the long journey down out of the mountains west. They sat on a low bluff above the river, having crossed before sunset, and watched the fading light turn purple and pink. To the east herons and cranes flew low above the sluggish waters, fishing for dinner.

"We'll be there by tomorrow noon," Ben declared after a long silence, anxious to engage an unusually quiet Willow in some form of conversation. "Then we'll know."

The sylph's voice was a soft, resigned sigh. "I already know. Nightshade has her. I can sense it. She wanted Mistaya from the very beginning, and she finally found a way to get her."

Her shoulder was touching Ben's as they stared off into the approaching dark, but the distance between them was frightening. All day long she had been withdrawing, closing herself away. Now she was someplace where no one could reach her if she did not wish it. Ben had waited patiently for her to work out whatever was disturbing her, hoping it wasn't him.

He cleared his throat. "She probably thinks of Mistaya as her property. Mistaya is payment for the debt she thinks she is owed for what befell her in the Tangle Box."

Willow was silent for a moment. "If it was only a matter of debt or even a claim to property, she would have stolen Mistaya away and been done with it. She would have ransomed her back or killed her, intending to hurt us by doing so. Instead, she concocted this elaborate scheme involving Rydall of Marnhull and his monsters. Mistaya is the prize to be won or lost, but she is something more as well. I think Nightshade has another use for her."

Ben looked at her. "What use?"

She shook her head. "I don't know. Perhaps it has something to do with Mistaya's magic. She was born in the Deep Fell, so perhaps they share something from that. Or maybe it is something darker. Perhaps she seeks to turn Mistaya's thinking so that it mirrors her own."

"No, Mistaya would never let that happen." Ben went cold all the way to his toes. "She is too strong."

"No one is stronger than Nightshade. Her hate drives her."

Ben went silent, a swell of horror rising inside at the prospect of Mistaya becoming like Nightshade. His good sense told him it could never happen. His emotions said otherwise. The two warred within him as he watched the shadows lengthen across the land, darkening the river and the hills.

"She would do that to hurt us, wouldn't she?" he said finally. "She would." He took a deep breath. "But how does that explain the Rydall charade?"

"Rydall gives her time to work on Mistaya. Rydall occupies us, keeps us at a distance and off balance. We don't realize the truth of things until it is too late."

Her eyes were empty and lost when he looked into them. "You've been thinking on this all day, haven't you?" he asked quietly. "That's why you're so far away from me."

She looked at him. Her smile was wan. "No, Ben. I have been preparing myself for tomorrow. There is a good chance I will lose Mistaya. Or you. Or even both. It isn't easy to accept the possibility, but it is there nevertheless."

"You won't lose either of us," he promised, putting his arm about her, drawing her close, knowing even as he did that he had just made a promise he might not be able to keep.

They slept poorly, made restless by anticipation of what lay ahead, of what they might find. They rose at sunrise, ate a quick breakfast, and were under way before the sun had fully crested the horizon in the mountains to the east. This day was steamy and suffocating as well, and they moved through it like swimmers on a sluggish tide. Bunion scouted ahead, keeping a wary eye out for any more of Rydall's monsters. Two remained to be faced, and Nightshade might choose now to unleash them. If indeed the witch was Rydall. Some doubt remained in Ben's mind, even if Willow was convinced. But by now he was doubting everything.

Ahead, the land stretched away in a ragged carpet of burned-out grasses and patchwork forest green, the line between foothills and plains blurred by the heat. He listened to the sounds of leather and traces as the horses plodded ahead resolutely. What would he do when they reached the Deep Fell? Would he go down into the hollow? Would he send the Paladin? How would he confront the witch? How would he learn the truth about Mistaya?

He glanced at Willow, riding beside him in silence. What he read in her face suggested that he had better find his answers soon.

—◁∞▷—

Nightshade knew of their coming long before they were in view. She had known of it almost from the moment they had left Sterling Silver and had kept careful watch over their progress. The confrontation she had envisioned from the beginning was fated at last to take place. Somehow Holiday had figured it out. She did not know how he had done it, but he clearly had. He was coming to the Deep Fell, and he would be doing that only if he knew the truth.

The seeming inevitability of things did not escape her. The Ardsheal had failed her, just as all the other creatures she had sent had failed her. Under Rydall's agreement she had two monsters left to send, but time had run out on that game and only one chance remained for her now. She had enjoyed playing with Holiday, seeing him struggle, watching him suffer as he fought one monster after another in an effort to survive long enough to rescue his beloved daughter. She had enjoyed breaking him down a little at a time, leaving him physically and emotionally drained by forces he did not even begin to understand. How could he know that it was Mistaya's own magic working against him? How could he realize what that would do to him? It had been satisfying, but the greatest satisfaction of all was yet to come.

The anticipation of it kept her anger and frustration in check, for although she would not admit it even to herself, she was disappointed that Holiday was still alive. Her expenditure of time and effort, of magic and power, could not be dismissed out of hand even with the argument that all was as expected. Nightshade hated to lose, hated to be denied anything, even where she could rationalize that it must necessarily be so. She wanted Holiday dead, and postponement of that result, whatever the justification, was difficult to bear.

Still, she had made her plan and believed it to be foolproof. Mistaya was hers yet, her unwitting tool, and she would be put to the use intended before this business was done. It was better, perhaps, that it happen now, before any more time passed. Mistaya was growing unmanageable, increasingly reluctant to engage in the practice of magic that Nightshade decreed, suspicious of the role in which she had been cast. It was bad enough that she had refused to help create another monster after the robot had failed. It was unbearable that she should dare to leave the hollow. Yet Nightshade had persisted. One more time she had found a way to use Mistaya, joining the girl's magic with her own to bring the Ardsheal back from the dead so that it could be sent against Holiday, but it had required great cunning and subterfuge on the witch's part to con-

ceal the truth of what she was about. It would be difficult to deceive Mistaya
again.

Yet she would be deceived, Nightshade promised herself. One final time.

She let Mistaya do what she wished with her magic and her lessons on the
first day of Holiday's journey to the Deep Fell. She let her practice what she
would, encouraging her, complimenting her, putting her at ease. Only one day
remained, Mistaya was told. One—and then she would be going home.
Nightshade prowled the hollow restlessly, barely able to concentrate on anything but the approach of the event she had schemed to bring about for two
years. She wandered off into the mists, playing out the moment over and over
in her mind, seeing it happen, anticipating the joy it would give her. Holiday
dead. Holiday gone at last. It had become for her the sole reason for her life,
the single purpose for which she existed. It had become for her as necessary
as breathing.

At night she went out in the form of a crow, flying over the land to where
the play-King slept in the company of the sylph and his Guards. She would
have lighted on his face and pecked out his eyes if she could have done so, so
great was her hatred. But she knew better than to take chances after employing so much care. She would not cheat herself now of the end she had devised
for him. She made certain of his distance from the Deep Fell, of the time she
would need to prepare, and flew back again to wait.

The following morning she waited until Mistaya had eaten her breakfast
before approaching her. Darkly sleek and vaguely menacing, she swept up to
the girl with a smile and a light touch of one slender white hand against her
cheek.

"Your father comes for you today," she advised in her most compelling
voice.

Mistaya looked up expectantly.

"He should arrive by midday. Are you anxious to see him?"

"Yes," the girl answered, and the undisguised anticipation in her voice set
the witch's teeth on edge.

"He will take you back to Sterling Silver, back to your home. But you will
not forget me, will you?"

"No," the girl said softly.

"We have learned a lot together, you and I." Nightshade looked off into the
trees. Mistaya had withdrawn from her since coming back down into the
Deep Fell. She had distanced herself as only children could, barely tolerant,
clearly marking time. It was a bitter recognition for the witch. She had expected better. "There are still many secrets to learn, Mistaya," she offered, trying to win back something of what she had lost. "I will teach them to you one
day if you wish. I will show you everything. You need only ask." She looked
back at Mistaya, eyes liquid. "This can be your home, too. One day you may
wish to come live here with me. You may decide that this is where you belong.

We are very much alike. You must know that. We are different from others. We are witches, and we will always be each other's greatest friend."

She almost meant it. There was enough truth behind the words to make it so. But fate had decreed long ago that it could never be. Her hatred of Holiday, so obsessive a presence, so monstrous and driving, had determined that it must be otherwise.

Mistaya's eyes dropped hesitantly. "I will come back to visit you. When it is safe to do so."

Nightshade's smile was cool and fixed. "That time may come to pass sooner than you think. I have arranged for Rydall to withdraw his challenge to your father. He will be here when your father arrives. Once he is gone from Landover, there no longer need be any barriers between us. Your father and mother will agree, I am sure."

Mistaya's brow wrinkled. "Rydall will withdraw? For good? He has given up completely?"

"I have persuaded him it is best for all concerned." Nightshade's eyes narrowed. "Magic can accomplish anything. This is what I have tried to teach you."

Mistaya looked down at her clothes and brushed at them while she spoke. "I have learned a lot from you," she whispered.

"You were a good student," Nightshade praised. "You have great talent. Do not forget that I first told you so, that I revealed to you what no one else would, that I helped you discover who you really are. No one else would have done that for you. Only me."

There was a moment of awkward silence. Nightshade could feel a shift in the balance of things. "I have something for you," she said to the girl.

Mistaya's eyes lifted. Nightshade reached down into her robes and brought forth a silver chain and pendant. The pendant was carved in the shape of a rose, the petals carefully detailed, the stem and thorns intricately worked into the metal. She took the chain and pendant and placed them about Mistaya's neck.

"There," she said, stepping back. "A gift to remember me by. So long as you wear it, you will never forget our time together."

Mistaya lifted the pendant from her breast and held it gently between her fingers. There was surprise and gratitude in her green eyes. Her child's face shone. "It is beautiful, Nightshade. Thank you very much. I shall wear it always, I promise."

A handful of hours will be enough, the witch thought to herself, keeping her smile carefully in place. Long enough to meet your loving father and embrace him one final time. Long enough for the pendant's hidden magic to cause the rose thorns to prick the play-King's skin and for their deadly poison to seep into his body. You can do what you wish with my gift after that. After it has served its purpose.

After you have served yours.

Questor Thews came out of the light of his magic in a wash of dizziness that very nearly toppled him. He staggered momentarily as the brightness faded, trying to gain his balance. Then, finding his feet on solid ground once more, he steadied himself, blinked away the last of his discomfort, and took a quick measure of his surroundings. To his relief he discovered that he was back in Landover. A scattering of pale moons dotted the midday sky, visible through the heavy screen of tree limbs. Stalks of Bonnie Blue poked out of scrub and from between moss-covered trunks. Familiar smells reached out to him. There was no mistaking any of it. But despite being back in Landover, he was no longer in the lake country. The look of things was all wrong for that. He was somewhere else, somewhere farther north . . .

"Jumping junipers, that is just about enough of that!" an irate Poggwydd snapped, grabbing a tight hold of Questor's sleeve. The wizard jumped at the unexpected contact. "I don't know what you did to get us back here, but I believe I'll simply walk next time! Next time, did I say? Bite my tongue! Next time? Beat me with a switch if there's ever a next time! Hah! Not likely! Not for this fellow!"

Scrunching up his face as if to cause his features to disappear completely, he released Questor and wheeled away in a snit. "Good day to you, sir! Good day, good day!" Then he stopped dead in his tracks. "Gracious me and mercy on us all, what's happened to him?"

He was looking at Abernathy. Landover's scribe sat on the ground next to an aging hickory, staring down at himself. He was a dog once more, a soft-coated Wheaten Terrier, shaggy and unkempt beneath his clothing, fur sticking out everywhere, ears perked, glasses perched awkwardly on his long nose. His liquid brown eyes seemed both startled and sad as he studied his human fingers, all that remained of his old body. Then he shrugged, looked up at Poggwydd, and sighed.

"What seems to be the trouble, Poggwydd? Haven't you ever seen a talking dog before?"

Poggwydd's wrinkled, furry face went through a series of bizarre contortions as he huffed and spit in an effort to speak. "Well, I . . . Well, of course, I . . . Humph! Mumble, mumble! Well, you certainly weren't a dog earlier!"

Abernathy climbed slowly to his feet and brushed himself off. "How much earlier do you mean?"

"Just a little bit ago! Just before we were gobbled up by the wizard's magic! You were a man, confound it!"

Abernathy's smile was rueful even for a dog. "That was just a disguise. This is the real me. Can't you tell?" He sighed again, and his eyes locked on Questor. "Well, you were right, Questor Thews. Congratulations."

Questor gave a quick nod in reply. "Yes, it appears I was, thank you. I must say again that I wish it could be otherwise."

"We all wish things could be otherwise, but this is the real world, isn't it? Or as real as it gets for us." Abernathy looked around in puzzlement. "Where are we, anyway?"

"I was just about to ask our friend," the wizard replied, looking in turn to Poggwydd.

The G'home Gnome seemed startled by the question. He glanced right and left momentarily as if to confirm his suspicions, then cleared his throat officiously. "We're right back where we started, is where we are. Well, back where I started, anyway. This is where that little girl found me, minding my own business, not causing anyone the least amount of . . ." He trailed off quickly as he saw a dark look creep into Questor's eye. "Ahem! What matters to you, I imagine, is that we're just a mile or so from the Deep Fell."

"I don't understand," Abernathy ventured, coming over to stand next to them. "What are we doing here? Why aren't we back in the lake country?"

Questor Thews was rubbing his chin furiously, twisting his whiskers into rat's tails while thinking the matter through. "We're here, old friend, because Mistaya's here—down in the Deep Fell with the witch. This is where Poggwydd saw her last. Nightshade took her back to the Deep Fell, and there's no reason to think she isn't still there. We've been brought here to save her, I believe."

"I don't understand any of this!" the G'home Gnome declared abruptly. "But that's fine, that's just fine, because I don't want to understand any of it! I just want to be on my way. So good-bye to the both of you and good luck!"

Once more he started away, this time heading east, away from the witch's lair.

"Don't you want to know what happens with Nightshade?" Questor Thews called after him.

"I don't want to know another thing about any of this!" The Gnome did not slow his pace. "I already know more than enough! Much more!" He scuffed at the dirt furiously, raising dust with his feet. "Do me a favor, please. If you find that little girl, give her my regards and tell her I never want to see her again. Nothing personal, but that's the way it is." His voice rose dangerously. "I hope she is a King's daughter! I hope she becomes a Queen! I hope if she ever goes for another walk, she does it somewhere else! Good day!"

He disappeared into the trees and was gone, a hunched ragtag figure leaving in his wake a scattering of rude gestures and indecipherable mumbles.

Questor dismissed him instantly and turned to Abernathy, eyes intent. "You know what we have to do, don't you?"

Abernathy looked at him as he might a small child. "I know perfectly well. Probably better than you."

"Then we had better hurry. I have an uneasy feeling about things."

And he did, too. It was hard to describe but impossible to discount. The feeling had been with him in the High Lord's old world: a need for haste, to get back into Landover as quickly as possible so that something could be done to prevent whatever it was that Nightshade intended. Now the feeling was even stronger, a growing certainty that the trap around Holiday and his family was about to close and that only he and Abernathy could prevent it. Perhaps it was a bit conceited and overdramatic to assume responsibility for so much, but Questor Thews needed to believe that there was a reason for Abernathy's sacrifice, that there was a greater good being served. His magic might have cost Abernathy his human identity, but it had gotten them back into Landover, to where Mistaya had last been seen and was probably captive still, and that had to count for something. Nightshade had told them that Rydall was her creature, that she had set in motion a chain of events that would crush Holiday, and that Mistaya would be the instrument of his destruction. Somehow the witch was using the little girl to get at the High Lord. If they could reach her in time, perhaps they could still make a difference.

They hurried away through the shadows and midday heat, off to the rescue. Gnats swarmed around them, drawn by their sweat, stirred by their passing. Questor brushed the gnats away, preoccupied with his thoughts. A horse would have been a welcome sight just about now, but then Abernathy wanted nothing to do with horses, so maybe going on foot was for the best. They crossed a stream and passed through a glade dappled crimson and yellow with wildflowers. Finches darted from cover and sailed off into the blue. Abernathy was breathing hard, but Questor did not let up on the pace. He was in some pain himself. He pushed his old bones harder, ignoring his aching joints. He forced himself to walk more quickly. He gathered up his robes and clambered down slopes and along pathways through the tall grasses and past the thorny scrub.

"Questor Thews, slow down!" he heard Abernathy gasp, for the scribe was trailing steadily farther behind by now.

The wizard never considered it for a moment.

Ahead, the mist and gloom of the Deep Fell were already in view.

HOLIDAY HEART

Mistaya was sitting with Nightshade on a grassy rise at the south edge of the Deep Fell when her father and mother rode into view. Bunion preceded them, edging out of the midday heat like a spider emerging from its hole, crouched down warily against the sun-scorched earth. King's Guards flanked and trailed them, armed with lances and swords, all metal and flash in the brightness. The company slowed as they saw her, reining in the horses, easing to a halt. Mistaya could see the tension etched on her father's face, could see the movement of his eyes as they swept the empty stretch of grasslands separating him from his daughter and came to rest finally on Rydall.

Marnhull's King sat atop his black charger a short distance to her right, concealed in his black armor and cloak, his visor pulled down, motionless in the shadows of a broad-limbed chestnut. He had been waiting there when Nightshade and Mistaya had climbed to the rim of the hollow. He had done nothing to acknowledge them. He had failed to move or speak a word since. He did nothing now. He was as still as stone, facing directly back toward Landover's King.

Nightshade rose, and Mistaya stood up with her. Ben Holiday's eyes flicked back to his daughter instantly. Mistaya wanted to run to him, to call out, to do or say something, anything, but Nightshade had forbidden it. *Let me speak first,* she had warned. *The negotiations between Rydall and your father are in a very delicate state. We must be careful not to disrupt them in any way.* Mistaya understood. She did not want to do anything to endanger her father. She just wanted to go home. She had been thinking about it since she had returned to the Deep Fell after meeting Poggwydd. She had grown steadily more anxious since, excited but a little afraid as well at the prospect of seeing her parents again after so many weeks. Now she felt a surge of emotion rise inside her chest, tightening her throat, bringing tears to her eyes. She had not realized how much she missed them, she guessed. She had not known how badly she would want to go home.

"High Lord!" Nightshade called out suddenly. "Your daughter is here with me, safe and well. She is ready to return home. I have gained King Rydall's promise that she may do so. He has agreed to withdraw from Landover. There will be no more threats, no further attacks. You need only promise that you will seek no retribution against him for anything that has happened."

Mistaya waited expectantly. There was a long silence, as if her father did not know how to answer, as if what he was hearing was entirely unexpected. She saw him look at her mother and her mother speak softly in response. Bunion moved restlessly between them, teeth gleaming, eyes fixed on the witch.

"What about Questor Thews and Abernathy?" Ben Holiday shouted back.

"They will be returned as well!" Nightshade answered.

Abernathy and Questor? Mistaya glanced up at the witch questioningly. What were they talking about? Had something happened to the wizard and the scribe? Weren't they safely back in Sterling Silver? Wasn't that what she had been told?

Nightshade smiled down, her face distant and shrouded within the hood of her black robe. Nothing to worry about, the smile said. Do not concern yourself.

"I will seek no retribution if everyone is well," she heard her father agree, but she did not miss the troubled tone of his voice. She looked back across the space that separated them, an empty, burned-out stretch of grassland fronting the shadowy depression of the hollow. Her father seemed a long way off.

Nightshade put a slender white hand on her shoulder. "You must go to your father now, Mistaya," she advised. "When I tell you to do so, walk out to meet him. Do not deviate from your path in any way. Go directly to him. No one else. Do you understand?"

Mistaya was aware suddenly that something was happening she did not understand, something hidden and possibly dangerous. She could sense it in Nightshade's words, in the same way she could sense so much about the witch. She hesitated, wondering what she should do. But there was nothing she could do, she knew. Nothing but agree. She nodded silently.

"High Lord!" Nightshade called out once more. "Your daughter is coming to you! Dismount and walk out to meet her. Come alone! That is the agreement I have made."

Again Mistaya could see her father hesitate, thinking it over. He was not sure of this, she could tell. There was something bothering him, something he could not seem to reconcile. She thought perhaps she should try to reassure him, then realized that she wasn't sure of things herself, that she was troubled as well. Her green eyes shifted to find Rydall. Marnhull's King hadn't moved. She looked quickly to Nightshade. The witch was still and expressionless.

Her father dismounted slowly and began to walk forward. Bunion started to go with him, but he sent the kobold back with a wave of his hand.

"Go now!" Nightshade whispered quickly in her ear. "Give him a special hug from me!"

Mistaya moved forward reluctantly, still pondering her confusion, still wondering what was wrong. She shuffled through the dry grasses with small steps, watching her father advance, watching him draw steadily closer. She glanced back at Nightshade, but the witch did not respond, a tall and dark etching against the hollow's steamy mist. Mistaya brushed at her hair where it fell across her face, and her green eyes flicked right and left. Her father came on, steady and watchful. She saw a worried, uncertain smile form on his lips. She could see his eyes clearly. There was relief mirrored there—as if he had not expected to see her again. A rush of confusion swept through her. Why was he looking at her so?

Suddenly she wanted to do as Nightshade had urged. She wanted to hug her father as tightly as she could, to hold him close, to feel the strong press of his body against her own. She wanted him to take her in his arms and give her shelter and reassurance. She needed to tell him how much she had missed him. She needed to be reassured of his love for her.

The day was still and hot, and the breeze that brushed her face was as dry as fly wings. "Father," she breathed softly, and hurried forward.

Then a sudden, desperate shout rose out of the silence. "High Lord! Mistaya! Wait!"

Questor Thews broke from the trees to her left, stumbling out of the shadows and into the sunlight. Disheveled and unkempt, robes trailing in tatters where the bright sashes had come loose and the seams had ripped, he raced toward them with his arms waving, his white hair and beard flying, and his eyes as wild and frightened as those of a creature pursued by hunters. Mistaya and her father both whirled in surprise, watching the ragtag figure come hurtling toward them. From out of the trees behind him, some thirty yards back, Abernathy appeared, huffing and panting and trying futilely to keep up.

Then Mistaya heard Nightshade's gasp of fury. The witch had gone into a crouch, looking like a cat poised to spring, arms extended as if to ward off something terrible. Her eyes locked on Mistaya's, as red as blood. "Go to your father!" she shrieked in rage.

Mistaya started forward in response, barely aware of what she was doing. But Questor Thews was still coming, running doggedly onward through the heat and dust, arms and legs pinwheeling wildly. Again, Mistaya stopped, transfixed.

"Mistaya, don't!" Questor Thews cried out. "It's a trap!"

Suddenly everyone was trying to reach her: her mother surging forward atop her mount with the King's Guards in close pursuit and Bunion racing ahead, Nightshade lifting her arms and spreading her dark robes like some great bird of prey, Rydall fighting to bring his rearing, panic-stricken black horse under control, Abernathy tumbling head over heels through the dry grasses as he lost his footing, and her father breaking into a sudden sprint.

But it was Questor Thews who reached her first, careening wildly across the last bit of space that separated them, snatching her up as if she were a rag doll, and crushing her to his breast.

"Mistaya!" he whispered in relief.

Then wicked green light flared between them, spraying outward from the pendant like shattered glass. Questor Thews grunted in shock, and the blood drained from his face. His grip on Mistaya weakened, and he dropped to his knees, barely able to cling to her.

"Questor!" she shrieked in horror.

She drew back as she realized where the light was coming from and peered quickly down. The thorns on the rose stem had grown impossibly long and jutted from the old man's chest like spikes. There was blood seeping from the wounds. Questor was shaking, and his fingers had tightened into claws. He was gasping for breath. Mistaya yanked the thorns from his body, tore off the pendant, and flung it away. Questor's eyes fixed on her without seeing, and he slumped to the ground and lay still.

"Questor!" Mistaya gasped. "Questor, get up! Please!"

Questor Thews did not move. He had quit breathing.

Mistaya leapt to her feet, sobbing with rage and despair. "Nightshade!" she screamed. "Do something!"

Her father came up quickly and reached for her, but she pushed him away. She rushed to where the pendant lay, looked down at it, then squinted out across the scorched flat. "Nightshade!"

The witch stood frozen in place, her pale, smooth face empty of expression but her eyes filled with terrible fury. Her arms swept downward, casting off the magic they had gathered.

"You gave me that pendant!" Mistaya screamed. "You made this happen!"

Nightshade's hand swept the air before her. "I am not responsible for this! Questor Thews shouldn't have interfered! He was a fool!"

"I trusted you!" Mistaya shrieked.

Now her mother was there as well, dismounting and hurrying over as King's Guards reined to a halt behind them, weapons drawn, and Bunion hissed at Nightshade in warning. "Mistaya, look at me," Willow ordered.

But Mistaya waved her away, picked up the pendant by its chain, and held it out accusingly toward Nightshade. "You intended this for my father, didn't you? You meant this for him!"

"I did not mean—"

"Don't lie to me anymore!"

"Yes!" The witch shrieked. "Yes, I meant it for him! The poison was meant to take his life, not that old fool's!"

Mistaya was shaking with fury. Her small body was as taut as a spear's wooden shaft, all straight and set to fly. Her hands were clenched into fists, and her face was streaked with tears. "I hate you!" she screamed.

She threw down the pendant. Her small hands came up, and fire lanced out of them, shattering it where it lay on the ground, turning the metal to dust. Ben and Willow shrank back in spite of themselves, startled at the power Mistaya possessed.

Abernathy finally reached them, panting heavily, tongue hanging out. He bent hurriedly over Questor Thews, dog's ear to the old man's chest. "There isn't any heartbeat!" he whispered.

Mistaya was stalking toward Nightshade now, all determination and iron will. "You're going to help him or else!" she hissed. "Do you hear me, Nightshade?"

The witch took a step back, then straightened. "Do not presume to threaten me, you little fool! I am still your mistress and your better!"

"You were never anything but a liar and a sneak!" the little girl snapped. "You tricked me! You used me! What else have you made me do? What of those monsters I helped you make? The earth giant and the metal man and the others? To what use did you put them?"

"They were sent to kill your father," she heard her mother say from behind her. "Ask her to deny it."

"Rydall!" Nightshade wheeled on Marnhull's King. "You wanted your chance at Holiday! Well, here it is! Kill him!"

Rydall was still struggling with his charger, barely managing to keep the frightened animal under control. At Nightshade's words, he twisted about to face her, menace radiating from his black-armored body. For a moment it seemed he might attack her instead. Then he reached for his sword, shouted in challenge, spurred his charger forward, and came at Holiday. But Bunion was quicker. The kobold rushed at Marnhull's King, teeth bared, a small black blur in the heat, and threw himself into the horse's face. The animal shied, reared, bucked, and threw Rydall from his saddle. Rydall's right foot caught in the stirrup as he fell. Burdened by the weight of his armor, he could not break free. He tumbled to the earth beneath the rearing, stamping horse and was hammered by the iron-shod hooves. The horse bolted, dragging his helpless rider across the flats. Bits and pieces of armor broke free, and blood stained the ground. King's Guards spurred forward to catch the terrified horse, but by the time they had reined him in, Rydall of Marnhull was a ruined, battered husk.

Mistaya continued to advance on Nightshade. "No!" the witch shrieked, clearly shaken. "We are even now! A life for a life! Rydall goes back to where he came from, and you and I do the same, little girl!"

But Mistaya did not slow. Her father and mother were hurrying after her, both of them grim-faced. Bunion came skittering like quicksilver through the brown grasses. King's Guards spread out all about them. Ben Holiday had the medallion out, and he held it up to the light in one hand. A streak of fear crossed Nightshade's face. She crouched to meet these threats, a feral look on her face, bits of green fire rising off her fingers. Instantly Mistaya pointed at her, crying out. Magic lanced from the little girl's hands and knocked Nightshade flying. The witch gasped in shock and tumbled backward. Then she scrambled up in rage.

"No! You cannot touch me! You have no right!" She whirled on Mistaya. Her pale face was contorted and ugly. Her self-control was shattered. "I will show you what magic can really do, little witch! I will send you back where you belong!"

Her hands came up, wicked green flames swirling at her fingertips. Mistaya locked her arms before her in self-defense.

Then, suddenly, Haltwhistle was there, materializing at the edge of the Deep Fell. Frost rose off his hackles and turned into ribbons of steam. Nightshade became aware of him an instant too late. She turned, but the mud puppy's magic lanced out and knocked her legs from beneath her. Flailing wildly, her conjuring out of control, she collapsed in a heap. Down came her magic, falling about her like rain.

Nightshade was engulfed. The strange mix surrounded and consumed her in the blink of an eye. She had time for a single quick scream, and then she was gone.

⎯⎯◦∞◦⎯⎯

For a moment afterward no one moved. They stood rooted in place, half expecting the Witch of the Deep Fell to reappear. But she did not, and then Haltwhistle came up to Mistaya where she stood transfixed before the smoldering bit of earth where the witch had stood. The mud puppy looked up at the little girl with soulful eyes and slowly wagged his tail. Mistaya broke into tears.

Her father came up, knelt, and put his hands on her slender shoulders, bracing her and looking into her eyes. "It's all right, Mistaya," he told her. "It's all right." And then he drew her close and held her against him.

Willow took her then, holding her as well, rocking her, telling her that it was over now, that she was safe. As she did so, Ben rose and walked to where Rydall lay sprawled in a crumpled heap on a patch of barren ground within a ring of King's Guards. He dropped to one knee beside the fallen King, lifted the black visor, and peered down at the face inside. Blood-filled eyes blinked up at him from beneath a shock of red hair.

Ben Holiday shook his head bleakly. "Kallendbor," he whispered.

The Lord of the Greensward coughed weakly. Blood streaked his face and beard and leaked in a steady stream from his mouth. "I should . . . have killed you that first day . . . on the drawbridge. I . . . should never have listened to . . . the witch."

He drew one last breath, sighed, and went still. His eyes stared sightlessly into space. Ben closed the visor once more. Kallendbor had never been able to accept the way things had worked out, it seemed. Only Ben's death would have satisfied him. He must have been desperate indeed to have allied himself with Nightshade. Now Ben knew how the robot had managed to get so close to them at Rhyndweir without being detected. Now he knew how the witch had been able to use her magic to make him think he had lost the medallion. Kallendbor had arranged it all. Nightshade must have told him Ben was coming, and he had laid his trap for Landover's King and waited for him to die. Now the Lord of Rhyndweir himself lay dead, and there would probably never be any real understanding of the madness that had allowed it to happen.

He rose and walked back toward his family, but Mistaya was already crouched over Questor Thews, surrounded by the others, her small face intent with concentration.

"He can't die," she was saying as Ben came up and dropped to his knee beside her. "This is my fault. All my fault. I have to make it right. I have to."

Ben looked at Willow, and she lifted her stricken eyes to meet his. Questor Thews was not breathing. His heart had stopped. There was nothing anyone could do for him.

"Mistaya, he came out of love for you," Abernathy said softly, reaching out to touch her shoulder. "We all did."

But Mistaya was barely listening. She reached down impulsively and seized Questor's limp hand. "I learned something from Nightshade that might help," she murmured fiercely. "She taught me how to heal. Even the dead, sometimes. Maybe I can heal Questor. I can try, anyway. I have to try."

She rocked back on her heels and closed her eyes. Ben, Willow, Abernathy, and Bunion exchanged hesitant, wary glances. Mistaya was calling on the magic Nightshade had revealed, and nothing good had ever come of that. *Don't use it,* Ben wanted to say, but knew he mustn't. The sun beat down on them, and the air was thick and humid with its heat. All about, the grasslands were still, as if nothing lived there or what little did waited as they did to see what would transpire. Mistaya shuddered, and a bright shimmer ran from her body down her arm and into Questor Thews. The wizard lay motionless and unresponsive. Twice more the shimmer of light passed from Mistaya's body into Questor's. The little girl's eyes fluttered wildly, and her head drooped forward, her hair spilling down around her face. Again Ben thought to intervene, and again he kept himself from doing so. She had a right to do what she could, he told himself. She had a right to try.

Suddenly Questor Thews jerked. The movement startled Mistaya so that she gave a small cry and dropped his hand. For a moment no one moved. Then Abernathy hurriedly bent down over his old friend, listened for a moment, and looked up in astonishment.

"I can hear his heart beating!" he exclaimed. "I can hear him breathe! He's alive!"

"Mistaya!" Ben whispered, and hugged his daughter to him.

"I knew I could do it, Father," she said. She was shaking, and he could feel tremendous heat radiating from her body. "I knew I could. I do have magic."

"You do indeed," Ben agreed, alarmed, and called immediately for cold water and cloths.

The others hugged Mistaya as well, save for Bunion, who merely gave her a toothy grin. The cloths were applied, she was given water to drink, and her temperature fell again. She seemed to recover. But the battle to save Questor was not yet over. His heartbeat was weak, his breathing was shallow, and he remained unconscious. The poison was still in his body, and while Mistaya had managed to negate some of its effects, she had not been able to slow them entirely. Ben sent several of his King's Guards in search of a wagon and had the others build a stretcher in the meantime. They secured Questor in place, tied the stretcher to Jurisdiction, and started slowly home.

Mistaya insisted on riding on the stretcher next to Questor. When a wagon was found, she rode next to him there as well. She held his hand the entire way. She refused to let go.

SPECIMEN

For six days after their return to Sterling Silver Mistaya sat by Questor Thews as he slept. She held his hand almost continually. She left only when necessary and then only for moments at a time. She took her meals on a bedside tray and slept on a pallet on the floor. Now and again Haltwhistle would appear, materializing out of nowhere to let her know he was close before disappearing once more. More than once Ben Holiday slipped into the bedchamber at midnight to cover his daughter with a blanket and smooth her rumpled hair. He thought each time to carry her to her own bed, but she had made it plain that she intended to see the matter through to its end. Questor would recover or die, but in either case she would be there when it happened.

Bit by bit Ben pieced together the story of how Nightshade had tried to destroy him. They elicited from Mistaya the Earth Mother's role in providing Haltwhistle to help disrupt Nightshade's plans and were then able to deduce by themselves how the mud puppy was meant to insure that even when separately deceived they might find a way back to each other and the truth. Abernathy filled in his part, trying to gloss over what the transformation from dog to man and back again had done to him, trying to downplay his role in saving Ben's life. But Ben would not allow it, knowing what it had cost his faithful scribe to give up his human form once again, painfully aware that Abernathy might never be able to return to who he was. They spoke quietly of Questor Thews and his determination to save Mistaya. They worried together what it might mean for the little girl if Questor died.

Willow spent long hours talking candidly with Mistaya of Nightshade and her experience in the Deep Fell, smoothing away some of the hurt and guilt that her daughter felt. It was not Mistaya's fault, she pointed out, that the witch had used her to get at her father. It was not her fault that she had not realized what was being done. She had not intended her father harm or meant to give help of any kind to the witch. In fact, she had used her magic in what she believed to be an effort to save her father's life. Given her position, her mother would have done the same. All of them had been deceived by the witch, and not for the first time. Nightshade's was a pervasive, devious evil that would have destroyed anyone with less character and courage. Mistaya needed to know that. She needed to accept the idea that she had done the best she could.

Her father, speaking to her alone at one point, said, "You must forgive yourself for any blame in this, Mistaya. You made a mistake, and that's part of growing up. Growing up is painful for every child but more so for you. Do you remember what you said the Earth Mother told you?"

Mistaya nodded. She was holding tightly to Questor's hand, one finger on his pulse where it beat softly in his wrist.

"Growing up for you will be harder than for most. Because of who you are and where you come from. Because of your parents. Because of your magic. I wish it could be otherwise. I wish I could make it so. But I cannot. We have to accept who we are in this life and make the best of it. Some things we cannot change. All we can do is try to help each other when we see that help is needed."

"I know," she said softly. "But it doesn't make me feel any better."

"No, I don't suppose it does." He reached over and pulled her gently against him. "You know, Mistaya, I can't afford to think of you as a child anymore. At least not a child of two. You've grown way beyond that, and I guess I'm the only one who didn't see it."

She shook her head and kept her face lowered. "Maybe I'm not so grown up as everyone thinks. I was so sure of myself, but none of this would have happened if I'd been a little more careful."

He gave her a small hug. "If you remember that the next time you decide to use your magic, you'll be grown up enough for me."

Ben sent word to the River Master that his granddaughter was safe and would come to visit soon. He went back to the work of governing Landover, although a part of him was always in the bedchamber with Mistaya, sitting next to Questor Thews. He ate and slept out of necessity and found concentrating difficult. Willow talked with him when they were alone, sharing her own thoughts, her own doubts, and they gave each other what comfort they could.

Several times more Mistaya used her magic to try to strengthen Questor Thews. She told her parents what she intended so that they could be there to lend their support. The magic shimmered down her arm and into the old man's body without apparent effect. Mistaya said she could feel it grappling with the witch's poison, could feel the struggle taking place inside. But there was no change in the wizard's condition. His heartbeat remained slow, his breathing was ragged, and he did not wake. They tried to feed him soup and water, and some small portion of what touched his lips was consumed. But he was skin and bones, all waxy and drawn, a skeleton flattened down against the sheets, barely alive.

Mistaya tried strengthening him with other forms of magic, giving whispers of encouragement, lending deep measures of her love. She refused to give up. She willed him to come awake for her, to open his eyes and speak. She prayed for him to live.

Her parents and Abernathy gradually lost hope. She could see it in their eyes. They wanted to believe, but they understood too well the odds against survival. The depth of their concern did not lessen, but the look in their eyes flattened out into acceptance. They were preparing themselves for what they saw as the inevitable. Abernathy could no longer speak to her in Questor's presence. Each of them was withdrawing, cutting ties, severing feelings, hardening. She began to despair. She began to worry that the old man would lie there like that forever, trapped between waking and sleep.

Then, on the seventh day of her vigil, as she sat with him in the bedchamber in the early morning light, watching the sunrise color the sky through the windows, she felt his hand tighten unexpectedly around her own.

"Mistaya?" he whispered weakly, and his eyes blinked open.

She hardly dared to breathe. "I'm here," she replied, the tears starting. "I won't leave."

She called loudly for her mother and father and, with the old man's frail hand clasped firmly in her own, waited anxiously for them to come.

Vince had completed his shift at the Woodland Park Zoo in Seattle and was on his way to his car when he impulsively changed direction and went back into the aviary for a last look at the crow. The damn thing fascinated him. It was right where he had left it earlier, sitting by itself on a branch near the top of the enclosure. The other birds left it alone, wanting nothing to do with it. You couldn't blame them. It was a mean-looking thing. Vince didn't like it, either. But he couldn't stop wondering about it.

A crow with red eyes. Not another one like it that anyone had ever heard of. Not another anywhere.

It had popped up out of nowhere. Literally. Same day as that incident at the King County animal shelter when those two nuts posing as Drozkin and some guy from U Dub had stolen that monkey or whatever it was. No one knew what had happened to them. They'd just disappeared into thin air, if you could believe the lies being spread around. Then, not two hours later, this bird appeared, right there in the same cage the monkey disappeared from. What were the odds of that happening? No one could explain it, of course. It was like one of those UFO stories, one of those sightings where weird things happened to the people involved but no one could prove it had really happened. Vince believed in UFOs. Vince thought there were a lot of things happening in the world that you couldn't explain, but that didn't make them any less real. It was like that with this bird.

Anyway, there's the bird, this crow with the red eyes, lying there in the cage, stunned. The animal shelter people were no fools. They knew a specimen when they saw it, even if they didn't know exactly what sort of specimen it was. So they hobbled it and brought it over for study. An exotic bird, so it belonged in the zoo. Now it was Woodland Park's job to figure out what it was. No one knew how long that might take. Months, he guessed. Maybe years.

Vince leaned against the wire, trying to get the bird to look at him. It didn't. It never looked at anyone. But you always felt it was watching you nevertheless. Out of the corner of its eye or something. Vince wished he knew its story. He bet it was a good one. He bet it was better than any UFO story. There was a lot more to this bird than met the eye. You could tell that much by the way it conducted itself. Aloof, disdainful, filled with some inner rage at life. It wanted out of there. It wanted to go back to where it had come from. You could see it in those red eyes if you looked long enough.

But Vince didn't like to look into the crow's eyes for too long. When he did, he could almost swear they were human.

Here is an excerpt from

A PRINCESS OF
LANDOVER

A new adventure in the
Magic Kingdom of Landover series!

Mistaya continued to climb until even the thinning winter trees hid all traces of the highway behind a screen of dark trunks and limbs and a thickening curtain of mist. The little falls had been left behind, and even the trickling sounds of its waters had faded. Ahead, the mist was growing more impenetrable, swirling and twisting like a living thing, climbing into the tree-tops and filling in the gaps that opened to the sky.

Had she not known what to expect, all this would have frightened her. But she had traveled between worlds before, and so she knew how it worked. The mists marked the entry into Landover, and once she passed through them, she would be on her way home. Others who found their way into these woods and encountered the mists would be turned around without realizing it and sent back the way they had come. Only she would be shown the way through.

Assuming she didn't get careless and stray from the path, she reminded herself. If she did that, things could get complicated. Even for her.

She pulled the collar of her coat tighter, her breath clouding the air as she trudged ahead, still following the path that had taken her up. When at last the path ended, she kept going anyway, knowing instinctively where to go, aware of how she must travel.

A wall of ancient oak trees rose before her, huge monsters casting dark shadows in the failing light. Mist swirled through them, but at their center they parted to form a tunnel, its black interior running back into the forest until the light gave out. Trailers of mist wove their way through the trunks and branches, sinuous tendrils that moved like huge gray snakes. She moved toward them and entered the tunnel. Ahead, there was only blackness and a screen of mist. She kept walking, but for the first time she felt a ripple of uncertainty. It wasn't altogether impossible that she could have made a mistake. There wasn't any real way of knowing.

The consequences of a mistake, however, were enormous. One misstep here, and you were in the land of the fairies.

She pressed on, watching the mist and the darkness recede before her at a pace that matched her own. She hugged herself against the chills that ran up and down her spine. Whispers nudged her from within the trees to either side, the voices of invisible beings. She knew those voices, knew their source and their purpose. Fairies, teasing travelers who passed through their domain. They were insidious, unpredictable creatures, and even she, who was born in part of their soil and therefore a part of their world, was not immune to their magic. Partly their child, partly an earth child, and partly a child of Landover—that was her heritage and that was what had determined who and what she was.

Her mother, Willow, had told her the story many times when she was small. Her mother was a sylph, an Elfish creature who transformed periodically into the tree for which she was named to take root and nourish in the earth. She had done so in order to give birth to Mistaya. In preparation, she had collected a mix of soils—from a place in Ben's world called Greenwich and from the old pines in the lake country and from the fairy mists in her world. But she had unexpectedly gone into labor and been forced to take root in a hurried mix of the soils she carried while she was still down in the dark confines of the Deep Fell, the home of the witch Nightshade. The consequences were unimaginable, and while Mistaya had been born without incident, she had also been born the only one of her kind.

You couldn't be more different than that.

But being different only got you so far. For one thing, you were never exactly like anyone else and so you never completely fit in. It was so here. Being part fairy was not enough to guarantee safe passage. Staying on the path and keeping your head was what would protect you.

So she did as she knew she must, even though the temptation to step away, to follow those intriguing voices, to try to find even one of the speakers, played on her curious mind. She pushed ahead very deliberately, waiting for the dark and the mist to fade, for the trees to open before her, for the passing between worlds to end.

Which, finally, it did.

Quickly, smoothly, without warning of any sort, the trees thinned and the curtains of mist lifted. She walked out of the darkened forest into a bright, sunlit day filled with sweet scents and warm breezes. She paused in spite of herself, drinking it in, letting it infuse her with good feelings.

Home.

She had entered at the west end of Landover, and the sweep of the valley spread away before her. Close by, just below, lay the broad, open grasslands of the Greensward; south, the lake country that was her mother's home; north, the Melchor Mountains where the Trolls lived; and east, beyond the Greensward, the wastelands and the fire springs where Strabo, last of the dragons, made his home. She couldn't see it all; the distance was too great, and when you reached the ring of mountains that encircled the valley, the mists cloaked everything.

As she scanned the familiar countryside, enjoying the good feelings that coming home generated, her eyes passed over and then returned to the dark smudge below the Melchor that marked the Deep Fell. Memories she did not care to relive surfaced anew, and she felt a twinge of regret. The Deep Fell was her real birthplace, dark and terrible, and though she would have wished it otherwise, it was a part of her. Nightshade had told her so. Nightshade, who had wanted her for her own child. For a while, she had wanted that, too. Treachery and deception had marked that period in her life, when she was only eleven years old. But that was finished now. Nightshade was gone, and she wouldn't be coming back.

She shifted her gaze, fixing it instead on the place where she knew Sterling Silver waited, not too far away now, less than a day's walk if she hurried.

She started ahead at once, moving deliberately down from the foothills into the valley, choosing her path almost without thinking about it. She breathed deeply of the scents of the valley as she descended into it, marking each of them in turn, identifying each one, able to separate them out and match them to their names. She had learned to do that a long time ago while studying under the able tutelage of Questor Thews, the court magician. Questor, ancient and amusing, held a special place in her heart. It wasn't just because he was so funny, frequently mixing up his spells and causing all sorts of minor catastrophes. It wasn't because he had always treated her like an adult and never a child, better attuned to who and what she was than her father. It wasn't even because he was the dearest friend she had, aside from her parents.

It was because he had saved her life and almost lost his own by doing so. It was because he had done so impetuously and without a second thought for the consequences. It was because he had dared to go up against a much stronger sorcerer in Nightshade, the Witch of the Deep Fell.

Mistaya had used her own magic to save him, a combination of newfound talent acquired from studying with the witch and her natural talent. Enraged upon discovering she had been deceived into using both to attack her father, she had lashed out at Nightshade in a red-hot fury. The two had gone toe-to-toe in a battle of sorceries that might have seen both destroyed if not for the timely intervention of Haltwhistle. Her spell had turned back upon herself, and Nightshade had disappeared in an explosion of green witch fire. Afterward, Mistaya had used her talent and determination to nurse Questor back to health. When he was well again, he became her teacher and constant companion.

Until her father had sent her away to Carrington where, he insisted, she would learn new and necessary things.

To his credit, Questor hadn't argued. He had agreed with her father who, after all, was King and had the final word on almost everything. He had told her that her father was right, that she needed to see something of another world, and her father's world was the obvious choice. He would be waiting when she returned, and they would pick up right where they left off on their study of the flora and fauna, of the creatures and their habits, of the world that really mattered to her.

Remembering his promise, she was suddenly anxious for that to happen.

Abruptly, a huge black shadow fell across her, a dark stain that spread wide in all directions, as something massive and winged swept overhead in sound-less flight. She gasped and dropped into a protective crouch, preparing to de-fend herself. A beating of great, leathery wings churned the sleepy air into a howling wind that threatened to flatten her, and Strabo hove into view. Body extended, the dragon banked into a glide that brought it about and down into a smooth landing directly in front of her.

She straightened tentatively and faced the dragon as it towered over her. "Good day, dragon!" she greeted bravely.

"Good day, Princess," the dragon replied in a voice that sounded like metal being scraped with a saw's sharp teeth.

She wasn't sure where this was going but decided it was best to find out sooner rather than later. "You seem as if you have a purpose in coming upon me like this. Is there a reason for your being here? Are you here to welcome me home?"

"Welcome home," he said.

She waited for more, but the dragon simply sat there, blocking her way. It was a massive beast, its weight something in the area of four or five tons, its body sheathed in leathery skin and armored with bony plating, its spine ridged with spikes, its triangular head encrusted with horns, and its legs as big as tree trunks. One yellowish eye fixed on her with determined intent while the other closed with languid disinterest. Neat trick, she thought, and wondered if she could learn how to do it.

"We have a small problem, Princess," Strabo rumbled after a long few minutes. "You have engaged in behavior that is forbidden to you. Are you aware of what that behavior might be?"

"I am not," she declared, wondering suddenly if it had something to do with Rhonda Masterson.

"You used your magic to create an image of me to frighten someone," the dragon said, confirming her suspicion. "This is not allowed. This is never al-lowed. No one is ever, ever, ever allowed to use an image of me, in any form whatsoever, for any purpose whatsoever, without my permission. Perhaps you did not know this?"

She took a deep breath. "I did not. I thought it was a perfectly acceptable usage."

"Think again. More to the point, don't do it again. I don't know what kind of manners they teach you at the castle, or what sort of behavior you have been led to believe is acceptable, but labeling all dragons as scary beasts is way out of line. Consider this fair warning. If you ever create an image of me again without my permission, you shall hear from me much more quickly than this and you will be made to answer for your foolishness. Am I clear?"

She tightened her lower lip to keep it from trembling as the dragon bent over her like a collapsing rock wall and she got a clear whiff of its incredibly rancid breath. "You are very clear," she managed.

"Good," he declared. When he straightened he was as tall as a three-story building and with his wings spread he was twice as wide. "I shan't keep you longer. It is good to see you again, and I wish you well. I have always liked and admired you and your mother; your father, of course, is a different story. Please do yourself a favor and don't take after him. Now, farewell. Take care to remember my warning."

Huge wings flapping with enough force to knock her sprawling, Strabo rose into the sky and soared away, flying east until he was little more than a dwindling black speck against the horizon. Mistaya stared after him from where she sat sprawled on the ground, aware of how close she had come to finding out a whole lot more about dragon breath than she cared to.

ABOUT THE AUTHOR

TERRY BROOKS is the *New York Times* bestselling author of more than twenty-five books, including the Genesis of Shannara trilogy: *Armageddon's Children, The Elves of Cintra,* and *The Gypsy Morph; The Sword of Shannara;* the Voyage of the Jerle Shannara trilogy: *Ilse Witch, Antrax,* and *Morgawr;* the High Druid of Shannara trilogy: *Jarka Ruus, Tanequil,* and *Straken;* the nonfiction book *Sometimes the Magic Works: Lessons from a Writing Life;* and the novel based upon the screenplay and story by George Lucas, *Star Wars®: Episode I The Phantom Menace.*™ His novels *Running with the Demon* and *A Knight of the Word* were selected by the *Rocky Mountain News* as two of the best science fiction/fantasy novels of the twentieth century. The author was a practicing attorney for many years but now writes full-time. He lives with his wife, Judine, in the Pacific Northwest.

www.shannara.com
Terrybrooks.net